G

A Deniable Death

ALSO BY GERALD SEYMOUR

Harry's Game

The Glory Boys

Kingfisher

The Harrison Affair

The Contract

Archangel

In Honour Bound

Field of Blood

Shadow on the Sun

An Eye for an Eye

The Running Target

Condition Black

The Journeyman Tailor

The Fighting Man

The Heart of Danger

Killing Ground

Dead Ground

A Line in the Sand

Holding the Zero

The Untouchable

Traitor's Kiss

The Unknown Soldier

Rat Run

The Walking Dead

Timebomb

The Collaborator

The Dealer and the Dead

GERALD SEYMOUR

A Deniable Death

Thomas Dunne Books
St. Martin's Press
New York

THOMAS DUNNE BOOKS.
An imprint of St. Martin's Press.

www.thomasdunnebooks.com
www.stmartins.com

Library of Congress Cataloging-in-Publication Data

Seymour, Gerald.
  A deniable death / Gerald Seymour.—1st U.S. ed.
    p. cm.
  ISBN 978-1-250-01880-9 (hardcover)
  ISBN 978-1-250-01879-3 (e-book)
  1. Assassins—Fiction. 2. Military surveillance—Fiction. 3. Terrorism—Prevention—
Fiction. 4. Suspense fiction. I. Title.
  PR6069.E734D46 2013
  823'.914—dc23

                                                              2012035956

First published in Great Britain by Hodder & Stoughton,
an Hachette UK company

First U.S. Edition: February 2013

10 9 8 7 6 5 4 3 2

For Nick and Jacqui

PROLOGUE

The bell began to toll, and Doug Bentley was one of the first to stiffen, straighten his back, and wipe the smile from his face. The sound always killed the quiet chuckles and murmured stories. The former lance corporal in the army's Pay Corps had come to do a job, as had the friends around him. It was the forty-eighth time he had been to the town's High Street in the previous eighteen months, and he had missed only a very few of the occasions when the tenor bell, cast in 1633, had been rung with the slow, sad beat that recognised the approach of death and its cortège.

The town, its bell, the church of St Bartholomew and All Saints, and the High Street had become part of Doug Bentley's life in that year and a half and, truth to tell, he wondered sometimes how he had found any purpose in his life, since retirement, before the opportunity had arisen to make the regular journey there. He knew all about the town: the coaching inns and the fine fossils that appeared in the mud springs, the unusual architecture of the town hall, built on columns more than four centuries before and donated to the community by an earl of Clarendon . . . He knew all of these historic points because the town was now central to his existence, and Beryl seemed not only to tolerate what he did but supported it. He needed her support each time they came on the number 12 bus from Swindon – no charge because they were senior citizens. This day, as on every day he came to the town, he had checked the varnish on the staff for his standard and satisfied himself there were no blemishes; he had renewed the blanco on the large gloves he wore until they were virgin-snow white; he had buffed his black shoes, shaved carefully, and put polish on the leather support for the bottom end of the staff. Beryl had pressed his grey slacks, ironed a shirt and inspected his tie; she had brushed dandruff flecks from his shoulders, picked fluff from his beret, and made certain that the bow of black ribbon that would top the staff was not crumpled. When the bus dropped them off, she would leave him to the company of his new veteran comrades, and he would not see her again until the ceremony was finished. The bell tolled and, as always at that moment, he felt his stomach tighten.

Doug Bentley lived in a village to the east of Swindon. Beside the infant and junior school a squat brick building was home to a small community of the Royal British Legion. It could support the part-time services of a bar steward, and they had a committee that had met there, eighteen months before, and agreed that Doug Bentley, volunteer, should go to Wootton Bassett, on the far side of Swindon, to represent the branch at the next repatriation of a serviceman killed in action. The former Pay Corps lance corporal, a member of the armed forces for two years of National Service in which he had never been posted overseas and – of course – had never heard a shot fired in anger, had preened with pride at the award of this honour. That he had never been in action, or 'up the sharp end', in no way diminished, in his eyes, his right to be regarded as a veteran; he had done his time, done what was asked of him. He had the respect of his colleagues in the Legion and they'd chosen him. The same pride captivated him on this summer's day as it had on the forty-seven previous times he had made the journey there with Beryl.

He was in a line with around a dozen others. They represented the Royal British Legion branches of towns and villages as far away as Hungerford, Marlborough, Bath and Frome, and RAF Associations, Canal Zoners, one-time paratroops and . . . They formed their line just on the road, off the kerb, and crowds had gathered to press behind them. Doug Bentley thought there were more photographers and cameramen than usual. He would not have admitted it to a stranger, but he always watched the TV news on those evenings after he had returned home to see himself, and was always pleased when he went down later to the Legion if members remarked that they had seen him. They made a neat line, old men re-creating parade-ground disciplines. He could be a tough old goat, had earned his living as a long-distance haulage driver, but would admit – only to Beryl – that when the tenor bell tolled and the line was formed, his gut churned, and sometimes there was a smear of wet in his eyes.

He had read of the one who was coming home. Aged eighteen years and four months, just accepted into a Guards regiment and killed by an explosion three days earlier in bloody Helmand Province, five weeks after arriving in Afghanistan. The family, friends and supporters were dribbling out of the Cross Keys public house and were crossing the road, weaving between the last traffic that the police would allow up and down the High Street before closing it. It was a good word that was used, *repatriation*, and he liked the thought of it for a fallen squaddie. The town, Wootton Bassett in Wiltshire, with a population of about ten thousand and nothing special to say for itself, represented – as the quiet fell from a sunlit blue sky – the mourning of a nation for a soldier who had given his young life that a greater number might walk in freedom and in peace . . . Well, that was what the tabloids printed.

No more traffic now. The relatives, friends and supporters were in place, and some of the kids among them wore T-shirts with a picture of what seemed to be almost a child soldier with a smiling face and a battlefield helmet that was a size too large. They all had flowers and some had already started to weep. Every eye, and Doug Bentley's, gazed left down the street, towards the raised town hall and the top of the hill, beyond the church and its bell tower, where the road came from the RAF base into which the coffin had been flown. He saw women in floral dresses, kids in jeans and sneakers, men standing straight and clutching shopping bags, the staff of shops, banks and coffee houses, and people with dogs that sat still and quiet at their sides. Early on, Doug had realised this was no place for generals, admirals, air marshals or senior politicians. The tabloids called it 'the tribute of Middle England'.

Three police motorcyclists led the convoy, coming at a crawl, heads appearing first, then the fluorescent yellow of the shoulders and last the blue lights on their machines. The bell had stopped and the engines made a mere murmur, but the sobbing of one woman was clear. The motorcycles went on past Doug Bentley and the others, then a marked police car, but the hearse halted to the far side of the town hall and the funeral director climbed out of the front passenger seat. The local man who did the drill calls for Doug and the standard-bearer party gave the command and the dozen were raised, the tips dropped into the leather case that took their weight. He felt the sun full on him and a bead of sweat trickled down his cheek.

The funeral director wore a top hat and a morning suit; he had a fine walking staff with a silver-topped handle. As he moved forward a woman opposite Doug Bentley seemed to contract in a convulsion of tears and a man beside her, who had pink knees below the hem of his shorts, rubbed her neck gently. As the funeral director reached them, top hat now carried, the command came – softly spoken – and the standards dipped. All those years before, as a lance corporal in the Pay Corps, he had loathed drill sergeants, had been clumsy and useless at the co-ordination required, but he could do this now. The hearse eased to a halt and Doug Bentley dropped his head, as if in prayer, but he could see, beyond the glass, the closely pinned Union flag over the new clean wood of the coffin. He often wondered what they looked like, inside the shrouds and below the lids: at peace and unmarked, or mangled beyond recognition ... It was those bloody bombs that did for them: what the TV said were IEDs – improvised explosive devices. Eight out of every ten who were brought through the town on their way to the hospital in Oxford, where the post-mortems were done, had been killed by the tribesmen's bombs. Doug Bentley didn't know about war, and his military service as a conscript had been about ledgers, officers' expenses and other ranks' salaries, but men in the branch in his village, who had been in the paras or the marines, spoke of the bombs and what they did to a body. Just eighteen years old the guardsman had been, and the picture on the T-shirts showed a face that was immature, arms and legs that had most likely been skeleton thin, all ripped apart by a bomb.

He saw the mother of the boy soldier, and the middle-aged man with her stood back a half-pace. He saw the father, with a woman in black behind him . . . It always struck him how few of the dead soldiers had parents who still lived together – he and Beryl had been together for forty-six years, had reared two kids and . . . Flowers, single roses, little posies of the season's last daffodils and pretty sprays of chrysanthemums were being laid on the bonnet of the hearse, against the windscreen and on the roof. The grief was naked and raw. It hurt Doug Bentley to watch. Some of the family had laid their open hands on the glass sides as if in that way they might touch the body in the coffin.

How long were they there? A little more than half a minute.

The funeral director, who had faced the hearse, now swung round, as if he had been a military man in his time, and waved his stick dramatically. He had the top hat back on his head and started to walk forward, up the empty High Street. The hearse nudged along after him, a few of the flowers sliding into the road.

The hearse left the relatives, friends and supporters clutching each other, wiping eyes and sniffling. It edged past old men who had brought out their medals for the day, the television satellite dishes, scanner vans and cherry-picker cranes. Another police car came behind it, a back-up hearse and a four-wheel drive for the Military Police. Some, he knew, had predicted that what they called 'grief tourism' would suffer from 'fatigue', that the crowds would dwindle – but they had been bloody wrong. The kid – the guardsman with a child's face and a helmet too big for him – had been shown the same respect as any serviceman coming through six months and a year before.

Up the High Street, the hearse again stopped briefly. The funeral director and the driver gathered up what flowers had not fallen away and laid them inside with due but brief reverence. Then the party drove at growing speed, with the motorcycle escort, down the road and towards the motorway.

In the first minutes after the convoy had cleared the town, the standards were raised, then lowered, and the command was given for the old servicemen to fall out. A few words of conversation slipped between them but the appetite for jocularity and the recall of times past seemed spent. Hands were shaken and they moved off to start the journey home. The family and its party had returned to the room at the Cross Keys, where the management provided coffee and biscuits, but a few lingered outside to drag on cigarettes. Most of the crowd who had borne witness to the sacrifice of a young life in Helmand Province stood around on the pavements, as if unsure what should follow: pensioners, veterans, shop workers and the idly curious seemed reluctant to break the mood of pensive resignation and quiet ... The traffic managed that. Petrol tankers, removal lorries, supermarket delivery trucks jostled to accelerate up and down the High Street. Doug furled his standard, collapsed the staff and threaded the parts into the canvas carrying bag. He said his goodbyes, almost stepped on a single red rose and went to look for Beryl.

He went past a dry-cleaner's, a bakery, a motor-accessories business, a fish bar, the Oriental Aroma, a picture-framer and a charity shop. He remembered what someone had said about IEDs – that the bombs were a new form of warfare, more deadly than anything the army had faced in the last half-century. He knew next to nothing about explosives, but could reflect on the T-shirts and the mother's weeping. He thought that by standing in the road with his lowered standard he had played his part. And he knew he would not be able to do so much longer. They were planning to move the repatriations to Brize Norton. He dreaded that: much of the purpose of his life would be extinguished when the hearses and their escorts no longer came through Wootton Bassett. The mood of the town would never be recaptured at another location. He didn't want to think about it.

He searched for Beryl and couldn't see her. She might be in the library, or in a bank, just window-shopping or— Damn near bumped into a woman on the pavement, tears streaming down her face. Quite pretty, she might have been in her early thirties. She had fluffy blonde hair in sort of curls and her mascara was smudged. She wore a scarlet skirt that Doug Bentley reckoned was some way short of decent and a white blouse that was not buttoned high. At her neck was a thin gold chain and a pendant that spelled out her name: Ellie. Ellie cried from her soul and gazed up the road where the hearse and its escort had gone.

'Are you all right, love?'

Just a choke, as if a sob was caught in her throat.

'It's these bloody bombs,' he said. 'The bloody bombs . . . Are you family, love?'

She sniffed heavily.

He produced a handkerchief, and she blew hard into it, then used it to wipe her face. She grimaced. 'They're all heartbreaking, love,' he said. 'I'm with the Royal British Legion, represent my branch. We're here every time to show our respect . . . It's a terrible loss to you and—'

'I'm not family.'

'Just came to give them solidarity. Most people do that and—'

'They're heroes, aren't they?'

'Serving Queen and country, making the ultimate sacrifice. Heroes? Yes.'

'The bravest of the brave. Heroes, all of them.'

Doug Bentley still couldn't see Beryl. He didn't know how to react to this woman's grief. His wife wasn't there to tell him, and he thought it was probably only five minutes now until the bus left. 'Just take it one hour at a time, then one day at a time, then one week—'

'They're heroes and their families must be so proud of them.'

He saw a broad wedding ring on her hand and with it a diamond-crested engagement ring, which looked expensive. 'Are you from an army family, Ellie? Is that why you're here?'

She seemed to snort, as if the question invited derision. 'Absolutely not – no heroes among my lot. His people must feel so honoured by him.' She shrugged.

He was confused now. 'It's none of my business, and I don't want to intrude, but did you come today to be with the boy's family, show your support?'

'No . . . God, no. I was filling up with petrol, at the Shell. The road was blocked and I wandered down. Seen it on the telly, of course, but it's different when you're . . . you know . . . I'm all right now. Thanks for your time.'

She wandered away without a backward glance, and he realised Beryl was now close behind him. Ellie's backside swung as she walked.

They went for the bus, where already a good-sized queue waited. His wife told him he had been chatting up a bit of a tart. He said that one minute the woman had been in floods of tears and the next quite off-hand but jabbering about 'heroes'.

Beryl followed her with an eagle eye. 'You know next to nothing about anything, Doug,' she said. 'Not that I'm holding that against you.'

They walked together to the bus stop, her arm tucked in his.

I

An unobtrusive man, he was noticed by few of the pedestrians who shared the steps with him that climbed to the pavements of Vauxhall Bridge in the November rain. He left behind him the cream and green walls and the darkened plate glass expanses of the building that those outside the disciplines of the Service called 'Ceauşescu Towers' – the headquarters of MI6. He walked briskly. It was his job to move unseen and not to attract attention, even inside the Towers. Len Gibbons was known to few of those who passed through the security gates, morning and evening, along-side him, or shared the lift to and from the third floor where his desk, East 3-97/14, stood, or waited in the canteen lunch queue with him. The few who did know him, however, regarded this middle-grade manager as a 'safe pair of hands' and in the trade that was about as good an accolade as could be handed out. As a 'safe pair of hands', he was entitled to trust and responsibility and he had received both that afternoon at a meeting with the director general: no notes taken.

The word of the day was *deniable*. The meeting in itself was deniable, the matter discussed was deniable, and the conclusions reached were deniable. The actions that would be taken were also deniable. Len Gibbons had been called to the upper floors and briefed over a pot of tea and a shortbread biscuit. *Take the bastard down, Len, would be the vulgar way to put it. Take him down and leave him on a kerb so that his head rolls in the gutter and the blood runs down the drain. Not, of course, that we like vulgarity. We might more politely call it 'interdiction'. Actually, I prefer 'take the bastard down'. It'll be deniable. My diary has me in the Cabinet Office fifteen minutes ago, and there all afternoon. So, go to it, Len, and know that many men*

– and widows – will be cheering you on. If you bring him down there will be cheering to the rafters. It's not the sort of thing we've done in years – a first in my time – but it has my total support . . . as long as it stays deniable.

Half an hour later he had cleared his desk and, with a filled briefcase, had allowed his assistant to leave ahead of him. He had switched off the lights, locked the doors, and they had gone down to the central hall in the lift. They had swiped their cards at Security, walked out into the rain and headed for the bridge. He did not look back at the building, did not know how many days he would be away from it, and whether he would win or lose . . . But the job would get his best effort. That, Len Gibbons guaranteed.

Across the bridge, he headed for the Underground station. He preferred to mingle with the masses that crowded the trains. He bought the two tickets and passed one over his shoulder, no turn of the head, no smile, to Sarah and felt her take it quickly, discreetly. Descending on the escalator he had the briefcase held tight across his chest, his coat sleeve hanging far enough forward to mask the chain linking the handle to the handcuff attachment on his wrist. Inside the briefcase were the maps, charts and lists for coded contact that would assist towards the state-sponsored killing of an individual whose life was considered forfeit . . . all, of course, deniable.

He wore the years well, fifty-nine, and was physically fit, mentally alert, with good colour in his face. His trade demanded ordinariness rather than eccentricity, and there was little about him that those on the platform would remember: no sign of the hairstyle under the trilby and behind the beige scarf, no sight of his shirt or tie because the raincoat was buttoned high. The brief-case bore no EIIR, embossed in gold, which would have shown he was a servant of the state. If any had noted him, glanced quickly at the trilby, they might have thought him a rather boring man whose employment shelf life drifted to a close. They would have been wrong. God, in the Towers, had known Gibbons the length of his professional career, would have judged him a man of insight and acumen, but handicapped by a throw of the dice: those damned events that could derail any intelligence officer's career. He might appear a buffoon, might cultivate that image, might use it as a cover to divert attention from the reality of a stiletto-sharp mind. He trekked into the heavier rain as the afternoon closed dankly on Central London.

The Underground behind them, they passed the entrance to the Ritz Hotel, then skirted the south side of Piccadilly Circus – neither looked up at the Eros statue – and turned down into Haymarket. She came level to his elbow and murmured the number they should look for. He nodded. They were a team. The rain's drips fell regularly from his hat brim and her hair was soaked, but they made no small-talk about the awfulness of the weather. Probably her mind was swamped as his was with the enormity of what they hoped to achieve in the next hours and days – not weeks.

There was a doorway and, inside, newspapers were scattered instead of a mat. A man in commissionaire's uniform sat at a desk but they were not challenged and declined to use the lift. Instead they walked up two flights and slipped along a corridor of closed doors, none of which boasted the legend of a company or business. She had a Yale and two mortise keys out of her handbag and he stood at the side while she unfastened the door. Gibbons did not know when the Service had last used the premises, whether they were regular or occasional visitors. He assumed that a front company held the lease and that all connections to the Towers were well disguised. Old procedures died hard. No interior lights were switched on until Sarah had gone to the windows of both main rooms, the kitchenette behind a partition, the toilet and shower room and pulled down the blinds. There was a room with a desk, a chair, and a small settee for him, and a room with a desk, chair, portable TV and a folded single bed for her; there were cupboards for each of them, a safe with a combination lock. Now, the reserve on his face faded: that buzz, the adrenalin flush and the excitement surge replaced it. He was a bureaucrat and a small cog – by fate of circumstance

– between large wheels and he accepted that, but he took pride in what he did. Usually he succeeded in providing what was asked of him. Bare walls confronted Len Gibbons and a wintry smile settled on his lips. She had emptied his case of photographs and the big folded map, and had the roll of Sellotape in her hand. She did not bother to ask him where she should display the images.

A ceiling light lit the desk on which were his phone, lap-top, notebooks, pencils and the paraphernalia that travelled with him. She chose the wall in his direct eye-line as the place to stick up the photographs. Some were classified and others were not. She fastened them in the same haphazard jumble in which they had been displayed before. There were pictures of armoured vehicles, all shapes and sizes, all wrecked – some turned right over, some on their sides and some left as debris because the wheels had gone, or the tracks. The craters in tarmacked roads leading straight across flat sand landscapes were great gouges – in some a soldier could have stood, the top of his helmet hidden. Still-frames, a quarter covered with Arabic text, showed a moment of detonation that had been downloaded from websites. There were clear portraits, taken with a macro-lens in extreme close-up, of the gear used in the bombs and their sophistication. He liked to know his enemy and thought it important to display the enemy's work and skills, to have them present around him at all times . . . There were photographs from the party last Christmas at a rehabilitation home where young men with military haircuts, all amputees, waved stunted limbs defiantly at the camera . . . and there was one magnified picture of a procession, slow and black, in the High Street of a country town. He had been with the operation from the beginning and thought now that, if his Maker was willing, it approached the end. At the beginning, two years and three months before, a man had sneezed.

He might have caught the mild dose of influenza from his wife or children. He had sneezed and gone back to his labour on the electronics bench.

He did not know that the sneeze would kick-start an operation launched from a far-away city. He had been bent over the bench and was wearing the magnification optics he used when working on the software he adapted with kit brought in from the United States. From the land of the Great Satan, he could obtain dual use passive infra-red devices or high-powered cordless phones with a range of near to seven miles from a base station, and dual-tone multi-frequency gear: the PIR, HPCP and DTMF, and the zappers for unlocking car doors and . . . The Engineer used them to provide the electronic signal to improvised explosive devices and to his design of explosive formed projectiles. From the safety and security of his workshop he created the bombs that would be carried along the rat-runs that criss-crossed the border of his country with Iraq to kill and maim. The sneeze had been perfunctory, and he was able to get his handkerchief out from his trouser pocket to smother the second. He had not stopped in his work and had not thought through the consequences of that minor eruption in his nose.

Had he done so he might have realised that a fine film had scattered from his face. Some minuscule droplets had wafted down on to the bench and a few had come to rest on the circuit he was putting together.

He had gone on with his work methodically and carefully. He had built the explosive formed projectile. He had a production line in a small factory area behind his workshop and the shaped copper charge was manufactured there to high-precision standards by experienced technicians. By his late-morning break, he had completed the electronics of a killing kit capable of defeating the electronic counter-measures of his enemy, and had begun on another, using the same procedures and techniques. They could almost have been described as a signature. The device onto which he had sneezed was now sealed, boxed and ready for transportation.

He did not know that the device had failed to detonate. A 'trigger man', as the Great Satan's troops described the bomb layer and the peasant charged with firing the device, had panicked when an attack helicopter had flown low over the sand scrape in which he had hidden himself, some three hundred yards back from Highway 6, the convoy route. He had broken cover and run. Later, to gain the reward of ten American dollars, he had fabricated a story of an advancing foot patrol, the need to destroy the firing software, its burial and his flight. The Engineer did not know that the sight of the man emerging from his hiding place and sprinting towards nowhere had alerted the Apache crew: a follow-up had been mounted and the abandoned device retrieved. That had been four weeks and two days after the Engineer had sneezed at his workbench and given forensic scientists something akin to gold dust: a sample for DNA analysis.

At a laboratory in the west of England, a woman in a white suit with a face mask over her mouth and her hair in a shower-cap, would say: 'Christmas has come early. It has to be the man who put it together.' There had been a meeting of ammunition technical officers and explosive ordnance disposal experts and the intelligence had been fed to them. One, who had been to the Palace for a gallantry decoration and was said to have exhausted more lives than any streetwise tom-cat, had said, allowing himself a gallows-humour grin: 'We chance our bollocks when we're out in the donkey shit trying to defuse these things in the hope that we can get fingerprints, anything, a speck of blood, because the trigger rag-head cut himself on a thorn – and that's just to identify a foot-soldier. Here we have the DNA of the top man in the chain. We've got it on a plate. That's a hell of a start.' The chair of a committee of intelligence officers and agent handlers, gaunt from the weight of responsibility, had briefed: 'I'm assured that only a small number of men, experts in micro-engineering, are capable of making these things. As you all know, but it's worth repeating *ad nauseam*, four in every five of our own and US casualties are laid at the door of these wretched things.'

The Engineer knew nothing about the basic information his sneeze had provided. He had gone on working through a full day until a car had taken him home. He had eaten with his wife and he had told his children, Jahandar and Abbas, the ancient Persian fairy story of Simorgh, and of God's three sons, Prince Jamshid, Prince Q-mars and Prince Korshid. He had not known of the chasm he had made in his personal security when he sneezed . . . Neither did he know that fifty-one days later a slim file would be handed to a journeyman intelligence officer charged with the co-ordination of an intelligence trawl.

She had to stand on tiptoe to fasten the top corners of the map to the wall with lengths of Sellotape.

He didn't help her, but sat down and swivelled away from the pictures of bomb damage. His shoes were on the corner of the desk and his chair tilted comfortably as he gazed at the map. Because Len Gibbons had never been to Iraq, let alone visited Iran, he had little understanding of the terrain, topography and general culture of the area. There were large yellow patches – desert – and a pair of narrow green strips that represented the cultivated, irrigated areas beside the Tigris and Euphrates rivers as they came to a confluence at al-Qurnah before going south as one. There was blue for what seemed to be great inland lakes with little symbols of marshland printed on them. Across the extreme eastern corner of the water-covered area was the bold mauve line of a frontier, and almost on that line, in what was marked as Iran, there was a bold cross in black ink.

She looked at him, and he nodded, all he would offer in the way of praise but Sarah would take no offence. He was, to her, a good man to work for, and she was on board for what the operation sought to achieve. She had no qualms about its morality. She stood for a moment, hands on hips, legs slightly apart, enough to tighten the skirt across her buttocks – but it would have taken more than that to awaken any interest in him. They shared the scent of pursuit and the excitement. She went to make a cup of tea, leaving him to stare at the map.

She could remember the day when his screen had exploded

into life, when a sparse file had started to thicken. No one forgot such rare, febrile days.

It was three hundred and nineteen days after Rashid, the Engineer, had sneezed over his workbench that a man walked into the lobby of the British Consulate in the Gulf Emirates city of Dubai and requested a meeting with a diplomat.

The Engineer had gone to work late because he had spent the morning with a doctor in the town of Ahvaz. His wife had been examined because of the persistent, but still relatively mild, head-aches that sapped her concentration at work. The doctor had prescribed aspirin and rest, so Rashid had taken Naghmeh back to their new home, then set off for his bench at the small factory. He did not know that an Iranian had requested asylum from the British authorities and would therefore be challenged to explain his value. He did not know that a spook attached to the staff, oper-ating under consular cover, would say, 'You claim you are a member of the Iranian Revolutionary Guard Corps – you said your unit was from the al-Quds Brigade – but I have to ask what sort of information you might bring with you that would justify from us your asylum and safety. Facts, my friend, are the currency needed.'

And, of course, Rashid, the Engineer, did not know that a traitor who had been assigned as a guard to an inner perimeter of an Iranian Revolutionary Guard Corps camp on the road south from Ahvaz, was now in flight, and faced – if again in the custody of al-Quds – either stoning to death or strangulation at the end of a rope. Perhaps Rashid, the Engineer, had seen this guard as his Mercedes swept him through the gates of the compound; perhaps the man had swung them open and saluted. Rashid did not know that the man had denounced him because death faced him in his own country: his crime had been to defile a commander's daughter – the girl had been a willing party but now cried rape.

The man said, 'I can tell you about the Engineer who made the bombs that killed so many of your soldiers, in Maysan and Basra

Provinces, and many Americans. I can tell you who he is and
where he is from, and where is the camp that he uses for the
building of the bombs.'

And he was left in the bare interview room, with a well-muscled
security guard, while the intelligence officer composed the signal
to London that would ask whether such information was indeed
sufficient currency for a promise of asylum – only a *promise*, of
course . . . And Rashid, the Engineer, knew nothing of this.

It was fifty-one days ago – two years and six weeks after a sneeze
– that the defining moment had been reached. Sarah did not have
a photograph of the features of the bomb-maker to fasten to the
wall on his right; instead a black outline of a head and shoulders
was superimposed on a white background with a name: RASHID
ARMAJAN. The moment, savoured with strong coffee, had provided
confirmation that the DNA sample extracted from the abandoned
workings of an explosive formed projectile matched that of a
target identified by a 'walk-in' at diplomatic premises on the Gulf.
Meetings had started and Len Gibbons had bustled between
them. He had contributed little but had taken brief notes. He had
learned the requirement of his seniors and how it would be
achieved. Matters had been moved forward at a location he could
not picture and was marked in his mind only by a crude cross on
a map, but that was immaterial to him. He could reflect, gazing at
the featureless face and at the name in her bold handwriting, that
the moment had brought him considerable satisfaction. The
collection of a used cigarette end, smoked only a third down and
tossed aside, had supplied the opportunity for the moment, had
involved considerable resources, a budget allocation – all handled
by Gibbons – and manpower deployment.

He told Sarah that the positioning of the sheet of paper on the
wall was excellent, and almost smiled . . . The child molester from
the al-Quds Brigade of the IRGC had said that the Engineer was
a prolific smoker. That had been enough to determine Len
Gibbons's course of action in confirming the named target.

*   *   *

They had told Rashid and Naghmeh that the tumour inside her skull was now the size of a songbird's egg. It cut across the nerve routes that controlled speech and mobility. Her condition had deteriorated over the previous weeks, with more intense pain in her head, increased dizziness, inability to move and great tiredness. She could no longer look after her children. The doctor in Ahvaz had realised the importance of her husband and had pulled strings to raise funds for the couple to fly to Tehran for more detailed scans and biopsies. They had stayed two nights at the medical school attached to the university. Rashid Armajan could not fault the treatment and respect they were shown: an official car had met them at the airport to drive them to their accommodation and had been available to take them back for the return flight. They had sat numbed and silent on the aircraft. The enormity of what they had been told had cudgelled them.

She had gone inside their house and would be with her mother and the children now. The Engineer walked on the concrete paving in front of their home. He could see out over the water in the lagoon to the reed beds. Where there were gaps in the reeds he could see more water and the berm, which was the border, hazed in the afternoon sunshine. He lit a cigarette and dragged on it. He smoked the Zarrin brand and had deflected or ignored his wife's pleading that he should give up. His concession to her was that he did not smoke inside their home. Many men he knew believed, and told him so, that he gave up too much for her when he went outside each time he needed to smoke.

He supposed that the two medical men who had faced them across the table in the neuro wing made a habit of telling patients and their loved ones the brutal news of imminent death. It had been suggested to him that he alone should hear their verdict after the test results were back, but Rashid and his wife had refused that option. They were a partnership and a bond of love held them. They had been together when the assessment was given them. It had been done without sentiment: the condition was inoperable, given the equipment and talents available in Tehran; the condition would deteriorate rapidly and she had a few months to live. She would be dead within the year. He was forty-one and she a year younger; they had been married for fourteen years.

Tears welled in his eyes and cigarette smoke ballooned in front of his face. He wore better clothes than he would have chosen had he been in the camp at his workbench. Good trousers, a good shirt and a lightweight jacket. The sun was tilting and much of its ferocious heat was now dissipated by palm trees to his left, just short of the small barracks where his own security was housed and border guards were stationed.

An old man came towards him, bent in the back and shoulders, harmless and feeble. He carried a plastic bag in one hand and a broom of dried fronds. He crouched to pick up unseen pieces of rubbish, swept the pavement and gutter, then cleared the dried leaves that had fallen. Rashid thought he was an Arab – there were many in the region of Khuzestan. They did the menial work and had no education. In Ahvaz, some police and IRGC members thought of them as terrorists, but this was an old man and . . .

He threw down the cigarette, turned on his heel and fished in his pocket for the packet and his lighter. He looked for a kingfisher over the water and saw a heron poised and still; a hawk flew low past him. He would not accept what they had been told in Tehran. His wife and he had gripped the other's hand and she had choked a little. He had sniffed hard. It was not right that a man who worked for the al-Quds Brigade of the Iranian Revolutionary Guard Corps should show emotion and fear of death. His own father, nineteen years before, had gone into an unmarked, unlisted minefield to rescue a pupil from his school who had wandered into it after a puppy. The dog had tripped an anti-personnel device. In the end, the puppy was dead, the pupil alive. His father had tripped another mine and had lived for four or five hours. He had shown no fear from beginning to end. The hawk had gone past the barracks and the heron was in a statue pose; another cigarette was thrown down, and another lit. He would not accept that the wife of an individual of his importance could be sent home to die because of the state's medical inadequacy.

His status? He was not praised or decorated in public. If a security chief, a brigadier or general came to Ahvaz, Rashid Armajan would be an invited guest. He would sip coffee or juice and describe his newest work, the research he did and the effectiveness of the killing devices he created. He built the best. He was, almost, the father of the EFP. Many coalition troops had gone home in bags from Iraq because of explosive force projectiles that had come from his workbench. The software firing mechanisms he put in place were ahead of and defeated the electronic counter-measures they employed. He was proud to be supreme in his field. Now that Iraq was almost purged of foreign military, he concentrated on developing the roadside bombs, of great sophistication, that would be issued to units of the Revolutionary Guard Corps if his country were invaded by Americans, their poodles or the Zionists. He was also called upon to instruct leaders of the Afghan resistance in the manufacture of simpler devices, and he had heard they had learned well what he had taught them; the best of his work, as used in Iraq, would repel any invader of his beloved country. He thought his status should afford his wife the help she needed. Another cigarette was thrown down, another pack opened. He heard his name shouted.

It was part of the Engineer's status that he was allocated a personal security officer. He turned. The officer was ten or a dozen years younger and walked with a limp, but would not use a stick or crutch. He had no love for the man, objected to his constant presence round their home. He would have thought the secrecy surrounding his name, his work, made protection unnecessary, but the man was evidence of status. A stream of apologies babbled from the officer's mouth: he had been told that the Engineer and his wife were due back on the last flight of the evening from Tehran.

He said they had caught the first, that two passengers had been dumped off the manifest. His face would have shown the grimness of his news. He walked back towards the house and heard the officer, Mansoor, yell abuse at the old Arab man.

His status permitted him to demand better. He did not know

that a cigarette end had already been picked up and placed in a plastic sachet to be taken across the frontier along one of the many smugglers' routes that passed through the marshes.

He did not know that the cigarette end, with his spittle on the filter, would be flown to Europe for examination, or that men and women, privy to the result, would clap and cheer.

Sarah had come off the phone and read to Len Gibbons the dishes on the takeaway menu from the *trattoria* at the top of Haymarket. Beyond the drawn blinds, the evening had closed quickly and he thought the central heating in the suite needed a tweak – there might be a frost before morning. He was on expenses and there was a quite generous allowance for evening meals on duty, but he had never been one to abuse a system's finances. Just a pasta dish with some chicken and tomato sauce, a bottle of Italian mineral water and . . . The matter of the Engineer had seemed to be stymied, and the momentum had seemed to have died.

He had not made the presentation, but had sat silently on a hard chair in the corner while men and women of greater rank did the talking. His own section head had read verbatim from Len Gibbons's brief. The great and the good, two weeks and a day before, had cringed.

'What – go on to Iranian territory? State-sponsored terrorism, by us, inside Iran's frontiers? Ask our Special Forces to violate that hornets' nest? They'd be entitled to refuse point blank. It would be an act of war, and the consequences of failure too awful to consider. I couldn't urge my minister to permit this action, however much of our blood is on this reptile's hands. Out of the question even to consider assassinating an Iranian on his own territory. Simply not possible.'

But a woman from the Foreign and Commonwealth office rapped her pencil on the table for attention. She did liaison between the Towers and government, had grey hair styled close to her skull, a lined face and wore a blouse that some might have described as stuffy with jewellery that had probably come from a grandmother. Len Gibbons noticed her beacon eyes, jutting jaw and narrowed lips. She spoke rather quietly: 'Any former students of ancient history here done Mesopotamia? No? Well, there was a king of Babylon, Hammurabi, powerful enough to have left a Code behind him, written in Akkadian. It was passed to the writers of Leviticus, Exodus and Deuteronomy. Broadly, all those years ago, it was stated, 'An eye for an eye, a tooth for a tooth.' Legitimisation for an act of revenge. Would it not send a message if it were done with discretion? Done "somewhere", wherever "somewhere" might be. My summary: we couldn't approve any act of extra-judicial murder and would wish to separate ourselves from any such folly. We would not wish to hear any more of this nonsense. And I'm as busy as the rest of you and have other matters more pressing to concern myself with.'

He thought she caught his glance and that she winked fractionally at him, the barest flutter of an eyelid.

All except his section head and himself had left the meeting convinced that a plan of outrageous folly and illegality had been roundly squashed by the lady from the FCO.

Back in his office that evening, the daylight ebbing, his screen had lit with a message relayed from another floor of the Towers. A man had, apparently, been selling dates at a border settlement. It was a good part of the world for dates and they were a local favourite: many sellers roamed communities for the opportunity to trade.

The Engineer saw the date seller when he came out of his home and walked towards the palm tree that threw shade on the chair that the security officer, Mansoor, used. The man carried a pair of baskets, each slung from the ends of a pole that he balanced on a shoulder. The Engineer saw that Mansoor had a handkerchief on his lap and it was loaded with dates. The seller had scored once at least. When he himself was approached he waved the wretch away. He had never, of course, heard of Abigail Jones – known to a choice company as Echo Foxtrot, a code-sign for the Eternal Flame – and had never, of course, imagined that an itinerant date seller could earn five hundred American dollars for each day he spent loitering at the border settlement.

He had come back from their doctor's surgery at the hospital in Ahvaz and had received the answer that had been telephoned from the headquarters building – in the former Tehran embassy complex of the Great Satan – of the al-Quds Brigade. He had told his wife the news he had been given and they had clung to each other. She had wept on his chest and he on her shoulder, and then he had sat her by a window where a light curtain would shield her from the sun. He had come out to smoke a cigarette and inhale the relief.

The date seller had heard part of what he said to Mansoor, but the Engineer could not know that: 'A second doctor, abroad, more experienced with the brain . . . as soon as arrangements can be made because time for her is so short and . . .' He could now cling to hope, and the security officer nodded, sucked another date, then spat out the stone.

He had never spoken to Echo Foxtrot – the Eternal Flame. Had he, Len Gibbons would have congratulated her without reservation, and if the information had come at a cost of five hundred American dollars a day then it was cheap. The Yanks would likely have paid five times that for it and thought it a bazaar bargain.

It was the end of their day. She would guard the phones during the night and use the collapsible bed, and he would go to his club: not the Travellers or the Reform or the Garrick, but one that specialised in discounts for couples from the old empire. Sarah had cleared away their supper and the tinfoil would go into a rubbish bag, which he'd take down to the security desk when he left for his accommodation. His last job before shutting down for the evening was to make phone calls. The list in front of him was written in her neat hand. The number of the American who would be waiting in his office on a side-street off Grosvenor Square and, further west, that of the Israeli in the fortified wing of their place in Kensington abutting the park. Both men would be similar to himself: facilitators, not movers and shakers. They were functionaries, the oil in the wheels that made things happen. After that

– their photographs were on his desk and later they would go on the wall – two more men would be contacted.

It was rare for Len Gibbons to entertain ideas that were not necessary to the business in hand. He lifted the photographs in turn, one of a younger man and one of an older, and held them where she could see them. Ridiculous, unnecessary, but he did it. 'For you and me, Sarah, our moment in the spotlight is nearly over. We'll be moving into the wings and it'll be their turn to hog the stage . . . If they're any good, we'll win. If they're not, we'll . . . I hate to think of the end game if they're not good enough and where they'll be. Anyway . . .'

'I'm sure they're good men,' she said gently. 'The best available.'

He reached for his phone. 'Which they'll need to be.'

He was a star, his exceptional abilities accepted by all who came into professional contact with him. He knew the range of his talents and treated less skilled 'croppies' with disdain, something near to contempt: he had childhood friends, no boozing pals. The best relationship currently in his life was with his 'oppo', Ged. There were some on the team who murmured, behind their hands, that Ged deserved beatification for tolerating 'stags' with that 'cocky little prick', but everyone acknowledged that Danny Baxter – called Badger to his face – was the bee's bollocks when it came to the arts of working in a covert rural observation post, where he and Ged huddled against the elements on a freezing night, halfway up a valley's slopes in the hide they'd built.

Aged twenty-eight, and still nominally a policeman, Badger had been transferred the previous year to the surveillance teams of Box – their call-sign for the Security Service. There was always work for the men, precious few women, who were best at 'shitting in a bag' and whose creed was to take in and take out: then excrement went into nappy bags, their urine into plastic milk bottles, and they left behind no sign of their presence. Badger and Ged's stag in the hide had less than fifteen minutes to run. Their effectiveness was already stretched to the limit and they had been there since a little before first light. The darkness was well set now and the rain was coming down hard. It buggered their efforts to keep the 'scope's lens clear, and the audio stuff was on the blink. He'd give the guy on maintenance, back in the police station at Builth, serious hassle for the audio's failure and won no friendships there, but he couldn't give a damn.

They were off the Beulah to Abergwesyn road and overlooked a track that led down to a farm that had a field with a half-dozen fixed-site mobile homes, holiday caravans. Three that week were taken by eight Muslim kids from north Luton. That day there had been physical-endurance stuff, filling big rucksacks with stones and cantering up steep fields, scattering the sheep, and they'd done jerks like they had a physical-education pamphlet around. They must be thick. The farmer who owned the caravans had a nephew in the Birmingham Police and had rung in to report his guests' behaviour . . . Always the way with town people, believed that the countryside had no eyes. They could have run round the streets of north Luton and not been noticed.

It had been a good stag for Badger and Ged. The hide was close to two hundred yards from the caravans, up the hill on the far side of the valley. They'd crawled into the gorse from where the sheep had grazed in summer and tunnelled through it – it was a useful hide because none of the outer foliage was disturbed. Both wore issue gillie suits that broke up the lines of their bodies, and similar headgear. Badger had made his own, and when Ged was assigned to him he'd told the man, four years older than himself, that what he'd concocted was crap and had made him a new one. The others on the team were astonished that the 'arrogant bastard' had done something for someone else, and the new camouflage headgear was best grade. Their faces, beneath the scrim netting that hung over their eyes, mouths and noses, were smeared with cream in green and black slashes, and the 'scope's lens had more scrim over it . . . The bloody rain dripped on them.

It had been a good stag – good enough to justify the damp and the hunger: they'd eaten only a muesli bar each over a fifteen-hour period and drunk minimum water. Badger had identified the natural leader among the Muslim kids – bad not having the audio working, but the 'scope lens was enough to sort out the men from the boys. There was one to whom the others seemed to respond: he gave the instructions, didn't do the runs up the hill with a weighted rucksack. He was a tall man, wore hiking boots, jeans and a heavy anorak; he didn't have the trademark beard of a jihadist or the close-cropped skull. He wore thick rimless spectacles and might have been a library supervisor or a junior accountant – could have been anything – which meant he had worked on his anonymity with the help of a razor.

Badger wasn't armed and Ged had a disabling spray canister on his belt under the gillie suit; the power of the 'scope's Leica lens, and the 500-ml one on the camera, meant they didn't have to be closer. There was support at the pick-up point, with Glocks and H&Ks, but that was down on the road and in a lay-by closer to Beulah than Abergwesyn. The kids from Luton would have been fired up with holy-war stuff, and the discovery of a covert team watching them would have bred – no argument – angst, and from angst came violence, and from violence came a knife and a bared throat when a victim's head was yanked back. The lenses they had been issued with meant they could stay a decent distance back, up the hillside, and do their business and . . . It was useful intelligence they had gained, and they had high-quality pictures and the number-plates of a Transit van that would be picked up when it was back on the road. Then it would be urban surveillance, and the guy with the rimless spectacles would be flagged for major attention. They'd each used a plastic bag, tinfoil and three bottles. Ged was wriggling to get them into the Bergen.

The leader guy and one of the others had been outside a caravan, had stood and shivered – the 'scope's night-vision attachment had shown this to Badger – and must have talked, something serious and not to be shared. Badger and Ged had identified a lieutenant, more trusted than the others, and could match up the night-vision image with the pictures taken in daylight so that he, too, could be marked out for extra attention. There was a scenario: in it, the leader and his right-hand guy did the speeches, talked of the sacrifice and might even have chatted up the prospect of the famous Seventy-two – the virgins waiting for a dismembered suicide warrior behind the gates into Paradise. Then they slid away and left the bastard dosed up with fervour to walk on to a train or a bus or into a shopping mall. Leaders and lieutenants did not do explosive vests wrapped round their own chests. The rest of the group would be fodder for the tailor who made the vests and wove into them the pouches for the ball bearings, screws, tacks and razor slivers, but they'd likely be rendered harmless if the top man and his bag-carrier were taken down at the knees.

Lights burned now in two of the caravans and the booking with the farmer was until the following day. He reckoned the lads would be gone at first light. There'd be one surveillance vehicle facing down into Builth, another towards Abergwesyn and a biker was floating.

They left the way they had come, and not even the farmer who had made the first call and who had worked that hillside with his dogs and sheep would have seen a sign of their approach or their departure, or noticed anything disturbed in the gorse.

In the back office of the police station, where local priorities were listed on a poster as combating anti-social driving and curbing speeding on the Llanwrtyd Wells road beyond Beulah, the staff had all gone home. They did the debrief and the pictures were downloaded on to a laptop and . . .

'There was a message for you, Badger.' The team was run by a an officer from the Box and he'd looked pleased to have the clear-cut portraits of the guy in the rimless glasses. The tails were waiting to track them back into Luton where the van had been hired. 'A call for you.'

He was looking for a shower, and a meal to warm his guts, and his bed in the small hotel where they were billeted – and where they were thought to be from a flood-prevention unit. He took the piece of paper from the hand offering it and shoved it into his smock's inner pocket.

'I'd read it if I were you, Badger, and I'd call them.'

He hadn't taken it out again. 'Actually, boss, I've done a bloody long stag – and a pretty good one for results. A wash, food and bed are my priorities. Who called?'

'I'm not your fucking answer-phone, young man. A guy from Six, actually. From the dirty-raincoat crowd south of the river. Maybe he wants to take you off our hands. I'd say that work from Six would suit anyone with as high an opinion of themselves as you, because it would be exacting and likely tax a genius. We'll miss you. Do me a favour? Just ring him.'

He called the number, and it was answered. He said who he was and that he was replying to the call. He'd expected to be told why he'd been singled out, but heard a monotonously flat voice tell him where he should be and when. There were no plaudits, just brusque business. He said, into the phone, 'If it's a job for crop-pies, I like to work with my mate as oppo. He's Ged . . .' The suggestion was ignored. The voice repeated where he should be the next day, and at what time.

Others around him drank gin, but Joe Foulkes stayed with the tonic. He had been invited to spend a full day with the battalion's Recce Troop, then stay the night in the officers' mess. He always enjoyed time spent with any of the Parachute Regiment's specialist units, found them receptive to the experience he had accumulated in a career of covert surveillance in UK conditions, through the four seasons, in rural and urban locations. They'd enjoyed his anecdotes over the meal . . . it had been a good day.

The man who called him gave no name but instead offered the Box's *poste restante* number, a code good enough to tell him the Secret Intelligence Service had sought him out. After a surpris-ingly brief exchange of pleasantries – barely civil – he was told he should be at Northolt main gate, the guardroom, no later than 07.30 hours. He had started to explain that the call had reached him at the mess of the Parachute Regiment, 2nd Battalion, which was – didn't the man know? – in Colchester, a hell of hike from the other side of London that would mean a bloody awful early rising, but his destination was repeated and the time at which he was expected. Then the call was terminated. He had not taken offence, and was more than interested that Six wanted his knowledge first hand.

He thought of himself, at fifty-one, as a bit of a legend in the field. Joe Foulkes had been a policeman since the age of eighteen, and a surveillance expert for more than twenty-five years; he had a good command of one of the more impenetrable languages on the planet and had, therefore, many seams of information ready for mining and extraction. That day he had been back to his first love. He seldom used it for real, these days, but he kept his veteran gillie suit in the boot of his car and always brought it out when he gave lectures and supervised field exercises. He had worn it when he had lectured Recce Troop, and his audience of young soldiers had been rapt.

He'd said, out in the rain and scrub beside the shooting ranges, that the basics should always be observed, and he'd used the buzz words that anyone attempting rural surveillance, in Iraq, Afghanistan or Northern Ireland, should have at the forefront of their mind. The outline of the human body was so distinctive that its *shape* must always be broken. *Shadows* were an aid, and should be hugged. The biggest giveaway, unprofessional and unforgivable, was the *silhouette*. Any kit *surface*, the bulk of binoculars or the length of a spotter 'scope, must be broken up. When a team moved, *spacing* was critical. The last of his six bullet points was *smell*: he'd talked of how long it lingered on open ground if there was no wind, and not just fags, toothpaste and weapons oil but the insect repellent you needed to keep man-eating Iraqi mosquitoes at bay. They were terrific, those young fellows, and they gave him respect.

He'd ended the outside session with a popular theme: how useless the Americans were – and the story of the FBI agent in the hunt for a red-neck abortion-clinic bomber in the mountains of North Carolina. The agent was supposed to be on a covert lie-up and had freaked out because he couldn't take the darkness or the silence. Another, from Alcohol, Tobacco and Firearms, had started to shriek because he wasn't permitted, in his hide, to smoke his daily ration of Marlboro Lite . . . And a sheriff's deputy, gone for a week's duty in a forest, had broken his spectacles on the first day out: he hadn't brought a spare pair and could barely see his hand in front of him for the rest of the stag. If Foulkes had been talking to an American audience, then FBI, ATF and the deputy would have become British, and if it had been Germans, the miscreants would have been Poles. It had been a good dinner and he had felt valued. At the table, they called him by the name he'd been given a couple of decades earlier: he was 'Foxy' Foulkes.

He'd wandered away from the group, had faced a fading print of paras in the heat of Aden, snapped more than forty-five years earlier before any of his hosts were born. He'd taken the call and felt perplexed by its brevity, the lack of information, but elated. The mood had stayed with him during the rest of the evening, but there was an early start and he needed some sleep before the wake-up call and the long drive. Now he thanked them, grimaced, and said something about an old dog needing its rest. A major asked him for his card: 'Difficult to get hold of you, Foxy, through the proper channels. Prevarication and obfuscation at every corner. We've really benefited from your time and would like you back. The boys enjoyed it hugely, and learned a great deal.'

'Delighted to.' He took out his wallet. He fingered in the pouches for his card and a photograph floated down to the carpet. A lad crouched, picked it up and glanced at it. There was an admiring nod as it was handed back to him. 'That your daughter, Foxy? Pretty girl.'

He flushed, then pride caught him. 'My wife, actually.'

'Lucky you. Congratulations.'

Foxy Foulkes warmed. 'Yes, we've been together seven years – second time round for me and the same for her. Frankly, we make a good pair. She works in navy Procurement in Bath. I think we can say, no hesitation, we're both happier than we've ever been. I've felt blessed every day since I met Ellie. We complement each other. As you say, I'm lucky to be with her. Anyway, time for bed, if you don't mind.'

He wouldn't call her that night – she didn't like to be disturbed late if he was away. He would call her in the morning. Truth was, he yearned to call her and drop a hint that it was secret business he was wanted for, but she'd be sharp with him at this time. She would have been impressed, of course, if he'd called her with his news, but it was too late. He couldn't imagine why he was wanted by Six at short notice and at an airfield. What for? Where?

2

A man with an angular face and a weary voice had greeted him. He seemed to have the organisation in hand and had told him, 'I understand people call you 'Badger'. If you have no particular hostility to the name then that's what we'll use. If you don't know somebody's name and title – and you don't know mine – what would you call them?'

He'd said that if he didn't know the name of a man who ran a show he'd refer to him as 'boss'.

'Oh, I'd like that . . . and over there, that's Foxy. I don't think anyone else will need identifying. Foxy and Badger. Very good. We'll talk a bit when we get there, but in the mean time I'd be grateful for your patience.'

They had been led by ground crew towards the Lear jet, its engines ticking over and the steps down. All bizarre, but Danny 'Badger' Baxter was not one to be fazed by lack of information. The flight was smooth, they were above the clouds and. . . .

He had shown his documentation at the gate, and the RAF police hadn't jotted down any of the details listed on his Box ID. He'd been told to park his wheels in a space outside the perimeter fence, like no one wanted to acknowledge that he had ever been here. Then he'd been taken in a minibus to a prefabricated departure annex. He was half dead on his feet, had left Builth before five, reached the airbase a half-hour before dawn and hadn't spoken to either of the other men waiting for the flight call. He had almost been asleep when the boss had spoken to him.

When he'd left home to take up the work in Wales, locked the door of his bed-sit in the hostel the police used in Bristol, he had been wearing clothes that could either be described as rugged or vagrant's gear, but he had clean socks and underpants that probably stifled most of the smell; he looked ragged, and felt out of sorts because of it. He'd noted that the other two had eyed him as if they expected dog-shit on his shoes and fleas in his clothing. He was unshaven and hadn't run a comb through his hair.

It was a black-painted American aircraft, with no markings that he'd seen. The pilot spoke with a drawl and dispensed minimal information. How long would they be up? Wasn't told. What was the flight's destination? Wasn't told. Would there be in-flight coffee and a bacon sarnie? Wasn't told. The boss sat in the front seats, and across the aisle from him there was a heavy-set guy, who also had an American twang but a more civilised one than the pilot's. There wasn't a girl with a coffee jug or anything to eat. The remaining passenger, Foxy, had what Baxter reckoned was a death pallor, and there were nicks on his throat, from shaving; one had transferred blood to the collar of his clean shirt. He wore a blazer, and the tie knotted at the collar might have been a military one; his hair was neatly cut and brushed, his slacks had knife creases and his shoes were polished. Badger didn't own a blazer, had precious few shirts that were smart enough for a tie, and the only one of those easily at hand in the hostel would have been black – for funerals. The man had looked exhausted in the departure area, out on his feet, and by the time they had been up a half-hour a gentle rhythmic snoring was coming from Foxy's den. Badger knew about foxes, had often enough lain up in hides at the edge of woodland to watch a remote house. The foxes, cubs and adults, would come close to him and scratch for worms or sniff around him. He was fond of them.

There weren't many that Danny Baxter was fond of. His father and mother lived in the shadow of the nuclear-warhead factory at Burghfield, near Reading, in Berkshire, had a bungalow there and a second-hand vehicle business. He reckoned the location, close to Armageddonville, meant they'd picked up a property cheap to live in and work from. He saw them no more than twice a year and there was nothing of his work he could talk about and nothing of their lives that he was much interested in.

No one at the hostel would have cared that he was being ferried – destination unknown – in an executive jet, and probably by now his regular oppo, the faithful Ged, would be heading east to Leeds in Yorkshire where he was based. He would be thinking more about how much of his gear he could get into the washing-machine than about where Badger was going.

No woman to care . . . There had been Fran – 'Frances' to her developer father who owned the harbour-side flat overlooking the water in the Bristol dockland. She'd been a third-year student, history of art, at the university and might have found him exciting, might have craved a bit of rough. They'd been together a bit more than six months but it was never going to last. No row, no flying plates: he'd left a note for her one day, propped on her pillow, which had an epic view over the water. *Keep safe, have happy times, and best luck, Badger.* He'd loaded up his big Bergen and a little rucksack, all he owned in the world, closed the door, locked it, put his keys through the letterbox and tripped down the stairs to the little van, nondescript, that he used, and driven out of her life to the hostel. A bloody awful exchange, but the time had arrived when she might have thought him right for moulding to her style or chucking out. He had done it in his own time and at his moment of choosing.

About the only thing that owned Danny 'Badger' Baxter was the job. It ruled him. It exerted enough of a pull that he wasn't concerned that no one had told him where they were going, when or why.

The man in front – Foxy – still snored.

He was woken by the steepness of the descent. They had come through the cloud, and there was a cross-wind, but the pilot flew as if he had the controls of a fighter aircraft. The lights for belt-fastening were late coming on, and Joe Foulkes was jolted forward in his seat, damn near catapulting into the back of the one immediately in front – the man sitting in it had introduced himself as Gibbons. He'd only given his name to Foxy, not to the fellow in the back who looked like a tramp waiting for a night shelter to open. He hadn't spoken to Ellie that morning – hadn't wanted to from the prefabricated lounge. He hadn't had the bottle to explain he was on a magical mystery journey to God alone knew where and wouldn't be home that night. If he had made the call, explained he would be absent again, he would have listened to the inflections in her voice, whether she seemed to regret it, whether she was indifferent or unable to disguise a riffle of anticipation because he would be away. But he had sent a text: *Tied up workwise/called away/will ring when possible/luv massive Foxy*. One had come back before they'd boarded: *Shame – missing you. Love, Elliexxx*. His phone was off now, would stay that way till whatever, wherever, whenever had been done.

He assumed he was to give a lecture. What else did he know? He knew that the greeter from Six might be the man of the moment and in charge, but he was shit-scared, halfway to terrified, of flying – Foxy could see the way the fists held the arms of the seat and the face was white. He knew that his best instincts were usually the first ones, and he had formed an immediate dislike of Badger, but that could be managed: his own age and seniority would determine they were not equals. He would have rank on the younger man, whose appearance was simply inappropriate and—

It was the sort of landing an aircraft might have made on a carrier's deck: abrupt, short on the taxi, jerking to a stop. The big sign over a distant terminus was just recognisable as 'Prestwick', and a helicopter was waiting close by on an empty desert of wet concrete. Its rotors idled, then picked up speed as the Lear's engines were shut down. The pilots came out of their cockpit door, and the main man – the one who'd have had battlefield wings over Kuwait or out of Da Nang – spoke briefly to the American passenger. He didn't make eye contact with any of the others. Joe 'Foxy' Foulkes had several failings but idiocy was not among them. The helicopter, like the Lear, was black-painted, he could see no flight-designation markings, and they were a hell of a way from the tower and the Prestwick buildings, out of sight and out of mind. He reckoned this was a flight that had never taken place.

They came on to the apron and scurried for the chopper. The rotors blew rain into their faces, and a crewman gave them a hand up into the hatch door. They strapped the harnesses into place. The military canvas bucket seats and the frames hurt Foxy's thighs. It was years since he had been in the close confines of a helicopter's cabin, with the noise growing until the ear baffles were passed to them – hadn't been in a helicopter since leaving the base at Basra after a four-month tour seven years back. A shitty place, horrible and . . .

A man who might have been Middle Eastern stared at him warily and didn't respond to Foxy's cautious smile: short, dark-haired, swarthy and stinking of cigarettes; the Six man, Gibbons, had tried to take the fellow's hand but it had stayed buried in a pocket. The other, taller and pale-skinned, with curly blond hair, lolling comfortably and chewing gum, was late thirties or early forties – Foxy recognised the military uniform of mufti: a double-breasted navy suit with a prominent stripe, black ankle boots and a waxed jacket that might have been useful out on a moor. The eyes seemed distant and didn't focus on trivia, such as what Foxy wore, Badger's messy hair or the white knuckles of the Six man. They lifted sharply.

They were in cloud, buffeted by winds, and the pilot made no effort to get below the weather, above or round it. They rocked and shook, and Foxy wondered if the intelligence officer might throw up. He played games in his mind. A business heavy in secrecy and international flavours: it reeked of deniability. He supposed that at Six, if they planned a deniable operation, they dusted down a cardboard file that would have been written in the fifties or sixties and dictated a quiet, remote location suitable for briefings, lectures and . . . The Mull of Kintyre helicopter crash had taken the lives of police and intelligence officers from Northern Ireland who were heading for a meeting at a garrison camp close to Inverness; the various arms had needed to be brought to neutral territory if jealousies and conceits were not to stymie co-operation. Perhaps tensions and stress points were yet to be revealed. Foxy almost chuckled.

The beast seemed to stumble through the cloud. Then – it might have been thirty minutes after take-off – light flooded through the small porthole windows, and rain distorted the view, but Foxy made out the shape of a castle keep in grey stone that matched the cloud. There was more grey from the breaking waves in a bay, and from the stones on a geometrically curved beach. Back from the sand and shingle, a field was half flooded, and behind it a grand house, on three floors, with a portico. Could they not have booked a house in south-west London – or anywhere north of the capital but closer? It spoke of delusions. They were down, but the engines were not killed.

He was last out of the hatch and the crewman steadied him as he jumped clear. The others were ahead and hurried between the puddles towards the main entrance where the rendering was chipped.

Out in front, moving easily and light-footed, was Badger. The American and the foreigner kept pace with him. Foxy felt the rotors' pressure blasting him from behind and staggered as the beast, anonymous and black, rose again and headed back over the bay. Gibbons was beside him.

'Why this place?' Foxy might have nudged a hint of sarcasm into his tone. The outside of the edifice seemed to drip water from roof gullies and guttering, and he expected that half as much again would be falling through the ceilings into the salons and bedrooms. He held tightly to his bag and thanked the Lord he always packed more socks, smalls and shirts than he anticipated needing. All of them had overnight bags except Badger, who likely stank and would be higher by the evening.

'Not down to me. He who pays the piper calls the tune – know what I mean?'

He blinked in the rain. 'I don't.'

'All in good time, Foxy – if you don't mind the familiarity. It's always best if names are in short supply. Our esteemed colleague from the Agency is paying the piper. The Americans are doing the logistics, which means their bucket of dollars is deeper than our biscuit tin of sterling. It's the sort of place that appeals to them.'

'And people live here – survive here?'

'There is a life form in the Inner Hebrides that probably needs to huddle for comfort in the kitchen. I'm assured we won't be disturbed by the family. Truth is, for this one the piper needs quite a bit of paying because it's not the sort of thing – Monday through Friday – we usually do. Let's get out of this bloody weather.'

They went in through the high double doors, but no warmth greeted them. Foxy had good eyes and a good memory, and his power of observation in poor light was excellent: he noted the washing-up bowl in the centre of the tiled floor, the portrait of a villainous-looking kilted warrior above the first bend in the stairs, the faded pattern on the couch, that the paint was off all the doors, the smell of dogs and overcooked vegetables, an older man in earnest conversation with the American and a woman with bent shoulders, a thick sweater and a bob of silver hair. The rain beat on the door behind them, water dripped into the washing-up bowl and Badger sat on the bottom stair, showing no interest in anything around him. Foxy noted all of it.

The voice of the greeter was soft in his ear: 'Their grandson was Scots Guards in Iraq, attached to Special Forces, didn't survive the tour. They'd want to help and, as I said, the Americans have a deep bucket. Improvised explosive device, on the al-Kut road. You're going to hear a bit about improvised explosive devices, but I'm getting ahead of myself.'

Foxy said vacuously, 'I have some experience, but this should be interesting . . .'

The man laughed without mirth, and Foxy couldn't see what had been funny about his remark – about anything to do with improvised explosive devices.

When the Engineer worked in his laboratory, or was on the factory floor checking the craftsmanship of the machine-tool work, he could escape from the enormity of the crisis that had settled on him. It was like the snowclouds that built up over the mountains beyond Tehran when winter came. When he played with the children he could briefly think himself free. When he walked on the track in front of his home and watched the birds hovering, swirling and wafting, there were moments when the load seemed to slip away. When he was at his bench, working on the use of more ceramic material to replace metal parts and negate the majority of the portable detectors . . . When he was out on the long straight tracks that had been bulldozed beyond the camp into wilderness and studied the capability of his radio messages to beat the electronics deployed against him, he sometimes forgot . . . The moments never lasted. There was laughter, rarely, and there were smiles, sometimes, and there were those times that the work was successful beyond dreams – countermeasures failed, detonation was precise and a target was destroyed in testing – but every time the cloud formed again, and the pleasure of achievement was wiped out. He could see the ever-growing weakness in his wife, the depth of her tiredness, and could watch the bravery with which she put on a show of normality. She was dying, and the process would each day be faster, the end nearer.

He could not acknowledge it to her, but he realised his fingers were clumsier and his thoughts more muddled. He suffered. He couldn't picture a future if – when – she was taken. Only once had he called in the debts owed him by the revolution of 1979 when the Ayatollah had left Paris and flown back to his people. He had been nine years old and had watched the television with his father, who taught mathematics in Susangerd, as the Imam Khomeini had come slowly down the aircraft's steps.

He had been three years older, and had wept when his father had dragged him back into their home: he had been about to join the child volunteers who would be given the 'key to Paradise' in exchange for clearing the minefields laid by the Iraqi enemy, making safe passage for the Revolutionary Guard Corps and the Basij militia. His father had locked him into a room and not permitted him to leave the house for a week. He had gone back to school and there had been many empty places in the classroom. It had been said that when they had ran across mined ground they were killed by the explosions, their body parts scattered, that rats and foxes had come to eat pieces of their flesh. It had also been said that on the third day of the clearance operation the children, his friends from school, had been told to wrap themselves in rugs and roll across the dirt so that their bodies stayed together, were easier to collect after the line had moved forward.

He resented not having a plastic key to Paradise. He did not believe the lie of foreigners that a half-million had been imported, at a discount rate for bulk, from a Taiwan factory.

He had been twenty-two years old, a second-year student of electronic engineering at the Shahid Chamran University in Ahvaz, when his father had died. The martyr Mostafa Chamran, educated in the United States and with a PhD in electrical engineering, had fallen on the front line and was revered as a leader and a fighter. There had been many around him to whom Rashid could look for inspiration, living and dead. He was the regime's child and its servant, and he had gone where he was directed, to university in Europe and to the camps in his country where his talents could be most useful on workbenches. This once he had called in the debt.

In the afternoon he would be on the road that led away from Ahvaz towards Behbahan. A new shipment of American-made dual-tone multi-frequency equipment had come via the roundabout route of Kuala Lumpur, then Jakarta, and he would test it for long-distance detonations. The Americans, almost, had gone from Iraq, but it was the Engineer's duty to prepare the devices that would destroy any military advance into Iran by their troops. He would be late home, but her mother was there – the message had come by courier the evening before.

Neither he nor his wife ever used a mobile telephone. In fact, the Engineer never spoke on any telephone. No voice trace of Rashid Armajan existed. Others communicated for him from his workshop, and he used encrypted email links. Messages of importance were brought by courier from the al-Quds Brigade garrison camp outside Ahvaz. One had come the previous evening.

He and Naghmeh should be prepared to leave within the week. Final arrangements were being confirmed. He was not forgotten, was honoured. The state and the revolution recognised him. At his workbench, out of sight of others, he prayed in gratitude. Was there anything another doctor, a superior consultant, could offer? Would a long journey weaken her further and bring on the end? But the courier had brought a message that gave hope. He saw death on Internet screens and from recordings on mobile phones. The killings were caused by his own skills. He lost no sleep over that knowledge, but had not slept well since the Tehran doctors' verdict when he had seen the bleakness in their eyes. Now hope, small, existed.

They would be in God's care.

'Before we concentrate on the individual who has brought us together today, who and where he is, there's something I'd like you both to respond to. First you, Foxy. In your long surveillance career, what was your most satisfying achievement?'

It was, of course, a trick question, and it was not unique to Len Gibbons. He'd heard it put twice during his thirty-five years at Six, in seminars when individuals were being evaluated. The answer usually revealed much about the subject.

They were sitting in a horseshoe on hard chairs, and no notes were taken, but away to the side a board was balanced against the back of an armchair, covered with a drape. He sat at the extreme left, and had introduced himself as 'Len'. The American was 'the Cousin' and the Israeli, from Unit 504 of Military Intelligence, was 'the Friend'. There was Foxy and there was Badger, and between them the tall, handsome, suited man, 'the Major'. There had been time for them to go to allocated rooms, have a tepid wash, meet a pack of Jack Russells and spaniels, and drink instant coffee from petrol-station mugs.

Then Gibbons had shepherded them into what might have been a ballroom – no water came through this ceiling – where the main furniture was cloaked in dust-sheets, but at the far end, to the left of a huge, unlit fireplace, there was a small table with a vase of flowers on it and a silver-framed photograph of a young face smiling above a Guardsman's ceremonial tunic. Gibbons thought it appropriate, and would refer to it. He had set out the chairs while the others were on the first floor – had borrowed enough from the dining room. He had gone to the sister service across the river, the Box, the anti-terrorist command and the Branch. The Box had come up with Badger, and Special Branch had said that Joe 'Foxy' Foulkes was the only one worth considering.

It was a good question because it gave a man enough rope either to climb to a higher level, or to hang himself. He saw Foxy – a capable man with a number of successes behind him – stiffen. Well, he would be evaluating the audience of Gibbons, the Cousin and the Friend, and wondering what Badger's take on it would be. Gibbons knew the record of Foxy Foulkes: a policeman of thirty-three years, a nine-year spell with Special Branch, four months in Basra, and a further seven years of lecturing in the arts of covert rural surveillance. He was a man who expected to be listened to and was.

Foxy's tongue flipped over his lips to moisten them. Gibbons saw that. The tie was straightened, which bought another few seconds, then a cough to clear the throat. The man was dependent on his instinct.

Foxy said, in a good clear voice, as if they were his students, 'Satisfying, yes? Interesting one. There've been a few – more than a few. Could be when I was with the Branch and we were doing the business on two Iranian attachés on a Manchester visit they'd made twice before. Our stake-out was on a golf course and there was snow on the ground. I had a youngster with me, didn't know his arse from his elbow, and we came in close enough to see the drops on their noses when they did their contact – a Muslim kid working in the club's kitchens. We did the approach so that not a flake of snow was disturbed within the arc of their vision . . . Yes, that was a pretty good one . . . And early in my time with West Yorkshire we had a budding PIRA cell on our patch. The Irish were clever by then and knew the procedures.

They had a meeting and stood out in the middle of a football pitch. There was no way we could get close enough with a directional microphone. I had the answer. I picked the lock of the groundsman's hut, took out the line marker after filling it with the white stuff and went right round them, then did the goal areas. By the time they were used to me I pushed the marker right up the halfway line and they actually apologised for being in my way and stepped aside. They'd been swapping phone numbers, so we had those and bust them up. And another. I did a hide in County Tyrone, up by the village of Cappagh, which was difficult country, populated with very difficult and very suspicious people. The hide was in a hedgerow and looked into a cattle barn where a Barrett .50-calibre was hidden. We thought it needed the human touch, not a remote camera. I'd dug the hide out and the first afternoon a sheep got caught in the hedge not fifteen yards from me. The farmer, a committed Provo, considered reliable enough to have responsibility for the weapon, came up to free the ewe. He walked right over my hide and his wellington boots would have been less than two feet from my face in the camouflage headgear. It was an exceptional hide and we were able to report when the weapon was moved, but the military weren't fast enough and lost its tail. Anyway, they were three of the best.'

Did the man expect a ripple of applause? He might have done and, if so, was disappointed. The Cousin gazed at the ceiling, the Friend at the floor. The Major had been paring his nails but now reached down to the case resting against his ankles and started to ferret in it. Len Gibbons wished fervently that Sarah was there, with her competence and reassurance. It was ridiculous that the players should have been carted up to this pile of old stone, but the Cousin must have felt this to be a once-in-a-lifetime opportunity for baronial glory, and the Friend had demanded remote anonymity. He thought the old couple would be rattling around in another wing, and had learned that a divorced daughter lived with them. She would have been the mother of the officer killed by a roadside bomb, and he wondered what delicacies would be provided at the lunch break. Time to ask the other man the question designed to disrobe, expose.

'Thank you, Foxy – very comprehensive. So, Badger, what in your professional career are the achievements that give you most satisfaction?'

The man looked straight at him, unwavering eyes, direct and challenging. 'None, boss, and I don't send hero-grams to myself.'

Silence. Len Gibbons realised he'd win nothing more from the younger man, no point in demanding it, and he thought Badger had played with Foxy's ego, tossed it up into the air, let it fall on the bare patch of carpet and ground a heel on it. The veteran had laid out the depth of his experience, put it in a showcase so that the rookie boy was bound to fall short. Each had done well and, like two dogs, they'd circled each other, hitched up a back leg and pissed on the available lamp-posts. He wondered how they would do together.

Gibbons said, 'A difficult moment now confronts us. We will soon enter realms of great secrecy. You will have seen its quality – the secrecy, this place, your journey here. You both come with your praises sung, but after we begin the briefing process it's too late for one of you to say, 'I don't think I really want to pull the shirt on for this game.' Put crudely, you either piss now or get off the pot. Are you in, gentlemen, or out? Foxy, first – are you staying or going?'

'You've put me in a difficult position. I don't know what you're asking of me. I'm a married man, the wrong side of fifty. I'd have appreciated the chance to talk to my wife but . . . I'm staying.'

'And you, Badger?'

'I go where I'm sent.' Again there was a spark in the young buck's face and a short, wintry grin.

Gibbons said, 'It starts now with a young woman, call-sign Echo Foxtrot, and those are the initials of Eternal Flame, which some colleagues call her because the Eternal Flame never goes out. It's a little joke – a joke because it's so inappropriate in her case. She's out a great deal more often than is usually sensible.

Step by step, gentlemen, but we'll start with her and she'll lead us to the meat. So, Echo Foxtrot . . .'

For her and for the guys with her, known to her inner circle – those entrusted with life-and-death confidences – as the Jones Boys, it was a half-hour of maximum danger. They had been at the roadside, in the shade of some trees, in excess of thirty minutes. Their two SUVs, Pajeros from Mitsubishi's factories in Japan, were battered and abused. They looked like heaps of sand-scarred, rusted crap but the armour-plated chassis, doors and windows were hidden from any but the most persistent observer. The vehicles were off the road but the engines murmured, and their weapons were armed.

She stood nearest to the road and the dust from lorries' wheels and pick-ups flew on to her *burqah*. The Yank was Harding and the Irishman Corky. They were close to her, *khaffiyeh*s draped round their faces and covering their hair. They had on dirty jeans, and jackets weighed down with grenades and gas in the inside pockets; each had a pistol at the hip, held in by his belt. In the Pajeros, with heavier firepower on the empty front passenger seats, were Shagger, the Welshman, and the Scot they called Hamfist. They were employees of Proeliator Security, a private military contracting company, and were paid to be bodyguards to Abigail Jones, a Six girl.

Without them – and their show of grudging loyalty – she would have earned the title 'Eternal Flame', the one that never goes out. She was far from her secure base in Baghdad's Green Zone, or the premises at the Basra airport complex, because she trusted, with a degree of fatalistic humour, the Jones Boys' dedication, the quality of their noses and their understanding of when stupidity overtook duty. She did not deal with them on a need-to-know basis but talked each move through with them so that Hamfist, Shagger, Corky and Harding were privy to the secrets of the Six operation that had now run for some two years – ever since an unexploded device had been recovered and subjected to analysis for the uniqueness of a man's deoxyribonucleic-acid deposits. She had been permitted two four-month extensions of her posting, almost unique, but she hoped to see the operation to its conclusion, to have a part in its death. The Jones Boys would be on the ground as long as she was. It was a commercial relationship that had become family, but they called her 'miss' or 'ma'am' and took no liberties of familiarity. Each time, though, that she went out and they hit the road, she took care to explain where they went, and why. Now it was to meet an informant.

He hadn't shown.

There should have been, approaching through the mirage mist of the road, a motor scooter with an old man astride it. The heat would have distorted their first view of him from perhaps a mile down the straight highway; and as it had cleared they would have known him by the matted grey beard. Many months before, the informant had gone through the marshes and along the berms crossing them, with the papers in his pocket to identify himself as a resident of the Ahvaz Arab community on the far side of the frontier. The scooter had been left well hidden and he had walked, waded where there was still water in the lagoons, and had cut old reed fronds to make a broom for sweeping. He had cleaned a road and a pavement, pocketing cigarette butts strewn behind a man who smoked as stress gripped him.

A few days before, the relative by marriage of the 'cleaner' had travelled as a pillion passenger on the same scooter with two baskets of dates. He had had similar identification papers – forged but good enough to pass a check by Iranian police, border guards, even men of an al-Quds Brigade detachment posted for the security of a valued man. He had asked vague questions in a coffee shop, had had gossip answers, and had overheard enough of a conversation to win the glowing smile of Abigail Jones, Echo Foxtrot. A fistful of dollars had been paid to the informants for the retrieval of the used cigarette filters and for a snatch of talk. She thought it most likely that either the informant and his relative had decided they had made enough money for their needs, had been intercepted and robbed, had unwisely shown a glimpse of riches in a coffee house, or had boasted and been heard by any of the myriad Ali Babas who lived in what was left of the marsh wilderness.

'Shit,' she said. 'But it was good while it lasted. Enough?'

Harding's eyes raked the road. 'Has to be, ma'am.'

Corky, wilting in the heat of over a hundred degrees, said, 'Too long, miss, that we've been here.'

'Shit . . . So, the heroes coming from home will have it all to do for themselves, without a local hand to steady them. No, guys, don't tell me this is lunatic. They'll have to go in there and do the business on their own. Shit . . .'

She walked to the lead Pajero. The two vehicles pulled off the dirt and on to the road, accelerating fast.

Five miles down the road, towards Basra city, they saw a huddle of men and a police car. An ambulance was coming towards them. They would not slacken their speed, and their faces were covered, to hide the pale Caucasian features, as were the automatic weapons, loaded and with the safetys off. Easy to see: a small scooter on the sand beside the tarmacadam, a body with its head covered but new shoes exposed. They would have cost in the city what a man survived on in the marshes for a month. A second body was covered, except for the head with its grey beard.

Corky, beside Shagger, said quietly, 'So they got greedy and were bumped. My thinking, ma'am, they were lucky. If the bastards of the VEVAK had picked them up, then to get robbed and shot would have seemed a blessing. The shoes will be gone before they get put in the ambulance, won't go to waste – but you had your money's worth out of them.'

She did not respond. Under her codename, Echo Foxtrot, she had her satphone out of her bag and was tapping out the numbers.

Badger listened as the call was wound up. 'No, I'm not suggesting there's anything else that can be done. I appreciate we're not talking about a flat tyre or an empty tank. I accept also your assurance that neither party would have been where hostiles could lift them. Paid too much – pretty ironic if you try to buy a man and end up going over the top of his avarice quotient. But it is still possible to go forward with this? It's a setback but not terminal – we are still on course? I value the reassurance . . . You will, of course, be given travel itineraries as soon as . . . Thank you . . . Stay safe, please.'

It was not possible, as Badger saw it, to conceal rank disappointment. It was in the Boss's voice as he spoke softly into the receiver. They had all watched him: they were the sort of men, himself and Foxy, the Cousin, the Friend and the Major, who made an art form of studying weakness, setbacks. Badger, briefly, let his imagination wander to the big map on the board propped on the easy chair that the Major had unveiled before uttering that first sentence: '. . . changed the outcome of a war from a triumphant . . .' That contact: a remote, clipped accent somewhere along Highway 6, between al-Amara and Basra, probably near the town of al-Qurnah – all marked on the map and linked by a ribbon of red – where the Tigris and the Euphrates met, fuelled his understanding of the heat, the hatred and the sheer danger of the place. The Boss sat very still and seemed to ponder. Then he shook his head, as if to clear his mind, and pocketed the phone.

He said, 'I can promise you, gentlemen, that in this matter you will not get half-truths and evasions from me. In the business that confronts us, we had a hope of local resources, but no longer. So, it is in our hands alone, which is probably a disappointment but perhaps a blessing. I apologise, Major, for the interruption . . . Please . . .'

They were no longer fighting cocks, Badger reflected, not pirouetting or prancing in rivals' faces. Linkage with a faraway place had rendered that sort of pride second-rate. On the map he could see the road, the line of an international border, the symbols of lakes and marshlands and . . . The Major breathed in hard, as if his mood also was altered. Before the call, he had started by saying that improvised explosive devices had changed the outcome of a war from a triumphant and victorious mission accomplished to something that was close to mirroring ignominious retreat. Then the phone had trilled in the Boss's suit pocket, and the Major had stood silent while the call was answered. The frown had set in his forehead and he had scratched the back of his neck.

'Back to where I began ... The improvised explosive device is the weapon that has snatched victory from the coalition and replaced it with a very fair imitation of defeat. It's a poor man's weapon, deadlier and more influential than the famed Kalashnikov rifle. I would like to quote from Kipling:

'A scrimmage in a border station –
A canter down some dark defile
Two thousand pounds of education
Drops to a ten-rupee jezail.
The Crammer's boast, the Squadron's pride
Shot like a rabbit in a ride.'

'Written more than a century ago, I suggest that the "education" was heftily expensive, and that ten rupees in the bazaar at Jalalabad or Peshawar bought something pretty cheap. Nothing has changed. We take the modern ten-rupee jezail – that's a long-barrelled flintlock or matchlock rifle – extremely seriously. How seriously?

'Between 2008 and next year, the United States defence family will spend in excess of thirty billion dollars – yes, you heard me – on all aspects of research to negate the effectiveness of these devices, from scanners, to detectors, and into the world of vehicles that can survive an attack. I said, "in excess of thirty billion dollars", and the principal parts of such a weapon can be bought for five or ten dollars in any Iraqi souk. More sophisticated parts are brought into the Middle East from American factories. It's a bewildering, crazy world. The most sensitive devices deployed in Iraq were to beat our strategy of putting a convoy inside an electronic counter-measures bubble that has a safety range of around a hundred metres. The enemy developed the technology of sitting off maybe a kilometre away and using combinations of passive infra-red and telemetry modules, and even such simple kit as car-key zappers, household alarms, the workings from inside a cheap wristwatch bought off a pavement stall. Right now, in Iran, they're ahead of the counter-measures. The roadside bombs, often deployed in a daisy-chain configuration – that's half a dozen devices linked over a couple of hundred metres – or in fake rocks made of *papier-mâché* or replacement kerb stones, create fear among troops. For every fatality, they knock down four, five, six wounded. They destroy morale and drive our armies into over-head flights by helicopter or overland drives in a truck with plate armour sides. Then along came the EFP, the explosive force projectile, which costs next to nothing to build and can destroy a main battle tank worth ten million sterling. The EFPs crushed us, and—'

The Cousin said, 'I know all this. I don't need a high-school lecture.'

The Friend said, 'We have experience of this. It is taught in military kindergarten.'

The Major's eyes narrowed. 'It's gratifying that some of you are so well informed. Is anyone not familiar with EFPs? Anyone?'

Foxy said he had served in southern Iraq, and shrugged, and the Boss smiled limply as if to show he was up to speed.

Badger said, 'I've never heard of an EFP, and if you think I should know – and it'll be important when you get around to explaining this business – then I'm all ears.'

'Thank you, Badger. Does anyone want to go and make coffee or walk in the rain? No?' He paused. He was a handsome man and would have fitted in on Horse Guards, or anywhere else in full dress uniform. Danny 'Badger' Baxter understood. There had been a time when he'd been on a week of stags watching a remote parked caravan where a nutcase guy was thought to be building a device to use against a supermarket chain. When the guy was picked up, the bomb-disposal people had moved in. Above the suit, the laundered shirt and the smart tie Badger had recognised the bleak, worn gaze. Maybe the Boss, the Cousin and the Friend didn't know about the people who did bomb disposal and made things safe. To be different was Badger's thing.

'Right, then I'll continue. The EFP involves a shaped charge, and we call that the Munroe effect. Charles E. Munroe, an American, worked out the theory of the shaped charge a hundred and twenty years ago while stationed at the Rhode Island base where they had a naval torpedo station. József Misnay and Hubert Schardian made refinements as they developed anti-tank weapons for the *Wehrmacht* in the 1940s. There is a metal tube, with a shallow copper bowl, factory-machined, at one end, and behind it explosives – perhaps military or perhaps triacetone triperoxide – a detonator, a trigger apparatus and a method of sending the signal for firing. The copper becomes a molten slug, travelling at a thousand yards per second, and will penetrate the armour of a tank, a personnel carrier, pretty much any vehicle on wheels or tracks. The EFPs are deployed at predictable choke points – where a road goes from four lanes to two, where there's a bridge, an elevated highway or repair work. The devices have been tested thoroughly across the frontier and inside Iran. The range of the radio signals will have been determined, and "dickers" will have been used on the Iraq side to watch the procedures used by the coalition and to report back on them. Several times the convoy will have gone by, not knowing it was under electronic surveillance, and the results sent back across the frontier. They're in no hurry. They have endless patience. They test and experiment and don't move until they're satisfied. Still with me?'

What could they say? The Boss nodded. The Cousin and the Friend forced a smile. Foxy shrugged. Badger said sharply, 'With you.'

The Major said, 'And I'm coming to the core. This is a peasant's weapon. I repeat, it's a peasant's weapon to deploy, to activate, to see it kill and mutilate. But it is not a peasant who builds the electronics that run ahead of the counter-measures, or who oversees the factory where the shallow copper dish is milled to high standards. The view is peddled by the Pentagon and the MoD that the bomb-maker is a low-life rag-head who deals in very basic science concepts. Such assessments are dangerous, misleading and wrong. A small number of clever, innovative men is capable of wrong-footing us so consistently that the body-bags keep going home, and the injured with wounds they'll carry to their graves. This particular individual – Rashid Armajan – is a man whose professionalism I would have, reluctantly, to respect. We know him also by the title given him by his employers and on the base where he works. He is the Engineer. Because I have looked at these people I feel free to offer a stereotypical image of him with some confidence. His family would be of huge importance to him. Alongside that we can say that religion is a major motivation, along with a profound love of his country. He's a perfectionist, and with that comes personal egotism. He believes himself the best. Religion and nationalism give him the right to butcher the troops of the Great Satan and the Little Satan – anyone on the wrong side of God's will. I'm not exaggerating if I say that this one individual is responsible in no small degree for the foul-up that is the coalition campaign in Iraq ... and don't forget how many casualties, killed and wounded, were caused by roadside bombs. We call an enemy a Bravo. Rashid Armajan is a big, bad Bravo, and we should take every opportunity to locate him and—'

The clap of the Boss's hands cut off the Major in mid-sentence.

Badger had been concentrating and hadn't anticipated the interruption. Then, as if satisfied that he had eye contact with the Major, the Boss softened. 'Thank you very much, Major, for that comprehensive and thorough study of our target. It's time for a break, and a sandwich.'

A frown settled on Badger's forehead, and he thought vaguely that part of an agenda had slipped by him, as if it flowed through a separate channel. His mind moved on because he had seen TV clips of the hospitals, clinics and rehabilitation centres where the amputees were taken, and of men struggling to hop along a corridor of parallel supports. He thought that after the sandwich he would be told what the mission was and what was expected of him.

★   ★   ★

She told her mother what had been agreed.

The children were at school and would not be home for two hours; her husband had been driven at dawn to the laboratory workbench. In darker moments, she would have said she competed with soldering irons, circuit boards, little silver detonators, alarm devices and . . . Mansoor, who oversaw the security at their home, had seen her husband taken away and the escort car that had followed, and would now be in his room in the barracks. She walked with a stick, held in her right fist, and her mother supported her left arm. She did not care that the sun was high and burned her face. Perspiration dribbled under the loose black robe and the scarf was tight round her head; she could feel, inside the material and pressed against the bone, the size of the growth.

She said her husband refused to accept the verdict of the doctors in Tehran.

Her mother walked with her, would not interrupt.

She said that her husband had demanded of senior officials that she be allowed to leave the country and visit a more advanced centre of medicine, that funds be made available for such a journey and that arrangements be made for her to travel.

They walked past the lagoon in front of their home. Birds flew low over the water and skimmed the tips of the reeds. The light played on the ripples where fish fed at the surface. She said that her work with the mine-clearance programme was not finished, and that if she was snatched away the deadly beasts would continue to take lives and maim children . . . She told her mother that Rashid could barely contemplate life without her. She urged her mother, now in her sixty-fifth year, to look after the children if . . . Then she smiled and declared she had faith in the consultant she would see.

Where? She did not know.

When? She had not been told.

Her mother cried softly, and the wife of the bomb-maker – who organised the clearing of old minefields for which there were no charts – tried to hold her smile. It had to be soon, she said, that the arrangements were made because she did not believe she had much time. She was in God's hands. And with her would be her husband, the only man she had loved, a good man.

She thought the ibis the most beautiful bird that flew over the reeds as it turned towards the raised island beyond them. To Naghmeh, it was frail and vulnerable, so delicate, and she scanned the skies for the eagles that swooped on the ibis.

In his experience, men who had been at risk of assassination for months or years became careless.

When they first believed themselves important enough to be targets of their enemy, they would slink in the shadows, but few could sustain the effort. Also, when the target was away from his base and the familiar streets where the safe-houses were, he would consider himself untouchable and go to cafés or restaurants if he were flush with his organisation's cash. He would sleep with his mistress in a hotel, hire a car and . . . To bring his mistress from Sidon in Lebanon and fly her on a budget airline to Malta International and have her share his double room in a waterfront hotel in Sliema was careless.

The man was not a fighter but a strategist and a tactician, and some in the higher echelons of Unit 504, intelligence gathering, believed he was among the principal architects of the hidden tunnels and underground strong points from which a blood-letting had been wreaked on the Israeli Defence Force among the bare, harsh hills in the south of Lebanon where the common border was. A target did not have to be a fighter. To be a strategist or a tactician was cause enough for a file to be lifted down and put into the tray of High Priority when an asset told of an extra-marital affair, the name of a mistress and her travel bookings. Few inform-ants were governed by ideology and principle; many were alert to good payment.

The target would have left the girl in bed. She would have screwed him until he'd wondered whether he was close to a coro-nary. Then he would have pushed her off, showered and walked to the Internet café. There, he would have finalised a meeting with a colleague now based in Tunis and another in Rome, and walked back to the hotel.

When Unit 504 went to war it was not with a straitened budget.

An aircraft loitered outside Maltese air space and held together the facets of the operation. The controller in the air was in communication with the slight young man who stood near to the taxi rank in front of the hotel, like any other hopeful stud waiting for his girl. At the end of the esplanade a motorcycle engine was ticking over, the rider helmeted, with a second helmet on his lap. Along the coast – two or three kilometres – a high-powered launch was moored as a concrete jetty. Further out to sea, on the edge of the radar horizon, a merchant ship registered in the port of Haifa was on course for a rendezvous. On occasion, the unit used a mobile phone loaded with enough military explosive to destroy the side of a man's head when he answered a call, or they might have built a bomb into the headrest of the driver's seat in a car, or put one under the nearside front wheel. They might attack with a commando squad of up to eight men, or there would be a single assassin with a short range 'Barak' SP-21 short recoil-operated and locked-breech pistol with fifteen 9mm rounds in the magazine; only two would be used. The target came close.

He was careless enough not to see the young man, wearing a nondescript grey T-shirt, lightweight windcheater and faded jeans, ease away from the lamp-post and wave to somebody down the road, behind his target, who did not look over his shoulder so did not see that no one was there. Carelessness killed.

Two shots to the head, one through an eye socket and one into the brain via the canal behind the ear as the target stiffened, went rigid, then sagged to the ground.

The target was in death spasms. Tourists and hotel staff ran up, then stood, petrified, as the blood came close to their feet. The young man was gone, and the motorcycle – stolen three days earlier – powered away. In the marina a launch revved its engines.

The older men who had planned the killing believed that a

message was given when a body bled on a pavement, and that such a message was always worth sending.

'You're good?' the Friend asked.

'Fine, thank you,' Foxy answered. 'Looking forward, though, to finding out what's asked of me.'

'We wouldn't be in this circus ring if it wasn't considered important.'

'It'd be more respectful if a man of my experience was brought inside the loop rather faster than this.'

Foxy had done enough buffet lunches to be able to balance a glass of mineral water and a plate of sandwiches. The Friend smiled with ice in his eyes. He'd met Israeli counter-terrorist officials at Special Branch meetings, with suicide bombers on the day's agenda, and had thought them unemotional, uncommunicative, untrusting and, above all, arrogant. He'd heard it said by a Branch veteran that the answer was to get them into a bar and force drink down their throats until they pissed their pants without knowing it. Then they might behave as human beings, as colleagues.

'You'll hear soon enough. When you need to know, you'll know.'

'If I don't like what I hear it'll be goodbye and I'll be at the bus stop, waiting for transport home.'

'With a broken leg, perhaps a broken neck – whatever needs to be broken to prevent you walking out of here. Walking out – you lost the chance hours ago. Does the rain stop? Do they grow rice here? You'll know soon enough and then, I guarantee, you'll be frightened – and so will your young colleague.'

'He's not a colleague – I know damn-all about him.'

'You will. You'll learn everything about him. *Everything*. And be frightened together. Fear is good. It bonds men and makes them effective. I think we'll go on, and then you'll understand why we're in this shit-heap, and what's required of you. Be brave, Foxy.'

Never before had he been spoken to by a foreign-agency officer as if he were of similar importance to a drinks waiter. His shoulder was smacked, water spilled from the glass, and the Israeli smiled coldly. He must have flinched, and he thought Badger would have seen him take that step back. They were led again into the briefing room. He believed the Friend. He didn't want to, but he believed that the time for quitting was long past, and that fear would be justified.

3

To Foxy, it was choreographed: nothing was here by chance. It was as if they had both – himself and Badger – been manoeuvred towards the proposition. And it had been done quickly, like he supposed a good hanging was, with a pretence of casualness.

'Times have changed. Things are different,' the Cousin said.

'Who can be trusted? Never many, but now the number has shrunk,' the Friend said.

'What I've learned, you want a job done well, you get your own people to do it. Then you know you're in the best hands,' the Boss, Gibbons, said.

They had been together in the afternoon, and the Cousin had talked – an accent that was distant tyres on gravel, pronounced but not harsh – and had shifted awkwardly on the chair. He seemed to come alive when he spoke of the marshlands east and west of al-Qurnah, and north and south of the town, the drought there, the dried, cracked mud and stagnant pools where water no longer flowed because of the great dams built far to the north in Turkey, Syria and Iran. He spoke of a cradle of civilisation and the location of the Garden of Eden – did it well – of cultures that stretched back several millennia and a people who had been bombed, gassed, hit with napalm jelly and driven from their homes. Then on to 'rat-runs' and the smugglers' trails along which the padded crates brought the bombs into Iraq. Through doors left ajar, and along corridors with stone floors, came the wail of a kettle boiling. That would have been the signal to the triumvirate – Boss, Friend, Cousin – that business should have been done.

Praise from the Boss: 'You're both the best in your field, excellent and professional.'

Admiration from the Friend: 'Your files tell us you're of high quality. This is not work for men at the second level.'

The proposition from the Cousin: 'We can identify, gentlemen, the target's location. He's about two kilometres inside Iran. He's protected – but he's about to travel away from his guards. We don't know where or when he's going. We think – are pretty sure – that you are the guys who'll give us the answers. That's what we're asking of you. Be there, watch, listen, and tell us what you see and hear.'

He was the older man. Predictable that their eyes should bead on him first. He could *see*, had adequate eyesight and wore glasses only for close work or with binoculars; he could *listen* because Six and the Agency, and whatever gang the Israeli was signed up to, would have top-of-the-range audio equipment; and he was almost fluent in Farsi, not interpreter standard but the level down from that. It would have been the language that had ticked boxes when they had trawled the files. He had also, rusty but never forgotten, the skills of a man trained in the techniques of covert rural surveillance. He had served a few days less than four months on attachment to the Joint Forces Intelligence Team at the Shaibah Logistics Base, where the questioning had been 'robust' or, in more legal phrasing, had involved 'coercive interrogation techniques'. His breath came harder and almost, he realised, whistled through his teeth. Did he want to go? Did he hell. Where did he want to be? The map was fastened with drawing pins to the board, then propped against the back of the chair. A dull ceiling light, economy bulbs, fell on it. Nowhere near east or west of Highway 6, or near the Hawr al Hammar marshes, or within spitting distance of those turgid, stinking cess-pool rivers, and the towns that smelt more of human excrement than of donkey shit.

He wriggled on the hard seat of the chair. He was given no help. Would have gone down on his knees in gratitude if he'd heard, 'Of course, Foxy, this is just a fishing exercise and if you don't want to bite we'll forget you were ever here.' In the Cousin, the Friend and the Boss, he saw no mercy. If he had been given further explanations, perhaps on the physicality of the operation, he might have been able to peddle excuses about the state of his hips, his ankles or the cramps he was subject to at night – but his file would have stated that his condition was first class, the product of gym work and, once a week, an hour's cross-country. He would have liked to be at home, with a malt in a crystal glass and Ellie in the kitchen, maybe humming to herself . . . He would have liked to be at a seminar, in a mess or at a conference, maybe, in Wiesbaden, or Madison, Wisconsin, with a spotlight on him and his words heard respectfully.

He wondered how long they would let him writhe before coming to his aid – 'Look, Foxy, if you're not up for crawling in the shit across the Iraq and Iran border with a directional microphone, your language skills, and that little creep alongside to carry the gear, you only have to say so, and there'll be no criticism of you.'

The room was at the corner of the building and the wind caught against the stone and howled. The branches of an overgrown shrub lashed the windowpanes. The wind came through and lifted the curtains, and there was the sound of waves on shingle. Two small truths gnawed at him. First, Ellie, his wife of six years, was less often in the kitchen now and his dinner was more likely to come from the microwave; also, the chance of sex had become remote. The second truth was that the invitations to talk and lecture and address were fewer and now he never had to concern himself with two clashing on one date. Allowing a pall of silence to hover was a tactic used at the Logistics Base by the interrogators of the Joint Forward Intelligence Team. Foxy, as the interpreter, had played the game. Silence disturbed men. He didn't know how to break clear.

Beside him, the quiet was broken.

The voice of the young man fucked Foxy: 'I'm assuming I'm next to be asked. So's we don't mess around till Christmas, I'm on. That's it.'

Smiles broke their faces and there was light in their eyes as they reached to shake Badger's hand – the Cousin and the Boss had to stretch across Foxy. If the bastard had asked about the positioning of back-up, what fee would be paid and how much up-front, what the insurance aspect would be, Foxy might have been able to keep the wriggle going and find a sticking point. Too late.

'Sounds important, sounds necessary.' He thought himself truly skewered, managed a thin smile. 'I'm taking it that the ground work's been done. I'm on board, of course.'

His hand was shaken: the heavy fist of the Cousin, the light, lingering touch of the Friend, and the cursory grip of the Boss. None of the bastards thanked him. It was like he'd jumped a river and there was no going back. He assumed they were unable to put a drone over a house and a barracks inside Iran, and that they didn't trust locally employed assets, or didn't have them. The three sat back, and Badger's arms were folded across his chest. He seemed relaxed.

Gibbons said, 'I think we might take a break now. Tea and, hopefully, cake. Plenty after that to push on with—'

'I said I was accepting your offer, but there are matters outstanding.'

'What matters?'

He hesitated – could have done with Badger's support, but was denied it. No damned response. Felt the loneliness. 'For a start, what's the back-up?'

'Very adequate, and you'll be well briefed on it before you're inserted.'

'Is that all I'm getting?'

'It's enough at this stage. Tea will be waiting.'

He blurted, 'The business of remuneration. Well, where we're being asked to go . . . am I not entitled to know the recompense?'

The Cousin said, 'We were under the impression that you were still, Foxy, a serving police officer, therefore salaried and liable for full pension if you care to quit and take it. Probably there's an overseas *per diem* allowance, disability stuff and widow's entitlements in the package. I'd say you're well looked after.'

The Friend said, 'Your remuneration is a great deal healthier than anything my government wants to or would be able to pay.'

The Boss said, 'If you're having trouble in the cash area, Foxy, I can always arrange for a diversion, on the way to the airport, via Headley Court. You'll get a chance to talk to amputees, victims of IEDs and EFPs, and see them learning to walk again or eating with artificial aids. You can discuss disability payments, your money and a soldier's wage.'

Badger gazed at him. No contempt there, but a dry smile.

'I was just checking because of my wife – because of Ellie. Tea would go down well. Thank you for your understanding. I suppose I'll want to learn about the target, his security and . . .'

He touched her hand. There were few gestures of intimacy between them when they could be observed. He did not care then that her mother watched as he let his fingers fall on her wrist. He saw the thinness of her arm under his fingers. He didn't care that Mansoor, the security officer, eyed them. Dark thoughts flitted in his mind. He could imagine her mother making love to her father when he was still alive – she had comforting weight about her hips and stomach, warm against a man, a sparkle in her eyes.

He couldn't imagine this for Mansoor, who limped from the rocket fired by the Americans' drone. Mansoor's wife worked as a typist for the intelligence officer in the Guard Corps barracks, the Crate Camp Garrison off the Ahvaz to Mahshar road – he had never seen her without her *burqah*. Mansoor seemed devoid of tenderness and without the need for a woman.

Rashid, the Engineer, yearned to celebrate triumphs with his woman underneath him, her nails in his back and her small squeals in his ear – not loud enough to wake the children – when his work in the factory and on the testing ground went well, or when she cleared a minefield sown three decades earlier or gained new funding from the provincial government. They would not lie again together. He did not believe that medical success could be snatched abroad . . . but he had demanded it. He smiled weakly. He said that very soon he would have the detail of where they would travel and the name of the expert she would visit.

He went again to read to their children and tell them more of the three princes. The story was about lions that terrorised a farmer's oxen and how Prince Korshid took the harnesses from the oxen, captured the lions, harnessed them to the plough, worked them and freed them. They went back to the hills and left the farmer in peace. It was a story his children loved. He saw the sad way Naghmeh watched him, sitting in her chair with her mother beside her, her eyes never off him. There had once been a girl, in Budapest where he had studied, who had terrified him with her openness. Memories of her and of that time reared more often now that he could only watch his wife's growing fragility. He would do what he could – he would fight, bluster and argue – for her, but he had no faith in the miracle required when they travelled.

It was 'interdiction'. Badger had heard the word spoken twice.

The evening session had been given to the Friend. The Israeli had talked of the al-Quds Brigade, its place in the ranks of the Iranian Revolutionary Guard Corps, its influence in Gaza and south Lebanon, its authority throughout Iran, the discipline, commitment and élitism of its members. He had talked like an academic, a schoolmaster, and had not used the rhetoric of an enemy combatant. It was relevant, hugely so, because the home of the target was under the protection of both the Border Guards and the al-Quds crowd. They lived beside the small garrison barracks because his wife, Naghmeh, was influential on a steering committee dedicated to mine clearance along the frontier. Her work would suffer if she was shut away in a guarded compound far from the ground where the personnel and tank mines had been laid, where children and adults died, or were mutilated, as regularly as once a week. He talked well, was interesting, and did not demean his enemy: he spoke of him with dislike but not contempt, vilified his cruelty, admired his commitment and gave respect. And if they, whatever organisation the Friend represented, knew so much, why did they not themselves provide surveillance expertise?

Badger had been to a moderate-performing school on the outskirts of Reading and had left with qualifications only slightly better than mediocre. He had been idle and unmotivated, had not gone to university. Lack of formal education did not make him a fool. Why did not the Friend's crowd do it themselves? Simple. They would have wanted a broad church, a coalition of the willing: they were akin to bookmakers who laid off the risk of financial calamity by slicing up big wagers. It had been a good talk. Then supper, no alcohol: a meal that must have chilled in the kitchens because it was hardly edible. It was brought in by the house owner – the grandfather of a dead soldier – and left on a sideboard. Most had not finished their plate of the main dish – stringly beef, boiled vegetables and heavy gravy. Some had toyed and the Boss hadn't tried, but Badger had done well. He wasn't fussy about his food. He'd heard little hisses of dissatisfaction from Foxy. While they ate, the Cousin had returned to the marshes, and the Major to the sophistication of the bomb-maker. Later the Boss had led them back to the lounge and the fire had been made up. Badger had done what he was good at, had sat, listened and watched. Twice he had heard the word 'interdiction'.

The Major had said to the Friend,' . . . care about passionately is interdiction. I used to lie awake at night, at the Basra Palace, dreaming of it. Better than a wet one. What needs to be done and . . .' The Friend had nodded in fierce agreement.

The Cousin had said to the Boss, '. . . every time it has to be interdiction so the mother-fuckers get the message . . .' And the Boss had sagely inclined his head.

It was a word beyond Badger's vocabulary.

Later, when Foxy talked to the Cousin about heat exhaustion when wearing gillie suits in the temperatures of the marshes, Badger had sidled towards the Boss, and asked what 'interdiction' was.

The Boss had said he thought it had stopped raining, and he wanted fresh air and the wind on his face.

They were outside, had taken faded old coats from hooks by the door. The wind had come on as a gale – there might have been hail in it – the seas crashed on the rocks, and he could make out the shape of a sheep flock huddled at an angle in the fence.

The hand pointed to the outline, indistinct, of the ruined castle keep. 'You know, Badger, there's history here and violent history at that. That place was the seat of clan mafia, gangsters and thugs, and they'd been there since the fourteenth century. There was a banqueting hall inside and, sunk in the floor of an annex, a dungeon that had a water level of three metres. There was a round stone in the centre that topped the surface. A prisoner consigned there had to sit on the stone and pray he didn't fall asleep after two days or five. He might stay awake for a week, but it was inevitable that he'd drown. I fancy they wouldn't have screamed, the victims, or begged. They wouldn't have given the bastard up above that satisfaction ... A serious place, and damn-all to do with this operation.'

'Yes, Boss.' Badger wanted to trust, to believe. 'What is interdiction?'

A pause. Badger couldn't see the Boss's face, and couldn't imagine why he had been brought outside to shiver.

The answer came. 'Latin stuff – something about hitting communication lines in a military context. But I think you're asking, Badger, what this plan means for our target, and what your role in this is leading up to. Am I about right there? A very fair question and one that deserves answering.'

'What it's about, yes.'

'I'm being very frank, Badger, and probably going past my remit. But where you're going and what you're doing entitles you to total honesty. We hope to track Rashid Armajan to a place where we can *approach* him. We can't do it where he is.'

'Have I been naïve, Boss?'

'Not at all. With your help, Badger, we get up close. That's an approach. You understand?'

They'd bung him, cart him to a safe-house and turn him. The Engineer would sing. 'I understand. Thank you.'

'That was indiscreet, and I'd get my wrist slapped. It's time to get back inside, and tomorrow's a hell of a day. What a dreadful wind.'

'You did absolutely right, Mr Gibbons.' He and the Major were in the hall, out of earshot.

'An untruth, but justified. He seemed to swallow "approach". '

The Major murmured in his ear, 'He's a young man, hasn't been where killing and mayhem are. Maybe he's good at his job, but he's not hardened in the way the older man is. He's going to be staring through a 'scope and binoculars at a target and he'll bond with him after a fashion. They all do. He'll get caught up in the trivia of the target's life, and the medical condition of the wife. There are kids, aren't there? He'll see them. He'll get to be, by proxy, a part of that family . . . at home, at his work. He's looking at a man who'll be arrested and sent to gaol. We're talking 'interdiction', zapping the bastard. Our Badger might not cope too well with that. You did right.'

'Which was why I did it. Serious business, killing a chap, don't you know.' A smile flickered at Gibbons's mouth.

Some days it was hard for him to remember his name. That day, his identity hovered between Gabbi who worked, occasionally, as an investigator into tax avoidance from an office near the Ministry of Finance, and Zak, and Yitzak, which was how the sailors on a freighter had known him, as well as the embassy people who had seen him out of the airport at Catania, in Sicily. He had many names. In the last year he had used Amnon, Saul, Peter, David and Jakob, and had seemed to have many places of work. On occasions his hair was blond but it could also be jet black or mouse, and cut short or topped with a flowing wig. The debrief would be the next day, and he had gone home and would sleep until he was woken by the clatter of keys in the door, the tap of her stick and her footfall.

He had been met at a military airfield. No trumpets. He had come down the short steps of an executive twin-engine plane and the unit's driver had had the front passenger door open. The woman, in an adjutant's role, was on the apron, her hand out for the passport with his last, now discarded, name and the photograph with the light hair. She had also taken from him the unused float for incidental expenses on Malta, and a mobile phone that had been operational. She had returned his own and asked if he was well. He'd said he was, and she had told him at what time he was expected at the unit in the morning. He had been driven to their home in the suburb of Ramat Gan. He'd made one call on his own mobile and had left voicemail for Leah, telling her he was back.

In the apartment – one living room, one decent bedroom, a small bedroom, a bathroom and a kitchen – he sprawled on the sofa with the bamboo frame. He had eaten yoghurt from the refrigerator and some cheese, and drunk juice. He might read later if he had slept and she hadn't come back from her desk at the defence ministry in the Hakira district. On the stairs to his second-floor door he had met Solly Stein and his wife, Miriam. They would have noted he was back and would have known that the apartment had been empty for four days. They would have thought he had been away on Revenue business, chasing a fat-cat crook who was – perhaps – a politician. The apartment was always empty when he was abroad because Leah slept at her mother's. Solly Stein did not know, never would, that the hand of their neighbour across the second-floor landing, the one Miriam held as they'd talked briefly – the weather, the price of milk – had the previous day fired two killing shots into the head of a Hezbollah strategist. If they had known, she would have kissed his cheeks.

He did not endure agonies of conscience as he lay on the sofa. He never had. Nor was he cold, unfeeling. He had been told that the resident psychiatrist attached to the unit regarded him as unique among his colleagues. Without remorse, rabid xenophobia, regret or triumphalism: like a man who worked in an abattoir and earned a monthly wage. An enigma, and not understood, but depended upon. There were some in clinics and others who beat

their women, and a few who thought themselves so above the law
that they hit banks and were now locked up.

He heard the tap of her stick against the door, must have dozed
but was immediately awake. He rolled off the sofa and his bare
feet slithered across the tiled floor. He heard the key go into the
lock. She knew what he did, but never spoke of it, or of her own
work at Camp Rabin, in Military Intelligence. She had been
blinded in Lebanon by the shrapnel scattered in the explosion of
an Iranian-built missile. The wounds inflicted were beyond the
skill of surgeons, and she lived in a world of black and grey
shadows. They hugged and the love shone.

'You're good?'

'I'm fine.'

'I brought supper.'

'Wonderful.'

They clung and kissed.

'Are you home for long – if you can answer?'

It was possible, in what she did at the ministry, that she helped
choose the targets allocated to him. She might have worked on the
selection of individuals of Hamas, Hezbollah or the Fateh Al-Aqsa
Martyrs' Brigade who were thought of sufficient importance.

'Perhaps, and perhaps not. Soon I will know. I am home tonight.'

They were lovers, and she was Leah. She could not have said
what name, in their bed, he would answer to.

The pool in the Zone had a bad end-of-season look about it. If she
had been a holidaymaker and paying good money to lie beside it,
with her book, she would have thought the place was up for sale,
or that the maintenance money had run out, or that this was
yesterday's destination.

There was a better-kept pool in the embassy's garden but she
preferred the dowdiness of this one. The weeds that grew between
the tiled and paved surfaces gave it more of an office feel and
negated any guilt at apparently skiving off for the day. She was
happy, anyway, to be far from her office in the secure section,
distanced from the interminable gossip of the diplomats and their

support staff. Her guards were not permitted at the pool and had to sit in an air-conditioned shed by the entrance to that sector of the Zone. The book, actually, was interesting.

On one side of her, quietly snoring, a towel across his face, was Hamfist, his flak vest beside him with the rucksack in which his gear was stowed, and an AK-47 assault rifle, with a magazine loaded and another taped to it. Her mobile lay on her thigh, the back smeared with sun cream. She took breaks from the book to make calls and check texts. Hamfist was a Scot, a 'clumsy sod' – as she called him – with any refined equipment other than one that fired a high-velocity shell. He had been in a Scottish infantry unit, had done nine years that included a spell in al-Amarah up on Highway 6. He had come through a mild load of post-traumatic stuff – better than the clap – but civilian life had not welcomed him. Instead he had signed for Proeliator Security and close protection for a Six officer. She thought he took more pride in wearing the newly washed and ironed T-shirt with the logo of the Jones Boys Band than almost anything else. She read about the birds in the marshes, on either side of Highway 6, that stretched in places to the border dividing Iran from Iraq. Pretty birds, majestic birds, endangered birds, some so small she'd need a tele-scope to spot them.

On her other side was Corky, not from the south-west of Ireland and County Cork but from the Andersonstown quarter of west Belfast, but there was no logic in acquired military names. He had been mentioned in despatches for his reaction in an ambush in Basra seven years back, and was in awe of her, but he allowed her to help him choose birthday and Christmas gifts for a son in Colchester aged eleven, and a daughter in Darlington, aged five. Her phone vibrated, and she raised her eyebrows – gold, the colour of her hair – lifted it, read the message and cleared it. She had organised the paperwork by which part of his salary was paid by Proeliator Security to each of the mothers. He had the same gear as Hamfist except that his rifle was an M16A1, with a muzzle velocity of 3,200 feet per second and a catastrophic hydrostatic shock effect on tissue when it hit, which Cork swore by. He wore a rumpled T-shirt, camouflage trousers, big wraparound shades, his boots, and was always a tousled mess.

Somewhere behind her, out of view, Harding and Shagger would be on plastic chairs or hunkered on their haunches, ready to go. She knew she merely had to hitch a leg off the lounger and drop the book – *Field Guide to the Birds of the Middle East* – into her bag, on top of *Birds of Iraq*, and they would be on their feet. By the time she had draped the towel around her legs and knotted it at the waist, all four would be wearing their flak vests and ruck-sacks, with their weapons in their hands. When she stood and lifted the bag, Shagger would come forward with her own vest and hold it up so that she could shrug into it. When she quit Baghdad, at the end of this show, took the Six shuttle flight down to Kuwait, then headed for the Towers, she reckoned they would be devas-tated. Not her problem, but it nagged. She thought often – with relief or ruefully – that the Jones Boys ensured her celibacy. It would be a rare bastard who ambled towards her and began a chat-up routine: *Hello there. Do you believe in love at first sight, or should I walk by you again?* Or, *Excuse me, I've left my wallet behind. Do you mind if we share an armoured personnel carrier home?* If an officer, American or British, Latvian or Australian, a diplomat or an administrator, had tried to get his hand in her pants, most likely he'd have ended in a Casevac tent. There were times when she ached for—

She had long legs, tight waist, fair bumps, pretty mouth and a good sun-kissed complexion, but no man. She called quietly, 'Guys, can you come over? Guys, please.'

She had the four around her. 'Don't get me wrong, this is serious and not bull. We're concerned about the survival pros-pects of the Basra Reed-warbler – smart name is *Acrocephalus griseldis* – the Black-tailed Godwit, the Greater Spotted Eagle, the Sacred Ibis, *Threskiornis aethiopicus*, and a few others, how they're dealing with drought and what effect renewed oil exploration in their habitat will have. Two supposed surveillance experts are taking off tonight and will hit here tomorrow. The ecogame is the cover. Questions?'

There never were. They relied on her to tell them what they needed to know, and she gave them more than was necessary, which showed her trust in them. In their world, and hers, trust was a big factor, sometimes the biggest.

'And there's people we have to see and bits of paper we have to collect. What do I think of it? Doesn't matter. We're back, they're forward and over the frontier, at what you guys call the 'sharp end'. We're supposed to be their support, but easier said than done. Rather them than me. It's all a bit old-fashioned, a bit of a shout from the past – but I'm up for it. Anyway, if the birds get oil on their wings, they're bollocksed.'

She went to get dressed in the female changing area, where they wouldn't follow her, and now felt challenged. She sensed she was heading, roller-coaster, towards an end-game more hazardous than anything she had experienced before, and that the risk factor had ratcheted.

The piper played what he assumed was a lament. Their host and his wife were on the front steps. In their foreheads, the positioning of their eyes and the push of their jaws, Foxy Foulkes thought he could read something of the grandson in the photograph. The old man and woman had shaken hands as they'd left. By chance Foxy was last out of the door, and they had gripped his. Might have been because he was the last, or that small morsels had dropped from the table and they knew a little of what was planned in the Iraqi marshlands. Maybe intuition told them that in their home an act of revenge was plotted against someone, anyone, who had worked to kill the grandson who might one day have taken over this pile of damp grey stone. It was grim stuff that the piper played. A light rain fell on his shoulders, and there was a stag in the field that seemed forlorn, lost. The dogs ignored the helicopter and chased furiously after crows that flew away from them. The grandmother held Foxy's hand and shook it. Foxy didn't know whether he should thank them for their hospitality or . . . They willed him forward. A murmur of 'God keep you safe' from her and a growl from him: 'Remember us, and go after them wherever you find them.' It was all theatre, had a majesty to it – decayed but there – and the piper's cheeks puffed with his efforts and the dirge was fit for a funeral but went mostly unheard as the rotors gathered speed.

He raised his voice: 'We'll do what we can.'

It was rare for Foxy Foulkes to feel that his words, drowned by the helicopter's engine and the piper's efforts, were utterly vacuous. Felt it then, could have bitten his lip. What he thought of as banal was a beacon to the couple. He saw their eyes blaze and wetness formed in the grandfather's. She stood tall and kissed his cheek – roughly shaven that morning in tepid water. He freed his hands and scurried past the piper. The crewman waited on the lawn for him, near to an old rose bed. The others had boarded. He thought the American would have paid in cash for the privilege of using the house and that there would be no paper trail. The helicopter's flight plans would have been listed as 'training exercises' and the flying logs would have perpetuated the lies. There would have been, Foxy realised, elderly men and women the length and breadth of the country who mourned grandsons cut down by the bombs left at the side of a straight road traversing a desert, men and women who had lost children, young women whose husbands had come home in coffins, and children taken to full military funerals who had no father. He was as trapped as if they had taken him to a pathology theatre at the John Radcliffe in Oxford where the corpses were brought, to the military hospital in Birmingham or the Headley Court rehabilitation clinic. He could never have refused. The crewman put a gloved fist under Foxy's arm and heaved. He flopped into the cabin.

The others were already belted to their seats, and he saw the looks of impatience because he had delayed them – for a minute and a half.

He wondered what he would tell Ellie, what sort of phone call was permitted, how long and how detailed . . . where the kit would come from, and what the duration of the operation would be. He knew so little and there was an almost infuriating calm about the little beggar sitting across the cabin from him. They were airborne, and there was a view of the once grand house, the couple on the steps who waved, the castle keep, the grey sea, the grey rocks and the shingle beach. Then they smacked into the grey clouds – and the little beggar showed no sign of letting the lack of information fester in him. Of course, he hadn't been there.

The helicopter shook and the pilot made no concessions to the comfort of his passengers. If 'Badger' Baxter had been to Iraq, he might not have been slumped in his seat, apparently relaxed about close support, how near they were expected to get and – Foxy's knowledge of the language raced in his mind – what the quality of the directional audio would be. Had he been able to reach across the width of the cabin, he might have kicked the little beggar's shin and wiped the calm off his face. It was his language skills that had done for him.

They powered through dense cloud. The Cousin and the Friend talked into each other's ears, protectors lifted. Foxy could not read their averted lips. The Boss, Gibbons, sat upright, hands tight on the frame of the canvas seat. Foxy met Badger's glance. Hadn't intended to. Was rewarded with a brief smile, as if they were equals and shared authority, responsibility. He wouldn't tolerate that. They were not equals.

He shivered. Couldn't help himself. He hoped the thick coat wrapped round him would mask it. He shivered at the thought of the reed beds, the water in the lagoons and channels, the heat and the hatred – and saw again the faces, some bloodied but not pleading, some bruised but not begging, in the interrogation rooms of the Joint Forward Intelligence Team. God help them if they were taken because of the hatred that had been incubated in that fucking place.

He was walking with his daughter when the mobile phone warbled. He let Magda's hand go, reached into an inner pocket, saw the number and did not recognise it. Few people had his personal phone details, and the majority of those he worked with did not. It was a way to protect his privacy. Had the number been generally available his phone would have controlled his life. He answered.

'Yes? Steffen . . .' There was a pause. A wrong number? He spoke again. 'This is Steffen.'

It annoyed him. He was a busy man, sometimes almost over-whelmed by the volume of work that his success and reputation brought him, and he valued the moments he spent with his daughter, who was seven. She had been talking about her day at school, the art lesson.

His own number was given by the caller, but not in German: the man spoke in the Farsi of his past. The caller waited.

He repeated, in German. 'This is Steffen, yes.'

The caller persisted, again in Farsi. Was he not Soheil, the Star? Was his name not Soheil? He called himself Steffen. He was married to Lili, who had been a theatre nurse at the Universitätsklinikum Hamburg-Eppendorf. From the day of their wedding, he had cut his links with an old world and his history. Lili and her parents had expected it of him, and his patients did not wish to be treated – at a time of personal crisis – by a specialist who was obviously an Iranian immigrant. He had a pale complexion and his German was excellent; the habits and culture of the new identity had been easy to acquire. His wife was blonde and pretty, and his daughter was not obviously mixed-race. They had settled, well into the prosperous society of the city they had chosen as their home. His daughter tugged at his arm, wanted his attention.

Again, was he not Soheil, the Star?

It was fourteen years since he had left Tehran. On the day he took the flight to Europe, he had recently qualified at the Tehran University medical school. His talents were such that he had been sent to the neuro-surgery wing of the UKHE to study under the tutelage of a *Chefarzt*. He had not gone home. He had married, changed his name, had believed he was forgotten – it was now four and a half years since the embassy in Berlin had last contacted him to make certain he was 'happy and content' and to tell him that his achievements were watched with pride by those who had provided him with the opportunity to go abroad. Magda tugged harder. He let go of her hand and she sagged back – he thought she might fall.

He could have cut the call. He could have switched off the phone, taken his daughter's hand, walked on beside the Hansahafen and put the contact out of his mind. He was asked if it was convenient to talk. There was an edge to the voice.

His thoughts meandered: to speak in German or Farsi? To answer to Soheil or demand to be called Steffen?

'The professor of oncology in Tehran, almost your foster-father, asked to be remembered to you. He is old now, and his wife is in poor health. Times at home are difficult, in what is their country and yours, Soheil. There is violence, and there are difficult people who exercise authority in some areas. The taint of treason is attached to those who befriend the few who distance themselves from the Islamic revolution. Is it convenient to talk?'

He asked for the identity of the caller, and was told he was just a humble functionary at the embassy in Berlin. Magda had gone to the edge of the quay, where there was a drop of three metres to the waterline. She was beside a gap between two traditional sailing boats. He could not shout at her because she might flinch and trip. He remembered the professor who had reared him from the age of nine after his parents, both doctors, had died in a forward medical post, under mortar attack during the battle to liberate Khorramshahr, when tending the wounded. The professor and his wife, childless, had taken the orphan into their home . . . He understood the nature of the threat to them. He did not contradict and give his German name . . . He had qualified with the highest marks, was the son of martyred parents and had practised for a year in a slum district of the capital. He had therefore been permitted to study abroad – but had not returned. He answered in his native language. His wife and daughter, his colleagues at the Klinik in Hamburg and the medical school in Lübeck, between which he split his time, understood no Farsi. His daughter reached into his overcoat pocket for the bread they always brought when they walked beside the harbour.

The blunt question: 'You work in the field of brain tumours?'

'I do.'

'There is a procedure called "stereo-tactic"?'

'It is in my field.'

'There are cases where a condition is inoperable in conventional surgery, but where stereo-tactic is an alternative?'

'There are.'

'You have a high reputation, but you have not forgotten your family's roots – your parents' heroism, your foster-father's sacrifices, the state's generosity?'

'What do you want of me?' His daughter threw bread into the air. Gulls flew close to her, screaming. They had huge predatory beaks.

'That you see a patient.'

'For whom nothing can be done in Tehran?'

'Nothing.' It was a cold voice. He presumed the patient, terminally ill without a procedure that was always a last resort and fraught with complication, would be a senior man in the clerical or revolutionary hierarchy. 'We are talking to you because nothing further is possible in Tehran.'

'The patient would come here or to Hamburg?' The bread was gone and the child was at his side, tugging his sleeve, and saying loudly that she wanted to go home. She started to pull him towards the Burgtorbrücke, and he let her take him.

'It is intended the patient would travel.'

'There are more experienced consultants in Frankfurt, Vienna, Paris and London, men better qualified than I.'

'We would not have the discretion that we gain from you, the confidentiality. There will be no electronic messages, only brief telephone communication. I will come to visit you, Soheil, when the travel arrangements are complete. I am so glad that I can report your co-operation.'

The call ended. He understood. *Discretion* and *confidentiality* were the keys. Perhaps it was a prosecutor with blood on his hands, who now faced his God, would imminently be with Him, and was important enough to demand the full resources of the state to buy him a few more months, or a general in the Revolutionary Guard Corps, or an imam. He could not run from them. He held tight to the little girl's hand as they crossed the bridge and headed for the fine villa that was their home.

His daughter – also perhaps vulnerable and a weapon to be used against him – sprinted ahead. He shouted at her to slow down, and she turned, wide-eyed, shocked by his anger. He accepted that even here, in his adopted town, he could not be free of them – ever.

He let himself into the office, closed the door behind him and locked it.

She was at her desk. Len Gibbons noted that, in his absence, she had turned her room and the one allocated to him into something that was as much a home as a workplace. She had arranged two small vases of flowers, one on his desk, which he could see through the open connecting door, and one on hers, and a tray for tea-making lay beside the electric kettle, with a biscuit tin. On a wall away from the photographs of bombs, the featureless picture of a target and the enlarged map of the marsh region between the confluence of the rivers and the frontier, she had hung a picture. He smiled as he dumped his bag down and shrugged off his coat. There was a big sky in which birds flew and a long meadow between forests, in which an elephant wandered, a scarlet parrot perched and a deer grazed. In the background, far down the meadow, a robed man led two naked – or near naked – figures.

'Enlighten me, Sarah.'

'It's the Garden of Eden. God's there with the two innocents. It's by Jan Brueghel the Elder, painted in 1607. Adam and Eve before the apple upset the cart. Appropriate, I thought. How did it go?'

'Well.'

'Are they all right?'

'We call them Foxy and Badger. They're probably just about all right.'

He was leaning over his desk, checking the notes she had left him and pitching them into the shredder.

'Is "all right" good enough?'

He looked up sharply. 'Has to be. We make do with what's given us. I must cut my cloth according to my means. Very thoughtful of you, Sarah, as always, and such an appropriate image.'

*   *   *

They were in business class. Foxy said that 'they' would have pulled a heavy one – a favour required – with the carrier. They would be up for around six hours on a non-stop flight to Kuwait City. Badger said nothing.

They took off.

Gibbons had seen them into the terminal, then shaken their hands and left. They had carried their bags of one change of clothes – dirty – and washbags to Check-in. Badger reckoned he was expected to carry Foxy's while the older man did the talking at the desk. He did his own talking, interrupted to make the point, left the bag on the floor and Foxy had had to go back for it.

They went up into the night, and Badger felt more gut knots than he'd ever known. Beside him Foxy was biting hard at his lip and was close to drawing blood. Badger didn't like to be afraid: it unsettled him.

4

A wall of heat hit them. Badger saw Foxy recoil from it. It seemed to suck the energy out of his own chest, his lungs – and he had walked only a few paces. The sun's light smacked upwards from the expanse of concrete, its force mocking the effectiveness of his sunglasses. Everything that was beyond a hundred metres away was distorted and bounced like a mirage. He could barely make out the distant terminal buildings, but the flags topping them hung limp. Foxy seemed to stagger – as if the wall not only surrounded him but punched hard.

Badger heard him: 'Fucking place, fucking weather. By the by, here, you're Badger and I'm Foxy. I don't want any mucking with proper names. Enough on our plates without chucking identification around. To whom it may concern, and us, those are our names . . . Nothing fucking changes.'

A fuel truck drove slowly towards their helicopter and a Humvee had parked on the far side of the cockpit – it would be for the crew. There were two Pajeros in front of them. A woman stood tall in front of one, scratching at her loose robe. She wore a head scarf close round her hair and Badger thought it was against the sun, not for modesty. There were two men in each vehicle; the windows were up and the engines were turning over, which meant they had air-conditioning.

Badger assumed Foxy was talking to him, not to himself: 'Nothing changes except the flags . . . My place was about a quarter of a mile the far side of the terminal. Any time after about seven in the morning and before five in the afternoon you could hardly walk that quarter-mile without dehydration. You'd need a couple of litres straight down, and if you walked it before seven and after five you had to wear a flak jacket and helmet and be listening for the mortar's whistle, or there were rockets incoming. I loathed it then and I loathe it now.'

Badger said, 'Nobody cares, Foxy.' He had stamped on the moan. Not the first, and it wouldn't be the last. During the long relay of their journeys, he had felt no inclination to humour the man. He'd seen Foxy crumple, as if the wind was squeezed out of him, when the request for permission to call home was curtly refused; he'd had to make do with a text of about five lines, and show it to Gibbons before he sent it. A poignant moment: Badger had been close by when the message was punched out and the mobile switched off. The Boss had taken it and put it, with Badger's, into a plastic bag, which he had pocketed. There was no one that Badger would have called. He had had his boots in the car and been able to bag them, but Foxy had only been carrying a pair of heavy trainers, which would not have been waterproof. Badger should have been sympathetic about it, but was not, and should have been grateful that Foxy had negotiated the fee with the Boss at the eleventh hour but he had not thanked the older man for winning payment over and above their salaries.

There had been the flight to Kuwait City, where they'd been met by a corporal, American, from a logistics unit, who had escorted them out of the civilian area to a military annex. They had spent three hours in a departure hut with air-conditioning chilling them and had been offered upright chairs. Foxy had sat in one with his back straight, but Badger had made a space on the floor, wedged his bag against the wall, lain down with his head on the bag and slept. Later, the same corporal had driven them in a minibus to the pad where the helicopter waited. There had been machine-gunners on the cabin doors, weapons armed, and they'd done contour flying, hugged the dirt, woven and come up where there were cables slung between pylons, but otherwise kept low. Badger had never been in a war zone, too young for the Northern Ireland experience, and he noticed that Foxy stared straight ahead, looking ill at ease.

Roads with occasional cars and ancient lorries. Homes were single-storey and surrounded by dumped vehicles and giant refrigerators. Kids waved, women ignored them and men looked away. Goats and thin sheep stampeded. A checkpoint where the Iraqi flag – red, white and black – fluttered briefly as the helicopter drove draught across it, and there were local soldiers or policemen. The gunner cleared phlegm from his throat and spat.

The sand stretched away until it reached green corridors that would have been vegetation alongside rivers. They went up one of the beds and were over mud and exposed wrecks. It was like the life had been taken from a waterway. They had not been issued with headphones and were given no commentary on the route, the security scene, the duration . . . nothing. Might have been junk and on the way to a refuse pit. They had come fast over a perimeter fence, and the huge scale of the base, the empire it had become, was exposed: a place built to survive for *ever*. As far as he could see, there were prefabricated constructions, hangars and maintenance bays, blast walls and stores warehouses. They had hovered, then the skids had touched and the heat wall had clutched them. When his feet had hit the concrete, Badger had wiped a handkerchief across his face. His body under the loose T-shirt was wet, but Foxy still wore his blazer and tie.

Foxy led; Badger let him.

They walked, him three paces behind, towards the woman and the vehicles.

He heard Foxy mutter, 'Could have opened his door – could have damn well stepped out to meet us.'

'Yes,' Badger said, barely audible. He was not used to meeting Six officers and didn't know what to expect.

'He'd better be bloody good, as good as he's arrogant.'

'Can't argue with that.'

'Do they think we're temporary staff for the kitchens, washing up or— Him not being here to meet us is just bloody ungracious. Discourteous prat. Christ, this bloody sun . . . I won't be quick to forget Alpha Juliet's breach of manners, and I expect your backing when I take him to task.'

They were close to her. Her hands were on her hips and she
swayed a little on the balls of her feet. Badger thought she had
control, and could have described it as authority. There was a
wildness about her appearance that appealed, a raffishness, and
he made that judgement in spite of the full robe, the trainers that
peeped out below it, the headscarf and the dark glasses.

'Welcome here, gentlemen, and thanks very much for making
yourselves available. I'm Abigail.'

Badger was alongside Foxy, and said softly, 'So that makes you
Alpha?'

'Alpha Juliet, correct.'

'I'm Badger, and he's Foxy.' He grinned. 'We're the sweepings
off the floor.'

'Pleased to meet you, Badger – and good to meet you, Foxy.'
She'd shaken Badger's hand first, briefly, then took the older man's.
Badger saw the confusion and near embarrassment in Foxy. The
cussed old thing would be wondering how far his voice had carried
in the stillness once the helicopter's rotors had shut down. There
was something about her mouth that was mischievous and he'd
have bet that behind the glasses there was a sparkle – might be fun,
amusement or even contempt. Before he had gone off to work for
the Box, and he'd been a croppie with his local force, a judge had
been under threat during an organised-crime trial. He was wanted
off the case and violence was in the air so the surveillance team was
holed up for days at the back of the property on the edge of a
Cotswold village. The judge had a younger wife with a flash of
cheekiness in her smile and she'd brought them, in the hide, at the
start of the second week of observing fuck-all, a tray of tea and
shortbread. She'd had that gravel growl in her voice, sort of husky
and deep. She hadn't cared that she might have blown the exercise.
The voice had said old money. It had been raining and Badger and
his oppo were well into their stag, cold and wet and . . . Old money,
good breeding and the rule of instincts. It was the only time he'd
ever climbed out of a hide in his gillie suit, pushed back his camouflage headpiece, sipped a mug of tea, dunked a biscuit, offered
thanks and told a woman to 'bugger off out of it'.

Foxy said, 'Good of you to meet us, Abigail. Appreciated.'

She took them to the vehicles.

Foxy said, 'We'd like a chance for a wash, maybe something to eat – light, a salad – then some sleep and—'

'Could be a problem, the bit about sleep.'

'We're very tired. I have to say, Abigail, that we haven't been treated well since being dragged into this mission. The briefings have been general in the extreme, all detail excluded. What's called for now is rest, then a comprehensive evaluation of the ground, the equipment, back-up and the time scales – that's after we're satisfactorily acclimatised and—'

'Sorry and all that, but those scales are pared down to the quick. I can do you the shower and some cam-clothing. Everything else is on the hoof.'

Maybe it was his tiredness, maybe the heat or the weight of the blazer, but Foxy barked, 'It seems pretty much of a shambles to me, and we deserve better. The man in UK – Gibbons, he called himself – who put this together, he warrants lynching. It screams wishful thinking and incompetence.'

She had the door of the back Pajero open for him. Foxy seemed to huff, then slid on to a back seat strewn with weaponry, magazines and vests.

She said, like it was no big deal, 'I put it together, it's my shout. If it fouls up and you lose your head, it'll be my neck on the block for decapitation. It's the best I can do.'

The door was slammed on Foxy. With a thumb she gestured for Badger to follow her to the lead vehicle. He had to burrow for a space on the back seat. When she was in and the doors were shut, they were driven away. He didn't catch her eye, didn't see the point in trying, and kept silent. Best to stay silent as he couldn't picture where the road led or who it led him to.

The Engineer's car had diverted in the city of Ahvaz, off the route that was shortest, quickest, to the camp. It had crossed the Karun river and gone to the principal clinic in the town where his wife's medication awaited collection. But the painkillers were not on the usual shelf and the man administering the pharmacy had not come to work that day. The woman who replaced him was unfamiliar with the stock held in storage, and there was a delay. By the time the plastic bottles containing the pills and capsules were in his hand, he had lost the first half-hour of an appointment awaiting him when he reached his workplace.

Not his driver's fault that they were late, but the man – his driver for nine years, loyal and fully aware of the importance of Rashid Armajan to the al-Quds Brigade – went now for a back-street cut-through to get them onto the main highway out of the city. They were away from the wider boulevards and the big concrete housing blocks, the post office and the railway station were behind them, and the homes were smaller, more roughly constructed. Cyclists, men on scooters, women walking with children and carrying water cans from or to the standpipes blocked and slowed them. The driver blasted the horn.

Rashid knew Ahvaz, had spent three years at the university in the city, but this was a district he had not been in, and the size of the Mercedes in the narrow streets made it an alien object. He warranted, as a senior man, tinted windows and blinds that covered the back windscreen: none of those who peered resentfully into the back of the car could have seen him, but the Engineer could see them, and when the Mercedes nudged the rump of a donkey or made children skip and women stumble aside. They would have known from the car that its passenger was esteemed by the regime.

At a crossroads, three policemen stood warily by an open jeep, holding carbines. Another was behind the wheel and had the engine running, fumes spilling out of the exhaust. The Mercedes braked sharply and the Engineer was jolted forward. Some of the papers he was trying to read spilled onto the floor by his shoes. Through the front window there was a brief exchange between the driver and the police sergeant, who pointed away from the direct route the driver was headed on. His arm made the sweep gesture of a long diversion. The Engineer could not hear them above the noise in the street, but the driver shook his head vigorously, as if rejecting advice, and the sergeant shrugged. The window powered up, and they went over the crossroads.

He asked what had been said.

The driver did not turn, was concentrating and weaving through obstructions. They were on the route to the gaol, the most direct way out of the city. There was a demonstration at the gaol, and they must pass it. To have taken the diversion would have added twenty minutes to the journey, and they were late.

A high-ranking official would be waiting for them, but the Engineer had been instructed never to use a mobile phone. There were satellites above that trawled for calls, did voice recognition and located the source of calls and their destinations. Mobile phones were the enemy of a man seeking discretion. The Engineer did not know of any specific threat to his life but the security officials had emphasised to him that anonymity was his best protection. The official who had come to see him from Shiraz would have to kick his heels and sip coffee or juice and . . . Why would there be a demonstration at the gaol?

The police had not said.

It was an Arab quarter they had been through. The street widened and they were edging clear of the alleyways. He reckoned his driver had done well to ignore the sergeant's directions. The gaol's wall was ahead and there was a rumble in front of them, like tyres on an uneven surface, but muffled because the windows were up and the air-conditioning was on. They came round the corner.

A crowd enveloped them.

He saw the faces through the windscreen. Arab faces, not Iranian. Ahvaz was the city of Arabs, and the Sepidar gaol was their prison.

It was as if the car was not seen and the mass of chanting, shouting men had their backs to the bonnet. The driver edged forward, and ahead the yellow-painted arms of two construction cranes jerked upwards. The men suspended from them kicked in their desperation but the arms rose until they were raised high enough for all the crowd to see them. A line of policemen, with riot shields and helmets, made a cordon between the crowd and the cranes, which were mounted on the flat beds of lorries: the gaol's gates were behind. The driver was able to go forward, slowly. The hanging was outside the gates, in public view, so the condemned were rapists, narcotics smugglers or robbers, and would be Arabs. The movement of the legs, had slowed, and the nooses had tightened. Rashid Armajan had never before witnessed a public hanging. He tried to bury his attention in the papers on his lap – but sneaked another glance at the bodies. The spasms had ceased now, and they spiralled on the ropes.

His driver murmured that they had been 'scum' and it was good what had happened to them. They were Arabs . . . The crowd, having watched the deaths noisily, seemed to the Engineer to be at a loss as to how to respond. Until some noticed the Mercedes.

He was an influential individual, a Persian, or he would not have had a big Mercedes with blackened windows, so he was a target. A fist beat on the bonnet, another on the front passenger window, then more on the other windows. Within seconds faces and bodies obscured the sky, the hanged men and the raised arms of the cranes. Faces pressed against the glass, and there was darkness. He could not see the papers in his lap. Hatred boiled around him. There were enough of them to lift the car, then let it fall and lift it again, higher. One more heave and they might tip it over. If the Mercedes overturned, he was dead— A gas canister exploded above the car and the crowd. The faces contorted in loathing as the white gas spread.

It came in through the air ducts of the Mercedes. His driver had spat on his handkerchief and held it as close to his eyes as he could while leaving himself a view of the open area in front of him. The crowd had melted away. Sandals lay crazily on the tarmacadam, with some shopping bags. A separated child howled. The crane arms were still high, the bodies still turned, and the gas dissipated.

He had never before witnessed an execution – but then, the Engineer had never made the journey over the frontier to Highway 6 and taken up a position to watch a convoy pass and the lethal force of his work. He had seen it only on the video screens of hand-held cameras and phones. He had never been close to death, never near the explosions, as he had been when the cranes' arms had been hoisted. He had never known how the soldiers of the Great Satan – or the Little Satan, also called the Poodle – were when they spilled out of their vehicles, or were lifted clear by medical teams, or were brought out as charred, unrecognisable shapes. He did not know if they screamed, or thrashed what limbs were left to them, or lay supine on stretchers, with their faces covered.

The windows were down. The gas was blown out of the interior and the driver swerved. A police officer shouted instructions as to which road they should take. The crowd had retreated to the edge of the square in front of the gaol, and the bodies would soon be lowered. Rashid Armajan would have said then, if asked, that the deaths of and injuries to soldiers in Iraq, foreigners or Crusaders, were matters for those in greater authority than himself, that his responsibility lay with the electronics on the circuit boards he manufactured. Some said, to his face, that he had done more to drive the Americans and the British from Iraq's cities and deserts than any other individual. He could feel pride in that accolade. They drove on, and left the gaol wall behind them.

He hoped that day to hear when he and Naghmeh would travel to visit a better-qualified consultant. Quite soon, breaking onto the main road and with the car speeding, he had forgotten the faces pressed to the glass. His mind was on his meeting – and when he would be told of his departure date. He felt calmer, the gas was gone, the windows were again sealed, and the little tremor of fear was lost.

She had left them to shower, and the Jones Boys had a bundle of kit for them. An officer who was more junior than herself, based at the Basra airport complex as Six's representative, had made himself scarce – run like a scared rabbit. With cause. Neither the junior, billeted on sufferance with the Americans and rarely allowed within the Agency's wire-protected compound, nor the

seniors in the Green Zone attached to the UK's embassy, nor the
team at the airport in Camp Cropper would have wanted to be
contaminated by Abigail Jones's mission. There would have been
no volunteers to step outside the protection of diplomatic status
that Six personnel enjoyed in this lice-blown, donkey-shit country.
But it was her shout, and Abigail Jones would see the thing through.
She understood the pitfalls of deniability and would live with
them; most would not. The junior wanted nothing to do with them
and had scooted as they'd pulled up in the Pajeros.

She called in, was connected to a Len Gibbons. She had taken
the incomers to the shower room and shown them how it worked.
The older one, Foxy, had waited for her to get out before even
starting to unbutton his shirt. Not the young one. Badger was
stripped down in seconds – muscled back, a close waist and clean-
lined buttocks – and had gone into the shower, turned on the
water and looked at her. There was soap but he didn't reach for it,
and she'd seen all of him. There was a store room off the office
area and Hamfist was in it with Corky and a heap of clothing, all
the kit they might need and the dinghy, everything, if they could
carry it.

Badger hadn't spoken. Foxy had talked for both of them, but
she had seen the light in the young man's eyes, and amusement.
He'd looked clean into her, through her.

On the link the voice was curt, clipped, as if Gibbons disbe-
lieved manufacturers' claims on scrambled protection. She said
that the younger one, Badger, seemed fit and was likely compe-
tent, but that Foxy looked on the edge of capability for where they
were going.

'You have to imagine the problem we had in locating covert
rural observation post experience, along with decent Farsi.
Doesn't grow on trees. For CROP, I had a half-dozen to choose
from, but Foxy's the best qualified. For the Farsi aspect, there
were no alternatives. It was him or we were into the business of an
interpreter listening and translating, then having that fed to the
rear, or of putting in someone like yourself, Alpha Juliet, who has
the language but no experience of sitting in hides. You are, anyway,

ruled out because you're on the inside. They're ignorant, they're capable and, most of all, deniable. They'll do because they have to. Time is not with us.'

She told him when they were leaving, and at what hour each morning and evening she hoped to make contact with him – *if* she had anything to report.

His response was sharp over the distorts on the link. 'Not "if" but "when". Please understand that a lot hangs on this.'

The call was cut. She looked through the door, not as a voyeur but to learn. The older man was in the shower now and the screen was misted so he was only an outline. The younger one was towelling himself hard, full frontal. He did not turn away from her. Not brazen, though. She saw that the soap was still in the bowl, seemed dry like it hadn't been used. She would have lathered herself from toe to scalp. She wondered how well, in London, it was understood what was asked of these two men, who already displayed raised hackles when confronting each other. In London, in an office that had been set up away from the Towers, would they have the slightest comprehension of the resourcefulness required? Easy enough to flick across files, draw out names and proposition in such a way as to make it near bloody impossible to back out with self-respect intact. They would have been skewered, those two, and . . . Her mind moved on. Did she have the slightest comprehension of how it would be to lie up in a hide while the clocks ticked, the hours dribbled by and they were beyond a frontier, out of reach of back-up?

Abigail Jones, career intelligence officer, was not certain she did. She called, loudly, for Harding and Shagger to get the vehicles ready, then to Hamfist and Corky to hurry with the kit. Foxy had hung his clothing on two wire hangers, except for his underwear, which he dropped into a paper bag. He put his wallet into his blazer pocket – he glanced wistfully at a photo – with his wristwatch, a fistful of loose change and his wedding ring. His shoes slotted into the bag, then went into his overnight grip. The younger one threw his clothing, wallet and watch into a plastic sack. All their possessions were secured in a steel locker. They trooped, the two of them, with towels round their waists, into the storeroom.

It was a long drive across bastard country. Nobody in their right mind would want to be on that road when darkness had come.

Where they were going, they might as well send a telegraph by Western Union if they took a lift in a helicopter.

The sun was sinking when they pulled away from the base. She thought the older man was steeled for a fight about lack of sleep so she put him in Harding's Pajero and let the younger man, Badger, ride with her. They were her eyes and ears. Without them the mission was doomed. With them it had a chance – not great, but a chance. They wore camouflage fatigues and Foxy had borrowed a pair of boots, and they had a bergen of food, water, medicines, whatever. A second bergen held the binoculars, the audio probe and directional microphone, the cameras, the batteries that everything needed, the radio, the sleeping bags, the scrim sheets, gillie suits – God alone knew how they'd get it off the ground and shift it on foot – and a shovel with a collapsible handle. They had flags, Iraqi pennants, on the front off-side wings.

When they were past the forward sentries, and the perimeter lights were drifting away, Hamfist armed his weapon. The rattle tore into Abigail's ears, and she thought that, beside her, Badger flinched. There were two handguns in the bergen with their supplies, ammunition for four magazines, flash grenades and gas. He'd looked at them carefully, then deliberately shaken his head. Was he firearms trained? He'd answered, almost apologetic, that he was not. She cocked her own weapon, a Browning 9mm pistol, and checked again, with her hand, that the rifle was on its clips along the bottom of the bench seat in the back behind her ankles.

She had done what was demanded of her, and a little more – and had no fucking idea if any of it was sufficient.

They hit the road and Shagger said they'd burn some rubber. They went north, and the sunlight, low, bathed her. If she couldn't comprehend what it would be like in the marshes over the border, who else could?

★   ★   ★

'Are you all right, Mr Gibbons?'

It must have been three-quarters of an hour since he had spoken with Abigail Jones on the link, and he had sat through that time with his chin on his hands, staring across the room at the map with the lines marking the rivers, the route of Highway 6, the edges of the marshes, the larger islands and the canals. The strongest line was the border with Iran, and his focus had been the cross in black marker ink that located the household of Rashid Armajan, the Engineer, a bomb-maker of great skill.

His head jerked up. She had allowed him his chance to reflect, had twice put fresh tea beside him, but neither mug had been touched nor the biscuit. She would have thought his mood had lasted long enough. He twisted to face her. 'Thank you, I'm fine, Sarah.' He grimaced. 'What do we say at these moments?'

'We say, Mr Gibbons, "on a wing and a prayer".'

'A dodgy wing and a big prayer.'

She turned to the window. The rain ran hard on it and seemed set in for the afternoon. He drained the lukewarm mug, then crunched the biscuit. He clicked on the memory of his phone and called the Cousin first, then the Friend.

The American told him that all was in place. 'Whatever we can give you, Len, we will, but at day's end your guys have to deliver.'

The Friend said his people waited to be told of developments. 'We're ready to go, but we need the ticket filled out, and that's for your people. At our end, we can run.'

Len Gibbons did not doubt what he was told, that the Friend could produce a killer.

Gabbi asked, 'Don't you have others?'

The man did not take offence at the challenge. 'There is a file. Read it.'

'Do you not have others?' It was not a complaint, more with amusement that he was asked again so soon.

'Do you want a state secret revealed? Do you wish to know how many competing operations are in discussion, development? Do you have to be told who has influenza, a hernia, who has a pregnant partner about to give birth? Do you concern yourself with who is tired, who might have lost the faith? The file is thin, but will thicken.'

He opened it. In the unit there were still older men, conservative, who preferred to use paper rather than rely exclusively on the electronic screen. The file contained four sheets of A4 – no photograph, no street map. He had driven in from his home, had dropped Leah at the defence ministry; they had talked about the coming public holiday, whether to go to the beach – not about choosing targets or killing them at close quarters – and why the refrigerator failed to achieve its maximum chill range. There was a concert at the end of the week, at the Mann Auditorium, and the Israeli Philharmonic would be playing Beethoven. They'd talked of that, and he had left her at the gate, seen the greetings of the sentries as she flashed a card at them and started to walk with her stick swinging in front of her. Many in the ministry, her section, would have wanted to bed her: only a few tiny fragments of the rocket's casing had blinded her and she was not scarred, her skin without flaws. Many times on his travels Gabbi could have called whores into his hotel rooms. He had not. He believed she had not. The file had a name, a cursory biography, a map of a border area and an Internet digest on 'brain tumours for beginners', dummy-style. The last sheet told him that the wife of the target was believed to be about to travel abroad for final efforts at treatment.

His smile never carried humour. A finger stabbed at the map and found a point fractionally on the Iranian side of the border with Iraq. 'I'm pleased to read this. I thought you wanted me to go there. How soon would I travel, wherever I travel to?'

'There are surveillance people who go close today or tomorrow to watch the house and try to learn. Perhaps it will happen, perhaps not. If word comes, there'll be a stampede.'

'And you are giving it to me?' He shrugged. He might go to a sales conference and he might not; he might be heading for a marketing seminar and might not; he might be called into a research-and-development brains trust and might not; he might be sent to shoot a man at close range but might not. He had been present at the killing of Moughniyeh in Damascus, of Majzoub in Beirut; he had been in Gaza, and in Turkey for a Syrian. That morning he had gone through the debrief and had told it factually, without remorse or triumphalism. He had reported that the pistol issued to him kicked to the left when fired. He had sat with the unit's psychologist, and they had talked of the programme the Philharmonic were offering at the Mann. The report the psychologist would write might have been dug from the records: it would be the same in essence as that produced after his return from Damascus, Beirut, Gaza City, Istanbul ... He changed little and was not scarred by his work.

'Stay close.'

'Of course.' He finished the glass of water offered him, and stood. He had heard it said that the man behind the desk, elderly, a little obese, bald and almost haggard, had been a junior on the planning team for the incursion into Tunis when the life of Khalil al-Wazir, who rejoiced in the title of Abu Jihad – Father of the Holy War – was taken, and the blueprint of the operation was taught to recruits as a model. Gabbi would not have considered flippancy with this man, who had much blood on his hands. It was the end of a long day: the dusk fell on the city, throwing shadows on the buildings. The last of the sunlight blistered on the sea beyond the empty beach. 'Call me.'

'We hope to hear soon. The Americans bring the money, the British bring the idea and the location. We bring you. It's a good arrangement, and gives us currency for the future, which is leverage. I do not know, no apologies, where you will go.'

'I have, my darling Lili, a problem.' He had been in Hamburg that day. He had operated. After seven hours in theatre – the patient was a prince from Riyadh who might, if he survived, buy a new wing for the neuro-surgery section – the consultant drove slowly and carefully home. He had been, unusually, complimented by the *Chefarzt* for the skill and precision of his work, but he could not be sure that the beast was fully extracted or whether enough remained to grow again beyond the most delicate reach of his knife. He had done his best and been praised. 'It is from Iran, from my past, and it pinions me.'

He came off the *autobahn* and turned for Lübeck. His pleasure at the praise was diluted. What he might say to his wife, after he had read a story to his daughter, as they sat at dinner and she poured wine, served the food she had cooked and told him of her day played on his mind. When he interrupted her, she would hear him out with a frown and an ugly twist at her mouth. Then she would snap, 'Tell them to go to hell. Put the phone down on them. Reject them out of hand. If they persist then call the Bundesamt für Verfassungsschutz. It's what they're there for, to deal with foreign threats. They're in the book. Are you intimidated by those people? Are you, Steffen? They're no part of your life.' She could not understand. He would not know how to explain to Lili – a little thicker on the hips since childbirth, and fuller in the bosom, with the first grey hairs that needed the salon's attention, dressed from the best of the shops in the Königstrasse – the power and reach of the al-Quds Brigade and what could be done to the elderly couple who had fostered and mentored him. They would end the meal shouting, and doors would be slammed and the little girl would be crying on the stairs. No one who had not lived there would understand.

He came off the big traffic circle and headed for Röckstrasse. Sleet was in the air, and there might be snow before morning.

She might throw at him, 'Are you not prepared to stand up to these people, tell them to go fuck . . .'

He owned a fine villa. Much of the old part of Lübeck had been devastated by British bombers in the spring of 1942, but the grand properties beyond the Burgtorbrücke had survived untouched. He was proud to have been able to buy a home on this street. It was an accolade to his work and endeavour. The light was on in the porch to welcome him, and the sleet flew in lines across it.

He would say nothing. She would not understand. Neither would her father, nor counter-intelligence officers. He thought himself alone, isolated.

He parked his car, went inside and told Lili of the praise heaped on him. He read the story to Magda, sat at the dinner table, complimented Lili on the cooking and asked about her day. He said nothing of the cloud hanging over him.

He had been dozing, might have been snoring gently, when the first shot hit the Pajero.

He was thrown forward, bounced off the back of the front passenger seat, then cannoned into the door. More shots followed.

Badger had woken fast. Since they had been on the big drag, which she had said was Highway 6, she had opened her window, unclipped the rifle and let it rest on her lap. The guy called Hamfist had a weapon peeping out into the growing darkness. He was awake. There were men milling in the road, lit by the Pajero's headlights and probably half blinded by them. One crawled and seemed to scream up into the night. He might have had a broken leg.

'What the fuck . . .' Badger murmured, for want of something sharper.

The road was clearing and the girl was shooting, Hamfist too. He heard her say it was thieves, and that Harding had hit one with his front fender. Corky might have winged another. They had gone straight over one of the tyres left in the road to slow vehicles down.

He could see the lights of the first Pajero, where Foxy was, then the flash and the screaming moving light – it would have been about a hundred metres in front. The light went past the front of that vehicle and carried on across black open ground. There must have been a berm or a dune because it exploded. Shagger swore and called it an RPG round. Hamfist matched the obscenity. They'd gone off the road into a ditch and Badger's elbow was driven sharply into his ribcage.

He thought they bucked over the sand and scrub for about a quarter of a mile. Then the wheel was wrenched again and they tilted, climbed and ground up onto the road. For a few seconds the two vehicles were side by side, stationary. The Six lady didn't speak, but there was a fast exchange between Harding and Shagger in a military *patois*. Badger deciphered enough to learn that thieves had put tyres on the road to slow vehicles, then stop them to rob the passengers of valuables and cargo. One thief had been run down, another had been shot. Around thirty bullets had been fired at the two Pajeros, and one rocket-propelled grenade.

Was it par for the course? Badger didn't ask. Neither Harding nor Shagger reckoned their tyres had been damaged.

Now she spoke: 'Can we, please, move off and get the hell out?'

They went on in darkness.

Mostly the road was clear, but a few times men emerge would from the dark, dragging along a pack-beast, and a few times great lorries drove towards them and made a chicken-game challenge. There were dull lights at a shack that seemed to serve food but had no customers, and there was a police road-block, but the Pajeros had their pennants up and were waved through without having to slow. Badger reckoned they wouldn't have slowed anyway, would have kept going and might have started shooting again.

They'd come into a town. She whispered that it was the Garden of Eden and Badger hadn't any idea what she meant, but again the windows were down and the guns readied. They crossed a bridge, and there was enough light for him to make out a sluggish, stinking flow of water. It looked a crap place, and he didn't see an orchard with apples, any naked girls or a fellow with a fig leaf for modesty. Out of the town, the bridge behind them and the road emptying again, they were on a track and the front Pajero threw up a dust storm they had to drive through. There was enough moon for the surface to be visible without the vehicles' headlights.

Badger closed his eyes, clamped them tight, and the pain lessened in his ribs and arm.

The end of a road, at a broken gate that had posts set into a sagging wire fence: through the gate there were heaps of discarded, rusted piping that went nowhere. He realised it meant oil and that it had been bombed. He'd carried his bergen, the fullest and heaviest, and had made certain he accepted none of the Jones Boys' offers to help. There was a single-storey concrete building with little compartment rooms that were filthy, shrapnel-spattered, looted. He'd taken one, and Foxy had been next door – but there were no doors. There was pain, though.

Badger was on the sleeping bag spread on the concrete floor. He didn't realise she was there. He could hear a constant drone of mosquitoes in flight but they had not bothered with him yet. There was no light, but the subdued sound of a radio playing soft jazz, maybe New Orleans – he'd have had to strain his ears to hear it better.

Staying still on the bag killed some of the pain. She was standing over him. 'Are you bad or good, hurt or in one piece?'

He blinked, tried to make her out in the darkness, couldn't. The movement he made in reacting to her voice hurt his ribs and he bit his lip. 'Thanks for asking. I'm fine.'

'Are you injured?'

'Bruised.'

'Does that mean "wrecked"?'

'No.'

'I have to ask.'

'I've answered.'

'Can I see it?'

'What for?' Badger shifted to face her. He had told the truth, and he would go on.

'Because I want to.'

He heard authority in her voice and doubted there was a future in argument.

'I want to know what state you'll be in when you go forward.'

'I won't be a passenger – not alongside him.'

'Open your shirt.'

He did. He could smell her breath and sweat – no deodorant. Excellent, professional. In this sort of place, Badger reckoned, you wouldn't know when you might have to burrow into a hole while the bad guys went by, and the smell of toothpaste or deodorant was the worst giveaway. Now he rated her higher than he had just on the evidence of her skill through the ambush, shooting well and fast, leaving the driver to do the driving and Hamfist to put down the main suppressive fire. He had the buttons on the camouflage top loose and rucked up the lightweight khaki T-shirt. He wouldn't show that it had hurt. She didn't use a torch but moved her fingertips across his skin, paused when he winced. Her face was close to his and the darkness was around them. A guy did a trumpet solo on the jazz that was playing, and he had to lift his arm so that she could get more easily onto the place where the elbow had hurt his ribs. He couldn't see her eyes, but her breath was on his face. The pain seemed to go.

She eased across him, slipped a leg over his hip and her fingers played on his skin.

Foxy Foulkes was dreaming. He had forgotten the name of the hotel and which junction he had come off at, and had forgotten the number of the motorway. He had forgotten, too, what the room had looked like, its décor, and what was in the chilled mini-bar. He had not forgotten, over seven years, that a lift had been offered from the training course for Greater Manchester Police, that she had been in the force's computing team and was going to a seminar in London. He was going south. She had put her hand on his thigh, and music had played. He'd wrenched the wheel at the junction, and they'd checked in without baggage. Both had been half stripped before they used the little key to open the fridge and take out a half-bottle of fizzy stuff. It was a hell of a good dream, him with Ellie, now his wife.

His blazer was on the floor, in the dream, and his trousers and underpants, her clothes scattered over them. It was passionate, even frenzied, at the start, but the second time had been calmer and quieter. He'd told her they were soul-mates, and in the dream they did it a third time – nearly bloody killed him – and she'd sighed . . . He had dozed, and then thought he was dreaming, but he was awake.

He heard a grunt through the wall and struggled to find Ellie. Then he sat up, listening. Bloody hell, were they at it?

Abigail Jones asked herself, 'What did you do that for?' And answered, 'God only knows.' She could have talked through a hundred reasons, or ten, and could have decided that none made sense. She used a tiny beam from a pocket torch to guide herself down the corridor, past the open doorway into the older man's room, and came into the big area where the gear was. She let the beam rove around. Shagger and Corky were on their sides, on the bags, and seemed to be asleep. Hamfist was hunkered against a wall, facing the outer doorway. He had an AK assault job, with two magazines taped, on his lap. He reached towards the small CD/DVD player to cut the music, but she waved a hand and he let it play on. Harding, the American, would be sitting on the building's outside step, with an image-intensifier sight on his weapon, watching the broken gate and the parked Pajeros.

A burr in the accent, and a whisper: 'They all right, ma'am?'

'They're fine.'

'They know what they're into, ma'am?'

'Probably as much as is good for them.' The torch was switched off and the jazz lulled them. She sat, cross-legged, with her weight against a loaded bergen.

'Rather them than me, ma'am.'

'A fertile imagination isn't called for . . . Foulkes – Foxy – told me what he regretted most was that I'd taken his wallet off him. He'd got a photo of his wife in it, and wouldn't have it with him. Maybe other aspects bothered him, but that was all he let on.'

'I don't have a picture of the wife, the ex, or the kids. I sent them money for new bikes last Christmas, didn't hear back. Doubt there'd be any tears if an RPG aimed straighter, except that the money would stop.'

'The younger one, Badger, reckoned I was good. Why? Because I hadn't used toothpaste or soap today or yesterday. His story – the best of the South Africans when they were fighting Cubans in Angola had their teeth falling out. Why?

Because they were the most dedicated covert-skills guys in the bush, and toothpaste is like soap – the scent lingers. No soap, no toothpaste, no cigarettes, no alcohol, no curries and nothing spicy. I suppose it was a little lecture in how serious the work is, the way that scent and smell last. I may just have been too damn idle to use toothpaste and soap. Oh, and armpit spray would be an appointment at Abu Ghraib. I learned that this evening.'

She asked herself again, 'What did you do that for?' And answered, 'God only knows.'

They were in grey light. Grey sky before the sun came up above a berm on the left side of the track, to the east of them. Grey water, brackish and stagnant in the centre of a lagoon, and grey mud with dark cracks that showed how far the marshes had been drained artificially, then flooded, then drained again by the dams upstream and evaporation; drought from lack of rain. The reed banks, also, had no colour – that would come with the morning.

Two Pajero jeeps, low on their chassis from the armour plate fitted to the doors and engine casings, the added layers of rein-forcement underneath, kicked up dust trails as they took a raised track between what had once been lakes, and went east. No radio on in either vehicle, and no conversation: the briefings were finished and had been reiterated over sips of bottled water before they had loaded up.

They drove along an old bund line, packed dirt and mud thrown up three decades before in the early months of the war with Iran, by bulldozers and earth-moving gear, for the convoys of Iraqi tanks to traverse the marshlands and reach the border for the drive towards Susangerd and Ahvaz. The four employees of Proeliator Security, the officer of the UK's Secret Intelligence Service and the two deniables had no interest in the history of the terrain they crossed.

There was no talk of them being in the lost Garden of Eden, or having passed alongside the Tree of Life in al-Qurnah during the night, or that they were where the Great Flood had occurred and the Ark had grounded. They did not observe that they were in the 'cradle of civilisation' where cultures had emerged five millennia before, and where a people, the Madan, had existed among the marshes since before history. Neither did they consider drainage, dam building nor drought. But they had gone by two tiny encampments, shanties with corrugated-iron roofing and other buildings in the traditional style of woven reeds, the *mudhifs*; children and dogs had chased after them but the thump of generators had not penetrated the thickened windows of the Pajeros. All of the buildings had been adorned with satellite dishes. The armies of the Medes, Persians, Greeks, Romans and Arabs had been here, and the Mongol hordes. British infantry had fought a battle close by ninety-seven years ago, and had struggled in the same heat that would rise later in the day. The marshes had been places of refuge for malcontents, rebels, insurgents, smugglers and thieves. There would never be, nor ever had been, allies here for a stranger.

Ahead, the grey landscape took on light colours – red in the sky, green in the reed banks, mud brown in the water – and dust coated the vehicles. Pigs and otters took cover and birds flew away from the intruders. They could no longer see the derricks of the oil platforms – discarded, damaged, awaiting new investment in the Majnoon fields, but ahead was a horizon.

The vehicles stopped. The dust settled. In the few seconds that it hung, obscuring any view of where they'd halted, two men pitched out, then the woman, and two more men, festooned with weapons, pulled the bergens clear and the small inflatable boat. No hugs, no exhortations about the importance of a mission across a frontier, just a brisk cuff from her on their shoulders, and a nod from the two armed men. The two slid down the bund line onto cracked mud and into crackling dead reeds. The others were back in the vehicles and the wheels spun, forward to the limit of the track's width, then reversing, and they were gone.

The dust clouds thinned.

Who might have seen that the Pajeros were lighter by two men and two bergens? No one.

The silence fell around them, a lonely quiet, intense and frightening, as it had always been for strangers who came unannounced and unwanted into the marshes.

5

They went forward, and were into the third hour since they had trudged away from the drop-off point. Foxy Foulkes still led. There were no maps to follow and this was ground that Ordnance Survey did not cover. Anywhere he had worked in Britain or Northern Ireland there had been big-scale maps with signs marking telephone boxes, churches, pubs and points of interest, like the summit of high ground. There were no buildings and no elevated terrain. He was slowing but he'd be damned if he'd allow the younger man to pass him and take on the role of pace-setter.

There was emptiness and stillness. Both, in Foxy's mind, were delusions and delusions bred a climate of danger. Among the reed beds and on the little mud islands that rose, perhaps, a metre above the waterline of a channel or an open space, or two metres above a dried-out bed, there would be the small villages of those marsh people who had survived the persecution of the dictator, the ebb and flow of the war fought along the frontier, an invasion of foreign troops, gassing, bombing and shelling, drainage, reflooding and drought. There would be tiny village communities that had TV screens but no schools or medical care. They could exist through murder and thieving, and by being paid for information. Foxy did not doubt that small craft, of which he had seen photographs in the intelligence reports at the interrogation centre seven years earlier, nudged through the passageways between the reed banks. He did not doubt that their progress, not as fast as when they had started out, left a track of sound. The sun was climbing.

It was now 'bare-arsed ground'. He and Badger had, an understatement, insufficient cover, and no map that helped; the GPS handset guided him. They had been through water to their knees, in stinking mud to their ankles, and in reeds that towered over their heads. The option now was to walk in more water or climb a bank, scramble to the top on all fours, and get on a bund line, or it might be a berm – there was a difference. A berm was an earthwork thrown up by bulldozers as a military defence or a flood barrier, and a bund was a raised road. To go up would make an easier route but they would be exposed – 'bare-arsed' – which would break every rule in the croppie's bible. He wanted water . . . Better, he *needed* water.

And speed. He realised he couldn't set the pace required. To get onto the flat top of the bund, or the berm, would ignore one of the core basics – Foxy taught them when he was out with recruits: Shape, Shadows, Shine, Surfaces, Space and Silhouette. If he went up onto the bund, and took the young'un with him, he would be silhouetted against the skies, the reeds and the mud – might as well have brought a bull horn with him and shouted that they were coming. He stayed down.

His boots went through the water. It was a small satisfaction that their prints in the mud would be hidden by the water.

There was clear, quiet breathing behind him, like the guy had no problems with the weight of his bergen. If they were seen, they would be at the mercy of thieves, who lived off what they could steal and sell on. They would be stolen and sold on, and then they'd be right for the orange jumpsuits, and for what used to be called 'the Baghdad haircut' in the interrogation centre. The sun's light and strength drained his energy, and the cloying mud sapped the muscle power in his legs. There would be plenty of groups ready to stand in an orderly queue for the chance to bid big money at any auction if a pair of Crusaders were up for grabs. Orange suits were the uniform for the camera shows where poor bastards pleaded for their lives and rubbished their politicians' policies: the jihadists put them always in the same colour as the Americans' prisoners wore at Guantánamo, as if that legitimised the killing. The 'haircut' wasn't a short back and sides but the head wrenched back and the throat exposed so that the blade had an easier cut . . .

and the same bloody camera would be running. The bastards in Luton and the West Midlands, Bradford and the north-west, who lived in the mean terraces and who – between their prayer sessions – flitted between the Internet sites that showed the beheadings, would likely get a hard-on if they had a fuzzy view of Foxy Foulkes's head going back and the flash of the knife . . . Damned if it was him who was going to stop first, and he didn't know how far they had still to travel to the frontier. The symbols and numbers on the GPS were blurred with the sweat dribbling off his forehead into his eyes.

They stayed in the lee of the bund, and there was a toppled battle tank ahead. His feet sloshed in water, and his stride was shorter. It was only the third hour and there might be another three to the border, then two more at least to where they would make the hide. He wore his gillie gear, and the bit that covered his head and face. A 'gillie' was a man who held the rods for the gentry on a salmon river, or guided marksmen towards deer; they'd been called up in the Great War from the estates to match the Prussian snipers with their skill in concealment, their knowledge of the elements and cover, and they'd developed their own suits, which gave them greater protection from searching eyes and lenses. The camouflage was good for the mud and dirt wall of the bund, but poor in the reeds. He listened for a gasp behind him – exhaustion, at the limit – but heard nothing.

Should have concentrated. Had the orange suit in his head and a man – himself – pleading to a lens for mercy. Guys were behind with rifles and one had a knife. He went by the tank. Its body was intact and he couldn't see the entry hole of an armour-piercing missile but one of the tracks was broken. It would have been a mine, then an internal explosion and fire. The plate on the turret was rusted by the wind and dark from the fire. It could have happened thirty years ago and they might still be inside. Thieves would have stripped the interior, the wristwatches and jewellery from the dead crew, if they were salvageable, but would have left the bodies. The thoughts of the jumpsuits and then the rotting dead brought him back to Ellie.

A car's wheels on the gravel, its door slamming. A key in the lock, her coming in.

Him: 'Hi, darling, where've you been?'

Her hesitating, then: 'Up to see Tash – didn't I tell you I was going?'

'Do I know Tash?'

'Course you do. She used to work with me. You never listen, love. Course I told you.'

'Made it home earlier than I'd thought . . .' He'd moved to kiss her, but she'd averted her mouth and he'd just caught the back of her neck, but he'd smelt the perfume, lovely scent. He couldn't see her face.

A sort of distant voice: 'I came back through Wootton Bassett, love, and got held up. They were bringing home one of the soldiers. The traffic was stopped. I couldn't go anywhere. I watched. They're all heroes, aren't they? His coffin had the flag on it. The Legion was there. Everyone stood to attention. Old blokes had medals on. There was a family with flowers, people crying, loads of them. It was for a real hero, fantastic.'

He'd said, 'Well, love, I'm not a hero but I negotiated the motorway all the way up from the far west and . . .'

It was a poor effort at a joke. She'd rounded on him and the rant had started. 'You don't bloody listen, do you? I'm talking about heroes; the bravest of the brave. Real men. It's about sacrifice – a man told me that at the petrol station. Giving their lives for us. He called it "paying the ultimate price". That's nothing to make some stupid remark about.'

And there had been a slammed door. The bloody irony of it. He was slogging through mud at the edge of a bund, had a bergen on his back and a gillie suit that about suffocated him, and he was doing hero stuff. His throat was parched, and he was dehydrating, and they'd not allowed him to send a decent text. Irony was cold comfort.

Two trucks had come off the bund and gone engine first down the sheer slope. Their bonnets were in the water. Maybe they'd been bulldozed off to make way for more tanks. The water was stagnant, and the smell was bad. He retched, and had to step further into the water until it was lapping his knees. He saw three legs of a creature stuck upright, and wondered where the fourth was. The carcass was of a water buffalo, and it was about fucking landmines. He was swaying. The heat and smell were destroying him. He started to sink.

'It's not the promenade at Bognor,' a voice behind him mocked. 'Shift it.'

He must have opened his hand, let it slip. The stink of the animal clogged his nose. He scrabbled for it, couldn't find it. The weight of the bergen seemed to pull him back.

His voice croaked: 'Give me a hand, Badger.'

'You a passenger, Foxy?'

'A hand.'

'Want me to lead? That it? Do a donkey's job?'

'I want to stop. Rest.'

'We have to get there before dark. That's what the boss lady said.'

'A drink, and some help.'

'Say it properly, Foxy.'

'Some help.'

'Properly, Foxy.'

'Please. Some fucking help, *please*.'

And his voice must have lifted. A flight of ducks lifted out of dried foliage on the far side of the lagoon, and he remembered what Alpha Juliet had said. He wondered, rambling, if they were Marbled or Ferruginous or White-headed Duck. A hand came under his arm. He felt himself propelled forward, and they rounded the sunken trucks, leaning behind the buffalo carcass.

With the hand in his armpit, the weight of the bergen lessened. They edged back under the bund. The mud seemed thinner now and the pace quickened. A water bottle was passed to him, and he swigged.

He couldn't hide it. 'Back there, I dropped the GPS. It sank. I lost it.'

No answer. Not even a look that killed. He passed the bottle back. He thought they were heading in the right direction.

The bloody irony of it. When could he have refused, stepped back smartly and walked away? The opportunities were never available for little people like Joe 'Foxy' Foulkes . . .

She was still in bed, alone. The central heating had failed in her workplace of the last two years, Naval Procurement in Bath, and the buildings on the hills south of the city were as little 'fit for purpose' as the communal boiler system. They'd shivered all through yesterday, and the decision had been taken to close down until the problems were fixed.

She heard, below the bedroom, the front gate squeal. It needed oiling. She'd asked Foxy to do it twice, reminded him only last week. A vehicle swung into the drive. Ellie got up, shivered, remembered she'd turned the heating up last night to twenty – Foxy didn't like that, and said sixteen was high enough. But Foxy wasn't there . . . She'd had the text.

There were footsteps on the gravel, and two men's voices. One was by the front door, the other beyond the gate. She hooked on her dressing-gown and parted the curtains. A man was leaning on her gate and his car half blocked the lane. Her eyes tracked across the drive, and there was Foxy's car. The bell rang.

She had had the text two mornings before: *Hi, love. In a hurry – have to be away, work, don't know how long. Verboten to phone. Luvya Foxy.* She had rung his mobile eight, ten, twenty times, but it was switched off.

She went downstairs. It was a decent cottage, in a country lane in a village outside the Wiltshire garrison town of Warminster, pretty with climbing roses over the porch, wisteria on the front walls, small mullion windows, a garden, three bedrooms, two bathrooms and a new kitchen she'd chosen. When they'd met, she'd been coming out of a divorce, with most of her savings gone in legal fees. She'd probably have ended up in a studio flat, if Foxy hadn't offered her the lift down from the north-west. No way she could have afforded a chocolate-box cottage in the country. She had something to be grateful to Foxy for, but over the last two years that 'something' had become vague – almost out of sight since she'd met Piers.

She opened the door. The man wore a white shirt, a chauffeur's style black tie, probably with an elastic band round the neck, and an anorak. He held out the keys. 'Your husband's, Mrs Foulkes.'

Half asleep, early in the morning and no alarm set: 'What?'

'Bringing back your husband's car. We picked it up from the car park where he left it. Sorry we couldn't manage it yesterday.' He was turning away.

It was a forlorn chance. 'And where is he? Where's he skived off to?'

In mid-stride he paused, angled his face to her. A laugh without a chuckle. 'Don't imagine they tell me things like that. Not for the likes of me to know. Just a thought – if he's away more than a couple of weeks, I suggest you turn the engine over, so's the battery's not flat when he gets back.'

She closed the door on him, failed to thank him. Upstairs, she checked an Internet site, a town hall's page, learned a date and a time, then called the guy who did accounts at the Naval Procurement offices.

He stood under a palm tree and gazed out over the marshes.

They were a source of fascination to him, an endless pleasure. He enjoyed little in his life. Mansoor was in his thirty-first year. He should, by now, have been prominent in the al-Quds Brigade, looking for further promotion and higher command, but the chance was denied him because of the explosion of the Hellfire missile fired from the Predator drone, neither seen nor heard, and giving a warning in fractions of a second as the light stream and the roar of power fell from the sky.

He could stare out over the marshes, watch the wind move the reeds and ruffle the trees on the island across the lagoon, see the hunting herons and kingfishers, the ripples on the water when the fish rose and always there was the changing weather – threatening, benign, calm, dramatic – and the light. No two days were similar.

He would not advance because of the injuries. Muscle, tissue, even some bone had been torn from the back of his left leg, above and below the kneecap. He would have recovered better if he had been close to medical aid: he had not. Numb with pain, Mansoor had been carried on a litter from northern Iraq across the mountains. The hospital where he had received the first serious treatment had been in the Iranian city of Saqqez. There had been traces of gangrene in the poorly bandaged wounds and the surgeons had deemed it necessary to take as much again of the remaining muscle, tissue and bone as the missile had. His limp was pronounced and his future as a combat officer was finished. He had been sent to the marshes on the border as security officer to the Engineer, Rashid Armajan.

He would not have believed it possible. He knew the names of the birds that flew over the water and nested in the reeds, those that were gentle and harmless and those that had sharp talons and wickedly curved beaks. He knew also where the otters lived and bred, where there might be pig with young, and which island had the greatest infestation of poisonous snakes. He also knew that in these marshes, half a century before, there had been striped hyenas, wolf packs and, rarely, a leopard. Crippled, he provided security for the Engineer and learned about the beauty and life of the marshes.

At first, while his wife continued to work as a computer operator at the Crate Camp Garrison, he had loathed the prospect of guarding this man. He had, almost, considered leaving the al-Quds. He had arrived at the house, had been billeted in the barracks that fronted onto the lagoon, had come to know the family, and the wild life of the marshes and could not have said now which mattered most to him.

There were godwits and a small swimming group of pygmy cormorants and babblers, and he kept Japanese binoculars hanging from his neck. It the birds panicked he would look hard to see if a pig had disturbed them, a large dog otter, even a leopard or a wolf. It might be pilgrims going to and from Najaf across the border, or smugglers bringing opiate paste from Afghanistan and crossing

Iranian territory. The birds were, almost, the sentries that watched over the little community, and more efficient than the men he commanded. With time, he had realised he was honoured to have responsibility for a man as important in the defence of his country as the Engineer.

That morning he had been called by his father, an informer for the Revolutionary Guard Corps. He was a part-time postal official and also helped with the executions at the city gaol. He was a man of few talents and many interests, who let it be known that his son had failed to fulfil expectations. His father would have expected to ride on the back of his son's successes; he had been uninterested in the medical prognosis after a section of his son's leg had been gouged out by a missile, and more concerned with his return to authority and influence. That day his father had telephoned him from the prison with details of the public hanging of two Arabs. He had been the link between the hangman and the crane drivers in their cabs, telling them when to hoist the arms. He had enjoyed the morning; it had gone-well. From his father's knee, through his time as a recruit of the Guard Corps, during his selection for the élite al-Quds, and lying on a makeshift stretcher to be hauled across mountain tracks, he had honed a hatred for all enemies of the state, whether Arabs in Ahvaz or the distant operators of the remote guided Predators. He could not salve his loathing of the Great Satan, take revenge for his damaged leg, but the Engineer had hurt them, which enhanced Mansoor's loyalty.

In the evening, he might bring out his fishing rod to catch a carp and then, too, he could watch the marshes. He was devastated by what he knew of the illness of the Engineer's wife. He was, he thought, almost a part of their family.

There was stillness in front of him, safety. The lenses of the glasses roved over the water and the flourishing reed beds. No creature moved sharply or thrashed to escape.

In the heat of the afternoon, the police came. They had two battered pick-ups. Corky had alerted her when the dirt trails were still more than a kilometre away. She had shrugged into a robe and her face was part covered with a scarf. Both Corky and Hamfist had done this territory with their regiments and would have regarded the police as deceitful and treacherous – they had probably sent a few to martyrs' graves. They had talked this through and the drills were understood. Two spotter 'scopes up on the bund line round the wrecked drilling camp looked down into the marshes that surrounded the site. Harding was behind one and Shagger had the other; both had bird books and pamphlets beside their stools. Abigail had not seen an individual come close to the camp, and none of the Jones Boys had warned her of a 'dicker' looking them over from cover. They would have been told, and they would have come. The routine was that she would explain in her halting Arabic that they were a part of a UNESCO-sponsored eco-watch, additionally funded by *National Geographic.* They had the full support of the ministry in Baghdad, and the provincial governor's office. She had the papers of each organisation to prove her point: a clutch of 'To Whom It May Concern' letters, all with impressive headings, a fifty-dollar bill attached to each one. She had anticipated that after each paper was examined the money would have gone. She knew what they earned, and remarked that she and her colleagues were grateful to the local police for watching over them. She could bore, and did so: her anxiety about the potential for oil pollution of this amazing habitat, unique in the world to Iraq; the species of bird and animal life here, needing monitoring, which were not found anywhere else in the world. Iraqis, from across the country, could be proud of it. Had they not been told she was coming with colleagues and an escort? She had the smile and her appearance was harmless, but the policemen would have seen the two men gazing out over the marshes through ' scopes, breaking off to write in notepads. They also had cameras, while two more carried automatic weapons and were in the shadow of the buildings. When she had bored them enough, they left.

She said to Harding, 'That was probably good enough for today, and maybe for tomorrow, but they'll be back. I don't think in a couple of days they'd manage enough links to unravel it at

Baghdad or Basra level. Three days, maximum four, would push against the limits.'

He nodded. Truth was, she liked him more than the others. The original quiet American, he spoke rarely but, of them all, he was the one Abigail trusted with her life.

She said, 'I doubt the Fox and the Badger will be in much shape after three or four days.'

Was it flawed? Two men who might have been inserted too late and find the bird flown, or had gone in too early and would be unable to sustain the watch. They might be there too long and show out. She had liked the scrapping between them. There was no way other than to have men on their stomachs, peering through lenses with earphones clamped to their skulls. It couldn't be done with satellites on the electronics in the drones. It would be their shout. The mission depended on them. She had thought the antipathy, at each other's throats, more likely to raise the competitive streak that would dominate their relationship. Too cosy, and they wouldn't be efficient. It was personal to Abigail Jones because she had examined Badger's bruising and had worked a leg over his pelvis to see it better. He had said something about the smell of her body, then the taste, and she had done as much stripping as he had. She had made a complication where there should have been none. She always kept a couple in her wallet, and when she had gone at first light to clear her system the condom had gone into the hole with their rubbish for burial. All a complication, but Abigail Jones did not do regret.

It couldn't last more than three or four days.

He met his wife, Catherine, in a coffee shop on Regent Street.

She told him what was in the bag. Two shirts, three pairs of underpants, four pairs of socks, and a new pair of pyjamas. Len Gibbons thanked her, awkward – he had been since they'd first clapped eyes on each other thirty-five or so years earlier.

He couldn't tell her how it was going. She could ask him nothing about what kept him in London, or why he needed changes of clothing. He couldn't tell her how long he would be there. She couldn't ask when he would need replacements and whether he would need another suit brought up, heavy- or lightweight. Nothing to say about the garden because of the weather, and she hadn't heard from either of the children, both students. The job ruled him, not that it had treated him well. Another woman, in her place, might have harboured doubts about her husband's staying up in London and sharing an office with Sarah, the faithful assistant. She didn't – had actually said so last year. Catherine Gibbons thought that, most days, he didn't notice what his assistant wore, probably hadn't registered what she, his wife, had dressed in. She was a widow to the Service. They sipped coffee and nibbled shortbread. He looked at his watch twice, and flushed when she caught him at it.

Naughty of her, but she challenged him: 'Important, Len, is it?'

He surprised her, didn't change the subject or sit in silence. 'Important as anything over my desk in years, and we have no idea how it will end or where. We've people out at the end of a line and ... Does that tell you anything?'

Her eyes were bright and mischievous: 'Is it legal?'

He didn't bat her away. 'Most would say it's illegal. No one would say it's legal. A few would say they don't bloody care ... Thanks for coming up.'

She persisted: 'Those people at the end of the line, do they know whether it's legal or not?'

'They know what they need to know. Yes, I appreciate your coming up.'

He left her, had already outstayed the time he should have been away from his phone. He knew Badger and Foxy had been dumped, would be moving forward towards their lie-up and soon be at the border – which was, sort of, a defining moment. Legal or illegal, he didn't bloody care – as long as it stayed deniable. It would be a huge step, as big as anything he had handled since he was a 'greenhorn'. Should it have been asked of them?

Bit bloody late, Len, to be worrying on that.

He was like a donkey refusing to go any further, its hoofs stuck into the mud. He thought of Foxy as a stubborn, thick-skinned ass, but the guy had stopped, and he was a hell of a weight – heavier when the momentum was lost. Badger swore softly. He tried to take the next step but couldn't tug Foxy forward. He turned. His face was in the older man's, whose lips moved.

There was more water ahead of them, but they had stopped on a small raised platform of mud and rotted vegetation. Foxy's right trouser leg was caught on a strand of barbed wire. His lips kept moving, but Badger couldn't hear what he was saying. He had been thinking about Alpha Juliet – and that their approach through the shallow water and scattered reed beds had been about the most feeble and unprofessional he had ever attempted.

Foxy's lips were still moving. Badger bent and freed the trouser leg, tearing it. The lips moved.

'If you've something to say, then say it.'

'Nothing to say to you.'

'Who to, then?'

'Myself.'

'How knackered you are, and unfit? Not up for it?'

'Something you wouldn't understand.'

'Try me.'

Foxy said, 'Try, smart-arse, "*Halae shomaa chetoreh?*" Answer, *khoobam mersee*. I asked how you are and you told me you're well and thanked me . . . We're at the border, and there's something called the Golden Hour, which you wouldn't know about. We're going to stop and rest for an hour, Golden or not. Got me?'

'We don't have an hour.'

'Then you can go on ahead, and when you find a friendly policeman you can say, "*Raah raa beman neshaan daheed mehmaan-khaaneh, otaaq baraayeh se shab*", but it's unlikely he'll drop you off at a hotel where you can book a room for three nights. It's – don't curl your lip at me – Farsi, which is spoken from where we crossed that wire. It's why I'm here: I speak the language. You're just the fucking pack animal that helps me to get close to the target. I matter, you don't. If I want to rest then—'

'Then you rest.'

It was a quick movement. A twist of the shoulders, a half-swivel of the hip and a step to the side. Badger extricated himself from Foxy's weight.

He took a pace forward, then another. He was over the wire – would have given a hell of a lot to have Ged alongside him, quiet, authoritative, more than able to take his share. He spoke not a word of that language, and neither did Ged. There was a channel in front, sliced through the reed banks, and open water beyond it. He thought it would be a kilometre and a half to where the cross had been on the GPS screen, their destination. He detested the man he was shackled with, but Badger had no Farsi. He took another half-dozen steps, stopped and heaved off the bergen. He tilted his knee, rested the pack on it, out of the water, and rummaged. He found the packaging, ripped out the plastic inflat-able and fired the air canister. It hissed, grew and floated.

He worked the bergen onto his shoulders again, turned and beckoned to Foxy. The heat blistered up from the water, and the gillie suit was one more burden. He didn't know how much more of his strength he could depend on – but he was not about to show weakness. Foxy came to him. Another gesture, for Foxy to get into the dinghy. The little craft – not much bigger than a child's on a beach – bucked under his weight. Badger lifted off Foxy's bergen and dumped it on the man's lap. There was a length of nylon rope, which he slipped across his shoulder and pulled hard. He walked, skirting the channel's edge. The water was level with his knees. They went by a collapsed watchtower, which would have been felled three decades before. Two of the wooden legs were out of the water and half of the platform. They rounded a sunken assault barge.

He asked, from side of mouth, 'What's the Golden Hour?'

'You want to know?'

'Wouldn't have asked if—'

'It's army speak. It's the time the back-up should take to reach an FOB – that's a forward operating base – when it comes under sustained attack and risks being overrun. The men know that back-up will reach them within the hour, by land or by helicopter.

It's the pact between the military units, an article of faith. At the
FOB they have to hunker down, hang on in there, and know that
within sixty minutes the cavalry will be coming over the horizon.
That's the Golden Hour – there's other uses, like getting treatment to the wounded, but that's the relevant one.'

'And her and her lads, they'd get to us inside an hour?'

Almost droll from Foxy, like he enjoyed it. Like he had hold of
the balls and squeezed them. 'Do you want it gift-wrapped? Grow
up, young 'un.'

'Meaning?' There might have been a tremor in Badger's voice,
but he swallowed hard and hoped it was hidden.

'They'd get to where that watchtower was, and the wire – the
border. They wouldn't cross it. That's how far they'd come forward
in the Golden Hour, not a metre further. They won't cross into
Iran. They won't discharge firearms at personnel inside Iran.
They'll lift us out from behind the border but won't come in and
get us. They'll be there within the hour, was the promise. Maybe
now you understand why I was reluctant to take the next step –
and why only an idiot would rush on. Got me?'

'Yes.'

'God . . . Did you take it all on trust? Didn't you think of asking
one important question? Like "Where's the back-up?"'

'Took it on trust.'

He started again to pull the nylon rope, and the water deep-
ened. It was at the top of his thighs, clammy in his groin. In
England, on operations, the back-up was never more than ten
minutes away. Here, to hold out for the Golden Hour, they would
have to retreat to the border, and there they would have handguns,
one each with three magazines, gas, fists and boots. It had an
emptiness to it, 'take on trust', that echoed in his head.

'I asked. It mattered to me because I've a wife . . . Didn't you
ask that woman, the clever bitch?'

'No.'

The van was driven into the car park at the rear of the hostel, and
a car followed it. To both drivers, it seemed a desolate place of

stained, weathered concrete and – late morning – it was deserted.
Most of the windows had the blinds up but no interior light on; a
few had the blinds down. They might have wondered whether this
anonymous block, with no name, only a street number, was the
correct destination, but a woman came out of the doors in part of
a police uniform, which matched where they were supposed to be.
The door clattered shut, and was self-locking. The van driver was
sharp enough to register the difficulty and called to her.

He'd brought a car back. And?

He'd need somewhere secure to leave the keys.

He had a name, Daniel Baxter.

Was she supposed to have heard of him?

He'd kick the door down, if he had to, to find somewhere to
leave the keys safely. The policewoman grumbled but took them.
They were attached to a ring with a picture of a badger's head.
She punched the door's code and dropped them into one for each
resident's locked boxes, and was thanked. She ran for her own
wheels.

The van driver said to his colleague, 'I don't know where he's
gone, Baxter, but I'd bet my best shirt that nobody here's even
noticed he's away.'

The consultant came out of the doorway, hoisted his umbrella and
started to run. He saw the man. His principal theatre was in
Hamburg, but he also had a clinic in Lübeck, at the University
Hospital and Medical School, with scanning equipment, where he
could see patients. His was a new block, but there were many old
buildings on the campus that had stood for more than seventy
years. On the far side of the street was the cafeteria to which he
liked to slip away in the middle of the day for a baguette and
coffee and to glance through the day's paper – the *Morgenpost*.
The football reports cleared his mind before he returned for the
afternoon. The man, not a German, was in front of the cafeteria.

It had been raining all morning. If the consultant had kept
running, heading for the café's door, he would have had either to
sidestep or collide with the man. He slowed in the middle of the

street and found himself anchored there. A delivery van hooted at him. The man had no umbrella, no raincoat. Water glistened on his short hair and the shoulders of his jacket. The shirt under the jacket had no collar and was buttoned at the throat, and the cheeks were swarthy. He thought the man was from the east, perhaps Baluchistan province. The trousers were baggy at the knees and the shoes dulled by wet.

The man had the appearance of a guest-worker in the northern German city. He could have been a bus driver, a plumber, a construction-site worker, or a book-keeping clerk in a warehouse – and would have been a ranking intelligence officer, working under diplomatic cover. He was rooted in the road, and a car swerved past to his left. A trio of students on bicycles trilled bells at him. The man had dressed, the consultant realised, to emphasise the old world of an orphan in Tehran, and of a student who had prospered because the state had paid his way.

There was a smile from the man, as if they were old friends. He came across the street with his arms outstretched. He ducked under the canopy of the consultant's umbrella and kissed Soheil on both cheeks – not Steffen. There was a whiff of a spicy sauce on the man's breath and a hint of nicotine. He would have been an official of Vezarat-e Ettela'at va Amniat-e Keshvar, and any official of VEVAK was to be feared. He had not told Lili of the call, and through that morning he had thought only twice of the contact.

He blurted, 'I've just come out for a sandwich. I have little time, and—'

'I have driven from Berlin and you have – distinguished Soheil – as much time as I need you to have. So, do we stand here and cause an accident or go somewhere? Your office? Can't someone go out and fetch coffee for you, juice for me, some food? Will you entertain me in the rain or in the dry?'

Would he take an Iranian intelligence officer into his sanctum? Hang up a wet jacket beside a radiator? Introduce him? *My friend here is from the Ministry of Intelligence and State Security in Tehran. Everybody knows – don't they? – that I'm not really German, that I'm*

Iranian by birth. My education was subsidised by the Ministry of Health in Iran, and now the debt has been called in. They want a favour from me. Please, make him feel at home and bring him juice and a sandwich – salad with fish would be best – and see if his shoes need yesterday's newspaper in the toecaps. He took the man's elbow and led him towards the café.

There was a table by the window, and three chairs. They took two and the official kicked away the third so they had the table to themselves. From the wet on the man's face, hair and jacket, the consultant thought he had waited for him for at least a half-hour, and knew he would have stayed there all day if necessary. No appointment had been made, but that screwed the pressure tighter.

He brought the tray with coffee and juice, a sausage baguette for himself and another with salad and fish. The man was reaching into his pocket and a cigarette packet emerged. The consultant – Soheil or Steffen – hissed that smoking was forbidden on all the university sites.

The man smiled. 'We can bring the patient at any time now.'

He was known for his cool head, and was said to be as sure as any in the big Hamburg hospital if he was faced with potential catastrophe in theatre. He stammered that he had not yet had the chance to check the availability of facilities. The stammer became meandering waffle: he did not know what was required, would not know until he saw the patient, had read the case history and examined the scans. The man let him finish. He might have fought, called a bluff, but he didn't dare.

What he did dare was to ask, 'My patient, who is he?'

The smile was laughter. 'Who? We have not yet decided on a name for them.'

The man took the consultant's hand. As a surgeon he was reputed to be slick and fast, which kept anaesthetic times to a minimum and lessened the dangers of internal bleeding. Now the pressure on his fingers showed him how vulnerable his talent was.

'I will see the patient.'

'I didn't doubt it.'

'And I will look into the availability of theatre and scan equipment. I know we are heavily booked, but I will look into it.'

'You will do what is necessary.'

His hand was freed. He was given a card. The man's baguette was finished, his own not started. The juice glass was empty, and his coffee cooling. They could come with a hammer, force his hand onto a table, or one of the low walls around the canals of Lübeck, and break every bone. They could destroy him. The man stood up. The printed card had a first name only on it, with the address and numbers of the embassy in the Wilmersdorf district of Berlin. The man put euros on the table, as if it would sully him to accept the consultant's hospitality, and slipped out through the door into the rain.

Back in his small clinic, the consultant checked the availability of scanners in Lübeck and the theatre in Hamburg. Then a patient was shown in. He forced a smile. His daughter had a toy marionette: he understood the way it danced to its handler's tune. If they had not yet determined the identity of the patient it was a security matter, sensitive ... He thought his life teetered as a chasm yawned.

It had been a day like many others. He had finished the debrief – had enjoyed the session with the psychologist – and had been shown a file that told him little. Then he had walked out of the building into the winter sunshine of the Mediterranean, pleasant and clean, and had gone to eat on his own.

Gabbi did not have a living soul in whom to confide. Had he been dependent on company – his wife's, the regulars in a bar, even others making up the numbers on the team – it would have been noted and the information tapped into his file. Any form of dependency, alcohol, bought sex or company, would have been noted and he would have been sliding fast out of the unit's building, down the steps, across the car park, past the sentries and into the street. It would have ended.

It would end one day. It was not a pensionable activity. Long before old age caught up with him, he would be gone from the unit. There was no 'former employees association', no reunions on the eve of public holidays, no gossip opportunities with veteran campaigners. It would end when exhaustion dulled his effectiveness, and the psychologist would call it 'burn-out'. He would be gone, and might get a job in a bank, or sell property, or just waste his days on the beach. His work for the state of Israel would be complete, and his pension earned.

He had sat on a bench and watched the sea, had had a book open on his knee but had watched the sails beyond the surf, the fitness joggers and dog walkers, the young soldiers who had their rifles hitched across their backs. He knew the case histories of the great failures of the unit's work – he knew more about the failures than the successes. He could talk through, if he had to, the minute by minute intricacies of Lillehammer in Norway: wrong man shot dead, the team captured by local police – catastrophic. Could relate the disaster of the botched poisoning of Khaled Mashal in Amman: a toxic substance, lethal, squirted into the ear, but the unit's people being held in police cells and their government having to deliver the antidote that would save the bastard's life – humiliating. A wry smile, because the killing of the state's enemies could be complex. But he did not make judgements, and the file he had been shown would carry the same importance as that of the man, buried the previous day in Beirut, who had stood outside a Maltese hotel. It was always best when he stood in front, blocked the path, looked into the face.

He headed for home and would reach it only a few minutes before she was due back. It was a day like many. The shadows fell, the sun dipped on a far horizon, and he would wait, as he did so often, for his pager to bleep or his phone to ring.

At last light they had their view.

Foxy was beside him.

It seemed so ordinary, so close and yet so remote. He could not have said, without hesitating, what he had expected.

'You all right, Foxy?'

'Fine.'

'Just that you sound clapped out.'

'I'll manage.'

'Good.'

'And don't bloody patronise me.'

The evening cool didn't penetrate the gillie suit. The hood was like a heated wet towel on his head, and his hair would be flat and wet under it. Not only ordinary, but dreary and cheap, the sight gave out no atmosphere of danger, or of a place where an enemy of importance was bedded in. An enemy. A target, like any other. Could have been organised crime, or a serial-rapist inquiry, or a training camp for the rucksack guys or the vest ladies. Just a target, and the only difference was that the Golden Hour would be a fine-run thing, if push came to shove.

They had come past a herd of water buffalo that had gone on grazing while half immersed, and there had been no herdsmen with them. They had seen small columns of smoke to the left, the north, and once there had been voices, kids', and the sounds of distant life carried across the marsh. He had dragged the inflatable, with Foxy and Foxy's bergen, and if he hadn't they would still have been back at the wire. They had gone slowly and twice he had been up to his chest in the water. Once he had gone out of his depth and had had to cling to the side of the craft and grip Foxy's sleeve. There was a narrow strip, going north to south, of land and they had come onto it. He had gone forward and dared to stand beside the sole tree there. He had gazed out and seen enough, then gone back for Foxy and found that the inflatable had been folded away and was tucked into the top of a bergen. They were together, on their stomachs. The tree was beside Foxy and they had a view that went through slow-waving reeds, then across water and over the brow of an island that was some eight or ten feet above the waterline. A lake stretched away, perhaps three hundred yards across and then there was a steep bank, palm trees and buildings.

To the right there was a group of huts, put together crudely with concrete blocks. Badger had his glasses on them, the start of his traverse, going south to north. There were men in uniform at the huts with infantry weapons. They wandered and smoked, sat and talked, hugging the shade. He scanned to his left and followed two children who kicked a ball without co-ordination. One of the soldiers joined them and squeals of delight carried to him. Tracking further left brought him to the mooring in front of the house where a uniformed man squatted and fished. The lenses picked up a little red dot on the water, a float. There was a block-house building behind the man, and its front was in shade, but Badger could make out a woman sitting in shadow. She was on a hard-backed chair and held a stick. The bright colours close to her were a child's plastic tractor and a tricycle. He thought where they were now was safe, a decent distance from the target zone. In the last light, a vehicle's headlights lit the dullness, and the man who was fishing reeled in his line, stowed the rod on the bank and hurried towards the single-storey house. The kids abandoned their game and ran to the woman on the chair. She pushed herself upright with the help of the stick. Where they were was safe, and useless. He didn't have to ask Foxy's opinion on it. It was useless because it was too far back, and they would have been voyeurs there, wasting their time.

'We have to do it now.'

'You asking or telling me?' A snarled whisper.

Badger said he was 'telling'. He was rummaging in a bergen for the audio-direction stuff and a spool of fine-coated cable when the car pulled up and they saw him.

Quite a good-looking guy, hurrying from the car to the woman and hugging her.

It couldn't be left to the morning. It would be hard in the darkness but he had to hack it, get closer to the guns and where the kids played and the woman had sat. He watched them and they had their backs to him. They went inside . . . a good-looking guy.

6

The dawn was coming up, and the niggle prospered.

The geography of the location dominated, as it always did when cameras or microphones were involved. Distances were crucial. A light wind in the night had rustled the reeds. Barely audible to the ear, they rattled – almost clattered – against each other when heard through the earphones.

Foxy whispered, 'The sound quality isn't good enough. I'm here for conversations, maybe half a sentence. The audio's beam is having to travel through the reeds and that's dominating any talk by the front of the house and the door inside. I didn't set the parameters of this caper. I'm the poor bastard that has to get here – wade, paddle, damn near swim. I didn't choose the ground.'

'Did I hear that right? "Wade, paddle, damn near swim"? You were on your backside, floating and being dragged along.'

The sun was a gold sliver peeping up, far away, above a flat horizon that was unbroken by trees or high ground, only by the reed beds that moved endlessly with the wind's force.

'What I'm saying is that where we are now is unsustainable. More important, where the mike's placed is—'

'By me, of course.'

'By you, yes. Where *you* placed the mike isn't good enough. If that's the best you can do we might as well load up, turn round and walk out.'

'Quit?'

'I came here to do a job, not for my health. I see little point in staying if I can't do the work.'

'So I have to go forward and move the mike?'

'About right.'

'And how close do you suggest I go – the front door, into the kitchen?'

Foxy could have stood up, stamped and shouted, but he didn't. One thing, verbally, to clip Badger's ears for his rudeness, but another to break the rules of thirty years' practice. Badger ought to show him respect for his accumulated knowledge. 'You should get the mike into a position where its beam doesn't cross a bed of reeds, so screening its access to the front of the house. Simple enough. You up for it, or do I have to do it?'

A shrug from Badger, sour little beggar. The sound was too poor for Foxy to identify more than occasional words. The one who fished had come by the house after darkness and spoken to a soldier, or trooper, or Guards Corps man, but the words had been muffled by the reeds' movement. The same man had again come into the magnified vision of the image-intensifier, and the night-sight had shown him talking to the target. Both had smoked and their speech had been distorted.

In a half-hour, the house and the low quay in front would be bathed in low sunshine and movement would be dangerous, or stupid.

They had good cover where they were. Off to the right, which was south, there was a bund line that bypassed the shallow island where the mike had been placed by the young 'un the previous evening. It marked a boundary to the lagoon onto which the target's house faced and came to the main shoreline on the far side of the buildings he'd identified as a barracks compound. The bund line was too far away for the mike to be set, but might make a better route onto the island.

More argument? Not then. Rolling away from him, Badger let his hands slide over his suit and checked it, involuntary and instinctive, then his headpiece. He put more mud on his hands and wrists and was gone.

What else had they bickered over?

The Meals Ready to Eat. One chicken and one beef, both with rice, and he had wanted the chicken. So had Badger. Foxy had insisted, had had the chicken.

The stags . . . He'd had to sleep, had been dead on his feet, but when the young' un did the watch Foxy had been woken five times. Hard to get to sleep in the scrape, but he'd been woken five times, and five times could hear sweet fuck-all because of the motion of the reeds. He had let Badger know he needed sleep, not the sound of a reed hitting another reed and a thousand more doing the same.

Using the bags had been a point of conflict. Badger had said they should carry them out. Foxy wanted to bury them. They had a dozen, enough for a little cache of excrement, and a couple of bottles to go with them. He hadn't done it for years, been a croppie in a hide, having to bag and bottle. He could lecture on it, could make men's faces fall at the thought of the bag and doing the business a couple of feet from an oppo. The bags were in a hole and covered over, but whether they'd be carried out was not yet settled.

They had stripped in the night, and that had made for more tension. Their gillie suits and the clothes under them were soaked. Their boots were sodden. Badger had lain on his back and wriggled out of his gear. His skin was white, had no cream or mud on it. It was too many years since Foxy had bared all in front of strangers, except in the changing rooms at the gym where he did work-outs. Inhibitions, which he would not have entertained ten years before, had stressed him. When he had slid off his boots, wrung out his socks, then pulled off his trousers, he had turned away from Badger – and criticised: 'You're stark bollock naked – what happens if we have to bug out fast?' He had heard the sharp breath and had known he was held in contempt, not given the respect he deserved. The boots had dried partially, the socks mostly, but the gillie suits were still sodden and heavy.

The light came on fast.

Foxy remembered that from his weeks in the interrogation centre. It came on fast in a surge and the shadows were shortening. He looked with his glasses for movement in the reed beds or ripples. He searched for Badger. He saw the target, in a vest and pyjama trousers, sandals on his feet, come out and drag on the morning's first cigarette, then go back inside. A car came, the

Mercedes saloon that had brought the target home the previous evening. It parked and the driver stretched, spat, then lounged. He saw two sentries on plastic chairs under the low trees but they stood, reluctantly, when the officer came by them. The children appeared in nightshirts and chased each other. One fell and seemed to graze a knee – there was wailing, which he heard on the headset. Everything he saw he noted in his log, and on the first page was his sketched map of the location.

The sound failed. There had been, quite piercing, the crying of the child above the reeds' motion, then silence. There was water in front of him beyond the reed beds, which were at the edge of the ground they had reached, and then there was the last island, lower and more exposed, without cover, then more reeds, denser than the others, and the lagoon in front of the house and the barracks. He had keen eyes. Ellie had told him his eyesight was above average. She liked to say, in company, that he could see a flea move on a carpet. Ellie's job at Naval Procurement kept her out of the house too long for her to hoover up any fleas. He ached for her, always had and always would. He'd never ached for his first wife, Liz, who might still be a radiologist in Yorkshire, he didn't know, with the two daughters, who'd been barely civil the last time he had gone up from London for a birthday ... A uniform, out of sight of the house, stood on the bank of the lagoon and urinated into the water.

Foxy brought the lenses off him and was traversing towards the house when he saw what seemed a snagged mess of dead reeds caught on a little promontory. There were two others out in the water, moving languidly with the flow, but the one on the promontory, which stretched out to form a mud spit, was anchored. He hadn't seen it before, and assumed that the wind, more powerful in the night, had dislodged it from the foot of the reeds.

His shoulder was tapped, and he started, half turned.

Foxy Foulkes's reactions weren't failing: his sight was good, and his hearing, and he would have claimed that his awareness was as sharp as it had been at any time in his life since he had been awarded his own Blue Book for passing out as a qualified CROP man. He had not seen or heard him.

'Come on.'

'Where to?'

'The mike's out in front. It's another fifty, sixty metres forward. We don't have that length of cable.'

'What are you saying?'

'You want to hear anything? We go forward. See that kind of island? It isn't one. We get to the far end of it on the bund line, and we can hook up. You'll have no interference there. We have to move *now*. Come on.'

'There's not cover there,' he said sharply, almost out loud.

'Then we make some.'

Foxy bit his lip and didn't say what he thought. It was too close. No cover. What the hell was he doing there? He didn't say anything . . . Thought plenty, though. Thought about the ground on which they would lie up and where he would have a decent link with the microphone, where the beam would be clear of obstruction, and about the sun's climb, the spreading light, the soldiers who were drifting from the barracks building and the faint smell of cooking. He was there because he couldn't have refused. The young 'un, Badger, had challenged him, and he thought one argument was settled: the shit would be left buried with the bottles.

He crawled away to get his gear together as Badger reeled in the cable.

If he looked for the target, and the target's home, he could see the weapons, and far out in front of him was the island-shaped platform on which there was little cover.

What to say? Nothing.

The Engineer had gone early. The sun had been barely up, and the heat haze had not yet formed when he had kissed his wife and waved briskly to Mansoor. The Mercedes had pulled away, and the day had begun.

A few months ago, before his new-found interest, Mansoor would have started on the many texts available to him on the types and maintenance of weaponry available to the al-Quds Brigade. He would have taken books on military tactics, particularly those describing the fighting methods of the Iraqi resistance, the Afghan Taliban, Hezbollah and the North Vietnamese from the library of his headquarters at the camp outside Ahvaz. In his convalescence he had read everything available on the methods used to defeat the American military, the forces of the Great Satan and its ally, the Little Satan. He knew what had been done in Falujah, Helmand and Beirut, where the marines had been bombed, and at the plateau of Khe Sanh. Then he had nurtured his new interest.

It did not make him less alert.

He would have said that his sense for danger or threat was greater than if he had been sitting in the shade with his head buried in a book or pamphlet. He knew about the battle of the marshes, the battle for Susangerd, the battle for Khorramshah and the battle for Abadan, and each move that had been made in the Karbala offensives, which were legend in the history of the Guards Corps. He had done that work, and had found a new focus.

He sat on a plastic chair in front of the Engineer's house – where the sentry would have been at night – and looked out in front of him. He had good binoculars.

His own wife, Golshan – *flower garden* – had told him, when she was angry and bold enough to speak directly to him, that he had come back from Iraq and the hospital a changed man, embittered. She worked long hours at the Crate Camp Garrison, and came home late on the bus to her room in his parents' house. He rarely saw her, so she had had no chance to learn of his obsession. He sat with his binoculars on his chest and waited for the movement of the birds.

He looked for the African Sacred Ibis. He could have seen it in East Africa, South Africa, Taiwan or on wetlands on the east coast of Australia, but he had never watched it fly low over the marshes in front of the house. They were there, he had read, but they were endangered and near extinct. It would be a cause for celebration if he were to see one, and even more so if a pair came close.

He had not yet seen it on this stretch of marshland. Naghmeh had told him she had watched one drift over the lagoon, but it had gone when he had come from his office. He watched, waited, and would break away only for coffee in the barracks, and his salad sandwich. Otherwise he would keep the vigil. He had his rifle across his knees and could tell himself – in true honesty – that he was conscientious in his work. He believed that the Engineer had told them so at the camp.

There were days when he thought he had seen one, neck extended, legs tucked up and powered by wide wings, far away over the reeds. Each time his excitement had surged as the speck had come closer, until he could see it was a slow-flapping heron. He looked also for the predator. Mansoor, the security officer, indulged himself with his search for the Sacred Ibis, but he was also on constant watch for the threat, for danger. The White-tailed Eagle had been up that morning, the hen, but he had not seen it now for an hour. The eagle had no equal, would swoop and kill the gentle bird.

If the Sacred Ibis came, if his hope was fulfilled, it would likely come low across the reeds, and he watched them closely. There were ducks and coots, and an otter. He thought them his allies. If the threat was alive, the waterbirds would panic and the otter would dive, telling him of a killer's approach . . .

The visitors arrived. Three cars had brought them from Ahvaz, Susangerd and Dezful. They would have gathered in Ahvaz and come in convoy into the border zone, which was under military control, and to which access was restricted.

He went to check the papers, to satisfy himself. He would get two of his men to move a table under the trees, set chairs round it and carry over a tray of glasses and a jug of juice. He would put more cushions on the chair for Naghmeh, whose pain was worse this week. Then, when the meeting had started, he would come back to sit and search for the ibis among the reeds.

Foxy listened. The sound was good – clear and clean. The technicians he had met on courses and field trials swore that this version of the shotgun directional microphone yielded quality results at three hundred metres, and he estimated it was now secreted no more than 240 metres from the front of the target house. He was using around a hundred metres of cable, sunken, from the microphone to where he lay.

No way he would say it. The position was good, the voices were crystal. He would have claimed they were exposed and at risk from being so close to the target's zone, and to the bastard who sat and tracked across the lagoon area, seeming to search it. The sounds of visitors and greetings were boosted by the walls and windows of the building behind where a table and chairs had been set, and bounced back.

He realised the skill Badger had shown to get forward to the lie-up, and more to go along the mud strand and place the microphone in the heart of what seemed to be snagged-up debris. He was so damn good – but Foxy wouldn't say it. Where they were had been dead ground to the view from their night-time position, and a track of sorts led off the bund line to the right. There were more reeds nearer to where he was – on his stomach; the bergens were hidden there and Badger slept there. Foxy needed to have a view of the target house. The weak point with covert listening gear, the technicians always said, was keeping the power going, having battery strength and replacement when recharging wasn't an option. What they used had Output Impedance of 600 ohms and a frequency range of 50Hz–10kHz and an S/N ratio of 40 dB plus, and he'd thought Badger hadn't understood any of the specifications. But he had done well to get them there.

He reflected: two kilometres across a hostile frontier, they were alone, exposed. He also reflected that the chance of success was minimal. He knew about the landmines sown in this area by the Iraqis during the war three decades earlier – the woman had a fine voice that commanded attention.

Naghmeh, the Engineer's wife, was at the centre of the table and around her was her committee. She talked of a village: 'The new well that was dug fourteen years ago was not deep enough and the water it reaches is inadequate. The answer is for the village to go back to the old well, but that is where the mines were laid. They are not mines against tanks and personnel carriers, but against people. They are the Belgian-made PRB M35 and the NR417. Also put there were the Italian SB33 and VS50, and there are the jumping American mines, the M16 A1 and the Bulgarian PSM 1. If – *if* – it is possible, I will go to Ahvaz with you to demand funds for the clearance programme. It is owed to the village, which should have decent water. I will go myself.'

Across the table from her, a man and a woman, representatives of a village to the east and a half-kilometre outside the border's restricted zone, wept quietly.

She spoke of the farmers: 'You have good sheep, of the best quality, and good goats, but the good land where your flocks and herds should graze is denied you by the mines. You have there the Yugoslav-manufactured PMA 3, which is primarily of plastic and rubber casing. It resists the pressure of flails to detonate it, but tilts on a foot's weight and explodes. It does not kill but takes a leg or a foot, or a manhood. The shepherd and the goatherd cannot use those fields, and cannot put their beasts onto them. You have waited too long. Too many of your families are crippled, and your children cannot be out of your sight. I will go to Susangerd and not leave until I have the guarantee of action. I can be formidable.'

The peasant farmers, who lived on a poverty breadline, wrung their hands and lacked the courage to look into her eyes.

She talked to the man and his wife, who had spent their own savings and their extended family's money, to buy a building and develop it as a hotel because they were near to a route used by the pilgrims going towards Karbala and Najaf – the shrine of Ali ibn Abi Talib, son-in-law of the Prophet, where each of the minarets was covered with forty thousand gold tiles. The side of the bund line that led to the border and crossed it, the tracks through the marshes on military roads constructed by the old enemy were mined, and the devices came from Bulgaria, Israel and China. The minefields were not marked and no charts existed to show their placement. The Iraqis who had put them in the ground did not care and the pilgrims would not walk or ride on a narrow track but spread across the elevated ground. Enough had been killed or crippled for no more to come. 'I will go to Tehran if I have to. Where there is oil there is mine clearance. When the drillers and pipe-layers have to come in, the ground is cleaned. Not only are people and animals killed but the potential wealth of the area is blighted. I will demand that something is done so that pilgrims can use that route and stay at your hotel. I will burn their ears, I promise.'

The couple choked back tears, and the woman let her hand rest lightly on Naghmeh's.

She turned to two younger women who wore headscarves but not veils. They would have come from a city and had education to go with their intelligence – as she had. 'I have complained frequently, and will continue to do so, against the corruption that afflicts the mine-clearance work. I will not tolerate it. Corruption is a stain on the Islamic state. We cannot get the clearance teams without bribing officials first – or giving them "bonuses". Then, when a contractor is appointed, has paid for that privilege, he cannot operate without further theft by officials. I will see whoever I have to see, and sit on their doorstep for however long I have to sit there.'

Her voice was quieter as if the effort of talking through the morning had exhausted her. She sucked in her breath and felt the pain. The silence was broken by a sob from the slighter of the younger women.

She could endure pain and extreme tiredness. She slapped her hand on the table. 'Now, where is our action campaign? Let us consider where we can advance.'

They all knew of her illness, and that the diagnosis was terminal. They also knew that she was due to travel abroad to consult with a foreign specialist, and that her life hung by a thread. She had their love and respect. Naghmeh could have made a short speech about her condition, telling them of her certainty that they would carry on with the work of mine clearance regardless of whether or not she drove the programme. She did not. None would have believed her.

She thought few of them reckoned there would be another meeting such as this, outside her home in the warmth beside the lagoon where the birds roamed. She faced the water. It jarred that the security officer blocked part of her view, and that his weapon was displayed . . . The pain throbbed, a drum beating in her skull.

They did the charade and logged birds; some species they could name but most they could not. The spotter 'scope, used by Shagger, stood high on a tripod, and Abigail was beside him with binoculars. The sun was high enough for the heat mist to have formed.

Where they were, the marsh waters were blocked and the ground around the raised walls, bulldozed to safeguard the oil-drilling site against flooding, was bare and cracked. There were precious few birds, endangered or common, to look for and she thought they might have to resort to throwing down bread if they were to get a decent entry into the log.

They were watched, mostly by kids, but there were adults, too, men. When the first half-dozen kids had turned up, seemingly materialising from open ground without warning, and the first couple of men, Shagger had murmured, 'Had to happen, miss, like it was written down on a tablet. Two sets of wheels and us, no escort, and out here, putting up the tripod and the telescope. Always was going to create interest . . . and the chance of acquisition. I don't know how long we can sweat it out.'

She had said, 'By now they'll be in place and will – I hope – have their eyeball.'

The sun beat down and she sweated. They were, predictably, the main attraction. She could have hoped that the area around the devastated drilling site had been abandoned by the marsh people – that the war and the draining by the dictator, followed by persecution and uncontrolled flooding, then four years of brutal drought, had driven them away. That would have been optimistic. Harding and Hamfist were sleeping, and Corky sat by the broken gate, his face half hidden by his wraparounds, the weapon lying on his legs. By the end of the day it would come to giving out sweets and they would be wrapped in five-dollar bills. Here, co-operation was bought with a high-velocity bullet and blood in the dirt, or by shelling out bribes. Might be why she detested the place and was counting the days till she was out of it – when this piece of work was finished, wrapped up. There might now be forty at the gate.

They stood and watched. She thought they had a degree of patience unmatched anywhere she had been by any peoples she had known. They stood in the harsh light without water or food. Their entertainment was herself, Shagger and Corky, blocking the easy way into the compound with his rifle. She did not think them hostile yet, merely inquisitive. Later, they might resort to showing pictures, blown up on the photocopier, of a bustard, a bittern or a darter. If they were lucky they had another day in place. If Fortune smiled, it might be three days. Out ahead the mist settled on a horizon of flat earth and reed beds, and far away there was water – where he was. She could remember each cadence of her voice: 'What did you do that for?'

And the answer had been that God only knew, an evasion. She did not, would not, make a habit of crouching over a strange man to check the extent of bruising and finding her hands, fingertips, running over a flat stomach and going lower, then grabbing one of his hands and dragging it behind her so that it was under her T-shirt and on her skin. Difficult for Abigail Jones to know why she had made a pitch for this quiet, sometimes taciturn, some-times mocking man who had walked into her life. It had been a compulsion. Regretted? Shit, no.

She had not met the guy in Basra, Six, Baghdad or her last London posting who did the business for her. There had not been a lawyer, a banker or an army man who had interested her. The last had been a teacher, mathematics for fourteen-year-olds, in a Lambeth comprehensive. She'd almost lived with him – three nights or four a week. He'd had no money and no prospects, but was fun and intense. He had jacked in the job, put the pension-scheme payments on hold and sold almost everything he owned, then gone to teach – mathematics or anything – in up-country northern Cambodia. He was Peter. He'd asked her, take it or leave it, if she wanted to come with him, but that would have meant resignation and a bust career.

There hadn't been another guy since, not in London and not here ... none of which answered her question. On top of a sleeping-bag in a ruined concrete office building with shell holes to view the stars and glass carpeting the floor, why had she hitched up her robe and lowered herself onto him? She didn't know. She could still taste him, or imagined it. No regrets, none. What was best, he hadn't thanked her. He hadn't assumed he was going into harm's way with the dawn, and this was a little boost to courage that might have flagged. He hadn't even seemed surprised, but had been deep in her and had said nothing. It had been good ... no regrets. He wasn't out of her mind – and was beyond the haze on the horizon. She wore a moulded earpiece that doubled as a microphone, and the transmitter/receiver was on her belt. It was her link to them, and she wouldn't anticipate the code message coming through unless their mission was complete and successful, or they needed to abort fast.

She didn't expect Shagger – or Hamfist, Corky or Harding – to remark on what had happened in the derelict building that night, but she wouldn't object to his operational input. He had the experience, which gave his comments value. He was the wrong side of forty, with a little weight gathering across his belt, and he came from the extreme south west of the principality. His parents had slaved through his childhood on a subsistence hill farm, breeding sheep, White Welsh Mountain ewes. He'd gone into the army on leaving the grammar school, joined a para battalion, whereupon his father had ditched his pride and gone bankrupt. Shagger had fought in Africa and the Balkans, done time in Ireland, had been in Afghanistan in 2001 and had left the army the next year, a sergeant. He was one of the drain who had quit to make big money with the private military contractors. He knew about every yard and feature of the road from Baghdad airport to the Green Zone, but he had never quite raised sufficient funds for his goal. He intended, one day, to have the cash in the bank to buy back that farm in the Preseli hills. With each contract he took, Shagger learned more. He gave advice only when it was asked for, and she never rejected it.

She said, 'They're fine for the moment. Nothing hostile.'

'They can see guns and it's daylight, miss. They'll chance nothing till it's dark. They thieve, miss. Always have.'

'To pull back is a last option.'

'It's the worst option, miss. Here, at least, we might be inside the Golden Hour, or on the edge of it. We have to sweat it out.'

'Would they know about the Golden Hour?'

'They know that back-up's guaranteed. Act of faith to them. Where they are, they'd need the faith.'

Badger listened as Foxy murmured translations and interpretations: 'He's the security man, the chief. Has a limp so he's been hurt somewhere. If he was hurt in an accident, it would have been on their roads. If he's a military casualty it would likely have happened inside Iraq or up in Lebanon. He's mumbling, doesn't know what to say, except that she should have faith in God.'

A benchmark of the work of a croppie, as Badger knew it, was to have binocular or 'scope vision, camera lenses or a directional shotgun microphone aimed at a target, eavesdropping, watching, noting, and be able to strip away the armour with which people tried to shield themselves if they expected to be observed. Few did. Not many understood the qualities he brought to his work, and the capabilities of the gear. It was a basic intrusion and he didn't care. His life was spent watching men and women, noting small private happiness, tension and moments of pleasure. He was a voyeur: he might have been standing on a street in darkness and gazing at the gaps in bathroom curtains as a target prepared to wash, or looking into lit homes and seeing bitter domestic arguments. He might have been watching a killer burn a victim's clothing, the sharing of the cash, the arming of a group on their way to a hit, a man weeping or a guard fumbling for words to a terminal patient. The gear enabled croppies to peer inside minds and souls. It didn't bother him. It was his work.

'She says her committee don't believe they can carry on without her. The mine programme will fold if she isn't there. She's the icon figure who demands action – she repeats that. He nods, doesn't answer, only says something about belief in God.'

They had developed the hide through the morning. It was as good as anything Badger could remember. Normal: go in at night and do the construction stuff under cover of darkness, be cosy and covert when the light came. Abnormal: to burrow out the scrape and cover it, do the work in the sun's glare, and have a man with security responsibilities sitting in a chair two hundred yards away. Something to be proud of. He had called the tune, and Foxy had stayed with the earphones clamped on, hadn't acknowledged that the work was well done – was brilliant. They were on the extremity of the reeds where they were thin, and had taken over a narrow strip of the bare ground, the dried-out mud. He had worked a shallow dip for them no more than fifteen inches deep, and had made a rim wall of the soil. All of it was covered with debris he had painstakingly collected further into the reeds, the same dead fronds that hid the microphone on the mud spit. More fronds masked the cable where it came up out of the water and ran across the mud towards them. A work of art, a collector's piece. Often the guard raised his binoculars and scanned. Then Badger had been statue still on his stomach, and the gillie suit was embedded with more reeds . . . There'd been no praise. He thought of Alpha Juliet. Difficult not to think of her. Impossible to imagine why she had done it, but he was glad she had.

'He's called Mansoor – that's what she calls him. He says he hopes God will watch over her. She says her committee depends too much on her. She says it's time to go and prepare the children's food for when they come back from school. I think he's near to tears. Right, she's gone, and . . .'

He was no longer listening. Fran had been good enough to run for a few months, but he'd left and she wouldn't have cried. There had been two girls while he was still at school, and he'd shagged one while her parents were out at the supermarket, every Friday evening, for a month, the other in the woods near the

nuke-weapons factory at Burghfield . . . And a woman PC called
Brenda, who ran the organisation side of the team that did surveillance on the gypsy camp where the tinkers who did the
country-house burglaries up and down the Thames-valley
corridor came from. Nothing important to him. She had been,
Alpha Juliet – and there was no one to tell him why she was locked
into his mind.

He wasn't handsome, had fuck-all talk. He felt the warmth of
her, and the moistness . . . He couldn't have said that any woman
before had mattered in his life. The heat burgeoned and his throat
was crisp, dried. His eyes ached from the glare of the water, and
the man sat in front of the house, the rifle across his legs. Badger's
head turned slowly as he watched, through his glasses, the reed
beds, the spit where the microphone was disguised and the open
ground into which he had scraped the hide. They were pressed
hard together, his hip into the slack part of Foxy's stomach wall,
and Foxy's hip bone sharp against his thigh.

Foxy whispered, 'It surprised me, how well my Farsi's lasted . . .'

If the man was fishing for a compliment, Badger wouldn't take the
bait. He answered, 'It's what you're here for – what you're paid for.'

'You know why we're here?'

'Are you going to tell me?'

'We're here because they – the spooks – don't have an asset to
put in here. They would have wanted a local, some guy who could
wander around and chat in the coffee house or the garage and talk
to the goon guards. They don't have one. So it's us. There isn't a
turned Iranian they could put in and trust, and there isn't a lieutenant of the Republican Guard, who thought Saddam was the
bee's bollocks, or a slimy little sod from the Ba'ath Party they can
rely on. They've reached down to the bottom of the barrel, and it's
us they've pulled out. It's crazy, daft, idiotic.'

'You volunteered so stop whining.' So close together, like lovers,
that the words barely needed articulation. Badger's murmur in
Foxy's ear, and the two camouflage head kits were almost meshed.

Foxy's response: 'We're the end of the road for them or the
barrel's scrapings, whichever. And they'll feel good. *They*'ve done

something – put two arseholes, daft idiots, into harm's way. It'll go on the papers they write and they'll get congratulated. What chance is there that the target will walk out of his front door and shout in Farsi I can understand and no fancy dialect, to the bloody sky, "Heh, anyone there? If you are, and you're upset about the growth in my wife's head, you need to know I'm off in the morning to Vienna, Rome, Kiev, Stockholm, any place where there's someone with good knife skills. Hear that?" We'll see him go, perhaps. Where to? We'll see farewells, tears et cetera. Where are they headed? We've no chance.'

'You could have refused.'

'And they'd have let me walk away? Grow up, young 'un. They'd have made sure it haunted me the rest of my days. No more work. Considered "unsuitable", branded "lack of commitment". You're held by the short and curlies. Didn't the lady tell you? Or wasn't she talking too much?'

'Best you shut your mouth.'

'But *they* can have their lunch and their gin, and can congratulate themselves that they tried, were audacious, and when we crawl out of here and get back, don't expect a load of back-slapping and gratitude. *They* won't remember your name. It has no chance.'

Badger murmured, 'Saying that because you're scared shitless? Or do you mean it – "no chance"?'

'What do you think?'

'I think you're crap. Try it again. I *know* you're crap.'

He thought Foxy was close to hitting him, and they both lay motionless. Badger watched as the security man roved the area with his glasses. He didn't know if Foxy had spoken the truth – that they had no chance, were small pawns and served other agendas.

'I will do it, subject to satisfactory arrangements.'

He was asked what arrangements would have to be satisfactory.

The consultant had gone out of the building and loitered in front of the café. He was not overheard. He had dialled the number given him, had been held at the embassy's switchboard for perhaps a half-minute, which he thought excessive, and when the call was answered he received no apology.

'The patient must have a name. There must be a date of arrival and—'

He was interrupted. The life of the hospital and the medical school flowed past him; the rain fell and snow threatened. There was often snow when the Christmas market began in Lübeck, in the square in front of the *Rathaus* and beside the Marienkirche. Then it was prettier and the traders coined cash. He was not, of course, a Christian but his wife went to services most Sundays and took their daughter, and on special saints' days he would attend with them. The patient would arrive as soon as it could be arranged, and the name would be given him when he saw the patient. Did anything else need to be 'satisfactory'?

'What would be the method of payment? These are expensive procedures. We require guarantees, money lodged in escrow, a banker's draft, a credit card or—'

A hardening of a faraway distorted voice. Had he forgotten who he was? What he owed? Did greed govern him?

'I'm not talking about myself. There are technicians, scans, X-rays. Assume that surgery is a possibility. Then you have theatre, and intensive care.' His temper was shortening. 'The patient cannot have that type of intervention, hours of it, then be put out into a winter's night.'

He would be told about financial arrangements when the timing and date of the patient's journey to north Germany were known.

The call ended. He pocketed his phone, went inside the building and sucked in a long breath. He wrapped a smile of confidence and competence around his face and greeted his first patient of the day.

His wife waved to him. From his car, he watched her go. All the sentries and security guards knew her. If they hadn't, there would have been bedlam at his stopping so close to the main gates and inside the concrete teeth placed to prevent access to a car bomber.

Gabbi watched her and, for a moment, almost unseen, his lips moved in to kiss her. She swung the stick in front of her legs and went to the guard who controlled the pedestrians' entrance. With her free hand, she would have gestured towards the ID in the plastic pouch that hung from her neck. All the sentries and guards would greet her – they saw her coming and going, swinging the white stick and getting to work or heading home, as if there were no impediment in her life. He shared her with many. He left the ministry building and took a route from the city to the south.

There was a complex at Giv'at Herzl that had a small-arms firing range, soundproofed, at the rear.

Those who used the range, as many women as men, were from the National Dignitary Protection Unit and the Secret Service, and there were soldiers who did bodyguard duties for senior military staff. The instructors knew most of the client base. Some fired at circle targets, others used life-sized figures. Gabbi had asked for a figure, a head wrapped in a *keffiyeh*. He did the fast slide of the pistol from a waist holster, then the double-tap shots for the head. They did not consider chest shots, or those aimed at the stomach, to be of any value. The instructors taught that bullets should be aimed at the skull. That day, his weapon was the Baby Eagle, the Jericho 941F, with a nine-shot magazine, manufactured inside the country. The instructors would never have been told of the role he played in the affairs of Israel – would not have expected or wanted it. They had seen the clients come and go, and could make judgements on the work the shooters did, what they trained for. Gabbi used a different technique on the range from that employed by protection or those who hoped to be close enough to take down a suicide bomber. They fired in screened booths, and only the instructors would have seen Gabbi with his back to the target shape, then producing the weapon from under his lightweight coat, spinning, whipping the pistol up, aiming, steadying it, holding it cleanly, doing the squeeze – and it was double-tap. The instructors would tell him, each time he fired twice, where his bullets had struck.

They had nothing to teach Gabbi.

He would not have claimed his skills were too great for him to need practice. Sweat ran on him, clogging at the edges of the ear baffles. He was a man apart and did not laugh with others and had no friends there, but he had the instructors' respect.

It was somewhere to go, somewhere to pass the time while he waited for the call – and he never tired of the cordite whiff or the rippling recoil through his wrists, forearms and elbows, and the kick of the Baby Eagle.

The instructors could have made a judgement on his work because he always fired at the head, was only interested in head hits that would drop a man dead.

Others would not have coped with the waiting, but Gabbi could . . . Later, after a wasted day, he would be at the ministry's gate, watching for the woman, pretty, with the white stick, and would pick up Leah. All the shots he had fired had been at the head, and all would have killed.

Time to think, time to reflect and time to brood. Len Gibbons waited and the phones stayed silent.

Other officers in the Towers, with time on their hands, would have been with Sarah in the single room allocated him at the Club. Not Len Gibbons and not Sarah.

She had made fresh coffee, and brought with it a plate of biscuits. He owed his wife, Catherine, too much – not that it made a jot of difference in Sarah's case as she rebuffed all advances from whichever direction and had done since a captain in the Life Guards had dumped her in favour of a girl from the Intelligence Corps – that had been after the first banns were read. He was hugely in debt to Catherine, and doubted he would ever pay it off. He was – to everyone who knew him in the Towers – Len Gibbons. When he was young, and Catherine was his new wife and the world had seemed at his feet, he could have anticipated that, within a few years, he would be *Leonard* Gibbons and on a fast track to the higher ranks. His career had come to a juddering halt and the scars were still on his back. But for that impact, he might have climbed to great things, and had not. By a thread, by a fingernail, he had survived – damaged – a professional débâcle and she had stood by him when the scale of his failure had made him nearly suicidal. With her encouragement, he had hung on, and had known that on his record was the condemnation of what had been codenamed Antelope, that the best he could hope for was to be labelled 'diligent' or, worse, 'conscientious'. The debt ran wider than his wife: it permeated the building from which he worked. He could, therefore, be given any bag of excrement and the safety of his hands would ensure that the job was done.

If he set his mind to it, he still had good recall of that bloody border, the watchtowers, the dogs and the guns.

He called through the door that the coffee was excellent, and thanked her for the biscuits. His phone stayed silent and he waited.

The Engineer explained to the brigadier the first principles of the bombs he had made, which were now stockpiled and kept in underground storage. They would use 'low explosives' and he spoke of TATP's contents: triacetone triperoxide had minimal scent, emitted no vapours, and would go undetected by even the best-trained sniffer dogs. He told the brigadier – who sat stern, rapt, not interrupting, as if he recognised the privilege of access to a man of renown – about the blast effects of the larger-scale bombs he worked on. There was, first, the 'positive phase', when the windows of buildings adjacent to the bomb were blown in, then the 'negative phase', when the debris and glass shards were airborne and dragged out again to refill the vacuum created by the blast. Calm, emotionless, he told the officer – who would have responsibility for the defence of the province if the troops of the Great Satan were unwise enough to invade the Islamic Republic with ground forces – of the effects of explosives detonating: 'blast lung' injuries from the thrust into the ears, nose and throat; more injuries from the high-velocity impact of the ball bearings incorporated into the bomb and the glass splinters raining down on a street or flying inside buildings. Further injuries, as soldiers of the enemy were thrown across a street and careered into buildings or cars, their brains bouncing against the inner wall of their skulls.

With a dry smile, he indicated a photograph on the wall of an American soldier's helmet: an arrow pointed out of a ventilation hole in its side. He said that such openings provided a conduit that concentrated blast into the hole, like the driving in of a nail. He spoke, too, of the medium-term damage to troops' psychology, if they had been exposed to situations where bombs were widespread, particularly if there had been casualties in their unit: a large number of enemy combatants in the Iraq war had gone home with post-traumatic stress disorder, as sick as if they had been severely wounded, and would not return. The brigadier grimaced as the Engineer finished and told him that he – almost alone – was responsible for the defeat of the coalition inside Iraq. His weapons had destroyed the will and resolve of the enemy. He had smiled and shrugged. Many this year had come to his office, had sat where the brigadier sat, and congratulated him on his achievement.

What news was there of the war in Afghanistan? Did it affect his work? the brigadier asked.

He said it was a low priority, that the devices used by the resistance were simpler than those employed in Iraq . . . They had been taught, had been supplied with chemicals and explosives, and he had written papers, but he kept them at arms' distance. It was Iraq that had mattered, where the true victory had been won.

Then they drank sweet tea – with cardamom, saffron, rose water and liberally spooned sugar – from small glasses, and smoked.

The brigadier raised it. He had heard of the illness of the Engineer's wife, and was privy to plans for sending her abroad for consultation and, hopefully, treatment. They talked about suitcases, what sort and size would be best for the journey. The brigadier had recently been in Damascus with new baggage and could offer advice.

When the tray had been cleared, the Engineer spoke to the brigadier of the theory of roadside thermobaric bombs, the ability of fuel-air explosions to devastate, and their potential inside trucks and saloon cars that could be driven by a 'martyr' into the doorway of a building. There, the blast would be confined and enhanced. He was working on that, on miniaturisation of the circuit boards for the explosive formed projectile, on extending the range of passive infrared beams and . . . He yawned, then flushed, embarrassed. He apologised.

He was told he had nothing to apologise for.

He said, confiding, that it was difficult to focus on his work.

He was asked if he knew an itinerary.

He hoped to hear that day, or the next, when he would travel with his wife.

It had simmered, but had been below boiling.

The spat stayed with them, but was carried along on whispers, almost soundless, and the voices played like soft winds on the front of their camouflaged headpieces.

Foxy said he needed water. Badger said he had drunk his ration for the morning.

Foxy said the biscuits tasted foul. Badger said he thought they were good.

Foxy said they should move to their right, maybe forty paces, and be deep in the reeds for greater protection. Badger said it was important they had an eyeball on the property and could ping the target.

Foxy had looked at his watch and wondered, barely aloud, what his Ellie was doing at that moment. He had started to relate how they had met and— Badger had cut him off, said he wasn't interested.

Foxy hissed, 'Are you contrary for the sake of it? You think I want to be here with you – the fuck I do – the most difficult, awkward oppo ever given me? I make a remark about my wife and you're not interested.'

'Correct. I'm not interested in your wife.'

'Who's special. Who I miss. Who I—'

'Not interested.'

And Badger, as usual, spoke the truth. He wasn't interested in Foxy's wife and didn't want to talk about her. He was interested in the one-storey house of concrete blocks, the big front windows, which were open, the door, ajar, the chairs and table outside in the shade. And he was interested in the guard, who sometimes sat on a chair and sometimes walked, sometimes coughed and spat, sometimes smoked, and who had now started to fish with a short rod, worms and a float. He watched the boat that was tied near the little concrete pier. He saw the wife, who was dying and walked with a stick, and the children who were chided by an older woman when they screamed too loudly and too close to their mother . . . If he and Foxy didn't talk, they didn't argue.

He knew that the long, motionless hours played havoc with Foxy's knee and hip joints, but couldn't bring himself to sympathise. Hours passed and the sun cooked them. He thought how vulnerable they were, vulnerable enough for him to bloody near wet himself . . . He would never again volunteer, never again shove his hand up.

The explosion burst in Badger's ears.

7

Foxy knew the sound of an artillery shell exploding. There had only been a slight squirm of the young 'un's body but it was enough to show him Badger was ignorant of weapons' detonations. It gave him pleasure. He twisted his head slowly, cranked his neck round far enough to see the smoke pall, first stationary, then climbing into the clear blue of the sky.

It was off to the right, near to the raised bund line. It rose, spread and began to lose shape. Silence fell.

He felt, now, a heavy pressure on his shoulder – as if a hand was spread wide and forced down. He could move only his head, not his upper body. Badger had hold of him. His pleasure at Badger's initial reaction had dissipated. He couldn't move, was treated like a passenger who wouldn't know how to react in a crisis and needed to be held still. What did the man think he was going to do – jump up, yell and bloody run? He couldn't free himself of the hand, but could manoeuvre his head, tilt his neck and look to the front. There was shouting.

The goon, the one he had identified as Mansoor – who had the rank of an officer and was in charge of security, obviously – was on his feet, out of the chair quick enough for it to have toppled behind him, and there were yelled instructions coming into Foxy's earphones. The guard was to be called out, weapons drawn from the armoury, the sergeant to be found, a patrol prepared. The pressure of the hand on his shoulder eased, a gradual weakening of the force.

He thought that Badger regarded him as old and second class.

The officer had stopped yelling and now stood rooted in front of the fallen chair. His binoculars were at his eyes and he traversed

up and down from the bund line to the reed beds and on to the far
end of the open ground. The lenses would have covered – with
each sweep – the apparently snagged mess of dead reeds in which
the microphone was hidden. They would have gone over the water
under which the cable was sunk, across the sand where it was
buried and travelled on to the heaps of dried leaves that the wind
would seem to have whipped together. In the lenses' view would
be the shoulders of the gillie suits, and the tops of the headgear,
and perhaps the hands caked with mud, and the optics that had
scrim netting round them and were tilted down so that the sun
didn't hit the glass. It was a test.

A good one.

Instinct told Foxy to duck his head further, chin against chest,
fill his face with mud and lower the headgear the last half-inch
that was possible. Not to look . . . not to dare to see whether the
glasses had moved on from the points that could identify him
and Badger.

They did. He watched and the glasses scanned where the
microphone was, the cable was buried and where they were . . . He
wriggled. Couldn't help himself.

It started as a moan, had gained in pitch and was now a scream.

He had to twist his pelvis, lift his hips and backside three inches,
get the bottle under his crotch and feel the relief.

The voice in his face had a harder edge. 'What the fuck's the
matter with you?'

'I was pissing.'

'Couldn't you wait?'

'No.'

'Not the best moment, under close observation, an alert. Tie a
bloody knot in it.'

Not the best moment. The scream had raised the birds in panic
flight, disturbing them more than the explosion had. He shifted
the bottle so that he could cap it, then pushed it back under
himself, using a knee to get it down by his boots. They were still
wet from the insertion march, but manageable – wet boots and
socks were the least of the problem.

Not the best moment because of the screams, now behind them, and the sight of troops jogging along the bund line. Could have been a half-dozen and the officer was on the low pier that jutted out into the lagoon, waving directions.

He had had to use the bottle.

Men were coming close and frightened little voices edged nearer. Carefully, minimum movement, Foxy raised a forefinger and eased one of the earpieces back. He had, now, the officer in his left ear and the noises off to the right, stumbling, curses and whimpers, in the other.

He could see the troops on top of the bund line. Most had rifles and two had machine-pistols.

The woman had come out and used her stick to take her weight as she made her way from the door to where the officer stood. She asked if a mine had exploded and was told that it was more likely an artillery shell, maybe 105mm calibre. She asked if pilgrims had detonated it – he heard the quaver in her voice and assumed it was concern, not the severity of her illness. The officer said it was more likely to have been thieves – there were dumps in the marshes from the old war and this one might have been stockpiled Iraqi munitions, perhaps for the artillery pieces of the Revolutionary Guard Corps. She knew of the abandoned dumps . . . He sent her away, but with courtesy, and urged that the children be kept inside: all the family should be at the back of their house, not by the front windows. That made sense to Foxy Foulkes, familiar enough with the ways of the world in Iran, or in Iraq, to comprehend why an educated woman and her young children should stay away from their windows and not see what . . . There had been enough of it in Iraq when he had served there, and the ammunition technical officers had spoken of it.

They said that the main targets for looters were the copper wires from telephone cables and the casings from artillery shells. If the shells were live they would reckon to know where the detonator was, belt it away with a sledge and free the casing. The casings made good money in the *souk*, and if a few entrepreneurs didn't make it to the market, God would take care of their families.

The ATOs said they saw too many broken bodies – limbs left up trees, guts smeared on walls – when the sledge hammer had hit the wrong part of the shell. The casings could be brass or chromate steel or anodysed aluminium. A primer and a propellant of black powder were inside the casing; at the tip, the warhead might have held high explosive or mustard gas.

The next scream was closer and the hushing increasingly desperate of those around the casualty. They might have been stampeding animals as they ran. Foxy had lost sight of the soldiers who had come along the bund line, and he realised that the fugitives were driven by a cordon of guns towards the reed bank that protected him and the young 'un, the open ground and the water either side of the raised mud on which they had their hide. Some luck, the way the dice came down. Foxy thought his freedom depended on the young 'un's skills. Might be more than his freedom: might be his life. The skills were those of concealment.

What Badger had done with the scrape in the mud and the camouflage covering it, the mud on what little of their skin might be visible, the weaving of dead foliage into the gillie suits and the headgear might be good enough to save him – and might not. It had been painstaking. At the time, before dawn, Foxy had thought it exhibitionist shit, pernickety little movements that tested the weight and colour of individual fronds before discarding them or threading them into the suits. If the work was not done carefully enough, there would be a rifle barrel against the nape of his neck. His bergen was on his right side and the other on Badger's left. He himself lay on the spotter 'scope and its small tripod.

The first of them, in flight, broke through the wall of the reed bed.

They stopped dead in their tracks.

They wouldn't have known where they were running to. They had lost cover, were in a cul-de-sac as far as flight went, boxed in.

The stomach wall of the one who had screamed was split open and his T-shirt was dragged up. He seemed to be trying to hold in his intestines with his crossed forearms. Another man had hold of his elbow and tried to support him, but scarlet fluid was running onto his trousers. Two more carried a dead man, who hung like a rag doll in their grip. Another, with ashen cheeks, hopped forward in their wake, holding upright a teenage boy in a long bright shirt. It was bloodstained from navel to knee. He had to hop because his left leg had been taken off immediately below the knee.

They would have seen the open ground, and the water, and they would have heard – those not screaming or moaning – the pursuit behind them in the reed bed, and might have seen, across the lagoon, the officer waving his little force forward, and heard the bawled orders. They crumpled, all of them, into the mud.

Soldiers came through the reeds, and hope died.

One walked so close that his foot must have come down on the young 'un's bergen. It was a dust-smeared boot and would have sagged as it stepped on the lower half of the rucksack, but the rifle was aimed at the gang, cowering, and the next step missed Badger's feet.

He took little breaths, just the barest amount of air, while ants or small spiders half drowned in the sweat on his face. He endured the irritations. He had forgotten, almost, that Badger was beside him. He didn't hear any breathing or feel any movement, but he heard the officer's shout across the water. He couldn't see him now but imagined that he cupped his hands in front of his mouth to give the order.

Foxy gagged. He had heard the order. It would have been faint to the soldiers, but it was loud and clear to Foxy.

He tried to swallow but there was no moisture in his throat. Worse, vomit seemed to creep up to the back of his mouth. Foxy had been with the army in Northern Ireland, in the bad days, when feelings had run high with the military, and he had been with the interrogators at the Basra airport complex when tempers were lost, but he had never heard an order given by a uniformed man such as the one that drifted over the still waters of the lagoon and was crystal sharp in his ear.

They were shot one by one.

It wasn't a killing where an automatic weapon was aimed in their general direction. Foxy couldn't see it but assumed that the sergeant – a short man with a machine pistol, in a tunic a size too small for him – had done the shooting. Single shots. A stench of cordite. A whimper from some, a curse from others, quiet from a few. Under any circumstances would Foxy have intervened? No. They could have been raping grandmothers, pushing down hooded prisoners onto soft drink bottles so that the neck penetrated, and he would have stayed silent.

The corpses were dragged away.

He heard the slither of the bodies on wet ground, then the cracking of reed stems as they were pulled through denser concentrations. Later, when those sounds ended, he heard the far-away splashes of burial in water, and wondered if they had found stones to weight them. They would have been Arabs, most likely from Iraq. They had come across the border because this was more likely to be virgin ground for the collectors of shell cases. Their crime was to have crossed the frontier, and what had made it a capital offence was that they had strayed into a most sensitive part of the restricted zone.

It was a dangerous thought, one he had not entertained during his four-month posting to the interrogation team. It risked sapping his commitment. What in God's name had he and his comrades been doing there? What were they doing there now?

What had they been doing there in days gone by when British squaddies had patrolled, Yanks had driven by in their armour-plated carriers, the foot-soldier was pleased to get a ten-dollar bill for putting the roadside bomb in place, and some damn man – who had glasses, good-features, a fine-looking wife who was dying and kids who were frightened – had laboured at a bench, making the bombs that took the lives in this place, which stank of donkey, dog, fly and human shit? The rant rioted in his mind. What were they doing there? The answer: would need a cleverer man than Foxy. He could have praised Badger for making the scrape, constructing the hide, saving them, but he didn't.

Perhaps he was too preoccupied to hand out praise. He would have given his left testicle bollock for the chance to hold on to Ellie, cling to her – would have given the whole handful of his tackle for the chance to hold her and be loved. Fractionally, beside him, Badger shifted, his arms moved and then his elbow dug sharply into Foxy's ribcage. He passed Foxy a flapjack. Foxy ate the flapjack, then said, wiping crumbs, 'Life's cheap, worth nothing, especially an Arab's. Iranians would see it like shooting a diseased dog. Don't expect there to be a court of human rights getting steamed up about it.'

Badger said nothing. They should have been bonded by the experience, but Foxy realised that neither would offer anything to the other.

The officer was back on his chair and his glasses were at his chest. The ducks and waders were again on the water, and the officer had his float out, watching it. The woman had come out from the house with her mother, who carried the washing basket, and the kids had their plastic toys. The guards had resumed their watch from the shade of the palm trees. Hard to believe it had happened, that anything had happened. He thought he and Badger would not have been so fortunate. It would not have been quick: interrogation, torture, slow execution – and not by a bullet. He had no idea what he was doing there, then and now, what was his business.

He would have liked to talk about Ellie, but the man beside him had no interest in her.

The washing was pegged out in the sunshine and the children played. The officer caught two small fish, which he unhooked and threw back. Nothing was said and nothing was learned.

Then the shivers started, rustling the old fronds that covered them, and he couldn't help himself – so nearly dead, and so damned isolated.

'The marsh area is one of the great wonders of the world. It is a unique and precious place. We're doing everything we can to protect your homes, keep you safe, and to maintain the habitat of many centuries . . .'

The crowd had more than doubled, might have trebled. Abigail Jones was at the broken gate. She had put a scarf over her hair and

still wore the loose cool robe. She had a bag, a local craftwork
effort, slung on her shoulder and in it were her communications,
her medical pack and her pistol, with two spare magazines, three
flash grenades and a purse with some money. She had reflected
that the bag contained all that the modern young woman needed
if she was promenading in sunny Iraq ... Different from what
would be in the bags of the girls she had been at school with or
shared benches with in college lecture rooms. She'd have said that
the comms, the pack with the dressings and morphine syringes
were the most important items – not the weapons because she had
Harding behind her: the M-16 would be slung across his chest, his
thumb would be on the safety, his finger on the trigger guard, and
there would be a bullet in the breach.

'...We're trying to let the whole world know how beautiful, and
how important, are the marshlands where you live. We want to
establish the extent of the wildlife that has survived the war with
Iran, the persecution by Saddam and now the drought. We need
to say with accuracy what birds are here and what animals. We
don't want to interfere in any way with your lives. The whole world
knows of the hospitality of the *madan* people, but we ask that you
leave us to count the birds and other creatures.'

If they believed that shit they'd believe anything. They didn't.
They were close to her. There was no hostility in the eyes, but the
sort of deadened dullness that came from poverty, hardship, and
the sense that an opportunity had presented itself. Two vehicles,
good for stripping; radios, binoculars and telescopes that would
fetch useful money in the *souk* at al-Amara; weapons that would
augment those filched from previous conflicts fought out in the
marshes – she had heard that old Turkish rifles retrieved after the
battle of al-Qurna, December 1914 and British-issued Lee
Enfields were still seen on a tribesman's shoulder. There were also
food, medical supplies and money. Little whistles of breath came
between Harding's teeth, his way when he was tense. He would
have known she was talking shit and convincing none of them, but
she had started and would finish, and her Arabic was fair enough
for her to be understood.

'. . . We ask you, please, to leave us so that the birds and the creatures are not disturbed and we can count and observe them. Later, when we have finished, we will reward your co-operation generously. We're doing this for you.'

She thought she had sounded so hollow.

They gazed back at her. They might decide that she and her guards were weak and rush the gate, might decide that they could shift around the fence – down in many places – infiltrate and over-whelm, or they might conclude it best to wait till darkness, not many hours away. The eyes stripped her. She had – like everyone who did a Baghdad posting – read the works of the explorers, mostly British from a half-century or a century before, who lauded the culture of the *madan* men and the lifestyle of many millennia. They would kill her, steal from her body – maybe rape her after death – and blood lust would determine that the bodies of Corky, Shagger, Hamfist and Harding were mutilated. It wasn't political, nothing to do with the offensive intrusion of a foreign army. It was all about the economic necessity of survival, requiring items of value to be taken to the *souk* at al-Amara, even Basra, and flogged off so that a new widescreen television could be bought with the generator to power it.

She smiled to the front and said, in English from the side of her mouth, 'Not an overwhelming response. I'm getting nowhere.'

'It wasn't my shout, ma'am.'

It had been Abigail Jones's decision to seek out the abandoned exploration site, and the more reliable maps showed no settle-ments near to it. There had been no alternative. Actually, she didn't know Harding's given name, and knew less about him than she did about any of the rest of her detail. She had never learned what military units he had been with – airborne, armour, marines, military police? He stayed apart from the banter of the others, but when he spoke it was worth her while to hear him out. All that was personal about Harding – who had been with Proeliator Security for eight years – was in his wallet, a photograph of a woman: a frail face under sparse grey hair, not his mother but the aunt who had brought him up in abject penury somewhere in the Midwest. She thought that, when this was over, he'd hit the Russian whores in the Dubai hotels. He was the smartest of the team, immaculate each day in his fatigues, and careful. She liked that, valued it.

'I don't see this as sustainable.'

'When they're hungry enough, ma'am, or thirsty, they'll come. Could be tomorrow or the day after, could be tonight or in half an hour. We'd have to drop a hell of a number of them to win.'

'Not what we're here for – it would be a disaster. Don't even think about it.'

She kept the smile fixed, but none of them stepped a half-pace back, and nobody answered her. If they'd heard Harding's voice, recognised him as American, he might not be killed but sold on. There were chickens in cages in the *souk*, waiting to be sold and slaughtered, goats and sheep that were worth good money. They'd get a better price for the American than they would for Corky, Shagger and Hamfist. She turned to Harding. 'Talk to me.'

'It'll be hard to stay here, ma'am, but *here* is within an accept-able distance of our people. Further back, wherever that's possible, is not acceptable. Already they're hung out, rags in the wind. I don't see an option, hard as it is staying our ground.'

'I hear you.'

'My opinion, ma'am, it's not possible – and the other guys would say it – to leave them out there beyond help. Wouldn't be able to hold my head high again.'

'Then we'll hack it. Somehow. Thank you.'

They might be lucky and they might not. They might have time, the angels singing with them, and they might not. She bit her lip.

'Have I spoken out of turn, ma'am?'

She shook her head. He had spoken with politeness, respect, but had given a clear message – *rags in the wind* – and two men far forward couldn't be left, after guarantees had been given. She had little sense of honour, obligation, when she gave the Service's word, but her men would have believed in necessary trust, and she had felt the younger man against her body, inside it.

'Hack it and sweat it out.' She walked away from the gate, and considered how many dollars to feed out now, how many later.

The consultant phoned Berlin. He leaned back in his chair and gazed through the window at the sleet spattering the glass. He gave the switchboard the name and was asked his own.

'My name is Steffen. I am calling from Lübeck.'

The connection was made. He didn't waste time on pleasant- ries. He began with the costs, in euros. There was the fee for his own time, for the clinic nurses, for the scanner, and the fee for X-rays, for the staff operating the scanner and the radiology team. He continued with the potential sums required if the examination showed that a stereo-tactic was possible and that an operation had a chance of success, then added, 'You should have no anxiety that we would conduct the procedure merely to gain the payments when we have no hope of a favourable outcome. We have a long waiting list. We only take a patient into theatre when there are grounds for optimism.'

The numbers were in front of him and bounced in his eyes. A consultation and examination – and a verdict that denied hope – would cost thousands of euros. Surgery, then close supervision in intensive care and a further period of convalescence would add up to tens of thousands. He said that debit cards could be used, in advance, but not credit cards or cheques; a money order taken out on a German bank would be acceptable.

Were discounts available to the Islamic Republic? He said that his own remuneration might be subject to a realistic adjustment, but all other fees were non-negotiable. He had made provisional reservations for facilities on the following Monday.

The fees were agreed.

He finished, 'Such a reservation will attract comment because, as yet, the patient has no identity. I am not interested in the patient's name, but would be grateful for one that matches a pass- port and the medical records brought from Tehran. I would suggest a name is furnished as quickly as possible, or suspicion will be aroused. We are talking about an initial appointment for nine in the morning, Monday.' He allowed a whiff of sarcasm. 'I trust that finding a name for the patient will not prove too great a problem.'

The consultant rang off. He had pushed to the limits, but he had won nothing, and danced to their tune.

In his office, Len Gibbons moved paper round his desk, sent it in clockwise circles, the other way, then north, south, east and west. The phone did not ring. The sheets were the contents of two files, cardboard and downloaded from the computer. The phone did not ring because there was – obviously – nothing to report from that far-away front line, nothing of *significance*. It was the life of intelligence officers, such as Len Gibbons, who handled men and women who were sent across borders and were at the extremities of survival, that the phone only rang when matters reached breaking point. He liked to have paper on his desk and regarded the screen as a poor substitute. Through the door, which was open, he could see Sarah was at her desk, typing briskly, not in the style of his own battering two fingers. She would be busying herself with the detail of the accounts for the operation – wise, sensible, and mind-destructively dull. Nor had there been contact from the Towers.

The paper he moved anti-clockwise was headlined *Joseph Paul Foulkes*. It wasn't the first time he had read the résumé of a biography, or the tenth, and wouldn't be the last. *Foxy* to his friends – not many of them. Aged *51*, brought up in West Yorkshire, grammar-school educated, joining the local *Police* at eighteen marrying *Liz (Elizabeth Joyce Routledge)*, a hospital worker, fathering two *daughters*, and specialising with the force in the élite *Covert Rural Observation Post* unit. Noticed. Advised that a career-enhancing move would be a transfer to the Metropolitan Police and *Special Branch*, then sent to *Northern Ireland* and given commendations for his work in dangerous country. A flair for languages. Courses at a language laboratory in Whitechapel, one on one, then six months of cramming in the culture aspects at the *School of Oriental and African Studies*, then *Bristol University*, and the military's *Beaconsfield camp*, culminating in a useful knowledge of Farsi, the principal tongue of the Iranian diplomats based in the capital. Where they met contacts – woodlands, parked cars, remote country hotels, restaurants and lorry drivers' cafés – he used the shotgun microphones or the larger parabolic versions and listened. Twice he had provided evidence leading to *conviction* and imprisonment. The marriage had not survived. Posted to Basra, *Nov 03–Feb 04* for work with *Intelligence and Interrogation*, utilising his language skills in Farsi. Second wife was *Ellie (Eleanor Daphne Wilson)*, now aged *33*, employed by Naval Procurement in Bath. Remains a serving police officer, with good reputation, running *CROP skills courses*. Summary: *Reliable, self-opinionated, wealth of experience*. Gibbons would say that Foxy Foulkes was as good as any spewed up by the computers – he was what he had, and almost as old as himself.

Gibbons could not imagine, or have survived, the privations of where he had despatched the man.

No call came through from the Towers. No colleague rang in to offer moral support. He was isolated. He could have contaminated others so they had, effectively, consigned him to the leper colony. He had the funds, the contacts, the links, and was cast adrift. If it all fouled up it would be *deniable* in the Towers, and a whisper would be passed that 'A junior official overreached himself, exceeded his powers, acted with no authorisation'. The great and the good would wash their hands of him. And if it succeeded?

The paper manoeuvred clockwise was headed *Daniel George Baxter*. It said he did not have friends, was generally known as *Badger*, and was *28 years old*. He had been brought up by his parents, *Paul and Debbie Baxter*, on the outskirts of Reading. His father sold second-hand cars and his mother took care of the books; they lived at *Burghfield* close to the Atomic Weapons Establishment. Schooled at a *comprehensive* and regarded as an *under-achiever*, criticised in school-leaving report as a *non-contributor*. Accepted into the Thames Valley Police in *2001* and initial reports described him as *quiet, resourceful and utterly dependable*. What had changed? Gibbons could almost have recited it – he'd read it often enough. One referee had been a doctor, an obsessional 'birder', who treated Baxter's parents. Baxter had taken him to flooded gravel pits west of Reading where he had led him, on his stomach, closer than he'd imagined possible to the perch from which a kingfisher dived; he had raved about the *mind-set and calm* of the applicant. A second referee had been a local accountant who prepared the business's final tax papers, and whom Baxter had taken to the Kennet where they had sat through a summer evening watching a female *otter* with her cubs, feeding and playing; he had written of the young man's *patience and dedication*. Had been taken into the force CROP unit at *22*, extraordinarily young, after three years as an undistinguished beat constable. Had found his vocation: court evidence for a narcotics 'untouchable' at Wantage, and the principal surveillance on a tinkers' site at Windsor, doubling as a thieves' kitchen. Had been drafted into the West Country regional office of the Box. Reported to have the *highest standards of professionalism*. Not academic, not particularly intelligent, but an *operator of genuine class*. Almost teetotal, does not smoke. *No known hobbies* but holidays are spent hiking, alone, in the west of Scotland.

If they won through – him on the back of Foxy and Badger, in co-operation with the Cousin and the Friend – he would be able to go back to the Towers, to a place dedicated to 'need to know'. Word would have seeped through the cracks in the walls and he would be the star of the moment. Few would know what he had done, what had been gained, only that a triumph lay at the Service's feet. For many years, almost the totality of his career, a catastrophe in the terms of intelligence gathering had dogged him. Triumph, wherever it was to be found, would help to wipe away dim memories of the watchtowers, fences and deceits of the trade ... but it would be on the backs of those two men, Foxy and Badger.

He was skilled at judging others, gutting their files, and could assess himself: he still suffered from a cruelty in the youth of his career, seemed to make a virtue of dullness and reliability, and kept his passions covert from work colleagues. He had the chance, now, to walk tall in the corridors of the Towers and take what he thought was his rightful place on the benches of those with influence . . . *if* two men performed, *if* luck favoured them, and *if* the dice rolled well, *if* . . .

The telephone didn't ring, and he moved the papers until they seemed to have little meaning. Then he looked at the pictures Sarah had pasted on the walls, and an outline of a face gazed down at him. It had no eyes, nose or mouth and was an enemy . . . He couldn't imagine where they were, Foxy and Badger, or how they were.

She was in front of him, inside the bakery, waiting to be served. He and Beryl were next in the queue, and he must have banged her elbow with the sleeve that held the two parts of the pole that carried the standard of his Royal British Legion branch. She turned, and he recognised her. She smiled, and he sensed that Beryl didn't understand.

'Hello,' Doug Bentley said. 'So, you're back again.'

'I come to quite a few,' she answered, and gave a little shrug. 'Afterwards I get some bread here.'

It had been a big turn-out that day. He and Beryl had done their usual thing. One bus from their own village into Swindon, then the 12 from Swindon to Wootton Bassett. They had met friends – the new colleagues they had come to know from their journeys to the town . . . too many of those journeys.

He did not think it impertinent to ask: 'Are you often here, in the town?'

She said, 'Only when they're bringing the heroes through. It's so moving, so emotional. I come when I can. I always see you.'

He had his position, with his standard, in the line and opposite the war memorial. He was well placed each time and faced the relatives who had brought flowers, usually roses from the florist behind the library. 'I wouldn't miss it,' Doug Bentley said. 'It's a responsibility I've been given by our branch to be here. The way I see it, I'd be letting them down, those coming through, if I wasn't here, if I just reckoned to be too busy. It's a responsibility and a privilege.'

'You're right.'

The customer at the counter had paid, picked up the paper bag with chocolate caramel slices and now eased out of her way. She asked for a loaf and he took a step forward. Beryl was fidgeting in her purse for coins. It had been a big turn-out because of the work the serviceman had done in Afghanistan. Ammunition technical officer – explosive ordnance disposal – down on hands and knees, defusing roadside bombs. Many photographs of him, young, a sergeant, had been held up by relatives, and posters with messages of love and admiration. So many of those who came through Wootton Bassett had been cut down by the bombs, and this man had lost his life in trying to make the wretched things safe. In his own military service – Pay Corps, National Service, never out of the UK – Doug Bentley had never come across any officer or NCO who would have attracted the level of support that the bomb men had when the bell tolled in the High Street, the hearse came up the incline and the funeral director walked with his top hat off and his staff in his hand. When the relatives had had their chance to put the flowers on the roof and touch the shiny black bodywork, that day, there had been rivulets of rain running down through the flowers, and tears cascading down faces. Doug Bentley had had his head lowered in respect and his eye had been on the black ribbon at the top of the pole above his standard. He did not know why good men, so loved and held in such regard, needed to chance their lives in defusing dangerous devices out in the middle of deserts, and in ditches beside fields.

She paid. She faced him and smiled. 'I've changed my hair. Fancy you recognising me.'

He'd known her because of the chain round her neck and the name in gold letters hanging above her blouse, resting on the skin where the cleavage started.

He lied, with a grin: 'I'm good with faces – and good with names, Ellie.' He didn't say he recognised her because the buttons ot her blouse, worn under an open winter coat, were out of order, as if they had been fastened in a hurry.

She was gone, and the shop's doorbell rang as she closed the door behind her. He asked for a loaf, a cob.

His wife's voice grated in his ear: 'She's been shagging again, hasn't she? It's that tart you spoke to in the summer. A woman can always tell. She's wearing a wedding ring, so it's a boyfriend she's been shagging, and she'll have a husband who's being two-timed and is too pathetic to know it.'

'Can you not, Foxy – for fuck's sake – stop your hand moving?'

'I'm trying.'

'Can't you try harder?'

Rare for Badger to criticise, and rare for him to be with an oppo he hadn't chosen, doing continuous stags with only faint chances of a doze, not proper sleep. Last time it had been like a holiday-camp talent contest, except that Ged hadn't been stripped down to a bikini. He had chosen his oppo after going to the line manager and complaining they'd shown out because George had coughed in a bush and they'd had to bloody run: George was dumped; feet didn't touch the ground. He would have preferred a rookie with him now, someone who had no knowledge of the tradecraft of covert rural work, who would take orders and do as he was instructed, and who had been there only to listen for Farsi talk. Badger had good hearing, and the shake of the hand beside him was an increasing irritation, like a dripping tap. They'd had the confession about the language.

'I can't stop it.'

'You're tired, I'm tired. You're hungry and thirsty, so am I. You're stressed, I'm stressed. You're shaking, I'm not.'

'I'm doing my best.'

'Not good enough. Try biting it.'

The confession had been the final issue. He could almost take the shake of Foxy's hand, with the rustle of the dead fronds. It was what he had said to Badger that had made a tipping point. He'd hidden it, and now he'd trotted it out.

A car, with a military escort riding inside the cab, had pulled up at the front of the house. A man had climbed out, then gone to the back and opened a rear door. He had extracted a bouquet of flowers, massive and colourful, then gone towards the officer, Mansoor. They had spoken, the man had been taken to the door and the wife had come out. She had accepted the flowers, and the car had driven away. Badger had seen in the glasses that she had had to fight to control her tears.

'What happened?' he'd asked.

'I don't know.'

'Isn't it working? Is the gear down?'

'Gear's great.'

'Why don't you know?'

'It's the language.'

The children were out again, and the officer had gone back to fishing, no bites, and smoking. Badger could see the flowers inside, through the open window. Hadn't anyone known? Not the Boss, the American, the Israeli, or fucking Foulkes himself? Had they known and kept quiet? In the confession the star word had been *dialect*. There were dialects in Farsi. Tribes had dialects, regions had dialects, the north and south had dialects, as did the east and west. There was the vernacular and there was the classical. Foxy had classical, but the vernacular was what the troops spoke and the officer spoke. In the confession it was stated that half of what came through the earphones was 'rough translation' and half was accurate. How had Foulkes managed with the interrogation team? He hadn't enough of the language to grasp the nuances that betrayed a man's lie. The diplomats he had tracked out of London, who had talked with young militants in students' unions, were educated and spoke classical. What could he not understand? He hadn't understood what the officer said to the man who brought the flowers, or most of what the Engineer had said to his wife, but he had been fine on the meeting she'd taken because that had been formal.

The hands shook.

They were together, hip against hip, shoulder against shoulder, two plastic bags by their knees and four bottles of urine. They might not even understand the mention of a destination, if they were lucky enough to hear one.

Badger said, 'You're useless, full of shit.'

'You're arrogant, full of conceit and piss. *You* – you wouldn't even have scraped through in my day.'

'I passed out well.'

'My day it was a proper test. Your day, Health and fucking Safety killed the hard bits. You wouldn't have come through.'

He was drawn in – shouldn't have been. 'I was top rated in marks.'

'Did you do the claustrophobia one, buried in a box with a pencil-wide air vent, in darkness, silence, and last thing you hear is the instructors walking away? Left for half an hour. You do that?'

'They'd scaled it back, wasn't permitted.'

'Send you up the Fire Brigade Tower, did they? The vertigo test. No restraint harness and lean over the edge of the tower's top to read the number-plate of a car parked right under you. How were you at that?'

'As you well know, it had been banned.'

'Dump you in a car boot, did they? Drive you over rough ground, bouncing, bashing? The boot opens and there's a German Shepherd looking to make a meal of you. Was that tough?'

'It had been ditched.'

'And isolation. What about water and a biscuit pack, driven to the far end of an airport fence, dropped off and told to sit against it, never lose contact with it. There's a car parked two hundred yards away and you have to log everything that happens to it, moves near it. The hazard lights might flash at midnight, a guy walks past in mid-morning. You're there as many as sixty hours, and you miss anything, you've failed. How did you do?'

'They've cut it back, it's not the same.'

'Did you do a run with a twenty-kilo pack, two and a half klicks in twelve minutes?'

'We did that.'

'Anyway, I did Claustrophobia, the Tower, the Boot, Isolation and Stamina, and I came out top in my class.'

'They give you a medal?'

'The training counted for something, and should be respected.'

Badger said, 'Assuming it's not the *wrong* dialect, and not the *wrong* tribe, and you can manage what you're here for, what's being said?'

They lapsed into quiet, and watched. The Mercedes pulled up, left the dust cloud to fragment behind it.

The driver was out snappily, came round the front of the car and opened the door for the Engineer. They had been together enough years for them to do small-talk on journeys: football teams that the Engineer had never seen and films he would never go to, but he valued the conversations. His own door was opened and he was handed the bag that held his laptop and the papers he had worked on. He stood, arched his back and stretched out the stiffness from the journey. The driver opened the boot and lifted out the new suitcase, carried it to the door, then bobbed his head dutifully, and was in his car, driving away.

Mansoor came to him. 'I think your wife is resting, and that her mother is with the children and their books.'

Mansoor's voice was breathy, hoarse, as if he had shouted and strained his throat. He demonstrated the wheels on the new case, ran them on the concrete of the patio in front of the door, showed how they went in all directions and grimaced. He asked what, that day, had happened, and was told men had been close, in the marshes, thieves, but they had been intercepted efficiently. How was his wife? he asked. Good, but tired.

He could smoke in his car but not in his house; he could smoke in his office and in meetings, but not in the presence of his children. She dictated the rules. He could not say how long remained for her – a month more, or the duration of his life. He did not know how long the rules she had laid down would exist.

There were two pigs in the water, near to a reed bed and close to the spit that came off the open ground some two hundred metres from their pier. He watched them, a full-grown boar and a young sow, emerge from the reeds and sink themselves into the water, only nostrils and eyes above the surface. Huge creatures, they moved effortlessly and with grace.

Mansoor told him that, before the thieves came, he had been watching for the African Sacred Ibis, but had not seen one. After the thieves had been intercepted, he had fished but had not caught a carp worth keeping, large enough to eat.

The Engineer had no interest in the bird, had less than no interest in the fishing. He did not share his cigarettes but smoked and walked to the limit of the small pier where the dinghy was tied. He was glad that Naghmeh was resting, that she had not been at the door to greet him and see the new case with the special wheels. Him bringing the case home marked a moment of virtual finality: when it was filled and they left, the road ahead might fork in two directions. They would head for recovery or death. There was no middle way.

Mansoor interrupted his quiet. He did not wish, of course, to intrude in private matters, but when was it likely they would travel? The Engineer said, distant and distracted, that the final arrangements were being put in place, but soon. *Soon.* They agreed it was a fine suitcase

Mansoor hovered behind him.

What did he have to say?

The voice was still throaty, as if there had been crisis and shouting here. The Engineer was told he should not permit his driver to take him through Ahvaz the following morning. There would be another hanging at the prison – a terrorist of the Ahvaz cells, an Arab. 'He confessed his crime, placing a bomb near the headquarters of the police, and named associates. The sentence of death by hanging will be enforced. Another was with him. He did not aid the interrogators and committed suicide. I am told there will be powerful emotions in the city tomorrow, and after the last experience ... There have been too many bombs from Arab terrorists. The penalty must be exacted. You should keep out of the city.'

He nodded, watching the pigs swim and feed. When the ciga-rette was finished he threw it down and watched it gutter in the

water. He went back to his house to find his children and show his
wife the suitcase he had bought for their journey.

Foxy whispered, 'Try this for a bedtime story to make you feel
good. The advice is to keep clear of the centre of Ahvaz tomorrow
because they're hanging a terrorist – sorry, probably a joker that
we or the Yanks shoved funds at so he's a *freedom fighter*. The Arabs
reckon they're third-class citizens in the blessed Islamic Republic
and risk their necks trying to blast the mullahs. Anyway, he's going
to be strung up and it's likely to make people angry. That tells me
the local good guys are infiltrated, compromised, have snitches
and touts in their cells, and aren't secure. That's why you and I are
here. There was another who would have been sharing the gallows
tomorrow but he topped himself. When the goon speaks to the
boss it's good, educated Farsi, and I can follow it.'
    'Have you anything else to say?'
    'Like an apology?'
    'For bitching, then sulking,' Badger teased coldly. 'You ready to
say sorry?'
    'No.'

The house was bathed in light from fittings screwed to the top of
the walls. It fell on the patio and across the track to spread over the
pier, where the dinghy was tied, and the water. The Engineer sat
on the plastic chair and smoked. He could have lived inside the
camp of the al-Quds Brigade, in a fine bungalow near to the
commandant's residence, or had an apartment overlooking the
Karun river near to the Hotel Fajr Grand. He might have been
accommodated in a government-owned villa near to the Ahvaz
airport, but he lived here. Her choice. It had been her decision
that, when the Americans began to crowd onto their aircraft and
head for home, taking with them the body-bags, so many of which
he had filled, they should make their home near to the water, the
marshes and old civilisations that captivated her, and where she
was close to her life's passion: the clearance of land mines. She
had supervised the renovation of the building, had bullied

architects and pleaded with builders, had created the world she wanted . . . and the pain had come. There was moonlight on the far water, the reeds and a spit of mud, beyond the throw of the security lights, and he saw the ripples, the movement of the birds and confusion where pigs browsed. He heard the racking cough of a sentry. He had thought he understood it, but he could not, now, imagine the future.

8

Foxy pinged her . . . He thought the temperature inside the gillie suit was in excess of 50 degrees centigrade – more than 130 Fahrenheit. He could have drunk water until his belly distended, but would not. They had carried in the water. Water, where they were, was more important than anything other than the audio-capture gear. They could survive on little food, concentrates with high protein, and minimal sleep. If the water was exhausted they would suffer dehydration, which meant muscle and stomach cramps, headaches, weakness, dizziness and heavy sweating.

Foxy had heard, on his Basra tour, that the body could lose a quart of moisture through sweat per hour. He lay still. *Ping* was croppie talk for having a close view of a target. Could have been *eyeball*, which was general for all police agencies on surveillance duties, but the guys who bagged the shit, bottled the piss and were an élite talked of *pinging* a target . . . It was the talk that kept Foxy alert. Good to think of himself as 'élite'. He deserved it.

She moved slowly in the sunshine at the front of the house. Her man was Tango One and she was Tango Two. Foxy reckoned her more important to their endeavour than the husband, and more likely to cough up the evidence of a destination. When she was outside, or when she was inside the room with the open window and he could see her shadow move or an interior light lit her, he eased the controls, lifted the volume and struggled for greater clarity in his earphones. He believed it was from her that he would break the damn thing, then get on the move, retrieve the gear and head for the extraction point. After this, Joe 'Foxy' Foulkes – not breaking any confidences, of course, and not spitting too much phlegm into the face of the Official Secrets Act – would be a big man, a valued man, a man in demand. 'Elite': he deserved that title, had done since the days he'd lain in the hide on the hill above the farm near Cappagh in County Tyrone and been there long enough to feed the warning that the Barrett 50 calibre was on the move. Guys from Intelligence, and special forces, had called his stake-out 'epic', and the battalion adjutant, the unit that had fouled up the cordon and missed the damn thing when it was moved, had made a personal apology, saying that 'such outstanding surveillance was short-changed'. This was beyond any category he had before been involved in.

The young 'un slept beside him.

There was more washing going out, more pegs slotting on the line, children's stuff and her husband's clothing. She would not, of course, hang out her intimate clothing where it could be seen by the guards from the barracks. Her mother followed her and carried the plastic basket with the shirts, shorts, socks, the kids' dresses, towels and washing-up cloths. He had the binoculars on her, 10×50, but didn't use the spotter 'scope. The visuals were of small interest compared to the audio system – wouldn't have said it into Badger's ear, but the microphone was well placed on the mud spit and well camouflaged. The gear was good and the sound quality was fine but their language was difficult for him because they didn't speak, mother and daughter, in the classical but in the vernacular. He understood each time she wanted another peg, that the small boy's shirt had not washed well, and that the girl had torn a skirt playing outside. He had to believe that the clue would be given him.

The young 'un slept. It was unequal. Badger could sleep for the full three hours while Foxy was on stag. When Foxy slept, Badger would elbow him if there was conversation on the patio. He had been woken when the Engineer had come from the house at dawn and paced at the water's edge, enjoying his cigarette and talking about football scores with two of the guards. He had been woken again when the car had come and the goon, Mansoor, had repeated the warning about keeping clear of the centre of Ahvaz, then asked about the Engineer's day. He had seen the shrug and heard a remark about 'meetings, all the day is meetings'. And a question was asked about the suitcase, but he had not caught the reply and had assumed that the wife approved of it. Then he had been allowed to sleep again. Twice he had received the elbow and been told that he was snoring. Foxy, as routine, dug his fist into Badger's hip each half-hour to wake him and then lie that he was talking or grunting in his sleep. If Foxy couldn't crash out for three hours, he was damned if Badger would sleep without interruption.

Yes, it would be good. There would be nods and winks, hints-offered, but the secrecy governing where he had been and why would be preserved. He would be introduced as the man who had gone into opposition territory, who had lain up in circumstances of quite extraordinary privation, had witnessed mass murder and delivered, had won through. He would talk about the skills and disciplines needed to achieve aims and ping targets. Who did he have with him, or was he alone? He might be asked that. He'd had a greenhorn, something of a sherpa, there – basically – to hump the gear. He'd enjoy that, and would be fêted. Ellie would be proud and . . . The washing was out on the line and hung limp; there was no wind. There were more flies than before.

The flies had been bad the previous evening, had disappeared during darkness and been replaced by mosquitoes. Now, in the full glare of the sun, the mosquitoes had gone and the flies were back – big bastards. They droned and probed at the scrim mesh on the camouflage headgear and they were on the mud-caked skin of his hands. He thought it remarkable that they didn't wake Badger, that he could sleep through their persistence. In the night, Badger had taken the shit bags and piss bottles out of the hide, wriggled on his stomach into the reed bed, dug a little pit – on the water line – buried the bags and emptied the bottles. Without the bags the flies should have been less interested. Didn't work that way. They'd come on in swarms and searched for routes through the scrim into his ears, mouth and nose, settling on his hands. He felt the prick as they bit, but he couldn't anoint himself with repellent: it would provide an alien scent.

She had the line filled with washing. Ellie often asked him to empty the washing-machine and put their things on a line when she was in a hurry for work and doing her makeup or running late. It was usual for him to iron his shirts and her blouses. He had learned to iron after he'd gone to London, leaving Liz in the north with the children, and did it well: Ellie was sometimes too busy with overtime at Naval Procurement to get home early and iron. Quite often, Foxy cooked the dinner.

He thought she'd have been a fine-looking woman if the illness hadn't ravaged her. She was quite tall, not dwarfed by her husband. The lenses showed her figure when she moved and the robe was pressed against her body. She would have seemed handsome from fifty or seventy-five yards, with a strong nose, good cheekbones and a chin that gave off authority ... Different when he watched her through ten times magnification. Harsher lines, a greater stoop in the shoulders and the wince at the mouth when she turned or reached up with the clothing or a peg. He sensed a steeled determination to complete the basic task. He watched her. It was what he did well.

Abigail Jones had not met Len Gibbons. She imagined, because he was 'old school' that he would have moved to a temporary billet, a London club or a camp bed wherever he had set up his operations centre, and that he paced, even chain-smoked, while he waited for a telephone call.

It would have been three years ago, just before she was shipped out to Iraq when she was coming to the end of her London duty, that she had been leaving the canteen area, and the older woman with her, whom she'd known from the Balkans, had stage-whispered a choice morsel about the man standing, seeming elderly and vacant, at the counter, then moving his tray.

The telephone would not have rung because she had sent no message. There was to be no radio traffic, and no satphone communication other than to transmit information categorised 'critical'. She had nothing important to report.

The woman, Jennifer, famed for indiscretion, had been in Belgrade while Abigail worked in the Sarajevo embassy and they'd become friends, distant, when sharing escape weekends on Croatian beaches. 'When you get down to Baghdad, darling, don't eff it up like that one did in his youth. In this hateful place they like to deal in one-chance-only scenarios. A good man, a nice man, and they said he was really capable. He was advanced, given responsibilities. Such a sad story. Never recovered fully, like blight in an apple orchard, and it was thirty years ago.' Gossip was forbidden, mortal sin. Abigail had asked what the man had done and where he had done it. Jennifer had chuckled and declined to expand on her story – except to tell her that the man was Len Gibbons, left for ever like a bit of driftwood, high and dry, when the tide slipped out. They had parted, gone off in different lifts to different floors, and she had forgotten about the tale until, six years later, she had been told Len Gibbons would field her reports when there was news worth imparting.

He was hardly going to want to know that she had lain in the sand, swaddled in a mosquito net, with her firearm on the ground beside her, fastened by a lanyard to her wrist. He was hardly going to be concerned that she had barely slept, and that Corky and Harding, Hamfist and Shagger would have slept less, that those she proudly called the Jones Boys had used two flares and a thunder flash and had maintained a perimeter of sorts. There hadn't been a charge but a creeping infiltration, the creaking of stressed wire as the fences, already sagging, had been flattened. The flares had stopped them, had held them in the shadow at the edge of the light pool. The thunder flash had scattered them, driven them back. Hamfist was the one who knew most of this sector and he'd claimed to read the *madan* mind. 'You can give the feckers – 'scuse, miss – a flash and a flare and we'll be OK. If it gets to us chucking about the lead we'll have to quit.' The flares and the flash had stabilised it during the night and, first light, Corky had urged her to get the treasury open. 'We can't shoot them all, miss, or it'll be worse than Bloody Sunday. We should try to buy them. Do it like an auction – start small and haggle like it's the bazaar. They're all Ali Babas, miss, and don't forget it.'

She could picture him: she'd seen him once in the canteen and a couple more times when he'd been near her as she'd come off a bus near to the Towers' entrance. There had been a weighted look to him, that of a man burdened: she'd define that as pallor in the complexion, straggling hair, a shuffle walk, clothing that was a little too loose and, above all, wariness, a sense of being left outside any loop that existed. Jennifer had spoken of 'one chance only'. It was where Abigail was now. The one chance to make it work – so she could justify rare interest in Len Gibbons, who waited for her call.

She had taken twenty five-dollar bills from her money belt, which she wore against the skin at her waist. And almost, taking the notes out and peeling them off the wad, she had giggled – but to herself. It had made a dent in his skin: she had not taken off her money belt when she had been over and across him. The buckle had gouged his flesh . . . Regret nothing. He had not seemed to notice that it had pressed into his flat, muscled stomach. She had gone down to the gate, Shagger yawning behind her, and Corky halfway between them and the vehicles. Hamfist and Harding had been near enough to the Pajeros to start them, and fast. She had called forward the twenty men she thought seemed oldest and had put, into each of the palms offered her, a five-dollar bill. Her own ancestors, a century before, might have given out beads or anything shiny . . . She'd closed each fist on the note. It had humiliated her, the crudeness. Then she had tried to persuade them to head home, get back to the huts built of reeds and the floating island shared with the water buffalo that gave them dung to use as their staple fuel for heating and the high-definition TV. Five dollars was meagre. None of them had shifted.

It had been Len Gibbons's turn, three decades earlier – if Jennifer's rumour was to be believed – to have 'one chance only' and to 'eff it up'. She thought she was now presented with a copper-bottomed opportunity to join his team. The crowd at the gate, in the half-day that had passed from her handing out the trifles, had doubled. The threat when the next belt of darkness came was, likely, twice as great. She couldn't get the boys to drive her back to al-Qurnah and try to rustle up rooms at the one building in the town, beside the big river and adjacent to the dead tree claimed as the 'Tree of Life'. One of the Shia zealot movements had control of that building. The alternative was to leave the site, drive onto a berm or a bund and park there where they were visible for ten miles or more. She couldn't call up a friendly UK platoon and have them do their security because the Brits were now in Afghanistan, and the marines, the Fort Bragg guys, too, had switched wars, had quit their last combat with a chorus of 'Fucking good riddance to a motherfucking place.' There was nowhere else to be. It was her 'one chance only' and she assumed that Len Gibbons, far away, doodling, would understand.

She asked the boys how much they reckoned she should shell out.

She went back inside, and hitched up her robe – did the act of a Basra tart – offloaded an additional two hundred and fifty American dollars and split the notes ten times. Twenty-five dollars each, and a demand for some action.

It was a weak hand, the worst.

This time she had Corky on her right and Hamfist on her left. Again she called out the oldest men, with those who wore clothing of the best material, and pleaded for the space they needed to monitor the wildlife successfully. Corky had said they could not be further back and do their job. Hamfist had said that any guy at the sharp end had to believe in the honesty of the people in support. She handed out money, repeated the pleading and went back towards the building.

She was a tough girl. Abigail Jones, convent-school educated, red-brick university, only took the bus in grim weather and ran to work most days in London along the Embankment, and home again. She could sleep on shit-laced concrete, hike and trek – and could almost have wept. There were more coming and none were leaving, and some now had rifles. In these parts any man with balls had access to a rifle.

Harding asked, 'How long do you think we have until we lift them out?'

She shrugged.

Shagger asked, 'What do we do, miss, when this crowd start coming?'

'Let me think about it, and give me some fucking space.'

There were two Black Hawks on the apron in the sun. One of the crews was in an annex where a room offered bunk beds and thick enough window blinds to blot out the ferocity of the sun's glare. They would be wearing ear baffles so that the roar of the aircon systems wouldn't keep them awake. The second crew, four personnel, was in the annex rest room and sprawled in easy chairs. They were in the dog days of the empire, and the final evacuation from the one-time colony was mere weeks away so little more than skeleton forces remained. The buildings they occupied were tired, the paint scuffed, and would not receive renovation. Inevitably they had caught the mood of 'drawdown', and had taped in their lockers at the Baghdad base a pencil picture of a snake divided into segments, one for each day they would serve on that posting. Most were now filled in and only part of the tail remained.

That crew who were awake, supposedly ready to kick themselves out of the chairs into the open-top jeep and have the bird airborne within three minutes of the bell going, found this assignment littered with unanswered questions. The four-blade twin-engine helicopter, with a lift classified as 'medium', was the workhorse of the American military, and carried stores – Meals Ready to Eat, the chemicals for latrines, home-town hacks looking for stories that didn't exist – and also flew special-forces units. It was reliable, flew like a dream, caused little hassle and less grief. But the American military effort was now scaled down, the troops reduced to spit-and-polish bull-shit in camps, so the guys in the two crews were generally just bored shitless. Each bird, each crew, could lift an additional eleven troops with full combat gear. They were on standby, but they didn't know when they would be called out or whom they would pick up; they had not been given an exact extraction point. New, out of the Sikorsky factories, the Black Hawk had set their taxpayers back, minimally, $14 million.

It was expensive hardware that sat on the tarmacadam outside the annex, and the 'ready' crew waited to be told *something*.

No one came.

Normally when special forces were involved – infiltration and exfiltration – herds of liaison men and women hovered, their cell phones ringing and their comms busy. There were none.

The pilot, Eddie, read a comic book and his co-pilot, Tristram, turned the pages of a Bible, the Old Testament. A side gunner, Dwayne – trained to use a 7.62 calibre machine gun – studied a puzzle book, and Federico, who had the weapon on the starboard side of the cabin, was deep in an aviation engineering magazine. They were not disturbed.

Any other time they had done the lifts for special forces there had been a presence alongside, checking every few minutes that their flight plans were ready and understood, that they knew where all the pylons with slack electricity cables were and which they could fly under, and that the fire power of Hellfires and machine-gun belts had been tested. They'd even demand a check on the fuel loads in the tanks. No one bothered them.

All they had been told was that a phone call would come through on the green handset, and a voice would give co-ordinates to an area approximately sixty kilometres away. That distance, going east, would put them hard against the Iran border.

They read, killed time, waited.

Badger had her in his glasses. Then, alerted, he swung them round, went through a full 90-degree arc with them, and picked up the bulldozer.

The big plant vehicle, with a bucket on the front, had come from behind the barracks and now powered along the bund line to the right. He fancied he understood. Past midday, with the sun at full strength, the smell was sweeter, more foul, and had seemed over the last hour to hang in the air close to him. The one they called the goon, Mansoor, hung onto the outer handles of the cab.

Badger had been up and awake most of the night, and had

allowed the older man to sleep from the time that the house lights had gone out until dawn, had let him sleep through for six hours before waking him and starting the routine of three hours on and three hours off. He had let him sleep except when the snores came on too fierce.

In the first light, grey and almost chill, with the sun not yet peeping up from a horizon of reed tops and water expanses, Badger had crawled out of the hide, taken care to rearrange the cover of dead reeds, then had moved away and scouted the bare ground, on his stomach. He had been in the reeds and had seen where a spur came off the bund line and towards where they had made the hide. Then he had reached the open water beyond and the little light flecked the bodies in the water. Already they were swollen, gross – the smell had been building and had not dissipated in the cool of night. Now, in the middle of the day, he imagined the corpses would be even more distended. He understood that men had been tasked to retrieve and bury them.

At dawn he had seen the bodies floating with clouds of insects over them, and in the middle of the day he saw the bulldozer. He didn't need to see much else. In this little corner of the world, far from anything he had experienced before, men could be shot dead, dumped and the evidence buried. The bulldozer went from his view and the sound drifted and was fainter . . . It was, after a fashion, what they did to their own. What would they do to those who intruded on their space and affairs, broke the boundaries of the borders and *spied* – he had read about spies. In the last war spies had been hanged in London, electrocuted in the USA, marched to the gallows in Syria, with a placard round the neck denouncing Israeli espionage, and to an execution chamber at the Sugamo prison in Tokyo: Richard Sorge, Communist agent, spying against Japan on behalf of Russian Intelligence, who denied all knowledge of him . . . *denied all knowledge*. It had a ring to it. Almost, in that heat, a shiver convulsed him. Fear? Apprehension? He put it down to the sweat running in the small of his back, where the fingers of Alpha Juliet had been. *Denied all knowledge*:

up in Scotland, with the theatre of that house and the bay with the waves crashing, the cold, the rain and the howl of the pipes, denial had seemed unimportant.

He had the flies and the smell, the sun flaring up off the water, dazzling him, and a mirage haze.

She came back out. His hand hovered, ready to shake Foxy awake.

Her mother followed her, but held back in the shade at the front of the house. Badger thought her beautiful, regal yet doomed. Through the glasses he could see the effort it took for her to walk from the patio to the water's edge, then little flecks of colour on the ground close to her feet: a flowerbed. Badger swore. She had made a flowerbed, and weeks before there would have been vivid colours in it. There was, against the house, a tap, and over the patio a discarded hose pipe. He thought it reasonable that the tap had not been turned on and the hosepipe aimed at the flowers – maybe his mother's favourite, geraniums – since her diagnosis. An ex-infantry soldier he had worked with had once said that shock spread in a life much as a hand grenade rolled, bounced and slid erratically across the floor in a bunker or a slit trench. It would have been like that when the news was given them. He thought it would have seemed a waste of time and energy to continue watering the flowers.

She captured him.

She sat alone in front of the water and close to the pier. The children were not back from school, the mother was inside the house and the goon was with the bulldozer. The guards would not approach her. Badger would have woken Foxy, given him a hard nudge in the ribcage – where it might hurt – if anyone had come close to her and talked.

She watched the birds. Did she know that men scavenging for artillery-piece casings had been shot – he assumed for being inside a restricted, sensitive zone – then dumped, were being retrieved now by a bulldozer to be clawed into a pit? Did she know that that was the price of keeping security tight around her? Her work was mine clearance. For Badger the world played at riddles.

What would happen to her?

He had not worked in Northern Ireland. He was too young, and the war there had lapsed to a ceasefire by the time he was trained and operational. He had come across enough who knew the Province. A paratrooper, off the hills above Brecon when Badger had been with them on exercise, had talked of doing back-up protection for handlers when they met with potential Provo informers – touts – in the shadows of pub car parks, in the empty darkened spaces of beauty spots. It always bloody rained, they said, when the proposition of betrayal was put, the approach made. Some, the paratrooper had said, spat it out, some hesitated, and some came on board – bloody ran up the gangplank . . . Then – this was the rub – they had to go back and tell the wife they were changing sides and taking the Queen's shilling. He hadn't forgotten that conversation long into a night. If her husband accepted the offer made, and she came through surgery, they would face a new life, and convalescence in an English seaside town or a suburb of any city in the United States. First, how would the man respond to *interdiction*, approach? Badger couldn't say, couldn't imagine it. But he was sure Mr Gibbons, the Boss, had his finger on the pulse of it.

There was, he decided, something totally elegant about the woman. Something utterly dignified. He would have been hard put to explain his thoughts.

She gazed out over the water. He watched her through the glasses, ten times magnification, and there were moments when he believed she looked straight at him, must see him. The heat in the suit sapped him and he fought to maintain his concentration. He had to make his water last – and in his ears were the sounds of the ripples against the pier's supports and the scrape of the dinghy against the planks. He reckoned, couldn't be certain at two hundred metres plus, that tears ran down her face.

Badger could not, in truth, take his eyes from her. He didn't know how her husband, assuming a surgeon could work a miracle, would respond to the approach.

$$\star \qquad \star \qquad \star$$

They had done more war games at the camp. Through the morning there had been a theoretical headquarters-command scenario of an American invasion pushing in from Iraqi territory on a front south of al-Qurnah and north of Basra. The Engineer's role had been to describe the new generation of explosive formed projectiles, their deployment, and effect against the enemy's armour, and the forces of any 'poodles' that the Great Satan could whip into line. They had not stopped for lunch, but took a break for coffee.

When would he be away?

Again, he found himself alongside the brigadier who had responsibility for this sector.

He grimaced. He had the suitcase, and they awaited final confirmation of the itinerary . . . very soon.

After the refreshment stop, they would move on to the area of counter-attack, and the Engineer had prepared a paper on the value of deflecting armoured convoys to specified roads where the bombs could be more effective and more concentrated. He would speak of the value of choke points into which armour would be drawn. He would quote the disproportionate success of the defenders of a Croatian city, two decades before, who had ambushed main battle tanks, hit the first in the convoy simultaneously with the last and then, at leisure, destroyed the wallowing beasts that could not manoeuvre. He would say this could be done by civilian fighters if they had only rudimentary skills in warfare. He would tell his audience of the effect that the explosive devices – manufactured under his direction with minimal metal parts, instead incorporating plastics, ceramics and moulded glass – had on units' morale, and give them, as a rallying cry, the conclusion that one casualty, without a leg or an arm, needed four men to bring him back from the explosion and a helicopter to fly him to the rear. Ultimately when one man hobbled down the main street of his home town and the civilians living there watched him, sympathising, support for the war would drain away. 'Let them come, let them face us, let them know the smell of defeat,' he would finish.

He was not an easy public speaker, and he tried to memorise what he would say and how he would deliver it, but the brigadier broke into his thoughts. Did his wife approve of the case?

She had not looked at it, had refused to open it, would not discuss with him what clothing she should take – whatever destination was chosen for them. She had sat in her chair in the kitchen for much of the evening after the children had gone to bed, when he had told them more about Prince Korshid and his brothers: the time he had gone to the bottom of the deep well and had found there a girl of unmatched beauty. On her lap was the head of a *deav*, a serpent, that snored foully. The prince would rescue the girl, but that was for the next evening. He did not say that tension cut the mood in his home, or confide that she had thrown back at him the riposte: 'If God says it will happen it will happen. Do you attempt to obstruct God's will with temporary relief? Better to die quietly, with love and in peace, than to chase a few more days of life. Are we justified in fighting it?' Her mother had watched them, silent, and he had not answered but had gone to tell the story to the children.

'My wife thought it a very fine case.'

'Her morale? Her attitude?'

'Very positive. She is focused on getting treatment she needs for recovery, and is most grateful to those who give her the chance of it.'

It was rare for the Engineer to talk on personal matters with a senior officer of the Revolutionary Guard Corps. He knew this man's importance in areas of military responsibility, and also because the papers regarding Naghmeh's illness would have needed his initialled acceptance. Just as this officer procured for him the most sophisticated and recent electronic equipment from the USA, reaching him via Dubai's container port, so he had the power to arrange the funding of such a journey and subsequent medical attention.

'You are important to us, brother.'

Others, in uniform, stood patiently behind the brigadier, waiting for an opportunity to speak with him, but he waved them away. It was a short, clipped movement but unmistakable.

'I know much about you, brother.'

'Of course. I accept that.'

'You live by the water, close to the border.'

'It was the home my wife chose, before the diagnosis, and a place of rare beauty, near to a command post. It is very peaceful, and—'

'May I offer advice, brother?'

'Of course. I would be honoured to receive it.'

Which was the truth. Advice would not be given lightly, or be ignored when offered by a man of such seniority.

Blunt words, the veneer of concern stripped off. 'You cannot return there.'

'I am sorry, did I misunderstand you? It is where my wife is—'

A searing interruption. 'Whether your wife is alive or dead, whether she is happy there, whether she likes to view the water and count mosquitoes is, brother, not of importance. A man of your value should be better protected. You will not go back there.'

This brigadier had been in place for some four months. The Engineer did not know him well. He could not argue, remonstrate or dispute. If she survived, she would be devastated. It was unthinkable that he should challenge a decision by so senior an officer.

'Of course.'

A wintry smile. 'I would suggest that if the Americans invade you go to the deepest hole you can find that a fox has dug and settle in it. Hide for as long as you can, and emerge when you have a new identity. If the Americans come, the shockwave will likely bring down the regime of the Islamic Republic. Revolution will rule. Do you watch CNN, brother? You do not. You are good, patriotic and disciplined. I watch CNN and I see the demonstrations in Tehran, Isfahan, Shiraz and Mashhad. We attack the websites and the mobile-phone links, but we cannot prevent the images escaping our borders. We can hang people, abuse them and lock them away, but when revolt has taken hold it cannot be reversed. There is an expression, 'a house of cards', and I fear that is what we will be. We conceive martyrs, we shoot at unarmed crowds but we do not cow the masses.

When their time comes, when our authority is fractured, they will rise up, as the crowds did in the last days of the imperial family. The officials serving the Peacock Throne were shot by firing squad, butchered with knives or hanged in the Evin gaol. If our regime collapses and I am still here, I imagine I will be led out to the nearest streetlight and a rope will be thrown up. I will be hanged, as will most of us gathered here today. We appear invulnerable but strength is often illusory. You, brother – maybe you would be on the streetlight beside me. If the Americans come, brother, how many will face the prospect of a rope over the arm of a streetlamp and will trade information to save their neck from being stretched? What better piece of information to give up than the identity of the man who designed the bombs that crippled the Great Satan's war effort inside Iraq? An American said once, of Serbs who were hunted and accused of atrocities, 'You can run but you cannot hide.' It was a popular phrase. It frightened men, intimidated them. You would be named, I would be named and most of the men in this room would be named.

'There is, of course, a solution to the problem of regime collapse and vengeance turned on former influential people. I can go abroad. I am authorised to fly to Damascus. Under deep cover I can travel to Dubai or Abu Dhabi. The American consulate in Dubai is in the World Trade Center, and the embassy in Abu Dhabi is located between Airport Road and Coast Street. They would not, if I walked in cold off the street, treat me like a friend, but they would show me respect, and I would avoid the rope suspended from the streetlamp. If you were to take a similar course when you go abroad, you also would be safe from the rope. Could you do that, brother, to save your neck?'

He saw that a trap yawned in front of him.

First there had seemed to be sympathy, then there had been honesty and, last, conspiracy. He was not one of them. He did not wear uniform, and was inside no inner circle. They were military men and he was a scientist in the field of miniaturised electronics. They used him. A trip wire might have lain across his path. If he had snagged it he would have gone into the prepared pit.

The Engineer said, 'I am completely devoted to the Islamic Republic, its leaders and its future.'

He was rewarded with a smile, slow but broadening.

He went on, 'I am devoted to my God, my country and my work.'

'I hope your journey is fruitful, brother. We will be waiting to welcome you home and pray God for the best outcome.'

The brigadier was gone from his side. He realised he had been taunted, also that he had been warned against making unwise contacts outside Iran. He could not remember when, before, he had felt such keen anger towards a senior officer of the Revolutionary Guard Corps. They mocked and threatened him. While they strutted on parade grounds, lined up their men across wide streets, then ordered baton charges or the firing of live rounds to disperse crowds who protested that an election had been stolen, he – the Engineer, Rashid Armajan – had been creating the weapons that defeated an enemy that was a super-power. He could not tell the brigadier to go fuck his own mother because that man had to initial the final authorisation for the journey in search of a consultant. He felt blood on his lip, and realised how hard he had bitten it, how much pain he had absorbed. He wiped his mouth with a handkerchief and hoped no stain remained.

They were called into the next session, and the brigadier did not catch his eye as they went back into the operations area.

Badger had rested, but not slept. He had eaten some biscuit and drunk sparingly, had defecated into a bag and urinated into a bottle. He had done all of that within six inches of Foxy, without disturbing the leaves spread over the hide. He had thought more about the woman in the plastic chair across the expanse of water than he had about Alpha Juliet.

She was still there. She might have moved, or not, in the three hours he had had his eyes squeezed shut while the sun was still crystal bright.

Her children were close to her. Their toys were out. He thought the kids more subdued, less raucous, than the previous day. Once, the girl fell and screamed and her mother did not move, but the old lady came out, waddled to the child, swept her up and cuddled her.

The smell hung rancid between them, around them, with no wind to drift it.

'Anything happened? Anything said?'

A slight shake of Foxy's head, insufficient to rustle the dead stuff over him.

'Nothing?'

The slightest nod.

The flies crowded above them and surged on his hands as Badger lifted his binoculars and adjusted the focus so that he could see the mess of reed leaves and stems where the microphone lay, then sweep on from the bund line to the barracks and a few of the soldiers playing basketball, then across the palm trees. He saw the head goon sprawled on a sunbed, and picked up the house and the kids, then the old lady who banged dust from rugs. He went by the flowerbed, abandoned, and reached the chair.

It annoyed Badger that he had twice asked the question and not been answered, annoyed him that he had felt it necessary to make bare, semi-civilised talk – like it was a weakness in him. He had ticks on his legs – could have been three bites or four. If he scratched hard, broke the surface and drew blood, the itch would be worse. They had to be endured. He would not fidget, give Foxy the pleasure of seeing his discomfort.

He wasn't proud of himself. He didn't ask, just pulled the headset from under Foxy's head covering. To achieve that he needed to get his fingers across Foxy's face, touch his cheeks, then go up to the crown and drag forward the arch linking the earpieces. His wrist was gripped.

'On induction courses, do they teach wet-behind-the-ears recruits, rookies, that courtesies matter?'

He had a hold on the headset.

'If they don't, they should run one for beginners in basic manners. Fucking ask.'

He didn't. A stand-off moment. Badger had hold of the headset and Foxy had hold of his wrist. Three seconds, five, ten. Badger let go and Foxy let go, and managed to choreograph it so that neither was the outright winner nor loser. He was given the headset and slotted it under his camouflage covering with small, slow movements. He thought he had lost high ground, which seemed – hard up against his oppo – to matter. What also mattered was his own inadequacy. He could watch the front of the house across the lagoon, and track the movement of the wife, her mother, the kids, the officer and the other guards, but if she spoke, and he was the one on stag, he must break into Foxy's rest time. It hurt him that he was reliant on the older man, hurt more than the tick bites bothered him.

She was very still.

There were birds on the water in front of her and they fed, ducking and diving. An otter swam close to the main wall of the reeds: the first he had seen that day. He knew otters from the islands off the west coast of Scotland. Only a glimpse, and then it dipped, showing an arched back and a stubby tail.

He didn't think she watched the birds or had seen the otter. On his earlier watch, a pair of pigs had crossed in front of him, would have swum over the sunk cable from the microphone, with just their snouts above the water.

The light had changed and was no longer on her face, but the sun's force was now more to her left side and her cheeks were not in its glare. Badger couldn't say whether there were still tears. Maybe earlier she had looked too closely into the sun's reflection from the lagoon and her eyes had watered. A woman who ran a mine-clearance campaign might be made of stern material – or might weep in private because of what had happened to her, to her man and her children. He didn't know.

Foxy farted. The foul smell hung around them, the residue of the last Meal Ready to Eat they had shared – beef in some congealed liquid. If someone had walked over them, he or she might have thought they'd picked up pig shit on a boot.

He reflected: there was no other way to do the job that the Boss,

Mr Gibbons, had set them. They had to be there, marooned and . . . He watched her.

She was not the woman of a drugs-dealer he had once kept pinged, day after day, while she lounged in a summer garden close to her pool, wearing not much on a rare warm week, and she was not one of the women from the tinkers' camp who had pegged out washing, lounged and smoked while the men planned thieving, and she was not the woman with the mousy hair and pale face, mistress to the man whose wife was under the patio extension and who would be led away, handcuffed, as the digger moved in. He had pinged many women who were consorts of a target and had not felt any of them were special or worth interest.

The Engineer's wife dominated any thoughts of Alpha Juliet. An instructor on the last week before Badger had been awarded his Blue Book, certifying his surveillance competence, had told the group that thinking of sex, stripping down women, doing business with them, was excellent for holding the concentration needed in a hide when paint drying might have seemed interesting. He had said that far and away the best shagging he'd had in his life was when he'd been lying on his belly, enveloped in a gillie suit, with nothing happening. It would have been good to remember Alpha Juliet – a fine, strong girl who didn't blather, didn't seem in search of commitment and seemed to have chosen him for better reasons than that she had gone without for a week: unfathomable – but he couldn't remember Alpha Juliet now. He stared through the glasses at the woman, and because he kept the focus on everything familiar about her, he knew which crow's feet were deepening at her eyes. Her breathing seemed harder, and her mouth would twist when the pain dug.

'You'll call me.'

'Yes.'

'Because without me you're worse than useless.'

He didn't answer.

Foxy went on, 'And keep watch all round.'

A point of principle: he didn't react and kept the glasses on her. He didn't take orders from the older man.

'Why are you only watching her?'

No response. He held the focus. Her hands were very still, and he thought she had a serenity.

'You gone soft on her, young 'un? Unprofessional if you have.'

Badger held his silence.

'If you've gone gentle on her, just remember who she is. She's the wife of Rashid Armajan, bad bastard, bomb-maker and enemy. She shares his bed and, before she went sick, used to spread her legs for the guy who spent his days planning the next generation of nasties to kill our boys inside Iraq. I feel nothing for her. She would have kept a nice tidy household for him, left him with no worries in his life other than working out the best way to blow up, mutilate and kill coalition troops. He was pretty good at it. Forgotten what the man said? 'A small number of clever and inno-vative men is capable of wrong-footing us so consistently that the body-bags keep going home, and the injured with wounds they'll carry to their graves . . . We call an enemy a *Bravo*. Rashid Armajan is a big bad Bravo.' That's what the man said. She's that man's woman and what she has in her head is immaterial to me. It matters that, because of what's in her head, he'll travel away from here. Nothing less, nothing more. In case you've forgotten it, young 'un, the ceremonies at Wootton Bassett when the dead come home didn't start with Afghanistan killed-in-action troops. They started with Iraq. We couldn't stay in Iraq because of the bombs, *his* bombs, bombs turned out on a production line to the Engineer's blueprint. My Ellie calls them heroes, the soldiers brought through that town. It's fantastic, such an honour to those soldiers, to have thousands line a street in respect. Only, sad thing, they don't see it. They're in the box. A good number of them were put there by that man and his talent for bomb-making. Because of him, all that the rest of us can do is stand on the pavement and give them respect, which is something but not much. A good number of the first heroes who came through were victims of explosions, his bloody bombs. And maybe by now his gear's in

Afghanistan, I don't know. So, I have no love for him, and I'm not going soft for her. My Ellie talks about Wootton Bassett and the heroes . . . Are you getting my drift?'

A crisp whisper. 'So much of an enemy that we're going to turn him.'

Surprise, a murmur. 'What the fuck are you talking about?'

'It's interdiction.'

'So, it's *interdiction*. Yes.'

'I checked it with the Boss. It's their way – spook jargon – of describing an approach. "Interdiction" is "approach". They hope to turn him.'

'Is that what he told you?'

'They're going to turn him, Mr Gibbons said – like it's a defection.'

Foxy muttered, 'Time for my sleep. Wake me when there's something you can't do.'

She had fine features and she sat so still. Her back was straight in the chair and she gazed ahead. Almost, her eye line was on him. Nobody came to her, she had no one to talk to, and Foxy slept. The wind had gained strength and he heard its rustle in the reeds.

9

'What the hell are you—'

'Wake up.' As normal, when Badger used his elbow to dig into Foxy's ribs, he held the palm of his hand across the older man's mouth, loose but a reminder.

'Where am—'

'In the hide in the marshes in Iran. What more do you need to know? Could give you the co-ordinates, except you bloody dropped the GPS.'

The voice whistled back, almost shrill, between the teeth: 'I was saying, before you fucking interrupted, "Where am I looking?" That was my question.'

'You don't have to look anywhere. Just listen.'

The headset was already off Badger's ears. He tried to pass it to Foxy. Foxy muttered that he needed a piss, always did when he woke up. Badger told him to wait. The cable was caught in the front of Badger's gillie suit, had fastened itself among the material strips sewn into it and the dried-out reeds. You couldn't pull a cable tight and hope it would free itself, and it was underneath Badger. They were in darkness, hip against hip, elbows locked and legs bloody nearly entwined. Their movements had roused the mosquitoes, and there were convulsions under the covering that shielded them. The cable wouldn't come free. Insults were swapped.

'Be careful, you clumsy bastard.'

'Use your fingers!'

'How did you snag it?'

'If you stayed bloody still I could free it.'

Badger laid down his night-sight kit. It was the hour before dawn. His fingers felt for the tangle in the cable. Foxy had his head down, grappled for and found the headset and put it over his ears. God alone knew how, but the cable's snag was near Badger's groin, and Foxy's head was halfway there. Time for a laugh? Foxy's head had moved to a comfort zone below Badger's ribcage. His fingers were under Foxy's chin and tugged gently. Twice Foxy gulped, then the cable came free.

He would be told, and didn't ask. To ask would demonstrate dependence on the older man. Nor would he get, now, a running commentary from Foxy.

He settled again as best he could. Difficult while Foxy used the bottle. There was no relief from the mosquitoes and when they crossed the moon, almost full, they seemed dense enough to throw a shadow. They had both been out of the hide during the night, and Badger had buried more plastic bags. He had gone as far as the wall of reeds to their right, where it bordered the open ground, and done exercises there, had moved his limbs and stretched his back. Foxy had gone further, almost as far as the mound of mud, but had stopped short of the bulldozer tracks. He could go further than Foxy. Anytime Foxy left the hide, the translation of remarks passed at the house was zero.

It was the time of morning that medics said was when people died – and well known to police crime squads as the best time to hit front doors, break them down and get up the stairs before weapons, narcotics or documents could be hidden. The target had emerged from the front door and started to pace.

She had joined him. He would have been well on with his first cigarette, a white glow in the dull greened wash of the night-sight lens. He wore cotton boxer shorts and a vest, and she had a shawl across the shoulders of her nightdress and was barefoot; he had put on sandals. The guard using the plastic chair by the pier had already scrambled away when he'd appeared, before she'd come – and Badger had woken Foxy.

It was going to be soon.

They had logged the carrying into the house of the new suitcase – black, with no motif that would stand out on a carousel. She had greeted him and her voice had been easy, clear, in his ears. He dreaded most that one dawn or evening, that day or the next, the black Mercedes would come, the driver would go to the door, bring out the case and lift it into the boot. The targets would climb into the back seats, the engine would rev, the goon – the officer – and the guards would straighten, the old lady would wave from the door, the kids at her knee, and the car would go. Where? Which airport, connecting with what flight? It was what he dreaded most.

The Engineer talked and his wife listened. He smoked, then threw the stub into the water. He walked with his hand under her arm and she had the stick to support her. There was no fat on the man, and Badger could see her contours, breasts, waist and hips, because a light wind was off the water. He would have had a better view, through the night-sight, if the moon had been smaller or had gone down over the horizon.

He dreaded most that he and Foxy would lie in the scrape with the bags and the bottles, their food; the bergens, the ticks, mosquitoes and flies, and the microphone would not pick up a remark on the destination. To have gone through this and not heard it . . . It was more than he could have endured.

They walked, and Badger watched.

He described the man, his arrogance and authority, and what the brigadier had said to him.

He explained his confusion. He asked her opinion: was he teased, tested? Mocked? Was it possible the Islamic Republic was a house built of cards and could be blown away?

He supported her and she followed his slow steps but was heavier on her stick.

Did they regard him with such contempt that he needed threats on the danger to him of defection? Was the regime's strength so fragile? He did not know, and there was no other person alive with whom he would have shared thoughts so heretical.

Why had it been said? Why did they doubt his patriotism and loyalty, the faith that governed him?

Why?

When he had nothing more to say, she dug in her bare heels, spread her toes in the dirt and twisted him to face her. The light came up off the water and bathed her. Ducks' splashes made ripples.

'It is unthinkable. You will see this Guard Corps officer today. You will not bow in front of him. You will stand your full height, and you will tell him his words are fit only for the tip where the city's trash is dumped. The thought of you betraying the nation is rubbish, and you will tell him so.'

'I will tell him, to his face.'

'It is rubbish because you would not leave me.'

'No.'

'Do they think that I, whether I am destined to live or to die, would go with you? It is inconceivable.'

'I shall tell him.'

'I would not go with you because I would not abandon my children. If I live a week, a month, a year or go my full span, I would not leave them. I would leave you before I would leave my children.'

'He said also that, because of my work, I would be hunted down and hanged if the regime should fall.'

'Is it more important what *might* happen to you than what *will* happen to me?'

She had shamed him and he lapsed into silence. He sensed that now she felt the chill of the night: she was shivering. He put his arm around her shoulders and started to lead her back to the house. He could feel her bones. Everything in his life revolved around the regime of the Islamic Republic that had come to power when he was nine years old. He had been to their schools; he had listened to their mullahs as a teenager; he had walked behind his father's coffin as a procession wound towards the cemetery. His father's life had been given in a minefield in defence of a child of the regime, and his mother had died of wounds received from shrapnel in the air attacks on Susangerd. He had struggled for the best results at university – electrical engineering – in Ahvaz, and for thirteen years had laboured over the workbench in the camp.

He had made the devices, done what was asked of him, and now he was teased, taunted. It was as if the suspicion of treason was laid at his door. She had hard bones now and they were angled against his hand. The weight seemed, each day, to drip a little more from her. He had only once been outside Iran.

He thought of that journey more often now, where he had been and whom he had met.

His journey had been to the Hungarian capital, Budapest, the course at the University of Technology and Sciences had lasted two years, and he had learned areas of electronic engineering that had served him well at his workbench. He could remember his fear at the levels of drug-taking and binge-drinking, the rampant sexual appetites of the students. As a defence against corruption, contamination, he had wrapped himself in work . . . and there had been a girl.

She was in his mind more often now because each time he touched his wife, Naghmeh, he felt the sharpness of her bones and believed her life was slipping away. He had little faith in a foreign consultant. Romance was gone. Lust and love were strained to breaking point. There had been a girl in Budapest, who had never aged because she was locked in his mind as she was then. It had been the one time in his life that he had felt weak. He had yearned for her, and had been a virgin, experiencing new longings. She was Maria, from Austria, studying industrial psychology. On some occasions he had sat, in great boldness, beside her for lunch in the canteen. They had been to films on the campus and had held hands, and they had gone once to hear a pianist play Chopin. She had come to his room one evening in April, when the days lengthened, flowers bloomed and spring burst. He knew her as a good Catholic, and that she drank alcohol. Her parents were divorced, and she would work after her degree, she hoped, in the Swarovski glass factory as part of the workers' support programme. She had come to his room in the students' hostel: her blouse had been low-cut, her skirt short, and he could smell the schnapps on her breath, and her perfume. She had reached up from his narrow bed, caught his arms and tried to pull him down. He had slapped her face hard. She had left him, face pale except where his fingers had met her cheek and a nail had scratched her nose. He had never seen Maria Ohldorf after that day and he had the picture of her face, frozen, in his mind, her shock and bewilderment. She had been pretty, and he had yearned to hold her, but had not dared. He thought often of her now as the weight slipped off his wife's bones.

He saw, on the edge of the shadows, Mansoor watching him. They went inside.

The Engineer cursed himself for thinking it – but she would not be saved. It was the stuff of dreams, false dawns. Sharp in his mind was the defiance, the extremes of rudeness, that he had hurled at the medical team in Tehran: almost the implication that they were peasants and ill-qualified. If he had listened, then had brought Naghmeh back to her children, there might have been a calm, loving parting, not preceded by a journey of desperation. But arrangements were made and could not now be cancelled.

The moon had gone, but first light was not yet on the horizon, above the far reeds and the water behind them.

Foxy eased off the headset, then pushed it across the little space to Badger. He expected to be asked what he had heard. No question came.

Had he been asked, he would have whispered, airily, that he had heard nothing of importance. It always threw interrogators waiting for an interpreter's translation of a suspect's fifty-word statement when a digest of around five words came back. He would not have said that the talk was of 'defection', rejected, and 'abandoning family', out of the question. He could have added that the Engineer and his wife spoke quality educated Farsi to each other. He could have latched onto a discussion, brief, that the Engineer would himself be a target if the regime failed and his association with the Revolutionary Guards Corps became general knowledge. He could have finished with an assessment, from the Engineer's voice pitch and the wife's, how their morale stood, and he would have assessed that her nerves were near breaking point and she was depressed. He said none of it.

It annoyed him that the query did not come – annoyed him enough him to hiss, 'Not interested? Don't you want to know?'

'If there was anything I needed to know you'd have told me.'

'I thought you'd want to hear their talk.'

'Only if I need to know it.'

The headset was taken. He felt the strength of the young 'un beside him, little bastard, eased over and broke wind again. The bloody flies were swarming over the scrim of his headgear.

Would they come to blows? Foxy reckoned there was a chance of it. He closed his eyes, thought about sleep, and more about Ellie. He wondered where she was and what she was doing. He could have drunk a two-litre bottle of water straight down, but it was rationed, a discipline that couldn't be broken. They had the water they had brought in – the greatest weight factor in the bergens was water. Only thinking of Ellie could clear his mind of the need for more water than was allowed. He rinsed some in his mouth, then swallowed it but eked it out. He couldn't think when he had last disliked a man – loathed or detested one – as much as he disliked Badger, and he thought it mutual. It was probably inevitable that they would fight. The quiet closed round them.

It was the last hour before the grey smears appeared on the horizon in the east. They were all exhausted and needed sleep. None of them would get it.

It was the crisis time. The Jones Boys had usurped her. She didn't give the orders, didn't open her mouth and make suggestions – she did as she was told. The extent of the crisis yawed ahead of her.

Each of them – Hamfist, Corky, Shagger and Harding – wore their T-shirts: they had gone into their bags, dug them out, stripped off what they already had on and had done a fast change. The extent of the crisis brought them together, made them a team, and a team needed a uniform: from a uniform came strength. They were paid to protect her, so they would. She had passed control to them. She knew them like the callouses on her hands, the virtues and weaknesses of each man, but she could not have said who among the four would emerge as the leader. None had. Interesting to her, because the sharing of their responsibilities showed – her opinion – stunning trust. But they were trained as fighting men, when trust was implicit, and now they were fighting.

She thought it medieval. Abigail Jones had childhood memories of traipsing around castles, mostly motte-and bailey, in the Welsh Marches – Ludlow, Caus, Wigmore, some that were shoulder-high ruins and others that were towering relics – and her father, the barrister, had lectured on battles, sieges, the storm tactics of attackers and desperate defenders, and she had imagined men-at-arms running from one battlement to another to stem the latest thrust, knowing that if the line was broken, the wall fell, they were gone, throats slit. Shagger had the vehicles, Harding had the door of the building, and Abigail tagged along with Corky or Hamfist.

They chased shadows caught in the beams of the big torches. It was not the ultimate attack, but probes – and if they found weakness they would come on, do it big-time. A mob always knew how to sniff out weakness, and she thought a crowd of men from out of the marshes – gassed, bombed, their habitat drained and their buffalo dead – would know how to scavenge for weakness, would be bloody near gold-medal standard at it. At first the shadows had kept back, hugged the no man's land between light and dark.

They were bold now, and the crisis had come.

They must defend the building alongside which the Pajeros were parked, and try to keep clear the approach ground between them and the broken perimeter fence. In front of them was the familiar track to the dragged-back gates, but behind them, inside the compound, was darkness.

The first blow was from Harding. His weapon was his M-16 Armalite rifle's stock. Two had come, light-footed and silent, from the shadows, and were a moment away from getting inside the building where the gear was, the water and rations, some of the ammunition and enough of the grenades. Abigail, chasing after Corky, had seen them and Corky had shouted the warning.

It was the crisis because Harding hit one in the testicles with the stock of his rifle, then struck the second across the face. A double-tap, of sorts – one movement, two casualties. The first went down and was retching at Harding's feet, might have thrown up on his boots, and the second was reeling back, clutching his mouth. Blood was easing out between his fingers, and she fancied he might have spat away a tooth. The first act of physical violence was the start point of the crisis.

She had ceded control.

It would have been the grossest impertinence for her to shout, 'Don't shoot! For fuck's sake, don't use live rounds.' A killing would be a disaster. A wounding and hospitalisation would be a catastrophe.

Bruising, missing teeth, abrasions were manageable.

Knives were shown at them when a larger group, six or seven, ran towards the vehicles from different directions – the nearest thing to co-ordination. If the first strike of a knife had hit, and one of them had gone down, they would have been dead – all of them. Dead meant Harding never getting back to see the aunt who had reared him in the trailer camp and never again getting value for money from the Russian whores in Dubai. Dead for Corky was a telegram to a housing estate in west Belfast, being opened by old people he had not seen in twenty years, and two kids who would not have a father. Dead in Shagger's world was a farm never bought and reoccupied by an elderly couple, pedigree sheep never grazing the fields that looked onto mountains. Dead was Hamfist's divorced wife getting a large cheque from Proeliator Security and maybe going as far as digging out a photo of him and putting it on the sideboard for a week. And, *dead* was Alpha Juliet – surrogate mother of the Jones Boys – never again looking into the face of Badger, deciphering nothing, learning less, and seeing in the eyes a message of self-sufficiency and reliance on no one. It had captured her . . . And *dead* was having the smelly rag-heads crawl all over her and likely shag her carcass. There were knives in the torch beams that might have been used to gut a good-size carp or skin a dead buffalo calf, or to slash the reeds from which their homes were built.

The alternative to being dead was to quit.

If they quit, they left behind Badger and Foxy, and a mission that had taken months to put together was aborted. She remembered the sergeant who had explained, shyly, that his work was routine, quite boring – he'd spent three and half hours on his knees while he dismantled a device left in a shallow hole near Highway 6, made it safe and gave the forensic people the chance to trace a DNA sample and to find the date-seller and the road-sweeper. She wouldn't quit.

Hands were on her. She smelt sour breath and felt long nails catch the waist of her robe, then the pressure pushing her downwards. Beside her a knife flickered in Shagger's beam, and might have been about to close on Hamfist's chest. Corky came. He had an iron bar. It might have been used once to support barbed-wire defences. Corky was from an estate where knowledge of street fighting came at about the same time as primary school and first communion. He lashed around him. There were groans, a scream. The hands were off Abigail. There were no faces, only hands, and some had their own blood on them. Three knives were lined up. They were at the edge of Shagger's torch light. She recognised it. They were together to feed each other the courage to charge forward, and the knives were raised boldly. If one of her Boys was down, it was over.

More had gathered behind the knives. They would swamp the Boys and her – there were so few of them, four guys and their ma'am, because the wisdom said that the fewer bodies on the ground, the greater the chances of going in and out without being identified. She hadn't argued with the wisdom – and the knives' blades flashed. She didn't know which, but either Corky or Harding threw the first gas grenade and it rolled among them. The smoke burst from the canister and enveloped them. They were pale figures caught in a white cloud and they seemed to dance as they choked. Another grenade was thrown and the cloud thickened. It was harder to see them, but easy to hear the choking and the coughs.

They took their casualties with them, five who were helped towards the gate.

She knew what she had to do. Her head ached, and the gas was in her eyes, making them water with needle pains.

Abigail walked away from her Boys, following the gaggle of men, towards the gate. She reached it and shouted, in good Arabic, what she wanted. She had resumed her role of authority.

She sat down in the dirt and folded her legs in the middle of the track. She waited for them to do as she had instructed. It was a gamble – as was the whole goddamn thing. She waited, and soon dawn would come.

When would he know? Mansoor asked him. And caught him flustered, having had to duck back into the house because there were papers he had been reading early that morning and he had forgotten to replace them in his briefcase. Know what?

Mansoor said it slowly, as if he talked with a demented man. When would he know the date on which he travelled, and when would he know where he travelled to?

The door of the Mercedes was held open for him and he threw the briefcase towards the far side of the seat. He said he would know that day – he had been promised.

A radio had been switched on in the house.

The security officer had fine hearing. He realised that the wife, Naghmeh, had not packed the new suitcase. He had been roused by a sentry in the night, and had gone half dressed from his room alongside the communal dormitory of the barracks. He had seen them – washed in moonlight – walking beside the water. He understood that the two were, almost, crushed. He had thought in the night that the wound on his leg was healed, and that the muscles and tendons that had been ruptured were knitting well. He had pondered, watching them walk together, that the time would come soon when he could apply for service with the al-Quds again, in Lebanon. It was an honour to be chosen to protect a man of the Engineer's prominence, and it could not have been said that he was careless with the responsibility, but it did not extend him. He was asked by the driver what the situation was that morning in central Ahvaz.

A news bulletin came on the radio.

He could answer. His father had telephoned that morning. The hanging of the terrorist the previous day had gone well. There had been militia and Guard Corps personnel on the streets; no live rounds or gas had been fired; the crowds had dispersed quietly after only one charge with batons. His father had said that the hanging had been witnessed by the family of a bystander who had died when the bomb the youth had placed had exploded; the mother had spat at the condemned as he was lifted, trembling, onto a chair with the noose round his neck and the hood over his face. The father of the bystander would himself have kicked away the chair if he had not been restrained. His father loved to watch the hangings . . . His father had said that the streets were calm. He said it was safe to take the quicker route through the centre of the city.

He was surprised. The question had shocked him. Never before had his charge, Rashid Armajan, made such a query. It had been asked from beside the open rear door of the car, as if an afterthought: 'Do you believe it possible that the regime governing us is, in fact, similar to a house built of playing cards that can be blown down, destroyed?'

The security officer, a true believer, gagged and must have betrayed his shock.

The Engineer was sharper: 'Could the regime collapse? Is internal dissent, external aggression – combined – enough to break us?'

He sensed a trap. The question was close to treason. Men, and women, were hanged for treason. Did the question test his loyalty? Was he doubted?

'Can the regime be swept away? Are we merely temporary? Are we like the Fascists and the Communists, the Ba'athists, the apartheid oppression in South Africa and the . . .?'

He stuttered it: 'The regime is strong, is a rock. Those who denounce it and look to betray it will fail. There are spies everywhere, and danger. Vigilance must be rigorous. I tell you, should I find myself confronting such an enemy, he would know pain the like of which he has never experienced before. We are strong.'

'Thank you. You are a good friend.' The Engineer sank heavily into the car, swung in his legs and the driver closed the door after him.

Mansoor pondered. He could – and most probably should – report such a conversation. Who would be believed? Himself, a junior functionary, or a man who was fêted by the high command of the al-Quds Brigade and who was about to travel abroad on the state's funding? Could he, by implication, accuse such a man of treason? The car turned a corner beside the barracks and disappeared, dust billowing behind it. Always it was necessary, if denouncing a man of prominence, to be certain. He was prepared to dither.

It would have been the wife's mother who had the radio loud because she was partially deaf, had been afflicted since the enemy's artillery had pounded Ahvaz.

He went to his chair in the shade and sat down with his binoculars. He wondered if this would be the day when the Sacred Ibis came over the reeds fringing the lagoon and settled on the exposed mud spit.

Foxy whispered brusquely, 'The radio knocked out the long conversation at the car. Before it was switched on he said he would be told today the "when" and the "where". That's about it. For me it'll be some sleep.'

Soon he would start to snore.

Badger felt alone. He had lost count of how many hours, days and nights it had been since they were scooped from their lives and taken north to the house facing out over the bay. The hours, days and nights since he had met the girl, Alpha Juliet, had merged too. He had taken the headset. Most of what it picked up was the babble of the radio. The heat inside his suit climbed, the sweat ran and he felt the weakness that lack of exercise produced. Those people at the house with the ruins of a castle and the pipes' wail were too distant: he could no longer put faces to them. Time dripped, the images blurred ... He couldn't bloody remember them.

'The carvery is always good value,' Gibbons said, 'and the fish is usually passable.' He played host to the Cousin, the Friend and the Major. It had been Sarah's idea. She had suggested it that morning, had made the phone calls with the invitations, had booked the table and appeared to believe he needed respite from sitting in the inner office, contemplating the wilting flowers, the pictures on the wall and the silence of the telephone. It had been sleeting in central London when he had walked from the office to the club.

A bottle of red was brought, a bottle of white and a small jug of water.

He smiled, a little deprecating. 'Always the hardest time for us, the waiting. We're all from that neck of the woods . . . I often think that others who are parked at their desks in our place and write those analysis pieces have little idea of the strains placed on us by our work in the front line . . . very little idea.'

Sarah had bundled a wad of cash into his hand, the implication being that she would lose it somewhere in the budget – elastic bands, highlighters, paper clips. In the club's restaurant, rarely used by him because of its expense, she had reserved a corner table where they could speak and be free of eavesdropping.

The Cousin remarked, 'There are people in Langley who drive up the Beltway before it's light for half the year, look at a screen all day, and it's dark when they're back in the car and off home. They tell the little woman, 'It's been a hell of day, sweetie, just one hell of a day.' They have no idea, and less concern, about the pressures we're under when we're running sharp-end stuff . . . But I take comfort from the feeling in my water that we've gotten close to the serious time. I'll start with the white, Len, thank you.'

The Friend said, 'I don't intend to badmouth my own people, but Israel has the world's highest proportion of jealous bastards who think they know better than the man of experience. We have awards that would fill a wall for interference and shit-chucking.

What we do is difficult and stressful and you can piss against the wind for all the appreciation you'll pick up. The red would suit me as a kick-off, Len, and I'm grateful for the invitation.'

The Major grimaced, smiled. 'I can remember a day when I'd been out on those open-sewer streets of Basra from dawn till dusk and I'd killed five IEDs. Each was complex and would have been shipped in from that bloody production line across the border, and one was for me and complicated. There were bad guys on a roof, watching to see how I went about it – hoping also to see the big flash and hear the bang. I went back to the mess. Believe it, please. There was a colonel in there – using the Basra Palace, Saddam's old watering-hole – for a farewell bash. He and his guests had put on their fancy-dress outfits and their gongs for smart dining. Flopped in a chair, feet on the table, beer bought me, and this bloody colonel wants to know why I haven't washed, shaved, changed before entering the mess. Didn't understand there was a life outside the limit of the air-conditioning system. I told him to fuck off – took my brigadier in Baghdad a week to smooth the waters. People have no idea about the real world. I'll start with the white and then try the red. Thanks, Len.'

They ordered, drank and ate. Another bottle of red was required, but the water lasted. In a vacuum of information, responsibilities were reiterated and guarantees given. Coffee was accepted, but no brandy – an indication of work taken seriously.

The Major said, 'I just want to put it on the record in this rather select company . . . People, these days, are pretty squeamish about what they call 'extra-judicial' interdiction. I think it an excellent way of dealing with an extant difficulty. Identify, locate and . . .' He slapped a broad hand – with chunky fingers that seemed to lack the sensitivity necessary for the dismantling of improvised explosive devices – on the table. The cups rattled in the saucers, the unused cutlery banged against the glasses, and he'd done a passable imitation of a shot being fired, and another. Then the Major wiped his mouth with his napkin, and dropped it as though business had been done and procedures agreed.

The Friend used a toothpick. 'We have a mantra that we neither confirm nor deny, and are consistent with it. It can, however, be let slip through many channels that the target was in trouble with his own people for fucking the wife of a man more influential, or for fabricating his expense accounts. That confuses the general public of many nations – but not the associates of the target. They know, they fear ... The greatest source of the fear is that their small corner, that most secretive part of an organisation where they exist, will be penetrated ... But we have to wait.'

He smiled and let slip a small belch, then meticulously folded his napkin and smoothed it.

The Cousin gazed around him wistfully, as if a small chance existed that, in a gentleman's club, he might be permitted to smoke a cigar. 'A Hellfire, if aimed accurately and carrying a punch of eight kilos of metal-augmented charge, can do a fair bit of 'extra-judicial'. We don't have – at this moment – a judge and jury sitting in north Waziristan, in the Haraz mountains of Yemen or in the sand round Kandahar, so what we do there has to benefit from lack of contact with a courthouse. I hear no great wail of protest. Go back two decades and a Canadian citizen was taken down, Gerald Bull, shot by – of course – persons unknown while earning big moolah for building the gun that was going to fire chemicals and biological out of Iraq and into Israel. Did the Canadians shout and yell? Deafening silence. The furore of the hand-wringers lasts a week at maximum – and it keeps the motherfuckers looking over their shoulders. There is only one law in this business. Don't get caught. It's a good one to remember. It has legs and has lasted years. A grand meal, Len.'

The Major and the Friend agreed. Gibbons raised an arm to motion for the waiter and his bill, then reached into an inner pocket for his fattened wallet. He said, 'It's not the easy time. When we have – and I'm confident we will – the direction to head in, it will all get easier. You've met the two men who are up front, know pretty much the same as I do about them. What I would like to say, though, the officer we have in support of them is first rate. Very dedicated. Yes – at the risk of landing hard on my arse – I'm very confident.'

The Cousin said, 'And you'd know about that, Len, as I hear it. You'd know about landing hard on your arse.'

The Friend said – and would have read the filtered reports reaching foreign agencies, 'Dogs a man, doesn't it, when he has to be lifted out of the shit?'

Gibbons offered no denials. 'Didn't like it, but lessons were learned.'

The Major, not privy to secrets of the trade and historic foul-ups, pushed back his chair and made ready to stand. 'I see, looking out onto the street, that nothing of the weather improves, sleet gone to snow. Hard to have a decent sight of them, in the mind, in the heat. It's merciless, the heat is. Brutal. Anyway, what interests me are your good words on the officer on the ground who directs all this, and your confidence.'

On her haunches, Abigail Jones sat alone. Behind her, fifteen yards back, was Corky.

He accepted, they all did, that she had taken control again, and would call the moves.

Somewhere under the robe she wore – now mud-stained and dusty – was the holster that hugged her waist. The pistol was in it and there was a slit at the side of the garment that her fist could be shoved into if she needed the thing. She had tucked her gas mask behind her backside so it was close to hand but not visible.

She had called for a leader to be sent. The rag-heads always liked – at a time of confrontation – to have a meeting, a conference; then they would hector and bluster, give themselves the opportunity to preen and usually to walk out. A meeting, at a time of substantial dispute, was the way they usually went. She sat in the dirt in the centre of the gateway and waited for a leader to come.

Corky could see, from the tilt of her head, that her eyeline was down. Her focus point would have been about half of the distance between where she sat and the line of men facing her. One had a scarf, bloodstained, across his face, and another could only stand with the help of two others; one had weeping abrasions on his shin

where the bar had been used on him, and another tucked his wrist
between his shirt's buttonholes and had a broken collar-bone.
There were others who might have fractured ribs or dried blood
on their scalps, but no shots had been fired and that was a miracle.
He thought they had done well.

His rifle was slung across his chest and he had two magazines,
filled, taped together. His flak vest was over his Jones Boys shirt,
and the gas mask was hooked to his waist. If any of them had run
at her, he would have dropped them.

Behind him was Shagger; Harding and Hamfist were at the
Pajeros. Pretty feckin' ridiculous but they still had the tripod up,
the spotting 'scope mounted on it. The identification pictures
were on the ground, held in place by a quarter of a mud brick: by
now Corky might have been able to spot a Marbled Duck. He
might have known the difference between a Ferruginous Duck
and a White-headed Duck, and definitely he could have said which
was a Basra Reed-warbler and which a Black-tailed Godwit. He
had a sunhat on, camouflage type, while Shagger and Harding
wore the Proeliator Security caps with the big peaks; Hamfist's
was from a pizza-delivery service in the east of Scotland. She wore
nothing on her head other than a wispy scarf. Her body threw off
no shadow because the sun was above her.

She waited. It was all bluff.

Harding's take on it was that had it been American spooks a
close-support airstrike would have been called in during the night,
and Black Hawks would have come to lift them out. Shagger had
said that if the mission had been run by any of the other Six
officers from Baghdad they'd have called a taxi and quit.

She sat very still. Corky couldn't see her face but thought of her
as serene, so calm.

The heat made him wobble on his feet, the shimmer came up
from the sand and the faces in front of him distorted. There was
pain in his eyes behind the wraparounds, he craved a drink, and
his concentration was going. Harding must have seen him rock.

The drawling voice was in his ear: 'Go get yourself a drink.'

'What about her?'

'Go close to her, break the mood she's set, you'll get bawled out.'

'I reckon.'

Harding murmured, 'She's remarkable.'

Corky did it side of mouth. 'No one like her, an ace lady . . . You have any idea how long this needs spinning out?'

'Beginning to think it's closing down on us. Don't reckon, up front, they have much more time. I saw how much water they took and it's the heat . . . I don't think they have a heap of time.'

He moved his hand and felt the coil.

It had been a better morning. The Engineer had gone. The goon, the officer, had driven his jeep away and might have gone to a village nearby to shop or to a town. The wife had not come out and the children had been taken to school by the older woman, in uniforms and with heavy rucksacks. The head of the guard who sat in the plastic chair with the rifle across his legs was lolling back. Badger had moved, at a slow crawl, to the reed beds. It was the first time either had moved in daylight, and it was incredible – like a liberation – simply to stand and stretch, arch and flex. He could move more than he could in darkness and was freer because he could see what his boots landed on.

There was the rhythm of Foxy's breathing beside him. He was asleep. Badger's hand had slipped underneath the folds of his gillie suit and rubbed – not scratched – one of the many tick scabs on his hip. The hand had come out and reached for the water bottle and he had felt the smooth, cold line of the coil.

He couldn't drink the water that lapped the bottom of the reed stems, but he could scoop it up in his hands, strip down to his boots and socks and wash himself. He saw the pocked skin of the ticks' bites and had prised others off his body, working as carefully as the contortion allowed to see that none of the bloody things was close to his backside. He was cooler and cleaner, a rare joy . . . It was the bottled water that would kill them: Badger reckoned there was enough for that day and one more, but he felt better for the wash, almost human. He had gone back on his stomach, doing the crawl that took him from the line of the reeds across the open ground. Then he had insinuated himself under the cover of the fronds, burrowed forward until his head and his shoulders were level with Foxy's and taken over the headset.

He flinched, drew his hand sharply back. The touch told him this was not wood, plastic or rubber. The coil might have been six inches across, but could have been as much as nine. It filled the gap between his body and Foxy's, was level with their hips. He thought his touch on it had been merely the gentlest brush. Foxy slept. Badger knew what he had touched. He had not seen it, but the texture against his fingertips was evidence enough.

Foxy had gone into the reeds with the collapsible shovel, had defecated, urinated, and buried the plastic bag and bottle. Badger had not known whether he had stripped down to his boots and socks or whether he had just wiped water under his armpits and in his groin. His breath had stunk when he came back. Badger's would have too, but the smell of their breath would have matched the general stench of the marsh and the trapped water of the lagoon. Foxy had been careful coming back, had taken an age, but had smoothed the dirt behind him and scattered more dead stuff, leaving it haphazardly put down – had done a good job. Together they had made an inventory of the water remaining: three bottles, and it should have been seven or eight in that temperature. After the exchange of the headset, Foxy had taken the watch and Badger had slept.

It could only be a snake. Badger had seen snakes in zoos when he was a kid, and there were snakes on the warmest days up in the Brecons that he had known about when stalking paratroops on exercise. There were also snakes in gaps in the heather and on flat stones, which he had seen when edging close to red deer in the Scottish hills, testing himself against their eyesight, hearing and the quality of their nostrils. Anyone who knew had told him that snakes were most dangerous when disturbed suddenly from deep sleep. Then they lashed out. He twisted his head, a considered, slow movement, and looked down into the darkened gap between his body and Foxy's. They were both in the scraped hole and across the top of it was scrim net, camouflaged and lightweight. Reed fronds were on top of the netting, and some light seeped through. The snake filled the space between their bodies, and it was coiled tight. Its tail was towards him and he couldn't see the bastard's head, where the fangs would be.

It had been another hand-over with nothing to be said, and Badger could listen to the breeze in the reed tops, and the charges of birds across the lagoon. Up to the moment when he had slipped his hand down in the hope that his fingers could massage some relief from the irritation of the scabs, he had been desperate for water. But the rules were that water should only be drunk when both were awake and the watch changed. He thought Foxy slept easily, head averted, breathing regular and with a light snoring in the throat.

It was important to him that Foxy slept easily. If he was restless, he might pitch over, roll onto the snake and panic it. It would have slithered into the place it now had, between their legs, and settled itself. If Foxy's arse landed on it, it would retaliate, it might go right and it might go left. It might go for Foxy's hand or arm, or try to bite through the suit and the lightweight trousers, or the leg below the suit and above the socks. It might launch itself at Badger. He lay so still, barely daring to breathe, and reckoned the head, with the fangs and poison sacs, was against Foxy but less than a foot from himself. He couldn't remember ever feeling so bollock naked with fear.

And remembered . . . Talk in the Pajero, not from Alpha Juliet but from the Welsh guy. All said with the lazy casualness that veterans use to frighten the guts out of rookies. 'Couple of years ago they was overrun with snakes. The marshes shrank and there was only a quarter of the water there had been. The snakes were disorientated and came into the villages, like they were looking for people and beasts. You watch out for snakes, bad bastards. The main one to watch for is the arbid. It's bigger than our Welsh viper, goes to about four foot in length. If you see it, you'll know it, and I hope you never see it. Thick body, black mostly but with red on it. I don't know about an adult, but I was told its bite kills a kiddie in around twenty minutes. Do we have serums? Sorry, no.'

Could remember it now, word for word. There was a knife in his bergen, but not on his belt. Badger tried to work out how much of an effort it would be to wriggle his body to where he could get down into one of the pouches and extract the knife, but didn't have a clear view of it. His mind seemed closed down, not functioning for solutions. Shagger had talked some more about the mosquito problem, the tick problem, the foot-rot problem. He had gone through the list of problems as the Pajero had driven north, and one had seemed much like another – until now.

How to wake Foxy? Not easy. How to wake him and not have him thrashing around? He checked ahead and there was no movement at the house.

He imagined the prick of the fangs. He would lash at the fucking thing, but it would be faster and would hit him again in the wrist – where the veins were – and the poison would start to flow . . . Maybe the morphine they carried would kill him. Couldn't have him standing up on the clear patch of mud, two hundred yards across the water from the target house, using what strength he had left to rip off the suit and his underclothing, because the pain of the venom was unsustainable, and howling . . .

He didn't know what to do. With his head tilted, he could see the coil.

Foxy didn't seem to move, but his voice was clear, soft, conversational: 'Is this, young 'un, what you're looking for?'

His hand came out and was close to Badger's. His hips rolled and his arse shifted. His legs twisted inside the suit and his body tipped. Badger tried to stop him, to arrest the movement, and hissed for him not to move, but was ignored. Foxy rolled onto the snake. His weight pitched onto it.

'Is this, young 'un, what you needed to find?'

IO

There was a low chuckle, no humour.

The clenched hand, three or four inches in front of Badger's face, obliterated his view of the house. He couldn't speak. He waited, in that moment, for Foxy's backside to heave up in the air, the gillie suit to convulse, a scream, and then for the body to heave away and the snake's—The chuckle became laughter.

The fist, under his eyes, opened.

The dirt was caked in the palm. Badger realised that what bound the mud, stopped it disintegrating as dust, was old blood. He thought the head was an inch long, the neck a further inch.

He couldn't have said how long it had been since the snake was decapitated – might have been an hour or done in the night, the carcass kept for the joke to be played. The lustre had gone from the wound at the neck and the tissue had whitened. He saw, protruding from the snake's mouth, open in death, the right fang. It would have been attempting to defend itself when it had died, and it was frozen in that last act of attempted survival. He tried to drag his face away from it, but the headset's cable trapped him.

Foxy, deliberately, let it slip.

The snake's head came to rest on Badger's hands where they held the binoculars, and he felt his temper go into free-fall.

Foxy said, 'You see, young 'un, you're so full of cock that you needed pegging down a notch, maybe four or five. I meet too many kids who reckon they're special and have achieved fuck-all that impresses me. I reckon then that it's as good a time as any to peg them.'

He had never hit a man, or a child when he was at school. In the police, in the years before he had gone into surveillance, he had never operated in a public-order environment when the order was given to display the batons and break up a crowd. People in the section house, and those on the team, would have called it 'red-mist time', but he'd despised that type of violence. If the psychiatrist who had an overview of them and saw the croppies once a year had known he was liable to the mist, the fast breathing and the burn in his brain then, likely, he would have been pulled out of the job and sent home. Might have been told to find a dark room, lie down and stay there till his head went cold.

'You were right for pegging, young 'un, because you have bullshit coming out of your mouth, ears and nose. When I get back I'm going to tell my Ellie about you, and we'll have a good laugh. Her, me and a bottle. I'll tell her what I did for a guy who thought he knew every answer to every question. Would you have wet your pants or shat in them? I'd like to know so I can tell my Ellie. You went into the reeds, down to the waterline, and I could see your boot treads when I went, where you squatted and where you washed. Some of the time you were about a yard away from where this creature was. It was asleep, and I'll bet big money you never saw it.'

They did unarmed combat training in the team, and there was talk that they might – soon – be issued with Glock pistols. Arming them was a divisive issue among the croppies, but there was anxiety that a jihadist, in search of the key to Paradise and the beauty pageant of virgins awaiting him, might get a strop if he realised he was under observation, come after the officer and put him – the image fitted – in the orange jumpsuit, then do the video. If there was a chance to go for suicide and the virgins, or the Central Criminal Court and thirty years banged up in Belmarsh or Long Lartin, it was likely he'd go for short-term freedom at the expense of the officer's life . . . But Daniel 'Badger' Baxter was not classified as violent, knew little about self-defence and was more likely to back off, sneak away. He felt it come to boiling point. He had about forgotten what he was there for and the purpose of the headset on his scalp.

'It was there – where you bloody nearly stepped on it, and that's from footmarks – and I had my old man out and was about to pee when I saw it. I took the knife out of my pocket, made sure my shadow didn't fall on it and did it first time. I can tell you it was one hell of a strike. The little fellow never knew what hit him. One minute he's dreaming of eating a rat and the next he's short of a head. One stab, straight down, a bit of sawing and the head's off. You didn't tell me whether you wet your trousers or shat them. I've a good mind, young 'un, an innovative one, and I reckoned the atmosphere in our little love nest was a bit too solemn, needed lightening up.'

They said that the two basics of managing building anger were to count to ten – or fifty or a hundred – and breathe in slowly. His fist was clenched. He was not certain what sort of blow he could land in the confined space. More of a gesture, but a good one. Worth it.

'So get off your high horse, young 'un, and stay off it. Hang around me and learn, think yourself lucky and—'

Something of a right jab. The punch only had some nine inches to travel. It would have been, if it had landed square on the cheek or on the forehead, little more than a slap, but it caught the end of Foxy's nose, and had enough force in it to make the older man jolt. There was a moment of shock in his eyes.

The blood came, not much, a run from the left nostril through the moustache, now ragged and untrimmed, to the upper lip.

Nothing was said.

He didn't know what he could have said.

Badger's father sold second-hand cars . . . not top-of-the-range but the sort that boys bought when they had their first job and that girls shelled out for when they worked at the Royal Berkshire Hospital and there was no bus route to bring them in. Paul Baxter did tight margins, bought cheap and sold cheap, was nearly honest and kept a couple of good mechanics working for him in the repair shop round the back of the show room. There was a warranty of sorts but difficult to enforce. Most of the cars stayed on the road long enough for his father not to be embarrassed by the sale, but a few did not. He never apologised and never explained – never said how sorry he was that the carburettor had blown up on the motorway, and never explained that a nine-year-old carburettor in that model of Fiat was a driving disaster.

Like father, like son. Badger didn't apologise for hitting Joe 'Foxy' Foulkes across the nose and making it bleed, and didn't explain that the heat and the dehydration were wrecking him, destroying him and that snakes were bad news for him.

He had his binoculars up.

If they had been in England, and it had been witnessed, there would have been a disciplinary hearing and a kangaroo court. Foxy would have been censured for the jape with the snake and Badger would have been suspended on full pay, pending further inquiries, for striking a fellow officer. It was, actually, quite a good joke with the snake.

They settled and the silence nestled on them. A good joke, yes, but he wouldn't say so, and Foxy wouldn't tell him he was 'sorry, and out of order, no offence meant'.

There would be another flashpoint. Badger did not gamble, but he rated it as a banker that they would explode again. No voices were on the headset and the thirst scratched his throat. They wouldn't allow themselves another drink for an hour, minimum. The sweat took more moisture from his body, and the house seemed to sway in the binocular lenses. The lagoon shimmered, and his eyes hurt. He had to grind his fingernails into his palm to hold some, any, concentration.

There was washing barely moving on the line, and a guard asleep. An otter swam by languidly, and time was running out for them. He didn't know what would cause the next explosion of temper.

Hamfist had come forward.

She hadn't moved, still sat cross-legged. He had brought a bottle of tepid water and put it down beside her hip. He'd seen that her gaze didn't confront the crowd but was on the ground a little ahead of her. The crowd had just done prayers, had swung away from the gate and taken a line to the east. The stand-off began again.

They reckoned – him, Shagger, Corky and Harding – that she had, temporarily, calmed the crowd. For all the broken heads and probably broken bones, the men seemed comatose. Might have been the heat. He'd had a company commander, up Highway 6 at al-Amara, who daily blessed the heat of the day and thanked the good Lord for any temperature above a hundred degrees Fahrenheit because it drained hostile energy out of the young bucks. The crowd had no shade. Neither did she.

He stood tall. If it had not been for the alcohol he'd have been promoted above his last substantive rank, corporal, could have made it up to platoon sergeant. The drink did him and there had, often enough, been that regretful look from officers when they'd busted him down. He denied to himself that he had a problem with drink: Hamfist had heard it said, and clung to it leech-like, that an alcoholic was a man who couldn't remember the last day on which he hadn't had a drink. It was yesterday, and the day before. If they had charged at her suddenly, he was confident of the quick reaction that would have dropped them on the dirt track before they were halfway. If the weapon on the strap across his chest had jammed, he had grenades – gas, blast and fragmentation – and a pistol. If the weapons had jammed and the grenades had malfunctioned, he would have used his hands and boots to protect her.

They would have had to take his life before they reached her. The other Boys were the same.

He was thirty-one years old, and his thirty-second birthday would come round in eleven days. She knew the date. Shagger, Corky and Harding didn't. She had known the previous year, his thirty-first, and he hadn't broadcast it but it would have been in the file she'd have flipped through before he'd joined her protection detail. God knew where she'd bought it. It was wrapped up in smart paper, and there was a little card on it, *Hamfist, Happy Day, Best, AJ,* and inside was a crumbling cake, with fruit and orange rind and sliced almonds in circles on the top. The best Dundee cake he'd ever eaten, for all it was damaged in transit. There had been nothing from his wife. He'd not shared the cake but had eked it out and made it last into a seventh week.

He understood what she had done and how she hoped to extricate them, her decision to use the site where there had once been oil-drilling exploration teams. Her decision, too, that they were close enough to the surveillance boys, and inside the Golden Hour of protection. Her decision, now, to sit in the dirt, exposed to the sun, face the crowd and wait. If it came to fighting, they wouldn't survive another night.

Hamfist couldn't know whether she had called right or wrong. If a leader came, she might have called right, and if there was no leader and only darkness, she had called wrong. It was a big call, and it would matter for the men up front. The hours drifted, and time passed. The sun had started to tilt and he no longer stood astride his own shadow – it had begun to nudge out towards his left side, and the soft shape of his body on the dirt was broken by the rifle's barrel.

Not for him to say that they walked a line, a high wire, and that maybe they headed for disaster . . . not for him to say that.

She didn't drink the water he had brought her. She sat and never moved.

They started up the engines every two hours. One Black Hawk crew would go through the procedures while the other rested, and an hour later it would be reversed.

Each had a pair of General Electric T700–GE–70 turbo shafts and each manufactured a power of 1890 h.p. While the pilot and his colleague sat up front and did their checks, the cabin guys did the look-over on the M240 machine guns. They were ready, and each hour a few of the men and women not yet due to return to the States – or to be shipped to Kabul – would stand in little huddles in what shade they could find to watch. Before the drawdown was well advanced, it would have been possible for the Black Hawks, with their unmarked black fuselages that were the signature of special-forces operations – the covert stuff – to be parked out of sight where only a chosen few maintenance technicians had access. Times had changed. The end-of-empire days dictated that a hefty chunk of the base was now in the hands of local forces and only an area inside a contracted perimeter remained for the Americans. Clerks, typists, cooks, marines off duty from security rosters would watch the exhausts spew fumes, feel the draught of the rotors and dream.

Inside every American compound life was now stultifyingly dull. No fire fights, no patrols, no finds of arms caches, and no bodies to be photographed They stayed behind the blast walls and saw nothing of the country but its skies, blue and merciless. They pumped iron, played basketball and smoked what they could find. The helicopters broke the monotony and intrigued them. On immediate stand-by. Prepared for a mission. Cloaked in secrecy. They attracted attention. When the cabin doors were pulled right back, medical gear and stacked gurneys were visible.

Tristram closed down the engines and Eddie did the calls as the switches were flipped. Dwayne wrapped a tea towel round the breech of his machine gun and the rounds in the belt, then secured it with tape. Federico aped him.

For those on the ground, the rubber-neckers, the attraction was that they might see – a final time – the birds take off and fly low over walls and fences, then across the desert and go into actual mother-fuck combat. The suppression fire of the machine guns would be called for, and there'd be blood on the cabin floor, lives at risk and . . . It was a dream, and good enough for the voyeurs. In draw-down days, excitement was sparse.

They jumped down, boots hitting the tarmacadam of the apron. A few pocket cameras were pointed at them, but their shades were good enough protection.

Tristram said, 'I got the whole lot of charts and the software fed for the Iran frontier.'

Eddie said, 'Up to the frontier, not over it.'

'I have that. The far side of the frontier and they're on their own. Not negotiable.'

'Wherever they're coming from, how far over the frontier, they have to get this side of it. For us to go over there is classified as an act of war. Into Iran, and when we land back I'm up for court martial, bet your life, and castration. No one will believe the navigation screwed me.'

'But it would be good to fly a last time.'

His voice dropped: 'Problem is, if we get called they're in deep shit out there. At the edge of survival. For the sake of those guys, I half hope we don't get to fly a last time.'

'I don't want state secrets, but are you any further forward?' She had come into central London carrying a plastic bag filled with clean clothing.

'Can't say.' Len Gibbons's shrug was expressive. 'Honestly, my love, I don't know.'

They were in the same coffee shop across Haymarket from his office, and she had already shown him the shirts she had brought on the train. Pity there were no shoes – the only pair he had with him were damp from so much rain and sleet, and now from the sprinkle of snow.

'Just trying to plan. Audrey said there's a meeting at the garden centre, advice on how to protect shrubs in winter. It's next Monday. I didn't want to accept her invite if you'd just come home that evening. Is it likely?'

He grimaced. 'In the dark and I haven't a candle. Be on the safe side, and go.'

They had been through much, had walked those routes together, and he'd valued her as a crutch when the world had caved around his shoulders. Her hand had come across the table to rest on his fist. Her rings were witness to the commitment they had made to each other before marriage and before the career setback. He would not have survived it without her, and he had often speculated which dreary branch of government he would now figure in if he had allowed himself to walk away from Six: Work and Pensions, Environment, Farming and Rural Affairs, Education and Sciences?

She had a habit of lowering her voice until it dripped conspiracy. 'Is it a big one?'

'By my standards.'

'People on the ground, at the sharp end, in danger?'

'I carry the responsibility.'

She looked far into his eyes. 'Is it like the old days . . . when you were young, tilting at windmills, the world yours, and me running to keep up? Like that?'

They might have been alone on a Suffolk beach, in a Scottish forest or on a Welsh hillside, and only honesty counted. Len Gibbons said, 'I can hide it pretty well, but I've not felt such excitement in thirty years. I'm alive with it. I'll go to the end of any road in front of me to see this one through and make it work. Three decades of sneers and titters, I've lived with . . . This sort of makes it worthwhile. All those bastards who put me down, I think I'm going to walk all over them. I feel blessed to be a part of it . . . Is it going to happen? God's truth, I don't know. I'm willing it to . . . Just have to believe it will.'

She smiled, would have tried to offer encouragement. 'It'll be all right, Len.'

'If it's not, and goes public, they'll crucify me at the Towers . . . but it'll be worse for those at the sharp end, on the ground.'

He lifted her hand, kissed it, passed her another bag, the dirty bundle, and was gone out of the door. The snow had eased, but the sleet drove hard. They were never out of his mind, those for whom he carried responsibility – and the man he targeted.

It was the end of his day. The Engineer stood in the anteroom outside the brigadier's office and the secretary gave him the fat envelope, telling him it contained his travel documents. He opened the envelope, glanced at the top sheet and said the itinerary would exhaust his wife. She shrugged. She reached down for the big envelope at her feet and said these were the X-ray and scan results requested from Tehran. She unlocked a drawer. From another envelope she took two passports, both bearing the crest of the Czech Republic. Finally from a plastic pouch she took a mass of euro banknotes and ostentatiously counted out a thousand in different denominations.

He read her attitude. Were there no better calls for foreign currency? Was there not a medical framework inside the Islamic Republic superior to any other? Why was so much deference shown to him?

The items went into his briefcase. She rang through, then indicated cursorily with her hand that he should go inside the office. He was greeted. Did he have everything? Was he satisfied? He did and he was.

He wondered whether this ranking officer knew of the questions put to him by a colleague and whether a crude trap had been set for him, or whether the regime was indeed a house of cards. But, that early evening, he was not to be tested and tricked.

'Come back to us soon and safe with the best news of Naghmeh . . . I would like you to consider who you are, and therefore understand the esteem in which we hold you. You are, to us, our Nobel or our Kalashnikov, even our Oppenheimer. You are the father of the bomb in the road . . . Do you know of a town in England, Rashid, that stops when the coffins come through, or of the crowds that line the bridges of the Highway of Heroes in Canada? Do you know of the communities in the United States that come to a silent halt when a local soldier is brought back? You sapped their will to fight, Rashid. You broke their commitment. When the time is judged correct your devices will be shipped to Afghanistan and the sophistication of the war raised. Afghanistan will be fertile ground for you. We will not tolerate the Great Satan's military – or the Little Satan's – against our borders. Our prayers go with you.'

He was kissed on each cheek and went out of the door. He hurried to the parking area and looked for his driver. He could not telephone her, never did, so he could not tell her what was in place until he was back at his home.

Stomach runs had arrived, one of the many strains of 'Basra belly'. It was early evening and the air was cooler, but without a wind, so the smell in the hide was foul. It had come on fast.

Bowel movements were not a chosen subject for conversation among croppies. Nor likely to be, Foxy would have said, among astronauts. How moonwalkers or surveillance men did their business was not big on the talk agenda among colleagues. One minute Badger had been lying beside him, on his rest time, and the next he had been squirming to turn over, and the top of the hide's camouflage, above the scrim net, had jumped. He had scrabbled for the plastic bags.

Not a smell for living with. Foxy – relief writ large – was more constipated than the other way. There was nothing he could have done – had he wanted – to help. Diarrhoea was part and parcel of a croppie's job. Foxy did not know how much was in Badger's trousers, how much in the bag and how much had spilled onto the earth of the hide. Badger was wiping hard, almost furiously. They had with them tubes of sanitary jelly that cleaned hands and that was next on Badger's list. Then the pills. They hadn't spoken since the punch was thrown.

On the headset there was only the crackled voice of a radio announcer and music. He watched the front of the house and waited for the car to come, for the children to run out and the target, the Tango, to get home. Strange old life he lived . . . Because of RIPA, Regulation of Investigatory Powers Act 2000, the trade of law-enforcement surveillance was watched, eagle-eyed, for abuses. Couldn't call a bad guy a 'target' in a briefing because it might come up in the legal process, and to name the accused, in court, as a 'target' was likely to be prejudicial. He watched for the target and the target's wife, and wondered whether she was resting or filling the suitcase that had been brought for her. The goon, the officer, had been on his chair as the sun had started to dip. He'd had the binoculars on his chest and seemed to use them to watch birds. Maybe birds were his turn-on . . . There was nothing for him to listen to but his nose was filled with the smell.

Badger did not apologise.

Perhaps it was not appropriate to apologise for diarrhoea. Maybe Foxy would have done if he'd had any other oppo. No apology . . . and no wind to freshen the air. Possible to go in reasonable secrecy from the hide after darkness came, but that was more than an hour away. Badger had swallowed Imodium, which would, sort of, plug him. Probably taken enough to stop Niagara in full flow. He hadn't asked what the correct dose should be. Foxy watched the goon, and couldn't get the stink out of his nose. When darkness dropped, Badger could move, with his bags, whatever was soiled and the collapsible entrenching shovel, to dig the pit.

The pig came, the sow. He knew stories about pigs, had heard them from the base medic, an orthopaedic specialist, who had talked about them after he'd put an interpreter back together – the man had been out in the marshes with a patrol when he was charged; a thigh bone had been broken and a knee smashed. When the big beast came out of the reed bed to the right of him and Badger and moved purposefully over the open ground, grunting, Foxy thought they faced a problem.

The problem worsened: the boar followed the sow.

Badger swore.

The sow led. Old teats hung slack from her underbelly and the mud glistened on her, was caught among the whiskers at her mouth. The boar had big bollocks and – more important – tusks jutting from the lower jaw. Badger thought the sow looked dumb, hungry, inquisitive, but that the boar was menacing. He could see why: at each side of his mouth, where the cheeks were, there were twin welts – the skin was broken and there were weepy patches. Badger realised that the tusks were in-growing and pierced the flesh, which would have been enough to make the brute mean.

They came closer, were within twenty feet.

They stopped. Now they were wary. Badger thought the sow might be the more cautious. The little eyes gleamed bright, tracking towards them.

In the last years, Badger had had birds come and perch on him, little songbirds, blackbirds and pigeons, and once a snipe had walked on elegant legs across his hands. Rabbits had played a few feet in front of him, and a fox had been over his back, jumping to clear it, as if his spine was a fallen log. Mice and rats had used his gillie suit for warmth. His ability to blend into nature made him good at what he did, as good as any – better than the old idiot beside him. A rat, heavy with the young it was carrying, had made a friend of him, enough for him to worry that he might be playing midwife when its time came. He could be still, and didn't know how still Foxy could stay.

There were flies round him.

Badger could accept rats, mice and birds sharing his space but the flies fazed him during the day, and the mosquitoes were worse in the evenings. All irrelevant. The sow mattered most. Badger thought that if she backed away, or lost interest, the boar would tuck along. Her interest was aroused but she did not yet seem to feel threatened. The boar's size was intimidating: he would have been more than a yard to the shoulder and the tusks were four or five inches long – the creature must live with perpetual discomfort.

Foxy had wriggled a little, making enough noise to raise the sow's ears. He murmured, 'I've a pepper spray.'

Badger thought he read it better. He had four plastic bags, all partially filled, one pair of fetid underpants and a body that stank. He flicked his eyes away. The kids had come out of the house with the old lady, and the goon was out of his chair. There was, far away, dust rising between the trees, where the road was, and guards were coming out of the barracks, rifles loose on straps across their backs and chests. The wife came, leaning on her stick. Foxy passed Badger the pepper spray, then clasped the headset tighter against his skull, tiny movements; he would have been straining to hear any remark made. Badger's own movement was to take the penknife from his belt and unclasp it; the blade was only two inches long but he thought it enough, and preferred it to the spray.

He saw the car, the Mercedes saloon. It was driven past the barracks and veered towards the house.

At that distance, the cries of the children were faint but clear. Their excitement carried.

He might as well have laid a trail of aniseed, grain or swill. The sow came forward. Badger could not stand up, clear away the scrim and the camouflage, get hold of the plastic bags, chuck them out and wave a deodorant spray to replace the smell of his shit with lemon fragrance. He thought, now, the pig knew he was there.

She was beside the edge of the scrape, where the scrim and the dead leaves covered his bergen. She was two feet, perhaps a few inches more, from him. She pawed the ground. The boar followed.

The target came out of the car and his driver carried his brief-case. The children were around him, and he lifted the little girl. The goon faced out across the water, and the open space that flanked the reed bed would have been in his view. It was the wife who saw the pigs and pointed at them. The boar was pushing at the shoulder of the sow, trying to come close. Badger saw the eyes and each whisker, each bristle, the sharp broken end of a tusk. The boar panted . . .

Now the boar led. He had pushed aside the sow. He drove down with his nose. The scrim snagged on a tusk. The snout pushed. The beast might weigh a hundred kilos, a hundred and fifty. It routed in the scrim for the bags and . . . Badger had the knife.

The boar's weight pressed down on him, and he used his left hand to hold the scrim tight, then jabbed the knife blade upwards and hit what felt like thick rubber or a leather wad. Blood spurted from the space between the nostrils. The pig reared back. The scrim ripped, the foliage fell away, and he let out a scream of pain, loud and shrill, parading that he was hurt. Maybe the boar didn't know what had made the pain, who had hurt him. He ran across the mud of the open ground, heading for the lagoon. The sow followed, seeming reluctant and confused.

They hit the water.

In front of the house, everyone watched.

The sow and the boar lumbered at speed towards deep water until only their heads remained visible. They seemed to make for the end of the mud spit where Badger had built the platform, with foliage washed away from the reed bed, where the microphone was mounted. In front of the house, they turned away as if the spectacle was over and Badger chose that moment to congratulate himself. The pigs swam towards the spit.

Foxy's head jerked forward. His turn to swear. The cable to the headset had tautened. The boar broke the surface close to the mud spit, kicked, rolled and tried to throw off an impediment. The cable was pulled up from the mud in front of the hide. Badger saw it rise in the water. There was a final convulsion and the cable from Foxy's headset went slack . . .

There were gravel pits out to the west of Reading and alongside the motorway. The teenage Danny Baxter had known them as well as any heron did. It was to one of them that he had taken his dad's accountant and brought him close to an otter's holt. The man had never seen the creature up close and was thrilled enough to become a referee of status when Danny had gone for the police job. Anglers patronised the gravel pits. Once, from the hide he'd made for himself, he had watched a bent, straining rod, a tight line and huge swirls from the depths. It had gone on for twenty minutes or more until the line had floated back, loose, nothing to hold it. The guy hadn't known he was watched, had sworn, kicked out and sent his stool and a rucksack into the water. It would have been a big pike that had snapped his line. Danny had seen it.

Now the line was exposed on the mud spit and floated on the water's surface. He saw where it ran up the spit and went into the mess of foliage where the microphone was.

It hurt to speak to Foxy, but he had to know. It was like he took a backward step. One question. 'Does it work?'

A nod, as if he were an interruption to concentration, therefore a goddamn nuisance. Then, 'Yes, but couldn't you have done a half-decent job with the cable? Bit bloody obvious, young 'un, because you didn't bury it properly.'

It was. The cable was a dark line across yellow mud, then a black thread over the water. If the goon, the officer, went back to his chair and used his binoculars to look again for the birds, the otters or the pigs, he must see, had to, the cable on the mud and where it floated. He thought he'd done well in concealing it and better than that in getting rid of the pigs, but his efforts had been ignored.

Everyone except the security man was now inside the house, and the light was failing. They had nothing. His throat hurt from lack of water. The irritation of the tick scabs and mosquito bites was acute, and the plastic bags were by his knees. The quiet came and – almost forgotten because of the sow and the boar – the smell returned. Time was running out, their covert rural observation post was near to compromised, and they had nothing to report.

There had been a re-evaluation, he was told. When he had been called to the unit's offices, he had brought his bag.

He was taken by one of their drivers to the airport.

It had been decided Gabbi should fly that evening to Europe. A neurosurgeon at Tel Aviv's Assuta Hospital – the most expensive and discreet in the country – had been asked, late, to advise. The medical opinion was that several European capitals had capacity beyond the best in Tehran, that a consultation at any one of a dozen locations might take little longer than the time needed for an examination, consideration and the decision to operate or not. It was explained that the couple could, within a dozen hours – twenty-four at most – be back at whichever airport they had flown into and looking for a flight home. The unit planned on the basis that information on a destination would be fed to them, and any who were privy to the surveillance mission mounted from the south-eastern Iraqi marshlands and harboured doubts did not share them.

He did not know whether Leah had worked on this last stage of preparation. She had been normal in bed the previous night, and over a light breakfast, then had left on the bus. He had planned a gym work-out, and the phone had rung: the call to come in, and the instruction that he should bring a bag. She might have known, she might not.

He would go to Rome. He had collected his passport: the Republic of Ireland was the flavour of that month. The days of big operations, he had been told, were over. There would never again be deployed as many as had gone down to the Gulf with tennis recquets and wigs. Nor did they look for the spectacular of the exploding headrest on a car seat, the detonating mobile phone when held against an enemy's face, or the poison squirting into an ear. One bullet, two maximum, was the day's order.

On arrival in Rome, he would be booked into an airport hotel, within sight of the terminals, and the call would come to send him forward or bring him home. He was not one to complain about the vagueness of the plans. He accepted what was put before him. If Leah had known, her kiss that morning as she went to work would have been no different.

They would not hold the El Al flight for him if he was late: to delay take-off could only draw attention to him. The car went fast on the airport road. A poem was in his mind:

> Breathes there the man, with soul so dead,
> Who never to himself hath said,
> This is my own, my native land!

He was the servant of the state, and did not doubt what the state asked of him.

> Whose heart hath ne'er within him burn'd,
> As home his footsteps he hath turn'd,
> From wandering on a foreign strand?

He would not challenge what was asked of him, and did not believe he could look into a face, see life and humanity, and hesitate. He liked the poetry of Walter Scott, but most of all he loved 'Patriotism', and he had faith. He did not query where the road took him.

When he'd boarded he would have forgotten the poem and would be engrossed in a business magazine.

★　　★　　★

The arrangements were in place.

It was a black-tie evening.

The consultant had used his authority to make the booking for scan facilities and X-ray without the usual requirement of a patient's name. It had, predictably, been queried. He had snapped back that there was more to medicine than filling in forms, and had seen a long-serving assistant wilt. He did not feel able to tell his staff that an unidentified Iranian, with the co-operation of the Berlin embassy and the likely support of an intelligence agency, suffering potentially terminal illness, was to be inflicted on them, so he had blustered and been unnaturally rude. His status at the university medical school was such that no complaint would be lodged.

Her parents would mind Magda for the evening. The black-tie occasion was a celebration of a local politician's birthday, an influential woman from the ruling party with the ability to dispense patronage. He and Lili would be with the great and the good of the city. In such company, his given name was Steffen and his family name was that of his wife. He was Steffen Weber, and soon there would be a prefix to his name, the title 'Professor'. He changed in the bedroom. Lili was at her dressing-table and sat in her underwear to apply her cosmetics. He could have said that until the last week he had been successfully absorbed into the German dream – the downturn in the economy seemed not to affect him – but he had brought the mood home.

If he had talked to her, it would have been a burden shared. He had not. He carried it alone. Easiest would be to look the patient in the face – he did it often enough – assume a look of principled sympathy, and say it straight: 'I am so sorry, there is nothing I can do. I regret that the question of surgery does not arise.' Those patients hurried away, and he had a cup of coffee, then carried on with his day. That evening in the *Rathaus*, there would be good food, fine wine and a string quintet. He would be among the élite and accepted . . . He sensed a shadow hung over him.

★   ★   ★

Dust trailed behind the big car. Abigail Jones had heard all four of her Boys arm their weapons.

It was a defining moment. The crowd ahead parted, the car was driven through it and came to stop in front of her – had to, or the BMW 7 Series would have gone right over her, squashing the life from her body. The driver braked with a certain flamboyance, and the tyres scattered dirt, some falling on her. It was about appearances and postures, and she took her time. She did not stand until the man had emerged from the darkened interior. It was a start, a good one. She had demanded that a leader come and he had. He was gross at the waist, wore a bulging *thobe*, long but cut like a white nightshirt, a *ghutra* on his head, chequered cloth with woven ropes to hold it in place, and sandals. He carried a mobile phone in one hand, his beads in the other. An assault rifle hung from a shoulder, and over the shirt he had a well-cut and discreetly patterned sports jacket that would have come from a London tailor, or from Paris. What else for Abigail to learn? He used a potent eau-de-Cologne. He had brought a youth with him, perhaps a son or nephew, who carried a briefcase – and two men for security, along with the driver.

As he approached her, she stood. Did it easily – did not betray exhaustion, dehydration or stiffness. It was Corky who had read it. The Irishman scurried forward with two old packing cases from the buildings. He put them down as if they were good-quality chairs, and used his sleeve to wipe them . . . The defining moment. She knew it, and her Boys. It was down to her skills as to whether they stayed or whether they were hoofed and in the process lost the mass of their gear. If they were hoofed, the guys up ahead were beyond reach.

She smiled – always did that well. Seemed to show frankness and honesty.

She called him 'Sheikh' and invited him to sit.

It was over water.

'You've had a drink.'

Only the quality of the microphone and its cable link were more important to them than water.

'I haven't.'

The light was sinking. Badger had been out of the hide and had gathered more dead fronds from inside the reed beds. He had waited until a rare cloud was over the last of the sun's brilliance, then had scattered pieces over the cable. He could not affect, without going far out into the water, the part of the cable that floated. Why not wade out? Too knackered. Badger had never known such tiredness. He could hike in bad weather, trek on moss and bog, and lose sleep. He didn't have the strength he'd needed those hours before when he'd scraped out the hide, moved the surplus earth into the reed bed, then gone out into the lagoon – his gillie suit absorbing water, weighing enough, almost, to drag him down – and built up the flotsam on the mud spit to hide the microphone.

'We're not due to have a drink for three-quarters of an hour – forty-three minutes, actually.'

'Don't make accusations, young 'un, that you can't prove.'

He came back, groped his way into the hide, and the cloud was now off the sun. One last beam of gold light penetrated the scrim, and he'd seen the glisten at Foxy's mouth, the dribble on his cheek.

The diarrhoea had weakened Badger. He had come back to the hide, crawling, feeling faint, worse shape than he'd known, and the job of hiding the cable only half complete. The exchange was in cutting whispers, neither voice raised.

'You've been at the water. It's on your bloody face.'

'You can't prove it.'

'We've enough for today, enough for tomorrow. We're supposed, in this heat, to drink seven or eight litres a day each. If we have a litre and a half each, we're lucky. It's despicable to steal water.'

'Shut your mouth, young 'un, before I shut it for you.'

He did so – but intended it to be temporary. He went into his bergen and brought out the bottle. He held it up and squinted at the level. It was about halfway down – he hadn't marked it. There was no indent on the plastic where his thumbnail had gouged a line. Had it been spit on Foxy's cheek? He reckoned not. His own throat was too dry for saliva, and he was dehydrated enough for there to be no sweat coming off him. If he'd tried to spit he would have scarred the skin in a parched mouth. Badger was sure. He pushed the bottle at Foxy, right up to his face. 'You want to drink, help yourself.'

'Don't bloody play with me, young 'un.'

'Go on, drink it all. Have yours and mine.'

'Watch it.'

'Finish this bottle and start the last. Swig your way through that too.'

'You're pushing me, young 'un.'

'And when it's all gone, we can fuck off out of it . . . if that's what you want.'

The scrim netting that held together the head covering he wore was gripped. 'You're shit, young 'un. When this is over I'll tell the world what shit you were here – tell all Gibbons's crowd. Tell them everywhere I get to take a seminar. I'll wreck you.'

Badger thought he was right, but the light had gone and he wouldn't know. Apologise? No. Might he have been wrong? No – and there was no worse crime than taking rationed water . . . The security lights came on outside the house. The goon paced, and the children came out to kick a ball.

Foxy said, 'My misfortune was to be teamed with a kiddie who was so ignorant, and had so little comprehension of the English language as to be at moron level. Know what "moron" is, young 'un, or is that too big a word for you?'

Again, he couldn't help himself: Badger did the short-arm jab.

The head was twisted so the blow cracked into the right side of the headset. It fell apart.

Foxy said, 'Not just a moron, but an ignorant one.'

The woman came out and Badger saw her through the glasses, a misted figure against the background lights. The children still played with the ball. She looked proud, he thought, and brave. She had dignity. He watched and admired her. She stood alone, leaned on her stick and didn't speak to the goon. He wondered how it would be for her: a sea change in her life, when it hung in the balance, was in a medical man's hands. He couldn't say how it would be for her if the approach was made and her man was turned . . . and he couldn't shift further from Foxy. It was as if he were anchored to the man.

They had drunk water, two mouthfuls each, and it had been Foxy's turn to finish the bottle. He had held it longingly to his mouth and sucked the final drops. One bottle remained. The silence wouldn't last through the night.

The moon climbed. Foxy, Badger realised, was exhausted and close to breaking point. He couldn't sleep. Not until the house lights were put out and conversations were stilled would Foxy pass over the headset and close his eyes. The anger each felt for the other was raw, of course. Badger was labelled a moron and ignorant, and Foxy was accused of being the cheat who stole water.

The light had gone; the moon was on the climb. The target, the Engineer, was out, smoked and walked, but he was alone.

There were birds in the water ahead, splashing, and Badger thought that once he heard the convulsion of a pig and wondered if the wound he had made in the nostril was infected.

He sensed Foxy would break the silence first, felt him to be increasingly restless. It was worse to be branded a cheat than to be called an idiot without education. Was he *certain* that the water level had been lower than it should have been? 'Certain': a big word. Foxy could not move from the hide and go into the reed bed to crap or piss. It was two full days since the new suitcase had gone inside the main door. It would not have been bought to be shoved into a corner but because travel was imminent. There would be – if fortune favoured them – one remark, half a sentence, or a throwaway comment.

He didn't think Foxy could last much more than the night and another half-day, and didn't reckon he himself had the strength to go on past the end of the following day . . . He hadn't seen Foxy's skin. He assumed it would be the same as his own, mottled with tick scabs and mosquito bites. Not possible to lie still because the itching was so great, and the flies came for their ears, noses and mouths, could burrow under the scrim net. Never again would Badger complain about a Welsh hillside: rain, a low mist, night frost, a view of a farmhouse with a field for campers would be paradise – if there ever was an *again*. He had twice punched a fellow officer, another croppie, and had allowed himself to be niggled by rank and personality. If it were ever revealed by his oppo that twice he had thrown punches, and had accused a colleague of cheating and stealing, there would not be an *again*.

The thought jagged his mind. What did a croppie do with himself after he was booted out for gross misconduct? For assault? For screwing up in the field and going unprofessional? He'd go to work for a local authority, tailing disability-benefit guys who did half-marathons and played golf twice a week after limping down to collect the hand-out dosh . . . He'd be on the phone, burning the ears of former policemen who ran PI firms and found evidence of marital infidelity, or did in-house security on companies that were leaking petty cash and equipment . . . He would have nowhere to go that was anything like satisfactory to him. Would he jack it in? He wouldn't grovel. He'd lose his job before—

Foxy broke. There was a trace of a whine: 'There was no call to hit me . . .'

Badger gave him nothing.

'. . . and no call to make that accusation.'

Badger thought Foxy had broken because, having barely moved since the hide was made, he would not be able to get out and do the legging back to the extraction point.

'I've tried to do a good job in extraordinarily difficult conditions and . . .'

Worth thinking about. The retreat from the hide – because the mission was fucked and the target had been driven away, or was complete because the information had been radioed out – was well worth consideration. A repetition in his mind of what he dreaded most: the car came, the new suitcase was loaded, and there might be a label on it they could not – with a 'scope or binoculars – read, and the Engineer and his wife, the goon, the wife's mother and the kids didn't say where they were going. To have done this for *nothing* would be the humiliation of his life, and he would stand accused of misconduct and professional failure because Foxy would nail him. Badger would make no apology, would not help in going to the extraction point in exchange for two punches being forgotten, and a cheating call being wiped off a slate.

'. . . and I've had no co-operation from you, no support, no comradeship.'

Badger watched the Engineer. Could have been his fourth cigarette. He was still alone and walking, no longer in silhouette from the lights behind him, thrown from the house, but moving away from the little pier where the dinghy was tied. He passed an old iron crane that in daylight seemed rust-coated – it was beside the water and might have dated back to a time when the water was the main highway – and went on towards the duller lights that fringed the area round the barracks. He was heading for the bund line to the right.

'Of course, I shouldn't have expected more from you. Too easy for you newcomers. And "too easy" makes for arrogance, and arrogance makes a kid useless. What did I say you were?'

Badger raked the shore with the binoculars, which were good for watching the house, but had the night-sight ready for when the Engineer was walking towards the raised track of the bund line. He could have scripted the line that would follow.

It did. 'I said you were moronic and ignorant. I had that right, double time.'

Hours of building resentment were over; a dike had been breached. Foxy had the verbal shits, Badger thought. He himself felt calmer and was not about to hit him again. It was *likely* that the water had been drunk out of hours.

'Did I say without good cause that you're moronic and ignorant? Are you fool enough to think that?'

His head was nine inches from Foxy's. Their shoulders touched, and their hips. Their smell mingled. The compulsion to scratch the scabs on his stomach was worse now, and the mosquitoes swarmed. If they made it out, reached the extraction point, loaded up the Pajeros, and 'Foxy' Foulkes – pompous, old-world – did not put in a career-killer report on him, his life would resume alongside Ged in hides, sodden ditches and damp hedgerows. He would tell the stories with relish. He followed the Engineer with his binoculars, then laid them down and took up the night-sight. The moon climbed higher and the birds were noisier on the water.

'How much of a moron? Enough of a moron to buy the shit they gave you?'

The goon, the officer, was out of the barracks and walking towards the house. The flash of a cigarette lighter burned out the night-vision image. He watched the security officer, used the binoculars. He felt tension coming in his shoulders, a tightening in his gut, and was confused.

'You bought it and believed it. They must have pissed themselves – Gibbons, the Yank and the Jew – laughing at you because of your ignorance. Back of the classroom, were you? Put your hand up, did you? "Please, sir, what's *interdiction*?" They gave you a bucket of shit, and you swallowed it. Want to know what "interdiction" means? Want to know that it doesn't mean an "approach" and turning an enemy? Want to know what you've signed up for, young 'un?'

All the muscles had stiffened, and his stomach had knotted. Cold had settled on the back of his neck and he held his breath.

'You volunteered for a spook-sponsored stake-out on what is bloody near enemy territory without the finesse of a war declaration. The target for surveillance is the man who makes the bombs that kill our boys, and he's right for *interdiction*, and you think that means some sort of cosy approach, a buttering-up in the hope the bastard will fall into our arms? You've all this shit about sitting in the countryside, wildlife around you, joys of bloody nature, and maybe you get to have a little cry because a deer's snagged on barbed wire, a rabbit's choking in a snare or a fucking

rat has a thorn in its pad. A wanking dreamer, that's what you are
. . . The military use of the word "interdiction" is about taking
down with the use of fire power. It's the destruction of the
enemy's potential to fight. How does it relate to this guy, the
Engineer, builder of bombs? "Interdiction" for him means that
he's killed. It's why I'm here, and why *you*'re here . . . Difficult
when you're ignorant, maybe a moron, to know what's real. He's
for killing, taking down, and you're a part of the process, a big
part.'

It was as though he had been hit in the stomach. But he held
onto the binoculars and could see the goon near to the house
speaking to a guard, an arm pointed away towards the bund line.

'In your education, the little of it you had, did they tell you
about killing? We use fancy words. We *harvest* fish, *cull* deer. When
we bomb a village and get the wrong target, that's not a screw-up
but *collateral damage*. It's bollocks, intended to soften actuality.
He's going to be killed. Didn't you know that, smartarse?'

The officer was striding out of the light, going at pace . . .

He could have been sick. It was that sort of blow that he'd taken,
the one that made a man double up, then heaved the puke into his
throat. He didn't know, now, how he could have swallowed what
he'd been told. He almost cringed.

Foxy warmed, would have sensed he'd hit home. 'It's deniable.
We finger the man. They move in a hit team because we've told
them where to look. He's stabbed or strangled, poisoned or shot,
and you're a part of it. Does that put you, young 'un, outside your
comfort zone?'

He had the binoculars down and held the night-sight hard at his
face. His eyeline took his head away from Foxy's mouth, but the
voice dripped on, and there was triumph in it. 'Don't think it
bothers me, young 'un, because I'm an old bastard and there's not
much can happen to me. Different for you. Your age, that stage in
a career when you reckon you're the dog's bollocks. Instead you
might just be in shit. An integral part in an extra-judicial killing,
which is at least accessory to murder. You're a part of it and your
defence is that you didn't know what *interdiction* meant. Reckon

they'll be queuing up to believe you? Extra-judicial is what you're into.'

He came level with him. For Mansoor, with the muscle wastage in his leg from the wound, it was a struggle to catch the Engineer.

It should not have happened. He had hurried, as best he could, from the house and past the barracks, then onwards until he saw the silhouetted figure in the moonlight high on the elevated bund line. The struggle to get the breath into his lungs, the pain from his leg and anger fuelled his aggression.

'You should not be here.'

Defiance from the Engineer, lit by Mansoor's torch: 'I walk where I care to walk.'

'My responsibility is to protect you. You ask me where you walk and when.'

Said softly, and with no trace of resentment: 'You forget yourself, Mansoor.'

'I do not.'

'You forget who you are and who I am.'

'I do not forget that it is my duty to protect you. I do my duty as best I can. I cannot protect you if you walk far from your home in the night and I am not warned.'

'Here – at my home – there is a threat?'

'There are thieves. There could be smugglers bringing drugs. There are the marsh people who would slit your throat for a packet of cigarettes or the coins in your pocket.'

'You are dutiful, and I am grateful. Do such imaginary threats equate with the threat to my wife's life? Call it a matter of perspective.'

'It is my duty.'

'And tomorrow – for how long I cannot say – you are relieved of that duty.'

'It is wrong that I will not be there. I should go with you.'

'Security, I think, is the smallest problem that faces Naghmeh and me. I wanted to walk and think. Now, to please you, Mansoor, we will walk back together.'

They did. The Engineer had lit another cigarette and Mansoor stayed a half-pace behind him. The moonlight was on the reeds and reflected in silver lines off the water; birds splashed and there were ripples from an otter's hunting. He apologised – it could go badly for him if the Engineer reported his rudeness. It was accepted and hand slapped his shoulder. It irritated him that he was not permitted, on the ground of cost, he had been told, to travel with them.

'And when we are gone tomorrow, Mansoor, what will you do?'

'Be certain that the old lady does not want for help . . . and I will watch for the ibis. I hope to see it . . . and my prayers will be with you. I will look for that bird. What else?'

It was, thought Harding, a master class from her in avoidance and evasion.

He was the only one of the Boys close enough to hear. He didn't understand everything because they flitted between English and local Arabic. The rest were back, relaxed now, and would have let their weapons hang loose across their legs.

It was a strange way to do business: he used English and most of her answers were in Arabic, but it helped Harding that he repeated most of what she'd said, translated it. In the business, she represented a charity from Europe of eco-freaks who wanted nothing more or less from their money than to have the most complete survey of flora and fauna in the marshes, with particular emphasis on the bird life. He did not contradict her, but pointed out that the area of the marshes she had chosen for her valuable, welcome research was not inside the triangle that had as its apex the confluence of the Tigris and Euphrates rivers and was the widest, most accessible part of the wetlands, but was hard up against the Iranian border. She spoke of the importance of the habitat. He spoke of the sensitivity of the frontier zone. She told him of the value placed on the wildlife of the marshes, its unique-ness and also its vulnerability. He told her of the suspicion, if her presence were known, of the Revolutionary Guards who patrolled a few kilometres down the bund line. She said she carried references and letters of introduction from people who were in the élite of government. He said it was 'interesting' that none had accompanied her on her research journey.

She held her line, Harding reckoned, and he held his.

She said she was trained in the preservation of wildlife. He did not accuse her of being in the employ of Britain's intelligence service.

She sparkled and flattered. He had mischief in his eyes and humour.

She remarked that the charity backing her could be generous to those who smoothed paths. He responded that the marsh people would always be grateful to those who showed meaningful generosity.

It was, to Harding, obvious that her cover story wasn't believed, nothing of it.

They liked each other. The sheikh let her know he had a brother who sold real estate in California, and that another brother had been hanged by order of the old regime in the Abu Ghraib gaol, that he himself had been imprisoned, then released, and allowed to return to lead his people but – of course – had never willingly served Saddam Hussein and the Ba'athists. Harding watched the dance played out. The sheikh could drive away, head for the army camp at al-Amara, report her presence and earn credit for future favours. Also, he could send someone across the border to the first road-block on the Ahvaz road and tell the men manning it that he had brought a message for an officer of the Revolutionary Guard Corps. That would earn him money and he'd be repaid also with safe passage for smugglers bringing him opiate paste for onward selling.

Harding, seven years with Proeliator Security and fourteen with the American marines, did not play cards for money – never had. The aunt who had raised him regarded any form of gambling as the devil's work. Card games, he assumed, were about bluff and trickery. Who, now, tricked whom? Who could depend on a bluff not being called? He watched, listened, and his mind flitted from the sheikh sitting on the crate and his Jones lady now cross-legged

in the dirt. His thoughts had moved on ... Strange guys, neither
to his liking. He didn't think that the older man or the younger one
would have joined him on the whore hunt in Dubai, or would have
been with him when he shivered at night on street corners or
shared the lie he lived. Neither would have made him laugh or
drunk with him until they were unable to stand, but he would go
to his Maker defending them. Why? Loyalty was the creed he lived
by. As loyal as the men from a marine platoon had been who'd
fought their way through towards four of them holed up in a
house as crowds gathered and cut off a retreat route. Loyalty was
a duty. Whether they could stay in place and exercise the loyalty
owed to the two men who were forward depended on her ability
to negotiate.

The radio stayed silent, and the guys up ahead had nothing to
report. Hours ticked by and little time was left. He could imagine
a scrape, the weight of the camouflage gear, the flies, ticks and
mosquitoes, the smells, hunger and thirst.

The sheikh might sell them to his own military or to the Iranians
across the border, and be well rewarded by either. She might buy
them time. They negotiated: a local leader of education and
authority over a swarm of peasants and an officer of an intelligence agency; they were equals. He didn't play card games but
had watched others: she had only a fistful of dollar bills and a
sweet, girlish charm.

He couldn't say how the game would play out. He thought hard
on the guys up ahead and the moon had risen high, and the
mosquitoes had gathered in droning clouds. If the sheikh reckoned a better deal lay elsewhere, pushed himself up off the crate
and walked back towards his car, then it was over for all of them,
and loyalty to the guys, far forward, was well fucked and bust.

'It is deniable because ... ?'

'It is deniable because it is illegal.'

'Who sanctioned it?'

'From high up, someone sitting on the top of the mountain, but
don't look for a written minute, young 'un. You'll not find an

electronic trail, and don't imagine there's schedules of meetings. Look back at it.'

'What am I looking back at?'

'Start with the people you met, the transport there and the place, then focus on the people. The transport was unmarked and you can lay good money, or bad, that somehow the flight records have been mislaid, and no flight path was filed or can be found for the chopper, and the big house takes guests but nobody signed a register. Anyone goes back to that house and tries to prove we were there in the face of bland denials, it won't be provable. Their grandson was killed by one of those bombs, side-of-the-road IEDs, and they'd rather like the bastard who built it to be killed, put on a flat slab of granite in a wilderness, left as carrion for the birds. Are you getting the picture?'

'What about the people?'

'Was there anybody of seniority, anybody who cut the mustard – had authority, was natural with power, expected to be listened to? If this had been a police operation there would have been a commander, perhaps an assistant chief constable. They weren't there. Nobody of rank was . . . Had one of them been allocated he would have called in sick. Any bastard with a career worth preserving, a pension to look after and the hope of a gong, would have stayed away – and they did.'

'You called him Gibbons and I called him "Boss". What was he?'

'A journeyman. They're stacked shoulder to shoulder, that type, at the Box and Six. They've reached a plateau of promotion, going no higher and too bloody frightened to quit, walk out and find a job in the marketplace. They hang about, do what they're told. They thank God they're still coming up to London on a commuter cattle truck, allowed to have a bloody briefcase with EIIR in old gold on it and still – just about – belong. Maybe, in his time – forgiven, not forgotten, held in the files – there was one of those messy little matters that he could be reminded of when they wanted someone to go down into the sewers. The American was Agency, would provide the cash and be looking for one last hurrah before heading to Florida and condominium life. Then there was the Israeli, humourless little bastard, the liaison for the hit – it's sub-contracted out and the Israelis are happy to slot Iranians of sufficient sensitivity, likely queue up for the chance. The major is exactly that, not a general or brigadier but a man who will have dirtied his hands in the sand defusing those bombs. What I'm saying, young 'un, is that these are the people who fight wars, not the ones who start or finish them. Then there's us.'

'What are we?'

'We're deniable. We never existed and never came here, and there's no record of us . . . And then there's only the lovely Alpha Juliet. I wouldn't hold your breath.'

'Hold my breath for what?'

'For the belief she's different from any of the rest.'

'Explain.'

'It's her shout. Miss Alpha Juliet's the instigator. Put it together. Give you a good ride, did she, young 'un?'

'None of your business.'

'My business, that she handled the recovery of a device from which DNA could be extracted, and put assets on the ground to verify that this target matched the sample. Why not have those same folk keep hanging round there and listening for the gossip, whatever? Because they're dead, and because the likes of them have fast burn-out. Luckily dead because they were thieved from, could have been worse. There's a security apparatus in Ahvaz, down the road from here, where they're skilled at doing things to fingernails and testicles. They know where the body shows up most for pain. In case you listened to the rubbish talked at home about torture, truth is that it works. Locals don't have fieldcraft – they don't have the backbone of training and skills, so they bring in you and me. I'm vain and like to be asked, and you're an idiot who doesn't know what questions to put. The whole operation is down to pretty Miss Alpha Juliet, who's hard as pig metal and would lie through her teeth for the cause.'

'What's the cause?'

'We came to Iraq looking for flower petals thrown under the tracks of the tanks. We were liberators. The politicians basked in it, and it lasted a few weeks, but we hung around a few years. We destabilised and put a new kid on the block as far as power went. We handed influence to Iran. They, the good mullahs, didn't want Caucasian troops right up close and personal on their borders and set their clever people to work on shifting us out. Their bombs did it. They reduced us to regiments of men and women cowering in barracks, and our military operations ended up as "force protection", which is army jargon for looking after your own arse and your own base and searching for an "exit strategy" with a whiff of respectability. But when that's inflicted on you it's predictable that you'll hate. Hate who? Hate the bastard that tweaked the old lion's tail. The lion now is moth-eaten, has bad teeth, and fleas crawl over him. The target had a hold of the tail and abused it. The lion wants to show it still has some useful claws.'

'Nothing to do with turning a scientist, bringing him over, getting him to switch sides and provide intelligence?'

'Nothing.'

'About revenge?'

'An act of vengeance. Some caution against, and others revel in it. But we're not, young 'un, in the hands of the cautious. The ones who've won the day would talk of "the long arm" and "making the bastards look over their shoulder". Most of all they talk about "sending a message", and the Israelis like sending them, and that's why they're on board.'

'You know all this because?'

Foxy growled, 'Because I'm smart enough to listen – and while you're chatting her up in the vehicle, then screwing her, I'm talking to her guards, rather sad guys who are growing old but don't know how to, who've gone out of the military family and can't replace it. They like to talk. I don't suppose you did much talking or listening while you were screwing her.'

'It's illegal?'

'Of course it is.'

'Under international law?'

'Under international law, and likely under the law practised on the High Street in Wolverhampton, Warrington or Weymouth.'

'That wasn't explained,' Badger said, flat.

'You seemed up for it, a chirpy volunteer.'

'I was.'

'Sow the seed and reap the whirlwind.'

'Yes. Thank you, Foxy.'

'Pity you never had an education, young 'un, and ended up so ignorant.'

It was time to open the last water bottle.

He packed the case. She sat on the end of the bed.

There was little talk between them. She spoke only when she needed to indicate to him which clothing he should take from the wardrobe, and which underwear from the chest. Earlier she had asked him what she should take, and he had replied that it would be better if she did not parade her faith: she should be modest but within limits. She had allowed him to choose what was appropriate. It was the only time in their married life that he had decided what she should wear. He was concerned that she had lost the will . . . Her last decision had been concerning the children. He was quiet as he moved about the room and his voice was subdued. The children, Jahandar and Abbas, were in his and Naghmeh's bed: he and his wife would sleep that night till dawn, when the car would come, with their children between them. It had been her decision. He had not argued.

The blinds were up and some of the glow from the security lights played through the open windows. She should have had the windows closed, the air-conditioning switched on, the flies and mosquitoes kept out – she would have slept better. He had not challenged her. A mosquito flickered close to Jahandar's face but she did not swat it away. He had suggested Naghmeh undress and get into bed, but she had shaken her head. It was because he, in the consulting room at the hospital in Tehran, had demanded more expert attention. Perhaps he refused to accept the inevitable, perhaps he denied dignity to her and heaped stress on her.

It was past midnight.

He closed the suitcase and applied the small padlock. He carried it outside the bedroom and put it by the front door. He looked out. There was purity in the silver strips of the moonlight, and crudeness in the bellowing of the frogs. It was said that the marshes, the waters and the reed beds were the cradle of civilisation. He felt humbled – and unworthy. It was the place of great artists and great scholars, great scientists and great leaders: he was the maker of bombs that killed young men.

He went back into their room.

She asked, 'How will it be in that town?'

'It is where they make the sweet that is marzipan, with the almond taste. They have been making it there for two hundred years. I saw it on the net. It is very famous, the marzipan they make there. We will bring some back for the children.'

He could say no more. He would have choked on his sobs. He turned from her so that she should not see tears on his face, and she held him.

It should have been a night of triumph but, with the food barely eaten, conversations hardly started, introductions not completed, the consultant had pleaded a headache.

He could not have said that his wife, Lili – elegant in a gown of understated expense – showed any sympathy. He said he wanted to go home, to the villa on Roeckstrasse. There was no headache. It did not concern him that she had entered this reception in her social diary some four months earlier, that friends and peers were there, and that it was an opportunity for her to show off her husband in an atmosphere of wealth and privilege. He held her hand tightly, said that the headache destroyed his enjoyment of the occasion and demanded that she accompany him home. She stood her ground, dug her stilettos into the *Rathaus* floor.

He did not belong. Never would and never could. In the afternoon, or early evening, of the following day it would be demonstrated to him that his life was not berthed in the pretty, affluent city of Lübeck, capital of the historic Hanseatic League of celebrated traders, home of the writer Thomas Mann, given the accolade by UNESCO of a World Heritage Site. It was not his home. It was where he lived courtesy of marriage, and where his name had been altered to make it more acceptable, his ancestry disowned. The next afternoon he was to be 'called back', as if a long unused door had been opened again. His home was not Lübeck – the restaurants, the beer, the river trips, the quaint passageways and homes so lovingly restored from war damage, the boutiques and the university – but was across continents. The man who had come from the embassy in Berlin, his cheeks encrusted with stubble, had dragged him back from the dream. He had no place here. He was from Tehran. His father and mother were martyrs of the war with Iraq, had given their lives to the Islamic Republic, killed in the front line while helping the wounded. He had been educated in Tehran; the state had trained him. A professor of oncology at the University of Medical Sciences had given him love and a family. He had shown his devotion to the state by working in the slums of south Tehran. He thought that a rope was tied around his ankle and he had been allowed a degree of freedom, as a horse was allowed to graze. Then the rope had been jerked and he was dragged back into a compound.

His wife, Lili, had started a strident conversation with the wife of a property developer who had big sites and big contracts for holiday homes up the river and at Travemunde on the coast. His headache mattered little. He could forget it, manufacture a smile and return to her shoulder, or he could walk out on her.

He went to his car. He had turned a last time in the hope that she would be hurrying after him, but her back was turned and her laughter rang out. He drove towards home and did not know how, if ever, he would regain his liberty. He did not even know the name of the fucking patient . . . and there was no headache, only anger.

The ring of the telephone would sign a warrant on a man's life – condemn him.

Gibbons yearned for it to ring, as if he was pleading for permission to kill the man himself. There were a few still left at Vauxhall

Bridge Cross – a little rheumatic in the joints, from a long-gone age – who would have understood his feelings. Not many. They were the unreconstructed warriors of the Cold War, and saw the bloody mess that was the Middle East as a self-inflicted wound that had bred many uncertainties. This band of brothers was left in the shadows of the corridors at the towers, and a younger generation – dressed down, more often than not, in jeans or chinos, shirts without ties or revealing blouses – preached an ethical manifesto, as if such a thing were appropriate in the new world order. Gibbons doubted it. Some shared his view; many did not. The arrangement for the communications was complex, but that was to hide them behind smoke. A message from the forward surveillance men would be sent on shortwave radio – brief transmission because to linger was to leave a footprint – to Abigail Jones and her back-up location. She would communicate with an Agency cell in Baghdad, who would onpass to the NATO base at Vicenza in the foothills of the Italian Alps. From there the message would go to technicians answerable to the Cousin in his service apartment behind Grosvernor Square. He would taste the message. A negative report would be transmitted electronically but an affirmative enough to kick-start the operation, would come through on the telephone. Complicated, but necessary for the process of denial.

He watched the telephone.

She had argued, but he had insisted. Len Gibbons had ordered Sarah to take his room key at the club and use the bed booked there. He had felt, increasingly that day, a point was about to be reached of success or failure, and he wanted to be present when the dice rolled, rattled, came to rest. He was now fifty-nine. His wife, Catherine, would have been disarmed to know that her bed partner, soul-mate, craved for a telephone to ring and therefore to consign a man to his death – not a fancy one in hospital with pain-relief drugs available, but in a street, spluttering blood as passers-by hurried on their way. She would not have believed it of him, that he tried to achieve anything so intrinsically vulgar as state-sponsored murder. She didn't know him, which was as well. If his children, at college, had known their father plotted a killing they might have disowned him and slunk away, ashamed. The neighbours, in a quiet road of semi-detached mock-Tudor homes on a suburban estate in Motspur Park, on the Epsom to Waterloo line, would have winced had they known what was done in their name, as would the members of the gardening club, and the choir he hoped to join at some future date. He willed the phone to ring.

He had a sandwich to eat and a Coke to drink. He sat at his desk and his universe was the telephone in front of him and its silence.

It had been a dream but was unfulfilled. He would have liked to visit ancient, historic Rome. He dreamed of walking on the old stones and being among the floodlit temples and squares; it would have been a pilgrim's journey for Gabbi.

He could not. Some of those attached to the unit who were sent abroad would have slipped out and taken a fast taxi into the centre of the old city, then walked to the tourist trail. He would not. The magnificence of a great civilisation was a forty-five minute ride down the road, a wonder of the world, but he was a mere functionary. So he did not leave his room, go to the lobby and shout for a taxi.

A message had been put under his door. He had not seen the courier. Neither had the courier seen Gabbi. From midnight, because time drifted fast, an executive jet aircraft was on standby. If it were needed, he would be told.

He sat in the darkness of his room, on the unmade bed, and waited.

She had said, with the light of the fire in her face, 'It's very important for the integrity of the survey, and its science, that we are able to work here undisturbed for three more days, maybe two, certainly one.'

He had said, the brightness of the flames bouncing on his jacket, 'What is "undisturbed"? How is that important?'

Abigail Jones said, 'The arrival here of a military unit would disturb the wildlife we're observing, and would obstruct our efforts at serious study.'

The leader of a marsh tribe, the sheikh, said, 'And your proximity to the border with the Islamic Republic of Iran, your work close to the border, does that require the co-operation of our Iranian friends?'

'Better that co-operation is not requested.'

'And better that information on your presence, as you seek the "integrity of the survey", is not passed?'

'Better.'

'So many of my people here are confused by your presence. Some who came innocently close have been injured, and some resent strangers near to their villages. These are difficult times for them, times of great hardship. I try to give leadership, but there will be some – younger than myself, with hot tempers – who will say that the military will pay for information about this expedition that surveys our wildlife, and others will believe that the Iranian authorities would also pay handsomely for knowledge of armed men coming close to their border for the purpose of evaluating the flora and fauna of the marshes. I have to lead, and I cannot lead if I am an obstruction to the young.'

Harding came past her with more wood, from broken packing cases, for the fire. She heard the bleating of sheep. The animals were behind the wall of men waiting close to the sheikh. There would be a signal from their leader. A knife waited in the hands of a man near to the front. Abigail Jones thought the operation hung now on a sheep's throat. If the signal were made that it be butchered, according to *halal* methods, negotiations had been concluded satisfactorily. If the sheep was led away, throat intact, and the knife was sheathed, the negotiations had failed and she doubted they would last there through the night. She was not about to back off, and there was in Abigail Jones a powerful sense of the value of retribution. She had served in Amman and Abu Dhabi, but also in Sarajevo as the second officer on the station. She knew the stories of the siege of Sarajevo and the atrocities inflicted, the massacre at Srebrenica and the close-run thing that had been the holding of the Muslim lines at Goražde; she had been involved with the teams of special forces who hunted down the war criminals. There

was, familiar to her, a small Serb town named Foča. She'd operated there openly and searched for the mean-minded bastards
who had done the bulk of the killings: two had been arrested, not
important enough to go to The Hague but convicted in local
courts. She thought it good that they whiled away their days and
nights in cold damp cells . . . There had been a fling with a Bosniak
artist down in Mostar, who had thought she was an aid worker.
He had painted well, but she no longer had any of his work – the
last had gone to the Christian Aid shop down the road from her
maisonette. 'Retribution' did not cause her any difficulty. He was
a man who made bombs. That was enough.

She asked, 'What is the cost?'

'The cost of what?'

She slapped her hands together as if the play-acting was over
and business was to be settled. She thought the change of mood
necessary. 'How much for allowing us to complete our survey
without interference from the military at al-Amara and al-Qurnah,
and without the knowledge of the Revolutionary Guard Corps
across the border? What will that cost me?'

The sheikh wetted his lips and the sheep bleated harshly – she
reckoned they had bloody good cause to. She might, then, have
killed for a beer.

Not much more to say, so neither had said anything.

Foxy slept now. Badger lay beside him and the other man's light
snoring was soothing, little more than the wind on the reeds. If he
grunted he made less noise than when the birds splashed. Best to
think about anything else . . . About the scabs on his hip, the back
of his thigh and his stomach, under which the wounds oozed and
might be infected. About the long and earnest-seeming talk
between the Engineer and the goon, which had been too far away
to be picked up. A little had: 'And when we are gone tomorrow,
Mansoor, what will you do?' Gone where? Not said. Foxy had
typed it onto the small screen he carried, his notebook, and pushed
it towards Badger for him to read. And under it was written, 'Look
for a Sacred Ibis [whoever that is, whatever].' The suitcase had

been packed in the front bedroom and a lamp had been on beside the big bed. Badger could see the children asleep in it. The gear was good, but it wasn't magic and they had no Merlin. The parents had kept their voices down so as not to wake their children. Nothing went onto the screen of Foxy's notebook. Twice Badger was passed the headset and was able to listen through the earpiece where he'd broken the plastic coating, but he couldn't make out the voices. The parents whispered, murmured, and the children slept.

It was the saddest thing Badger had ever seen. Nothing in his life compared with it. The parents had packed their case and made ready to fly – *somewhere* – in the morning, and she was dying and the children were being left behind. They had decided – the mother and father – to have the kids in their bed with them this last night. He could look through his life, like a drowning man was supposed to, and he could not recall anything as gut-wrenching as what he saw in the lit bedroom. His mother and father, Paul and Debbie Baxter, had good health except that he'd had a hernia operation four years ago and she had pain in a knee if she walked more than a couple of miles. A grandfather had died on one side and a grandmother on the other, but they'd had good years, good lives, and it had been welcome at the end to both. No car accidents in the family, and no cancers. He had no best friend, so no one he was close to with a crisis to face, and Ged, his best oppo, was fit, and Fran, whom he'd lived with, was in good nick and her father worked out at the gym three days a week. He had been out of general uniform duties too long to remember how it was when he'd been sent, blue lights and sirens, to an RTA and found a guy's head splattered across the windscreen, or a woman thrown off a bicycle. What was different when he had been at the roadside was that he hadn't seen the victim before, hadn't witnessed the man kiss his woman on the step, hug his kids and drop down into his car. He hadn't had the ringside seat when the woman came dripping out of the shower and her man was giggling, tickling and flicking at the knot that held up the towel. He hadn't seen them wolf breakfast or make sure that the bills were out of sight and not spoiling their precious time together. They, the bomb-maker and the bomb-maker's woman, were the saddest couple he had ever watched.

He could see the hands of his watch. If the case was packed they were going early. When they had gone, it was over. Nothing to stay for. Failure. If they went and there was no destination, it was down the pan – and had failed. The message would be sent. He would retrieve the microphone and draw in the cable. The Bergens would be packed and he would likely carry Foxy half the fucking way to the extraction point. What would he remember of her? Maybe when she'd sat on the bed, the kiddies slept and the case was filled – or when the committee of de-miners had come to the house, sat in the shade to say farewell, and some had cried . . . or when she'd stood alone in the light by the pier and the dinghy, leaning on the stick and watching the birds. Perhaps she saw an otter or followed the pigs with her eyes and enjoyed the peace.

It was illegal.

Danny 'Badger' Banks had put up his hand, volunteered, had signed up, and it was deniable, outside the law. Not about harvesting and not about culling, and not about the blank images, unseen, between the animals in the market pens and the meat hanging from hooks in a butcher's shop. About an illegal murder. They had talked of the bombs in the shit beside the road, and the mutilations. The major had said, *The improvised explosive device is the weapon that has snatched victory from the coalition and replaced it with a very fair imitation of defeat . . . There is a small number of clever, innovative men capable of wrong-footing us so consistently that the body-bags keep coming home and the injured with wounds they'll carry to their graves . . . We call an enemy a Bravo. Rashid Armajan is a big bad Bravo and we should take every opportunity to locate him and . . .* It would be murder, and those helping in the killing would be charged as accessories.

The night was quiet around him.

The lights inside the house were out, and the curtains were drawn at that bedroom window. He had not seen her undress, didn't know with what intimacy her husband might have helped her with straps and fastenings. The man was not a jihadist who would explode himself in a carriage in an underground tunnel, and he was not a smuggler of Class-A stuff, polluting streets and youngsters and breeding addicts. He was not a break-off from a splintered Irish republican team. The man, the Engineer, did not threaten Danny 'Badger' Baxter, or anyone he knew.

They had talked about the town the coffins came through, the military wing of the Selly Oak hospital, of the place in Surrey where the prosthetics were fitted and mobility was taught again. It was not his agenda.

Badger reckoned he walked at others' beck and call. Like he was a dog and a whistle blew. Foxy had told him he was deniable and an accessory, that it was illegal, and he had answered, 'Thank you.' What to do?

His mind churned, and his eyes hurt from exhaustion. The scabs hurt worse, and the last water bottle was dry. The mosquito bites itched and his guts were full but he couldn't empty them. He didn't know where to find answers.

It was the last morning. He had the headset on and waited for the first light to be switched on in the house. Then he would wake Foxy, whom he had thanked. He saw the flash of a cigarette lighter to the right and the goon came out of the barracks. There was a slight smear on the horizon, and the day started.

12

When it had the light to see where it flew, the bird left its perch on a broken tree. Its place, a favourite for two years, was now dried out, and the mud under it had become a wizened mosaic so it could no longer wade there and hunt. It had not fed for three days, but the bird was a creature of close-governed habits and its instincts preserved its loyalty to that place. Hunger drove it to abandon its perch.

It laboured into the air, weakened by lack of food. It was up before the dawn light had spread, and before the eagles had soared high to search for prey. It worked hard to get elevation and to feel the draught of wind under its broad wings.

It went over areas of sunbaked mud, once covered with a film of water, and over what were now narrow drains and had once been deep waterways, and skirted a collection of huts that would have been in danger of annual flooding when the bird was young but now were marooned. Below it a few skinny, undernourished water buffalo meandered in search of lakes and lagoons.

The ibis flew towards water, to the east where it would find food: small fish, frogs, mice or immature rats, beetles, spiders, butterflies and moths. The bird was female. The last year, her eggs had addled. Hunger had driven her from the stick nest in the tree and she had spent too many hours away, looking for the food that would sustain her. The ground had been arid and without life, and the village where in previous years she had scavenged was now deserted. Once she had seen the carcass of her mate but she had not fluttered down to feed off it, had left the mess of bones and feathers for the crows to peck at.

She had broad wings, white with black-tipped feathers. As she flew, climbed, a rhythm returned to the flaps that took her forward.

It tired her to fly any distance, but she would go as far as her strength permitted in her search. A column of smoke spiralled near to some buildings and she saw people there, swung away and did a half-circle around them: she had no love of people.

When the sun edged over the horizon, she felt the first of the day's warmth on her wings and back, white-feathered, and on her neck and head, black-feathered and with a black beak. The sun encouraged her to beat her wings harder, and soon she found a rivulet to follow. Then it became a stream, and a different smell seemed to come from the ground. There were reed banks.

She flew lower.

Beyond the reed banks there were expanses of water, not clear and dark as it would have been if the level was deep beyond the length of her wading legs. She looked for water that reflected the skies and in which she could see the mud bottom, not thick weed.

She saw a building that had small lights around it, the green of the reeds and a bare space of dried dirt on which debris had accumulated, and she saw a little promontory just above the water and at the end a mass of dried leaves. She made a clumsy landing because of the time she had been flying. She settled, had barely steadied herself, then readied to strike. She was listed as a bird deserving the status of 'conservation concern' and 'threatened'. In the last survey of the marshlands, while warfare raged around the dedicated lovers of the ibis, it was estimated that only twenty-six adults lived in this habitat. She hit with her beak. The strike was brutal, fast: she had a frog.

It was a fat frog and it struggled, but its existence was already forfeit. It was put down on the reed fronds, and held by the beak until the claws at the foot of the bird's left leg could pinion it down.

It was eaten, swallowed whole and alive. Digestion would take time, and the water level around the place where she settled was good for her wading.

She squatted, preened herself, pecked at insects real and imagined. She gazed around her and felt comfortable.

★   ★   ★

Badger watched. He had had the glasses on the bird as it circled the landing place twice, each time lower on the circuit. He wondered what species it was, but thought it pretty – and effective in the art of killing.

The bird, hunched down, lancing its body feather with its beak, was welcome – a relief to Badger from the *options*, from breaking disciplines and scratching bites. The mosquitoes had gone now, the flies were gathering, and the wind coming from Foxy was foul. Twice he'd elbowed the man's ribcage to stop the snoring, but then the options had been uppermost.

A man of ethics? A police officer bred on morality? Badger didn't know if he was or not. He believed in getting a job done and not much more. He had never fabricated evidence, had never claimed not to have seen another constable strike a man with a baton, and had never fiddled expenses. He had never done anything he would be ashamed of, had never risked his career with a criminal action. The rip-off culture at the police station in Bristol where he had started out had passed him by. Almost, in fact, he had been bollocked for insufficient arrests, relying on cautions and verbal warnings rather than hoicking the arrest statistics for the division. He had a moral code, not flaunted when he was in uniform or out of it, not based on any religious teaching and not worn on his sleeve. The code gave him – he recognised it now – a sort of naïveté. Maybe the naïveté had come on heavier since he had gone into rural surveillance and after he'd nagged Human Resources for the chance to go on the CROP course. Options? They had nagged at him through the night, while Foxy slept, and the one factor making the matter bearable was that nothing had materialised for him to report. He was watching the bird scrabble with its big feet for better grip on the reed fronds he had put there. More serious than 'options', it was kicking at the camouflage he'd made.

The bird hacked hard, thrust dried stuff back and seemed anxious to work down to a hard surface. The glasses showed him the slim, long body of the microphone and, once, the drive of the right foot lifted the cable ... If the bird kept going, the microphone would be pushed into the water. Down to options that mattered. Out of his mind went *I was, sir, only following orders that I believed to be legitimate.* No more baggage about *I'm not prepared to be involved, Foxy, in extra-judicial murder. I'm not some fucking Israeli. I will not allow any message that contributes to the target's killing to be transmitted.* Pushed down the agenda was *I'm walking out now and having no further part in this*, and at the bottom of the heap was *I'm a moron and ignorant, and I didn't understand.* More important, top of the pile, was how to stop a pretty bird – a bloody nuisance bird – kicking out the micro-phone and drowning it. Couldn't stand up and shout, couldn't go walkabout to look for a stone and lob it. Once more it scratched. The shape of the microphone was clear now and the cable was well visible and . . . It stopped, seemed to compress itself down.

The door opened – the front door.

The goon was walking from the barracks towards the house. Lights had been switched on inside and, faintly, a radio played. The door was wide open and the kids spilled through it. Then the case was lifted out. Maybe it was the Engineer who brought it, maybe the older woman.

The case didn't bulge. It had a green ribbon tied to its handle. Badger saw that the small girl was crying and the boy went to the water's edge, threw in a pebble from the track, watched it bounce. The bird was hunkered low on what was left of the foliage. Maybe it thought this was a place to stay, where frogs were available on order. Maybe it was not about to shift out. He jabbed Foxy.

Him and Foxy? Between them now a sort of tolerance existed, like a ceasefire. Not peace and not war. When the car came, the suitcase was loaded and they drove away, the mission was done, whether they had anything to radio or not. He doubted he and Foxy would speak much on the way back to extraction, or while they were driven to the base, and not at all when they were heli-coptered to Kuwait City. Likely they'd be in different rows on the flight, which Foxy might demand and he himself might insist on. There might be a handshake at the terminal but it would be transitory and neither would go on the other's Christmas-card list. They'd never meet again.

One jab was enough. He passed him the headset. When the bird had kicked, noise, explosions, had been in his ears, but the bird's chest – small mercy – did not cover the microphone tip and he could hear the little girl crying.

There was more wind, then a murmur about needing to piss, then the question: how much water was left? None. Then the statement: without water they were screwed. The headset went on Foxy's ears and Badger whispered about the bird. '. . . and can't do much about it. The goon has it in his glasses, looks excited enough to do a jerk-off. What is it? Not anything I've ever seen.'

'It's called an African Sacred Ibis. Pretty rare. Big in Egyptian mythology. Do me a favour, just shut up.'

Foxy looked wan, weak, about played out. A day wouldn't have gone by in the last ten years without him shaving and examining his moustache in a mirror, without him putting on a clean shirt and polished shoes. He looked sad and a frown cut his forehead. Then he grappled in his pocket for the notepad and flicked the switch to light the screen.

The wife came, and the children ran to her. The Engineer peered up the track and past the barracks, then looked down, savage, at his wristwatch. The goon gazed at the bird. She had the children against her knees and bent awkwardly, held them tight and tried to comfort them. What comfort, Badger wondered, could she offer?

The car would come and the bird would fly. The noise of the car and the crying of the boy would be too much for it. Many weeks, several months, Mansoor had dreamed of seeing the bird, *Threskiornis aethiopicus*, merely fly low over the reeds and be in the lenses for a few seconds, half a minute, but it was down and he had a fine view of it, and could not believe that the moment would last, but she comforted the child.

He heard her. He had no children. He did not know if it was his fault that his wife was barren or hers. She said, in their bedroom at the back of the house that was owned by his father, in a low voice, so she should not be overheard, that he was responsible for her inability to become pregnant. He could not believe that. He refused, of course, to go to a doctor and have tests done on his wife, Safar, and himself. So, with no child to look after, she went each morning on a shuttle bus from their home in Ahvaz to the Crate Camp Garrison on the road to Mahshar, came back each evening and helped his mother to prepare a meal, then did cleaning and went to bed. They had sex every weekend, quietly so as not to disturb his parents, but her period never missed. He saw how Naghmeh, wife of the Engineer, comforted the children. He had looked away from the bird that was on what seemed to be flood debris that had snagged at the end of a mud spit.

'You should not be frightened.' She held tight to the children. 'There is nothing for you to be frightened of.'

He thought she did not cry because it would have frightened the children.

'We go to see a very clever doctor, and he will make me better.' He looked up but the bird had not moved.

He did not know if he would ever see her again.

'We will bring you back sweets, because you will be very good when your grandmother cares for you . . .' If she died in Germany, the children would go to her mother, and their father would be found an austere room in the Crate Camp Garrison. He would visit them only at the end of the week and on public holidays, and would bury himself in the papers and circuit boards on his work-bench. 'The reward for being good and brave is very special sweets.'

Then Mansoor would be recalled to the ranks of the al-Quds Brigade and most likely a desk would be found for him, papers to process and a keyboard to hit. He might be in Tehran or Tabriz or in the mountains on the Afghanistan border . . . if she did not come back. She had quietened and calmed them. The car was late. It reflected on him. It should by now have been at the house.

'We are going to a far-away country, to Germany. There is a

town in Germany where they make wonderful marzipan . . .' The sun edged higher and he saw that Naghmeh no longer shivered. Its first warmth fell on him – and on the bird. It was a clear two hundred metres from him, but he could sneak the binoculars to his eyes and see its markings. It had been venerated in ancient Egypt, had been thought so valuable that it was sacrificed to appease gods, and in one archaeological site the mummified remains of a million and a half ibises had been uncovered. He believed himself blessed, and turned away from it. The weapon hanging from his neck clattered against the magazines in the pouches of his tunic. '. . . which is made from almonds and sugar.'

She looked up at him sharply. He had not seen it before. She seemed to despise him. It might have been the weapon that caught her attention, or the magazines into which the bullets were pressed, or the two grenades at the webbing on his waist, or the flash of the al-Quds shield sewn on his olive sleeves. It might have been because she knew his father helped to hang men, or because his wound crippled him – or because he had produced no children. He wanted them gone, but the car had not come.

'The best marzipan is made in the town we go to, Lübeck, and there we will go to the shops and buy marzipan sweets for you, because you will be good and you will look after your grandmother. Your father says Lübeck is a very pretty town, and is famous for the marzipan we are going to bring home. You will be very good.'

He walked away from her and the children, and went to the Engineer. He shrugged and said that the car was not late for its departure time, but should by now have arrived. If a few minutes more passed without it coming he would get on the radio and demand an answer. The Engineer looked at him as if he was dog's mess on a shoe heel. The sun rose, carrying the day's warmth with it, and the bird was still on the mess of leaves. He thought he heard a car, far away.

It was repeated by Foxy, the third time. 'I heard it. I don't doubt what I heard. "The best marzipan is made in the town we go to,

Lübeck." She said that. Also she said, "Your father says Lübeck is a very pretty town, and is famous for the marzipan we are going to bring home." About as clear as it could be.'

'You going to send it?'

'Of course I'm fucking well going to send it.'

It was like a new man had materialised beside Badger. A bloody kid had scored a goal. Foxy had learned where a targeted man could be killed, and Badger wondered if that counted for more than scoring the goal.

'Illegality, deniability, extra-judicial killing.'

Dismissively: 'Do me a favour, young 'un, and pass the kit.'

His hands burrowed into the bergen beside him and Foxy was flicking his fingers in front of his face, as if time was not to be wasted. Badger felt dazed. A moment of truth had come, missile speed, from the clear blue skies above the scrim net. There were the seconds when a crisis developed – armed police had told him – when anticipation and training were overtaken by actuality. One thing to think about it, talk about it or practise it, another when it happened. It had been Badger's job to look after the communications: the comms should have been ready, kept in place for immediate transmission, only needing the battery to be activated. They were not. Foxy's snapped fingers and the irritation said they were there, flying high, and his voice had been quiet but he had made no effort to hide his elation: *I heard it. I don't doubt what I heard ... Of course I'm fucking well going to send it*. Badger had the comms gear in his hand and was levering it out of the bergen.

'What's the matter, young 'un? Just shift it.'

He had to push aside a bottle half filled with urine, and two sheets of the tinfoil that was there in case the Imodium wore off. He brought the kit up under his stomach and then his chest.

Badger could have done it himself – could have thrown the button, let it warm, made the link, sent the stuff, like passing down a death sentence. The kit would have been snatched from his hands. Foxy would not give up the glory moment. He could see the man: another cigarette, another glance at his watch, another

spin on his heel to show anger that the car hadn't come. The goon
was on a radio or a mobile, had it clamped to his face, his weapon
and binoculars bumping on his chest as he bent some poor
bastard's ear about the car being late. She stood with her mother
and the kids were calm. The bird was still in place.

Emotion melded with the professionalism dinned into him.

His eyes flitted from the distance view of the woman and her
husband to the near ground where the bird squatted, part
covering the microphone. The length of cable that was exposed
before it went into the water snaked out from under its tail
feathers.

There was a soft whine in his ear as the comms kit gathered
power. A red light glowed, and he sensed Foxy's exhilaration. He
felt a sort of flatness.

They had the link. Foxy murmured his call sign, Foxtrot and
something Badger didn't catch. A query on Alpha Juliet, a pause.
Badger sensed that Foxy was at bursting point, and it flushed out
of him.

The town was named. It was spelt out. Lima – Uniform –
Bravo – Echo – Charlie – Kilo. They were 'leaving any time now,
route unknown'. Badger turned his head away from the house,
the family, its guards and the bird, and stole a look at Foxy's face.
Something almost manic, something of achievement not reached
in a lifetime before, and he could see a clenched fist, the knuckles
whitened. Then, an afterthought, Foxy said something brief
about recovery of kit, a further transmission about extraction,
and cut it.

The car came. It was the Mercedes. The goon bawled at the
driver, who pointed to a tyre and bawled back. The case was
carried to the car and the boot was sprung open. The kids had
started to cry again. The bird was sitting on the microphone. He
could imagine that pandemonium had broken out on receipt of
their report, and he had done nothing about agendas, had failed to
scour the options.

He and Foxy had done something huge and the response would
be awesome. He knew it. Foxy might have forgotten himself: an

arm had snaked out and was around Badger's shoulders. 'We did it. Against everything, every count of the odds, we did it. We scored.'

There was a photograph. The frame was expensive enough to have a hallmark stamped in it, which guaranteed its pedigree. It was on a table beside the bed.

The photograph had a message handwritten in heavy black ink: *Ellie, With love to my darling girl, Foxy.* The picture in the frame was of Joe 'Foxy' Foulkes with camouflage cream daubed on his face and wearing a gillie suit, but not headgear. He was grinning. It was a portrait of a man of action.

Neither of them, in the bed, were embarrassed or distracted by its presence. It was face down.

'I'm not having him giving me a cold eye, the old bugger,' Piers had said.

'About all he's capable of, these days, is watching,' Ellie had said.

He'd arrived late at night, and his car was parked down the side of the garage, well inside the gate. It was pretty much hidden from a casual glance. She'd thought that a bottle of wine, on the carpet in front of the fire in the sitting room – Foxy's chair pushed back to make more room – would ease them into what was a momentous time in the relationship. It was the first time he had been there. They'd been at his place and in the pubs there, where she was anonymous, on the far side of the motorway beyond Bassett.

It hadn't worked out as she'd planned. Time had not been wasted on Foxy's rug in front of a fire blazing with logs that Foxy had cut, and none of the wine had been drunk from the bottle that Foxy prized. Straight up the stairs, past the collection of cartoons, police stuff, that Foxy had collected, into the bedroom and onto Foxy's bed. They'd stripped, and the light had been on, and he had crawled over her and looked up into Foxy's face. His hand had come from between Ellie's legs, reached for the frame and flipped it. Her hand had come off the small of his back and

given it a shove. Now it was mostly hidden by the clock radio
that had woken Foxy when he was at home. It had been Ellie's
decision that Piers come to the house.

Where was he? She didn't know. What was he doing? She'd
only had a text. What had she been told? Pretty much nothing,
and the guys who'd brought the car back had just been peasants.
Would he just turn up? Always rang first, something about getting
the wine to room temperature or decently chilled.

They'd slept, knackered, and the dawn had come and she'd
woken him.

Rain beat on the mullions. It was a grey dawn, a miserable one.

'Not to worry,' Ellie said. 'You're back here tonight.'

'Am I? You sure?'

'Too bloody right.'

It was eleventh-hour stuff, and she had jack-knifed up when the
chimes had gone. She'd had to rummage in the robe to get the
receiver, would have shown a mass of leg and didn't care. The
haggling, pure bazaar, had gone on through the night and into the
small hours.

She had nothing in her hand except money. Probably they
could have ignored the bartering and come and taken the money
by force, and would have lost a few, or several in the fight. She and
her guys, if still upright, would have been unable to prevent it. So,
money had been on the table and the sheep had gone quiet – they
might have thought, as the night wore on, that their throats were
safe. And had been wrong.

There had been a bare apology, first light and a grey mist over
the desert dirt, and she had been listening to the fucking thing,
and then had run to the front Pajero, and her laptop.

The sheep had been skinned, then skewered and cooked over
the fire. Bowls of rice were passed round, and bread brought
from a village. The sheep had been slaughtered when the deal
had been closed. Not an easy one for her: no chance of getting
on a satphone and calling up her station chief in the Baghdad
compound and asking him what ceiling she could reach to: he

was outside the loop and would want to stay there. It was her decision alone, and she had pledged the lot. Her bundle of dosh, each last dollar, would go into the sheikh's pocket. It carried no guarantee of honesty – he could trouser what she gave him, then drive away, call his friend, who would be a full colonel, and pass on information about Jones and her Boys to another colonel on the far side of the frontier. No guarantees, except – she had the laptop out and it was powering up – she had dropped in an aside. Ground troops of the coalition no longer did grunt work in the field, but the firepower of the air force was still available. She *might* be able to call out an F-16 Fighting Falcon with a load of missiles and maybe a pair of CBU-87 bombs.

She had power up and the satellite signal was locked.

It would have been in her eyes – lit by the fire: she had co-ordinates of where the sheikh lived and where his extended family were gathered, and the implication would have been that a bomb could go astray and she would give not a flying fuck if it did . . .

Abigail Jones opened a link to the Agency in the communications area of the station, in the fortified, sanitised sector of the capital. She was answered. Could she identify herself? She was Alpha Juliet. She gave her message, spelled it out again, but with a codified alteration. Kilo – Tango – Alpha – Delta – Bravo – Juliet. She added one word, 'Enroute', then '0647'. The cut-out process had begun. She didn't know to whom she spoke, and a technician didn't know who had sent him that brief message, or the identity of the receiver at the Vicenza base. Cut-outs bred deniability and fogged a trail.

She turned off the laptop and walked back towards the fire. Abigail Jones might have welcomed the thought that word of this would seep through the firewalls of need-to-know inside the Towers. It would be the same for her as for old Len Gibbons; whispers, nods and no complete picture. She would be noticed in the atrium hall, the canteens and corridors. She felt a little whiff of pride.

Shagger broke the indulgence. He asked, 'When do they come out?'

'They have to retrieve the gear, then shout and start moving. I don't have a time yet. Now let's get these bastards on the road, and what's left of that mutton. The big part's done and we know where he's headed. It's a fantastic result.'

He came into their darkened bedroom, hoping she was still asleep, but Lili's voice was sharp: 'Steffen? How is your headache?'

When he had come home from the *Rathaus*, alone, her parents were already in bed. He had gone to the remaining guest room, where he had tossed and turned. He had heard the crunch of tyres, long after midnight, on his drive, then laughter – hers and a man's – talking and finally the key in the door. The car had driven off. Perhaps a man she had known from childhood had brought her home.

The bedside light came on and she sat up, her back against the pillows, the sheet tight to her throat. She wore nothing.

He had been nine when his father and mother had been killed in the battle for Khorramshahr. They had died in the liberation of the city after nearly a year of Iraqi occupation. He had been told they could rejoice in martyrs' deaths. He struggled to remember them, to picture their faces and hear their voices. His father had told him once that there was never a good or bad time for confession. It had involved him taking a handful of piastres from his mother's purse to buy sweets from another kid at school. His father had told him that confession was a fine purging agent. He had gone to his mother, interrupted her work on medical case histories and seen her brow furrow with annoyance. He had said he had taken some money and bought sweets. She had shrugged and returned to her work.

Now he said, 'There was no headache.'

'What, in God's name, were you up to?'

'I did not want to be there.'

'That is pathetic. It was important – we talked about it.'

Something of his pain would have been in his face. He was

wrapped in a bathrobe, had come to their bedroom to find clothing for the day: he wore a suit, shirt, tie and polished shoes when he saw patients; he dressed down only for days with his students. He sat on the side of the bed. He took a deep breath – he was not Steffen but Soheil. He was not from Lübeck and German, but from Tehran and Iranian. He spoke the truth, bared himself.

He spoke of a phone call from Berlin, a meeting with an Iranian, who might have been an intelligence officer of the VEVAK. He said he had cleared facilities for a patient to come for consultation, and had been rude to his staff who had queried why he had agreed to see a nameless patient with no medical history. He said he was trapped, that his past and origins had claimed him.

The sheet dropped. Her hands reached out and gripped his shoulders. 'You are German! You do not have to—'

'Wrong.'

'You are German. You are Steffen Weber.'

'I was, but am not now. I am Soheil – I am my father and mother's child.'

'You do not know who you are treating? You do not know who their secret police are bringing?'

'I do not.'

Her back arched, and he saw the upper curve of her chest, which had been on show at the *Rathaus*. It would have been covered only with a loose wrap on the ride home.

She shook him. 'Call the police or the security people. This is not a banana country. You cannot allow thugs to manipulate you.'

'I—'

She flared, 'Are you married to me? Yes. Are you their servant?'

He could not answer her. He pushed himself up from the bed and went to the wardrobe. He took out a suit and a folded shirt, fresh socks and laundered underwear, a quiet tie and shoes that glinted with the polish the maid had applied. He closed the wardrobe, turned and knew what he would see.

His wife, Lili, held the sheet high, covering herself. He thought that a woman would always cover her body if confronted by a stranger. He went to dress. He faced a long day in Hamburg before he returned to the medical school at Lübeck for his evening appointment with a patient whose name he had not been told. He did not think, then, that her marriage to a stranger could be saved.

He reached the door and said. 'They would hunt me, track me, find me if I refused. They will have chosen me because of my birthright. I assume that the patient is someone of military importance or in intelligence gathering. If you wish, Lili, to condemn me, you could lift the telephone and speak to the police or the security apparatus. I ask you not to . . . They have a long arm and a long reach, and I would spend the rest of my life searching the shadows at my back.'

He closed the door after him.

Sarah knew.

The telephone on the desk had rung. He had been sitting on his desk, feet dangling, when it had screamed for his attention. He had picked it up.

She knew the story.

His face had seemed to contort as he'd listened. A greyness came to his skin, followed by pallor, and Gibbons's tongue had flipped over his lips. She understood that a location had been given. Then Gibbons shook, as if throwing off an unwanted skin, a burden, and his back straightened. His only question: which airport were they going out from, City, Heathrow or military? It was as if, by the time he hung up, he had regained control.

She was in the outer office and it was not her place to pressure him for the information so she'd kept her head down.

He called to her that the town named as the target's destination was Lübeck. She asked if the transport was taken care of, and he nodded, but without excitement. Well, perhaps anticipation of 'excitement' was unrealistic, she thought, as she looked through the open door at Len Gibbons, whose office – and professional life – she ran. She knew why the name of Lübeck had stopped him dead in his tracks. She knew the story.

The story held in the Towers' archive was titled *The Schlutup Fuck-up*, and not many knew it, but she did.

When Sarah had gone to work for Gibbons her friend, Jennifer, had quietly let her know about the Schlutup Fuck-up and its effect on his career, the struggle the man had put in to shift it off his shoulders. A veteran in the archive and able to ferret in restricted areas, Jennifer had unearthed the story. To Sarah's knowledge, Len Gibbons had never been back to that northern corner of Germany, up by the Baltic coast and close to the Trave river. Small wonder the poor wretch had blanched. The pain of the Fuck-up would have been acid-etched in his mind.

She disguised her privileged knowledge with apparent indifference: 'Will you be wanting me to come with you, Mr Gibbons?'

'I don't think so, Sarah, but thank you. A pretty ordinary place, Lübeck, and unlikely to present problems. Not a place to be mob-handed on the ground.'

She wondered how he would be – in a modern world of supposed integrity – when he was there, in Lübeck, and deniability might be hard to rustle up. And she wondered, all those years ago, how much tittering there had been behind hands in the previous home of the Service, and how much a Fuck-up of dynamic proportions would harden a man – a man such as Len Gibbons. He had not mentioned the men in Iraq, not expressed praise or admiration for their work, nor sympathised with the conditions they would have operated under, nor referred to the back-up team. She could do jargon with the best of them: Sarah considered the lack of praise, admiration, of any acknowledgement for what others had achieved to be part of the 'collateral' of the Schlutup Fuck-up and the scars it had left.

'Whatever you say. I asked . . .'

'Good of you. Pretty straightforward stuff, and an experienced team around me.'

It was a cold morning in the city but the early sun gave beauty to the skies. The blue was cut by the exhaust fumes spewed from the engines of a Boeing 737, bound for the Swedish ferry-port city of Malmö. Gabbi did not query whether the most effective route had been chosen for him, or the quickest, or the one that would provide greatest security. He would land by noon, would be met and driven to the departure point. Layers of people worked on the problems and came up with answers that he would not second-guess. It gave Gabbi satisfaction to reflect that so many laboured behind him. He was launched, and had no thought for those who had gained the information that had set him on his way.

The car had taken them.

There had been a further delay when Mansoor had looked down at the nearside rear tyre of the Mercedes and thought it too smooth, barely within legal limits, not fit for carrying passengers of such status. He had queried the tyre's safety. He had almost accused the driver of taking a good tyre to the market in Ahvaz, selling it and replacing it with an inferior one, then pocketing money. They had argued, until the Engineer had clapped his hands and demanded that he and his wife left.

The dust cloud thrown up behind the car had thinned, and the children had left cheerfully enough with their grandmother for school.

The bird had stayed. He had as good a view of it as he could have hoped for. He did not tire of watching it. His father would not have understood, or his wife or his mother. Himself, until he had been allocated to the security of the Engineer, he would not have believed that a man could watch a bird that sat across a hundred and fifty metres of water from him, and pray that the moment would not pass. The focus of the glasses was on the feathers of the wings and neck, the clean lines of the beak – and on the expanse of mud behind it that was broken only by the debris of dead reeds.

'What's special about that bird?'
'It's endangered, rare – his obsession.'

'We're screwed. We can't move while he's there.'

'State the obvious, young 'un.'

'We can't leave it but we can't go to get it.'

He couldn't leave the scrape and move in the gillie suit across bare ground to the reed beds, then go into the water, wade to the mud spit and give the bloody bird a shove while binoculars were on him. He couldn't tug out the microphone because the cable would be out of the water and visible. He couldn't leave it there either, because that would break the disciplines. It would be the equivalent of leaving a semaphore sign that 'UK was here' when the microphone was found – as it would be.

'Then we stay put. Night follows day, right? We go at dusk.'

'That's a whole day to kill.'

'So sleep a bit, think of water.'

'We haven't got any.'

'You ever get tired of stating the obvious, young 'un? Apparently not.'

'I have to go forward and collect the stuff. I have to get ...' Badger didn't finish. Foxy had grunted, sighed, turned his back on him. Maybe it was nine hours before he could move out to collect the kit. He could reflect and evaluate. He could count the flies that swarmed above the scrim net. He could watch the goon in the plastic chair and wonder how a grown man had such an empty skull that he needed to sit with a rifle across his knees and watch a bird that was not much different from the herons Badger had seen in Wales, and half as interesting as the eagles he knew from Scotland. He could think of Alpha Juliet and holding her, of sending the call-sign code back for a meeting at the extraction point, and ... Time for interrogation.

Badger asked, What was our justification for coming here?

He answered himself: They said it was a rogue state and reckoned there were weapons that could nuke us, gas us, poison us.

Were we surprised that they wanted us out so shot at us and blew us up?

He answered himself, Gob-smacked.

Did no one question the inevitable bit? That clever bombs

might be provided by a neighbour and laid by a local? he asked. Did no one reckon it might be none of our business?

He answered: Plenty did, but they were ignored, out of step with policy.

Us coming here, was it done in my name? Badger asked.

He answered, and his words rang in his mind, Who needed the opinion of a moron? The big people knew what was in your best interest.

The big people – were they right to say that the man I fingered was our enemy?

Irrelevant. It's done, can't be undone.

Badger asked, Do I take pride in what I did – getting here, surviving here, fulfilling the mission – or am I ashamed?

He paused, then answered, A luxury and an indulgence. A waste of space – and breath. Done and impossible to undo. You are, Danny Baxter, the little fellow who is told what to do and does it. A man will have his head blown off and a good woman who clears minefields – who is dying – will be widowed. *You* are a part of it, and it's done in *your* name. Perhaps they'll give you a fucking medal to polish.

The sun was higher, and his need for water was cruel. His stomach was distended by the Imodium tablets, and the sores were suppurating. Their mission was complete ... except that the bird sat on the microphone. There was nothing else for Badger to look at. He could see the bird's back and fancied that a small loop of the cable had hitched up and was near to its folded legs.

The goon sat in his chair. A guard had brought him coffee and a plate of sandwiches.

Hours to kill before he went into the water. They had done their work and should by now have been with the guys in the Pajeros and Alpha Juliet. Congratulations should have been gruffly conferred and he might have had cream on the scabs and sores. He worked out which route he would take, and considered how dark it should be before he moved. The time dragged and Foxy slept. Then the pigs came and an otter passed by. Ducks were there, and coots, and the hours crawled. Badger's body was racked with pain. He knew each step he would take when he went into the water.

13

The sun had dipped and started its slide.

Badger moved. When he shifted it was better for some of the sores and worse for others. The flies still swarmed and it was not yet dark enough for the mosquitoes. He could see the face of his wristwatch.

'Not long, thank God,' he murmured.

'What?'

'I said, "Not long."'

When he was out of this hell hole, Badger reckoned, he'd want to shout. He would need – maybe at the airfield at Basra, or at Kuwait airport – to get up on a table in the spooks' office or in a coffee lounge and bawl the roof off, yell, scream, shake the walls. He'd shout in the shower, and louder in the surgery when the medic examined the wounds that the biting creatures had given him. He craved to shout now at the goon who sat in the chair, facing the lagoon and the still water.

Another thing he'd do, when he was back at any imitation of civilisation, was take the gillie suit, and the vest he wore under it, the pants and the socks, maybe even the boots, and chuck it all into one of those oil drums used as an incinerator, spill some fuel in and throw into it a lit roll of newspaper. They'd burn: the lice and fleas, ticks, ants and little red spiders. It would be sheer pleasure to watch them. Through the day, the thought of stripping off that gear and of the flames leaping in the drum had been companionship for Badger. He envied little about Foxy but his ability to sleep wherever and whenever.

He squirmed a little. Any movement seemed to set off the irritation of the insect bites. The next evening, those that weren't lodged in the gillie suit would turn up and find the meal ticket had moved on. His mind jostled between reality and fantasy, as it had done to kill the hours: fleas, ticks and ants who found the empty hide should consider themselves lucky not to have been in the suit when it went into the drum … Maybe he'd gone a little mad. Maybe 'a whiff of insanity' was part of a croppie's job description. But it was good to let the madness take hold because then anxieties about *it's in your name* and *it's done, can't be undone* were pushed back. He stretched his legs to the limit and his left thigh cramped.

'About another hour, then I'll be moving.'

'That so, young 'un?'

'The bird's awake, seems it's getting some life back.'

'Should be hungry. It'll need to go and feed.'

'The further away the bloody better, and him with it.'

The goon, the officer, had finally stood. He took a last cigarette and tossed the empty pack onto the ground beside the quay. He stretched and walked to the far end of the short pier, but hardly looked right or left. His eye line stayed with the bird. Now it was upright and seemed to test the ground and the debris under its feet. It stamped a little and eased the weight from one leg to the other. Then its head lifted, its neck straightened and it croaked, a harsh sound. The wings opened and flapped.

'Go on, you bastard. Get yourself up and away.'

It subsided again.

'Whether he's there or not,' Badger muttered, 'I reckon in an hour I can go and get it.'

'You got eyes, young 'un?'

'Yes.'

'See anything with them, or are they crap?'

Badger bridled. 'I can see better than you.'

There was a silence, and self-satisfaction on Foxy's face. The silence meant there was something he should have seen but had not.

Badger backed off. He was not prepared to beg for an explanation. He bit his lip and looked again. The bird hopped twice, then came down heavily. The goon was most of the way through the last cigarette and kicked the packet along the edge of the quay. For the first time in that long day he did not seem totally engrossed in the bird. The woman – the mother of the Engineer's wife – came out through the front door with a glass in her hand, went to the goon and gave it to him. They talked. The children might have had a meal or a story, might have watched the TV. They had been lively when they had come home from school in the middle of the day – one had played with a ball, the other a skipping-rope.

The shadows lengthened

The heat of the day dissipated.

His throat was dry.

Foxy was now fully alert and used his glasses to rake over the bird, the house and the goon. His view slid between the pier where the dinghy was tied, and the barracks and the bund line beyond.

'Where all this began . . . I said that in an hour it'll be dark enough for me to get forward and bring back the microphone and the wire. Are we arguing?'

'Heard you the first time,' Foxy said.

Many hours dead, one more to kill, then the journey to the extraction point.

He was breathing hard.

He threw down the cigarette, stamped on it.

There had been months of boredom in Mansoor's recent life, weeks of tedium that had seemed to drift on with neither high spots nor low moments, merely ordinariness. He had to stifle the panting. Tension gripped him.

He could not show it.

His back turned now to the lagoon, as the light fell and shadows stretched far behind him, he walked with a clipped, slow step – as if he had no further interest in what he had turned away from – towards the door of the house. He took the mother back her glass, then called to the kids. One was playing football with two of the guards and the other had a toy pram. He took them inside and tried to suppress any hint of authority in his voice that might frighten them; he gave no appearance of uttering an order.

With the children inside, he told their grandmother to keep them there, to wait two or three minutes and then to close the door. He thought her a strong woman – anyone of her age would have lived through the battles in either Susangerd, Ahvaz or Khorramshahr and would not have survived if prone to panic: they had been vicious battles with few prisoners taken – women had been killed, women had been raped. She should close the door, bolt it, move the children to the back of the house, but leave the radio or TV on in the front and not draw those curtains.

He walked now across the dirt, saw the cigarette packet, picked it up and headed for the barracks. He did not speak to the two guards who were still sitting in the shade of the trees. He would not have trusted either to act out the relaxed and typical scene – its tedium – if he had spoken to them of a security alert. They would have run round like headless chickens. He kept to the tree line where the shadows were thickest and would go to the barracks by the side entrance. He would not be seen and would give no warning to a watcher.

The bird had moved, had stood.

The cable had been pulled up and had made a loop. He would not have seen it unless his glasses had been on the bird. The loop had raised a length of black-coated metal, which he estimated at between thirty and forty centimetres long.

Mansoor had been in Iraq. He had been there during the difficult days when the troops of the Great Satan had attempted to load maximum pressure on the resistance and on the al-Quds teams sent to guide and advise. He and his colleagues had been lectured that they must always be vigilant against surveillance: no use of mobile telephones, no meetings with sensitive personnel outside buildings where they could be identified by the drones in the skies – the precaution of changing meeting points so that patterns were not established and bugs installed – and he did not think his eyes had deceived him. He had seen a loop of wire and a length of tube, and they were among the dead leaves on the mud spit. How long had the debris been wedged there? Two or three days, no more. Had there been, three or four days before, a sufficient storm to flush out those leaves and dump them high and dry? There had not.

He went into the barracks and woke the men who were sleeping, tossed those who played cards from their chairs and switched off the television. He told the armourer what he wanted and how many rounds of ammunition should be issued to each man. The light was slipping and the high lamp on the post by the barracks, where it ran alongside the far end to the quay, had lit. Evening was coming, and he had only glimpsed the loop and the tube. He did not feel confident enough to demand reinforcements from Ahvaz, and did not wish to hand over the matter to a more senior officer.

He could hear, down the corridor, the chains rattling as the rifles – Type 56 assault weapons, made in the People's Republic of China – were freed from the armoury's racks.

'Do I take a Glock?'

'You won't need one.'

'It'll be out of your weapon's range.'

'I won't be behind you.'

Badger spat, '"Won't be behind you!" Great. I seem to remember I half carried you here.'

Calm, authority, a voice used to being heard, not contradicted: 'You won't need a Glock. And I won't be behind you.'

'I don't understand what shit you are coming with.'

'It's about the quality of the eyes.'

'Mine are as good as any – all the tests show it.'

'It's what you didn't see, young 'un, when the bird moved.'

'The bird moved, didn't take off, settled. Perhaps, last light, it'll get a frog and—'

'You saw nothing. You don't need the Glock and I'm not behind you. You're not as good as you thought you were.'

'Which means?'

'I'm going forward – and I'll decide when – and I'll retrieve the microphone and the cable. Clear?'

'It's my job.' The calm fazed Badger, made him uncomfortable – always difficult to argue when a man refused to be riled. He wondered if the older man was capable of getting across the clear ground, through the reed beds, then wading fifty yards and doing the reverse trip. Badger reckoned, when they came out, he would be carrying two bergens and likely have Foxy hooked on his back. 'I'm going.'

'I make that decision.'

'No. I do that sort of thing. It's for me to do.'

'I'm going to tell you two things, and do me the courtesy of closing your mouth and listening. If I could square it with any last vestige of professionalism that I have, I'd get you to load up the bergens – now – and we'd sneak out. We'd leave in place the microphone and the cable. They're found and the balloon goes up. The effect of that is that calls are made and they end up in Lübeck, having been processed through every floor of the Ministry of Information and Security. He will be pulled out, meaning that everything we did was for fuck-all of nothing, and he can make some more of his little toys. Hearing me?'

'That they'll find the gear within the next twenty-four hours? A big ask.'

'You don't know what to look for – and you're blind. It's already been found.'

He might have been punched in the crotch. Badger folded. He could still see the bird and it could not have been famished sufficiently to go hunt another frog for itself, and the feathers on its back were pink from the last of the sun that would be down, buried, in the next fifteen minutes. Changeover time coming. The flies would have been exhausted after bombing the scrim net for all the daylight hours and the mosquitoes would have rested and would be hungry for flesh and would be coming out, hunting. He stank. His stomach was bloated from the tablets, could hardly make wind, and precious little of his body was free of the bites and the scabs had bloody grown and the sores oozed. He looked for the goon and couldn't see him, then for the cable and couldn't find it.

'Are you sure?' he asked.

'If I wasn't, I wouldn't have said it.'

'If they know about it, why you? Why is it your job?'

The shadows were on them and he couldn't see Foxy's face. He thought he heard a sob, not a choke, but something softer, sadder.

Foxy said, 'It'll take me a while, young 'un, to think through what I want to tell you.'

'I'm the one who's supposed to have all the answers,' Abigail Jones said.

Corky was beside her. 'Why haven't they come? That it, miss?'

'It'll do.'

'They have kit in front of them and can't retrieve it till dark. Would that fit?'

'Snugly, Corky. Hard, though, isn't it? More than us, they want out. We want it badly, they want it more. A whole day to wait.' It was unusual for her to muse in public, wear frustration on her sleeve. Normally she bottled such feelings, which might have been partly why she lived alone, when based in London, in her two-bedroomed maisonette. It cost her a fortune, and it would have been useful to have a guy living there, on her terms, to chip in with the expenses. She didn't know one she could allow to copy her front-door key, and have access to her space. A man who had been a senior clerk in the old Bank of Iraq now looked after the incidental finances of the station in the Green Zone. He had supplied her with the dollar bills she had given to the sheikh. He also did invoices for food, fuel, clothing, and could switch handwriting patterns effortlessly. At the end of the tour she would take a bucketload of cash to a respected dealer in gold and precious stones and buy items of quality but not enough to attract the attention of a Customs nerd. She'd be wearing them, looking expensive, when she came back through Heathrow, and would sell the stuff on in London. That way, Abigail Jones could afford a maisonette with a view over the river. She'd learned the methods on her first trip to the Gulf and on the posting to Bosnia.

It was coming up on her fast, the bug-out from Baghdad. Soon enough there would be the round of parties – her people, Agency staffers, the embassy, hand-chosen Iraqi army officers and intelligence men, and a general mêlée of multi-national spooks. The best part would be the knowledge, shared in a tight circle, of the 'taking down' of an Engineer. It would be a pleasure to know he was dead, and that she had played her part in it. There would be an office car from Heathrow to her home, and she would sign the docket and have the driver lift the bags to the front door, then fish out her keys and step inside her home, alone. She wondered if that evening, when they hit the Basra road, Highway 6, there might be a swap of mobile numbers, done in the lead Pajero, if he would be there – giggles about where it had been last time and . . .

Corky said, 'Because their gear is forward they need darkness to get it back. Shouldn't be long.'

'I have to say it, Corky – I'd have been tempted to ditch the stuff, and we'd have been out of here seven or eight hours ago, if they'd made good time.'

The crowd had gone, drifting away in the wake of the dust cloud from the big BMW in which the sheikh rode. There would have been what Corky called 'dickers' who watched them, but for now the wads of banknotes had bought emptiness round the perimeter. The light on her communications kit hadn't flashed. No message from London, no acknowledgement and nothing to tell her that a hit was on course. Nothing from ahead, from beyond a horizon of dirt and soft-coloured reeds.

They had spent their day cleansing the building they'd used. Now it was as they had found it, every fag end picked up and bagged. The vehicles were loaded with the sleeping bags and mosquito nets, the spotter 'scope for bird-watching, the spare weaponry and ammunition. She had done the rounds and was satisfied. She had paused in the doorway of the room where he had slept and seen a smooth part of the concrete flooring where the dust had been swept away by the motion of his hips. She regretted nothing.

'Only thing, miss, that's worse than ditching gear and leaving it behind is doing that to a comrade, your mate.'

'I think I understand that, Corky.'

'You don't, young 'un, interrupt or contradict me.'

Badger reckoned he was composed now, ready. 'Heard you.'

'You'll watch my back and I'll retrieve the stuff.'

Badger didn't interrupt, or contradict.

'I'll go in about fifteen minutes when the light's gone. It's not acceptable to leave the gear, so we won't. We get the stuff and leave the hide covered. We have to hope it'll stay that way long enough. The goon's watched the bird all day. He'll have seen the cable and now he's gone back to where his guys are. His own people are poor quality, but I doubt he is. You saw the limp, which means he's been injured – I'd imagine it was a combat wound. He may act with his own people or, more likely, he'll have sent for decent back-up from down the road. When it's dark, I'm going.'

Badger lay on his stomach and listened. The sun tipped the tops of the reed beds in the west, and the skies over the palm trees across the lagoon and the house, where nothing moved and few lights showed.

'When I come back to you, I may be coming fast, and we don't fuck about, young 'un. We're going for speed and distance, and I'm thinking that the first quarter of a mile is the critical bit. We manage that and use the comms. We try to find, without bloody drowning, the extraction point. That's what's going to happen.'

Still no contradiction, no interruption.

'I'll go forward to retrieve the stuff because I don't know what'll be waiting there. When I don't know, I won't ask anyone else to do what I should be doing. In case there are any misunderstandings between us, young 'un, don't ever forget that I'm in charge. I lead and I decide. You don't. Before you ask, my memory of the plug from the cable into the microphone is that it's a straight socket, not robust. Giving the cable a yank will do the business and they'll come apart – surprised the pigs didn't manage it. I'm going, and you'll have everything, the bergens and the rest, ready for a fast break-out.'

'You're not capable of it.'

'I'm going forward – it's the burden of leading.'

'Because getting a cable and a microphone back from fifty yards is dangerous? That's rubbish.'

'It's dangerous – which you'd know if you had eyes. And—'

'And what?'

There was a pause.

'It's better that I do it.'

'For Christ's sake, Foxy – you've got a wife, a home, respect. Love.'

'Wrong.'

'My home's police quarters, a dump. I'm a squatter. I don't have a woman.'

'You have Alpha Juliet and something might just—'

'You have a wife – a *wife*. A home and a wife. Why—'

'Try this proverb by John Heywood. He wrote it in 1546, which was the last year in the life of Henry the Eighth. "An old fool is the worst kind of fool – as in, he's marrying a woman fifty years his junior." Actually only eighteen years, but I'm the worst kind of fool.'

'What're you saying, Foxy?' Badger cursed himself. He knew what Foxy meant and should have buttoned his lip.

A quaver in the voice. 'There's an ex-policeman who trans-ferred a few years back to Ministry of Defence security at Bath. He told me. The guy she's with is in Accounts. All of Naval Procurement knows, and probably most of Accounts, but I was one of the last. She's shagging him. You want some more, young 'un? My wife isn't likely to be at home, sitting in front of the TV with a supermarket meal for one, yearning for me to be home. She's more likely to be in my bed, drinking my cellar dry with her legs spread. It hurts more than anything I've known. I pretend, I talk about her, and it's all lies.'

'You didn't have to tell me, Foxy.'

'They watch me at work, people who know I'm married to her and who've seen her picture. I know I'm drawn, pale, and they snigger that it's because I'm getting it night after night. But they're not from Naval Procurement – they know. It'll be their daily soap-opera episode. She goes to Bassett – you know what I mean? Wootton Bassett. She sees them bring the soldiers back from Afghanistan, up the High Street, and uses it to taunt me. These are "heroes", and I'm the old fool who gives lectures and is half buried in the bloody past. I think they have sex when she's claiming to be sick and doesn't go to work. She goes through Bassett on the way home. It's like she thinks you're not worthwhile unless you've earned a Bassett job for yourself. Don't ever forget it. No fool like an old fool. I think that's enough, young 'un.'

'You didn't have to.'

'I'm grateful to you for listening.'

The light had slipped some more.

The binoculars no longer showed him the bird, and the dim lights on the far side of the lagoon only outlined the walls of the house. The big lamp, the high one in front of the barracks, had come on, but there seemed to be no movement. Badger wondered if that indicated the guards' mealtime. He didn't know whether he had missed things he should have noted, or whether Foxy had lost his marbles through heat and dehydration. No one, before, had confided in him like that. He felt uncomfortable. They would get to Kuwait City together, then split and be in different rows in the aircraft. They'd head for the Green Channel separately, and cars would take them in opposite directions. He thought also there was an evens chance that he'd be going into the water to get Foxy back. No one, before, had ever talked to him with such raw unhappiness.

He wriggled over to lie on his side, his back to Foxy, and started to search in the bergen beside him for what he might need when Foxy went to get the microphone and the cable.

They had reached Frankfurt. There was fog over Hamburg and the airport there was closed temporarily, but would reopen within two hours.

She was exhausted. They sat on the silent stationary aircraft, with a full cabin of other passengers, and waited for the announcement that the pilot would soon be starting up the engines. They were now on their fourth leg. Ahvaz to Tehran. Tehran to Vienna with the national carrier. Vienna to Munich with the Austrian airline. Munich to Hamburg. She was tense and quiet. There was little the Engineer could do to comfort her, and old inhibitions died hard in him: he thought it would be 'unseemly' if he held her hand, with every seat occupied and a feeling that he was watched. Paranoia – what else? She was dressed as he had never seen her before. She had been given, in the toilets off the VIP lounge at Tehran's Imam Khomeini International, different clothes to wear, which she had protested she had never seen before. Now she sat in a skirt that reached a little below her knee, a thick cotton blouse and a solid jacket of deep green silk. It had been suggested that she no longer needed to wear a headscarf. They had Czech passports. She had whispered hoarsely, 'Do I have to renounce my nationality, of which I am proud, and my religion, to which I am devoted?' He had said, hesitantly, that concerned officials in the ministry considered she would attract less attention if she was not an obvious Iranian citizen. 'Is attracting attention so important? Are we ashamed of ourselves?'

Now her breathing was forced. He rang the bell above his seat, and when the stewardess came, he asked for water for his wife. It was brought, without grace.

Through the porthole windows, the Engineer saw that lights glistened on the apron and that rain spattered down. He looked at his wristwatch and made the calculations. He said that by now, at home, it would be dark. She swallowed hard and said she hoped the children were in bed and would sleep well and . . . There was little to talk of that could be, in any way, appropriate. His only previous flight abroad had been as the student who went to Budapest. She held on her lap a briefcase that contained a full digest of her medical history with X-rays and printouts of scans. Abruptly, the music cut and a woman's voice boomed. To ribald cheering, the plane shook as the engines ignited.

'I think it is an hour to Hamburg. We take the local train to the centre of the city, then the faster one to Lübeck.'

They were good boys, peasants, but not trained like the men of the al-Quds Brigade.

He had drilled into them three times what they should do, where each would be. They were from the ranks of the Basij and they looked at him with the sort of awe that was predictable in simple youths who found themselves under the command of a war veteran of an élite force.

They sat on the floor of the main communal area in the barracks and asked no questions but seemed to absorb what he told them.

'It was always the duty of the defenders of the state's frontiers to be on constant alert to prevent incursions from spies, terrorists, criminals, anyone who sought to undermine and betray the revolution of the imam. Perhaps, tonight, such a risk exists from our enemies, but we are ready.' He dropped his voice, a trick he had learned many years earlier when he had been attached to Hezbollah, in the Lebanese Beka'a Valley, from a Syrian intelligence officer. 'I could delay, do nothing, send for help from Ahvaz, and the senior men there would know I had no faith in you, that I did not think the Basij capable of confronting the spies, the terrorists, the criminals. If the threat is there, we will destroy it, and in the morning we will send for help from Ahvaz.'

He had made a plan, on the table using sand from a fire bucket and coloured sheets of cardboard, that showed the house, the quayside and the pier, the lagoon, the barracks and the bund line that ran along the southern edge of the water. He used grass where the reeds should be and blue card for the water. He had been through the plan three times. He thought his wife, working on the computer at the al-Quds camp, would hear him praised.

It was a simple plan, and he thought it a good one. The boys listened intently and held tight to their rifles.

★　　★　　★

The landfall was lost behind them, taken into the mist.

The ferry carried long-distance lorries and their trailers and was en-route from the Swedish port of Trelleborg, to the south of Malmö. It would reach its destination, Travemünde, after a 16.00 departure to sail across the Baltic, at 23.00 hours. It had been a close-run thing, but a representative in the Swedish capital had achieved, in eight hours, what had been asked of him. A passport had come from an embassy safe, and Gabbi's photograph put in place. He was Greek Cypriot, living in Norway and working in the haulage industry. He was a driver's mate for a shipment of bulk timber. To have created the passport, the biography and gained the necessary seat in the cab was a triumph for the representative, and the driver's mate had a foot-passenger ticket to return on the ferry the following morning or on the additional sailing in the late afternoon. He would not have said it himself, but the representative, who had met him at Malmö's airport, Sturup International, had told him that no other intelligence-gathering agency in the world could have put together such a package so quickly. They liked cargo ferries, from which cars and holidaymakers, passengers not connected with long-distance business, were barred. Customs and Immigration checks, and those for embarkation, were bare formalities and the representative had said it was a perfect route.

Gulls wheeled over him.

He stood at the rail, in fading light, and watched the long, straight line of the boat's wake. He shivered, sucked in air and used his tradecraft. He wore a long-peaked baseball cap, a scarf covering his mouth, and gloves, and would spend the entire sailing on deck, not inside where it would be noticed if he kept on the cap, scarf and gloves – and on deck no cameras would record him. The wind was brutal and there was sleet in the air, but he stayed at the rail.

The men were in place where he had positioned them. He was ready. Mansoor's last action was to take out from a shed behind the barracks a small inflatable dinghy capable of carrying four men.

He did not have night-vision – such equipment was kept by combat forces – but he had good eyes, and the moon would be up soon. He had good ears too.

He watched and listened. He did not know what he might see or hear, but he felt confident. If he saw and heard nothing, if he had imagined the loop of wire and the tubing on which the bird sat, then he had not called out a platoon from Ahvaz and could not be ridiculed.

The dark had come and sounds rippled from the lagoon, from the birds and frogs and the pair of pigs, and he believed – concentrating his gaze into the darkness – that the Sacred Ibis, a bird revered for three millennia, had not moved. It was the key.

He stood in the middle of the road and gave his memories full rein.

The road – once the northern trunk route from old West German territory to the German Democratic Republic – ran between Lübeck and Schwerin. East and West had met here, separated by a white line that had been painted across the tarmac. It was natural that Len Gibbons should come to the village that straddled the road and was called Schlutup.

He stared into the middle distance. The dusk was coming slowly and the wind whipped him. He saw only desolate heathland, where no trees grew: dead ground. It had been his place, his territory. He had been 'Gibbo' then, and considered bright enough in his twenty-ninth year to be sent from London to join the Bonn station and be given responsibility to run assets in the northern sector. Not as exciting as Berlin, but good work that would have been the envy of the peers who had joined the Service with him. The man had been codenamed Antelope.

Where he looked now there had then been the Customs post and the base from which the Grenztruppen and the Staatssicherheit had been deployed. It had been a complex of buildings, reached by a corridor between high wire fencing, a minefield, dogs, watchtowers – all the paraphernalia that awful state had needed to keep its citizens from flight – and now was levelled. The barracks of the border guards from which they deployed to the watchtowers and patrols in the killing zones had been flattened; the cells and inter-rogation rooms of the Stasi had been bulldozed. It had been Gibbo's ground when he had run Antelope. He accepted that a bewildering coincidence had brought him back to Lübeck, extraordinary and unpredictable. He thought that the Fates had dealt him a fine hand, the chance to obliterate old memories and wounds. A successful killing would wipe clean the slate of the Schlutup Fuck-up.

They had travelled – himself, the Cousin and the Friend – on separate flights. His had taken him via Brussels and then a connec-tion to Hamburg. The Cousin had also gone to Brussels, but had had a fixed-wing charter bring him on to the smaller airfield outside Lübeck. The Friend would have travelled in his own mysterious way, by his own routes and channels. Another hired aircraft, most likely, and documentation that would fool most experts and certainly would have been accepted by local officials. They had met by the canal in Lübeck, near to the gardens between the Muhlen and Dankwarts bridges and sat on a bench. The Israeli had smoked cigarettes and the American a small cigar – Gibbons had yearned to ditch his abstinence. The pieces of the jigsaw had come together.

It was where the story of Antelope had been launched by a pastor. The young Gibbons, fresh-faced and revelling in a job that brought him to the cusp of Cold War action, had been standing almost at the point where he was now and had been staring up that road past the barriers. Dogs had been leaping on their leashes at him and he would have been under the gaze of half a dozen pairs of binoculars. Three or four Zeiss and Praktica cameras would have been focused on him. He had known, then, so little of the East. He had once been on an *Autobahn* drive direct to West Berlin, and on the military train that ran across communist terri-tory to Berlin from Helmstedt in the West. There was little to learn from watching the empty road, the ground where no cattle grazed and the expressionless faces of the guards, so he had turned and walked down the hill.

The pastor had approached him, sidled to his shoulder . . . The pastor had a friend who was trapped in the East. There was a café down the road from which the old border had run and they had gone there. The Pastor had refused alcohol and drunk tea. He had talked more of his friend. Where did the friend work? At the telephone exchange in Wismar – where else? Trumpets had blasted, excitement had gone rampant. Soviet military formations were close, naval forces had moorings on the Mecklenburgerbucht to the north and at Rerik and Warnemunde to the east, and the telephone exchange had the potential to offer up the pouches of gold dust so coveted by the Service. He had filed his report of the meeting for consideration in Bonn and London. With reservations, and instructions for due care on Gibbons's part, Antelope had come alive.

He stood in the road and was oblivious of the traffic. The dusk had arrived sharply enough for the oncoming lights to dazzle him. Cars, vans and lorries swept past, the slipstreams buffeting him. He stood his ground. The jigsaw's pieces had slotted together well. He had remarked, without apparent humour, that the marzipan factor had clinched the location, Lübeck. The Americans had the database, and were able to name an Iranian-born neurosurgeon resident in Lübeck who practised there. He performed complicated surgery either in the city's medical schools, or in Hamburg; there was a home address on Roeckstrasse. The Israeli said that a man would come from Berlin and would have with him necessary equipment. The facilitator was in transit and would reach the city late in the evening, but had not volunteered details of the man's travel plans. They had gone their ways and would meet again in the late evening. Hands had been shaken. A course of action had been launched and would not now be revoked. They had stood, and the Cousin had remarked, off-hand, 'I say this, Len, with real pleasure. Your boys who went forward – that old guy and the youngster – they did us proud. My sincere congratulations to them.' He'd answered that they were unable to beat it straight out because there was kit to recover, but about now they would be on the move and, yes, it had been a first-class effort. He had not thought about them before or since the Cousin had spoken of them.

It was, in a sense, a pilgrimage that Gibbons had made to Schlutup, straight from that bench in his hired VW. There was a small centre, deserted, but dominated by the church where the pastor retired now, had stood in while the incumbent was away. Then there were residential streets of bungalows with a sprinkling in the gardens of the winter's first snow. He had parked and walked past a lake – ducks had scattered off it. He had remembered the lake, and there were concrete bunkers that British military engineers had put in place when the borders were defined and the barriers had gone up; the structures were now collapsed and overgrown. There was a paddock with horses. One was old, a skewbald, and had had its head down with tiredness. There was a trace in his memory of a young horse, roan on grey, possibly. He had walked onto the death strip where there would have been smoothed sand, firing devices and patrols, and the bankruptcy of the regime was on show. He had found an apple tree. A few rotten fruits had survived the autumn and he imagined the bored young guard, a conscript, far from home, who had tossed down a core and bred the tree. The death strip was now in the possession of hikers and dog-walkers, and he had met children out with a teacher, a man with Schnauzers and a woman with a yellow Labrador. He had walked along the strip where the fences and towers had been dismantled two decades earlier, where few signs survived to corroborate his past and the Schlutup Fuck-up.

The place, and Antelope, had governed his life, fashioned and shaped it, and had made him the man he was. So much had been expected – based on recommendations from young Gibbo – of a traitor working inside the Wismar telephone exchange. Few escaped their past, and actions of many years ago, and Len Gibbons was not among those who did. The pastor had introduced him – tantalisingly brief – to a man in the café, and had murmured that he was indeed from the exchange, allowed across the frontier to watch a football match between Dresden and Hamburg. Bundles of phone dockets were passed, with red crosses on them if they were between military units, and spools of tape. He had been with the man no more than fifteen minutes and had thought him brave, committed and, almost, a hero. He had seen him walk to the pastor's car outside the café and be driven away. The pastor then had access to the East and became a regular and reliable courier, until his health was said to have failed. The question was raised: did the Service have potential couriers in the East, men and women who could be trusted? The question had been answered, and the Schlutup Fuck-up was born. They were old wounds but had not healed.

It was an indulgence for Len Gibbons to have come here. He knew all the escape stories from this section of the Inner German Border: home-made balloons, gliders built in garden sheds, tranquilliser pills buried in meat and thrown to the dogs, then payment to the traffickers, who would attempt to hide a client under the back seat of a car, with sedatives for a child, and bluff a way past the border troops and the Stasi. One appealed to him hugely. The next day, while the hitman worked and while his own presence on the streets was unnecessary, he would go a little to the north to where he had walked for comfort and peace thirty years earlier, and he would think of Axel Mitbauer of the East German national swimming team. He would be there the next morning because it was unnecessary for him to witness a killing, merely to have a role in its organisation.

He turned away. A car blasted its horn at him, but he ignored it and began to walk to Schlutup's church, dedicated to St Andrew. He had spent much time there and thought that being there had sculpted him, made him the man he was – whom some hated, some despised and few admired.

'You didn't have to,' Badger whispered.

Low, but almost brusque from Foxy: '"Didn't have to"?'

'About you and her. You didn't have to tell me.'

'Don't remember telling you anything.'

'Please yourself.'

'I usually do.'

It was enough and couldn't be put off longer. Did he regret the agony-aunt session now? They hadn't spoken in the last quarter of an hour and the light had failed. Badger would have gone out, loosed the cable, then faffed about until he found the microphone. He would have come back, reeled in the cable and not thought too much about it. Foxy had made it a big deal: he had talked about danger, and the wire, and suggested the goon had seen and noted. God's truth, Badger had observed nothing that rang alarm bells, and he'd thought he had a good nose for them.

'And you don't have to.'

'"Don't have to"?'

'You don't have to go. I can do it.'

'Far as I'm concerned you can barely wipe your arse. What I told you to do, do it and be ready. Then we shift straight out.'

'It's done and checked.'

'Well, check it again.'

Foxy started the slow wriggle backwards, using his elbows and knees to move himself, and his head went past Badger's chest. Badger ducked – shouldn't have spoken, but did anyway. 'Is it her badmouthing you, sneering about heroes and Bassett, letting you know you're second-rate, that hurts?'

'You're out of order, young 'un, and taking a liberty. I don't remember telling you anything. Reckon I'll be about fifteen minutes.'

He was gone and Badger was alone. The space beside him gaped. He began to clear out the inside of the scrape and shove their rubbish into his bergen. He took out the Glock and could do the business by touch: he checked the magazine and felt that the safety was in place. He heard, very faintly, Foxy's crawl towards the reed beds. He pulled their kit out of the hide, lay in silence on his stomach and waited.

14

Foxy went forward. No call for farewells: no last handshakes, no clenched fists punching against shoulders. He crawled to his right, leaving the mass of dried fronds behind him, and used his finger-tips to guide him. He reached ahead to check for obstructions, anything that would break as he went over it.

The moon would be up later. Now it was not much more than a silvery wedge behind the mist that came up off the lagoon. It was the best time to be on the move, and the creatures in the water helped him: the frogs, the birds, and the pigs that had moved on and were almost up against the raised bund line that divided the lagoon beyond the beds. Croaks, splashes and grunts broke the quiet, and he felt good with the noises around him – not that the goon or the guards, who were more than two hundred yards away, could have heard the crack of a twig breaking.

He went into the reeds, and wriggled on elbows, stomach and knees. He felt a great stiffness in every joint. He had assumed it would be hard to get his muscles supple again after the hours in the hide, but hadn't imagined it would be this bad. He had never done such a long stint in a cramped lie-up before. It would make good copy in a lecture hall, with the same old curtains drawn as before: 'Sorry and all that, guys, but I'm not at liberty to tell you which corner of the world I was in – enough to say it was hot and the donkey shit smelt recent enough. I hadn't moved more than a handful of yards before every muscle had seized and . . .' Couldn't say where, but his audience would be total pillocks if they didn't understand he'd been behind enemy lines, alone, and going forward. Ellie was forgotten, and Badger, as was a monologue that had demeaned him. He thought about faces in grey light stretching away from him in an auditorium. A spotlight was on him and the men and women in the audience – from an infantry unit, a logistics regiment, the cavalry or the intelligence family – would listen to what he had to say. There would be no when or why but they would finish up with a good idea of what it was like to lie in a hide in the thick fabric of a gillie suit. At the end, there might be a little hint of what it had all been for: 'You won't, of course, expect me to break the Official Secrets Act, but out in that dismal wasteland, where the sun shines and we've had few thanks for the sacrifices made, we lived with the curse of the IED, that wretched little package at the side of the road, in the body of a dead dog, behind a kerbstone, and always cleverly made. Let's just say that one man who made the damn things is now pushing up the daisies. Thank you all for your attention.' He'd smile a little, and take a step back from the lectern, and they'd have learned about the privations of being a croppie. He would expect a brief moment of stunned silence. Then a colonel or a brigadier would stand and lead an ovation.

He was where the reeds thinned and there was open water ahead. He didn't know – hadn't asked Badger – how deep the water was, or how far he had to get from the hide to the mud spit. Most of the time he had held the binoculars in front of his face and the magnification had foreshortened the distance to the concealed microphone. The water lapped in his boots and saturated his socks. So damn tired because they had finished the drinking water some twenty-two hours before and his body had no more moisture to lose in sweat. His mouth and throat felt like sandpaper, and his muscles were slow, unresponsive. He was wading. He made each step forward with huge effort, which became greater with each step he took. He could see the back of the bird ahead, a slight blob of soft colour. If, then, Foxy could have found the cable, he would have yanked it.

He would have ditched the old discipline that said all gear should be brought out. He would have dragged at the cable, broken the connection and abandoned the microphone. The bird would have flown, spooked by the commotion. He would, too, have made some excuse about having the microphone on the way back, stumbling and dropping it. But he didn't have the cable in his hand.

Foxy would not turn around, retrace his steps through the glue that the mud made, and return to the hide – acknowledge failure, exhaustion, fragility – and ask Badger to do the job. He couldn't. He had opened his mouth and blurted stuff, made a fool, big-time, of himself. He struggled to get the boots moving again and the water level was past his waist. His stomach growled for food and his throat choked for water. He had weakened enough to spill the story of his marriage, then weakened further and done a volunteer. Now the mud was above his ankles and the gillie suit was a lead weight. The smell of the mud was in his face and he thought he was making more noise than the pigs when they had stampeded. Coots ran from him on the water surface and took flight, screaming.

Far in front of him, past the outline of the mud spit – his target – was the house with its security lamps, and away from it the old lamp-post on the quayside in front of the barracks. When he rested and was quiet, he could hear a radio playing softly in the barracks. It had been folly to say he would do it. He was bloody near marooned, unable to move.

He took another step. Abruptly he was in open water and the reed beds were behind him.

Foxy realised he should have discussed with Badger how best to approach the spit where the microphone was. He should have worked his way further to the right and nearer to the bund line where he would have avoided the deeper water. But he hadn't – he had been too proud.

Another step, and he lost his left boot.

He could have screamed, but took another step.

The church was a fine building of weathered red brick. Len Gibbons had walked down the hill from the old border-crossing point, past homes with gardens scoured by frost and a snow shower. He had hugged shadows and felt that the journey to

Schlutup was a demonstration of indulgence and weakness. He remembered it so clearly. Sometimes Len Gibbons would meet the part-time pastor, status never quite defined, inside the church, and sometimes outside. They would talk close to the old lifeboat, preserved and mounted on wood blocks above gravel, and the renovated clock, with gold-plated hour symbols and hands, would chime. The church of St Andrew had seemed a safe, reliable, *trustworthy* place to meet, and the pastor had seemed a man of integrity . . . The young Len Gibbons had seen an opportunity for advancement and had wanted to trust. He went into the churchyard and passed ancient headstones. There were lights inside, a final blaze of organ music. He had wanted to believe, and urged his seniors to accept his judgements. Many said later that it was against their better judgement that they had acquiesced, and had shifted the blame for the catastrophe to the slight shoulders of the young Len Gibbons. But an asset in the telephone exchange at Wismar was of prime importance. An old lesson had been learned; great danger hounded intelligence officers if they believed only what they *wished* to believe.

The clock struck the hour, the doors opened and light flooded out. The music was finished but voices came through the doorway, clear and bright.

He could not have said why he was there, why he had driven out from Lübeck to the place that had altered his working life and reconstructed his values. At first, the pastor had been able to travel into and out of the German Democratic Republic. Stories had been planted of elderly parents living behind the Curtain and to the south of Schwerin, and passes being issued by an official who was a long-standing friend of the family. The pastor had brought back printouts of the numbers called by units of the Soviet Army, Air Force and Navy. Useful? It had hardly mattered. The presence of the agent, Antelope, in such a sensitive position, was important.

He watched the doorway, and the first of that evening's congregation emerged and stood for a moment on the step, their breath vivid in the cold. They shivered but did not break off their conversations.

There had not been sufficient rigour applied to the asset and the story he had told. The pastor had announced, one May day, that he would no longer be able to travel back and forth into the East, as the official had been transferred. Was it possible that the asset, Antelope, could deliver his stolen material to a courier regarded as honest and reliable by the spy masters? Over the following five months, three couriers were identified, then names and addresses given for the pastor to pass them to the asset.

The man came out of the church in a small group, talking earnestly. Gibbons stayed back, let no light fall on his face. The silhouette of his body was masked by the trunks of the plane trees. Then, the man had always shaved closely and his hair had been cropped short. Now he wore an old coat against the evening chill, and his hair was in a ponytail held by an elastic band. His beard grew randomly across his face. The last he had heard of the man, still recognisable, was that he had started a sentence of six years' imprisonment at Hamburg's Fuhlsbüttel gaol. The end of the first week of October was Republic Day in the East. On that day the decision to arrest a pastor had been taken after joint consultation between British and German intelligence officers: the British in Bonn had gone cap in hand to their ally and grovelled on the failure of an operation that had cost the freedom, perhaps the lives, of four couriers. The information had been unwillingly accepted that Antelope was a sting operation conducted by the Stasi from Berlin, that a treacherous telephone operator in Wismar had never existed. Maybe the gullibility of Gibbons's seniors had saved his own skin. Others would have gone with him to the guillotine had he been too heavily punished for the capital crime of naïveté. He had survived by a thread, but was an altered man.

He did not spring forward to greet the man: *How the devil are you? Looking well, considering. In work, or dependent on hand-outs? Do you still believe in the clapped-out empire that faded to dust overnight? Was it all worth men's lives, the ones you condemned to years in cells or for hanging?* He watched the man, once a pastor, go out through the gate, and those around him laughed at something he said . . . All so long ago, but relevant to Len Gibbons.

That night, he had met the man, had walked away with a package in his hand, then lit a cigarette, which was the signal. German police, plain clothes, had come forward and snapped on the handcuffs. He had killed, in his soul, any last trace of humanity. He no longer believed in mercy. Now, a servant of the Service, he obeyed orders. It was why he had been chosen. All agencies in this field of work needed men like Len Gibbons.

He turned on his heel and went back to the car park where he had left the VW.

Foxy reached the mud spit. He had fallen once. The booted foot had tripped against the one that wore only a sock and he'd gone down into the water where it was shallow. His head would have gone under if his hands hadn't found the bottom, but water – foul-tasting – splashed onto his face.

He was there. Foxy sucked in air. There was a flap in his face, desperate. The bird's wings beat, but it failed to launch itself. There was no one for Foxy to ask what the fuck was happening. He had no idea why the bird just flapped its wings hopelessly. He might have figured it out if his mind had been clearer.

It gave a croak, like a death rattle, and he had his hand up, protecting his eyes from the wings. The cable whipped against his cheek. His fingers found it and ran along its length, then collided with the bird's body. It went into spasms of action, then was still. The beak hit him.

The African Sacred Ibis was snagged by the cable. He let go of it and the bird rose a foot off its perch. The cable tautened. The ibis croaked, and the claws on its feet came against Foxy's hands and ripped at them. The flesh tore. The beak came back at him, was used as a spear. He grasped the cable again and the bird hung from his arm.

Foxy lashed out with his free hand. It didn't matter to him that the bird was endangered, that its presence was a jewel in the eco-system of the marshes. He struck out, used full force. He couldn't see it beyond the vague shapes of the wings as they beat at him but he recalled a long, slender neck – he had seen it when the bird had flown in, and while it had cleaned the feathers on its chest. He knew that his target was the neck, and the blow was hard.

He was Joe 'Foxy' Foulkes: he had taken on the full might of an African Sacred Ibis, worshipped as a deity in the civilisation of the Pyramids and pharaohs, and had broken its neck.

It hung from his hand. There were no reflexes, no shuddering death throes. Foxy had killed it. It hung from the entanglement of the cable. It had seemed large when the wings had beaten, the feet slashed and the beak stabbed, but now it was shrivelled.

He heard only the lapping of water, maybe against the reeds behind him or away to his right. He heard rippling. Maybe the wind had risen with the darkness. He tried to pull the cable free but it gouged against his palm and the limp carcass prevented him tugging it free. Foxy knelt on the mud spit. He could hear his heart, his breathing and the rippling of water, but could see nothing except the patch of white, the wing feathers and the back of the bird. He started to disentangle the corpse from the cable. It would have realised it couldn't lift off and had sat still, hoping that the approaching beast would somehow avoid it. Only at the last, when the cable around its left leg and body had tightened, squeezing air out of it, had it reacted.

Foxy didn't know how long it had been since he had left the hide, not even how long he had been on his knees on the mud spit. A degree of tenderness held him as he slackened the cable and started to free the bird's body. He found the microphone wedged among the reeds and branches Badger had used to give it stability. When he had freed the bird he laid it down and put reed fronds over it. He took a deep breath, and slipped the microphone into the poacher's pouch inside the gillie suit. Then he began to coil the loose cable.

He didn't know why, then, the frogs' croaking was silenced, but he could hear the water rippling.

'Did you think it would be like this?'

'I did not,' the Engineer answered.

A shuttle bus had brought them from Hamburg airport, and they had been dumped with their bags on the pavement outside the *Hauptbahnhof*. The rush-hour crowds surged past and towards them. His experience of a European main-line terminus had been in Budapest as a student in his early twenties. He knew crowds from Tehran, but there he had command of language and the status of chauffeur-driven transport; Naghmeh flinched away from the press of people around her.

He had seen her gaze, mouth slack and eyes wide, at the prostitutes outside the station and under the street-lights, waists exposed in the cold, skirts barely covering their upper thighs, their faces painted. He had said nothing; neither had she. They had come inside the high arched building and loud music had greeted them. He had known it was Beethoven. She had asked why they played it so loudly in the station.

'It keeps away the drug addicts – I read that. Users of heroin do not like such music,' he had said.

'Why do they allow those people on the streets in a public place?'

He had studied the board, searched for the train going to Lübeck. She leaned on his arm, needing its support. He said it was the way matters were handled in Germany, France, Spain and Britain. She had snorted.

Had he known it would be like this?

He did not lie: he had not.

'Do they have no respect for us?'

'I cannot argue with them. We are here. We will take the train to Lübeck. At Lübeck we will go to the hotel. I can do no more. Would you have me rant at the embassy, call the ministry or the commanding officer of the al-Quds? Would you have me complain?'

She looked into his face but could not meet his eyes, which were locked on the departures board. 'We should not have come.'

He said what platform the train would leave from and started towards the steps going down to it, pulling their bag.

'Did you hear me? We should have stayed where our own God is.'

He told her how long it would be before the train left for Lübeck. It was heresy to suggest they might turn back, and they went slowly down the steps.

He had started on the return.

Impossible to go quietly now. Each stride forward taxed him to his limits. He gathered in the cable and looped it on an arm. Badger would maybe have to pull him the last few yards into the depths of the reed bed, and he might need, there, to flop and rest. Before he accepted any help, or rest, though, he would get there. He had a stubborn pride.

The light came on.

He was too exhausted, his mind dulled, to realise in the first seconds what the light that trapped him meant.

No panic, not in the first moments after the beam caught him. For Foxy, it was a time of innocence. To him it lasted an age but it would not have been longer than five seconds. Then the panic broke, and he started to thrash. He was up to his groin in water and the weight of the gillie suit tugged him down. He had one boot for a good grip in the mud and one foot with a sock that slithered and gave no purchase. He flailed his arms as if that would help him to go forward, but the mud had trapped him as effectively as the beam. There was shouting from close by, near to the source of the light, and answering calls from away to the right, where the bund line was.

The beam closed on him, and he heard the splash of paddles, then the guttural cough of an outboard. Foxy understood. A craft had been paddled towards him, then allowed to drift closer. If he could reach the reed beds there was a chance . . . He dragged his knees up, one after the other, tried to stamp, but the water held him, the gillie suit dragging, and the mud oozed deep beneath his feet. Foxy had done time in the Province, had been on attachment to 3 Brigade, Armagh City, in the ditches, the winter hides, and camouflaged in thick summer scrub, sometimes with an oppo beside him, sometimes reliant for his safety on back-up that would be 'down the road'. There was fatalism in all of those who did the work that the guys supposedly watching their backs would never react in time if they showed out. He wrestled with the suit, hitched it high and was able to get his fist into the poacher pouch. His hand locked on the microphone. He dragged it clear and dropped it. He felt it knock lightly against his knee, then his ankle. The bootless foot trod it into the slime.

The beam of the light was off him. He splashed, heaved, charged and thought each step the last he was capable of. The light raked the reed beds, then passed over the open ground and the hide. Nothing there. He didn't see Badger, crouched, holding the Glock locked in both fists for a steady aim. Neither did he see Badger in the throwing position to arc smoke or gas in his direction and towards the boat. He saw only a scurrying pair of coots, then a drake stampeding clear.

He dropped the cable.

His feet tangled with it, then he was beyond it, one more step. The light swept off the open space and across where the hide was, tracked over the water and locked on him. Two shots were fired.

In the Province, it had been taken as read that a croppie who had shown out to PIRA would be captured, tortured for information on his work, call-signs and targets, then trussed, blindfolded and put in the back of a van. It was assumed that the last sound they'd hear would be the scrape of metal on metal when a handgun was cocked, and that death would be 'a bit of a bloody relief' after what had gone before. That had been drunk talk, subdued and slurred. No bastard would find the microphone, and the cable had gone down. He'd lost sight of it.

Where was Badger, and where was the fucking cavalry?

Two more shots fired. Could have been from a rifle or carbine, but not a pistol. The light lit him well. The bullets were aimed close enough to him for a spatter of the lagoon water to come up and into his face. The engine had power and the light surged closer. He heard the shouting more clearly.

He should keep still. The voice was shrill and he sensed that adrenalin surged. It would be the goon, the fucking officer, who sat in the chair and watched the birds. Wrong: watched one bird. He took a deep breath and flopped down into the water. It came over his stomach, then his shoulders. His head went under and the foul stuff was in his nose, mouth and ears. He tried to push himself away and the light was over him.

Foxy used his hands on the mud and pushed the cable aside. He felt the air forcing itself free of his chest. It was lodged in his throat and he knew he couldn't hold it longer – and didn't have to.

A hand clenched hard into the gillie suit. It had been pathetic: he would have been, when he reckoned he had dived, no more than a foot below the water's surface, moving at the pace of a bloody great slug and kicking off a trail of mud. The hands had him, heaved him up, and his head was clear of the water. He heard laughter – not of humour but of contempt – and the breath spurted from his mouth. Then he cried out because he couldn't replace it fast enough and panted.

The light blinded him. He couldn't see who held him, who laughed at him. The laughter was killed, and the shout was of real anger – as if he had inflicted pain – the reprisal a blow to the side of his head. He didn't know what had aroused the anger and stifled the laughter.

A rope was looped under his arms and across his chest, then drawn tight, with a jerk that squeezed more breath from his lungs. The pain pinched, and another hand had caught at the neck of the suit. The engine pitch rose and the boat gathered speed. He was dragged through the water. If his head had not been held up by the fist he would have been swamped and gone under.

He wondered where Badger was, what he had seen.

The engine noise softened. He felt his feet, one in the boot and one in the sock, scrape over the mud. The engine was cut and the big light went out but a torch was in his face and he squeezed his eyes shut. He didn't know how much time was needed, but thought it would be many hours.

The rope was used to pull Foxy over the quayside and onto the ground. He was on his stomach, but a boot went into his ribcage and pushed him over. He rolled on his side and came to rest on his back, like a fish hauled by anglers into a boat, then left to gasp on the deck. There was a jabber of voices around him and rifle barrels close to his face.

Many hours were needed, and Foxy didn't know if he could give them, in Lübeck, enough time.

He sat in his office.

To those around him, who worked late in the treatment rooms at the university's medical school, he was Steffen Weber. To himself he was Soheil, in Farsi, the 'star'.

He did not need to ask. He had seen three patients that day and conducted lengthy examinations of their conditions. One he could help, with surgery, but two had conditions beyond his skill. He would deliver verdicts, positive and negative, the next afternoon. He had seen the patients, been in and out of the office and had gone past the desk his secretary used. She had left no note on his own desk to tell him: *Your wife rang and requested you call her. She will be at home.*

He had not telephoned her.

He could have; she could have; neither had.

What should he do? He did nothing. He did not call his home and tell her he was sorry for their argument, that he loved her, and their daughter, that nothing should be allowed to come between them. He did not ask her if she had had a good day, did not apologise for being late that evening. The consultant, a man revered in his circles, did not lift the telephone on his desk. She could have rung, spoken of her love for him and her gratitude for him working his fingers to the bone to buy their home, that kitchen, that life for her, and she might have said she accepted his judgement on what he could do and what he could not avoid. She, too, had done nothing.

Around him he felt a growing tension among his assistants, as if they believed him responsible for a situation in which an unidentified patient had obtained an appointment without the prior submission of X-rays and scans. It insulted them.

He could not respond.

As the hours of the day had gone by, his temper had shortened. The last of his patients – the forty-nine-year-old senior officer from the fire station in one of the Baltic coast towns north of the city – had been clearly beyond help, but the visit to the consultant, with his wife, would have marked a closure point from which the patient could prepare for death. The man should have been treated with courtesy, sympathy and understanding. The examination had been short, almost brusque, and the patient had been told that the consultant could offer a final verdict the next day but he should not hold his breath. He had noted that a nurse had stared into his face as the couple had left, showing rank hostility. The distrust proved widespread among his staff. The next target for a vicious response was a mild-mannered clerk from the fees office. There was a hesitant rap on his door. He waved the man in. 'Yes?'

'You have a patient visiting you tonight, Doctor?'

'Yes.'

'Facilities were originally booked for next Monday morning, but have now changed?'

'How does this concern your office?'

'The patient as yet has no name, address or—'

'Correct.'

'We have no record, Doctor, of how the account will be settled. We have no debit-card number, no banker's order.'

'No.'

'Please, Doctor, how will the account be settled?'

'I have no idea. We will wait and see. Now, fuck off out of my room.'

The clerk did so.

He saw Foxy on the quay and the guns pointing down at him. There were torches and a flashlight on Foxy, and the picture in the view-finder of the image-intensifier was pale green, washed out at the fringes and burned through on the focus point. Badger watched.

What could he have done? Could he have intervened? Might he have saved Foxy? He slapped it from his mind. Badger thought it indulgence to consider what he might, could, should have done. He had done nothing. It would have been dishonest to claim he'd liked Foxy, been fond of him, even that he'd acquired a degree of respect for him. He was not dishonest, never had been. To a fault, Badger spoke it like it was. He couldn't have said it was anything other than gut-wrenching to see, through the lens's soft focus, the man he'd shared the hide with – had slept alongside, had eaten, defecated and urinated next to, and from whom he'd been given the big confession of life with a woman who shagged around.

On the quay they were searching Foxy, had the suit pulled up, his legs, arms and chest exposed. Then hands seemed to go down into Foxy's underpants and scrabble there for anything hidden. The boots came at him to pitch him over, and they did his backside, searched in there. He couldn't have done anything because he had seen little of Foxy being taken – he'd been on the far edge of the clear ground, away from the hide, and had the bergens beside the small craft, with the air cylinder used to inflate it. He'd reckoned that he'd pull and Foxy would ride. He hadn't seen the light come on, and had become aware of the crisis only after the shots were fired. Then he had scrambled, leopard crawl, and seen the scale of it. There had been a light on the boat and more lights along the raised bund line out to the right. They would have had automatic weapons, assault rifles, with an accurate killing range of four hundred yards, and he'd had a Glock with an effective hit chance of thirty yards. He had seen, with the image-intensifier, Foxy ditch the microphone and the cable.

Badger thought they were like kids up early on Christmas morning. The goon strutted around his prisoner, and the older woman had come out of the house.

He went to work. The cable came easily. He drew it out of the hide and pulled it up from the slight trench in which it was buried. The main length came sparkling from the lagoon water and made a little wave, which was sufficient to draw in the bird's carcass. It was dead and he didn't know how it had died.

The old woman came close to Foxy, who was near naked now, on his back and exposed. She gave a keening cry and lashed out with a foot. Badger saw Foxy's head jolt. She managed one more kick before she was pulled off him. Two guards escorted her back to the house. He felt sick. He went on with the work. He coiled the cable, walked across the open space and down a shallow slope, hidden from the lagoon, and stowed it in the bergen that was in the inflatable. From the other, Badger took out his own Glock and the spare magazines, the gas and flash grenades. He didn't know what he would do with them. If Foxy had had a Glock, grenades and the gas it was unlikely he'd have made it back from the mud spit.

When there was no more to be done, he sat down. With the image-intensifier, he had a poor view of the quay, the buildings along it, the lights and the cluster of men standing over the stretched-out shape. He reflected on the scale of the catastrophe. A word kept coming into his mind: *deniable*. He saw a bruised face, bloodied, one or both eyes closed, the broken look of a man without hope, and a voice in monotone denounced a mission of espionage. Hardly, not at all, *deniable*. Time to tell the news.

He had the communications, made the link, said it like it was. Didn't expect a coherent answer from Alpha Juliet and didn't get one. Silence hung. After a few seconds he thought the connection had already been open too long.

Her voice, strained: what did he intend to do?

Badger said, 'Hang around, while I have darkness cover. See what happens, what shows. Not come out till I have to.'

They would be on stand-by for an extraction, but on their side of the border. The shit was in the fan, she told him grimly – unnecessarily.

'Plenty of it,' Badger said, and cut the link.

★   ★   ★

They read their stuff.

When the door of the ready-room opened, the co-pilot, Tristram, did not look up from the Old Testament. Dwayne allowed his puzzle book to drop into his lap and chewed his pencil stub. The side gunner, Federico, was deep in *Aerospace & Engineering* magazine, but shifted his feet without taking his eyes off the pages to allow the pilot to go to the door where a communications technician handed him the scrambled receiver-transmitter.

When he came back in, no more than a minute later, Federico again swung his legs to give the pilot, Eddie, space to pass. Dwayne and Tristram did not look up but waited.

The pilot said, 'We can go at any time from now. If we go it'll be into a hostile environment and close up against the border. There are two guys up there and right now it's a bad time for them. It'll be us that goes in for extraction – if that's the call – and the others do top cover. It won't be a night for sleeping.'

The pilot, his side-kick and the gunners looked up from their reading matter and sat taller in their chairs. They peered through the open window and could see the helicopters, floodlit, on the apron, fuelled and armed.

The old woman, the mother of the Engineer's wife, had shown them the way. When Foxy was dragged off the quayside, kicks were aimed at him. He was cursed and spat at.

All his senses reacted. He could feel pain from the kicks and the wetness of spit. He could smell the sweat on their bodies and the food they had eaten on their breath, and he could hear them. Not easy to understand because they used the vernacular of country people from the south, and he thought they'd have been recruited from farms and villages, not a major town. He was dragged. They had stripped the gillie suit off him and he was left with his underpants, socks and his one boot. The rope was still below his armpits and across his chest, burning the skin. He was on his back and more of the flesh was stripped raw on his buttocks and the back of his thighs. He reckoned the heel without the boot bled from the sharp stones embedded in the ground.

They thought he was a spy. They didn't know if he was alone. Some said he was because no attempt had been made to rescue him or to shoot at them as the boat had closed on him – they argued about it. He could measure the excitement of those who had taken him. Was he American, British, or a pale-skinned Iraqi – a Sunni bastard from Baghdad or a Kurd from the north? That was also an area of debate. The goon, Mansoor, strutted beside him. Foxy was bumped along the dirt track away from the house and he saw the old crow woman, in her black, framed in the window, watching. His eyes met hers and he read hatred. He felt a growing numbness to the pain.

It wouldn't last. He had seen men who had been taken.

The rope was tight on his chest and seared him. He had seen men taken in the Province, had stayed on in the hide and used his encrypted communications to guide in the arrest team. He had had image-intensifiers if it was dark and early on a winter's morning, or binoculars if it was summer and already dawn. All of those taken had been experienced men, well practised in the techniques of resistance. All would have regained composure within a half-minute of the door being flattened, the kids starting to bawl, the dog kicked into the kitchen by troops and the woman scratching at the faces under the helmets. All – by the time they were brought out of the door into the fresh air, frosted or already warm – were calm and their composure came from the knowledge that they might endure a kicking or a slapping, but not much worse, then go into the cages at the Maze and mark time until freedom came. He had not seen one Provo plead and weep – they'd had no cause to: they were not about to be killed or to undergo severe torture. They might have done at the start, in the old days when the war was coming up to speed and when 'robust methods' had brought PIRA to its knees, but a halt had been called long before Foxy's time. And he had watched once from a distant ditch, in the Somerset hills west of Taunton, the Quantocks, when an animal-rights activist had been taken from a cottage at dawn: he had burned a laboratory to the ground and driven the scientists working there close to suicide, but he had seemed to think little of going into custody. He had not been about to go through any hoop, and had known it.

It would be the goon's finest hour. What every security man dreamed of.

Foxy's head bobbed, rolled, and the back of his skull found stones to bounce off; some of the chips were razor-edged and slashed him. He could be thankful that the pain, for now, was numbed. He had done time with the interrogation unit at the Basra base. He had seen Iraqis brought in from the cells of the Joint Forward Intelligence Team – a separate camp within a camp, not answerable to local commanders: those men had known fear, and had cowered. They had had the scars to show what had been done to them. Foxy had sat at bare tables alongside the men and women who organised the inflicting of pain. He had been opposite prisoners who shivered and mumbled answers that he had had to strain to hear, then dutifully translated. It could, of course, be justified. The men under interrogation knew the inner secrets of the enemy's principal campaign weapon: the improvised explosive device. They might know who made them, who trafficked them, who laid them, and their answers could – a big word, *could*, often used by the team – save the life of a nineteen-year-old rifleman, a teenage driver's limb, or a lance corporal's sight. People said, from far away in the safety of London, that torture did not provide truth. Foxy would have said they were wrong. He would have claimed that, delivered as an art form and from manuals, it made a man cough. He was not given the freedom of the team's mess, but they couldn't operate without his language skills so he had been tolerated, given an occasional beer and told that information extracted and translated had led to the finding and defusing of a weapon, or a raid on a safe-house, or the interception of a courier.

He knew that pain worked miracles.

So Foxy understood what was coming to him. When his head twisted, lolled, he could see the barracks, and the light shone down from the street-lamp and fell on the door. The rope went loose and the goon called for a rag to be brought. A guard ran inside.

Foxy kept his eyes closed. There were Escape and Evasion people at the base and they said eye contact was bad, that being a sack of potatoes was best. They did the SERE courses, and talked of Survival, Evasion, Resistance and Escape. Few people listened closely because the lectures seemed to add to a nightmare – as they had when men talked in the canteens about what to do if PIRA took them.

Foxy's head was lifted and a hand tried to get into his hair for grip but could not, so grasped his ear, lifted, and the cloth covered his eyes. It was yanked tight and the knot hurt at the back. His ear was let go and his head hit the dirt. Then the rope bit again under his arms and he was dragged some more.

They went onto concrete. He rocked on a step after the top of his head had cannoned into the raised bit – that provoked laughter. There were no more kicks, and he thought that already he was less cause for amusement. There was a fucking cat that lived two doors down from his home, and it liked to come into his garden, pull down songbirds and disable them. Then it would walk away, interest waned . . . He was pulled down a corridor, then to the left. A door was unlocked. Predictable that they'd have a lock-up: for a criminal, a miscreant on a discipline charge or a foreign-born agent who was deniable.

He lay on the floor and the concrete was cool. He waited for the pain to start, and wondered how long, in Lübeck, they would need him to resist, and how long he could last. A match was scraped and he smelt cigarette smoke. It came close to him, closer, past his head and over his chest. The agony was on his stomach as the lit cigarette touched. Foxy screamed.

'He's switched the damn thing off,' she said.

'Well, he would, miss,' Corky said.

It was the fourth time she had tried, the fourth time she had been answered by a crackle of static. The weight lay on her shoulders. She would carry the glory of success and bear the burden of failure. It was a problem with these wretched deniables that the responsibilities were not shared. There was much that Abigail

Jones now regretted. She had agreed that he should stay in place, watch and learn, and not come out. Not shared, because there was no bank of bureaucrats in an open-plan office who all owned a piece of the operation. She had it on her own. She could talk only with her bodyguards – not her mentors or her think-tank: none of them had a degree from Warwick in politics, economics and modern history, or Six's training on grappling with the 'consequences of actions' or 'cutting and running on the Iran-Iraq border'. Had the problem concerned single-parent fatherhood from a distance, Hamfist might have contributed, and Corky if it had been regeneration of Provo heartlands (West Belfast). Shagger was big on the economics of hill farming, and Harding on trailer-park life.

It had been sharp of Corky, close to insolence.

She was curt, as if her control was ebbing: 'What does that mean, exactly what?'

They could play dumb, be on the edge. 'He would switch off, wouldn't he, miss?'

'Why? It's hardly professional.'

They had a fire in the scorched oil drum, and there was enough timber from the buildings to keep it burning. They were sitting around it, and she reckoned that the crowd would be back at the gate in the morning, and that the bribe chucked at the sheikh hadn't a long life. There was a grunt, almost derision, and she reckoned it was Shagger's. Was any of it professional? Any of it?

She said, 'It's unprofessional to switch off communications. Is that an area of debate?'

Hamfist was quiet, reflective: 'His partner's been taken, miss, and if he'd left the radio on, the chance is you'd have ordered him out.'

Shagger had a good voice, might have been to the standard a choir wanted: 'He'll go when there's nothing else he can do. Won't be before he has to. He'd think, miss, the most unprofessional thing he could do is to turn his back on a mate, go before it's time.'

From Hamfist: 'He'd have to live with it the rest of his days. And it would track him every hour of every night.'

She snapped, with bitterness: 'But there's nothing he can do.'

From Harding: 'It's like keeping a vigil, and it's what a man owes to another. First light, ma'am, he'll come. Forget about Badger, think about Foxy. Badger'll be good, but Foxy'll have it bad. How much time is needed in that German town? How much is that time going to cost him? The time Foxy buys'll come expensive. You with me, ma'am?'

She felt small, shrunken. They'd swamped her irritation at a radio being switched off and turned her attention, four-square, to the man with the trimmed moustache and the clipped voice, who was beyond reach and in need of prayers. The flames played on her face, and she shuddered.

15

He said nothing.

The questions came in Farsi and Arabic, in halting English and Pashto. English was always the last of the series.

He answered to none.

Who was he? What was his name? When the bedlam of languages had been used, and he'd answered none, he was beaten.

The goon did not use any special weapon: there was no hardwood truncheon, no lead-tipped baton, no leather-coated whip. The instrument was a length of builder's wood. Nothing refined.

His underpants had been taken off him. They stank. He thought they would be soiled. His boot, also, had been dragged off, but his socks had been left. They, too, stank, and were sodden and tight on his feet. He could see. The blindfold had been removed. The room had no window and a light burned in a ceiling recess, covered by a wire-mesh grille that soaked up some of the bulb's power so the room was in shadow. Two guards stood by the door. He reckoned they'd have been Basij, conscripted, part-time warriors and the lowest of the low – Home Guard stuff. They had automatic rifles that they held warily. There was a ring on the wall, and a rope was tied to it. The far end was lashed to his right ankle. He was no threat to them, and had no chance of escape. He couldn't have risen to his feet, bullocked past the goon, incapacitated or disarmed the two guards, opened the door and charged off down the corridor. Even so, the guards were tense, and armed. He couldn't have done anything because his arms had been pulled behind his back, and his wrists were bound together with farmers' twine, the knot tight enough to restrict blood flow.

He didn't answer, and couldn't protect himself.

When he was beaten, if he tried to wriggle away, get onto his side, face the wall and present his spine, his head or his upper arm was grabbed. He was pulled back and turned, with a boot, onto his back, his privates and lower stomach targets for the wood. Twice more he had been burned.

Who was he? What was his name?

There was blood on his face from the cuts on his cheeks below the eye sockets and from his nose – already broken, he thought – and from the split on his upper lip. He didn't answer, although he could have done. *I am a detective sergeant of the Metropolitan Police Service and currently attached to Box 500.* His name was *Joseph Foulkes, born 8 April 1960, married first to Liz and second to Ellie, two kids the first time round.*

It would have been hard to answer, though: bits of his teeth lay on the concrete floor and his tongue had swollen to double its size. Had he given his name, it was likely that more of his teeth pieces would have worked loose and had to be spat clear.

He said nothing. Defiance was natural to him. So far – cigarettes stubbed on his stomach, blows from the wood and kicks – he could absorb it. Bloody pain was manageable. It wouldn't last long. The defiance was melded with sheer obstinacy. He was of the age when kids had gone to see black-and-white films, had read close-print books and knew of Odette Hallowes, and Yeo-Thomas, who was the White Rabbit, and of Violette Szabo. He was of the age when he had passed judgement on naval personnel captured in the Shatt al-Arab waterway who had seemed to thank the bastards of the Revolutionary Guard Corps for the humiliations and mock-executions and had almost apologised for navigation cock-ups. The stories of childhood had stayed with him. The memory of news bulletins, and older men's disgust, was sharp. He told the goon nothing.

There was a table in the room. There had been a moment when the blindfold had been stripped off and he had seen a clean notepad on the table, with two pencils. The top page was blank. The bastard expected to fill it when he, Foxy, did the canary bit. The page stayed blank. It was his target to keep it so.

The goon did not know who he was. The goon moved on. What was his mission? He was asked in Farsi, Arabic and English, then again in Farsi and finally in Pashto. The wood was raised as he was given a second to show willingness to answer. He could see the wood but his eyes were misted and narrowed from the blows. He could have said: *A colleague and I are on a deniable mission to observe the home of Rashid Armajan, bomb-maker, and using techniques of surveillance as practised in covert rural observation post procedures, with a shotgun mike. We learned that Armajan and his wife were headed for Lübeck where she has a medical consultation and he has an appointment with . . .*

It was about time drifting, and he didn't know how much was needed. What was his mission? Maybe, already, the Engineer had reached Germany. Maybe, the following morning, afternoon or evening he would be targeted – if Foxy answered the question *What is your mission?*. Telephone or radio calls, text messages or emails would fly, and a shield would be placed in front of the man. He would be inside a security bubble and the chance would be gone. A shite-face would say that Foxy Foulkes had not delivered and there'd be a cock-sucker on hand to agree. Pig obstinate, and knew it because Liz – first wife – had told him so.

The wood came down. The goon bastard swung it with full force. Foxy's problem – there were many but the one topping the list: he didn't know where the blow would land and couldn't wriggle to avoid its impact. It was on the shins. No flesh there, just skin on bone. Done with the flat of the wood to inflict pain, not the edge, which might have broken the tibia. He might not say anything but he was near to screaming.

The wood was lifted again. Foxy looked up at the face. He didn't see hate, only frustration, and the wood came down. He jack-knifed because it was in the groin, on the shrivelled little thing that Ellie – two months back – had laughed at when he'd walked naked into the bedroom from the bathroom. She'd turned her back on him and gone back to her book. Great waves of heaving, wanting to vomit, convulsed Foxy. The wood went up again and he couldn't help himself. He no longer had the strength to cross

his legs.

...

Mansoor had no doubt that pain loosened tongues and broke resolve. The frustration: he did not know who he had.

Mansoor had assumed that the man now stripped and spread-eagled in front of him, unable to protect himself, would talk after a brief display of defiance. The message sent by radio to the security section of the IRGC had not identified him as an al-Quds Brigade officer, although his name was on it, and his location at the border post on the sector that faced the Iraqi town of al-Qurnah. There, *An intruder has been apprehended. Investigations are ongoing, and an officer with an escort should be sent tomorrow morning to take the prisoner into custody in Ahvaz.* All deliberately vague.

The frustration grew with each blow he struck, and the silence that followed it. Twice, he had crouched beside the bloodied face and put his ear near to where the front teeth had been battered out because he was certain the man would answer him. He had heard coughing and groans. He did not know the identity of the man, or the purpose of his mission. It would have helped Mansoor had he gone outside, into the evening air, taken a chair close to a fire that would disperse the mosquitoes, and not allowed anyone close to him. Had he sat, sipped some juice and calmed, matters now clouded would have clarified. He stayed in the room, used the wood again, and yelled the questions. Who was the man? What was his mission? No answer came.

It had been a dream of glory.

In the dream, men came from Ahvaz in the morning. A prisoner would be brought from the cell at the back of the barracks and given to them. With the prisoner there would be an envelope containing a full confession, listing his name, his operation, his controller. The light would be coming up. His men would be armed, ready, and he would tell the senior investigators who had travelled from Ahvaz that he had no more time to talk with them as he would now be making a complex search of the area and would conduct a thorough follow-up. In the dream, he was congratulated for his diligence, and shown deference. In the dream, later, further praise came from his own unit. He had dreamed of the praise, had even recited in silence the words of congratulation showering down on him.

He hit the man again, and again, and again, drew more blood and darkened more bruises. The control had gone from Mansoor's voice and the questions were no longer soft-spoken but shouted, high-pitched.

He lit another cigarette.

He started again, at the beginning, and asked the first question: who was he? As he had at the beginning, he dragged on the cigarette, let the tip glow, then bent over the stomach. His hand crossed the skin and went towards the hair. The urine ran. He pressed the cigarette down. The man screamed.

Badger heard him.

The scream – Foxy's – was a knife cut in the darkness. Before, there had been the dulled sounds of the frogs, the coots and the ducks, and of the pair of pigs that still rooted in the edges of the reed bed. There were sprints by water birds and territory scuffles, but Foxy's scream was a slicing wire, and another followed it.

He sat very still and very tense.

Badger would go when he had to. Then he would switch on his communications and make a last staccato call. He would give an 'expected time of arrival' at the extraction point, but not yet.

He expected that the dawn would come, the sun would poke up, announcing one more stinking hot day, and he would see – in the magnification of his binoculars – the arrival of military transport, lorries and jeeps. Soldiers, not these crap guys but trained men, would spill out and the search would begin, with cordon lines and others sent forward at the sides to give cover fire. Then it would be right for him to quit. He might also see, before he slipped into the water behind him and the forest thickness of the reeds, them taking Foxy away. He might be on a stretcher or might be dragged. If he was upright, his head would be slumped and a cloth bound around it. The blood, the cuts and bruises would be easy to see, even at that distance. He would have done what he could, stayed to the limits of obligation, and he would track back towards the extraction point. He was confident he would be ahead of the follow-up force – and two things were certain.

Two? Just two.

First: no bright young spark from the Prudential Insurance sales team was going to write a life policy for Foxy. A slow smile played on Badger's face. There had been a funeral for a CROP technique instructor, young, killed by stomach cancer, before Badger's time but still talked of. When the coffin had been carried out of a packed church to go to the crematorium, a crackly recording of Gracie Fields doing her hit song, 'Wish Me Luck As You Wave Me Goodbye', had played and the whole congregation had begun to clap. Many were weeping buckets, and they'd kept the nearby pub open till past midnight. It was said to have been the best funeral moment ever. Badger always smiled when he thought of it – he wondered if Foxy had been there.

Second: an operation was unravelling and its security had been breached. There would be *Cancel* flashes and *Abort* instructions. Humour was good for squaddies and croppies, fire teams and ambulance people, but outsiders – other than the psychiatrists – reckoned it offensive and loutish. They understood fuck-all.

The scream came once more.

Fainter, with a blunter cutting edge. That would not mean that the pain was less: it was a sign that his strength was down, and the fight was draining.

He had no protection now from the mosquitoes. The clear ground where the hide had been made was around four foot above the water level. Badger's place now was on the reverse slope from where the hide had been and his boots were just clear of the water. His body was on the incline and only his head, covered in camouflage scrim net, broke the top line. He had the binoculars with him and the night-sight. One of the bergens was against his boots and the thin rope, holding the small inflatable, with the second bergen in it, was round his ankle. He was ready to go, but not before the time came.

Badger remembered when he'd been a young police officer and they'd escorted ambulances into Accident and Emergency with knife and gun victims. He would see men and women sitting on plastic chairs in the corridors and know that behind doors or screens a life was ebbing; they were there to express solidarity, a sort of love and friendship. He would stay as long as he could. Badger could picture them now: they had politeness and dignity, and seemed grateful to him for his concern. There was often a bit of a choke in his throat when he slipped away to resume his duty, and went out of their lives. It was an obligation to stay – here and at the Royal Bristol Infirmary or the Royal United in Bath.

When he left, the location of the hide would have been cleansed. He had used reed fronds to brush around where the hide had been, smoothing out boot and handprints, then scattered the reeds they'd used for cover. He'd gone over the footfall into the reed beds, the clear ground that led over the rim where he was now and down to the water. The microphone was buried in mud and the length of the cable had been retrieved. The bird's carcass was beached in front of him.

There was nothing more he could do.

It had gone well – well enough for the spats between himself and Foxy to have been dismissed – and now it was worse than anything imaginable. Foxy taken. He would talk, of course he would. The screams he had heard said that Foxy would talk. In a week's time, or two weeks, Badger would be in his room at the police hostel and the TV would be on in the corner, half hidden behind a hillock of kit, and he would hear the voice, and look up, and Foxy's face would be on the screen. He would hear Foxy's confession in a flat, rehearsed voice, and would remember the screams. The screams said he would talk.

Didn't like him, did he? Never had – not that, now, it mattered much.

Foxy could barely see. The swelling under and above his eyes had almost closed off his vision. Difficult for him to hear anything because his ears had been beaten and sound was dulled. But he was lucid and could analyse the pain. The cigarettes were worst. The beatings were repetitive and taking their toll of him. What had made him scream was when the cigarettes scorched his skin. Each time it was done he had wet himself. They were the worst because his eyes could pick up the flash of the match and his nose could smell the smoke and he could make out the descent of the hand that held the cigarette. He had started to scream before the fag's tip had touched him.

An image came into his mind, was clear, then hazed and faded. It was of a small, cramped-up guy who had been brought to speak to them in the base outside Basra. He had been an expert on SERE, American. He wore US combat fatigues and had a flash on his left arm. It showed a shield and a double-bladed military knife, vertical, that cut two lengths of barbed wire. The man said, in a deliberate, far South accent, that the symbol was of Survival, Evasion, Resistance and Escape through the wire barricades of the enemy's gaols and territory. He had gestured towards the shield, and his right lower arm and hand had been missing, replaced with a multi-purpose hook.

None of the Brits had come into the lecture hall if they were off-duty; the only ones there were happy enough to have a minor diversion from their work. The others, who were resting or in the canteen, hadn't thought it worth their time. Foxy had been at the back of the small lecture hall and had listened, half awake; like most of them he had not rated it likely that he would face a situation where he needed to know how to Survive, Evade, Resist and Escape. The start was *clear*: the man, the shield insignia, the hook, and the introduction by a British officer, and the story of how a man, now in his mid-fifties and therefore a veteran, had lost an arm three decades earlier and learned enough lessons from it to have been kept on in the military well past all normal retirement dates.

The next part of the memory was *hazy*. Something about being the number-two flier in an F-4 Phantom and hit by surface-to-air near Hanoi, limping back and getting close to the DMZ, then having to bale out, and being captured with a broken arm and escaping before the local medics had fixed the damage. He'd been with the air-force pilot, walking and getting gangrene, then the pilot, using a sliver of glass from a broken bottle, washed in a stream, had amputated at the wrist. They had come through.

The guy was a primary expert in his field, but an audience had been pressed into attending and had thought what he said irrelevant to life in the base. What had *faded* was what the guy with the hook had said. Foxy struggled for recall, and watched for the fucking cigarette packet to be dragged out of the pocket.

The goon would lurch towards him, drag up his head, get a handhold on his hair or ear, then use the fist on his face.

Foxy struggled to remember what the SERE guy had said, but the memories were gone. The goon, Mansoor, limped. He could give no indication that he understood a word of Farsi. Nor could he give any hint that he had watched the house and listened to conversations. He was in the business of buying time.

The time between each cigarette seemed the most important measure. Not the hands of a clock or watchface, but the time between the last cough on the cigarette, then it being dropped and stamped on, and the next brought out from the pack, put in the mouth, the match scraping the box, sometimes failing to ignite, and the delay while another was pulled out. For fuck's sake, Foxy, not a fucking laugh. Get out of this fucking place and apply for the franchise to build a decent factory in these parts for the manufacture of good-quality matches, By Appointment to the Ayatollah. A business opportunity – for fuck's sake, Foxy. The goon had a bad chest and had had, also, a bad wound.

Much had been lost, but not the *logic*. The view Foxy had of him was difficult through swollen eyelids. The goon leaned on the table and gazed down at his prey, seeming to consider how next to inflict pain and win answers. The pages in the pad stayed clean, the pencils unused. Logic told Foxy that a military casualty was posted away and out of sight. No army unit wanted disabled men hobbling about the garrison. One had ended up with the work of overseeing the security of a bomb-maker, was posted in Nowheresville, off the map, and forgotten. Good name for him: 'Backwater Boy'. The Backwater Boy wasn't stupid, was switched on enough to pick up whatever signs had been left for him. He had made the trap and left it on a hair trigger. Foxy had gone into it, led by his bloody chin. Logic said, also, that Mansoor, the Backwater Boy, had been tardy in calling for back-up and the big fellows from Headquarters. He wanted to book into the limelight, courtesy of a prisoner and pages filled with confession. He might have allowed vanity to cloud good sense. But they would come. In the morning, they'd be there. He'd bought a little time, but didn't see how he could buy enough – needed a sackload of it.

Questions . . . Who was he?

The struggling English with a pupil's accent . . . What was his name?

Temper rising . . . What was his mission?

And logic said – because the big fellows were not already there – that he would be sweating on his failure. It didn't help him. It achieved confusion and scrambled clarity. Foxy clung to his silence. There didn't seem to be an alternative. He couldn't believe that any crap about being a bird-fancier, an anthropologist or an eco-scientist would carry weight. He'd been caught floundering in darkness close to the home of a security target, wearing a camou-flage gillie suit, designed for a sniper or for rural surveillance. He didn't know for how long he could bottle the admissions.

Not long . . . He was naked except for his socks. His arms were knotted behind his back; a rope shackled an ankle to a wall ring. He had wet himself and lay in a pool of it. Mucous stuff dribbled from his backside, and among the mosquito bites and tick sores there were the new burn marks from the cigarettes.

The packet came out, was shaken, the filter ends bouncing up . . .

Foxy cringed away and hugged the wall, twisting his stomach to keep his privates from the goon. He tried to remember what the man with the insignia on his arm – the knife and the split barbed wire – had said of *Resistance*. He could not, and struggled.

. . . and the filter went between the lips. The matchbox was out. Foxy felt the scream welling. He was pressed hard against the wall, which gave him no sanctuary. The match flared and the cigarette was lit. The glow came, the smoke billowed, and Foxy saw that the man panted, with anger, tiredness and frustration. He came forward and the bad leg trailed on the floor. There was rage in the eyes. The man, Mansoor, crouched. There was no pity. A big drag on the cigarette and the tip burned. Foxy didn't have the strength to fight, couldn't worm clear.

The hand came low. Foxy screamed before the pain, and the scream still had a voice when the pain flushed in him. He didn't think the scream was heard, and didn't care.

He'd come late, bad traffic on the road and a meeting that had overrun. The rain had been sluicing on the path. Ellie had shrugged, explained, and he did what was asked of him.

She'd told him where Foxy had stacked the logs when they'd been delivered last August, behind the garage, and she'd given him the basket to fill. When he'd done that, she'd told Piers to fill the coal bucket from the bunker Foxy had spent an afternoon putting together on the far side of the garage. She'd explained she would have done it herself but the rain had been so fierce.

The fire burned.

What had changed that evening was that his car was not down the side of the garage, near the coal and out of sight from the lane. He'd told her he'd have been half drowned if he parked where he had last night. She'd said it didn't really matter.

There was a meal for two from the supermarket on the table. Foxy didn't like pre-cooked, packaged meals and bitched if they were offered him and she hadn't cooked his supper. The bottle had come from the wine store Foxy kept topped up. A pair of candles had been lit. It didn't really matter if the Noakes woman from down the lane walked her dog last thing, saw the extra car and only a light on upstairs, or if the Davies man went out with his, saw Piers's car and knew she was being screwed. It didn't matter: Ellie wasn't staying.

Would she be going with Piers? Setting up home with him? Maybe, maybe not.

It was a decent Chilean wine: Foxy rated Chilean vineyards and said they were sensibly priced. They ate and drank; their tongues loosened. The storm brewed and rain lashed. Twigs, from the leaf-less trees, were blown onto the slates and rattled as they fell to the paved path. She said where she would be in the morning and that she'd already phoned them at work, pleaded the throat infection that was her most used excuse, and he'd asked whether they still bought it. She'd shrugged, like it wasn't important.

Piers asked, 'You going to pack it in, the job?'

'I might.'

'If you wanted out, you could transfer internally. I could – end up at the same place.'

'Like where?'

'Edinburgh, Preston, Plymouth? Two wages. Wouldn't be a place this size. You'd be shot of him.'

'Worth thinking about.'

'You could tell him. What's he going to do? Bite your head off? Just tell him.'

'When?' She gazed at the front door and the wind rattled it. For a moment she listened hard, as if expecting the crunch of tyres on the gravel. 'I might and I might not.'

'When? When he comes back? Do you know how long it'll be until . . .'

'Don't know when he's back, or where he is, or why . . . Are we going to talk about him all night? That what you want?'

Her eyes danced. The candle flames lit them and she held her glass across the table. He filled it and she raised it as if in a toast. It seemed a waste to have lit the fire, then abandon it. She left the plates on the table and led him by the hand to the stairs. She might stay with Piers and she might not. What was certain for Ellie, she would be on the pavement tomorrow, mourning the homecoming of a hero. It seemed important to be there each time, as if it was a drug. She was not ready to wean herself off it. She took him up the stairs and he was pushing her. They almost ran the last few strides into Foxy's bedroom.

Had there been a fly on the wall, it might have noted that Len Gibbons, at a corner table of a restaurant down by the Holsterhafen

– one bottle killed, another damaged – Len Gibbons said, 'I just cannot credit it. We set up a most successful operation, and the whole thing is put at jeopardy because one of them is idiotic enough to go back to collect a microphone and some cabling. I'm almost apoplectic. We get back, garbled, an interpretation that says it would be unprofessional and against regular procedures to leave the gear behind. Does it bother the Iranians if their DNA is on the bombs that mutilate our soldiers today, and have done for the last eight years? Of course not. They couldn't give a toss. One would have thought, given a modicum of common sense, that they'd have upped sticks and done the fastest possible runner, but that's not the case. Result: disaster. The other is hanging about there, can't do anything, and should have high-tailed it hours back. I tell you, whoever gets back from this is going to have their arse kicked the length of Whitehall. How could they do it to us? And I'll you something else, my friends, it won't be Len Gibbons – faithful dog in Her Majesty's darker affairs – who takes the rap for it. Sorry to rant, but I just cannot comprehend how such imbecilic things can happen ... Well, it's what comes of using increments, getting in casual labour. So much work done and all of it wasted.'

Had there been a bug in the socket beside the table, it would have been able to pick up and pass on the quieter tone of the Cousin. 'I would hesitate, of course, Len, to gainsay you, but, forgive me, I will. Where are we? We're in Lübeck. Also in the town, or soon to be, are Herr Armajan, the bomb boffin, and his *Frau*. Now, halfway to the other side of the world it's the middle of the night, and in some bog a group of peasant militia have their hands on a high-importance target. They get on the phone, are connected to some idiot manning the switchboard, who knows his commander will kick his balls in if he's disturbed. What I'm saying is that the local man will fail, during the night, to raise anyone of real import. That's the way those places work. Some time tomorrow morning, there's a possibility that it might land on the desk of a man who knows who Armajan is, where he is, who is responsible for him. Very few in VEVAK will know, and perhaps only one man in the embassy in Berlin. My analysis, if we get close tomorrow, we'll have a clear run in.'

Had there been a waitress who hovered at a table further out in the restaurant and who was blessed with sharp hearing, she would have eavesdropped on the quiet voice of the man called the Friend, who said, 'I'm more inclined towards the optimist than the pessimist, the glass half full rather than half empty. I think we'll have him tomorrow morning. We go, gentlemen, and stake out. We're old men but a bad evening in Lübeck is a good enough opportunity for old skills to be dusted off. I'm confident we'll locate him and then the opportunity will present itself for the strike. The morning, tomorrow, would be best. I would like to say that it's been a real pleasure to be a colleague of both of you. If we travel tomorrow, early, there will be no chance of farewells. I do it now, gentlemen.'

They went out into a bitter night: one to go to Roeckstrasse, one to the medical school on the university campus, and one to meet the ferry from Telleborg to greet a man considered expert at his work.

They came to Lübeck. It had been a slow train with stops, and the carriage had been crowded. For part of the journey he had stood and she had sat. For the first twenty-five minutes out of Hamburg she had been sandwiched between a black-skinned girl, who ate pastries, scattering crumbs, and managed to talk continuously on a mobile phone, and a youth with orange-dyed hair in a standing strip over the crown of his head, the sides shaven, metal rings in his ears and eyelids. When they'd left the carriage, the girl had brushed the remainder of the crumbs off her lap, but the boy had said something politely that she did not understand as he had stepped over her feet.

She was exhausted. He had looked for a lift to take her from the platform to the concourse, but there was none, and it had been a laborious effort for her to climb the steps.

The Engineer had sufficient English to ask for the hotel, at an information kiosk. He said that the hotel into which he was booked with his wife was on Lindenstrasse. The woman had been filing her nails and looked at him as if he were an interruption; she had pointed out where they should go, and passed him a small map with the street heavily underlined.

His wife asked if they could take a taxi, and he said it was, on the map, only a hundred metres or so . . . They should have used a taxi. She leaned more heavily now on his arm and the case squealed on its wheels. There was sleet in the air and a thin film had settled on her shoulders and in her hair. They passed a bench where a bearded old man sat with an opened bottle beside him, then statues to Wilhelm I and Otto von Bismarck. He did not know who they were or why they were commemorated. He looked again at the map and realised he had gone too far along the street and must turn to the right. She sighed heavily, blamed him.

They had to cross a major road but went with other pedestrians, and then they were in Lindenstrasse. The hotel was an old, white-painted building. He had expected something modern, glass and steel. He helped her up the steps and bounced the case after him.

They were at Reception. A girl was there, young and blonde. She wore a low-cut blouse and leaned towards him across her desk. He sensed Naghmeh's recoil. She queried his business there and he answered that he had a reservation. She asked, of course, in what name. *In what name?* He turned away from her. He felt a fool. He had to reach inside his jacket pocket, produce the Czech passports, flick one open and look at the name. He should have memorised it on the first flight, the second or third, or on the train. He grinned, played the idiot, and displayed the page of the pass-port that carried a name and his photograph. Both were taken, photocopied, handed back. Registration forms were given to them. He said, in his difficult English, that his wife was not well. He made a meaningless scribble on his form in the signature box, and asked for the key. It was given him, with a sealed envelope.

They took the lift, went along a corridor and heard TVs. He unlocked the door. It was an ordinary room, with a double bed and a wardrobe, a small desk and a television on the wall. A door led to a bathroom with a walk-in shower.

She looked around her and sagged. In the hotel in Tehran there had been a bowl of fruit and a vase of flowers because of who they were. Not here. He opened the envelope as she sat heavily on the bed. It was handwritten, not signed, on the hotel's paper, and said at what time they would be collected. He checked his watch. They had an hour and ten minutes to pass. Was she hungry? She shook her head.

She lay down, eyes closed. Pain seemed to cramp her. He had created her exhaustion, her loss of dignity, because he could not face life without her. Her breathing was ragged.

The Engineer found a magazine and read about Lübeck, what an old Hanseatic trading city offered the visitor and where marzipan could be bought.

How long could he hold out? Two more cigarettes had been lit but he had seen at least another six in the packet. He might hold his silence for the next and perhaps the one after that. Foxy didn't know how long his body would allow further resistance. Pain travelled from the burn points, the cuts, the bruising, the splits and the wrecked gums to his brain.

The goon, Foxy realised, was not trained. He had no experience of the dark interrogation arts. He understood only physical force and the infliction of pain. But men would come, elbow him out. They would have the same skills as the interrogators from the Joint Forward Intelligence Team in Basra, whom he had sat alongside and done 'terp' work for. All the basics were used by the Brit interrogators: sleep deprivation, stress postures, hours under the hood that was a thick hessian sack made for sandbags, slaps, kicks and shrieking in the ears. Big, proud men were broken by them, as he would be. Foxy would be broken, lose the resolve . . . so what had all the pain been for? Might he not at the start have coughed who he was, his name and mission . . . He had bought time.

He didn't know how much more he could buy. The man across the room from him, exhausted, breathed heavily. His eyes were wide and bloodshot. His fingers trembled and the wood shivered in his hand. Frustration, obvious, built in the goon's head. The next spate of violence would be uncontrolled aggression and Foxy would suffer ... knew it. But didn't know how long it mattered that his silence held. When he had been the interpreter for the JFIT people in Basra, he had never seen one of them show anger, lose their cool. He knew the routine: questions, silence, beating and kicking, silence, burning – knew it and waited for it. How long did they need? More than an hour? More than one more beating and two cigarettes? Foxy couldn't remember what the gaunt little American, with the hook for a hand, had said or what was called a 'code of conduct' with a prisoner.

He lay on the cell floor, trussed, roped to the wall and knew it was coming soon: a bad beating and kicking, and a burning.

A decision that only Mansoor could make: to give up on him and wait for the senior officers to come, or to try one more time.

He had been exhausted and had spent time leaning against the table – not sitting. He had been brought a glass of juice by one of the Basij peasants; the guard had had no stomach for what he had seen, the prisoner on the concrete floor, and had vomited his last meal. He had drunk the juice, which had refreshed him, given clarity to his thoughts. The two guards inside the cell, minding the door, had not spoken during the long hours. He thought they were terrified by what they had seen. He knew they looked away when he used a cigarette to burn. They did not interrupt the growing understanding he had.

When his mind cleared it was as if he had slapped his own face hard. He was, himself, exposed. He could have been naked, lain alongside the man on the floor. He could have been beaten and accused.

It was about the man he was tasked to protect – clarity came in a burst. A puzzle that had been obstinate slid into place: so simple. Some who examined his actions might find it hard to credit that mere enthusiasm, and vanity, had led him to create circumstances where the prisoner remained in his custody and not in that of officers with experience and rank. He was tasked to protect Rashid Armajan, a man of great sensitivity. He had pulled from the water an agent in a camouflage suit who offered no explanation and he imagined that the couple now travelled anonymously, without a cordon of guards. He thought he had put them at hazard – perhaps killed them. Some would say – suspicious men with the cold eyes of investigators – that the denial of information about the capture was itself an act of treason.

He could go from the cell, down the corridor and into his office, slap on the lights and telephone to the Crate Camp Garrison. He could demand to speak first with the duty officer, and then that the commanding officer, from the al-Quds Brigade, be woken and brought to the telephone. He would tell of an arrest made five and three-quarter hours earlier, a failed questioning, and no message of such an important matter passed up any chain and . . .

A great sigh. Almost a sob of desperation.

He dropped the cigarettes onto the table, pushed back the flap of the packet, flicked the box of matches and reached for the wood.

Mansoor believed that salvation, for him, lay with a confession from his prisoner. Then he would telephone the Crate Camp Garrison and get the connection to the duty officer. He steeled himself, took rambling steps across the cell, away from the table, and towards the man on the floor.

The scream went to the marrow of Badger's bones. He looked again to the east, away into the blackness of the night, and did not see the dawn's first softening. He would not go until that early light signalled the day's start.

Until his death, he would hear Foxy's screams, never be free of them. There would be, even in a deniable world, an inquiry – like a fucking inquest – and the questions would be asked by those who had never been in a shallow scrape, covered with scrim net and watching the movements of the guard detail around the home of a target who made the bombs that killed the guys brought back through the Wiltshire town. Likely the questions would be asked by those who had never gone without water when the thermometer hit 110 degrees plus, had never lain in a scrape and pissed into a bottle. They would not know of a meeting of a landmine clearance group with a terminally ill woman, who stood tall with courage, and did not see small kids kick footballs and ride tricycles, unaware that their mother would soon be dead but that their father would beat her to the grave. They would know nothing, but would demand answers to their questions.

Wasn't your job, Constable, to get Sergeant Foulkes into position, then support him in every way possible and do the donkey work of extracting him? ... You were aware, Constable, that Sergeant Foulkes was nearly twice your age? ... How was it, Constable, that you permitted Sergeant Foulkes, an older and less fit man than yourself, to go forward to retrieve the cable and microphone? ... Did you not feel retrieval was your job? ... Did you, Constable, pull your weight on this mission?

The shout came from deep in his chest, rose in his throat, burst from his mouth, was silent and hurled towards the coots, the ducks, the marauding otter and the browsing pigs on the edge of the reed bed.

'You weren't fucking there. If you weren't there, you don't know.'

He would stay until dawn, but there was no light yet, no smear, to the east.

16

It was like an afterthought. The goon, Mansoor, paced a path back and forth in front of where Foxy lay and lashed the wood against the wall. Once a guard had flinched away but had been belted on the shoulder and cried out. The pacing had gone on, the blows had been struck and paint chipped off the concrete. Then had come, no warning, the assault, and a new level of violence.

Different: the lashing with the wood first, not the questions. He tried, logic scrambled and confused, to anticipate where the next show would strike him, what part of his body. Foxy no longer had the ability to plot the patterns, and he couldn't wriggle, curl himself into the foetal position, because the blows were random.

There was more blood and another tooth had dropped from his mouth. The wood had to lash through the swarm of flies that now flew over him. Between each blow they came in to settle – each time bolder – on the newest wound.

How long? He was hit across the cheek. How long needed to be bought? The little air in his lungs was knocked out. He was bent and winded. He remembered . . . He was hit on his right kneecap, then on the left ankle. The beating had reached a frenzy and the goon grunted.

He saw light on the hook: the hook had caught the sunlight that filtered through the windows and spread across the auditorium, and Foxy remembered the words of a Code . . . and no one in the room had taken seriously what was said. There had been an almost audible titter, laughter behind hands, when the American had spoken of the Code. An awkwardness, because each time the SERE man had talked of the United States of America, there had been a pause and then the sentence had been remade with 'United

Kingdom' inserted; where there had been 'American' there was
'British'. It was resurrected. He could focus on a sentence that
survived the beating and the pain, had it sharp: *I am British,
fighting in the forces that guard my country and our way of life. I am
prepared to give my life in their defence . . . I will never forget that I am
British, responsible for my actions, and dedicated to the principles that
made my country free. I will trust in my God and in the United
Kingdom.* Some had said the man was naff, others that he spoke
crap. One had stated the little guy had the relevance of a Disney
cartoon cut-out . . . More blows landed. None of those who had
sniggered were here and hurt, not knowing how much time needed
to be bought.

He had gone through too much to lose now. The questions
came.

Different questions.

Shouted. *What did he know about the Engineer and his travel?*
Yelled. *Did he know the destination of the Engineer?* Shrieked. *Was
he with Mossad or the CIA or the British agencies?* Hoarse. *What had
he learned of the Engineer? What had he reported?* They dinned into
Foxy's head. Then there was quiet and he could hear the goon
panting. The two men by the door fidgeted, barely breathed, and
the hush settled. Foxy couldn't say where in his body there was no
pain. He heard the strike of the match, and it was repeated – as if
the first strike had not ignited the cigarette. There was the rustle
of the foil being loosened, then the noise of the pack dropping
back onto the table. Foxy knew there were more than two cigarettes in the pack and knew he couldn't survive, and hold to the
Code, if he were to be burned more than twice. He cringed. The
men and women who had used him as a terp in the JFIT team at
Basra had liked to say there was a certain way of breaking the
strongest man, the one most determined to fight.

The environment was where no hope of rescue existed, or
liberation, but most important was that no sympathiser was on
hand to witness and give comfort. The degradation of aloneness
broke men and women. Foxy couldn't feed off another prisoner
– no name necessary, no prior contact required – in an adjacent

cell who went through similar hell. He had no clothes to cover himself so his shrivelled penis and shrunken testicles couldn't be hidden. He could scream with the pain of the cigarettes and no one would come. So alone . . . He remembered the little man who had told the guys how they should behave, respond – and had been there, done it and survived – and could recall the flash of light on the hook, hear again the titters.

It was as if Foxy reached out to the stunted guy, hoped the hook would close on his hand and grip it. The whiff of the burning cigarette was closer again, and he awaited the pain. There was blackness.

In the blackness, no noise in his ears, no cigarette smoke in his nostrils, he couldn't see the glowing end coming closer to his stomach. And the sense of time, bought at such a price, was lost.

'You are Iranian. That is such a comfort to us. We need comfort . . . At home it is now past midnight and we were awake at five this morning, had hardly slept. Three flights, a train journey, we are so tired. It is a great comfort to know that we are with an Iranian, speaking our own language, and meeting a man who has the support of important people. Are you from Tehran? Or Shiraz – or, perhaps, Isfahan? We packed so quickly that I never thought to bring you something from home, some cake or—'

'So that there is no misunderstanding, I am now German. I live in Germany, my wife is German. I do not expect, ever, to return to Iran.'

'But if you are born Iranian you are always Iranian – and not one of the traitors, the monarchists, or we would not be here. I do not understand.'

'What you should understand is that I, too, have had a long day. I am tired as your wife is tired. I do not want to sit here and gossip about life today in Iran, and how many demonstrations have been broken up this week by the Basij, how much tear gas has been fired by the Guard Corps in Tehran this month and how many have been arrested on the university campus.'

'Why are you seeing us?'

'Because threats were issued, and I feared for my family. Because the regime in which you, no doubt, have a senior position, with influence, is known in Europe for its brutality and its long arm. We do not, whatever the blood connection of nationality, have any bond other than that I am a man of medicine and your wife is to be examined by me. You will guarantee the remuneration that is necessary under German practices.'

The consultant turned to the wife. He thought her an attractive woman, but bowed with exhaustion and illness. He reckoned her to be around forty. He smiled and asked her quietly, 'Is there a name I can use?'

'I am Naghmeh.'

The man interrupted, 'We have been forbidden to travel under our own names.'

He said, the smile hardening, 'I could ask what is the nature of your work that prohibits the use of your own name but it would shame me. You are not the patient. Your wife is. Naghmeh, you have brought documents, X-rays? Yes?'

His wife was about to answer but the man's intervention was faster. 'We have the X-rays from Tehran, from the university hospital, and the most recent haemoglobin checks from the laboratory. The name has been cut off, but they are ours.'

An envelope was passed. The consultant did not open it, but laid it aside on his desk. 'They are giving you steroids to combat the headaches?'

'They increased the dose for her last month, but last week when we went again to Tehran they confessed they were not expert enough to offer further treatment and—'

'Have they told you, Naghmeh, what condition they believe you suffer from?'

'They have not told her. They did a biopsy, then told us that new procedures were not possible and—'

He said, 'Would you, the anonymous man, wish to be afflicted with a brain tumour? It's about the size, I imagine, of a pigeon's egg. Would you care for it to be inside your skull? If not, please allow your wife to answer when I address her.'

'You insult me.'

'In Germany women are entitled to speak for themselves. Please . . . Naghmeh, the procedure is this—'

'You show me no respect.'

'I speak to my patients with great respect – and with little respect to those too frightened to give me their names.' The consultant, feeling he was now Steffen, and not Soheil, was conscious of victory, a cheap one. He said, 'Naghmeh, we will need to do more X-rays and also an MRI scan – that is, magnetic resonance imaging. It identifies the hydrogen atoms that lie in soft tissue, and will show what is there. For that you go into a scanner and lie full length. You do not move, very important, and will have removed all jewellery and metal objects. We are told then what we need to know. Naghmeh, I am being frank. We will look and see. I know my skills and what is beyond them. There are two stages. On the basis of what I find tonight I will know whether I can operate. I may believe I can but I offer no guarantee of success if I decide to do so. If I do not feel I have anything to give you, I will tell you so, with honesty. They are waiting for you. Maria will escort you. I assume, Naghmeh, that you do not speak English or German.'

She shook her head. He tried to smile, and reassure her. Why? They came through his consulting rooms at the university in Lübeck every week, people who were frightened, defiant, clinging to some small hope and trusting in him. Why? It was about the dignity of her face, about courage, and there was something of the Madonna in her features, as depicted in the statue that his wife and daughter knelt before each Sunday during services at the Marienkirche. There was depth in her eyes, and majesty. He had no mother or anything of her to treasure beyond vague memories from when he was a small child; a few photographs had been left behind in Tehran and would now be lost. He thought Naghmeh was how he would have wanted his mother to be.

The nurse came, took the wife's arm and led her out of the room. The husband began to follow but was brusquely turned away by the nurse. The door closed.

He said, with aggression, 'What work do you do in Iran that warrants such secrecy – or am I not to be told?'

Already he knew part of the answer. The man did not have the stature of a soldier. He was not old enough for high rank in the Revolutionary Guard Corps, and did not possess the chill in the eyes that the consultant presumed would be evidence of work in intelligence. When he himself had spoken of MRI scans and hydrogen atoms, there had been no confusion on the man's forehead. He was a scientist or an engineer.

'My work is to ensure the successful defence of my country – of our country.'

The patient would be gone for three-quarters of an hour. The consultant sensed he kicked an open door. 'Nuclear work? Are you a builder of a nuclear weapon?'

'Not nuclear.'

'Chemical, microbiological? Do you work with gases, diseases?'

'No.'

'What is left? What is so sensitive that you travel across Europe with false papers and have no name, with embassy people running errands for you? What else is there?'

'My wife is a good woman.'

'Obvious.'

'She heads the committee responsible for clearing minefields in the sectors of Ahvaz and Susangerd.'

'Fine work.' He had not expected to confide, was drawn to it. The Farsi bred confidence and suspicion ebbed. 'My father and mother were killed during the recapture of Khorramshahr. They were together, both doctors, treating front-line casualties. They were martyrs. Your wife does noble work . . . And you?'

The man hesitated. The consultant had noted his fingers, the stains. He asked the man if he wanted to smoke, accepted the nod – there were days when he himself yearned for the scent of fresh tobacco smoke – and led him out of the office, past the empty desks of the support staff. He took him to the back fire escape and let him out onto a steel-plate platform. A cigarette was lit and smoked. Sleet spattered their shoulders and ran on their faces.

'What do you do?'

A simple and unemotional answer: 'I make the bombs that are put beside the road.'

'Good bombs? Clever bombs?'

'I am told the counter-measures, electronics, are difficult, that I am ahead of the American scientists, and the British. I am told I am the best.'

'I understand why you travel in secrecy, then, and have no identity.'

'To what purpose to be the best while my wife is dying?'

'You are right to go in secrecy, without a name. Iraq and Afghanistan?'

'More sophisticated in Iraq, but we teach the Afghan resistance about basic devices. There, they do not need such advanced devices as I made for the Iraq theatre, my best work, but I have influence on what is used in Afghanistan.'

'And we see on the television many funerals in NATO countries because of the bombs beside the road. If they knew of you they would kill you. Do I approve, disapprove, of what you do? I do not interfere in matters I cannot influence. You should have no fear that I will allow any feelings to dictate my decisions concerning your wife. Thank you for allowing me to breathe the smoke.'

The moon was at its height and there was good light over the clear ground. Badger caught two rats on the periphery of his vision, extreme right side of the 150-degree arc he was capable of. When the moon went down past the horizon, Badger would take the two bergens and leave nothing to show he had been present, a witness to the place. The rats came from the reed beds to his right and straight towards him.

There were people who did not like rats, and people who were scared shitless by them. There were people who saw rats as vermin, to be slaughtered.

Badger did not feel strongly about them. They scurried towards him and the one behind gave slight squeaking sounds. He couldn't have said if it was twenty minutes, half an hour, longer or shorter, since he had last heard the scream – it had been weaker the last time. The lights in the house were out, but the security ones were lit. There was no movement beyond the pacing of the two guards who watched the single-storey building, and another guard – uniform and assault rifle – who sat under a tree. One more leaned against the outer door of the barracks. He could see the guard at the door clearest because he was in the range of the most powerful light, which beamed down from the lamp-post.

They came towards him.

The smaller one, greyer than the other, came to Badger's side, skipped onto the small of his back and was over him and gone without a backward glance. He had barely felt its weight. The other had a more russet coat and a longer tail, well scaled and as long as its body. It was down to training that Badger could observe and note every moment of an event that seemed, at the time, insignificant. They said that, in the world of the jihadists and of the high-value targets in organised crime, the little moments that seemed to hold no significance were those that might put a puzzle piece in place. Unlikely that there would be importance in the movement of a rat across his body, but he noted it. It came on a slightly altered track and had veered towards his shoulders. It came onto Badger's arm, went over his armpit with a brief sniffing stop, was on his right shoulder, then the nape of his neck. It paused there, was close to his ear, and there were the sounds, faint, of its breathing. It went forward, crossed the crown of Badger's head and a claw seemed to catch in the netting of his headpiece. It came down onto his forearms, then his hands, covered with camouflage cream, which held the binoculars. It stopped there, he saw the glint of its eyes, a yellowed amber. Perhaps it was aware, at that moment, of larger eyes watching it or felt the beat of Badger's heart, but it was not fazed. It moved off him and went by the image-intensifier, laid on the ground, and was gone. He had had many such encounters and—

The scream came.

It didn't matter to Badger that the sound was even fainter than before. He clutched the binoculars, had nothing else to hold on to.

The rats, together again, were exposed on the open ground in front of him and the moonlight was on them. The difference in colour was lost, their size seemed to merge and the length of their tails. Badger could have sworn that both rats stiffened at the scream, like it was a sound alien in their world.

He listened for the scream to come again, shared the pain a little. And he saw the faraway lights across the lagoon. Then his attention was taken by the rats: they had found the carcass of the bird. It was tugged between them and feathers flew. He watched them maul and mangle it, but another scream did not come.

He understood that he had fainted. He had no sense of time gone. His first image was of the bucket. The goon held it, swung it, and the water doused him. It would have been the second or third bucket because water cascaded off him towards a growing pool in the corner. It was aimed at his head and came in a wall towards him, splashing hard. It went up his nose, into his mouth and some forced a passage into his eyes, which were slitted with the swelling.

Foxy must have lifted his head. An automatic reflex gesture, not one he controlled. His vision was distorted, and although he looked up into the face of the goon he couldn't see the expression: anger, frustration, panic that his prisoner might have croaked on him? There was laughter. Foxy didn't know whether it was humour, or manic.

A barrage of questions was thrown at him, none new. He didn't know how long his fainting had protected him. The questions bludgeoned him, but he had no chance to reply. He thought the goon as weak as himself and . . . The cigarette was on the table, laid across the packet. A match was out of the box, and on the piece of wood he had been clubbed with. He would have fainted as the cigarette was about to be lit – as if he had been granted a stay, because the pain was not worth inflicting if he was unconscious.

Questions, and their answers: *I am Sergeant Joseph Foulkes of the Metropolitan Police Service. I am on a deniable mission put together by the Secret Intelligence Service of Great Britain. As an expert in covert rural surveillance, I was tasked to observe Rashid Armajan, the Engineer. I have a good working knowledge of Farsi and deployed a microphone directed at Armajan's home. I heard it said that Armajan, the Engineer, travelled to the German city of Lübeck with his sick wife. I relayed that information to my back-up team who are across the frontier in Iraq. I do not have a schedule, but in the next few hours an operation will be launched to kill Armajan in Lübeck. I am told that the killing is justified because of Armajan's talent in constructing the electronics of roadside bombs.* They were the answers he had not given, would give. There was a threshold.

He saw the cigarette picked up, the filter lodged in the goon's mouth. A match was raised and the box was lifted.

He had been to the threshold of pain, and could not go there again. Through the swollen lids, tears ran . . . They would be in an officers' mess, after dinner had been served with drinks: *What I heard, not for repeating, we had their stellar IED boffin in our sights in Europe after a clandestine operation on the Iran border, and that guy, Foulkes – self-styled surveillance wizard – was captured, interrogated, only had to hang on a few hours, keep his mouth shut, but spilled the lot. We didn't get the boffin, which would have been worth popping corks for.* A variety of the theme would have passed between beds and cubicles in a ward at Selly Oak where the military casualties were cared for: *What I was told, the bastard was damn near in the gun sight, but this guy talked* . . . And in a gymnasium at the place south of London where they taught the amputees a degree of mobility: *He talked a good talk about himself, but he spat it out and didn't give our people the time they needed.* That was what they would say and where they would say it.

The match flashed and the cigarette was lit. The goon had taken a handkerchief from his pocket, stained, and Foxy knew it would be used to wipe a place on his privates, make it dry, so that the cigarette was not extinguished by the water that had been thrown at him.

Foxy did not cringe and didn't attempt to bury himself in the angle between the concrete of the floor and the cement blocks of the wall. He knew the threshold would be crossed when he was burned. Everything he would say when the pain scorched his skin was in his mind.

The goon came close, limp prominent, and bent over him.

Foxy's arms were tied behind his back and his right ankle was fastened by rope to a ring in the wall. He was very calm. Foxy was on his back and seemed to spread out his left leg. It was as if he exposed himself further, was more naked, could not defend himself and was close to the cracking point, the threshold and denial of the Code's principles. He needed only to be tipped.

The goon was over him. Damn little strength left, and all of it so precious. The bruising, the cuts, the burns, the insect bites, now infected and raw, seemed less alive. He flexed the muscles of his left leg. The goon, Mansoor, crouched, and the handkerchief came down towards a place an inch or so above the hair at the pit of Foxy's stomach. His skin was rubbed hard, dried and smoke poured from the goon's mouth. The handkerchief went back into the pocket. The cigarette was taken from the lips and went down towards the skin.

It touched. Foxy reacted.

Didn't feel the pain, not that time. It took all of his strength, and more, from reservoirs he hadn't known existed any longer. His leg came up straight. Then he swivelled as best he could on his backside, the leg bent sharply at the knee, and the impact pitched the goon over. His weight would have gone onto the damaged leg and he stumbled. The cigarette dropped, he lost his balance and sprawled.

Foxy locked him with his leg.

He had no weapon. His arms were behind his back so he couldn't punch. His ankle was roped so he couldn't kick. He couldn't grapple with the goon's belt or get to his throat. He did the head-butt.

A young policeman, called to closing-time fights in pubs and late-night brawls in the streets, had learned that back-street combat was with a broken bottle or the bone at the front of the skull. He had seen it done, and known of the pain it inflicted on hard men. He held the goon close with his legs around the man's waist and slammed his head into his face. He heard the squeal.

The pub and street fighters he had seen as a young policeman went for the nose.

Foxy hit again and again. The guards had come from the door and his ears were gripped. The small of his back was unprotected and boots lashed the bottom of his spine. For a moment the goon's ear was close to Foxy's mouth.

It was hard for Foxy to speak through the split lips, swollen gums and the gaps where teeth had been. He spoke in good, correct Farsi into the ear: 'Who is fucking your mother tonight, Mansoor? Who is riding her? Is there a queue round the block waiting to fuck your mother? What do you do, Mansoor, while your mother is fucking the street? Do you get kids to suck you off?' Vile language, learned well. He was dragged clear and his face was hit. His leg was bent back so that the goon could be pulled off him. He knew those sentences, in Farsi, by heart and had often spoken them. It was under instruction by the interrogators of the Joint Force Intelligence Team, when he'd done terping, that he had mastered the lines guaranteed to make an Arab prisoner or captured Iranian lose any vestige of cool. The interrogators knew their work, and Foxy had seen its success many times.

The goon was on his feet. He flailed his arms to drive back the guards, his chest heaved and blood flowed from his distorted nostrils. His feet stamped, and the bar of wood was in his hand.

The first blow struck him – Foxy would have been at the threshold if there had been another cigarette – and more deluged down on him. He saw nothing in the cell. The table was gone, and the cigarette packet, the matchbox, the chair, the guards at the door and the light in the ceiling. There was darkness. Foxy no longer fought the beating. He was overwhelmed, and his strength had gone.

He saw, at the last, a man in a darkened street. He wore a black frock coat and carried a top hat in one hand, a cane in the other, and walked proudly. It was the last thing Foxy saw – and the man's head was lowered in respect.

★   ★   ★

'Still a good turn out, is there, Doug?' he was asked.

They were lucky in his village to have their own British Legion branch and the building was adequate, in need of repairs but the fabric was sound. Doug Bentley always came for a drink, or three, on the evening before a repatriation.

There were four beers in his round, all low-strength, which reflected the ages of his friends. He was standing and collecting the glasses to take them back to the bar. They couldn't afford a paid steward any longer, and it was accepted that glasses were reused, not clean ones for when each drink was poured. 'Still plenty there. It's held up well.'

'Third in a fortnight? Right, Doug?' From an old Pioneer Corps man.

He paused. 'That's right, the third. It's five have come through. Anyone want any crisps or peanuts?'

'My Annie won't watch it.' From a paratrooper who had done Cyprus and Aden. 'Upsets her. I used to watch regular, but I don't now. It's bad enough seeing it on TV, but it must be pretty difficult, Doug, week in and week out – for you, I mean. Yes, nuts, thanks.'

It wasn't talked about much in the bar – it was in the early days, but it had been running for three years now. Doug Bentley had carried their standard for all of that time, and no one else had jostled him for the job. He didn't talk about it unless another raised the subject of Bassett and the hearses coming up the High Street. He would have liked to share it more often – not just with Beryl – and the opportunity yawned. He took it. 'It's a damn sight less upsetting for us than for the parents and the grannies, the brothers, the nephews, all the kids from the family. One last week, a woman cried her heart out. All quiet except for her sobbing. It went right through to your guts. She was weeping her eyes out in the road. We all felt it, all of us in our line. What I remember, the week before, was all the hands that were just laid on the glass of the hearse, the nearest they could get to the coffin with the flag on it, and that same one – a big family and friends group had come over from the east of England – an older man shouted, "Well done, boys," for the two of them going through, and others picked it up. "Well done, boys," and they were all clapping. It gets in your bones, like rheumatism does. I wouldn't miss it. I say that in honesty.'

'I'm the crisps, the bacon ones, Doug.' He was a veteran of Suez, artillery. 'Do they really like it, being out there and having the world watching them? Nothing like that in our day – were popped down out there. Seems unnatural to me, like it's a spectacle – I'm not criticising you, Doug.'

'Fair enough. I was chatting with a sergeant from a unit last month, and he said the military and the families appreciate people being there – like it's recognition. Could be called appreciation. It's what's said ... I tell you, when they finish coming through Bassett I don't know what I'll do with myself ... Right, four pints, one crisps and we'll have two nuts.'

He went to the bar.

His neighbours thought it was morbid, and had told Beryl so, him and her going off so regular on the first bus to Swindon, the second bus to Wootton Bassett, and the long reverse journey. While he was down at the Legion, the night before a repatriation, she would be running the iron over his charcoal slacks to get a decent crease and brushing the shoulders of his blazer, the one with the Pay Corps badge. If she'd time she'd polish his three medals, and before he'd come out he'd do his shoes so that they gleamed and put the whitener on his formal gloves. Last thing, she'd check there were no crumples in the black ribbon she tied with a flourished bow at the top of the standard pole. His neighbours had empty, vacant lives and nothing to lift them. Doug Bentley thought himself blessed, and also that a hole, wide enough for a volcano to spew from, would be left in his remaining years when the repatriations stopped coming into the Lyneham base, and the hearses no longer drove up the hill into the town.

He brought the drinks back to their table, with the crisps and the nuts, and the artillery veteran asked if there was time for a cribbage game, and the paratrooper – who had last jumped thirty-nine years before – said there was; the Pioneer Corps man, who had spent two years digging latrines on tank ranges in Germany, agreed. Then they'd all three looked at Doug Bentley for his opinion: time for a cribbage game? They had to nudge him.

He'd been far away, just down the High Street from the Cross Keys, waiting for the command to raise the standards and . . . He said he'd enjoy that.

Len Gibbons watched.

Too many years since he'd been in a long raincoat and a trilby, hugging shadows in a doorway and listening: it was enough to make a new man of him. He saw the target, the target's wife and the medical man. They paused on the step and the sleet had eased. He saw also the car across the width of the pavement close to the kerb. The driver reached back and flicked open the rear passenger door.

The car had been there, on a restricted-parking line, all the time Gibbons had been in place, but the opening of the door, and the flooding of the interior with light, enabled him to see the driver: hardly a taxing identification. Dark-haired, swarthy, stubble, and a shirt buttoned to the throat without a collar. The car, an Opel saloon and granite grey, did not have *Corps Diplomatique* plates, but Gibbons reckoned it was an embassy vehicle. He had, of course, done his discreet walk round the block, the café across the campus street. The car was all the security offered to the target and his wife. He used a little of a veteran's tradecraft. He had good ears, could hear – Catherine said – every cat that came into the garden to scratch up the new bedding plants; he wore a hearing aid. It was a tip he'd picked up from the Provos: they had worn them when their hit teams advanced on potential attack sites and needed to know if they were covered by military or police guns; with an aid, they could hear better when a weapon was cocked. Gibbons had borrowed one from the technical people in the base-ment annex. It fitted comfortably, and was good value.

It was said first in German, as if the consultant made his point in that language, then repeated in English, but not in Farsi. The

consultant had personally escorted them to the doorway, and said,
'I shall look at the MRI and the X-rays overnight. Tomorrow I can
tell you what is possible and what is not. Please, your appointment
with me is at eight thirty. You understand that I can promise
nothing.'

He was gone. The target supported his wife down the one step
and across the pavement, then helped her into the car. Gibbons
saw her face, haggard, and saw the target's, numbed. The door
slammed, the light was cut, and the car drove away, no ceremony
. . . Incredible. The lack of security, the absence of a full escort,
astonished Gibbons. It told him that as yet the authorities had not
reacted to a capture in the marshes. Extraordinary. He didn't
follow the car and had no need to know where the target would
sleep that night. He didn't want to test the professionalism of the
driver and give him the opportunity to recognise a tail in place.
But it had been a satisfactory evening that nothing had blighted.
He had gained the knowledge that would facilitate a killing, its
location and time. His step was almost jaunty as he walked to his
own vehicle.

The Cousin was across the street and low in his car – it was near
to the bus stop where parents were waiting for their youngsters to
get back to Roeckstrasse. He attracted no attention. He saw the
big car, symbol of an individual's triumph in his chosen field,
sweep off the road into the driveway, the tyres scattering gravel.
The house was dark, obviously empty, and offered no welcome.
The car door was swung shut.

The breadwinner was home and no one greeted him. That
stirred a chord with an old warrior from the Agency: he was now,
most of the time, out to grass, and would only be dragged back –
not, of course, inside the Langley complex – when deniable work
was called for. In his own life, before she'd finally quit, there had
been times enough when he had come home late, tired, to find
she'd decamped to her mother, her best girl friend, her worst girl
friend, any fucking place. He understood. Woman trouble: couldn't
live with them, and couldn't live without them. He saw the

consultant, who hadn't drawn the curtains or dropped a blind, pace in a room on the ground floor and eat what looked like a slice of cold pizza. He had no more, there, to learn.

The Friend took the young man into the city, parked near to the cathedral, then invited him to walk.

Had he had a good journey on the ferry? He had. Had the weather been bad in the Baltic? Not a problem. How had he passed the long hours? On the deck, reading. What had he read? Just a magazine. That had settled the Friend's opinion that the spear-carriers of the state were best left to themselves, and that banal conversation was meaningless.

Both wore caps with deep peaks and both had scarves over their faces, but that was natural in the cold cloaking the city that night, with the threat of the first severe snowfall. They went past the cathedral, with its massive floodlit sharp-tipped spire. The streets were narrow, and old houses pressed close to them. Little side turnings went into brief cul-de-sacs with small homes that might have dated back four centuries, when his own country had been sand, camels and migrant Bedouin. He did not tell the man that the apparent age of the streets they walked was bogus, that the British bombers had come at the start of an Easter feast and destroyed the city with incendiaries: that Lübeck had been rebuilt with care for its history. They went by the modernised church of St Anne, a Franciscan building, and he stopped to gaze for a moment through an iron-barred gate that was unlocked and slightly ajar. At the end of a paved path was the door to a brick building and above it a dull light burned. He said it was the synagogue of Lübeck, and led the way.

At the door, he rapped the knocker, then pressed the bell. Feet padded noisily towards the door, a bolt was drawn back, a key turned. Sparse light fell on them, and they were admitted to a wide hall.

The Friend said, 'Anyone you see here is Russian. There are no German Jews in Lübeck, only Russians. Yeltsin sold the Jews to the German government. They are here and few speak German. They have made another ghetto, where we are. The few who know you are coming believe you are a political activist of the Jewish faith, hunted by extremists and needing refuge. A man will arrive from Berlin later tonight and bring . . . well, he will bring what you need. I will collect you in the morning. What you do and how is for you to decide. Then we get the fuck out. I shall be here at seven. Sleep well.'

The caretaker, an old man, had directed them to an office where a camp bed had been left, with two folded blankets and a pillow. The Friend touched the young man's shoulder. It might have been a gesture of encouragement, of support, but that was so obviously unnecessary. He had met – in his life with the unit – many men and women who killed for the state: some talked incessantly, others were silent, as if their tongues had been torn out; some were restless and fidgeting, others coldly still. All were touched by what they did, altered. Not this young man. There was a nod, a murmur of thanks, Hebrew spoken, then the back was turned, as if an audience was completed.

The Friend let himself out, walked away down the street towards Königstrasse and the *pension* where he would sleep, if it were possible. He did not doubt the killer would sleep well on the collapsible bed with the wire frame and the wafer mattress.

Harding said, 'They're back again, ma'am, and the numbers are building.'

She answered with irritation: 'I've eyes, I can see.'

In truth, Abigail Jones could see little beyond the broken gate. Shadows flitted forward. There was thin moonlight, which gave the shadows a wash of pale colour. The American had the best eyesight of them all and probably knew how many were armed with rifles or shotguns and how many had come back with clubs or the spears they used for fishing where the lagoons weren't drained. She should have apologised for her tone, did not. He did not seem to take offence. Maybe he understood how the tension swarmed in her head.

'We could be getting into problems when the time comes to get out of here, ma'am.'

Obvious. At that time, past midnight and well into another day, she alone carried responsibility in this little corner of the world – her sphere of influence. She had responsibility for herself and the four men paid to protect her, and for the situation further forward – a black hole of information, cut off from contact. She had helicopters on stand-by that could be utilised once only. She couldn't call up the Station in Baghdad and request guidance: *Sorry, Abigail, don't know what you're talking about. That's nothing that's flown across my desk. What to do? The best you can.* And neither could she make a sat link with London and the Towers. Call her home desk: *I'm just the lowly minion, the night duty officer, and I'm not permitted to contact your HDO before 06.00 local ... Anything I can help with, or will it keep for the next seven hours?* And she could hardly raise Len Gibbons, likely in Germany and leading the charge on a target: *No way I can contribute, Abigail, because you're there and I'm not, which means your judgement will be the one that counts. I'm sure whatever decision you take will be the right one and will stand up to scrutiny.* If she asked for the advice of Corky or Shagger, or went to Hamfist and dropped the matter in his lap, if she looked up into Harding's face and asked what she should do, she would lose authority.

'If they're in the way when we need to get out, we'll go over or through them – whichever.'

He shrugged, acceptance. These men were happiest when told what to do and when. They would drive hard and shoot straight, and it would be for her – Abigail Jones – to face the wrath of the aftermath. Fuck it. The problem was that the money had been handed over and had bought a few hours but not enough. The radio stayed silent and she had no word from forward, the other side of the border. She could rail, stamp, blaspheme and swear, but the radio stayed quiet. The number of men from the marshes now outside the gate had increased through the night, and by the morning they would again be boxed in, and the dollar bills were exhausted. It had been a short window and they hadn't used it. *Fuck it* was about the best answer she could muster.

'If that's what you want to do, ma'am, that's what we'll do.'

She smiled, grim. 'Settled, then. Harding, one of your Rangers told me when I first came here that his father had been with a paratroop unit of the South Vietnamese army and had done time as an adviser in the Central Highlands. The old guy had told his son that what made the early days there 'comfortable' was the certain guarantee that if he had been wounded or killed, heaven and earth would be moved to lift him out, on a stretcher or in a bag. Might take the services of a platoon that needed reinforcing with a company that then had to call on a battalion to be moved, and a flight of helicopters with a wing of air support. Whatever it took, it was available, and the guys on the ground knew it, so they were 'comfortable'. I can't go and get Foxy, and can't go as far as Badger likely is, but I'll sit on the extraction point for him – and we'll move before dawn whether I've heard from him or not. Like I said, "over or through them". A coffee would go down well.'

It was fraying, might already be unravelling.

'I'll get you a coffee, ma'am.'

'And we can—'

He interrupted her, almost kindly, like he tried to share – but could not. 'Packed and ready to burn some rubber. We'll go when you say, ma'am.'

'Hang him up, like a pig, hang him high.'

The officer gave his order. He thought his men barely recognised him. Not long before, he had led the killing of the Arabs who had crossed the frontier in search of abandoned military material, and his men – from the ranks of the Basij – had shown no hesitation or emotion in shooting, then digging the pits. They were frightened of him now. He was down on his haunches and his back was against the wall. The prisoner was on the far side of the table and chair. He realised that so much would have confused them. Why were senior men from Ahvaz not here? Why had they not been given custody of the man? Why had the man been beaten so savagely that he lay prone, unmoving? Why was the top sheet on the notepad clean, and the pencil laid neatly beside it? Why did they not know who they had captured and why had they not been praised for the success of their efforts? Why did their officer hug the floor and the wall, his head bowed? He was panting in spurts, and he clasped his hands together but could not stop them trembling. Why? The enormity of what he had done engulfed the officer, Mansoor. He did not turn towards the men who crowded in the doorway.

'Get him out. Hang him up.'

They hesitated. All of them, not merely those who had guarded the doorway, would have heard the prisoner's screams, and his own shouted questions, the thudded blows with the wood, and the water splashed from the bucket. The Basij were the arm of the regime: they broke up demonstrations against the authority of the state; they made the cordons on arrest operations; they kept back the crowds at executions; they enforced the edicts on dress and music. They hesitated to go close to the man. Mansoor did not know who he was. The man wore no chains, no rings; his one boot had no label and the one in his underpants had been cut out. Only at the end had he spoken and then with such insults that . . . His head was on his knees and he recognised the enormity of disaster brought on him by his loss of temper. The man, prone, terrified them.

His hands scratched at the wall. His fingernails gouged the plaster over the concrete blocks and he pulled himself upright. He went past the table and kicked the chair from his path. He stepped over his prisoner and did not know if the chest moved but he saw no bubbling in the blood at the mouth. He could not look into the man's eyes because the swelling above and below had closed them. As he bent to reach past the man and loose the rope from the ring on the wall, he saw the wounds and bruises he had inflicted, the scars of the insect bites and the sores that ticks had caused. The man had destroyed him. He felt – almost – wonderment, a confusion. His face was very close to the man's and he murmured the question he needed answering more than any other: 'Why did you come to this place, which is nothing? Why were you here? Why was it worth it for you?' He freed the rope, dragged on it and the man slid across the floor, through the blood, urine and water, on his back and buttocks. His other leg was bent but he did not cry out. Mansoor threw the end of the rope into the doorway, where it was caught by a guard, and gave his order again. The body was heaved past him and jammed in the door. It was freed, and then had gone down the corridor.

He slumped again, and his hands held his head.

Badger watched. Perhaps the coots did too, the frogs and the pigs. He hadn't slept, eaten or drunk. He had been without sleep, food and water for more hours than he could calculate. He was close to delirium, on an edge.

They brought Foxy out. There were two on the rope and they went at a good pace, Foxy bouncing along behind them. They had come out of the main door into the barracks and had turned towards the water. They went into the pool of light thrown from the high lamp. When a stone caught at Foxy's shoulder or hips and he got stuck, he was kicked free by those who flanked him. If his trailing leg snagged, he was kicked again. Badger saw it through his binoculars so he lived with each jolt of Foxy's head. One of those who followed kicked at Foxy whether he was caught or not; another bent every three of four paces to scoop up dirt and pebbles, then threw them hard at Foxy's face. Badger, with his lenses, could see the wounds, the cuts and the drying blood. He could also make out – among the scabs – the red marks where the skin had been burned. Now he knew why Foxy had tortured the dark with his screams of agony.

He looked for the goon, for Mansoor. He didn't understand why he, too, had not come outside.

But Badger – on the edge of control – understood little.

The rope was thrown up and looped over the arm of the lamp, a strip of ironwork welded to the main pole. Its free end was caught, tugged down, and a gang of them took the strain. Foxy's head bounced a last time in the dirt, then the body was up and clear. The light shone on the rope's knot around his ankle, and onto the leg that took the weight. The other hung angled and crazily. The arms were loose in the shoulder sockets and the wrists brushed the ground. He turned slowly, gently.

Badger watched.

He watched for more than a minute and saw some of the guards punch the body, or kick at the head. He waited until their tiredness took over and they drifted back towards the barracks. The shadow under Foxy turned slowly, then went back on itself. Badger went to the bergens and took from them what he would need. It did not seem to be a matter for debate.

17

He had sent the message, then, again, switched off the kit. He had no wish to be burdened with an inquest.

He went into the water. The gillie suit billowed out and the cool settled on his legs and stomach. He had done what he hoped was sufficient to protect the Glock and the four magazines he had taken from the bergens, and had sealed them in the plastic bags that the Meals-Ready-To-Eat had been packaged in. The gas grenades and smoke were in other bags and all were knotted tight. The moon did not now have far to fall and sent a spear of light across the lagoon. There was a place, near the far quay, where it merged with another, duller, strip. The silver and lustreless gold met and sliced through each other, near to the quay and about midway between the house and the barracks. The moonlight was stronger and uninterrupted, but the high lamp's was broken by the shadow, always spiralling, of the shape suspended from a rope.

Badger left behind him, on the far side of the clear ground, the bergens and the craft, ready and inflated.

He went into the water beside the wrecked carcass of the bird; the rats had left nothing worth returning for. He waded the first few paces and was soon up to his chest in water, the weapons, ammunition and grenades under the surface and deep in the suit's poachers' pouches. He had tried to evaluate what was ahead of him. Wasted effort. It mattered little. There might be a company of infantry, equipped with modern gear, all fed, watered, rested and alert, dug in with slit trenches and sandbagged sangars between the quay and the high lamp from which Foxy was suspended. He was on the move because he was obligated. It was no big decision for him. To retire, do nothing, to turn his back on

Foxy – rotating in the light breeze from the rope – he didn't consider it.

He came to the mud spit, lay on his stomach and used his elbows and knees to propel himself over the open ground, past the small mess of leaves, branches and dirt that he had used as the hiding place for the microphone. He allowed himself a brief thought that it had been well done. The arrival of the bird, the beautiful leggy creature that had so entranced the goon officer, had probably fucked them. If the goon's attention had not been on it, where he must have seen *something* – a flash of light off the gear or a kink in the cable – they would have been out, clear, and gone . . . He went down again into the water. Ducks came from the dark to his left, were spooked by him and stampeded across the water, struggling for lift-off. The noise seemed loud enough to rouse the dead. But they were up, away, the ripples subsided, and the dented silver and old gold lines of the reflections calmed.

The bed of the lagoon seemed firmer. It might have been an old waterway, and the bottom was settled, weathered down. While he was within his depth he made good progress. Badger had no idea whether he would be able to wade or have to swim. The natural light was good and he could see well. Of course, he could also be seen. He moved steadily and left a wake behind him.

Badger would have appeared, had he been seen while he waded or swam, as detritus that floated on gentle currents. He kept away from the lines of light thrown by the moon and the lamp. Through the scrim netting of the headpiece he looked hard for the guards, their positions, their readiness. One was near the house, close to the front entrance, and illuminated by the security lights; in his view was the short pier to which the dinghy was tied. Another was sitting on a plastic chair by the entrance to the barracks, rigid and upright. His head was still, as if in shock, and he was heavy-built. Badger thought he was the one who had kicked Foxy's head as they'd pulled him across the dirt. He hadn't seen the goon emerge from the building. Another guard was further to the right from the barracks, close to the raised bund line that bordered the lagoon.

Police lectures on surveillance in siege situations emphasised
that the numbers of hostage-takers must be logged. Why? Because
the Germans had screwed up big during the Munich Olympics,
and a lesson learned from mistakes of thirty-nine years before
were still valid. The point was that German police on the walkway
in front of the Israeli team house in the athletes' village had seen
the Palestinians in doorways and windows, and politicians had
gone inside the house, but no proper count had been made of how
many guys were there with their assault rifles. The rescue plan was
based on the premise that there were four armed men – but when
the helicopters brought the athletes and their Arab captors to the
military airbase where the shoot-out would happen it was realised
that there weren't four targets to neutralise but eight. A recipe for
a screw-up. Badger had counted three guards outside, which
meant there were five more inside and the goon. Important.
Strategies played in his mind . . . The first dawn light would come
soon.

An otter swam alongside him – ten or a dozen feet away – for a
half-minute and showed no fear of him, but then dived and he saw
it once more, fifty or sixty yards away. After it dived the second
time he didn't see it again. Coots skirted him but didn't bluster
away. It was good that he could walk on the bottom . . . Badger
imagined there had been trade through here a century before, and
a crossing point at the frontier for pilgrims and traders, smugglers
and traffickers. That was why the quay had been built, but then
the waterline would have been a yard higher, lapping near the top
of the structure.

The light on the water was brighter, the silver and gold mixed.
He moved more slowly. He now tested each step so that he didn't
slip and splash. If the level was up to his lower chest, he crouched
in the water and only his headgear would have been visible. He
could see Foxy clearly. The free leg was bent at the knee, askew at
the hip and seemed to wobble, as if with spasms of life, and the
blood had dried on the wounds.

It was what he might have called – like the retrieval of the microphone and the cable – the 'rules of the trade'. It was not about

emotion. He would never have said he was 'fond' of the old bastard, that he had enjoyed Foxy's company.

He went under. No warning. Took a step and plunged. The water was in his nose, his throat and his ears. He couldn't thrash, daren't. Darkness was around him and the cool of the water was on his face. He went down further, the weight of the suit dragging him. Pain built in his chest, and he tried to come up.

There was light. He gasped and trod water. None of the guards had moved or shouted . . . Foxy turned on the rope.

'When, miss?'

'When we have some light,' Abigail Jones answered Shagger.

It was the third time he had asked the question and been rewarded with the same answer. It was with increasing concern that Harding, Hamfist, Corky and he had watched the crowd of young men growing at the gate. Five minutes before, Corky had revved up the lead Pajero and gone onto full beam; the headlights had lit the crowd. It was predetermined that Corky would drive the front vehicle, Hamfist the second. Both had plotted how they would get through because there seemed to be junk – wood pallets, an old refrigerator, some rusted oil drums – blocking in the road.

'Thank you, miss. We're ready when you want it.'

'Nice to know,' she said evenly. Brutally, they had no more cash to shell out. They didn't have a hundred dollars between them, and might have needed a thousand to get shot of the place. 'Not yet, but soon.'

She swivelled, turned away. She thought it was too early. Here, they were boxed in but had the freedom to go for a break-out, could drive hard and straight. To hell with what they hit – a barricade or a host of shouting men – but if they were too early at the extraction point they would be stuck on a raised road with nowhere to go except back because in front was the border.

A bleep on the machine in her inside pocket. It was repeated. She hauled up her robe, flashing ankles, knees and thighs, had a hand in the pocket and the machine out. More bleeps and she was all thumbs and almost cut the connection. The screen showed the message: *Gone forward to get Foxy, then pushing for home.* Nothing else. She had gone back to 'Transmit', had powered in the necessary codes that did the scrambling and been rewarded with the ongoing whine that said the recipient of her call had switched off. She had stood in the darkness and howled in frustration – like a hyena or a wolf. Was she any more of a lunatic for howling than her Jones Boys? Unlikely. They'd have understood. They wore their T-shirts, with the band's logo, and were a brotherhood. They'd have known why Badger had sent the message, then refused to accept any call that might query it. They'd be rooting for him. And Abigail? There had been a depth in the eyes, a sort of abyss and going far . . . She said she hoped they would go, come hell or high water, in an hour, and it would be a few minutes before dawn. Shagger left her. She would be under the gun and care of Corky while he went back to the Pajeros to tell Harding and Hamfist that they wouldn't move for at least an hour.

If they made it out – *if* – they would disperse that evening, dawn the next morning at the latest. She doubted that ever in her life again would she recapture moments such as being with Badger; fighting off the marsh people at the oil-exploration compound; negotiating with the sheikh; running agents across a frontier, knowing them to be condemned by their greed; and seeing the two figures move off towards a hostile frontier; to have been responsible and to have waited too long outside the Golden Hour for their return. It wouldn't happen again. There would be a junior at Basra, sent down from Baghdad, who would collect the gear and spill out the advances on salaries for spending money. Another guy would be there from the security outfit, and the Jones Boys' T-shirts would go into a bin as first stop on a journey to the incinerator. Then they'd split. She had lived with them for many months, most of a year, and there would be a brisk, embarrassed handshake, a little formal. Then she'd be gone. It didn't matter if it were with Badger and Foxy, or if she was alone. They'd be on another flight to Qatar and then a shuttle to the Gulf. Hamfist would go to his room with six-packs and drink himself insensible in private. Corky would shop for rubbish and send parcels, costing a fortune in postal charges, to the woman in Colchester with the eleven-year-old son and the woman in Darlington with the five-year-old daughter. Shagger would walk on the beach and look at the sea, ring his bank to check out what he was worth, eat fast food and spend as little as he could. Harding would be in a six-star hotel, in a room with the curtains drawn against the sun. He would sit on the carpet in a corner and shiver. They did not, any of them, do ethics; they did the job. She would miss them, would never fill the hole they'd leave for her. In common, they were all rootless, playing at soldiers, refusing the advance of age. They were counterfeit . . . She loved all of them.

Shagger was back. 'All done, miss.'

'In an hour go for a broke, and find what we can.'

'Whatever you say, miss.'

'It's a shit world, Shagger.'

'Same as before, miss. Whatever you say.'

They would have to fight their way out to get to the extraction point. She made a further call, had the connection and voiced fears.

They sat, fully dressed, on the bed.

The Engineer said, 'He seemed an honest man.'

His wife said, 'A decent man.'

'A man to be trusted.'

'Without arrogance. He did not treat us merely as customers.'

'I was rude to him and will apologise. Tomorrow will be the start of the future, and we may believe again.'

'How will we sleep, waiting for a verdict?'

'We are in God's hands.'

'Always . . . It is a long night.' A smile, rueful and almost brave. 'For the children it is tomorrow and soon, for them, it will be the time we go to see him, to be told.'

'You should eat.'

The man from the embassy had brought them back to the hotel in Lindenstrasse, near to the *Hauptbahnhof*. He had seen them to their room. His eyes had roved over the interior and he'd glanced dismissively at their luggage, at what she had unpacked. Then he had gone to the window, flicked back the curtains, examined the vista and drawn the curtains again. He had remarked that they should not stand there with a light on behind them and look out. The Engineer's wife knew nothing of security matters: Why? she asked. He had rolled his eyes at the Engineer, as if he expected him to educate his wife. They should not leave the hotel during the night, should not be out of the room unless a matter of urgency demanded it: a fire alarm ringing. They should not answer the telephone or make any calls. Then he had left them. He would have been, the Engineer believed, from VEVAK, a man used to exercising authority. Most would have been fearful of him. The Engineer dealt with such men most weeks of his working year. He was called the Kalashnikov, the Nobel, and doubted that a bureaucrat from VEVAK had ever been so praised.

He said, 'I will make a proposition, Naghmeh, if you will listen to it.'

'We will go home,' she said. 'We will finish this and go home.'

'You will not listen – not now, not ever?'

'If the physician, tomorrow, tells us he is not a miracle worker, we start for home in the afternoon. Should he be blessed with the skills, we will stay for the operation. I will convalesce, and we will go home the first day he allows me to travel. I will hear nothing else.'

'Yes, of course.'

'We will go home, whatever time is left to me. To our children, our family, our work.'

'Yes.'

'I will not listen to any proposition other than that I can go home tomorrow or when it is permitted.'

A church clock chimed, the sound muffled by the double glazing of the window and the drawn curtain. He was sure he could have picked up the telephone and in his halting English, asked the reception desk to patch him through to the American consulate, likely to be in Hamburg, or the British. He could have made his pitch . . . but he lacked the courage, facing her across the bed, to make the proposition. He smoothed the bed, and saw her wince. He switched off the bedside light, lay back on the bed and held her.

Neither would sleep that night.

He was at the side of the quay.

It had been hard not to splutter and cough up water. The rope sang, almost a moan, as it twisted under the strain of the weight.

The dousing under the water and the struggle to regain the surface had cleared Badger's head, purging the exhaustion. He was alive to what he would do. First, he had moved, slow steps, on the bed of the channel, which was littered with stones, broken concrete and ironwork, to the outer end of the pier. He had ducked his head, keeping his mouth and nostrils above the water, and had loosened the knot that held the dinghy to a prop supporting the pier's planks. He had laid the bag with the Glock and the magazines on the single wood seat. He had worked his way along the length of the pier, under it, then had been against the side wall, made of rotting timbers and concrete blocks. He had allowed himself brief glimpses over the edge, had raised his head high enough to catch snapshots. The three guards hadn't moved. Foxy hung from the lamp-post and turned in the slight breeze. He did not see the goon or any more guns.

Ahead, there was silence. Behind him, he heard the night sounds of the birds, their splashes in the water, and the incessant frogs' croak. He coiled himself. His hands went down into the pouches and took out the plastic bags. He prayed that the water had not saturated the grenades.

A post held the timbers in place and had been sawn off some inches above the top of the quay. The high lamp left a small space of dense shadow beside the post. He stacked them there: the grenades and the short-blade knife. He coiled himself tighter, his hands on the top of the quay. He would be fifteen or twenty feet from where Foxy hung, forty-five or fifty from the guard who sat by the door into the barracks. That would be the closest weapon to him, and there were two others within two hundred feet that

had a killing range of more than a thousand feet. Behind the
entrance to the barracks men would have rifles close by. Badger
recalled what military people had told him. On the Brecon mountains, in Wales, he had been with paratroops; in the heather, gorse
and bracken of Woodbury Common, south Devon, he had been
with marine commandos. He had done surveillance on them to
challenge his own skills. He had won their respect and they had
talked to him late at night in their bivouacs. They were attack
troops and he was a croppie, a voyeur, who should not get involved.
The message paras and marines preached – rare for them to agree
on something – was that an assault would always achieve short-
term aims if launched at ruthless speed, with the devastating factor
of surprise. It had hardly seemed appropriate to a guy who made
his living by moving with a stealth that did not disturb wild creatures attuned to danger.

'What are you?' Badger murmured. 'Foxy, you're a stupid
bastard.'

He loosed the spring. He had bent his knees, straightened them
and, in the same movement, had heaved himself up with his arms.
His knees landed hard on the quay. Water cascaded off him, and
more sloshed in his boots. He tried to run fast, straight, but his
movement would have been that of a shambling bear and he was
huge and wide-bodied in the gillie suit. He threw the first of the
grenades, the 'flash and bang', which did the stun job, and saw it
fly forward as the guard fell back in his tilted chair, then pitched
sideways. He had dropped his weapon. There was bright light,
white, and with it came the deafening noise that ripped through
his headpiece, under the scrim. He reached the door, and the
guard was on his side, clutching his head. Badger threw two more
flash-and-bangs into the hallway, and followed them with two gas
ones. If they'd done their job they would have deafened, blinded,
induced vomiting and put up a smokescreen that men would
hardly want to charge through. Another, gas, went towards the
guard who had sat close to the house. He hurled two more flash-
and-bangs in the direction of the man beyond the barracks towards
the elevated bund line. He himself had some protection from the

scrim that dripped water and covered his face. Enough? He didn't know – would find out soon.

He kicked the weapon away from the guard at his feet, who was trembling, and heard volleys of screaming – in terror – from inside the barracks. He turned his back and ran – shambled – towards the lamp.

'You know what you are, Foxy? I'll tell you. An idiot.'

The hands hung a foot, or a foot and a half, off the ground, the head level with Badger's waist. Foxy was a bigger man than himself. Not even on tiptoe could Badger reach the rope knotted to Foxy's ankle. Nothing to step on so he jumped. He caught the leg. He had the knife in his hand and sawed hard at the rope.

He didn't know how long he had – seconds, not minutes. The gas inside the barracks would be good, but the one he had thrown towards the guard by the house would drift and thin, and the blind-ness from the flash would be short-lived. Seconds left, and he had no free hand to throw more grenades. He saw the rope fray.

There was shouting – might have been the goon, the officer, or one of the older guards.

They fell. He was on top of Foxy, and Foxy's body took the weight of his fall, but the wind went from his lungs and he had to gasp. 'Bloody idiot, you are. Nothing else.' Almost slapped Foxy's face. Badger tossed the last grenades: a smoke one towards the barracks, one flash-and-bang in the direction of the house and the other towards the last guard who had been outside. He hoisted Foxy onto his shoulder in the fireman's lift and staggered.

Badger couldn't run. He managed a crabbed trot, but not in the straight line that would have gone direct to the pier.

It seemed to him that he went slowly, and his back was exposed. He didn't weave because he sought to break a rifleman's aim but because of the weight of the man – the *idiot*. And Foxy was a *stupid bastard*. He expected to hear the drawl put him down, counter him with contempt, but heard only the shouting behind. He went down the pier.

He dumped Foxy. He dropped his shoulder and let Foxy fall into the dinghy. The impact shook the craft and water splashed into it as it rolled. He pushed it away from the pier and went into the water, which was at his waist, reached across, snatched the Glock that was under Foxy's back and pulled it out. He had the twine at the front end of the dinghy in his hand and struck out, best foot forward. He couldn't have said how long it was till he was beyond the flood of light from the high lamp, when the first shots were fired at him, not aimed but a wild volley on automatic. Then he was out of his depth and used the side of the dinghy to support himself, kicking with his legs and paddling with his hand.

'A fine bloody mess you've put us into, Foxy. *Idiot.*'

There were more shots and two came near. Water spouted in front of the dinghy. Badger groped behind him, didn't turn. He found Foxy's hand, took hold of it, squeezed the Glock into the palm and told Foxy he could help. He could either shoot back or he could use his hands to propel them. They had reached a fair speed now, and there must have been a suspicion, in Badger's mind, of hope. He thought his aim would take them close to the mud spit where the bird had been and across or around it. Then they'd hit the shallow water and wade through it, get over the open ground and reach the inflatable and the bergens, and—That was a lifetime ahead. There were no shots from behind him in the dinghy, but that didn't bother Badger and he thought Foxy would have enough nous, experience, to shoot when required to.

He knew it would not be long before organisation was regained behind him. He stamped his feet to get a better grip but the water was up to his chest and the bed below him was mud.

'It'll be bad, bloody, Foxy, when they get it together. How did you get me into this? Don't sulk on me.'

He could see the spit, and it wouldn't be long before they were organised.

With boots, fists and the butt of his rifle, Mansoor drove his Basij peasants out of the barracks and onto the quay.

It mocked him. He was an officer of the al-Quds Brigade, a veteran of undercover operations in occupied Iraq. He had been wounded in the service of the Islamic Republic and bore the scars of it. Neither his rank nor his experience could alter the enormity of what he saw. It laughed at him. It was a length of rope with untidily cut strands that hung from the lamp-post. It was well lit and the wind stirred it a metre above his head. There was more than a slashed rope to mock him. The pier, away to the side where the dinghy should have been moored, jeered at him, too.

Lashing furiously around him, Mansoor created a fear of himself that was greater than the fear brought by the grenades. He beat his authority into them, and broke off only once. He had gone into the communications room, made the link, sucked in the air to give himself courage and reported that a prisoner had escaped, that his barracks was under attack from a special-forces unit that had now retreated towards the Iraqi frontier. He and his men had beaten off the assault but the prisoner, believed a casualty, had been taken. He had cut the link and gone back outside. His eyes wept and his hearing was damaged, but the scale of the catastrophe inflicted on him ensured that Mansoor regained control. It could not have been otherwise: if he sank into a corner and shivered, he would be hanged as a traitor.

He punched hard, kicked hard, hit his men hard with the rifle butt. His voice was hoarse from bellowing, and he rasped instructions.

The jeep had come forward and he had to swing the wheel because the driver cowered from him. When the vehicle faced out into the lagoon, and the headlights were on full beam, he could see the low outline of the dinghy and a slight wake drifting from it. The outline was visible on the extreme edge of the light thrown by the vehicle.

The shooting was ragged. The Basij, as Mansoor knew, could not have hit a factory door with rifle fire at a hundred paces. There were the Austrian-made Steyr sniper rifles, which had been purchased by the IRGC, and the copy of the Chinese long-range weapon that was in turn a copy of the Russian Dragunov – the Iranian military called it the Nakhjir – but Mansoor had no marksman's weapon in the small armoury. He had only the short-range assault rifles. They emptied a magazine each in the direction of the dinghy. He snatched at one, took it from a guard. He had seen how the resistance inside Iraq fired when at the edge of accuracy. He wedged himself against the lamp-post. There was no optical aid to the rifle sight, only the forward needle and the rear V for him to aim through. He did a calculation and set the sight's range at two hundred metres. Squinting, Mansoor could see the dinghy. He thought a naked arm was draped over the side and made furrows in the water, adding to the wake, but he couldn't see the man who propelled it away.

He twisted the lever, went from automatic fire to single shots. It would have been a difficult shot with a Steyr or a Nakhjir; with an assault rifle it would be worse than difficult.

He had not fired seriously on a range, watched by an expert instructor, since before he had been sent to Iraq. He struggled to remember old lessons of grip and posture, the settling of weight. His breathing slowed, and he began to squeeze the trigger bar. Old memories died hard. He could recapture, with extreme concentration, everything he had been taught on the range used by the al-Quds élite outside Ahvaz . . . but Mansoor was no longer a member of that élite, the special forces. His body was damaged, he had not slept and his temper was torn.

Single shots, three.

The first was short, the second wide – no more than two metres wide and two metres short – and the target was a dark, low, hazed shape. He had to squint to see it with any clarity. He believed that the third shot bucked the shape of the dinghy and that it reared a little.

More orders, more blows and kicks. He put his men into the two jeeps. Their lights speared off past the barracks as they headed down the track towards the elevated path of the bund line flanking the lagoon. He reckoned he had scored a hit, that the jeeps would take him past their flight line, that he would block them . . .

It was the town that had shaped Len Gibbons, made him the man he was – not the man the neighbours saw on a weekend morning when they walked their dogs, pushed prams or promenaded on the cul-de-sac off the railway line between Motspur Park and Epsom.

He sat in his *pension* room, on Alfstrasse, with the lights off and the curtains open. He had worked the small easy chair close to the window. The drunks had dispersed and the late-evening stall-holders had cleared up and gone. He had used this lodging house on recommendation from a secretary in Bonn when he had travelled north to the town, on the business of Antelope, and had usually been in this room, with the same pictures hung over new but similar wallpaper, the same chest and wardrobe, but a more modern chair. He would have looked out over the same view, the same towers on the great church.

To the neighbours in the cul-de-sac – all of whom knew Catherine well and expected to speak to her if she was out at the front, gardening, or unloading the ecobags she took to the super-market – he would have seemed a remote sort of man, distant, with little conversation, but harmless. He might have been washing an unspectacular Japanese car, using an electric-powered mower on the small patch of grass beside the path, or retouching the paintwork. He passed the time of day with them, and would smile at their dogs or their children. His conversation would range over the state of the weather, the reliability of the trains into London, and the price of fuel . . . What did he do? They were accountants, salesmen, teachers, hospital staff, widows who stayed at home and retail workers. Him? Some dreary job in London. It was never quite explained whether that meant Work and Pensions or Environment, Food and Rural Affairs, but that was enough to satisfy them, and reason for him to be away on an early train on Monday and back late on Friday. Most would have thought it 'sad' that 'old Gibbons' slaved away at the expense of leisure and enter-tainment, and most would have felt sympathy for Catherine who existed alongside such a dull man with so limited a horizon. His suits were grey, unremarkable and bought from a chain, and his ties were those given him at Christmas. What did they know, the neighbours and the casual friends of his wife? They knew nothing. Neither did the mass of those going to work each day in the Towers have a more comprehensive profile of him. Some had made hobbies of archaeology or bell-ringing or whist, or did convoluted jigsaw puzzles, and thought themselves fulfilled. Len Gibbons successfully lived a local lie. Well hidden from view, there was a restless energy in him that a few recognised and some utilised. Now it contemplated, without qualm, the killing of an enemy. The Schlutup Fuck-up, in this town, had marked, moulded and fashioned him: he was a man in the shadows, but possessed of a ruthless determination.

He sat in the chair, listened to the great clocks of Lübeck. He did not think of the prevailing weather, or commuter train timetables, the cost of petrol, or holidays. He did not think of how Catherine would be that evening or whether his son and daughter prospered at their different colleges. He considered, instead, all that had been done to guarantee the death of a man. He thought enough was in place.

Had they known the work of Len Gibbons, his neighbours might have wondered if conscience afflicted him, if that night – in the certain knowledge of what would happen later in the morning, at his own hand, removed but culpable – he would find sleep hard to come by. The neighbours did not know the man living at the mock-Tudor semi-detached home in a safe corner of suburban South London. Any thought of conscience had been gouged out of him when he had worked in this town, listened to the chimes and handled Antelope. No second thoughts, hesitation. What mattered was not the snuffing out of a life but the effectiveness of his work, and the satisfaction that would come from a job well done. There had been brave words in the damp heap overlooking a Scottish sea loch, but they had been for the benefit of the outsiders. The big picture was wiped, and the little picture was paramount: it showed a man, with his wife, coming across a pavement on the campus of the university's medical school, and another man closed on him. It was the limit of the picture, and he was not troubled by it. He could have slept had he cared to. The Marienkirche was a principal church in Lübeck, rebuilt with extraordinary dedication and skill after the war. The great bells, shattered and lit by a single candle, that had plummeted down from the spires, were off the main body of the nave. They had been there when he had come to Lübeck thirty years before and they would still be there. They were supposed to grip the visitor by the throat and condemn the atrocity of violence. Gibbons didn't care what would happen later that morning. Neither would the crews of the Wellington and Stirling bombers – who had made the firestorm, brought down the bells and filled mass graves – have been troubled.

He sat alone and watched the skyline – and his phone, with the encryption software, bleeped. Not Sarah – asleep, no doubt, on a fold-away bed – but the Cousin. He glanced at the little screen: something about exfiltration in hand. He cleared it. *Infiltration* and *exfiltration* were history. The job had moved on. For a moment, Gibbons tried to remember the faces of the two men, but could not and gave up: they were from the past, not the present, and did not affect the future.

He smiled to himself. He had decided where he would be in the morning, when the strike went home.

Low voices alerted him. He didn't understand the speech, but thought it was Russian.

There was a light knock on the door. He came off the bed, slipped on his trousers, went to the door and opened it. The synagogue's caretaker shuffled away. Framed in the doorway, a man gave a warm smile and had a large old leather bag hanging from his shoulder. A hand was offered. He took it. He had never met the man, and offered a formal greeting that betrayed nothing.

The man spoke in their own tongue, used the word that in their language meant 'engineer' and smiled again. He had a light, tuneful voice.

The transport would be outside at seven that morning, in four hours. Gabbi nodded. There would be the two of them, for the wheels and the hit – not five, not ten or twenty-five. A sneer curled the man's lip: it told Gabbi that this one – from Berlin Station – had had no dealings with the unit in the Dubai business. He was shown a photograph, taken in poor light, and it was explained that the woman was the Engineer's wife. The shirt-sleeved man was the neuro-consultant. In the foreground of the picture there was a car with a rear door open. He was told the registration number and make, that only one security man was used for the escort. He looked hard at the photograph and saw the face, eyes, the shape of the spectacles, the cut of the hair and the clothing, and memorised it. His hand never touched the photograph, and when the man's fingers held it, Gabbi made out the fine texture of the latex gloves he wore. It was assumed that the entry of the Engineer, his back to the street, would be a difficult interception, but when he left, it would be an easier shot, into the face and stomach. Then the man shrugged, as if he had realised he should not presume to lecture an expert in techniques. On the likely schedule, he would be on the return sailing of the ferry in late morning. He had faith in the arrangements woven around him and did not query them.

Gabbi was asked if he was comfortable. He said he was. Did he need to know more about the target, why the target was identified? He did not. Was he satisfied with the arrangements in place? He was.

Anything he needed would be brought to him. Gabbi said he had found a book of drawings by a girl who had been a witness inside the camp at Theresienstadt and had survived. He said he had had family there who had not lived. He did not say it was his wife's grandparents who had been incarcerated in the camp and had died of starvation.

The bag was opened. A package in greaseproof paper, held together with thick elastic bands, was handed to him, with similar gloves. He knew the Beretta 92S, and a little grin flicked at his mouth when he was told that this particular weapon, and the ammunition it was loaded with, had been sold to the Egyptian armed forces: a small matter, but likely to cause confusion in an investigation. There were two magazines, eighteen bullets in all, and he would use two. It was wrapped again, and put on the table beside the bed.

The man reached forward, gripped Gabbi's shoulders and gave him a light brush kiss on each cheek. Then he was gone and the door closed on him. Gabbi heard the slither of the caretaker's slippers, then the thud of the outer door being shut. He went back to bed and hoped to catch more sleep.

His shoulder was shaken gently. The pilot, Eddie, jack-knifed up on the cot bed. His co-pilot hovered above him. 'Thought you'd like to know that we're fuelled, armed, all the checks done, ready to press the tit and lift. And likely we may be lifting.'

'Why didn't you wake me?'

'You were sleeping like a baby – would have been a crime.'

'Fuck you.' The pilot rubbed the sleep from his eyes. 'What we got?'

'Could go around first light. As we thought. A covert team up on the frontier, and maybe there's casualties coming with them. The other bird is getting herself to speed. We go together.'

He could hear the rotors of both birds turning over, and the ground-crew people would be crawling over the Black Hawks. It would likely be the last mission of interest that Eddie flew before the draw-down sucked him in. Then he might go home, or might be packed off with his guys and his machine to Afghanistan. He'd like to finish well. He tightened his boots.

'Oh, and Eddie . . .'

'What?'

'We don't exist, and any flight we make is classified as never happening. It's likely the mullah-men will be powerfully angry if we do get called out and are up close on their ground.'

'Fuck them.'

The birds' engines sounded sweet and the windows shook. If an exfiltration needed a helicopter lift-out, they'd be in trouble, deep stuff, and it would be close run. It was good of the guys to let him sleep and recharge. Might have been their own survival instincts that had allowed it. Spooks, the pilot reckoned, were mad – not people you'd take home to your mother – and he'd go as far as he could to save them.

★   ★   ★

Badger hissed, 'How you put yourself in this place, Foxy, I don't know.'

The dinghy was holed: a bullet had pierced the metal hull about an inch below the waterline.

It went down a few yards short of the mud spit, where the water was up to Badger's waist. He had time to hoist Foxy onto his shoulder, as he had before. The skin, against the stubble on his own face, was wet, clammy and seemed white in the darkness, as if there were night-lights under it – like the ones used in nurseries and hospital wards. He went over the spit and past the heap he had made of dead foliage then slipped back into the water.

'Don't ask me how I'm doing. Actually, I'm doing fine. Just don't bother to ask.'

He could hear the jeeps' engines on the bund line away from him, but he would have been masked by the reed beds. It was as well that he was. He could stand upright, which was best with the weight he carried. The level dropped and lapped at his knees, the birds thrashed for take-off and he plodded on, the mud under his boots clinging to them. He was taking deep breaths, struggling to suck the air deeper into his lungs. His legs were leaden. He had not begun: Badger was only at his start line. He came out of the water and was on the open ground. He went by the carcass of the bird, unrecognisable now as a creature of beauty. Badger didn't do bird-watching, he wasn't eco-obsessed, but he had learned to respect nature when he was in hides and when he hiked, testing himself, in Scotland or in the Brecons of Wales. He knew the range of the small songbirds that would come from the heather and bracken to filch crumbs, and the predator hobbies, peregrines and eagles; he knew also the divers on the lochs. There had been a poem drilled into them by a teacher about a bird a seaman had shot with a bolt. He was cursed for it, his mates too. That was what Foxy had done; he had killed the ibis, made it into rats' food.

'Shouldn't have done it, Foxy. Look what it's done to us, with you killing it . . . You could say something, Foxy, not play bloody miserable.'

He went as fast as he could, and his boots went into the side of the scrape where the hide had been. He lurched out of it, and Foxy's weight shifted on his shoulder. Badger gasped and swore softly. It had been a sizeable piece of his life, important, and might be memorable, a bit of ground two yards square that had held them both, and the bergens, for hours, days and nights. He would remember it. Badger couldn't have said then how long his life expectancy was, but the image of the scrape, the net and the camouflage, the smell of the bags, the piss bottles, Foxy's body and breath, and Badger's own would stay with him until the last. That might be when a firing squad was given the order or in a far distant bed in whatever home was then his. He went by the scrape and it was behind him. He would never see it again, but he wouldn't forget it, ever.

'Good riddance, Foxy, eh? How you doing? We're getting there . . .'

He staggered a bit going down the slight slope. He came to the bergens and the little inflatable. For a moment, he considered whether to tip Foxy into the inflatable along with the bergens. Only a moment. There were reeds off to his left and behind them the clear space used to bury the poor bastards who had come scavenging, and then – across more water – the elevated track. He could see the lights of the two jeeps. They were going slowly but making progress, and there would be a place ahead of them where they could swing to their right and either drive over mud, or trudge to get across the route Badger intended to take to the extraction point.

'I reckon you're better with me, Foxy. The bergens can get the ride.'

He didn't hear agreement or criticism. It was best to have Foxy on his shoulder – if there was a crisis, anything near to catastrophe, Badger didn't want to be crouched over the inflatable, heaving his man onto his shoulder. He cantered into the water, which splashed up round his ankles, into his boots, and up the hem of the gillie suit. The weight was fierce on his shoulder. There was a string at the front end of the inflatable and he had it in his free hand. The other steadied Foxy, was on his buttocks and had a grip there. Foxy's head bounced on the back of Badger's hip, and his knees were over Badger's heart. The feet kicked his stomach with each step.

'Not going to be fun, Foxy, the next bit – and it'd be good if you helped yourself a bit. Know what I mean?'

He went deeper into the water. The level rose. He realised that Foxy's head, upside-down, would go under. He didn't break his step and the mud gave him a useful grip. He twisted Foxy a bit so that his head lay on the side of the inflatable. They went further out, and he could follow the path of the two jeeps' lights, bouncing. He thought they were now on a rough track that, maybe, hadn't been used for many years – the longer the better – and was crumbling. They were moving slowly. If he was ahead of them, for all his burdens, when they swung and came after him, he reckoned he had a chance – slim but a chance – of reaching the extraction point. If they were in front blocking him, and the dawn light came up, he didn't feel inclined to make any bets on himself coming through, not the chance of a cat in hell. He had seen Foxy's body, and had heard his screams, and the two encouraged him to keep going forward. His breath sang from his mouth and each step was harder, the burden heavier.

'Don't get it into your head, Foxy, that I'm doing this for love of you.'

He was out of his depth. His feet flapped and had nothing to grip against. The weight of the bergens steadied the inflatable, which had to take most of his own weight, and Foxy's. It didn't seem possible to Badger that he should tip the bergens into the water and rid himself of them: instructors always talked about the *requirement* of bringing back kit and in Stores they grumbled if it wasn't accounted for. It was an *obligation* to return it after an operation. Requirements and obligations were part of the bible he worked to.

The lights of the jeeps were harder to see. Important? Yes. It told him that dawn was coming, not there yet but not far away. If they blocked him when the dawn had spread its light, it had all been for nothing. He thrashed his feet, and attempted to paddle with his free hand, and they went forward. If they were blocked . . . Who was listening? Maybe some pigs were, an otter, the birds, but the men in the jeeps wouldn't hear him.

Badger said sharply, 'Not for love of you, Foxy, no. I don't even like you. And you're a fucking passenger hitching a ride.'

Twice they went under. Twice he choked and cleared his throat, then spat out the marsh water. But he kept the pace. Had to.

18

A wind had risen. It came from the south, perhaps the south-west, and ruffled the water Badger waded through. It was a warm, vigorous wind. It flapped the tips of the reeds off to his left. The bed below him was uneven. Sometimes his boots found a grip and then he was able to lurch forward faster with the inflatable and the weight over his shoulder. He used the craft's rim for buoyancy when the bed fell away under him. The wind helped to drive him on.

Little white crests were now whipped up and water splashed over the sides. He fancied that the bergens shifted because they were floating in the bilge. The wind brought the sounds closer of the two jeeps' engines. If the wind, steadily strengthening, had been from the north, or the north-east, he might not have heard them straining in low gear on the the bund line that was little more than loose-packed sand. Had he not heard them and been able to plot their position, he might have slowed and clung to the rim of the inflatable, let his legs dangle in the water.

The engine noise drove him forward. If the jeeps could get past him, then swing to their right and come from his left, his route to the extraction point was blocked. Rest was not possible. Badger could not have said when, if ever, he had felt so tired, so hungry and thirsty. He thought once, very briefly, of pictures he had seen on television screens: refugees on the move pushing prams laden with possessions or carrying little suitcases, or the skeletal figures of men gazing at an eyewitness from the far side of a barbed-wire fence. Mostly his mind was blank, as if the screen had been switched off, and the matter of the moment was getting the next secure hold for his right boot on the mud, then following it with the left. Crisis was when the right boot, or the left, slipped and pitched him forward, Foxy's weight dragging him down. Triumph was when the left boot, or the right, had good grip and he seemed to surge. It was like the flight of a wild animal. Maybe a deer, isolated on Bodmin moor with hounds closing, would have understood what drove Badger on.

He wasted breath on speaking aloud. 'Don't help me. Don't do anything. You're Foxy, the big man. Leave it to me. I'm the boy, there to do fetching and carrying, the one who has to graft. You're the top beggar, Foxy, right? Please yourself. Leave it to the boy.'

It might have been clever of Badger to strip off the gillie suit and go on in his pants, socks and boots, but he could not. It was about his culture: he had to bring back two bergens, a gillie suit, headgear and Foxy. Badger no more considered ditching the suit than leaving either bergen to float on the water, or dropping Foxy in the hope of increasing the possibility of his own survival.

'Do I like you, Foxy? No. What did I get? I had the short straw. I was in the wrong place at the wrong time, and some shitface had written the wrong stuff in my file, and the computer chucked me up. You don't deserve me, Foxy. There are some God-awful people who do my job, guys I wouldn't take water off or a biscuit, guys who are crap. They're the ones who should have been here, watching over you. See if any of them would have lifted you up and kept going with you. You're a lucky bastard – say it, Foxy, say, 'I'm a lucky bastard.' Better, shout it. Foxy, shout, 'I'm a lucky bastard to have Badger with me. I didn't hear you.'

The whipped reeds sang in his ears and he heard the splash of the small waves he breasted, the little thuds when the inflatable bounced on the crests, and – clearest – the jeep engines.

He fell.

He tumbled forward and was buried below the surface. For a moment the great weight kept him down. He struggled to draw in his knees, bend them, then raise his body. His head broke the surface.

Water fell off him. Algae and weed were in his face. He understood. The bed sloped upwards. He had tripped because it was no longer flat. The water was at his knees, not his waist or chest. He was in the shallows. He still had Foxy on his back and he was left with one free arm to drag the inflatable. It grounded, then came free again. When it grounded the second time it took a greater effort to free it. He could see the headlights and hear the engines better. He could also see ahead.

The first minutes of dawn made grey and indistinct shapes: might have been raised ground, another bund line or another bed of high reeds. He had gone before on instinct, taken the direction he thought was the most direct path to the extraction point. The light had washed through pastel shades and no clarity. The jeeps were ahead of him, and they swung. The headlights didn't reach him, but if they kept their course they would stay ahead. He crested a slight slope.

In the last minutes of the old night, Badger would have seen nothing ahead of him. The first minutes of the dawn, and the new day, showed him an outline of the ground ahead. He tried to remember, and failed. He couldn't remember the ground between the hide in front of the house and the half-sunken strand of barbed wire that was the border. Close to it was the toppled watchtower. He could recall the burned-out tank and its broken tracks, could picture where the trucks had gone down off a bund line and into the water, contaminating it with old engine oil. He could remember and picture what was on the far side of the border, between the line marked by the rusted wire strand and where the Pajeros had brought them, but couldn't recall what they had crossed, skirted, waded through to get close to the target location.

He went over 'bare-arsed ground', no cover, and broke the laws that were carved on the tablets of the croppies. He did Shape, Silhouette and Sound, because the inflatable scraped on the dried mud and broke across reed stumps, and Space because he was bunched with the inflatable, which was more of a sledge than a water craft. He didn't do Shine – he'd broken every other law – but they hadn't been teaching 'flight for life' when they had made the laws of covert surveillance. He went on. Badger thought that within a few minutes, three or four, they would be across his route out and a line of them would be confronting him. They would have the first of the low sunshine on him – easy shooting, clear.

'Didn't think of that, did you, Foxy? Didn't reckon on the trouble I'd have getting you clear, did you? All right for you up there – but I'm bloody nearly on my knees. I'm suffering, Foxy. Have you nothing – anything – to say?'

Moments returned, filtered in his memory. There had been buffalo in the water, and a settlement – too small for a village – with concrete-block buildings and TV dishes. They had made a wide detour, but that had been daylight and this was dawn.

Different noises. Engines revved. It was the sound there had been on the roads north of Bristol during the winter before last. Ice on the roads, snowdrifts on the verges, too much for the gritting trucks to cope with. Badger was in the southeast of Iraq, in the marshlands where the temperature would soon top 110 degrees Fahrenheit, and he remembered the ice and wind-chill of a West Country winter. Tyres spinning, no traction. The racing and shrieking of the engines, the snow, ice and refrozen slush spitting out behind the wheels. Badger understood. The headlights, to his left, were static. No snow, no ice, but drifts of fine sand that would have come in on the winds and caught the top of a bund line. They were loose enough, and deep enough, to block the axles and spin the wheels.

The light grew. So little time was left to him. They would abandon their jeeps and run.

The inflatable split and air hissed from it. Badger had Foxy on his shoulder. He heaved on the thin rope and went forward, pulling the bergens. The raised area he had gone over would have blocked off the ground from the water, and might have given – in a long-ago war – tanks the chance to manoeuvre in battle formation over what had been marshland. He had no cover, and the light was coming. Badger did not know whether he would be ahead of them and their line or too far in front of them for rifle fire to be accurate.

Dead in the mind now, only a wild creature's demand to survive, but the weight on his shoulder, and what he was pulling, meant he couldn't raise his speed. Away to his right, the east, the sky lightened.

'Fuck you, Foxy.'

The jeeps would go no further.

Mansoor yelled, lifting his voice over the screaming of the engines. At first he could not be heard and the men sat tight, the sand spewing back to coat the windscreen of the second jeep. He hammered the butt of his rifle on the dashboard, and was heard. He yelled to them to kill the engines.

Silence fell. The officer of the al-Quds Brigade could not have said when he had last slept or eaten. His recall of the night went back no further than the frenzy with which he had struck his prisoner. He had hit, kicked, used his fists and had not backed off. Fear overwhelmed him now. He could look into the darkness and towards where he believed the fugitive was. Beyond the black of the night – with the moonlight long gone – and away to the east he saw a sliver of morning light, lines of subtle colours that ranged through deep grey and soft gunmetal, to silver and the narrowest strip of gold.

He had his men out of the jeeps. He strained to see movement in front, and cursed. There would be on the road between the small settlement and Ahvaz, reached through villages of farmers and minefield amputees, a convoy of at least one black saloon, filled with intelligence officers of the Brigade, and two trucks of fighting men. He could not consider how it would be for him if the car and the trucks arrived and he had no prisoner. He strained and saw nothing. He gazed at the darkness, blasphemed, and was alone.

'Why were you here? Why did you come to this place? Why could you not have gone to another sector? Why here? Why mine?'

He thought himself destroyed. He could imagine the faces of the men who would have sat in the car at the front of the convoy. They would show him no sympathy, no understanding. His father in the gallows shed at the gaol showed no sympathy or understanding when a condemned man was led in to stand beside the stool on which he would be perched. Neither did he show it when a man was brought out through the gates and placed under the crane's arm. He did not know of one officer in the Brigade who would offer understanding. Despair washed around him – and the shout was in his ear.

A guard, from the Basij, pointed. All of them followed his finger – and saw nothing. The guard was a peasant, one of a line of subsistence farmers. Perhaps he had been sent out to sit on the hillsides north of Ahvaz and watch the sheep, be certain the lambs did not stray. The guard called that he could see a man, carrying another and dragging a load.

They ran towards the dawn, in a chaotic stampede, but Mansoor, with his damaged leg, could not keep pace with the younger, fitter men and bellowed that they should slow, go only at his speed. He sucked in air, filled his lungs, went as fast as his leg would carry him. They were off the bund line and on flat baked ground. The strip of gold widened below the silver.

He saw the man. Why had he come? He was alone, carrying the body on his shoulder and dragging what seemed like a khaki litter behind him. He moved at snail speed. For a moment, Mansoor believed fortune favoured him. Then he looked ahead of the man and saw the reed bed that stretched in front of him. He saw also that the first light of day had made a mist shimmer in it.

The distance to the target was some three hundred yards, and the light was poor and— He demanded rapid-fire bursts on automatic – but they were men of the Basij, not of the Brigade.

He had no cover. His goal was the reed bed where, perhaps, an old watercourse had run and enough seepage had survived the drainage programme.

Badger couldn't see beyond it, didn't know how wide it was, but was aware of the mist. It crept towards him, and meandered among the clumps of reeds, some thick, others collapsed: it was a refuge and a goal.

He heard the crack of bullets going above him. They thudded into the hard mud and made dirt puffs. Two shook him – they would have struck the bergens on the holed inflatable. Some were close but more were high and wide, or short and no threat to him. They gave him incentive. A paratrooper, a sergeant, had said to him on the Brecons, 'I tell you, kiddo, nothing gets you moving better than live rounds when they're headed at you. They clear the bowels and get you up to pace.' He seemed now – with the whine overhead and the patter into the mud – not to feel Foxy's weight over his shoulder, or the pain of his palm, which was raw where the rope attached to the inflatable chafed. With the light came the flies, but the shooting kept Badger going, and there were distant shouts.

He remembered nothing of this place.

He could have been here before or not. He had no recall of the berm he had come across and the bund line to his left, or the dried-out plateau and scant reeds in front of him. All croppies hoovered information. From anywhere and any source, information was gold dust. It might come from a lecture hall or a chance encounter, but all of it had value and should be squirrelled into storage. A driver had taken a team of them, in a police wagon, out onto the Pennine moors for a CROP on what might have been a jihadist training camp. He'd talked of his time in the United Nations police force in Croatia; there had been a story of a breakout from a besieged town and the likely result of failure was being massacred by their enemy. Those Croats had tried to go across country the fifteen or so miles to the nearest haven, and some had been captured – slaughtered – because they had ended up going in circles, all sense of direction lost. They were so weak from lack of sleep and food that they had doubled back on themselves and, two days later, had been where they'd started out. Not a story that was easy to forget. Badger remembered the trite laughter among his fellow croppies. Now he had no compass, but he had the growing light in the east. He, too, was clapped out from exhaustion and hunger.

He would get to the cover of the reeds and the low mist and would push through. He wouldn't see the Pajeros in front of him but the house, the kids playing with a football, the barracks and the lamp-post from which a fraying rope hung. It was a night-mare. He shouted, 'We going right, Foxy? You'll tell me if we're wrong? Least you can do, stuck up there, is tell me if I'm off course.'

There seemed to be an answering yell, but not from Foxy.

Badger twisted his head. He could see over the skin of Foxy's buttocks. The officer limped among his guys, ranting at them. The shooting stopped and he made a line of them, then brought them forward.

'Foxy, is there any excuse for dumping the inflatable and one of the bergens?'

The line of guys, with their officer, was around two hundred yards from him, and more shots were fired, but wide. He had fifty yards to go until he reached the reeds, but the mist came towards him – might last thirty minutes, but every other morning it had burned off quickly. Might be too quick for him.

'There's the one with mostly clothing, not that we've used it, some of the kit and the last of the grenades. The other's where communications is. There's not much in it either. What you reckon, Foxy?'

More yelling from the officer, and they veered away from the direct line, turned a sharp angle and went into the reeds. Nine men with their officer. The foliage swallowed them. They would have seen, from where their jeeps had stopped in loose sand and they had elevation, how far the reeds went, and would have judged they could make their cordon line on the far side.

'I'm going to dump both bergens, Foxy. Goes against the grain, hurts, but at least it's all sanitised. Don't bloody critise me.'

Badger hit the reeds. They lacked the life of the beds beside the hide and were diseased, stunted. He could hear, to his left, shouts and dried stems breaking. He thought – so far – that a fragile curtain of morning mist might have saved him. Useless things now played in his mind. There had been big estates above the Thames, outside Reading, and kids he had known had earned cash from beating: they had been paid to drive reared birds, most of which could barely fly, into the cordon where the guns were.

When they came out of the cover they were blasted. He was down on his knees and still carried Foxy, didn't allow him to slide off his shoulder. He dragged at some broken reeds and made a shallow pile of them over the two bergens. He had, now, only the pistol, the magazine already in it and one more, and he had short-range communications that would link with Alpha Juliet. Everything else that should have been brought home and returned to Stores was in the two bergens. It hurt him to abandon them. Badger pushed himself up and turned his back on them. He began to thread through the stems. The light was growing.

'Worst thing I've ever done, Foxy, is dumping that kit. What I do reckon, though, is that she'll be at the extraction place. We have to get there. She won't ditch us like I ditched the bergens. She's the sort of girl who'll be there. She's great. Foxy, all that shit you told me about your woman, about your Ellie, I've forgotten it. I'm going to get you to where Alpha Juliet is, Foxy. That all right?'

He went carefully, and the light grew. He could do a better pace without the backpacks to pull, but he knew the cordon line would be in front of him, and the guns. Who knew where he was? No bastard did. Who cared where he was? Alpha Juliet might. No other bastard would. He was deniable. No reason for any bastard to know or care.

Gone2work. A cryptic text to Len Gibbons had shown up on his mobile. It was as if one of the last pieces of the jigsaw had slotted together. Not the final one, but one of the most important.

He was not a grandstander. He didn't expect a seat where he could sit and watch the deed done. It was still dark on a late November morning at the leisure resort of Travemünde, up the river and north of Lübeck, facing into the Baltic. The text had been sent by the Cousin. The message told Gibbons that the consultant had left home, had arrived at the university and gone into the block where his offices were. Good enough. It seemed to indicate that no security alert had been launched.

Further up the floodlit quay, out towards the groyne on which the lighthouse flashed, there were piers on wood piles and cormorants gathered on the hand rails – black, with long necks, big beaks and the lungs to give them diving time when they hunted. They had been perched on those hand rails when he had been here thirty-something years before. Then there had been a winter morning when he had waited for the first ferry to return across the river from the village of Priwall and bring with it the workers who had jobs at Travemünde or Lübeck. He had last been here a few weeks before the collapse of the Antelope operation. It was, for Len Gibbons, almost a pilgrimage and he might have brought flowers with him if a kiosk had been open. Had he done so, it would have been because he cared to remember the lives that had been lost because of his trust in a man he had met once and so briefly and seen once from a distance. To make this journey, come here and wait in the bone-piercing cold, with the wind snapping off the sea, was of greater significance to him than when he had loitered outside the church of St Andrew and watched the man who had been a pastor.

The ferry came towards him. As he remembered it, there was a café on the far side of the river. He would buy himself a hot breakfast – eggs, sausage, a heated pastry and coffee. He was savouring the thought when the phone bleeped again.

Both arrived, all in place. Warm congrats, your favourite Cousin.

He read it twice, then deleted it. Not quite the final piece, but so close.

He had believed in confusion and a complex chain of command, had dared to hope that the terse message, passed through many links in a chain, reporting the capture of Foulkes did not mean that a protective net would be tossed over the target. The Engineer and his wife were now at the consulting rooms and the building was not flooded with detectives and armed uniforms. By a miracle, word from that distant corner of Iran had not seeped out, A cargo ship, monstrous in the dark, passed in front of the ferry.

He shivered, from the cold, nerves. He could absorb the Baltic's November chill. Len Gibbons had done time as maternity cover in Estonia's capital city, Tallinn, and a decade earlier he had been the second man in Stockholm. Had it not been for the Schlutup

Fuck-up he would never have been sent as a fill-in to the former Soviet satellite, and if he had gone to Sweden it would have been as the station officer. The boat laden with containers had passed, the ferry had come in and the ramp was down. He walked on board, as he had done three decades before. Then he had left the pastor on the quay. Now he stood with a few hardy spirits on the deck.

The ramp was raised, and he felt the shudder of the engines below his feet. His mobile bleeped again. His 'Friend' was in place.

Len Gibbons switched off the phone, opened its back section and removed the chip. He dropped the phone first into the white wake of the water that was pushed aside by the ferry's passage, then the chip. It floated for a fraction of a second, then was swamped. He had broken all contact with the conspiracy. In a minute they were at the Priwall ramp.

He felt calm, comfortable, and satisfied with a job well done. He had brought them together and they would face each other within the hour. He had no doubt that the assassin in the pay of a semi-friendly government would show the necessary skills and take the life of an engineer who served a semi-hostile state.

Late that afternoon he would drop off his hire car, fly from Hamburg to Brussels, take the last Eurostar connection into London, then a bus to the Haymarket. He would climb the stairs of what would be, probably, a deserted building, but Sarah would be there, and he'd give her the present he would buy before leaving Lübeck. Perhaps she'd blush a little, and murmur something about his 'thoughtfulness'. The office would be cleared and ready for them to move out. She would have known the outcome of the operation by listening to any news bulletin, and he might invite her for sherry in his club's bar. Then they would go their separate ways.

The following morning he would leave his train at Vauxhall and walk to the Towers. It would be well known that a prominent Iranian weapons scientist had been 'taken down' in the German city of Lübeck the previous day – it would have been broadcast widely and reported in the newspapers. A minimal minority would find the opportunity, out of sight, to press his hand. Only later would rumour and gossip spread: he would then be a noted man, respected. He chuckled.

He came off the ferry at the side of the ramp. The cars sped past and threw up the puddles' water. He went to the café for his hot breakfast.

It was right that he had made the pilgrimage.

The Cousin, too, had no more use for a mobile phone. The main part, not the inner brain, was tossed casually into the back of a corporation rubbish cart as it cleaned streets before the rush-hour began; the brain was wrapped in the paper bag that had contained the pastry he had bought from a stall by the Mühlenbrücke. He dropped it into a bin in the park off the Wallstrasse. He felt bullish.

Like Gibbons and their Friend, the Cousin expected to stay in the city for the next hour, no longer. There was nothing he could do in that time, and his connections were now broken. He would then drive south, fast, to Hannover. He would leave his hire car there and pay his bill – false name and cards – and a military driver would take him far to the southwest, towards Kaiserslautern. By late evening he would be on a military flight out of the Ramstein USAF base. Those who disapproved of extra-judicial killing would not know about it, and those who did not would pump his hand and slap his back.

He was in the park, and shared a bench with a derelict guy. He bought the man coffee from a stall and a pastry with a custard centre. The derelict had few teeth and bobbed his head in gratitude. The Cousin felt no need to communicate any more than his general sense of well-being. It was not every day there was a chance to waste the bastards who had done the damage in Iraq, and were in the process of getting devices into Afghanistan. Christmas was coming early.

The images in his mind were of bombs detonating in those far-off places. He had forgotten them since he had left the rendez-vous city of London. As if why they were in Lübeck, and what they were doing, had no relation to the deserts and mountains where the young guys were sent. As if he, the Friend and Gibbons had lost sight of the reasons and been buried in the detail of it. He laughed, and the derelict cackled with him. The Agency man came from small-town Alabama where there were good fire-and-brimstone preachers. Ten years earlier he had visited an elderly uncle; it had been the fourth Sunday after the planes had been flown into the Twin Towers. He could not remember where the text had come from, which Old Testament chapter, but the preacher that morning had said, "'If I whet my glittering sword and my hand take hold on Judgment, I will render Vengeance on my enemies and will reward them that hate me.'" Fine stuff. Allelujahs to go with it, and plenty.

The rain had started to patter on his shoulders. There were, of course, the two guys who had gone forward, identified the destination and hit trouble, but an alarm had not been raised and the hit was in place. The target faced Judgment, was adjacent to Vengeance. The two guys were blanked out of his mind, deniable, and he laughed again, then walked away, leaving the derelict with the last of his pastry. He would have time for a quick walk around Lübeck, the renovated historic buildings, before driving away.

He laughed because he thought vengeance a fine rich dish, best served as a surprise.

He sat in the van, and did not smoke or drink take-out coffee. Instead he read. Gabbi's choice was to be among favourites.

Just as his driver, who had brought him the weapon during the night, did not know his name, so Gabbi would have been kept in ignorance of the driver's – except that his wallet had been flipped open, a euro note extracted, and he had seen the plastic-fronted pouch inside it with the ID that would take the man, in the name of Amnon Katz, into the car park of the Embassy of Israel, 14193 Berlin. Little escaped Gabbi. Probably, when he was back in Tel Aviv tomorrow, and had his debriefing, the day after tomorrow, he would mention that the embassy's man had not satisfactorily hidden his identity or troubled to disguise his workplace.

He thought the man with him, Amnon Katz, squirmed too often in his seat. Maybe the people who should have escorted him were on holiday or had made excuses. After the chaotic affair of the Emirates killing, intelligence-gathering officers had sought to distance themselves from the work of his unit. He had Amnon Katz, who had been calmer in the night and had spoken coherently. Perhaps he had not slept. Perhaps he had a knotted stomach. Perhaps he had doubts, now that he was up against the place where a man would be killed. They had a view of the steps leading up to the main door of the block and of the lit windows on the first floor. A saloon car was parked at the kerb. The top of a man's scalp showed above the driver's seat headrest. There was no other security in sight. He coughed hard, cleared his throat. He had not drunk any coffee because it would be unprofessional to be stuck outside on a cold pavement and need to piss. He could feel the weapon lodged in his trouser belt, under the overalls. He reached to open the van's passenger door.

The man, Amnon Katz, gave him his hand. For encouragement? Gabbi ignored it.

He closed the door quietly behind him and went to the back of the van. He took out a road-cleaning brush and a couple of bin liners, and smiled ruefully. He would be fucked if there were no leaves to collect and no rubbish to sweep up. He had a shovel and thick, industrial gloves.

He did not look behind him but walked towards the parked car and the steps. The wind blew harshly down the road in the centre of the teaching-hospital complex and buffeted his face. His baseball cap was well down over his eyes and a scarf closely wrapped at his mouth. The cameras would be rewarded with little. And the van? He heard its engine start. It reversed, and would be driven away. Somewhere behind him, watching him, was the stubbily built man with the old face, the bright eyes of youth and the coldness at the mouth who had met him off the ferry. Gabbi trusted that man, and regarded him as a friend. He was the one who would take him away when it was done.

He began to sweep the gutter – slush from the salt put down, a few leaves, some soil washed off the frozen shrub beds. He went slowly, had no wish to be close to the saloon car in front of him. He had seen his target go inside, with his arm around his wife's shoulders, but the target's back had been to him and he had seen little of the face. The condition of the wife, and the verdict she would be given, did not concern him. Each time Gabbi pushed the broom, he could feel, against his belly, the stock of the pistol – and now his mind was closed.

They sat very still, and close. The Engineer did not speak and neither did his wife, Naghmeh.

They were in the waiting room. The door to the office was shut but they heard his voice and thought he made telephone calls. Men in loose-fitting, unbuttoned white coats crossed the waiting room, knocked and went inside, then nurses in starched white trousers and figure-hugging white jackets. There was a woman at a desk close to the door, a gatekeeper. She did not make eye contact with either of them but kept her face bent over her screen. Soft music played from high speakers. There were magazines but they did not read them. They had nothing to talk about. His wife would not have wished to hear about the progress he was making in extending the range of electronics that could transmit the signal to the receiver fitted in the device, and do it from further outside the bubble that protected the enemy's convoys from remote detonations. He had no interest now in which block of land beside which length of raised road leading to which village would be granted the necessary funding for a mine-clearance team to begin work.

Their lives were on hold and they barely dared to breathe. Neither could read the faces of those who went into the consultant's room or left it. He could not be pessimistic or optimistic, and she could do no more than hold his hand.

It was sudden.

The door opened. He was shirt-sleeved, but with a tie in his collar, well shaven and looked to have slept. His face gave no clue. The Engineer had heard it said that an accused could always tell, from the moment he was brought back into the courtroom and confronted the judge, whether he would hang or take the bus home to rejoin his family. He felt his wife's hand stiffen in his. She clung to him and their fingers locked.

There were X-rays in a pouch in the consultant's hand and he spoke quietly to the gatekeeper, who nodded. Neither gave evidence of what was said, and he waved for them to follow him inside.

They crossed the waiting room shakily, did not know what awaited them.

Presence and courage radiated from her, as they had on the previous evening. In his experience, talking to patients was more difficult than performing complicated surgery on them, and he had been told that his manner was not always satisfactory: he should curb brusqueness when the news was bad and elation when it was good. He was tired and had slept poorly. Lili would have fled to her mother, taken their daughter with her, would have poured into her parent's ear a litany of his craven acceptance of a call to old loyalties. She might come back to him, might see that his affluence would not easily be replaced on a divorcee's circuit, if he made a call and grovelled – he accepted that their lives were altered, that a crack had appeared that would not easily be repaired. She might not come back.

They intruded into his life.

If they had not come to Lübeck, he would have slept well and been against the warmth of his wife's body. He would have been woken by his daughter climbing across him . . . but he had woken cold. She looked into his face. He indicated the chairs, but they stood in front of him, silently demanding his answer.

He said, 'There is much to talk of and I ask you not to interrupt me but to listen carefully to what I say. I have identified a glioblastoma, grade two, which is confirmation of what you have already been told by your consultants at home. The tumour is close to what we call an "eloquent" area . . .'

Having intruded into his life they had derailed it. He held up the scan images. 'I want to show you what we have learned.'

★   ★   ★

'Time to go. Hit the road, guys.'

She thought she sounded authoritative and that her voice had a crisp bite. The light was up. Dawn slipped into day. Abigail Jones's last birthday had been her thirty-third, which should have marked her out as being at the peak of her powers. She did not believe the crap about veterans' experience outweighing youth's innovations. All she had worked at now hung precariously on that day's events. She couldn't escape it. The sun was low, bright on her face. It threw grotesque shadows.

Those shadows were edging nearer to her. She couldn't say how fast they advanced with each minute, but at first light they had started to form, nudging through the broken gate to the compound. They were now well up the track towards her, and if she didn't take control, get the show on the road, they would be tripping against her feet. Hard for her to see the men because the sun was behind them, but there would be a hundred, perhaps more. Nor could she see what weapons they carried. Some of the money she had paid out to the old bastard, the sheikh, would have been distributed but more would have gone into his own biscuit tin, and a suggestion would have been made that there'd be more where it had come from. She heard the sound of the big engines behind her. It would be about bluff, always was. Either the sea would part or it would not. If it did they would be fine, dandy, and on their way. If it did not, they'd be swamped and drowned. The Boys would have sorted it out for themselves: Corky in the first Pajero with Harding riding shotgun, and she would be with Hamfist, close behind – like up against the fender. Shagger would be alongside Hamfist, and they'd try to do it with gas, and if not, it would have to be live rounds – and if it was live rounds, her career was mired and she would be gone.

She'd had no communication with Badger, had tried enough times for a link. He was not switched on, maybe had not the time, or inclination, to talk. Maybe he'd been taken . . . and was dead. Her obligation was to be at the extraction location. If she held her hand above her eyes, down almost to the bridge of her nose – where her freckles were thickest – and squinted hard, she could see a wall of men, not soldiers or police but marsh men, the *madan*, from the cradle of civilisation. Ninety years before – she had read it in the digests preparing her for service in Iraq – they had been described by the British military as 'treacherous and deceitful'. They lived in the shelter of the marshes from which they 'looted and murdered indiscriminately', and the last invader to have taught them a degree of discipline had been Hulagu, grandson of Genghis Khan, eight centuries back. They would be formidable but bluff. An appearance of unshakeable will and unstoppable force might win through. She did no more pep talks. If they went into the crowd and broke legs, tossed bodies, crushed teenagers, and fired gas, but did not break through, they would be torn limb from limb, like the security people trapped by a mob in Fallujah. They were all good at the wheel, her Boys, but she was happy, in difficult times, to have Hamfist driving. The first Pajero was level with her.

She couldn't speak to Harding because his head was encased in his gas mask and he had canisters across his lap. Corky's gas mask was on his forehead, and the engine was revved. She hitched her loose skirt, climbed up and into the back seat of the second Pajero, Hamfist's. Whatever the outcome, she would have diplomatic immunity, but they would not: the immunity once enjoyed by men working for private security contractors had long since been withdrawn. They might face big problems. Not her. Had she said, then, that the issue was ridiculous and given an instruction for a route across the sand onto Highway 6 and the road south to Basra – and safety – she would have been ignored. Abigail would have lost her credibility. She sat in the back, with hardware around her and had her pistol on her lap, cocked. She hooked the straps of the mask into place.

They surged.

Would the waters part? Would the fucking Israelites stay dry or get soaked? Time to get an answer.

Corky threw some, and Shagger did, then zapped up the windows. Harding and Hamfist had thumbs down hard on the horns. Inside the armour plate and the blast-resistant glass, she could hear the thud of the grenades letting out the gas clouds, the thundercrack of the flash-and-blast ones, the banshee bellow of the horns. She held the pistol tight. Some scattered in front of Harding, but others were thrown sideways. Hamfist's went over something that might have been a leg, a stomach or backbone. If Harding stopped, or Hamfist, they would be ripped apart, cut into small pieces, and the men would lose their balls. Fuck alone knew what they would do to her. Her own people lived among the Lancashire county set where they hunted, shot and regarded themselves as affluent country heroes. They always preached that a driver should never swerve to avoid wildlife on the road, or for a domestic cat or dog, but should go straight through it and so retain control. Harding did, and Hamfist. They were through the gas clouds, the crowd was thinner, and they hit the barricade.

It would have been built during the night. Old wire, rusted and sharp – good for getting up against the axles and snagging them – some collapsed fencing and a couple of oil drums. That was the first. The road was raised and the banks fell away and the local Clausewitz would have thought it good for blocking the milch-cow run. They went through it. The wire sprang up and thrashed the windows. Hamfist nearly stalled, which gave the young bloods the chance to get close and their fists were against the windows. Abigail saw the faces and the hate: she knew what would be done to the Boys and didn't care to think what would be done to her. They were through the first block.

The second was more of an art form. The first would slow them, but the second would stop them, and then they were fucked. She hung on to the back of the seat in front. A gang of twenty or thirty were either side of the second block, and had axes, hammers, spades and firearms. Maybe the worst thing would be fire. They could be burned out. If they were stopped and the engine was lit, they would have to come out, as rats did when smoke was pumped down their hole.

Harding swerved. In the lead Pajero, he would have used all his strength to swing the wheel. The vehicle swayed, made like it would overturn, and went down the bank. About six foot down,

Abigail reckoned. She thought they were going over when Hamfist followed. Went down on two wheels, then crunched back onto four, and the Boys were shrieking, as if it was a victory moment. They bounced on the dirt below the road and went through what would have been a disused irrigation channel. The wheels took traction again. She had no idea how many injured they had left behind. They bumped back onto the road, where the bank was less steep, and stripped off the masks. She didn't like triumphalism, but it was as if she'd loosed her dogs.

A half-mile down the track, astride it, was the sheikh's big car. The man himself was sitting on a collapsible chair beside the road. The kid with him held an umbrella above his head to shade him from the sun. Corky went straight on, did not swerve out of the impact. He hit the BMW 7 series a full power blow in front of the left side wheel and sent it off the road. The track ahead was clear. She wondered where they stood, as regards the time and the Golden Hour.

She uncocked the pistol, put it back into her inner pocket.

Quiet, a little stunned at the violence she had unleashed, Abigail said, 'That was burning bridges, and no going back over them.'

Hamfist answered, 'It was called for, miss.'

They drove hard, and she didn't know what they would find. She made a link with the operations people at the Basra air base and promised co-ordinates. It had been necessary, but ugly . . . and it might be that everything she had started had turned to ugly. They went, trailing sand, towards the extraction point – could go nowhere else.

It was ground he could handle and Badger made good progress through the reeds. The stems were close set, but he had the skills to insinuate himself, and Foxy, between them. He took each step carefully, tested the weight and kept his boots off the dry, brittle fronds. It was an illusion of success, and he knew it.

Ahead, already, light filtered through – not from above but from the front. Following this line, he would come within the next several minutes to the edge of the reeds. They thinned fast and the sunlight came into them. It was the same when he looked to the sides. The reed beds, and the soggy mud in which they thrived, were a fool's sanctuary, Badger knew ... He could hear them around and in front of him.

He thought they had boxed him, two at each side and the officer, Mansoor, and the others behind him. There were shouts from the officer. He had regained control and had them organised as he wanted. More were out ahead. He heard the answering calls from the guards and the orders from the officer. Badger was at the limits of his endurance, on the edge of what he was capable of doing, bent by a burden and exhausted. But his mind worked. He realised he was being herded towards the guns, same as the pheasants.

He went on. He told Foxy why he pushed forward towards the ever sparser reeds where the light shone brighter. 'Better that way, Foxy, on our feet and going towards where we belong ... Better to be moving than on our backs when they close round us, us looking up at them, scared, and them pissing on us. Better going forward, Foxy.'

He heard other noises, clumsier and heavier, and couldn't place them. He was bent low, found it easier to get a right boot in front of a left boot if his spine was tilted forward. It seemed to spread the weight better.

They were closer behind and the reeds were thinner ahead and the sun came on brighter and the near dark of the thickest part of the beds was gone. He couldn't control the depth of his tread and the mud between the stalks of the reeds left perfect indentations, as good as any scenes-of-crime officer would want. The mud was uniform. He couldn't find wider stretches of deeper water, to his knees or his thighs where he could go to hide the trail. Neither was there a way through where the ground had dried out. Screwed, yes. They had his trail now. Their calls to one another were growing in excitement and he thought them louder to give each other confidence. The shouts of the officer were more frequent as if he, too, sensed an end game was near. Twice more he had heard louder sounds of surging movement, and had heard also a snort of breath. He thought that among the guards there must be one perhaps more obese than the others, winded from his efforts and . . .

He heard the men coming nearer to him, driving him towards the voices at the front. They would have their best marksmen at the front. Badger wouldn't be able, when he was flushed out of the reed beds, to run, weave and duck. With the bergens dumped, he could manage a crabbed trot, barely faster than when the paras did forced speed marches on the Brecons with eighty pounds of kit on their backs.

'Foxy, what do you weigh? Must be a hundred and fifty pounds. Don't worry, I'm not dumping you.' Important to say it. Foxy wondering whether he was going to be ditched and left to face them again.

'We're going out through the front of these reeds, Foxy, and it'll be breaking cover. I don't know what we'll find, except there's guys out there in a cordon line waiting for us. I've got the Glock, and a full magazine in it, but I don't know how far we'll be from the extraction place, and whether we'll get any help from them. The border's ahead but I don't know how far.'

He couldn't hide and they had his bootprints to follow. The camouflage of the gillie suit was wrong for the reeds – good for sand and dried dirt. They were close to coming out of the cover and the light around him was more brilliant. Maybe it was that time the squaddies talked about, when they said they thought of their mothers and fathers, the girls they'd been with and babies they might have made. The bloody flies had found him and were striving to break into the headpiece. Maybe it was the time when squaddies decided whether they wanted Led Zeppelin or the Rolling Stones to play them into church – and maybe it was the time when squaddies became angry and wouldn't accept the obvious. In half a dozen paces he would be out of the reeds and guns would face him.

'There may be good ground for us and there may not. I just don't know. I'm saying, Foxy, that we aren't taken – not prisoners, no. You up for that? Whatever I shoot, there'll be two rounds left.'

He heard the crashing and breaking of stems, and didn't under-stand it.

'That's one for you and one for me. You know what, Foxy? We could get a Bassett job for this. Be good, wouldn't it? But I'm not lying down and rolling over yet. We're going to give it a go. You up for it?'

The scream was close. A man cried out, first in fear, then in terror, then in shock, and last, in pain. Badger was at the edge of the reeds. The scream cut his ears, louder and shriller than any of Foxy's had been. He saw the boar break from the reed bed, blood on its tusks. The men in front of him, who had had their rifles ready and had seemed alert to their main prey, were now running to the edge of the reeds and Badger's right. He understood. A huge thing. Maybe twenty stone of it, maybe more. As big as the one that had sniffed him in the hide and had had a short blade up its nostril. He understood that the guards at the back, behind him, had driven the beast before them, as they'd driven Badger, but a guy on the flank of the box had been in the way of the boar's flight. Not a clever option – he might have had his bowels and intestines ripped out of his stomach wall by the tusks. He screamed again, and, likely, they had no morphine. It ran, and shots were fired at it, would have been well wide. The guy kept screaming, and the boys he slept with, served with, went to him. It gave Badger a chance. He went where the boar had, on dried dirt towards the next raised berm.

19

Badger had changed the outline of his body. There was open ground ahead of him. Once there had been lagoons and channels, but the water flow had been blocked off and the sun had baked the mud during four or five years of drought. The eco-system in place since the marshlands had been claimed as civilisation's cradle was wrecked. If a river source, or a filled canal, was left untouched, the marshes survived; if they were all dammed, the reeds died and the water evaporated, the ground dried and life failed. Behind him, the reed bed had taken a last hold in what would have been, once, a wide, deep channel. Now he faced a gradual incline that stretched to the far distance. Where there had once been channels that must have been far outside Badger's depth, there was now a tacky damp surface below a fragile crust. He couldn't see where they had come in, but off to the side – too far away to be of help – there was a shimmer that might have been water. He thought himself near the approach route, but not close enough to recognise its landmarks.

He had no cover other than the low wisps of mist that were being steadily burned off. There were indentations in the ground, little scratched paths where water had once run, and stumps of reeds, broken off six inches above the mud. The stems and leaves were long rotted, and there was the ribcage of a boat, overturned and half buried, not protruding more than a few inches. There were, too, slight tumps where silt had once gathered and perhaps the current had been forced to gouge a way to the right or left. The sun was higher, clear of the horizon, and the heat built. He knew in which direction he must go, and remembered a single strand of old wire he must reach. On his own, he might have used his skills to cross the open ground. He would have reached the horizon and found the wire, part buried.

Badger had changed the outline of his body. In doing so he could no longer hug the ground, make it his friend.

With the screaming of the guard gored by the pig, the yells of the others and the shouts of the officer bringing chaos, Badger had taken Foxy off his shoulder – but had not rested. The beast had gone, had careered away and found sanctuary from its enemy in the wafting blocks of ground mist. Badger had not taken the time to rest his shoulder but had hitched the suit up, and heaved Foxy's body onto his back, then drawn the arms forward until they fell over his stomach and the head rested on his neck. He had let the gillie suit drop over two of them. 'It's going to be hot in there for you, Foxy, a steam bath, but it's the way it is. Nothing I can do about it.'

He was bringing Foxy back. He had said he would, and there had been no complaint from the old bastard. He couldn't see behind him, and to twist his head might dislodge Foxy. In front of him was a short horizon – much less distance visible than when he had stood at the edge of the reeds – he knew he must trust in his ability.

He could hear shouts still but the screams were fainter. He would crawl for the time it took him to count to a hundred. He would stay statue still for the time it took to count to another hundred. He was on his stomach, legs splayed. His knees took some of the weight as he edged forward but his elbows took more.

'The problem, Foxy, is that I don't know whether one of them has us, whether the rifle's up, whether it's a game they're playing. I don't know what's behind and I've not much idea what's in front. I just have to go forward. You up for it?'

He thought it right to tell Foxy what he was doing and why.

'They could have a gun sight on your arse, Foxy, and mine, and we won't know it.'

Badger went on as best he could, his knees and elbows scraping the ground. He moved and counted, then lay, barely daring to breathe, and counted again, and he thought Foxy stayed quiet and

still and Badger could not have asked more of him . . . and when
the next problem came in his mind, a realisation, he did not share
it, like Foxy deserved a reward . . . the next problem was their feet
and their boots. Badger's boots and Foxy's feet. He did not know
whether they stuck out from under the hem of the gillie suit: might
just be that a heap of mud or an accumulation of silt, whatever the
appearance his gillie suit left for the searching eye, was spoiled,
blasted apart, by the sight of a pair of boots and a pair of feet stuck
out from under it, and not possible for him to know the answer.

He reckoned he had done a hundred yards from the reed bed
out onto the open ground, and reckoned there might be a thousand to cover. Then he'd have to hope he found the single strand
of rusty barbed wire.

His skills would count for something, but luck might count for
more. They said – smug, complacent beggars – that luck had to be
earned. Men with towering self-esteem didn't accept that luck
played a part in success. He was going forward again and he didn't
know how much of a trail he had left, where it was wet or where it
had dried out, and didn't know whether his camouflage was good
or useless or how many were looking for him. He had gone past
the boat and was level with a buffalo's white ribs. Immediately in
front of him there was a small raised patch of sand that might
offer slight cover. The sun climbed above him, and the heat grew.

He didn't know if a rifle was aimed, whether the adjustment to
the sights had been made, whether a safety was off, whether a
trigger was squeezed, whether a bullet would kill or wound . . . He
went forward.

He could have treated it as mutiny. If it was mutiny, he was entitled, as an officer of the al-Quds Brigade, to shoot them. Then the
proper course of action, if his orders were repeatedly disobeyed,
was to report it to his superiors and the guards would face military
courts and punishment. But Mansoor did not treat it as mutiny.

Three times he had demanded that these Basij kids – peasants
from the fields and the back streets of Ahvaz where there was no
education – should form the line and advance with him. Three

times not one had moved. It was their NCO who had been gored, raked from groin to upper chest by a tusk. Had it been one of them, a teenager, the NCO might have known how to talk to them, used a language they understood, and they would have followed him. Mansoor, an officer from an élite unit they feared, did not possess such skills. They were crouched around their man. None would leave him. It would not be possible to carry him back to where the jeeps had stalled: the wound was too deep. They held his hands, and there were sobs. His screams had sunk to the moan of the dying.

Mansoor had left them.

First, he had walked along the edge of the reeds. He had found, easily, the cloven-hoofed tracks of the boar. It had run away at its maximum speed, throwing up mud. He had found, after a more thorough search, the route the man had taken from the reeds and forward across open ground. He had seen him going like a stack of hay towards the reeds, upright, carrying the man Mansoor had interrogated and killed, and dragging the little blown-up boat with the military backpacks.

He could see, where there was still a sheen of damp on the ground, the marks where elbows, knees or boots had pushed the man forward. There were places, beyond the mud, where he could find no trace of a track. Then there would be brittle crusts of baked dirt where the surface had been broken and he could pick it up again. How the body was carried, he didn't know. In his mind, Mansoor was certain that it had not been left in the reed beds. The man in the camouflage clothing would not have come through the water of the lagoon to the barracks, then thrown flash and gas grenades and taken down his comrade only to leave him, when pursuit closed on them, to the rats and pigs. The man carried his comrade and was in front of him. He watched.

He had an impression that the man was using what tactics of evasion were open to him, not going in a straight line, but cutting from one side to another, breaking any pattern of movement. Mansoor tried to imagine what he would have done. He went back to the days before the shrapnel injury had crippled him, thought of how he would have attempted flight across open ground, with the positive of a sniper's costume and the negative of a burden. He had come away from the reeds, and the anger had left him with the tiredness and the sense of abject failure. It was as if a new contest had started.

New and fresh, without past history, the game would be played out to the death.

He did not know if his thoughts had logic. He had taken himself away from his job as security man to the Engineer, away from his father and from his wife. He thought he walked alone, that the slate was clean. He searched the dirt ahead for the fugitive. He no longer cared whether success would absolve past failure. Near Mosul, he had been shown a parcel of desert, without features, and had been told that an American sniper and his spotter were there, and had killed an hour before. He and many others had raked the sand with their eyes and the aid of lenses and had not found him. The marksman had killed again as the dusk settled. But then there had been no track to follow.

Mansoor went warily, roved backwards and forwards, found a trail, lost it and found it again. He was distracted. As the heat built, the haze grew and the mist went. A bird flew across him, went from his left to his right. He stopped, moved not a muscle. A smile softened him. The ibis went far to his right, towards where there was still water, an old irrigation canal with a bund line beyond it. He knew this territory, had made it his business to learn it since his posting to the Engineer's home. He knew where trucks that had gone off the bund had slid down, where there was a burned T-74 main battle tank, and where a border watchtower was toppled. The bird headed for the water and his eyeline followed it. Small splashes of white caught his eye, and he lost the bird.

Where the ground was highest, three or four metres above where he stood, almost a kilometre away, there were two white vehicles, four-wheel drive. He knew where the man, with his comrade, his brother, headed to.

He remembered the bird: its grace, and its death.

Where he was, the ground was dried, dust, and it was easy for him to hold the man's line but then it petered out. He lost it beside a buffalo's bones. He started, again, to search for it. If the man reached the white vehicles, Mansoor had lost.

'Did you see the fucking bird?' She had her binoculars locked over her eyes.

'Yes, ma'am,' Harding said.

'What is it?'

'It's the African Sacred Ibis, miss,' Corky told her. 'Logged, of course, for our eco-study of flora and fauna.'

'It's pretty,' she said, then lapsed back into quiet.

She could hardly stand. The Boys were a few paces behind her at the Pajeros. The track petered out here and the only way they could go was back. They didn't like it when she swore – she thought it interfered with their image of themselves as protecting a maid in peril, that sort of shit. When she was tired or a fair bit pissed off, she swore and blasphemed, trying to break the image they had of her. It usually screwed up.

'They're endangered, the ibis. We used to see them down by Basra,' Shagger told her.

Abigail Jones thought it wrong that she should slouch or lean against a wheel hub, and out of the question that she should climb inside and get comfortable – ask to be woken if anything showed. 'Anything' did show. A single man was out of a reed bed, a wavering line of soft green in the light and heat. He wore combat fatigues, and when her eyes could get decent focus she fancied there were rank flashes on his shoulders and dark stains on the front of his tunic.

'What am I watching?' she asked.

Hamfist said, 'When I was with the battalion we used to patrol up past al-Amara, then go east to the border because it was a rat-run for arms shipments, as important as the one down here. There's a Revolutionary Guard camp at Mehran, a big training site, and a transit for hardware resupply. If we were close to the border they'd come out and eye us. We might wave, and shout something to spark a contact but they never responded. That's their uniform, Iranian Revolutionary Guard Corps, and they're serious. They don't do fun on a Friday night. He's looking for him.'

She turned her head away, swallowed hard.

Shagger said, 'It's down to you, miss. What are our rules of engagement?'

She attempted authority, didn't know how good a fist she made of it. 'We can fire in defence of our own persons. We can fire, also, in defence of those working with us, assuming that the threat comes from inside the territory we are currently operating in. What we cannot do is to fire live rounds into Iranian ground. Under no circumstances do we shoot, to kill or wound, across the border. What I'm saying is that he has first to reach wherever we establish the border to be and if they – in hot pursuit – cross that line, real or imaginary, we can blast the shit out of them. Conclusion: there can be no Iranian casualties, at our hand, on Iranian territory. Understood?'

She thought she would crumple in the heat. She could have found some shade by the body of either Pajero, but then she could not have watched the ground where the man came, careful, following a zigzag path. She could not have been inside, with the engine and the air-con on, because she would have ceded control. They nodded, no enthusiasm. She might have lost them.

'The one you say is an officer, coming forward, talk me through it.'

Hamfist, towering over her: 'He's following Badger's trail, miss, like a tracking hound does when it has a scent.'

'Where is Badger?'

Shagger: 'Out in front of the officer, miss, and coming.'

She saw nothing: nothing with her own eyes and nothing with the aid of the binoculars. The haze seemed to ripple on the ground and it hurt her to look. She saw nothing except the man who advanced, taking his time, patient.

'I can't see anything.'

Harding: 'If he's as good as he's talked up to be, you won't.'
Corky: 'If you see him from here, miss, he's as good as dead.'

Around him there were occasional stunted heaps of dirt and he hoped he made another of them. He saw a broad-winged shadow pass lazily in front of him and lifted his eyes, not his head: an eagle turned on a wide circle. He knew eagles from Scotland, and kites and buzzards, big birds of prey but slighter than eagles, from Wales. He didn't think its vision would be impaired by the haze coming off the mud now that the mist was gone. He thought the bird's sight would be perfect, and that it would have noted him and therefore had made a pass above him. It had in effect checked him out and moved on. If the man following him had had an eagle's eye, and its vantage-point, it would have been over long before. Badger kept to the routine he'd set, and stayed motionless for the count to a hundred, moved for the next hundred, and tried to merge with the heaps and humps. He found more often now that he lost track of how far he had counted, and had to start again. The weight of Foxy grew, as if the man had weights fastened to him.

'I reckon I have to see where we are, Foxy. If I don't, way I feel, I could go off course.'

He had worked himself around one of the heaps and stopped when it was behind him. There was another to his left, level with his hip. He had Foxy across his back. His legs were slack between Badger's, and his head was draped on his shoulder. His arms were tucked down over Badger's chest and wedged there. He thought the two heaps, augmented by the bulging gillie suit, would appear to be one larger hump that had been dumped by storms, erosion and, once, by a water channel. He started, very slowly, to turn his head.

'Were we right, Foxy? Don't they say, in combat, you have to believe in the cause and that God walks alongside you – just war, and all that? What d'you think, Foxy? Is He alongside us? Don't you understand that I need an answer, and you're the only fucker right now that can give me one?'

He shifted his head, changed his eyeline, half-inch by half-inch. A small bird, pretty plumage, pecked in the mud not a foot from his face. The sun beat down, and the heat chiselled him. His eyes ached from the brightness. The man tracked him: the officer, Mansoor, came slow and steady after him. The rifle was in his hands and could go quickly to the shoulder. For Badger, to grab for the Glock would make a convulsion of movement, and the game would be over.

'She's a good-looking woman, and she's a lump in her brain. Likely it'll be today she hears whether anything can happen or she's being sent home to tick off the days. Also likely, this'll be the day her husband's hit – what they called *interdiction*, and I was too ignorant to understand. Were we right, Foxy, to widow her and kill him? Are you going to tell me, Foxy?'

The man was still about a hundred yards behind Badger. He had veered off to the right, straightened, then taken another half-dozen short paces. Now he had stopped. He searched the ground, unhurried, and traversed. The rifle was raised. The officer, Mansoor, took a stance with his legs a little apart, his boots steady. He aimed and peered through the V sight. He had the needle steady on a target, and fired. One shot, and the songbird fled. Badger understood.

'It's us that did it. We take responsibility. It's not those people up in the north. Not the Boss, the Cousin, the Friend or the Major – and not the Jones woman and the guys with her. We did it, like we were faithful servants – did as we were told, touched forelocks, didn't bitch. Couldn't have happened without me putting the audio in place and without you hearing their talk. Can we live with that, Foxy?'

A second shot was fired. The impact, the dirt spatter, was further from Badger. Two shots fired and two heaps of earth hit. Perhaps the man had similar torments of exhaustion, the injury in his leg ached and he wanted out. Anger built in him, and frustration. That was good for Badger, because a cold-minded man was a more formidable opponent. He talked softly and Foxy's ear was an inch from his mouth.

'Different when you look into their faces, right? When you see them playing with the kids, doing everyday life.'

If he had been alone, Badger would have backed his chance of crossing the open ground as better than even odds. But it was not only himself. There was a quaver in his voice now, annoyance. 'What are we doing here, Foxy? What are we doing on their ground? What were we ever doing in this God-forsaken fucking place? Please, Foxy, I have to be told.'

Another shot was fired. He saw the flash as the cartridge case was ejected. The report echoed away from him. He didn't think the man would turn, head away, lose all heart, but he did believe that the firing of three shots showed frustration and anger, which would destroy concentration. Badger moved his head, lost sight of the man. He saw two white shapes on a horizon. They were minimally small. He wondered if it was there that the wire strand lay and if the burned tank was to his right, and the trucks that had skidded off the bund line into stagnant water, and the fallen watchtower. He needed an answer from Foxy but was denied it. He started to move again, and the silence was back, no wind blew and no cloud protected him. The heat haze was his friend.

'Us coming here, it wasn't in my name. Us walking in here – tanks, bombs, guns – that wasn't in my name. Up in the north, should I have thrown it back in their faces? I'm a policeman, Foxy, not a fucking soldier . . . Give me an answer that works, please.'

He thought he heard Foxy, thought the clipped, nasal voice told him about casualties and rehabilitation clinics, about the coffins coming in shiny hearses up a High Street in the blazing sun or when there was snow piled at the kerbs, or when rain drizzled to reflect the misery. It told him about the 'national interest' . . . He could only hope that the haze would hide him.

'They're waiting for us, Foxy, the girl and the guys are.'

Corky gestured ahead, past the expanse of open ground and past the solitary man who tracked his target. She refocused the lenses. The binoculars found them.

Abigail Jones saw a jeep and two lorries. They were short of where the first two vehicles had lost traction in the sand. She wouldn't have seen it with the naked eye, but the glasses pulled the scene into her face. A cluster of men stood around a casualty, but the new troops who had reached that point didn't stop to help, merely paused long enough to be given the general direction of the flight and pursuit. She could pick out different uniforms, good camouflage patterns and a different scale of weaponry. She recognised three RPG-7 launchers, and a machine gun. She turned to Corky, raised an eyebrow.

'That's IRGC, miss, Revolutionary Guards, not the riff-raff. But you knew that, miss.'

Her name was called, Shagger's voice, behind her. She swung on her feet. He pointed away, down the track they had used. In the far distance the sunlight blazed off the windscreen of the BMW saloon they had tipped off the track into shallow water. Dust billowed. There were three or four pick-ups, crudely painted in olive green, and a Land Rover among them. Two of the pick-ups had machine guns fastened to cross-bars behind the drivers' cabs. Her lips must have pursed, and maybe she cursed quietly. Shagger had an answer for her.

'That's Iraqi Army, likely from al-Qurnah – and that's heavy fire-power they're carrying. We're between a rock and a hard place, miss, or a lump hammer and an anvil.'

She said that the Black Hawks were in the air, which meant little. She was shivering, couldn't halt the tremors, and no longer had certainties.

A truth had come to Mansoor. The quiet allowed his thoughts to collect. Truth won through against his exhaustion and hunger, the heat of the high sun, and he realised the enormity of his failure. He saw the Engineer, whom he had been ordered to protect, leave home with his wife to go abroad in secrecy and on a journey where, if his arrangements were known, he would be vulnerable to attack. He saw, also, the man in camouflage who had been dragged from the water and had resisted interrogation. He could not justify his failure to alert senior officials immediately after the capture. Who would understand his motives? He doubted that, in the length and breadth of Ahvaz or from one end to the other of the garrison camp, he could have rooted out one man prepared to say that his actions had been reasonable, given the pressures he faced.

He was like the dog that searched for a rabbit's scent. Had it, held it, lost it and searched again for it. He could not see him. The fierce light mocked him. Often he would have sworn an oath on the Book that he saw movement in the heaps and humps of dirt that stretched away from him. Three more times he fired and heard only the report of the bullet.

The man he hunted had destroyed him. He might as well have exposed himself and urinated on Mansoor's boots. The heat of the day had come and the shimmer of the ground made a greater confusion. He sank to his knees. For a minute, no more than two, he had lost the trail. Here the ground was dry dust and he had to search for a place – no larger than a piastre – where the crust was broken. He followed a new line and went closer, imperceptibly, to a raised spur on which two heavy white vehicles waited. He saw a woman there, whose skirt moved in the wind, and men, all with the same T-shirt decoration, stood around her.

They pointed beyond him, and when he turned and saw the extended cordon line approaching, he knew little time was left him.

'You have been most patient.' The consultant leaned forward, his elbows on the desk, and peered into the face of his patient. 'A few of those who consult me are able to match your patience, but not many. I have explained in detail the size of the tumour, where it is located, what it is adjacent to and the importance of those areas in terms of speech, mobility and quality of life. You have listened and not interrupted. For that I am grateful. You will appreciate that it is my duty to take you through these matters. Now I can conclude.'

He smiled. It was the first time he had allowed any signal of his professional opinion to be on display. He saw her jaw drop.

'I would use what we call the gamma knife – more simply, that is surgical radiotherapy – to extract the problem area under general anaesthetic. It is a technique that we have used with good results in Germany.'

Her husband had caught her arm and seemed to crumple in the shoulders.

'Nothing is foolproof and nothing is guaranteed. Success is based on skill and experience. Enough to say that we feel optimistic of a good outcome. When I was called out of here, while I was explaining our diagnosis, it was to hear the opinions of others to whom I had given access to the scans. Their opinions, broadly, matched mine. We can do the operation. The alternative is that you will be dead within two months.'

Why did he persist? Easier, by far, to say that surgery was no longer an option and tell the patient to go home and spend her remaining days with her family. He could not have been gainsaid. But there was about her something magnificent that had captivated him. He had thought her husband a rat-faced bastard, and a regime man, but the man's face was wet with tears.

'We would start the necessary pre-operative examinations tomorrow, and I believe I could have access to surgery time, at the university medical centre, in Hamburg-Eppendorf, within a week.'

Had this been a German woman, she would probably have reached out her hands, held his cheeks and kissed him. It happened often. This woman's expression remained stoic and her fingers stayed clasped on her lap. He thought her beautiful. She might have been the price of his marriage and have cost him a place in the upper echelon of Lübeck society. Others now would be sitting in his waiting room, showing, perhaps, less fortitude.

'If you ring my receptionist this afternoon she will advise you of a schedule. We will need details of how the account will be settled and will give you a breakdown of costs. In the meantime, you should hope the weather clears so that you can enjoy the old quarter of the city, but do not tax yourself too greatly. I will see you to your car.'

He stood. The man – an Engineer who made bombs that killed and mutilated troops far from their homes – blubbered like a child, but she was composed.

★   ★   ★

The tide was sliding away and the beach showed a damp ribbon of sand. He stood where it was dry and could see miles along the coast line . . . as he had that day. It was where the border had run from alongside the Dassower See, and its shore, then cut across the peninsula at its narrow point, leaving Priwall in the west, Rosenhagen and Potenitz in the east. It had come down from the sand dunes, now a nature reserve: *Naturschutzgebiet – Betreten verboten.* Then, the wire, the minefields and barricades had crossed the beach and gone far out into the waters of the Lübeckerbucht. It had been an early-summer day, with a brisk wind but clean sunshine.

The pastor had brought him.

The Lutheran priest had worn jeans, an open-necked checked shirt and heavy sandals, while the youthful Len Gibbons had dressed in grey slacks, lightweight brogues and a sports jacket of quiet herringbone. It had been the pastor's invitation. *He wants to see you once more, see the man he works for whom he trusts. His friend's cousin is a border guard and it is arranged, but you must give no signal, and you will see him only very briefly, but it will be, for him, as if you touched hands.* They had walked on the beach and had gone towards the fence, where it dropped down into the dirty Baltic water. A watchtower overlooked that section, and a patrol boat was out in the Bight. It had been a naturist's beach, and they had gone among the flapping bosoms and shrivelled members of elderly males and had seen the guards, behind the fence or up in the towers, clicking their cameras; there had been a joke about porn stocks in the guards' camp being low. They were the only clothed people on their side of the wire.

On the far side, every man was uniformed and armed, big dogs had howled at them, and Gibbons had seen him. Maybe for a half-minute, and at a distance of some three hundred yards, a young, slight-built figure had come from the gorse behind the dunes and walked towards the sea with a guard. Antelope had stopped close to the waterline, and gazed towards the barriers, then turned away. Gibbons and the pastor had gone back through the naturists and the young SIS officer had felt bonded with his asset, more trusting.

Two months later, the message had come through that new courier arrangements were required and Gibbons, to his desk chief, had spoken up on behalf of the asset's request. Contacts had been supplied. Three at least, because of Gibbons's naïveté and his superiors' lack of due diligence, were dead, and their lives would have ended unpleasantly. The experience had made Len Gibbons – surviving by fingernail grip – fight as he had been fought. He had been taught, in a front-of-the-class seat, the value of ruthless application of his government's policy. No sentiment intruded into his professional life, no qualms were permitted. Morality? He wouldn't have known how to spell it.

So cold. Near his feet there was an old, pockmarked railway sleeper, with heavy chains nailed to it. It would have been a tiny part of the underwater system with which the East German state had sought to defend itself. Pathetic people, wiped from history . . . Eleven summers before Len Gibbons had come here, a teenage international swimmer from the east, Axel Mitbauer – 400-metres freestyle – had gone into the water up the coast, having anointed his body with petroleum jelly, and had swum fifteen and a half miles before reaching a bobbing buoy in the Lübeck Bight. Gibbons always took that story as proof of the superiority of his country, his creed, his calling. He still felt it as strongly as he had when he had last been on this beach those years before. He had never worn patriotism on his sleeve, but it was warming to be on a winner's team.

The wind whipped him. Pretty shells crunched under his feet. He looked at his wristwatch. It might already have happened, or would be about to happen. He thought it time to start the journey home. He had done well. It was a triumph and would be recognised as such by the few inside the loop. Good to have been at this place of failure when a success was acted out.

Deutsche Presse-Agentur
Lübeck 24.11.2011 09.12
Police report fatal shooting on the campus of the university medical school.

The Cousin heard it on a news flash on the local station – he had tuned in on his car radio for that purpose. 'That's my boy,' he murmured. He ignored the No Smoking sign in the car, lit a cigarillo and drove a little faster down the wide highway. He felt good – like after the best sex or a decent dinner – and he'd stay with the station for updated news.

Deutsche Presse-Agentur.
Lübeck 24.11.2011 09.29
Eyewitnesses at the university medical school of the UNESCO heritage city of Lübeck report two dead and one injured in a gun attack outside the neuro-surgery unit of the teaching hospital. A confirmed fatality is Steffen Weber, a consultant at the hospital, who was shot on the building's steps. An unidentified gunman fled from the scene of the attack. Police have now cordoned off the hospital grounds.

The swap had been done, vehicles switched – the clothing and the weapon would go back to Berlin for disposal – and the Friend drove carefully within the speed limit towards the ferry port on the road to Travemünde. He knew these people, had had experience of them for more than thirty years of his working life. He had been on the periphery of the teams that had gone into Beirut for the revenge killings after the Munich Olympiad, and those hitting targets in North Africa, Rome, Paris, London and Damascus. He would have said he could read the feelings of the trigger men, whether they fired pistols at close range or detonated bombs remotely. This one was extraordinary. The man beside him was quiet, relaxed and had yawned a couple of times. He showed no sign of having spent a bad night on a cot bed in an outer office at a local synagogue. It was on the radio, made a news flash and interrupted an item about the preparations for the Christmas fair and the hope of a boost to the city's economy.

'They have not spoken of him yet.'

'They will. Give them time.'

Deutsche Presse-Agentur
Lübeck. 24.11.2011 09.43
A Lübeck police spokesperson said that Steffen Weber, consultant in neuro-surgery, was pronounced dead at the scene after being shot on the steps into the building where he had his office. Also killed, she said, was a foreign national, as yet unnamed, and a driver from the Iranian embassy in Berlin was wounded – but with no life-threatening injuries. The unidentified gunman is believed to have escaped from the hospital grounds in a commercial black Nissan van driven by an accomplice.

She sat on a hard chair in a corridor. Her husband's body and that of the consultant were beyond swing doors. Twice she had tried to breach them and twice she had been gently, but firmly, refused entry. No one spoke to her. If she spoke to them, her language was not understood. Many hurried past and the swing doors flapped open for them, but not for her. There were policemen, doctors in gowns, nurses. She was not offered tea, coffee or water. She was forgotten. A woman came past her, escorted by uniformed men and bureaucrats in suits. She was blonde, expensive and boot-faced. Naghmeh assumed her to be the wife of the man who had tried, and failed, to shield her husband. Her head hurt, where her hair had been wrenched and there was blood on her face and hands, but no one seemed to see it.

Deutsche Presse-Agentur
Lübeck, 24.11.2011 09.58
A police spokesperson has confirmed that the fatalities following a shooting in the grounds of the university medical school were a neuro-surgery expert, Steffen Weber, married with one child, and a foreign national, believed to be an Iranian male, who was escorting his wife from the building following a consultation with Dr Weber. An Iranian embassy driver was shot twice as he attempted to block the gunman's escape. Across the street at the time of the shooting was twenty-three-year-old Manfred Hartung, a student: 'The two men and the woman came down

the steps from the doors. They were smiling and radiant, laughing. The driver of the waiting car opened the back door for the lady, and a short man, young, wearing workman's overalls, laid a shovel on the pavement and stepped forward. I saw he held a handgun. He aimed at the man who held the woman's arm, but the other attempted to put his body in the line of fire. The gunman shot four times. Two bullets hit the one I now know to have been a doctor, and when he fell, two more were fired at the man who was with the woman. The first put that man onto the steps and the woman fell over him, but the gunman pulled back her hair with one hand, placed his weapon against the man's forehead and fired again. The driver put himself in the way of the gunman and was shot at close range. It was very fast, like a film, and I doubt it lasted more than fifteen seconds. It was an assassination. The gunman did not run but walked at a brisk pace up the road and a van drove him away.'

The talk was of cuts, small neat slashes to the budget on which his empire depended. The director general had Human Resources, Finance, Overseas Stations and Purchasing in his office and they nit-picked around costs and outgoings. Fiefdoms were defended and ... He had the text on the television screen that was on the wall behind his department managers. The politicians demanded savings but were wary of the power he exercised. If he were to leak that the nation's security was threatened by penny-pinching, the Westminster crowd would capitulate. He played the game, went through the processes. Something would be offered, but not much. They were on the matter of foreign travel – business class or cattle truck – and he read the text reporting an incident in a distant town in northern Germany. It was enough for him to collate the sums: three plus three made six.

Take the bastard down, Len, he had said, and the head had ducked in understanding. Gibbons, always described as 'a safe pair of hands', had delivered and might get a minor gong out of it for long service, but not much more, and there would be no meeting in this office with congratulations bouncing off the walls and no pumped handshake. It was *deniable*, and would be kept that way, but he felt a frisson of excitement and his blood flowed faster. Matter closed, business completed. He switched off the television screen. A good outcome.

'Miss, are we fucked?'

Not a question that Abigail Jones needed to answer. Pretty bloody clear. She strained to hear better. Sounds filtered in her ears. There was the light wind that ruffled her hair, the fullness of her skirt, the scarf at her throat, and sang a little against the radio antennae on the Pajeros. Harding had a hacking cough. Hamfist had the habit, when tension rose, of slapping the palm of his hand across the stock of his weapon and making a rhythm of it. Corky kicked stones he found on the bund line. Some went off in ricochets and a few cannoned against the bulletproofed sides of the Pajeros. Shagger sang a hymn, barely audible – it would have been one he'd learned as a kid in chapel, in Welsh.

Hamfist asked again: 'Are we fucked, miss? If we are, what can we do about it? Put it this way, miss, I'm not going into the hands of the crowd in front or the crowd behind. No chance, miss.'

Abigail Jones thought of all the women in the SIS, those who did power-walking up and down the corridors, jogged in the midday break, were shagged by line managers and desk chiefs to get up the ladder faster, contributed at seminars and think-tanks, and wanted responsibility. They would sweat for it and spread their legs to be given it. She hadn't sought it and it had landed in her lap. 'Where are you, girls, when you're needed to share the load?' More important: where was Badger? Prime importance: where was the chopper?

'Nearly fucked, but still a little slack to wind in.'

She listened for the Black Hawk, but didn't hear it. She knew it was coming, was airborne and had the co-ordinates. She knew also that the crew would have flown special forces, done difficult stuff, was experienced in extraction, but it had not, yet, showed.

'Minimal slack, but a bit. You meant that, Hamfist, about not going into a cage?'

She didn't know where he was, how far forward. Didn't know how far he had to come. The Iranians, described by her guys as IRGC, were in a cordon line and coming through. They were some four hundred yards from her, her Boys and the two Pajeros. They had good firepower – her team couldn't match the hardware – and came steadily towards the single man in the olive green, with the officer's flashes, who tracked Badger.

Of Badger, there was neither sight nor sound. She had powerful binoculars, and the Boys did. They also had trained eyes for watching ground and the subtle changes movement made. Abigail had not seen him. Neither had Shagger, Corky, Hamfist nor Harding, who had the best eyes of them all. It was as though he had disappeared, burrowed into the ground and gone. The cordon line came to the officer. She couldn't know what was said but saw the little cameo played out: authority gone, rank lost, humiliation on show. He was spoken to – the line had stopped – and his head didn't lift. He might have mumbled an answer. A more senior officer's hand thrashed across his face, and there would have been a drawn pistol in it. Her lenses showed the grey, or white, flashes of teeth falling, then the blood drops. He was hit again, was on his knees and kicked. How would it have been in her own crowd? If she failed to bring Badger home, and Foxy, if they were paraded on state television – dead or alive – and if a government had to squirm out apologies, how would it be? Not kicked, not losing teeth, not pistol-whipped, but out on her neck, erased from memory. She'd be – to those who knew – a cult figure of ridicule and hate. Perhaps better to be kicked.

'Miss, their cage isn't for me.' Hamfist said it distantly, as if – each minute – her importance counted a little less.

She looked into their faces. Harding's was impassive, told her nothing. Corky wouldn't meet her gaze. Shagger murmured that goddamn hymn.

'Could we go across country?' It wasn't rhetorical: she didn't know the answer.

There was a chorus, but clearest was Harding: 'We can't, ma'am. Go down, get round the firepower in front of us and trek into Iranian territory. Go right or left and we hit water. We wouldn't do a half-mile and they'd take the vehicles out with the weaponry they have. It would be a shooting war and not on ground of our choosing . . . and it does nothing for the reason we're here – for the guys, Badger and Foxy. If you've looked behind you, ma'am, the outlook is worse.'

Behind was the hard place, the anvil.

The elevated track on which they had come was blocked by the Iraqi vehicles. The mounted machine guns had men behind them, and she could see the layers of belt ammunition, lit by sunlight. They were .5 calibre weapons and the Pajeros would not be able to go down into the dirt and survive that sort of attack. They were around two hundred yards behind her and the Boys. Local people, local troops, loathed the private security contractors. They might have had a decent relationship with their mentors in the American or British Army, but the private soldiers – not answerable to civilian or military law – were detested. A single shot was fired, from a rifle. She ducked, then focused. An officer in a swagger pose, legs apart and barrel chest pushed forward, stood in front of the Land Rover's bonnet, held an AK and had it pointed to the sun. A warning. Near to the officer, gesticulating, was the sheik who had lost a BMW top-of-the-range saloon.

She turned. Looked the other way. To the front. The IRGC men and their officer were closer now, and the beaten, kicked man lay in the mud far in their rear. The first shot was answered. She heard the crack of a bullet going high . . . between a rock and a hard place, a lump hammer and an anvil.

She searched the ground and couldn't see him.

Two forces and two shots. She had nothing sensible to say and left her Boys hanging on her silence. If they were taken she would have a fair chance of not growing old in either the Evin gaol of Tehran or the Abu Ghraib lock-up in Baghdad. The Boys might have a poor chance of ever smelling fresh air again, particularly if an Engineer had gone into a gutter and bled his life away, and especially if tribesmen from a marsh village had been killed in the break-out with the Pajeros.

She searched again, every damn stone, every rotted reed stalk, a buffalo's white bones and a frame for a boat encased in mud. She saw a movement and thought it was a rabbit. The lump hammer and the anvil came closer – maybe less than a hundred metres to each side of them. She heard the scrape as one of her Boys armed his weapon.

'For fuck's sake, miss, what now?'

It was because they had come back for him, for Badger. It was because Badger had gone to get Foxy. She could have screamed it. All bloody sentiment, the crap about going the extra yard to retrieve a colleague, obligations in a world she didn't inhabit. She sucked in her breath and would scream that the bloody hole they found themselves in was *their* fault. Blame should not be levelled at *her*. She bit it down, clamped her teeth on her tongue, felt blood on her lips – and heard them.

The big blades were spinning pretty circles and the two came, dark and fast, with the profile of killer dogs over the last of the bund lines. There were no pylons here and no phone wires slung from poles. The Black Hawks could have been twenty feet above the ground, could not have been more than forty. She had no more strength and her knees buckled. She could see, when the Black Hawks were above them, the faces of the cockpit crew, then the hatch gunners. They slowed and banked a little, then hovered and she saw that one had taken a position towards the anvil and the other faced the lump hammer. In addition to the firepower from the hatches there were rockets on pods slung forward below the stubbed wings. The rock had stopped and the hard place stayed static.

Abigail Jones was trembling and could barely stand upright under the down-draughts. She cupped her hands and screamed his name.

Futile.

The Boys took a cue from her. They all screamed, five feeble voices against the thunder of the engines. She had no link to the pilot but she could see him clearly through the shield of the cockpit. He pointed to his wristwatch and tapped it hard, like this was no fairground joyride and time was precious. The rotors kicked up dust.

The dirt and sand swirled round them and it was in her mouth and nose, flattening her loose clothing against her torso and legs. The Boys were spewing, coughing, and there was a curtain round them of sand, dirt, debris, stones that scoured their faces. The curtain was dense enough for her not to see, any longer, the lump hammer or the anvil. She lost her view of the rock and the hard place. She was choking and her screams had died.

He came through the curtain.

She didn't know where from. He was low, bent, and shuffled. The down-blast of the blades rocked him. It was Shagger who reached him first – ten paces from her and now clear of the curtain – then Harding, who dragged off the headpiece. He was huge in the gillie suit and seemed to understand little. His eyes were glazed and without recognition. First, Abigail Jones saw the bare white feet trailing from the bottom of the suit, then the head that lolled on Badger's chest. Corky had her, no ceremony, and one Black Hawk came down. The skids bounced once, and the other flew cover above. Corky had hold of her collar and his other hand was between her legs and she felt herself airborne, thrown high and forward. The gunner's gloved hand yanked her into the interior. Badger came next, and it was a struggle for the crew to get him up. He neither helped nor resisted them. Hamfist followed, then the rest . . . and they climbed, steeply. Her guts dropped lower than her knees. Before they pulled away – flew for safety – the two gunners had a moment of fun: they shot up the Pajeros until the flames started and black smoke spiralled. They went out fast.

Shagger shouted in her ear, competed with the engine power, 'He won't let go of him. He has Foxy.'

Harding yelled in her other ear, 'Cold, dead, been gone for hours, but he's not loosing him.'

She said, with a wonderment, 'All that time, through all that, carrying him, already dead, with what was chasing him – it's incredible . . . a miracle.'

A gunner – had the name 'Dwayne Schultz' stamped on his jacket – passed her a headset and she heard the pilot. They were to overfly Basra and go direct to Kuwait City. She shrugged, not her decision. She twisted in the seat and could see back up the fuselage and past the gunner's squatting body. Badger wore the suit and his hands were wrapped across his chest. Through the open flap she could see Foxy's head and arms, a little of his shoulders; she could see also some of the wounds on his body. The responsibility weighed on her, and the cost.

'Good to have you back with us, Badger. To have both of you . . .'

20

He was early, and confused. It was pretty much like being a national serviceman, new to his corps, not daring to be late on parade and standing by his made bed with the folded blankets on it, waiting for the sergeant to pitch them onto the drill yard. Doug Bentley was early because he hadn't known how long it would take him to get to the town at that time of night. He was confused because no one he'd met or spoken to had seemed to know the form. Just 'Best bib and tucker, Doug, and all the gear.'

It was past eleven and, other than on a British Legion night, that was way past Doug Bentley's bedtime. Most of the pubs had closed, the Chinese was only doing slack trade, and the last bus had gone through. He stood outside the Cross Keys and it was cold, properly cold, with no moon to speak of, a clear sky and a hard frost forecast. He'd taken the precaution of wearing a wool pullover under his white shirt, which made his blazer tight, but better a little discomfort than being seen to shiver.

There had been a phone call, taken by Beryl and passed to him, from their local organiser around the time they were having their tea. That was all the warning he'd had. 'And, of course, Doug, completely up to you as to whether you turn out but others will be there. Don't ask me any more because I don't know anything.' The big decision was made to go, even if it meant a taxi fare to get home.

Others came, looked as lost as himself, men from Bath, Melksham, Frome and Chippenham, two from Swindon, and the Hungerford fellow who'd been cavalry. They all wore their polished shoes, the usual slacks and blazers, and had their white gloves and their standards in the leatherette cases. Well, obvious that a hearse was coming through, but no one knew the name on the box, or where he'd bought it.

He was glad of the company, and them being there made it real. They formed a casual line, as they always did, a little down the street from the big pub and opposite the war memorial. He didn't like to show off his ignorance so didn't quiz his colleagues, but he realised they were all in the same boat when questions were put to him. Answers were in short supply. So be it. He followed the actions of others and put his pole together, letting the standard hang free. He checked that the black bow at the top wasn't creased, and started to hear voices. If he tilted his head a little and looked back to the arched entrance of the Cross Keys, he could see people emerging.

A man in a striped suit, with an open camel overcoat and a trilby low on his forehead, said, 'Bit of a dump, don't you think, Bob? Probably all right on a spring morning, certainly not a November evening. I suppose if that's what was wanted it was right to do it. It'll bring closure. It was a good result and achieved at a rather low cost ... Can't ask more than that.' The thick-set man with him might have been, Doug Bentley thought, a body-guard. He nodded his head, on which the hair was almost shorn, and might have murmured, 'Yes, Director.'

They crossed the road, had to wait for an old saloon, speakers thumping. A young woman, with fine golden hair hanging loose and bright under a street-lamp, parked up the High Street and came at a jog towards the Cross Keys. She met a man – another suit, but creased and with shapeless trousers. 'It's Len, isn't it?'

'And you're Abigail? Good to meet. Funny old place this, but a funny old occasion. Don't get me wrong, I'm not against it, only that it's a bit left-side, irregular, sort of off the beaten track. What is it – a week since you were back?'

'A long week.'

'And the colleague?'

'Bizarre. Out on his feet when he went into the chopper, and wouldn't let go of Foxy – you remember they were Badger and Foxy? – and was talking to him, soft and quiet, all the way to

Kuwait, a lengthy flight even in a Black Hawk. When we landed
Badger had to be separated from the body – it was stark bollock
naked. Weird. It took two of my escort to get him to free it. The
corpse went into the care of the ambassador, formalities to be
gone through. We had to quit sharpish, and did. We were out on
the first London flight, straight after he'd had a medical. What did
I expect? That he might sit with me, put his business seat flat and
sleep? He went into Economy and I never saw him until Heathrow.
Frankly, Len, I might have enjoyed a drink with him at the airport
and we might have shared a ride to ... God, we went through
tough times in a tough place, and in a sense were together – don't
quote me or I'll throttle you – but he walked past me in the
concourse and said not a word – like I didn't exist. The last I saw
of Badger he was at a bus stop, waiting for the shuttle – creepy.'

'It all went well. I had time for a quick shop on the way out for
some marzipan, useful as a present for home and my office. Then
it was a cloud of dust and gone. I assume he knows how it all
turned out.'

'I don't know who told him, if anyone did. We sent a message to
the opposition.'

'Sent it in clear and loud.'

'Will it be listened to?'

'What matters is that we sent it, and it'll hurt them and bloody
their nose. I value that as justification.'

'Good. Where should we be standing? Is this right, or should we
be on the other side?'

'Where he is, I suppose. But ... Can you believe it? That big
bastard cut me dead in the bar, didn't know me. We stand near to
the director but on pain of death we don't speak to him. We don't
show the world we know him. Did I get a glass of sherry? Did I
hell. Did I get a nod and recognition? Not yet. I think it was something to be proud of.'

'I'll catch you.'

The one she'd called Len crossed the road, now empty, and
took a place a dozen steps from the director. Doug Bentley's eyes
darted. She had a pretty face, with frankness in the eyes and a jut

at her chin. Her cheeks were red and the freckles alive. She wore old jeans and a quilted anorak, and every few seconds she swept the hair off her face. He realised she needed a moment of privacy from view – and lit up a cigarette.

He looked the other way, up the High Street, not down it, and saw the woman. He recognised. Gagged for a moment. Saw her and wondered about her blouse, the buttons on the front. Another woman was hurrying down the High Street with two girls, skinny teenagers, in tow. So much for Doug Bentley to absorb – and a guy was hovering behind Ellie . . . Ellie wore black, and her blouse was white but not buttoned high. He could see the ornament she wore and wanted to stare, had to force himself not to. He was uncertain whether the buttons were out of order.

The other woman caught up. 'You're Ellie?'

'That's right, and you are . . . ?'

'Liz – and these are my daughters. It wasn't a pretty divorce, but I was told this afternoon what was happening – wasn't told much else. Wasn't really told anything, except that I might want to be here. I took the girls straight out of college and we hit the road. I've moved on but that doesn't mean I don't remember the good times with him, and I respect him. You have my deep sympathy.'

'Thank you, Liz, that's really kind. I don't have any answers and I don't even know where to go to get them. I'm utterly devastated. He was such a wonderful man, so caring and kind. All I feel is emptiness. This is Piers, from the office where I work, Defence, and he's being very supportive. Foxy was such a generous man and so much loved. What's happening here tells me he died a hero, and this is the least he can be given, what he deserved.'

So much to tell Beryl, might keep her up half the night. Smug little sod, Piers. He was standing too close to Ellie. The bell sounded. Doug's line shuffled, straightened, and the bottom piece of the pole went into the leather slot above his privates. His hands, immaculate in the gloves, took the strain of the standard. A policeman had walked out into the High Street and was waving brusquely at a car to go through and leave the road clear, like they always did. He could see, across the High Street, the women, the top man and his minder. Bikers had joined them and they cupped cigarettes, which glowed in the near darkness. Lights were coming on in the upper rooms above Doug Bentley's line of colleagues and the war memorial. Further up the pavement a man was in a heavy tartan dressing-gown, with his pyjama trousers and bedroom slippers; a woman on the other side of the street had put on a quilted dressing-gown but a nightdress hem peeped free. The bell tolled from the tower of St Bartholomew and All Saints, and more came out. The town seemed to wake. The pavement was well lined opposite him, could have been two deep, and plenty more on his side, but no reporters, no cameras and none of the satellite trucks the television brought.

The blue lights came up the hill, flashing garishly. It would have passed the Pheonix Bar and the Methodist church, the entrance to the Rope Yard and the front of the dental clinic. It would now be level with the Wagon and Horses. The lights were on a police motorcycle. They had the standards high. Doug Bentley was next to a Canal Zoner, and beyond him was a para from their association. A man slipped into place beside him. He gave him a glance, fast. Scruffily dressed, what Doug Bentley would have called out of place, in old cord trousers that had smooth bits above the knees, a T-shirt, a windcheater, and a casual acrylic beanie hat. He hadn't shaved. The police motorcycle came level with the standards and crawled. He looked again to the side. It was wrong that a man should stand close to their line and be turned out like a vagrant. The blue lights went slowly and lit the face. He blanched and the standard rocked. The face was burned, might have had a blowtorch at it. There were big circles where the flesh was raw and the skin was broken, and they were coated in a cream that glistened. He thought the man had been under attack by mosquitoes or flies. The face was gaunt. The hearse came.

A funeral director walked ahead of it. He had a good stride and swung his stick with practised ease. Doug Bentley recognised him from some of the daylight repatriations. The escort was not what he was used to, no police car, no military Range Rover, no back-up hearse, but in essence it was the same, and the Legion people gave it reality, with the gathering opposite, the crowds who'd abandoned their beds or the late-night stuff on television and the bars. They dipped the standards. He should have hung his head and looked at the pavement, but he could tilt a little and it would not be noticed. He knew who it was – would have been an idiot not to have known. The face was ravaged, as if the man had starved, and the pocked cheeks were sunken. He wondered where it came from, the name 'Badger'. His neck had the scrawniness of an old man's, and the coat hung loose. The man, Badger, had his hands in his pockets and kept them there while on both sides of the street men stiffened and stood erect. Doug Bentley did not feel the hands in the pockets showed disrespect. Likely they had been so close that respect was proven.

He could see into the hearse, but only a little of the box was visible. Normal times there was a tight-pinned Union flag on it. It was shapeless and camouflaged. There seemed to be a thousand tags of green and black, soft brown and sand-coloured tabs of material woven into it. The dirt was obvious and the mud stains and . . . The woman, Liz – first wife – held her daughters close to her, all weeping, and Ellie had stepped off the pavement into the road and put the palm of her hand on the glass. Abigail had her face turned away as if she couldn't halt the tears and didn't want it known. Len stood tall and the director was at attention, stiff. His man had slipped on an old military beret and saluted. Doug Bentley's arm was dragged down and his standard shook. He realised he had the weight of Badger to support, and did it. He thought the man so wrecked that he should have been in a hospital bed, not cold on the street of Wootton Bassett.

The stick was swung, the feet pivoted, the top hat went again onto the funeral director's head, and he walked. The hearse followed him.

There were little shouts, could have been from the bikers: 'Well done . . . Well done, mate . . . Well done, my boy . . . Well done.'

A few clapped.

The voice beside him was soft, little more than a murmur: 'Not in your name, Foxy, and not in mine.'

The standards were raised and the order was given for them to fall out. He could take the pole from the slot without toppling the man, but the weight slackened. He separated the pole into its sections, furled the standard and stowed it. He heard little bursts of talk. The blue lights were down the street and moving away, and while he watched them they seemed to speed. The pavements were clearing fast, and there was the roar of Harleys, BMWs and Triumphs as the bikers went. The women were arm in arm, coming back to the Cross Keys and the bar and . . . He'd lost the others, Abigail and Len, the director, and the bodyguard that an important man warranted, and the policeman who had done the traffic control.

The one he had supported, Badger, threaded his way through the thinning crowds and walked badly, as if he had big blisters. He seemed to sway and the light lessened on his back.

Doug Bentley watched him as far as he could, then headed for the car park behind the big supermarket and the library, where his taxi would be waiting. He felt he had been there, wherever it was, and that he had lived through it, whatever had happened there, and was humbled to have been a part of it. He imagined sand and dirt and burning heat.

The clock on the tower struck midnight. A new day had started.

The man was gone, like it was a job done, and the High Street was empty. The night closed on him.

GOD,
The DEVIL,
and
HARRY POTTER

Also by

JOHN KILLINGER

Ten Things I Learned Wrong from a Conservative Church
Enter Every Trembling Heart
Lost in Wonder, Love, and Praise

GOD, The DEVIL, and HARRY POTTER

A CHRISTIAN MINISTER'S DEFENSE OF THE BELOVED NOVELS

∞

JOHN KILLINGER

THOMAS DUNNE BOOKS
ST. MARTIN'S PRESS ❦ NEW YORK

THOMAS DUNNE BOOKS.
An imprint of St. Martin's Press.

www.stmartins.com

Title page photograph courtesy of freestockphotos.com

Book design by Jonathan Bennett

ISBN 0-312-30869-8

First Edition: December 2002

10 9 8 7 6 5 4 3 2 1

For
Arthur and Charles Salutksy
and James D. Smith,
my good friends when I was
Harry Potter's age,
and
Thelma Hayes Herrin,
who was our devoted teacher
and has faithfully kept up
with all of us ever since

CONTENTS

GOD,
The DEVIL,
and
HARRY POTTER

INTRODUCTION

The appearance of Harry Potter has been one of the most exciting events in publishing history. The first Potter novel, *Harry Potter and the Sorcerer's Stone,* was turned down by several publishers for being either too literary or too long or both. But when it appeared in bookstores it became an overnight sensation, and was the first children's book to make it onto the *New York Times* Best-Seller List since E. B. White's *Charlotte's Web* in 1952. In 1999, after the publication of *Harry Potter and the Prisoner of Azkaban,* the Potter tales were numbers one, two, and three on the *Times* Best-Seller List. When *Harry Potter and the Goblet of Fire* came out in 2000, it sold an unbelievable 3 million copies in the United States in a single week. Children and their parents actually camped out overnight in front of bookstores to be sure to get their copies.

On December 18, 2001, *USA Today* announced that J. K. Rowling's Harry Potter books had made her the best-selling author in the world, surpassing the record previously held by mystery writer John Grisham. On that date, the four Harry Potter books in print were firmly entrenched on the best-seller lists, having been there for months and showing no signs of fatigue. They had been translated into more than 30 languages in more than 130 countries. The movie of the first novel, *Harry Potter and the Sorcerer's Stone,* was then opening to sell-out crowds around the world, and many children were standing in line to see it a third, fourth, or even fifth time. Stores all over the globe carried Harry Potter pop-up books, coloring books, trading cards, eyeglasses, watches, dolls, games, posters, magic wands, and other Potter-phernalia. Even the giant retailer Wal-Mart sells drapery material bearing the crests and names of Gryffindor, Hufflepuff, Slytherin, and Ravenclaw, the four student houses at Hogwarts School of Witchcraft and Wizardry. Author J. K. Rowling's agent in London, Christopher Little, has said he receives more than one hundred inquiries a day from people wanting to use Harry Potter's name and image to market various kinds of products.

All of this in spite of opposition from the Muggles—a word Harry's creator adapted and softened from "mug" (someone easily fooled) to designate the mundane, noncognoscenti populace that doesn't understand or sympathize with the world of wizardry—and can also well relate to the militant objectors purporting to represent the best interests of the Christian religion. Typical of these is a woman I know in Michigan who has forbidden her grandchildren to read the Potter books because of their "wicked" picture of "a world filled with wizards and goblins." She hasn't actually read the books, of course; but the word is out on the conservative grapevine that they are dangerous and unfit for public consumption. Many conservative Christian parents have led vigorous crusades to have the books banned from schools and libraries. James Dobson's Focus on the Family organization, one of the most powerful citizen groups in the United States, opposes the novels on its website. A massive protest in Columbia, South Carolina, orchestrated to coincide with one of Rowling's American book tours, argued that there is too much evil and darkness in the Potter stories, and that they promote witchcraft and wickedness. A minister in Alabama wrote to *USA Today* objecting to the attention the newspaper paid to the movie of *Harry Potter and the Sorcerer's Stone*. It was a nasty, evil film, he declared, despite the fact that he boasted of having neither seen the film nor read the novel from which it was made. Another minister, Pastor Jack Brock, of Christ Community Church in Alamogordo, New Mexico, had a "holy bonfire" on the Sunday after Christmas 2001, in which he publicly torched the Potter books, declaring them "an abomination to God and to me"!

There is a handsomely published book called *Harry Potter and the Bible,* by conservative Christian writer Richard Abanes, which assembles most of the pharisaical arguments against the Potter literature, blasting its supposed ties to the occult and to new-age philosophy, assailing Harry and his friends for the way they break rules, and insisting that "the books clearly present far too much moral subjectivity and patently unbiblical actions to be of any ethical value."[1] The author says *Harry Potter and the Goblet of Fire* "glamorizes dishonesty," and he criticizes Dumbledore for saying it is his belief that truth is (only) "generally" preferable to lies. He extols Percy Weasley as the kind of role model children should have, contends that scripture "tells us to behave in a way that is diametrically opposed to how Harry Potter" and his friends comport themselves, and accuses Rowling of catering to children's natural desire to be "grossed out" by unsavory descriptions of body fluids, crude jokes, and vulgar acts such as belching, vomiting, and "accidentally cursing."

Abanes also defends the conservative idolization of J. R. R. Tolkien and C. S. Lewis, insisting that their writings, which he dubs "mythopoetic," are not harmful to children because they create settings of complete imagination instead of interweaving fantasy and real life as Rowling does—something he is sure confuses Harry Potter fans into wanting to become witches and wizards. He praises Tolkien for his "masterful" tales and his "expansive imagination and brilliant mind," and extols Lewis because he "authored numerous books explaining and defending Christianity." Their Christian theology, he insists, is "veiled beneath various characters," while Rowling provides readers with "a *direct* link" to "current" paganism and the practice of witchcraft. There is indeed a witch in Lewis' Narnia stories, Abanes admits, "but she is evil and based on age-old and widely accepted symbols and illustrations of evil."[2] Apparently it is *attractive* witches who are out, for the conservative mind-set!

Perhaps nothing in *Harry Potter and the Bible* reveals the conservative way of thinking more than Abanes's advice to parents whose children must choose between remaining in a classroom where the teacher is reading from a Harry Potter story or suffering the embarrassment of asking to be excused. It may be better for them to remain in class, he concedes, than "being made to suffer the taunts of other children." But the parents should conduct "follow-up discussions" at home, and they might take the opportunity to introduce their children to "godly fantasy such as C. S. Lewis' Narnia series or J. R. R. Tolkien's books about Middle-Earth." The experience, moreover, "might open up witnessing opportunities for a child to share Christ's love with classmates."[3]

There is another, much more balanced, book by Connie Neal called *What's a Christian to Do with Harry Potter?* Disturbed by the controversy among Christians over the possible subversion of faith in the Potter stories, Neal takes a conciliatory approach, quoting both sides of the argument and pleading for a gentler, kinder, and more civil agreement to disagree. She admits that Rowling's narratives create *curiosity* about witchcraft among the young, and concedes that this can be disturbing to Christian parents. But she herself doesn't appear to regard the books as inherently evil, and suggests that they can even be employed to generate conversations with children that will prove helpful and enlightening. When a friend impugned Neal's faith for working on a book about Harry Potter, she says, she mollified the friend by telling her how she had "shared the gospel with a family friend by using the Harry Potter story as a redemptive analogy, and how he became a Christian shortly thereafter."[4]

One chapter in Neal's book is titled "What Would Jesus Do with Harry Potter?" It is an intriguing question—at least *I* found it so—and one the conservative religious mind will surely find central to any argument about the adolescent wizard. But Neal uses it craftily, suggesting that individual Christians will answer it according to their particular likes and prejudices, and that, because there can be no objective answer, it is important not to "turn it into a rhetorical question to tell someone else what Jesus would have *them* do."[5]

Let me be clear at the outset: I too am a Christian. In fact, I am an ordained clergyman and have in my lifetime ministered to six parishes, spanning the continent from Massachusetts to California. It has been my privilege to teach in four of the finest theological seminaries in the United States—the longest at Vanderbilt Divinity School in Nashville, where I was professor of Preaching, Worship, and Literature for fifteen years. I have spent the last seven summers as minister of a picturesque little church on Mackinac Island, Michigan, which is visited by thousands of worshipers from all over the world. I have written many books on the Bible, prayer, and various inspirational subjects. I have preached or lectured in many of the great churches of the world, as well as on campuses of seminaries and universities from Maine to California.

But in spite of all this, I confess to a very strong enthusiasm for J. K. Rowling's books (her name, incidentally, is Joanne Kathleen Rowling, and the last name is pronounced "rolling"). In fact, I could easily say, in the words of the old popular song, "I'm just wild about Harry." I remember when I first read *Harry Potter and the Sorcerer's Stone,* which I discovered on the shelves of the charming little public library on Mackinac Island. I found it hard to put down! When I absolutely had to, because of the press of duties, I kept thinking about it. The scenes scrolled through my mind as vividly as if I were watching a movie. No, it was better than that, it was a *virtual reality* movie. (After writing these lines, I was gratified to hear a youngster on CBS's *48 Hours* for February 3, 2002, say that, because Rowling tells her stories so well and in such vivid detail, he feels that he is *watching* them like a movie instead of *reading* them.) I *lived* the story of Harry Potter, the extraordinary young boy who, without a trace of personal hubris, becomes the primary nemesis of the evil Lord Voldemort and his nefarious Death Eater disciples.

Like the nine-year-old boy my son and his fiancée encountered in the theater, who was seeing *Harry Potter and the Sorcerer's Stone* for the fourth time and declared that he *was* Harry Potter, even lifting a shock of errant black hair to reveal a lightning-shaped mark on his forehead, I identified with Harry completely. I too had been a nerdy child, weak, bony, bespectacled, and completely unimpressive, with clumps of unruly hair. I never lived in a closet under the stairs, but my bedroom was in an unfinished attic space where I could look into the open roof trusses and got splinters in my bare feet from the rough, unfinished flooring. And I felt totally at the mercy of the selfish grown-ups and Dudley Dursleys in my life. When I read *Harry Potter and the Sorcerer's Stone,* I was whisked magically back to my boyhood and *became* Harry Potter, no question about it.

That, as I see it, is the essence of J. K. Rowling's skill as a storyteller. Of course she isn't C. S. Lewis or J. R. R. Tolkien, or, for that matter, Charles Williams, the third and lesser-known member of their coterie. (Am I permitted to offer a repressed "thank God!"?) She isn't male, she isn't an Oxford don, and she doesn't hang around the Eagle and the Child fetching beers for her companions and talking about English literature, medieval pageantry, and philosophies of linguistics. But she can tell a story with the best of them. Even Michael Dirda of *The Washington Post*, who worries that the Harry Potter books are keeping children from reading other things they should be reading, speaks of Rowling's "storytelling magic." Her narratives are transparent to the lives and actions of her characters. The glass is so clean, so absolutely devoid of smudges, that we look through it and are immediately caught up in the narrative. We duck when the owls begin flying everywhere, we fall in love with old Hagrid, whose hands are as big as the lids of dustbins and whose feet are like porpoises, and we suck in our breath when Harry gets on his Nimbus Two Thousand (later his Firebolt) and begins soaring like a miniature jet plane around the Hogwarts playing field.

Rowling's plotting is fantastic. Margo Jefferson said in *The New York Times* that "J. K. Rowling can plot as well as any thriller or television drama writer."[6] Small, apparently gratuitous details in the first novel show up with marvelous consequences in the later stories. And the writing! I have been a writer for years and years, and I find myself pausing to *envy* the way Rowling has described something, the crisp, efficient way her sentences propel the reader along, the sheer, beautiful economy of her prose. People are prone to think of books that receive so much hype and huckstering as potboilers—flimsy, airily fabricated stories written to please the masses and make a buck. The Harry Potter novels are anything but that. They will stand the test of decades—even centuries—as well contrived, carefully articulated stories with highly memorable characters.

And Rowling has this deliciously childlike appreciation for the simple way good and evil are juxtaposed in the world. Adults don't always see it. They have been trained not to look anymore—to pay more attention to so-called ordinary things like gas bills, frozen dinners, and NFL games. But children know better. They can still *feel* the existence of bad things in their universe—contrary spirits, hulking presences, the shadows of baleful intelligences all around them, threatening to do in the ordinary world, especially if it ever becomes conscious of them.

Maybe kids get it from reading comic books about superheroes who are always fighting Armageddon-like battles. Or maybe, as Wordsworth suggested, they are really parents to the persons they will become, and know more about spiritual matters as infants than they will remember when they have grown up. Either way, they often have a sensitivity to important conflicts that their parents dismiss with a frown or a shrug, the way Ebenezer Scrooge dismissed the early signs of his approaching visitations as indigestion from eating a bit of beef or a bad potato. They know, even when their parents deny it, that there are more things in this world than the philosophers have dreamed of, and that these things portend both danger and excitement for youngsters willing to pay attention to them.

Thank God, I say, the Harry Potter stories will keep alive for a whole generation, even in this age of microchips and supertransistors, a sensitivity to the spiritual realities that lie at the heart of what it means to be human and inhabit a universe of competing energies such as the one in which we dwell. I, for one, salute J. K. Rowling and her glorious imagination. She is helping to save millions of youngsters from a sterile, passion-less childhood, and from the grip of a video society that has long and fervently intended the demise of book publishing altogether. Someday, old and decrepit readers will arise and call her blessed, attributing to her and her alone their sum-mons to the pleasures of the printed page, and a consequent lifetime of delight in books, first awakened by the Harry Potter series when they were young.

That is something a lot of Rowling's detractors miss, I fear, or simply don't care about—the way she has stimulated thou-sands of children to read who might never have read without her. The publication and distribution of her books has been nothing short of a miracle. To think that she was an out-of-work secretary and secondary-school teacher, lining up for her monthly assistance check, when she was first writing these bril-liant stories! And then, once she came to the attention of an agent and a publisher, the books took off like an unquenchable fire, selling millions of copies in every language. It was as if the kindling had been laid in every hearth in the world, and sud-denly the magic flame ignited it, so that the *whoof!* of it was astounding, was breathtaking—and we haven't begun to see the waning of the conflagration! Maybe that is what the detrac-tors fear or envy—that their own notions of what people should be reading and talking about have not swept the globe with such speed and passion—indeed, haven't swept *anything* with speed and passion, even their own households, congrega-tions, and communities.

Anyway—there are two basic premises in this book, *God,*

the Devil, and Harry Potter. The first is that the detractors are wrong and that the Potter stories, far from being "wicked" or "Satanic" (one widely quoted e-mail accuses Rowling of having written "an encyclopedia of Satanism"), are in fact narratives of robust faith and morality, entirely worthy of children's reading again and again, and even of becoming world classics that will be reprinted as long as there is a civilization. And the second premise is that much of that faith and morality is derived not only from the archetypes and legends of world literature, combined with Ms. Rowling's own fertile imagination, but from the wealth of Christian tradition that has spawned the author and her hero—a tradition that her detractors in their mean-spiritedness and narrow-mindedness (someone once spoke of an acquaintance so narrow-minded that he could peer through a keyhole with both eyes at the same time!) apparently do not know or else fail to appreciate.

Most of my attention shall be paid to the latter premise, as I attempt to suggest to the open-minded reader a few of the various ways in which the Potter mythology—for that is what it is, an expression of a *mythos* or worldview, regardless of critics like Abanes—is not only dependent on the Christian understanding of life and the universe *but actually grows out of that understanding and would have been unthinkable without it.*

It is true, as Elizabeth Schafer argues so well in her book *Exploring Harry Potter,* that the Potter stories are filled with classical allusions and shades of fairy tales, legends, and British history. J. K. Rowling took a double major in French and Classics at Exeter University, and both subjects have paid off handsomely in her stories. Hogwarts, for all its sounding like "hog-wash," is a kind of Olympus, where Dumbledore is Zeus and Professor Minerva McGonagall is Athena. Hagrid is Orion, the wild hunter born of three gods' seed planted in the earth in the hide of a sacrificed bull, or Zagreus, the Cretan equivalent whose name sounds more like Hagrid and also represents the Titans. Professor Quirrell is Janus, the god with two faces, and the egotistical Gilderoy Lockhart is Narcissus, in love with his own image. The Forbidden Forest contains centaurs and unicorns. There are basilisks and hippogriffs and other mythical beasts in the stories. As Harry discovers in *Harry Potter and the Chamber of Secrets,* Hogwarts even has its own version of an underworld.

Dumbledore is also a kind of Merlin, who mentors Harry the way Merlin guided the young Arthur. Percy Weasley is Percival, King Arthur's loyal, punctilious knight. Merlin once disguised himself as a stag, the way James Potter, Harry's dad, was an Animagus who could transform himself into a stag. Harry quests for the Sorcerer's Stone the way Arthur sought the Holy Grail. As in Greek myths and Arthurian legends, the Potter stories are filled with special caves, stones, dragons, magical cloaks, and trees. The dreaded basilisk in *Harry Potter and the Chamber of Secrets* recalls the monster Grendel in *Beowulf.* Harry is a kind of Cinderella, who graduates from living under the stairs to being a prince among men. Hermione is put to sleep the way Snow White and Sleeping Beauty were. The living, dueling chessmen in the Hogwarts game are reminiscent of creatures Alice meets in Lewis Carroll's *Alice in Wonderland.*

Many of Rowling's characters and happenings are in fact quite polysemous—a word Dorothy Sayers employed to refer to the many layers of meaning in Dante's *Inferno*. Dumbledore's name, for example, is a British word for "bumblebee." It is equivalent to the Scottish *cockchafer*, which means "a May bug or beetle." The beetle was sacred in ancient Egyptian religion, which held that Khepera, or the scarab, rolled the sun into the sky each day the way a dung beetle rolls up little balls of dung in the sand. Blue or green beetles were enclosed in almost every sarcophagus. This becomes interesting when considered in reference to the opening scene of *Harry Potter and the Sorcerer's Stone*, where Professor McGonagall waits for Dumbledore outside the Dursley house in the form of a cat. The cat was also special in Egyptian mythology and was related to the moon because of the way moonlight shines in its phosphorescent eyes. It was believed that a female goddess named Bast took the form of a cat and sat with her foot on the head of the reptile Night, the enemy of the sun, until Khepera rolled the sun back into the sky at the start of the day. As Schafer says, the reason for the success of the Harry Potter series may well lie in J. K. Rowling's remarkable blending of archetypal patterns with the very imaginative symbols she herself has concocted!

But there are Christian references in the Potter novels as well, and a generally Christian structure to Rowling's understanding of the world. It is true, as Schafer notes, that "Harry does not attend church in either the Muggle or magical worlds, nor do any of his friends, teachers, or family."[7] It is also true that Halloween at Hogwarts bears little relation to All Saints'

Day, Christmas is a totally secular holiday (except for the singing of carols), and Easter "is referred to mostly as a way to note advancing time in the school calendar."[8] And yes, Harry and his friends, like ordinary children from any background, sometimes fudge the truth and break the rules to get their own way in a society controlled by grown-ups. Yet the world of Harry Potter would be inconceivable apart from the structures of Judeo-Christian theology and a very traditional Christian conceptualization of human existence and the way it should be approached by every follower of Jesus.

Beginning with Harry's miraculous survival as a baby (which is more like the survival of the infant Jesus than is usually noticed) and proceeding to discussions of the conflict between good and evil and the ethical considerations entailed by such a struggle, we shall in this book reflect at length on the possibility that Harry Potter, like Dostoevsky's Prince Myshkin, François Mauriac's Xavier Dartigelongue, and John Irving's Owen Meany, is a witting or unwitting Christ figure who actually battles the forces of darkness for the souls of the faithful and wins a place in readers' hearts because he so admirably conforms to our expectations for such a redemptive figure. If this possibility is true, and I believe it is, then what Ms. Rowling has furnished us, besides what the Brits call "a good read," and a whopping good one—maybe one of the best of all time, as millions of readers will attest—is a modern interpretation of the gospel, the wonderful news that "God was in Christ, reconciling the world to himself" and making sure that the goodness of creation would never be obliterated by the forces of darkness and evil.

MYSTERIOUS BIRTHS
AND MIRACULOUS CHILDHOODS

CHAP. 1.

T WAS LOGICAL for the producers to select *Harry Potter and the Sorcerer's Stone* as the first of J. K. Rowling's books to make into a movie, for it is the first of the novels and the one in which we are introduced to Harry as a baby, a foundling, actually, around whose delivery to his foster home occur several portentous and supernatural happenings. There is a downpour of shooting stars. Owls begin flying everywhere in the daytime, so that even the weather forecasters are talking about it. Inhabitants of the wizard world are standing around in little gatherings on street corners and outside pubs, so that the Muggles—the ordinary citizens—spotting them in their brilliantly colored cloaks wonder if it isn't "some stupid new fashion" or "some silly stunt." And one of the Hogwarts professors, Minerva McGonagall, parades around outside the Dursley home as a cat, who from time to time is seen studying a map to be sure she is at the right place.

Harry's parents have just been killed by Lord Voldemort, the dark wizard, whose name sounds a little like that of Vortigern, the evil king in the Arthurian legends who planned to kill Merlin, and may mean "the Flight of Death" (from the French *voler*, "to fly") or "the Will of Death" (from the Latin *volo*, "to will or be willing"). But Harry has miraculously survived. In fact, the Avada Kedavra, or Killing Curse, Voldemort pronounced on him actually backfired on the Dark Lord himself, nearly annihilating him, so that the good wizards of the world rejoice in the hope that he is gone for good.

Anyone familiar with the narratives surrounding the birth of Christ must surely feel a tingling of the skin at this point, recalling not only the acts of sympathetic magic in the universe when he was born but the wicked attempt to exterminate him and the godly presence he represented. While the angels heralded his arrival (like the mysterious appearance, in Harry's case, of the owls), the wicked King Herod sought the location of his birthplace, and, failing to secure it from the magi who discovered it by following a star, dispatched his soldiers to slay every Jewish male under two years of age. It was to escape this infanticide that the angel supposedly warned Jesus' father in a dream to "take the child and flee into Egypt."

The theme is, of course, not confined to early Christian legend. Moses, the leader of the ancient Hebrews, was also hidden at birth to save him from the wrath of an enemy. And as for Harry's power to resist Voldemort even at the age of one, there is a story about the Greek god Apollo in which he slays the giant Tityus for attacking Leto *immediately after he is born,* and another in which he kills a large serpent with bow and arrows while still in his mother's arms.

Harry is said to bear a peculiar reminder of his encounter with Voldemort—a jagged scar on his forehead similar to a bolt of lightning. At various times in Harry's life it will glow with an unearthly radiance and cause him excruciating pain when Voldemort is near or is contemplating some terribly evil deed. This is a nice touch, possibly more reminiscent of Batman films than anything in ancient mythology—Batman and Robin often had devices that warned them of the approach of crooks. It serves to identify Harry both as an extremely special person and as a survivor of his initial meeting with the powerful Dark Lord.

The mark of course becomes integral to Harry's character, the way Robert Graves in *The Greek Myths* says Odysseus' being gored by a boar when he was a young man led to his essential character. The Roman name for Odysseus, Ulysses, means "wounded thigh." And Marie-Louise von Franz begins her important work *Individuation in Fairy Tales* with the ancient Spanish narrative of "The White Parrot," which was originally Indian, then Persian, and tells about twin children, a boy and a girl, each born with a star on his or her forehead.

It is interesting that Rowling made Harry Potter's mark a lightning bolt. When the Torah describes the initial encounter between Moses and the divine, Moses asks God for his name so that he may cite it to the Egyptian pharaoh. God says it is Yahweh, which in most biblical versions is translated "I am who I am." Yahweh is actually represented in the Hebrew text by the tetragram YHWH, as traditional Hebrew uses no vowels. Among ancient Jews, it was an extraordinarily holy name, one never to be employed lightly. According to legend, it was spoken only once a year, on the high holy day of Yom Kippur, the Feast of the Atonement, and then only by the ritually purified high priest when he entered the Holy of Holies. And the thing that makes Rowling's choice of the lightning bolt for Harry's special mark from the encounter with Voldemort is that some Hebrew scholars believe the name YHWH originally meant *a flash of lightning*!

FAMILY CONNECTIONS

As in the case of Jesus, Harry's strongest connection to the supernatural comes from his mother's side. At least, it is her strong maternal love that saves him from Voldemort's power. His father is of course a blood wizard as well. But Harry's being taken by Dumbledore, McGonagall, and Hagrid to grow up in the Muggle household of the Dursleys is a potent reminder of his humanity as well, his relationship with ordinary mortals, or, in Christian terms, his incarnation in human flesh.

The Dursleys are caricaturish human beings. I suspect, in fact, that J. K. Rowling found the inspiration for Petunia Dursley, the sister of Harry's deceased mother, in the popular British TV comedy figure Hyacinth Bucket, the pretentious middle-class social climber who always insists that her name is actually pronounced *boo-KAY* and reminds people that her sister Violet lives in a mansion "with a Mercedes, a sauna, and room for a pony." Like Hyacinth, who tries desperately to conceal her relationship to her less affluent sisters Daisy and Rose, and especially to Daisy's neanderthalian husband, Onslow, Petunia (whose name is also "flowerful") doesn't want anybody to know about her controversial sister Lily (again, the name of a flower) and her husband, James, or that the skinny little boy with the unruly dark hair, so unlike her precious, chubby, blond-haired son, Dudley, is in any way related to her and her family.

The Dursleys, we are told, "had everything they wanted"; but they also had a secret they didn't want anybody to know, and that secret was Petunia's relation to a witch. The Dursleys and Potters hadn't seen each other in several years, and Petunia Dursley simply pretended to everyone that she didn't have a sister. Like Hyacinth Bucket, who shudders whenever she sees her sister Daisy and her family arriving in their backfiring old car, the Dursleys "shuddered to think what the neighbors would say if the Potters arrived in the street."[1] The Dursleys knew that the Potters had a young son, though they hadn't seen him, and this was another reason they wished to keep the Potters away: "they didn't want Dudley mixing with a child like that."[2]

When Harry shows up on the Dursleys' front stoop, they have to take him in because he is family. But he is treated like Cinderella, and given a closet under the stairway for his room. While his cousin Dudley gets birthday parties and incredible arrays of presents—at one birthday he counts only thirty-six presents and complains that he received thirty-eight the year before—Harry is barely tolerated in the Dursley household and is treated with undisguised contempt by both Dudley and his parents.

In spite of pious attitudes toward Jesus and the holy family, it should be recalled that he and his earthly family were not always on the best of terms. The one instance in which the Gospels speak of him as a youth occurs when he was taken to the temple at the age of twelve, probably for his bar mitzvah. It contains a chiding from his mother for an inconvenience he occasioned his parents. The parents had gone a day's journey away from Jerusalem when they discovered that their son was not in the caravan. Returning to Jerusalem and searching for three days, they eventually found him in the temple talking to the rabbis. His mother said, "Child, why have you treated us like this? Look, your father and I have been searching for you in great anxiety."[3]

Later, all three synoptic Gospels record an occasion when Jesus' mother and brothers came to a place where he was teaching, desiring to see him, and were left standing outside. Jesus reportedly said, "Who is my mother, and who are my brothers?" Then, pointing to his disciples, he answered his own question: "Here are my mother and my brothers! For whoever does the will of my Father in heaven is my brother and sister and mother."[4] It was a curious response, perhaps signaling a greater distance between him and his family than we usually imagine. Some scholars point to a preceding verse in the Markan passage as a possible explanation. There is a suggestion there that people were saying Jesus had "an unclean spirit"—that he was possessed by a demon and was ill or mad.

Having heard this, his mother and siblings might have come to fetch him home, and he possibly knew their motive in coming.

(Popular thought about Jesus and his mother is undoubtedly strengthened by the report in the Fourth Gospel that when Jesus was being crucified he consigned her to the care of John, the youngest apostle, saying that John was to consider her as his mother and she was to think of John as her son,[5] and also by many well-known artistic images of the pieta, or the grieving mother tenderly cradling her crucified son. But the Fourth Gospel is hardly the most reliable for historic detail, as much of it was contrived for rhetorical or theological reasons, and the pietas are obviously the products of later artistic imaginations.)

In addition to Harry's living with the Dursleys, there is, in the course of the Potter novels, another important reminder of his "earthly" connections. It has to do with the Sorting Hat's almost putting him into Slytherin House when he enters Hogwarts School of Witchcraft and Wizardry. The hat hesitates, then places him in Gryffindor House only because Harry has begged *not* to be put in Slytherin. Slytherin was founded by Salazar Slytherin (Rowling may have called him Salazar because Antonio de Oliveira Salazar was the name of the unpopular dictator of Portugal from 1932 to 1968, and she lived for a while in Portugal as a teacher), a dark wizard who spoke Parseltongue, or serpent language. It was also the house to which Voldemort belonged when he was a student at Hogwarts named Tom Riddle. Later, in *Harry Potter and the Chamber of Secrets*, Harry reflects on his having almost landed in Slytherin, and on the fact that he too speaks Parseltongue, like Voldemort. He even comes to the realization that his encounter with Voldemort when he was a baby left "a bit" of the Dark Lord in him. Dumbledore tells him, though, that he is *very different* from Voldemort because of the choices he has made about his life. It is our choosing that determines who we become.

When the young Jesus of Nazareth was baptized at the River Jordan by John the Baptist, it will be recalled, he was driven by the Spirit of God into the wilderness, where he spoke with the devil and endured three temptations to fall down and worship the evil one. Each time, he chose not to do so. Similarly, Harry converses with Voldemort in serpent language and rejects the Dark Lord's rule over his life. Jesus' choices determined his destiny as a redemptive figure and his eventual death on the cross. Harry's choices will lead him into direct conflict with Voldemort's purposes and, in *Harry Potter and the Goblet of Fire,* to the experience of the dreaded Cruciatus Curse, obviously so named because it causes its unfortunate victim to undergo a torment like that of a person being crucified.

The symbol of Gryffindor House is a lion. It is an image packed with many meanings, including the fact that the lion was the symbol of the tribe of Judah, to which Jesus belonged, and also of England. Richard the First of England, noted for his Christian faith and courage, was called Richard the Lion-Hearted. And in C. S. Lewis' Narnia tales, the Christ figure is the Great Lion, Aslan, son of the Emperor Beyond the Sea.

The emblem of Slytherin House, on the other hand, is the serpent, the traditional enemy of Judaism and Christianity. It is also the symbol of the Dark Lord, whose mark is a skull sprouting a tongue like a serpent, and whose "pet," in *Harry Potter and the Chamber of Secrets,* is the dreaded basilisk.

Harry Potter, like Jesus, has a foot in two realms. While he represents the lion, the noblest of beasts, he is also somehow related to the serpent, the lowliest of beasts and the enemy of all. But the allegiance he chooses—and Rowling gives great emphasis to the matter of choice—is to the lion, not the serpent. Like Jesus, he refuses to bow his knee to evil, and steadfastly pursues the higher path to righteousness and compassion. He is of the earth, earthy. But he is also destined for nobler things.

THE CINDERELLA MOTIF

It is perhaps the Cinderella motif itself—the beautiful person in disguise who will one day triumph over his or her surroundings—that immediately endears Harry Potter to J. K. Rowling's readers. As Professors Dumbledore and McGonagall discuss the death of Harry's parents while they wait outside the Dursleys' house for Hagrid to show up with the baby, they provide liberal hints of Harry's illustrious future. "He'll be famous—a legend," says Professor McGonagall, "—I wouldn't be surprised if today was known as Harry Potter Day in the future."[6] And later, when Hagrid has arrived and the baby is left on the doorstep, Rowling says, "Harry Potter rolled over inside his blankets without waking up. One small hand closed on the letter beside him and he slept on, not knowing he was special, not knowing he was famous."[7]

Professor McGonagall also unwittingly provides a clue to Harry's identity when she expresses astonishment at Albus Dumbledore's report that Voldemort was unable to kill Harry. "It's just astounding," she says, "but how in the name of heaven did Harry survive?"[8] It is all, of course, *in the name of heaven*—like the newborn Christ, Harry represents a supernal power at work in the world to defeat the spiritual wickedness that seeks to control everything.

Harry dwells beneath the stairway for the present, as Christ lived in a peasant home in Galilee. But one day the world will know, and, when it does, he will become the stuff of myth and legends!

Rowling may not have intended it, but her pairing of Professors Dumbledore and McGonagall at the Dursley home to see the baby safely deposited there is reminiscent of the aged couple in Luke's Gospel, Simeon and Anna, who see the baby Jesus when he is brought for presentation at the temple:

> Now there was a man in Jerusalem whose name was Simeon; this man was righteous and devout, looking forward to the consolation of Israel, and the Holy Spirit rested on him. It had been revealed to him by the Holy Spirit that he would not see death before he had seen the Lord's Messiah. Guided by the Spirit, Simeon came into the temple; and when the parents brought in the child Jesus, to do for him

what was customary under the law, Simeon took him in his arms and praised God, saying,

> *"Master, now you are dismissing your servant in peace,*
> *according to your word;*
> *for my eyes have seen your salvation,*
> *which you have prepared in the presence of all peoples,*
> *a light for revelation to the Gentiles*
> *and for glory to your people Israel."*

There was also a prophet, Anna the daughter of Phanuel, of the tribe of Asher. She was of a great age, having lived with her husband seven years after her marriage, then as a widow to the age of eight-four. She never left the temple but worshiped there with fasting and prayer night and day. At that moment she came [forward], and began to praise God and to speak about the child to all who were looking for the redemption of Jerusalem.[9]

When Dumbledore has carried the sleeping infant to the Dursleys' doorstep and laid him there, he, Professor McGonagall, and Hagrid stand looking at him for a minute. "Well," Dumbledore says finally, "that's that. We've no business staying here. We may as well go and join the celebrations."[10] Celebrations indeed! The sway of the Dark Lord is believed to be at an end. His little nemesis is sleeping peacefully. It seems a lot like the first Christmas Eve!

When the others have gone, Dumbledore produces his silver Put-Outer, with which he earlier doused the street lamps on Privet Drive, and clicks the lights back on again. Then he murmurs, "Good luck, Harry," swishes his cloak around him, and is gone.

It isn't quite a *Nunc dimittis*. But it doesn't miss by far!

CHILDISH POWERS

While the canonical Gospels are judiciously silent about Christ's doing miraculous things as a child—the miracles take place only in the world around him, in the appearance of angels and in the baby's surviving the threat of King Herod—there is no shortage in other places of legendary tales about his displays of childish powers. A. N. Wilson, in *Jesus: A Life,* refers to apocryphal Gospels that had him proclaiming his godhead, predicting the future of the world, and discoursing on the mysteries of creation—all while still in the cradle! He supposedly had the capacity to blink his eyes and bring the world to a stop, just as he had been present at the creation of everything.[11]

According to the Gospel of Thomas, a fourth-century Coptic Gospel, Jesus was two years old when he and his family arrived in Egypt. As they were passing through a field of corn or wheat and his childish hand reached out, he plucked some grain and chewed it. After that, the field yielded a number of bushels of wheat equal to the number of grains he had eaten. During the year that the holy family resided in Egypt, the infant Christ came upon some boys playing with a basin of water. He took a dried, salted fish, placed it in the basin, and ordered the salt to be expelled. The fish instantly came to life and swam about in the basin, striking fear into the other children, who ran home to tell their parents.

There is in the apocryphal book of James a famous story about Jesus when he was five. He made some clay sparrows as playthings on the Sabbath, and several of the adults, including Jesus' earthly father, Joseph, reprimanded him for making something on the day of rest. The child nonchalantly waved his arms and sent the sparrows flying into the air, telling them they would not meet death at anyone's hands.

Other stories in the Gospel of Thomas have the Savior-child making people blind or deaf for his amusement, or in some cases even killing them, only to restore them at his whim. Wilson mentions an Arabic Gospel that tells of a time when some children ran away, refusing to play with Jesus. He chased after them, and came into a woman's house where they were hiding in the cellar. He heard them moving about and asked the woman if they were in the cellar. She lied, saying no, those were only some goats. He replied, "Let the goats out." And when he opened the door to the cellar, she saw with horror that he had transformed the children into goats! Later, when the children's parents begged Mary and Joseph to get their son to restore their little ones, he happily did, and asked them once more to play with him. This time they were only too glad to do so![12]

Rowling attributes similar magical qualities to young Harry Potter. Once, when Petunia Dursley cut off most of his unruly hair, leaving only enough "to hide that horrible scar," Dudley

laughed at Harry's near baldness, and Harry went to bed
dreading school the next day, knowing the children would
tease him mercilessly. But when he got up the following morning, his hair was exactly as it had been before his aunt cut it off!

When his Aunt Petunia attempted to put one of Dudley's
old sweaters on him, which he found revolting, it grew smaller
and smaller until she couldn't get it over his head, and she
decided it must have shrunk in the wash. Another time, when
Dudley's gang at school had been chasing Harry, Harry tried to
leap over some trash cans to hide, and inexplicably found himself sitting atop the chimney over the school kitchen. Like
Superman, he had been able to "leap tall buildings with a single bound"!

But Rowling's favorite story, and the one played up in the
movie of *Harry Potter and the Sorcerer's Stone,* is the one
about Harry in the reptile house at the zoo. It was on Dudley's
birthday, and the Dursleys were taking Dudley and his friend
Piers Polkiss to the zoo. They wanted to leave Harry behind,
but had no one to leave him with and were afraid he would do
something horrible to their house if they left him alone, so they
ended up taking him with them. After lunch, Dudley headed
for the reptile house, which was his favorite place at the zoo,
and soon found the largest snake in the place. It was so huge
that it could have wrapped itself around the Dursleys' car and
compacted it into a trash can. But at the moment the snake was
fast asleep. Dudley stood with his face pressed against the
glass, wanting it to move. "Make it move," he whined to his

father. But his father's rapping on the glass produced no effect, so they walked away.

Harry stood looking at the snake. As he did so, it slowly opened its eyes and raised its head until it was staring right at him. Then it *winked* at him! Harry winked back. The snake jerked its head toward Dudley and his father as if to say: I get that all the time. Harry agreed that it must be very annoying, and the snake nodded. When Harry asked where the snake came from, it pointed to the sign that said, "Boa Constrictor, Brazil." As they continued to converse in this strange manner, Dudley's friend Piers turned and saw them, and shouted at Dudley and his father to look, saying they wouldn't believe what the snake was doing!

Dudley came waddling back and pushed Harry away so he could have an unobstructed view. He and Piers were leaning close to the glass when suddenly it was no longer there and the huge snake came slithering out onto the floor beside them. They howled with fright, but it merely snapped at their heels and kept right on going. People in the reptile house were screaming and running every which way as it slithered along. As it passed Harry, still sitting on the floor where Dudley had pushed him, he heard it hiss, "Brazil, here I come. . . . Thanks, amigo."

The Dursleys weren't sure how, but they knew Harry was somehow to blame for what happened. So he had to endure the longest time he had ever spent confined to his cupboard under the stairs. When he got out, the school term was over and summer vacation had started.

As in the case of the apocryphal stories about Jesus, the main purpose served by these stories about Harry is to underline his fantastic powers and foreshadow the much more important things he will do in the future. He might live among ordinary people, the Muggles, but he himself is clearly much more than ordinary.

THE UNKNOWN YEARS

Much has been made, over the centuries, of Jesus' so-called unknown years, the long span of time in which nothing appears to be known about him, except, of course, for the apocryphal stories. It is believed that he was about thirty years old when he began his public ministry, appearing to John the Baptist at the River Jordan and asking to be baptized, following which he entered the wilderness for forty days and nights and underwent the ritual of the three great temptations. But, with the lone exception of Luke's tale about his lingering in the temple with the rabbis when he was twelve, there is no word about his life from the time the family returned from Egypt, presumably when he was two or three, until that dramatic appearance some twenty-seven years later.

There are, of course, many tales and legends about Jesus during this interim period, one of which involved a boyhood visit to England. The poet William Blake mentions the story in his long poem "Jerusalem." Apparently it was widely held that Joseph of Arimathea, not the father of Jesus but the wealthy man mentioned in the Gospels as the owner of the tomb where Jesus was buried, had made trips to England as a tin merchant. On one of these trips, he brought along the young Jesus and his mother, and they landed at St. Michel's Mount, off the coast of southwest England. After Jesus' death, Joseph was rumored to have brought the Holy Grail, the goblet from which Jesus and the disciples drank at the Last Supper, to Glastonbury, in Somerset, where he buried it. There was even a wrinkle in the story that said the original church at Glastonbury had been built by Jesus as a monument to his mother when he was a teenager.

There are, certainly, great lapses of time in Harry Potter's life when we are not told what was happening, but it would not have served J. K. Rowling's purposes to skip over his childhood and present him to her audience as an adult. She began the Harry Potter series, after all, as a collection of stories designed for and about children—even though she has confessed that she wrote them for adults as well. What we get, instead, after a rather brief description of Harry's infancy and a little of his unpleasant existence with his Dursley relations, is the narrative of the incredible barrage of mail about Harry's enrollment at Hogwarts School and then, when he is eleven years old, his actual departure from the Dursley household to take up life as a student at Hogwarts.

The mail barrage is a very curious episode, pivoting on Uncle Vernon's refusal to allow Harry to have the letters that arrive addressed to him. The letters come thicker and thicker, necessitating Vernon's nailing up the mail slot to keep them out of the house and eventually leading him to take the family to a broken-down house on a barren island off the coast where there is no mail service. And there, in the middle of a terrifically stormy night, the giant gamekeeper Hagrid appears, bends the gun Vernon waves at him into a pretzel, informs Harry that he's a wizard, and presents him with a letter stating that he has been accepted as a student at Hogwarts School of Witchcraft and Wizardry, thus marking the end of Harry's period of waiting.

Still, there is one similarity to Christ's coming of age and being baptized by John at the start of his ministry. It was at this point that Jesus' being chosen by God was first made plain, when a *bat qôl,* or "daughter of a voice," spoke out of heaven to say, "This is my beloved Son, in whom I am well pleased."

Harry has not known, until Hagrid appears on the island with the letter, that he is a wizard or that he has any future other than an extension of the same miserable life he has been leading under the Dursleys' stairway. Hagrid becomes furious with the Dursleys for having hidden the letter Albus Dumbledore left with the child on their doorstep and kept from him the information that his parents were wizards and were killed by Voldemort. They had told him, in fact, that his parents died in a car crash. To which Hagrid exploded, "Car crash! How could a car crash kill Lily an' James Potter? It's an outrage! A scandal! Harry Potter not knowin' his own story when every kid in our world knows his name!"[13]

As Hagrid recounts Voldemort's killing of Harry's parents and attempting to slay Harry in the same way, only to be unsuccessful and managing merely to leave the scar made by his powerful curse, Harry remembers clearly what he had not been able to remember well before—a blinding flash of green light and "a high, cold, cruel laugh." He asks Hagrid what happened to Voldemort. Hagrid says that nobody knows. Some wizards speculate that he had enough humanity left in him to die. Others say no, he is out there somewhere, merely biding his time before he strikes again. Whatever happened, he met his match in Harry, even though Harry was only a baby.

Hagrid regards Harry with "warmth and respect" approaching adoration. But Harry is so stunned by the announcement that he is a wizard that he can't really take it in. His whole life, practically, has been spent with the Dursleys. Dudley has battered him regularly, and Aunt Petunia and Uncle Vernon have treated him like an outcast whom they could barely tolerate in their home. If he is really a wizard, then why haven't they turned into ugly toads every time they've locked him in the closet under the stairs? It didn't make sense. When he says this to Hagrid, Hagrid only laughs. And, after a scuffle in which he turns Vernon Dursley into a pig, Hagrid carries Harry off to London to get him ready to go to Hogwarts.

Devoted Christians, prone to read an imperialist theology back into all the details of Jesus' biography in the Gospels, think of his wilderness temptations—to turn stones into bread, to worship the devil in exchange for a kingdom, and to throw himself down from the pinnacle of the temple to test whether God would not bear him up[14]—as evidences of his strength and determination as the Savior of the world. But is it possible, if only barely, that it was the other way around—that instead of being confident of himself as the chosen of God, he could not really believe it any more than Harry could believe he was a wizard, and went into the wilderness as an attempt to clear his head and get his thinking straight? Was he only *testing* the voice that had pronounced him the Son of God, the way Harry tested Hagrid's announcement that he was famous in the wizard world and that everybody in that world was expecting great things of him?

In both cases—Jesus' and Harry's—they must face what they are about in the world, namely, that they are instrumental in the age-old conflict between good and evil powers, and are about to embark upon remarkable careers filled with good works, formidable opposition, and an eventual struggle to the death with the wicked force seeking their destruction. And it is to the similarities of those careers that we must now turn.

THE STRUGGLE
BETWEEN GOOD AND EVIL

CHAP. 2.

HERE HAS BEEN only one great plot engine for all fiction since the coming of Christ, and that is the struggle of good to overcome evil. Before Christ, in the eras of great Hellenistic and Roman literature, this was not true. There was struggle in *The Iliad, The Odyssey,* and *The Aeneid,* but it was not about the conflict between good and evil; this essential ingredient in all great Western literature (and even many of the lesser writings) is derived from Hebrew and Christian theology, and especially the Gospels, with their portrayal of the battle between Christ and the forces of darkness. Today, whether we are reading Agatha Christie, Tom Clancy, John Grisham, P. D. James, Barbara Delinsky, Toni Morrison, or Barbara Kingsolver, we expect our interest to be aroused and maintained by an honest-to-goodness contest mimicking that of Christ and his mortal enemies.

J. K. Rowling does not disappoint us. The major plot

device in the entire Harry Potter saga is the dangerous, abiding menace of the Dark Side, as we met it in *Harry Potter and the Sorcerer's Stone,* which is forever attempting, out of its evil, malicious nature, to annihilate the good in the world. We have barely turned a page of the first Potter novel when we learn of the dastardly attack of Voldemort—whose very name is so terrible that most wizards refuse to speak it—on Harry's family, and that Harry wears, throughout the saga, the jagged mark on his forehead that is the residue of that fateful encounter. As surely as Sherlock Holmes was destined to battle the villainous Moriarty, Harry is bound to mortal conflict with the great Death Will, whose lesser adumbrations, Draco Malfoy, his father, Lucius, and Professor Quirrell, are only minions in his kingdom of darkness and hate.

Briefly, here is the story of the first novel: Harry's parents have been killed by Voldemort, the primal villain. When Harry goes to Hogwarts, the wizardry school, he learns that a Sorcerer's Stone created by one Nicolas Flamel (a real historical character, by the way) has been moved from Gringotts Bank, where Harry's parents left the money he inherited, to a secret location in the school where it is guarded by Hagrid's great three-headed dog named Fluffy (which sounds much nicer than Cerberus). The stone has two incredible qualities: It can create all the gold its possessor desires and provide its owner with the Elixir of Life— the possibility of never dying. Harry and his friends Ron and Hermione suspect Professor Snape, who is an unpleasant wizard and seems to have it in for Harry, of plotting to steal the Stone.

One night Harry, Ron, Hermione, Neville Longbottom,

and Draco Malfoy are being punished for being caught in an off-limits area after hours. Their punishment consists of being led by Hagrid into the Forbidden Forest, which is a frightening experience, and a dangerous one, because something in the forest has been killing unicorns. The "something" turns out to be Voldemort, who is drinking unicorn blood to maintain his strength until he can get his hands on the Sorcerer's Stone. He and Harry almost have an encounter there, but Harry is saved by a centaur named Firenze, who frightens off Voldemort and carries Harry back to Hagrid and the others.

Learning that Professor Dumbledore has been lured to London by a false message, Harry, Ron, and Hermione rush to the Stone's hiding place, hoping to save it. After a gauntlet of obstacles, Harry reaches the hiding place, and finds, not Professor Snape, but the stuttering Professor Quirrell. Quirrell is in the service of Voldemort, and it was he who was drinking the unicorn blood, in Voldemort's behalf. When Quirrell removes from his head the turban he always wears, Harry sees that the back of his head is occupied by Voldemort's face.

Voldemort must have the Sorcerer's Stone in order to become strong again. But he and Quirrell have not been able to find it. The Mirror of Erised, which is supposed to reveal what the viewer wishes to see, is there. Quirrell has been staring at it, trying to read the location of the Stone. Voldemort tells him to have Harry look into the mirror; perhaps it will yield its secret to him. When Harry looks, he feels the Stone slipping magically into his pocket. Voldemort orders Quirrell to kill Harry, but when Quirrell touches him, his hands are sorely burned. Harry grasps Quirrell and holds him tightly, thinking it the only way to survive. He passes out, supposing he has lost the battle. But he awakens in the hospital, where Dumbledore sits by his side and explains everything. It was Harry's mother's love that was still protecting him when Quirrell tried to harm him.

Dumbledore, having arrived in London and realized the call was a hoax, rushed back in time to intervene and save Harry. Quirrell died, but Voldemort escaped. And Dumbledore, in conference with his old friend Nicolas Flamel, decided to destroy the Stone so it would no longer be a temptation.

There are several subplots to the story, of course, including the friendship of Harry with Ron, Hermione, and Neville; the young wizards' efforts to master curses, potions, and simple magic; the rivalry between Harry and Draco Malfoy; the softness of Hagrid's heart, especially for Harry, Fluffy, and a fledgling dragon named Norbert; and the yearlong battle among the four student houses, Gryffindor, Hufflepuff, Ravenclaw, and Slytherin, for the prestigious house cup awarded at the end of the last term. But the master plot, the one underlying the entire novel, is the critical struggle between good and evil—the one in which Harry, the often unwitting Christ figure, aided by Professor Dumbledore, who is a kind of God the Father watching just offstage most of the time, ends by defeating Voldemort, the personification of all that is wicked and unholy.

(Is it only an accident of Rowling's narrative art that Harry is in a coma for three days following his supreme exertion with Quirrell and Voldemort, and then returns to consciousness with Dumbledore looking over him and answering all his questions about what has happened? Or is this a subtle allusion to the three days Christ was in the grave following his death on the cross and preceding his resurrection?)

It is unfortunate that fundamentalist Christians have been put off Rowling's novels by all the talk of witches, goblins, spells, incantations, potions, dragons, invisible capes, and magic stones, and reacted by branding such harmless devices as "Satanic" and "anti-Christian"; for the story Rowling tells, again and again, is the one so basic to Christian belief, of a cosmic battleground on which the servants of God are continuously engaged in mortal combat with the forces of evil, and of the way characters define themselves and their eternal fate by identifying with one or the other of these eternal armies.

THE MIXED FIELD

What is the righteous hero to do in a world where evil, like the Devil's Snare plant guarding the way to the Sorcerer's Stone, is waiting to entrap the unwary victim? Can the evil be uprooted, burned, destroyed? Not in this world, unfortunately. That is the theme of a parable told by Jesus in the Gospel of Matthew:

> The kingdom of heaven may be compared to someone who sowed good seed in his field; but while everybody was asleep, an enemy came and sowed weeds among the wheat, and then went away. So when the plants came up and bore

grain, then the weeds appeared as well. And the slaves of the householder came and said to him, "Master, did you not sow good seed in your field? Where, then, did these weeds come from?" He answered, "An enemy has done this." The slaves said to him, "Then do you want us to go and gather them?" But he replied, "No; for in gathering the weeds you would uproot the wheat along with them. Let both of them grow together until the harvest; and at harvest time I will tell the reapers, 'Collect the weeds first and bind them in bundles to be burned, but gather the wheat into my barn.' "[1]

Good and evil are a complicated business. Good sometimes looks like evil, as in the case of Professor Snape, whose dislike of Harry makes Harry and his friends think Snape is on Voldemort's side; and evil often masquerades as good, as it does in the case of the stuttering Professor Quirrell. And weak persons, like young Ginny Weasley in *Harry Potter and the Chamber of Secrets,* sometimes vacillate between the two and, for one reason or another, such as ambition or greed or love, permit themselves to be drawn into evil's web and employed by it to achieve its own ends.

Jesus' parable of the field makes it clear that in this world the two are really inextricable. The complete destruction and eradication of evil would destroy much that is good as well. So good people must be prepared to deal with evil over the long haul. They must learn patience and wisdom, and equip themselves to exist in a land where the wicked may strike at any moment, and from the most unexpected quarters.

The fatherly Dumbledore understands this, and tries to explain it to Harry when he sits by Harry's bed in the hospital. Harry already suspects it, and asks if Voldemort won't make another appearance sometime, some way: "I mean, he hasn't gone, has he?"

> "No, Harry, he has not [says Dumbledore]. He is still out there somewhere, perhaps looking for another body to share . . . not being truly alive, he cannot be killed. He left Quirrell to die; he shows just as little mercy to his followers as his enemies. Nevertheless, Harry, while you may only have delayed his return to power, it will merely take someone else who is prepared to fight what seems a losing battle next time—and if he is delayed again, and again, why, he may never return to power."[2]

Dumbledore's statement that Voldemort isn't truly alive is interesting, and is consistent with Voldemort's name, "Flight of Death" or "Will of Death." It is as if he is a condition or a disease rather than a real person. He is a negative value corrupting the world, like the weeds in Jesus' story. And he will not be eradicated until the world itself comes to an end. He *seems* to be eliminated at the end of *Harry Potter and the Chamber of Secrets*, after his third attempt on Harry's life; but the reader cannot doubt that he will be back again in another guise. And the reader's fears are of course confirmed by his strong resuscitation in *Harry Potter and the Goblet of Fire*.

When we reflect on Jesus' encounters with evil in the

Gospels, they boil down basically to four. The first was in his infancy, when Herod attempted to get rid of him by slaying all males under two years old. The second was in the wilderness temptations immediately following his baptism and preceding his ministry. The third was in all his niggling confrontations with the Pharisees and Sadducees throughout his ministry—people he called evil because of their hypocrisy, pretending to be righteous when they were not. The fourth and final encounter was at his capture and crucifixion by the Romans, when darkness spread over all the earth at midday, symbolizing the momentary flickering of the Light that had come into the world at his birth.

Harry Potter experiences the first type of encounter when Voldemort attempts to kill him at birth, and the fourth in the fight over the Sorcerer's Stone, in the chamber of secrets, and in the cemetery at the climax of *Harry Potter and the Goblet of Fire*. A case might be made for his undergoing the second type of encounter, the temptation, as well—especially in the summer he spends with the Dursleys in *Harry Potter and the Chamber of Secrets*, when he is sorely tempted to use his magic but faithfully restrains himself because he is not supposed to use it away from the Hogwarts campus. But it is the third type of encounter—the small, everyday confrontations with minions of evil—that constitutes the bulk of the novels, just as it accounts for most of the narratives in the Gospels. This is the stuff of daily life—the slow, grinding struggle against evil that consumes us all our days, often undramatically, always wearing, and eventually flowing, like rivers to the sea, into the pure concentration of evil that exists as an onto-logical threat to all civilization.

The Voldemorts, Lucius Malfoys, and Barty Crouches add high drama to Harry's tales. But it is the Draco Malfoys and Professor Snapeses who constitute the major drain on his energy, because they are so relentlessly there, so regularly in his face, so consistently teasing, jealous, insulting, and malicious in their dealings. Just as the Pharisees and Sadducees were always needling Jesus, probing for his weaknesses and undermining him with other people, the Malfoys and Snapeses are the daily pain of a good and idealistic person like Harry.

What J. K. Rowling sees, and faithfully conveys in her narratives straight out of her Christian catechism, is the way people like Malfoy and his friends Goyle and Crabbe *lend themselves* to evil and, in the end, whether through weakness or greed or personal ambition, become part of the corrosive force of evil in the world. They are little fish, hardly worthy of being called wicked in and of themselves. But they are part of the circulating evil in the world that contaminates the atmosphere for others and thereby spoils what might otherwise be a kind of paradise. They are the unwanted weeds that cannot be uprooted without destroying people and things around them, and as such they are a judgment upon themselves.

A CONTINUING BATTLE

Each of the Harry Potter books is an episode in the constant struggle with evil. Harry doesn't seek evil. It simply finds him, in the way evil has of zeroing in on those who represent goodness and innocence in the world. He would like nothing better than to play Quidditch, enjoy his friends, and get on with his life. But Voldemort's failure to kill him when he was an infant has made him famous as a resister of evil, and, just as the old Western films often turned on the motif of the wicked gunslinger who wanted his chance to gun down some mild-mannered hero who was known for his prowess with a pistol, Voldemort and his followers keep circling and returning to Harry, wanting to destroy the very symbol of their opposition.

Harry Potter and the Chamber of Secrets is the chronicle of Harry's twelfth year on earth, and is, for the first hundred pages or so, a very funny book, with lots of humorous characters and incidents. We meet Dobby, for example, the self-flagellating little house-elf (Elizabeth Schafer calls him a kind of leprechaun) who comes to the Dursley home to warn Harry not to return to Hogwarts, and we follow Harry to the Weasley home, known as the Burrow, which is the first wizard house Harry has ever seen, filled with strange artifacts and fascinating witching books. When Harry and the Weasleys travel to Diagon Alley, where the Hogwarts students purchase their school supplies, they go by Floo powder, and Harry gets off at the wrong grate and winds up instead in nefarious Knockturn

Alley. And when, for an unknown reason, Harry and Ron Weasley can't enter the usual way into track nine and three-quarters at King's Cross Station, they fly to Hogwarts in Mr. Weasley's enchanted old Ford Anglia, a car extremely reminiscent of Herbie, the Walt Disney VW with an attitude. (Rowling says the real prototype was a turquoise Ford Anglia that belonged to her high school chum, Sean Harris.) The car develops trouble near Hogwarts and crashes into the Whomping Willow Tree at the edge of the Forbidden Forest, which nearly beats both them and the car to death. It is all lots of fun, and the reader begins to wonder if Rowling has turned entertainer in her second novel and is no longer concerned about the great existential and ontological conflict that marked the first one.

But then hints begin to coalesce, confirming the prediction of the house-elf Dobby that something terrible is in the offing. Draco Malfoy has become the Seeker on the Slytherin Quidditch team, because his father, Lucius Malfoy—whose first name links him with Lucifer, the enemy of God—bought the entire team new Nimbus Two Thousand and One broomsticks. Draco calls Harry's friend Hermione a *Mudblood*—an opprobrious name for wizards born of Muggle parents. Harry begins hearing a strange voice in the hall—"a voice of breath-taking, ice-cold venom." It says, "Come . . . come to me . . . Let me rip you . . . Let me tear you . . . Let me kill you. . . ."

All these things are intertwined. Lucius Malfoy, like Salazar Slytherin, for whom Slytherin House was named, wants to eliminate all students who are either Mudbloods or semi-Mudbloods. A series of mysterious petrifications begins to occur—first a cat, then some students—and it is clear that they are somehow connected with a monster that lives in a secret chamber created years ago by Salazar Slytherin somewhere in the bowels of Hogwarts.

In a women's bathroom presided over by a ghost named Moaning Myrtle, Harry finds a diary that once belonged to T. M. Riddle, a student at the school fifty years ago. Although it is blank, Harry discovers that if he speaks to it, it will talk back to him. And, on the page for June 13, he watches as the little square for that date becomes a miniature TV screen. Putting his eye to the space, Harry watches as his friend Hagrid, at that time a student at Hogwarts, is accused of releasing the monster, and is expelled from school.

As fear stalks Hogwarts, Lucius Malfoy shows up with an order from the board of governors for Albus Dumbledore to step down from the headmaster's job. At the same time, Hagrid is taken away to Azkaban, the wizard prison, on suspicion that he has let the monster out of the chamber again.

Harry's friend Hermione is petrified by the monster. When Harry and Ron visit her lifeless body in the infirmary, Harry notices a piece of paper clutched in one of her rigid hands. Prying it out and reading it, he discovers that it is a page from a book about the deadly basilisk, legendary King of Serpents. Suddenly everything becomes clear to Harry: The mysterious voice he has been hearing in the corridors is a serpent's voice. He could hear it, while others couldn't, because he speaks Parseltongue—snake language—his means of communicating with the serpent at the reptile house in *Harry Potter and the Sorcerer's Stone.*

But where is the basilisk? At the end of the page in Hermione's hand, she has scribbled the word *pipes.* Harry remembers the toilet, and realizes that Moaning Myrtle, the ghost, was killed by the basilisk. Perhaps the monster dwells in the pipes beneath the bathroom, and Myrtle lives there because that is where she was murdered. Just as Harry is coming to this conclusion, the stakes are raised: Ginny Weasley, Ron's little sister, has been abducted by the monster and taken to the chamber. With Ron and Professor Lockhart, Harry hurries to the bathroom and says in Parseltongue, "Open up!" A sink begins to writhe and shift, and soon opens to reveal a large pipe. "I'm going down there," announces Harry, in an action reminiscent of the *descensus ad inferos* of Jesus.

The long trip through a dark tube ends in the chamber miles below the school. There Harry finds Ginny, petrified, and a tall, dark-haired boy standing near her, who identifies himself as Tom Riddle, the owner of the diary. Harry asks if he is a ghost. He says he is a "memory." Harry says they must get out before the basilisk returns. Tom says it won't come until it is called. Tom is not merely Tom Riddle; he is Lord Voldemort, Harry's archenemy, and he has been scheming to get Harry alone in order to kill him. He and Tom Riddle, he says, have been one from the first—the name Tom Marvolo Riddle is an anagram of "I Am Lord Voldemort"—and brags that he is the greatest sorcerer in the world.

He isn't, says Harry; Albus Dumbledore is.

Voldemort becomes angry.

Music begins to erupt in the chamber—eerie, unearthly music. Suddenly a majestic bird the size of a swan appears, with fiery red feathers and golden tail and talons. It is Albus Dumbledore's phoenix, named Fawkes (for Guy Fawkes, the gunpowder plot conspirator, whose day is celebrated with bonfires in England each November fifth), which has just been reborn from its ashes and is extremely powerful. It has come to help Harry because of his faithfulness to Dumbledore.

Voldemort orders the monster to appear and kill Harry. The chamber wall parts and the giant basilisk emerges, its yellow eyes flashing ominously. Harry keeps his eyes shut so that he won't be paralyzed by its gaze. He hears sounds of a tremendous thrashing. When he dares to peek, he sees that the phoenix has pecked out both of the basilisk's eyes. Voldemort commands the monster to *smell* the boy and kill him. But Harry has become miraculously armed with a sword, and, like St. George, he plunges it into the serpent's mouth. He is wounded in the act of doing this, and appears to be dying from a great poisonous fang embedded in his arm. The phoenix hovers over him, weeping tears into the wound, and it is miraculously healed. Outraged, Voldemort raises his wand to destroy Harry. But the phoenix flies over Harry's head and drops the diary in his lap. Harry plunges the basilisk's fang into the heart of the diary, and Voldemort screams, collapses, twists on the floor, and—disappears!

This is all highly fanciful, of course, but no more so than

the great drama in the book of Revelation when God's angels bind Satan and cast him into the lake of everlasting fire. Eschatological battles require apocalyptic language and images. They cannot be described by ordinary pictures. Something far more vivid and outsize is necessary. Consider this passage from Revelation, in which Satan is expelled from heaven:

> And war broke out in heaven; Michael and his angels fought against the dragon. The dragon and his angels fought back, but they were defeated, and there was no longer any place for them in heaven. The great dragon was thrown down, that ancient serpent, who is called the Devil and Satan, the deceiver of the whole world—he was thrown down to the earth, and his angels were thrown down with him. . . .
>
> So when the dragon saw that he had been thrown down to the earth, he pursued the woman who had given birth to the male child. But the woman was given the two wings of the great eagle, so that she could fly from the serpent into the wilderness, to her place where she is nourished for a time, and times, and half a time. Then from his mouth the serpent poured water like a river after the woman, to sweep her away with the flood. But the earth came to the help of the woman; it opened its mouth and swallowed the river that the dragon had poured from his mouth. Then the dragon was angry with the woman, and went off to make war on the rest of her children, those who keep the commandments of God and hold the testimony of Jesus.[3]

The sweep and the imagery are not that different from those employed by Rowling. In fact, there can be little doubt where Rowling got the idea of the King of Serpents for her story, whether she did so consciously or unconsciously.

And if it is true, as I earlier suggested, that Albus Dumbledore is a kind of heavenly Father watching over Harry Potter as a Christ figure (why else did he stand outside the Dursleys' home that night when Hagrid arrived with the baby?), is it not also possible that Dumbledore's great phoenix somehow symbolizes the Holy Spirit that often came and ministered to Jesus during his years of ministry? Rowling's description suggests as much. The phoenix arrives with the sound of "unearthly" music and is seen first in flames that erupt at the top of a pillar. The music grows louder and louder, until it lifts the hair on Harry's head and makes his heart feel as though it is swelling to twice its size. Then the bird shows itself with magnificent crimson plumage and glittering, golden tail feathers. When the disciples of Jesus were gathered on Pentecost, following his crucifixion and resurrection, they first heard "a sound like the rush of a violent wind," which filled the entire house where they were sitting. Then "divided tongues, as of fire, appeared among them."[4] Perhaps the similarities are only coincidental—if anything in this world really is.

Afterward, when Harry and Dumbledore are reviewing what has occurred, Dumbledore hands Harry the bloodstained silver sword with which he dispatched the basilisk. Harry turns it over, its great rubies blazing in the firelight. And then he sees the name engraved on the hilt: GODRIC GRYFFINDOR.

Godric is a great old Anglo-Saxon name. But is its meaning—"God-rich"—an accident?

Will this be the end of Voldemort? Has Harry truly vanquished him for good? Not unless the world has come to an end. The wheat and the weeds must continue to grow together. Lucius Malfoy is dismissed from the school's board of governors, and his son Draco has to stop swaggering about as if he owned Hogwarts. Of course, Dumbledore returns in glory, and Hagrid comes back to his gamekeeper's cottage at the edge of the Forbidden Forest, to be made Professor of the Care of Magical Creatures in the next novel. Harry tricks Lucius Malfoy into freeing Dobby, his house-elf. There is a great celebration for the end of term, and Harry thinks he's never been happier.

But we know the lull in hostilities is only temporary. Evil has been defeated once again, but not permanently. There will be another story, and another battle.

SAME WAR, ANOTHER BATTLE

The whole creation, wrote St. Paul, "waits with eager longing for the revealing of the children of God," so that it too "will be set free from its bondage to decay."[5] For the Jews and early Christians, the Creation meant especially the nonhuman living things in the world—birds, animals, fish, reptiles, and even insects. The Bible is filled with references to them, from the serpent in the Garden of Eden (and in stories about Moses and Jesus) to the doves, lambs, and oxen of the sacrificial system, the great beasts of Job's vision (probably a hippopotamus, a crocodile, and a whale), the lion that was the symbol of Judah, the ram and the goat of Daniel's apocalyptic passion, the donkey ridden by Zion's king in the prophecy of Zechariah (and later by Jesus in the Triumphal Entry), and the leopard, horses, dragons, and of course the Lamb in the book of Revelation.

Birds and animals figure prominently in Rowling's work as well. Owls, cats, dragons, unicorns, and hippogriffs, like their biblical predecessors, are a reminder of the connection between the natural world and the spiritual world, and help to heighten the sense that a cosmic battle is taking place. In none of the novels is this more true than in *The Prisoner of Azkaban,* where several of the characters themselves are Animagi, able to transfigure themselves into animals at will.

Azkaban is the wizards' equivalent of Alcatraz, a rocklike prison surrounded by water, from which escape is almost impossible. The prisoners are guarded by *dementors,* ghoulish beings who kiss their unfortunate inmates and suck the minds or souls out of them. In *The Odyssey,* Mentor acts as a wise and faithful counselor, helping his friends Odysseus and Telemachus to make up their minds. In *The Prisoner of Azkaban,* it is the other way around: The dementors *take away* people's minds.

One renowned prisoner, however, has been at Azkaban twelve years without losing his soul to the dementors. He is Sirius Black, named for the Dog Star, who can transform himself into a large black dog, and is reputed to have betrayed Harry Potter's parents to Voldemort. We learn early in the novel that Black has escaped from Azkaban and is on his way to Hogwarts, apparently to kill Harry. The entire novel turns on this threat of harm to Harry, whose father, we learn, was also an Animagus.

In the complicated denouement, which follows the usual array of delightful sideplots, fascinating gadgets, and thrilling Quidditch matches, we learn that James Potter had three close friends at Hogwarts: Sirius Black, Remus Lupin, and Peter Pettigrew. Lupin, now a professor at Hogwarts, is a werewolf (his name means "wolf," and Remus was one of the twins suckled by a wolf in Roman legend). James, Sirius, and Peter mastered the skill of transfiguration in order to accompany Lupin when he turned into a werewolf and see that he came to no harm. James became a stag, Sirius a dog, and Peter a rat. Their nicknames were, respectively, Prongs, Padfoot, and Wormtail.

At the climax of the story, as the dementors are closing in on Sirius, Harry and his friends make the discovery that it was Peter Pettigrew, not Sirius, who betrayed Harry's parents. When Sirius afterward hunted Pettigrew down on the streets of London, Pettigrew attempted to blast him with a curse, striking and killing twelve Muggles in the vicinity. Then Pettigrew changed into a rat and slipped away, leaving Sirius to be apprehended for the crime. The dementors had been unable to rob Sirius of his soul because he was innocent—and because he could transform himself into a dog, and they had no power over animals. Several times in the novel Harry sees a black dog in the distance, and fears it is a Grim, or terrible omen. But it is only Sirius, watching over his old friend James' son while he searches for Pettigrew. And Pettigrew, in his rat form, has been hiding out as Ron Weasley's pet rodent.

Harry and his friends are in the Shrieking Shack, "the most haunted house in Britain," when they learn all of this. With Pettigrew in hand, they are heading back to Hogwarts when the clouds part, the moon appears, and Professor Lupin is suddenly changed into a werewolf. This produces a lot of confusion, and in the midst of it Pettigrew manages to slip away. Sirius is captured again by the dementors and placed in the tower. Harry and Hermione rescue him with the aid of a hippogriff named Buckbeak, who was reared by Hagrid and is himself under threat of execution. Sirius then flies away on Buckbeak, and the two of them go into hiding. Pettigrew doesn't appear again until we meet him as a servant of Lord Voldemort in *Harry Potter and the Goblet of Fire*.

Discussing the whole business with Dumbledore afterward, Harry expresses his impatience with the reality of things—that Black and Buckbeak, though innocent, are in hiding, and that he himself, at one moment in the Shrieking Shack, stopped Lupin and Black from killing Pettigrew, which means that, in some sense at least, it is *his* fault if Pettigrew somehow helps Voldemort to come back. Dumbledore reminds him of how complicated and diverse the consequences of all our actions are, and says, "This is magic at its deepest, its most impenetrable"[6]—a marvelous statement about the tangled mystery of existence, and a reminder, to us, of Jesus' parable about the wheat and the weeds, and how they must grow together, inseparable until the end of time.

If the existence of hippogriffs and other magical beasts in the Potter narratives bothers Christian minds, it should be recalled that so-called *bestiaries,* or collections of stories about various beasts, both real and mythical, were extremely popular among Christians in the Middle Ages. The earliest of these books that we know is the fourth-century *Physiologus,* variously attributed to an unknown scholar of that name, to St. Jerome, translator of the Vulgate, and to St. Ambrose, bishop of Milan. Drawing on descriptions of strange beasts from Hebrew, Indian, and Egyptian lore, as well as the classical reports of such figures as Aristotle and Pliny, it gave very imaginative accounts of the creatures' appearances and used them to frighten people and (hopefully) increase their faith in Christ.

The genre developed rapidly as a form of Christian education and remained popular until the time of the Renaissance and Reformation. The fanciful beasts were widely used in the art and iconography of the period, decorating churches, cathedrals, Books of Hours (prayer books), and even Bibles. Most of the creatures, such as the gryphon (part lion, part eagle), the unicorn (part horse, part goat), the hippocampus (part horse, part dolphin), the yala (part lion, part elephant), the basilisk (part bird, part reptile), the aphisbaena (reptile heads at both ends), the mermaid (part fish, part woman), and the merman (part fish, part man), were imbued with Christian qualities and used to instruct people in Christian virtues. The unicorn was especially sacred as a representation of Christ. According to popular belief, it was attracted by the Virgin Mary; so hunters used portraits of Mary to try to lure it into the open and take it captive. Only the dragon was considered unredeemable by Christian artists, for it was supposedly derived from the devil himself, and from the serpent that enticed Adam and Eve in the Garden of Eden. Therefore it was invariably represented as an enemy of human beings, and was shown either threatening them or being slain by Christ or St. George.

The countless saints' legends that developed as part of Christian lore in the Middle Ages were likewise filled with allusions to strange creatures imported from secular sources. The famous St. Anthony, for example, was said to have been assisted once by a centaur (half man, half horse), and to have been fed by a satyr (half man, half goat).

With her use of centaurs, unicorns, hippogriffs, and other fanciful beasts, J. K. Rowling is only reminding us of our very colorful past, which, like any past, always consciously or unconsciously impinges, often in important ways, on the present and the future. When Lord Voldemort feeds on the unicorn in *Harry Potter and the Sorcerer's Stone,* for example, the gruesome image is tantamount to a recrucifixion of Christ. Voldemort restores himself by drinking the blood of Christ. Evil regains its strength by feeding on all that is good and holy.

ONCE MORE, WITH PASSION

In the fourth novel, *Harry Potter and the Goblet of Fire*, which Rowling has confessed was her most difficult to write and is pivotal to the three remaining narratives, we learn how truly interwoven good and evil are as Lord Voldemort recovers vitality and calls on his hidden disciples to join him in his bid to take over the world. Weakened at the beginning of the novel to the point of possessing no bodily vitality, and completely dependent on the aid of his servant Pettigrew (from the third novel), now always called Wormtail, Voldemort schemes his total revitalization, including having his own body again.

Central to his plan is a fabulous international Triwizard Tournament, planned with great secrecy by the Ministry of Magic, and held at Hogwarts. Each of three great wizard schools, Beauxbatons in France, Durmstrang in Germany, and of course Hogwarts in Britain, will put forth its champions, of which one from each institution will be selected by the Goblet of Fire to represent that school in the actual competition. The judges announce that candidates must be at least seventeen years of age, as the contest will be very dangerous and require advanced competency in wizardry. The goblet selects a famous Quidditch star, Viktor Krum, from Durmstrang; a tall, beautiful girl, Fleur Delacour, from Beauxbatons; and Cedric Diggory, a modest, handsome young Quidditch player, from Hogwarts. Then the goblet confounds even the judges by spitting out the name of a fourth contestant, Harry Potter. No one appears to know how Harry's name even got into the goblet, as he is three years under the age requirement, but the goblet's will is honored and he is accepted as a bona fide contestant.

There are three trials for the participants, spread over the remainder of the school year, and each is a race against time. First, each contestant must successfully remove a golden egg from the nest of a fierce, fire-breathing dragon. Second, each must rescue a person of great meaning to him or her who has been captured and is bound in the land of the merpeople, deep under the school lake. And, third, each must thread his or her way through a large maze filled with hazards (dragons, a troll, Blast-Ended Skrewts, boggarts, and giant spiders) to reach the Triwizard Cup at the center and lay hands on it before the others, thus claiming victory.

Unknown to the judges, however, Voldemort learns about the contest and uses one of his followers, Barty Crouch, son of a prominent wizard minister and one of the competition's judges, to make sure Harry wins. The reason he wants Harry to win is that the Triwizard Cup has been transformed into a magical Portkey, so that the moment Harry touches it, it will instantly transport him to the cemetery where Voldemort's father is buried and many of his servants have gathered. But Harry, trying to help his fellow competitor, Cedric Diggory, allows Cedric to touch it with him, and they are transported together to the cemetery. Surprised to see Cedric there, Voldemort executes him on the spot.

Following a magical rite which requires some of Harry's blood, Voldemort is restored to power, and his followers all give a great cheer. It is now Voldemort's intention to kill Harry and let the world know that he has triumphed over the adversary who nearly destroyed him thirteen years earlier.

But Harry, angered by the death of Cedric as well as those of his parents, resists. He and Voldemort simultaneously exchange curses. Their wands contain feathers from the same phoenix, however, and are so mystically akin that they cancel one another out. A golden filament springs from their tips, encircling the two opponents, so that Voldemort's supporters cannot get close to help him. Then the ghosts of Voldemort's victims materialize out of the end of his wand—including those of Harry's parents. They encourage Harry to hold fast to his wand and continue the duel. He does so, and the force of the contrary curses raises both contestants into the air. Suddenly, Harry is able to break free. He quickly recovers the cup that is a Portkey, and, bearing Cedric's body with him, escapes to Hogwarts.

There, we discover that Professor Mad-Eye Moody, who has been Harry's friend, is not really Moody at all, but young Barty Crouch, who has transformed himself into Moody by taking Polyjuice Potion. The real Moody has been locked up in his own magic trunk. There is a tense confrontation between Albus Dumbledore, who sees the crisis clearly, and Cornelius Fudge, the Minister of Magic who always wants to compromise or "fudge" things, over what must be done to contain Voldemort's power. Dumbledore wants to approach the giants and enlist them in the fight against the Dark Lord, but Fudge, a purist who has never liked dealing with nonwizards of any kind, refuses. So *Harry Potter and the Goblet of Fire* ends with everything resolved except the future, and the stage is clearly set for terrible battles with Voldemort in the next three novels.

Once more Rowling has underlined the real nature of evil in the world. It is never a simple matter, with a satanic power pulling the strings on millions of selfish, churlish minions. Voldemort is indeed satanic, but his power waxes and wanes according to the fidelity of his followers. And the followers themselves are not always faithful. Professor Snape, head of the Slytherin House at Hogwarts, bears Voldemort's Dark Mark on his body, but has successfully resisted the call to return to him. So has Professor Karkaroff, the suspicious-acting head of the Durmstrang delegation, who flees into hiding when he realizes Voldemort is trying to reassemble his forces. And poor Barty Crouch (the elder), a wizard bureaucrat who has developed a reputation for scrupulosity in searching out and punishing Voldemort's followers, the Death Eaters, becomes hopelessly entangled in evil when he saves his son from Azkaban and then realizes his son is instrumental in helping Voldemort return to power.

Even Harry Potter himself is tangentially involved in Voldemort's resurrection, for his blood was an essential ingredient in the formula for the Dark Lord's restoration in the cemetery. Harry knows this. He feels guilty for having suggested that he and Cedric Diggory claim the Triwizard Cup together, thus involving Cedric in the journey with the Portkey and ending in his death. He refuses to keep the thousand-galleon prize money, and gives it to Fred and George Weasley to open a joke shop, which he sees as a small antidote against the gloom produced by evil in the world.

A friend asked me if Harry really grows in the novels. Of course he does. When we meet him in *Harry Potter and the Sorcerer's Stone*, he is a naïve eleven-year-old whose real knowledge of evil is limited to the crass, objectionable qualities of the Dursley household. At the end of *Harry Potter and the Goblet of Fire*, he is a somber, wary young adolescent, cognizant of the innumerable dark strands woven into the pattern of life. "We could all do with a few laughs," he tells Fred and George. "I've got a feeling we're going to need them more than usual before long."[7]

THE GAME
OF LIFE

CHAP. 3.

 UIDDITCH IS SURELY one of the most fantastic inventions of J. K. Rowling's always imaginative and innovative fiction. A game easily worthy of witches and wizards, involving lightning speed, dexterity, teamwork, racing brooms, and not one but *four* balls, three of which are aggressively *alive,* it far surpasses football, baseball, basketball, soccer, hockey, horse racing, and car racing, all of whose actions it at least partially imitates, combines, and sublimates. Nor is it extraneous to the fateful struggle between good and evil, for it always stands symbolically at the very center of that struggle, so that it both mimics and actually becomes the struggle. Its very name is brilliant: Quidditch, from the Latin *quid,* meaning "what," and instantly recognizable for its relationship to one of the great terms in Western philosophy since the Middle Ages, and especially since the advent of the modern existentialist movement created by Martin Heidegger and Jean-Paul Sartre. The *-ch* at the end bestows a certain chthonian flavor on the name that is most appropriate for a game played by witches and wizards.

Quiddity or *quidditas,* whose pedigree goes back at least to Duns Scotus, a philosopher from the little town of Duns, not far from Rowling's Edinburgh, is the *this*ness of things, the essential, undismissable reality of them, as opposed to mere dreams, fantasies, and the imagination. It is simply the way things are in their irreducible being, the unadorned, unavoidable haecceity or uniqueness of existence. And Quidditch, with its remarkable imitation of life, in which its fans are caught up in life and its players actually stand at the precise, existential center of the game of life, is the essence of quiddity. When it is happening, as is true to only a slightly lesser degree in most major sporting events today, it is hard to distinguish between it and life itself; in fact, it represents life so quintessentially that it actually becomes *larger than life*! It isn't any wonder that, as Rowling says in *Harry Potter and the Sorcerer's Stone,* "Everyone from wizarding families talked about Quidditch constantly."[1]

There are seven players on each of two teams in a Quidditch match. Three of the seven are called Chasers, and they spend their time chasing a red ball about the size of a soccer ball called the Quaffle and trying to put it through one of six hoops mounted fifty feet in the air. (Harry describes the Chasers' actions as "sort of like basketball on broomsticks with six hoops."[2] One player on each team is a Keeper. It is the Keeper's job to fly around the hoops and prevent the other side from scoring. There are two players on each team called

Beaters. The Beaters serve two functions: They rocket around the playing area trying to knock opposing players off their brooms, and they attempt to deflect the Bludgers, the two lively black balls, slightly smaller than the Quaffle, which zoom about dangerously toward the players during the contest. There is a seventh player on each team called the Seeker. This is a smaller, lighter player who buzzes about, often high above or around the periphery of the other action, looking for the Golden Snitch, the small fourth ball, which has wings and darts about so quickly that it is difficult to see. The game of Quidditch isn't ever over until the Snitch is caught by one of the Seekers, so games have been known to go on for months. Harry Potter shows such amazing talent with a racing broom the first time he rides one that he is instantly marked for a Seeker.

It is highly interesting that Rowling calls this seventh player a Seeker, a word often applied today to persons whose concern for true spirituality leads them from religion to religion and philosophy to philosophy, rarely resting long in any one place but always searching for the essence of a higher humanity. (Such activity is of course considered a no-no by most conservative Christians. Richard Abanes, in *Harry Potter and the Bible,* for example, pillories "the current atmosphere of 'spirituality' where occult-related ideas and values not only are accepted, but also often are viewed far more positively than Christian-based beliefs and concepts of morality."[3]

Rowling's use of "Snitch" is also worthy of attention. Although lexicographers are uncertain of its origin, it is probably related to the word *snatch,* from the Middle English *snacchen,* which meant "to give a sudden snap" to something, or "to seize peremptorily." (The use of *snitch* to designate a tattler or betrayer probably derives from the idea that this person "snaps up" the perpetrator of a crime or misdemeanor.) The Snitch, whose sudden capture by a Seeker ends a game, may be symbolic, in its goldenness, uncanny speed, and almost total elusiveness, of the essence of life itself. Life at its best is hard to capture and pin down. Only the most talented persons—or the luckiest—manage to catch it during their days on earth. Harry Potter, as one of the most talented Seekers in the history of Hogwarts—in one game he sets a new record by catching the Snitch in only five minutes—is a rare personality, embodying the finest traditions of the search for a golden existence.

The question of how one finds and seizes the good life has occupied human philosophies from time immemorial. It is central to all the great religions of the world. And in the Harry Potter tales, the answer to the question is identical to the answer given by the Judeo-Christian tradition: It consists of obedience to God and faithful service to the community. "[God] has told you, O mortal, what is good," says the Hebrew prophet Micah, "and what does the Lord require of you but to do justice, and to love kindness, and to walk humbly with your God?"[4]

Contrary to conservative Christian complaints, the entire system of ethics in the Potter stories—Richard Abanes refers to it contemptuously as "Potterethics"—is perfectly congruent with the ethics of Jesus in the Gospels. It pits goodness and mercy, as exemplified in the behavior of Harry, Ron, Hermione, Hagrid, Dumbledore, and the good wizards, against greed, selfishness, and contempt in the Dursleys, Voldemort, Quirrell, Malfoy, Crouch, and all the bad wizards of the various novels.

Consider the character of the headmaster. Dumbledore, whose last name may seem puzzling because it means "bum-blebee," as I pointed out earlier, has a giveaway first name. Albus is surely related to Albion, the poetic name for England, which was in turn derived from the name of one of Poseidon's sons in Greek mythology. But it is even more obviously borrowed from the Latin *alb* and the French *albus,* which mean "white" and provide the name "alb" for the tunic or vestment worn by a priest. Also, in the early church, albs were worn by baptismal candidates from the Saturday before Easter until the Sunday after Easter, which is sometimes called Alb Sunday. A saintly man who is both wise and compassionate, Dumbledore could hardly be more selfless and godly.

On the other hand, Draco Malfoy, who is Harry's nemesis at the school and in the Quidditch matches, has a first name that in Latin means "dragon" or "serpent." His last name aptly means "bad faith," from the French *mal foi*—a term used even by the atheistic Jean-Paul Sartre to describe the behavior of those who exist without authenticity and spiritual awareness. Malfoy is snide, conniving, and totally untrustworthy. Even the youngest children reading about him in the novels or seeing him on film take an instant dislike to him, for they recognize him as a contemptible, despicable human being. And when we meet his father, Lucius, in *Harry Potter and the Chamber of Secrets* and subsequent novels, we realize that the apple hasn't fallen far from the tree—he is perhaps even more unbearable than his son.

There are clearly two ways in Rowling's novels, one good and the other bad. One leads to life and the other leads to death. The contrast could not be more vividly delineated.

THE MODEST HERO

One reason Harry is so endearing to the hordes of children who love him is his invincible modesty and humility. He can never get used to the way he is instantly recognized by other wizards and fêted for his survival of Voldemort's attack on him when he was an infant. Typical is the description of the way he is received by Gilderoy Lockhart, in *Harry Potter and the Chamber of Secrets,* when he and the Weasley family go to buy their schoolbooks at Flourish and Blotts. Lockhart recognizes him immediately, and, being an inveterate self-publicist, maneuvers Harry into a photo with him and uses Harry to curry favor with the crowd in the store.

Lockhart, whose first name means "gold king" or "gilded king," is the very picture of a blowhard, one who constantly puffs himself up. As the new Professor of Defense Against the Dark Arts at Hogwarts, he never misses a chance to toot his own horn or shower himself with confetti. An author who has traveled the world appropriating the stories of real heroes who defeated werewolves and various curses, then performing a Memory Charm on them so that they didn't remember that the stories were theirs, he has concocted a brilliant false pedigree for himself to go with his wavy hair and thousand-watt smile. In the end, he proves to be a coward and an impostor, and, when one of his own Memory Charms backfires on him, can't even remember who he was.

Harry, by contrast, is a shrinking violet, and prefers never to be in the limelight. When he first meets Ron Weasley, who becomes his closest friend at Hogwarts, Ron is frightened and impressed by Harry's saying Voldemort's name aloud. When he tries to say something about it, Harry remonstrates: "I'm not trying to be *brave* or anything, saying the name, I just never knew you shouldn't. See what I mean? I've got loads to learn. . . . I bet," he adds, voicing for the first time something that has been worrying him a lot lately, "I bet I'm the worst in the class."[5] When the gibbering house-elf Dobby visits Harry at the Dursleys' and fawns over him because of his greatness and goodness, Harry becomes red in the face and protests, "Whatever you've heard about my greatness is a load of rubbish. I'm not even top of my year at Hogwarts."[6]

"Harry Potter is humble and modest," says Dobby in reverence. "Harry Potter speaks not of his triumph over He-Who-Must-Not-Be-Named."[7]

And when the obsequious, adoring, first-year student Colin Creevey follows Harry everywhere, taking snapshots of him, Harry cringes and attempts to dodge out of sight. At a

Quidditch training session, the arena is filled with the sound of clicking, coming from somewhere in the stands. The coach and players look up and see Colin shooting away.

"Look this way, Harry!" he calls. "This way!"

"Who's that?" asks Fred Weasley.

"No idea," Harry lies, putting on a burst of speed that carries him "as far away as possible from Colin."[8]

Walking humbly with one's God, as the prophet Micah recommended, is a sign of inner goodness. Harry's head is not turned by recognition and popularity because he knows these do not in themselves constitute worthiness. His own worth—for he is not, once he gets away from the Dursley household, a particularly self-doubting boy—stems from a sense of being in tune with goodness, not from possessing or exemplifying it.

The same could obviously be said of Jesus, who chided one admirer, "Why do you call me good? There is only one who is good, and that is God,"[9] and who on at least one occasion when a crowd was so excited about him that they wanted to make him a king, slipped away and returned temporarily to obscurity.[10] The Fourth Gospel operates from an extremely high Christology, of course, depicting Jesus as the cocreator of the world who came among human beings with omniscience, self-awareness, and the clearly defined purpose of becoming the Savior of the world; but in the Synoptic Gospels, written several years before this more sublime interpretation emerged, Jesus is the humble Galilean chosen by God for a mission that carries him into conflict with the political and ideological powers of the day, and he never loses the rough, country simplicity of a man who is in love with God, not with himself.

A COMMITMENT TO RIGHT

Another thing children have said they like about Harry Potter is that he lies or fudges the truth when he has to, but only in the service of a right action or a good purpose. Professor Snape constantly accuses him of bending or violating the Hogwarts rules to suit himself, and this he certainly does. When he is forbidden to go to Hogsmeade, the wizarding village that upper students love to visit on special days, because he did not secure Uncle Vernon's permission, he dons the Invisibility Cloak he inherited from his father and goes anyway. And he often uses the cloak to get him and his friends Ron and Hermione around the halls of Hogwarts or down to Hagrid's cottage by the woods after hours, when they are sleuthing for clues or simply want to visit Hagrid. He comes into possession of the magical Marauder's Map, developed by his father and a little band of friends, which not only shows all the hidden passages of the Hogwarts castle and its environs but reveals, at any given moment, where everybody in the castle is. Such instruments are strictly forbidden. But Harry delights in the map and uses it frequently—though only in the service of good.

It is this kind of disregard for the rules and regulations that is assailed so vigorously by Richard Abanes in *Harry Potter and the Bible*. Assiduously chronicling the lies told by Harry and his friends, and the number of times they fracture regulations, Abanes accuses Rowling of extolling "deceitful behavior" as "a valuable tool for successful living," and deplores the model this sets before young readers. He and his conservative friends obviously much prefer the anal behavior of Percy Weasley, whom he exalts as a good character for zealously following the rules.

What conservative Christians often forget, however, is that Jesus, the founder of their religion, invariably exhibited a healthy disrespect for rules and regulations, especially when they were followed for their own sake or stood in the way of some worthy goal or achievement. He called the Pharisees "whitewashed sepulchers," who made the outside of their lives appear clean and inviting, while inside they were filled with death and putrefaction. They were always straining at gnats, he said, and swallowing camels. They liked to be seen standing on street corners praising God, when in fact they should be fleeing from the wrath of God. They were always looking for specks in their neighbors' eyes, when they could hardly see for the great planks in their own. It was Jesus' healthy disregard for the rules—healing people on the Sabbath and letting his disciples pluck grain on the Sabbath, among other things—that alienated the Pharisees and led eventually to their insistence that the Romans crucify him. Not once in his ministry, if we disregard Judas' betrayal at the end, did Jesus have problems with the *'am ha'aretz,* or ignorant and nonobservant Jews of his time. On the contrary, it was the scrupulously educated and strictly observant Pharisees and Sadducees who dogged him relentlessly and brought about his death.

It is therefore highly ironic—and tragic—that a certain strain of Christianity in our time should loudly proclaim its unyielding loyalty to Christ and his religion while so flagrantly disregarding the actual character of the man himself and the way he consistently opposed a religion of rules and hypocrisy. I cannot help agreeing strongly with Professor Marcus Borg, who says, in *Meeting Jesus Again for the First Time*, that Jesus came not to remind us to be holy as God is holy but to be *compassionate as God is compassionate*.[11]

Despite his propensity for dealing loosely with truth and regulations when it is convenient, Harry is invariably oriented toward the service of goodness and high ideals. His father, who was high-minded and courageous, and his mother, who was loving and protective, have passed on to Harry their best qualities, and those who knew James and Lily Potter when they were students at Hogwarts a generation earlier often express pleasure at the way the son embodies the parents' noblest traits.

Rowling is fully conscious of the way she sets forth Christian ethical priorities in her books. In *Harry Potter and the Chamber of Secrets*, when Harry is debriefing everyone in Professor McGonagall's office about what happened in the chamber between him and Voldemort, McGonagall eagerly prompts him to continue his story by saying, "Very well, so you found out where the entrance was—*breaking a hundred school rules into pieces along the way, I might add* [italics mine]—but how on *earth* did you all get out of there alive, Potter?"[12] Rowling gives children the credit for knowing right from wrong about infractions of rules. She knows they bend and break the rules all the time. What is important is not how punctilious they are in observing rules but what their real character is, and what they do with their lives.

Like the Jesus of the Synoptic Gospels, who "set his face to go to Jerusalem"[13] as the political currents flowed against him and he could almost certainly anticipate imprisonment or death, Harry stubbornly moves on toward any important confrontation, regardless of the pain or danger involved. When he knows Hagrid is suffering in his gamekeeper's cottage, he sneaks out to see him despite the consequences if Harry is caught. When he is warned not to return to Hogwarts because something terrible awaits him if he does, he goes anyway. When Sibyll Trelawney, the professor of Divination, predicts Harry's death on an almost weekly basis, he waves it off with a shake of his head and pursues his path as truly as if she had foretold only success and happiness.

His courage and determination are symbolized by his behavior in a Quidditch match with the Slytherin team after Lucius Malfoy has bought the entire Slytherin team "the fastest racing brooms gold could buy." The match has hardly begun when a heavy black Bludger comes hurtling toward Harry with such speed that he barely avoids it. George Weasley, one of the Gryffindor Beaters, gives the Bludger a powerful whack in the direction of a Slytherin player, but it changes course in midair and shoots straight for Harry again. Harry drops quickly to avoid it, and George hits it again, this time toward Draco Malfoy, the Slytherin Seeker. Again the Bludger acts like a boomerang and heads toward Harry. Harry puts on a burst of speed toward the other end of the pitch. But once more he hears the Bludger "whistling along behind him."

What is happening? Bludgers never behave like this.

Fred Weasley, the other Gryffindor Beater, is waiting at the end of the pitch, and Harry ducks as Fred sends the Bludger away. "Gotcha!" yells Fred. But the Bludger, as though "magnetically attracted to Harry," heads for him again, forcing him to fly away at full speed.

The Gryffindors call time out. Wood, the player-coach, wants to know what's happening. George Weasley says that somebody has tampered with the Bludger. The Slytherins have obviously bewitched it so it won't leave Harry alone.

A few minutes back into the game, just as Harry spots the Snitch, the Bludger hits him at last, smashing his elbow and breaking his arm. The pain is dazzling. Harry slides sideways on his rain-glazed broom, barely managing to hold on. His useless arm dangling by his side, he swerves once more to miss a frontal assault by the Bludger. Then, edging toward the Snitch, he takes his good hand off the broom, gripping the shaft only with his legs, and seizes the prize. Riddled with pain, he lands his broom, says vaguely, "We've won," and faints.[14]

It is the kind of courage that leads people forward despite powerful opposition—even to a cross!

DECENCY AND FAIR PLAY

Part of the age-old formula of the battle between good and evil is that the good always play fairly and honestly, while the bad use any means available to win. As Professor Quirrell sums up the evil viewpoint for Harry in *Harry Potter and the Sorcerer's Stone,* "There is no good and evil, there is only power, and those too weak to seek it."[15] But unlike the followers of Voldemort, Harry is committed to fairness and justice, as are all his friends and most of the students at Hogwarts.

As Madam Hooch, the referee, says to the Gryffindors and Slytherins at the beginning of Harry's very first Quidditch match, "Now, I want a nice fair game, all of you."[16]

But, of all the four Hogwarts houses, Slytherin, whose emblem is the serpent, is most inclined to play unfairly. The game has been under way only a few minutes when Harry spots the Golden Snitch and zooms toward it. He almost has it when *wham!*, a Slytherin player named Marcus Flint rams him, knocking him off course. A still inexperienced player, Harry holds on to his broom for dear life.

"Foul!" cry the Gryffindors.

Someone in the stands, familiar with soccer, cries, "Send him off, ref! Red card!"

Even the game announcer finds it difficult not to take sides. "So—after that obvious and disgusting bit of cheating—," he says. Professor McGonagall growls to him that he is to be impartial. "I mean," he continues, "after that open and revolting foul—"[17] We understand, because our instincts as readers are always with those who play fairly and against those who don't.

Fairness is as natural to Harry as breathing. He never considers taking unwarranted advantage of other players. In the great Triwizard Tournament in *Harry Potter and the Goblet of Fire,* Harry has learned from Hagrid that the first trial of the tournament will involve dealing with enormous dragons. He also knows that both Madam Maxime of Beauxbatons and Professor Karkaroff of Durmstrang are aware of the dragons, and thus infers that their champions will likewise be informed. The one contestant who would not know is Cedric Diggory, the other Hogwarts champion. So Harry contrives to get alone with Cedric and tell him.

"They've got four, one for each of us," he says, "and we've got to get past them."

"Are you sure?" asks Cedric.

"Dead sure," says Harry.

A minute later, Cedric asks, "Why are you telling me?"

"It's just . . . fair, isn't it?" he says. "We all know now . . . we're on an even footing, aren't we?"[18]

Harry's sense of fairness and loyalty extends to almost anybody who deserves it. He cannot stand Draco Malfoy and his bullying friends, who sneer at others, skulk around like young Death Eaters, and can be trusted only to be untrustworthy. But to everyone else—Ron, Hermione, Dumbledore, Hagrid, Mr. and Mrs. Weasley, Mad-Eye Moody, even Hagrid's big hippogriff, Buckbeak—his fealty is never questioned or compromised. His sense of right is as unfailing as the magnetic needle that finds true North.

It isn't something Harry works at. He never sits and thinks, "Now, I must behave this way in order to fulfill my duty to Hogwarts and wizardry in general." It is simply instinctive in him to be honest, fair, and faithful.

The same is true of his close friends. Ron is perhaps more prone than Harry to cut corners. But both he and Hermione have an innate sense of decency and fairness. In Hermione's case, it comes out particularly in *Harry Potter and the Goblet of Fire,* when she takes up the cause of the house-elves who prepare the meals and keep Hogwarts clean. We met the first house-elf, Dobby, in *Harry Potter and the Chamber of Secrets.* Harry was instrumental in setting Dobby free from his indenturedness to Lucius Malfoy. In *Harry Potter and the Goblet of Fire,* we meet Dobby's friend Winky, a female house-elf who belongs to Barty Crouch of the Ministry of Magic. When Crouch fires her for being involved in a fracas at the Quidditch World Cup, she shows up at Hogwarts as part of the house-elf team that does the menial work in the castle.

Hermione is present when Crouch fires Winky and becomes immediately incensed at the wizards' treatment of her.

"The way they were treating her!" Hermione said furiously. "Mr. Diggory, calling her 'elf' all the time . . . and Mr. Crouch! He knows she didn't do it and he's still going to sack her! He didn't care how frightened she'd been, or how upset she was—it was like she wasn't even human!"[19]

"Elf rights," an issue similar to black rights or women's rights, becomes one of Hermione's themes in the novel, and she sounds off on it at every opportunity. When Ron Weasley says, "We've been working like house-elves here!,"[20] a phrase reminiscent of the derogatory term "house-niggers" common in the U.S. South until the late twentieth century, she becomes upset and reveals to him and Harry a box of badges she has fashioned with the acronym S.P.E.W. on them. The letters stand for the Society for the Promotion of Elfish Welfare, and signal the beginning of Hermione's campaign to free the Hogwarts elves, and pay them for work performed. Echoing the conservative voice in the battle for racial integration, Ron insists to her, "Hermione—open your ears. They. Like. It. They *like* being enslaved!"[21] And it seems to be true. On more than one occasion, Winky cries, throws herself on the floor, and protests that elves *want* to work and aren't interested in being paid for what they do. But Hermione is determined. She will not be happy until the elves' slavery is ended and they begin to receive representation on various wizards' boards and agencies.

All of this is integral to the plot of the novel, as we learn, because Winky's fidelity to the Crouch family has caused her to keep a secret that, had it been revealed, might have saved the wizard community a lot of grief. But the importance of the issue to Hermione is revelatory of the decent inner nature of those who belong to the forces of good in the world. Perhaps it is not to Harry's credit that he isn't as perturbed about the freedom and compensation of the house-elves as Hermione is, although his maneuvering of Lucius Malfoy into giving Dobby his freedom indicates that his heart is in the right place. And Ron, at times, looks positively selfish in his interest in the food provided by the house-elves and in his twitting of Hermione about her campaign.

But their varied levels of concern for the house-elves is a fairly accurate mirror of Christian compassion toward the Negroes during the struggle for integration in America, and probably in South Africa as well. Some Christians campaigned tirelessly for human rights. Others believed the social system was working well as it was and that only the radical young blacks really wanted equality with whites. And some, of course, actually resisted change, believing God had ordained the system as it was.

There is little doubt where Rowling's sympathies lie. With the all-seeing eye of the novelist, she understands the nature of the house-elves and their desire to live in a menial capacity. But she also cares about those who serve—she herself has been a secretary and a secondary-school teacher—and obviously sympathizes with Hermione's passion to bring liberty and equality to those who work so tirelessly behind the scenes at Hogwarts. When Hermione becomes exasperated with Ron and pleads, her eyes flashing, "*House-elves!* Not once, in over a thousand pages, does *Hogwarts, A History* mention that we are all colluding in the oppression of a hundred slaves!,"[22] she is speaking for Rowling and all decent people everywhere who care about the way history and cultures often forget enslaved or abused people.

Whether at Quidditch, in the classroom, in the social structures of Hogwarts, or in the mixed world of Muggles and wizards beyond Hogwarts, the good people in Rowling's narratives never move far from the reminder of Jesus: "In everything do to others as you would have them do to you; for this is the law and the prophets."[23]

A READINESS TO SACRIFICE SELF

"This is my commandment," says Jesus to his disciples at the Last Supper, "that you love one another as I have loved you. No one has greater love than this, to lay down one's life for one's friends."[24]

Self-sacrifice may have occurred in people before the Christian era, but never with the recommendation and frequency it enjoyed after the example of Christ on the cross, who willingly tendered his life "a ransom for many."[25] The theme of giving one's life in behalf of others became common in early Christian culture, and through the intervening centuries the church has continued to honor the love and courage of those who rise to the call for such an action.

Jaroslav Pelikan, Sterling Professor of History at Yale University, says in his widely read *Jesus Through the Centuries— His Place in the History of Culture:*

> The followers of Jesus came very early to the conclusion that he had lived in order to die, that his death was not the interruption of his life at all but its ultimate purpose. Even by the most generous reading, the Gospels give us informa-

tion about less than a hundred days in the life of Jesus; but for the last two or three days of his life, they provide a detailed, almost hour-by-hour scenario. And the climax of that scenario is the account of Good Friday and of his three hours on the cross. The Apostles' Creed and the Nicene Creed recognized this when they moved directly from his birth "from the Virgin Mary" to his crucifixion "under Pontius Pilate." What was said of the thane of Cawdor in *Macbeth* was true preeminently of Jesus: "Nothing in his life/ Became him like the leaving it."[26]

If there is indeed a Christ-likeness in the Harry Potter stories, it must somehow involve the theme of self-sacrifice—of the hero's willingness to brave threat and danger for others, possibly even undergoing self-immolation. Harry is of course a child in the stories—only eleven at the outset and eighteen at the end of them—and it is still anyone's guess whether Rowling will have him die at the conclusion of the final book. But again and again he proves his readiness to risk everything in behalf of others, fulfilling Christ's ideal of laying down his life for his friends.

In *Harry Potter and the Sorcerer's Stone*, Harry and Ron come to the aid of Hermione when she is endangered by a giant, loathsome troll. Professor Dumbledore has warned of the troll's presence and ordered all students to their rooms. Harry and Ron are en route to their dorm when they remember that Hermione wasn't present and didn't know about the troll, so they go to look for her. On their way, they catch sight of the monster. It is twelve feet tall, with "a great lumpy body like a boulder" and "a small bald head perched on top like a coconut." Its short legs are thick as tree trunks, and it carries a huge wooden club, which it drags along on the floor because its arms are so long.

The troll enters the girls bathroom. The boys see that the door key is in the lock. They edge toward the door. Harry leaps forward and turns the key. Happy with their success, the boys turn and run back down the corridor—until they hear a scream from the bathroom and realize Hermione is in there.

Returning to the bathroom is the last thing either wants to do. But they have no choice. Harry opens the door and they run inside. Hermione is against the far wall, looking as if she will faint. The troll is advancing toward her, knocking sinks off as he passes.

"Confuse it!" Harry yells to Ron as he seizes a loose water tap and throws it at the monster. The troll turns, stares at Harry, and starts toward him. Ron throws a metal pipe at it, deflecting its attention. Harry runs around it, grabs Hermione, and tries to propel her toward the door. But she is frozen with terror and cannot move. The troll roars and starts toward Ron.

Harry does something the author calls "both very brave and very stupid." He takes a running jump and manages to fasten his arms around the troll's neck from behind. The troll doesn't notice the frail boy's presence until it suddenly shrieks with pain from the wand Harry has thrust up its nostril. Howling in agony, it now twists and flails its club, trying to throw Harry off or catch him with a blow of the club.

Hermione sinks to the floor in fright, as Ron pulls out his own wand and cries the first spell that comes into his head: *"Wingardium Leviosa!"* The club flies out of the monster's hand, rises in the air, and then descends with enormous force on its head. The troll staggers, then falls flat on its face with a thud that causes the whole room to shudder.

Moments later, three professors arrive. "What on earth were you thinking of?" asks Professor McGonagall. "You're lucky you weren't killed. Why aren't you in your dormitory?"[27] Harry doesn't answer, of course, for they should have been obeying the rules. But in this case a higher rule applied: He and Ron had returned to the bathroom to save Hermione. And they were all disregarding the rules for a simple reason: They were trying to prevent Voldemort from getting control of the Sorcerer's Stone.

Later in the same story, when Harry, Ron, and Hermione think Professor Snape is in league with Voldemort and is trying to secure the Sorcerer's Stone for him, Harry says he is going to get to the Stone first—which means disobeying Professor McGonagall's orders not to enter the dungeons where the Stone is, getting past the three-headed dog guarding it, making his way through the Devil's Snare plant that stands in the way, and finding the magic key that will open the final chamber.

Ron says he is mad. Hermione says he can't—he'll be expelled for doing it!

"SO WHAT?" Harry shouted. "Don't you understand? If Snape gets hold of the Stone, Voldemort's coming back!

Haven't you heard what it was like when he was trying to take over? There won't be any Hogwarts to get expelled from! He'll flatten it, or turn it into a school for the Dark Arts! Losing points doesn't matter any more, can't you see? D'you think he'll leave you and your families alone if Gryffindor wins the house cup? If I get caught before I can get to the Stone, well, I'll have to go back to the Dursleys and wait for Voldemort to find me there, it's only dying a bit later than I would have, because I'm never going over to the Dark Side! I'm going through that trapdoor tonight and nothing you two say is going to stop me! Voldemort killed my parents, remember?"[28]

As Christ's sacrifice was infectious among his followers, several of whom were supposedly slain for their faith, Harry's bravery rubs off on Ron and Hermione, who finally accompany him on the quest for the Stone. When Harry's ability as a Seeker has enabled him to spot the right key flying around the room among hundreds of others, and they have entered another chamber on their way, they see that they have to get past an astonishing, lifelike chess set, whose players are taller than they are and come to life as they accept the challenge of crossing the board. Ron, who has been more attentive to chess than Harry, takes the lead. Walking up to a black knight, he reaches out and touches the horse. The horse begins to paw the ground and the knight turns his head toward Ron. Ron tells Harry to take the place of a bishop and Hermione the place of a rook, and he himself leaps astride the horse, as the former pieces move off the board, relinquishing their roles.

The game begins, with Ron directing their moves. "Harry— move diagonally four squares to the right." He does, and the other knight is taken. The white queen smashes him to the floor and drags him off the board, where he lies quite lifeless. The slaughter continues. Every time the white pieces have the opportunity, they ruthlessly take their opponents. A pile of black players lies slumped beside the board. Ron ponders what to do next.

"Yes," he says softly, "it's the only way . . . I've got to be taken." "NO!" shout Harry and Hermione.

"That's chess!" says Ron. "You've got to make some sacrifices! I take one step forward and she'll take me—that leaves you free to checkmate the king, Harry!"[29]

Ron steps forward and the white queen pounces on him. She strikes him across the head so hard with her stone arm that he crashes to the floor. But Harry makes his move and the white king takes off his crown and throws it at Harry's feet. The chessmen part and bow, clearing their way to the door.

Harry himself will of course face Professor Quirrell and Voldemort when he and Hermione get to the Stone. We have already discussed that encounter. But it is heartening to see what a powerful influence for courage and sacrifice Harry has exerted on his friends and disciples.

In *Harry Potter and the Chamber of Secrets*, the house-elf Dobby tries to warn Harry away from Hogwarts because of "terrible things" he knows are going to happen there. Dobby's master was Lucius Malfoy, who is one of Voldemort's faithful followers, and Dobby is torn between his earlier fealty to Malfoy and his affection for Harry. His feelings for Harry win out because Harry's earlier victory over Voldemort gave hope to all good elves and wizards that the Dark Lord's power was broken. But Dobby knows that awful things are being planned against the Mudbloods, or Muggle-born wizards, and wants Harry to leave.

Harry protests that he is not Muggle-born and therefore has nothing to fear. When Dobby insists that he leave, Harry says one of his best friends, Hermione, is Muggle-born, and he will not leave her.

"Harry Potter risks his own life for his friends!" moans Dobby. "So noble! So valiant! But he must save himself, Harry Potter must not—"[30]

Harry of course ignores the warning and does indeed risk his life for his friend—the very action recommended by Jesus at the Last Supper. And not only that, he soon afterward risks his life for another student. Draco Malfoy has conjured up a huge black snake during a demonstration by Professors Lockhart and Snape at the Dueling Club. When Lockhart makes a clumsy attempt at making the snake disappear, it flies into the air and falls back to the floor at the feet of a student named Justin Finch-Fletchley. Enraged, the serpent raises itself, fangs exposed, to strike.

Without pausing even to think, and completely unaware of the danger to himself, Harry instinctively rushes forward and shouts at the snake, "Leave him alone!"[31] This is the episode in which we learn that Harry speaks Parseltongue, the language of snakes, which explains his understanding the ominous voice breathing death through the hallways of Hogwarts and his ability, at the climax of the story, to address the monstrous basilisk in the secret chamber. This snake is easily dispatched by Harry's command. But not so, unfortunately, the terrible basilisk under Voldemort's control.

I have already referred to Harry's eager descent into the pipes leading to the secret chamber to rescue Ginny Weasley in terms of Jesus' *descensus ad inferos,* or Descent into Hell. The Descent into Hell, which was mentioned in a sixth-century Gallican creed that expressed the ideas later embodied in the widely used Apostles' Creed of about 750 C.E., pictures Jesus descending into Hades during the three days (or parts of three days) between his death on the cross and his resurrection. In the Middle Ages, it was known as the Harrowing of Hell. Christ supposedly assaulted the gates of hell to free the souls consigned to Satan's power. There were many popular woodcuts of the imaginary event, and, later, many stained-glass windows depicting it.

"I'm going down there," declares Harry when he and Ron behold the bathroom pipe twisting and becoming enlarged, revealing a tubular entrance to the secret chamber below.

"He couldn't not go, not now they had found the entrance to the Chamber, not if there was even the faintest, slimmest, wildest chance that Ginny might be alive."[32]

The way down is "like rushing down an endless, slimy, dark slide." Harry sees more pipes branching off in all directions, and knows he is "falling deeper below the school than even the dungeons." At the bottom is a "dark stone tunnel large enough to stand in"—and it is there, in the inner bowels of the secret chamber, that Harry confronts the hideous basilisk and his old nemesis, Lord Voldemort. Once more, he has risked his life for another without thinking of the danger to himself.

In *Harry Potter and the Goblet of Fire,* Harry not only risks his life to rescue his friend Ron from the merpeople deep under the school lake, but shows his complete disregard for himself when others are at risk of any kind. For the second task of the Triwizard Tournament, the champions' friends have been captured and are being held under a spell by the merpeople. Each champion must elude the giant squid in the lake, a troll, the boggarts, and the horned water demons, or grindylows, and rescue his or her friend from the underwater captivity. But when Harry reaches Ron, he finds not only Ron but Hermione, Cho Chang, and a small girl he recognizes as Fleur Delacour's baby sister. Having used a jagged rock from the bottom of the lake to cut Ron's bindings, he begins to hack at Hermione's too, afraid the other champions will not reach them.

The mermen grab him. "You take your own hostage," says one of them. "Leave the others . . ."

"No way!" says Harry furiously.[33]

Cedric Diggory, the other Hogwarts champion, shows up and cuts Cho loose. He tells Harry that Krum and Delacour are on their way for the others. Krum arrives and helps to free Hermione. But Delacour still has not come. Harry attempts to free her sister but is threatened by the mermen. He pulls out his wand, warns them to fall back, and finishes freeing her.

Holding her around the waist and grabbing the neck of Ron's robes, he kicks off from the bottom. It is difficult going, bearing two captives instead of one, but he eventually makes it back to safety. Fleur Delacour, he learns, was attacked by grindylows and could not make it to rescue her sister.

Professor Dumbledore, sizing up the situation, crouches at the edge of the lake and has a conversation with the chief of the merpersons. He reveals to the other judges what transpired beneath the water, and they award Harry forty-five points out of a possible fifty, for displaying "moral fiber," even though he returned last from the mission. The amount puts him in first place with Cedric Diggory. But Harry has shown no concern for his standing in the contest—it was the lives of the captives that really mattered to him.

LOVING OTHERS

"No one has greater love than this," said Jesus, "to lay down one's life for one's friends."[34] Love and sacrifice are intimately connected, and the bottom line of the whole Christian message is love. God sent his Son into the world, says the Gospel of John, because God loved the world.[35] And the writer of the Epistle of 1 John says:

> Beloved, let us love one another, because love is from God; everyone who loves is born of God and knows God. Whoever does not love does not know God, for God is love.

God's love was revealed among us in this way: God sent his
only Son into the world so that we might live through him.
In this is love, not that we loved God but that he loved us
and sent his Son to be the atoning sacrifice for our sins.
Beloved, since God loved us so much, we also ought to love
one another. No one has ever seen God; if we love one
another, God lives in us, and his love is perfected in us.[36]

When Harry asks Dumbledore, at the end of *Harry Potter
and the Sorcerer's Stone,* why Professor Quirrell could not
bear to touch him when Voldemort was demanding that Quirrell kill him, Dumbledore says:

"Your mother died to save you. If there is one thing
Voldemort cannot understand, it is love. He didn't realize
that love as powerful as your mother's for you leaves its own
mark. Not a scar, no visible sign   to have been loved so
deeply, even though the person who loved us is gone, will
give us some protection forever. It is in your very skin. Quirrell, full of hatred, greed, and ambition, sharing his soul with
Voldemort, could not touch you for this reason. It was agony
to touch a person marked by something so good."[37]

In the Christian tradition, all of those who belong to God,
and live in God, are transformed by love into a vast commonwealth of souls, a heavenly kingdom, in which love continues to
grow stronger and stronger. Because they have been touched by
this love, Christians still alive pray for the dead, and it is believed

that the dead pray for them as well. Charles Williams' novels *All Hallows' Eve*, *War in Heaven*, and *Descent into Hell* are about this invisible but extremely powerful community of love.

In the dramatic scene in *Harry Potter and the Goblet of Fire* where Harry's and Voldemort's wands clash, producing an amazing gold filament between them, the ghosts of Voldemort's victims begin issuing from the end of his wand—first Cedric Diggory, whom he has just slain, then Frank Bryce and Bertha Jorkins, and finally Harry's parents, James and Lily Potter—and each in turn has words of encouragement for Harry.

"Hold on, Harry," says Cedric's shade.

"You fight him, boy," says Bryce's ghost.

"Don't let go, now!" cries the ghost of Bertha Jorkins. "Don't let him get you, Harry—don't let go!"

"Your mother's coming . . ." says James Potter quietly. "She wants to see you . . . it will be all right . . . hold on. . . ."

"When the connection is broken," says Lily Potter—the golden filament temporarily binding the two wands— "we will linger for only moments . . . but we will give you time . . . you must get to the Portkey, it will return you to Hogwarts . . . do you understand, Harry?"

"Do it now," whispers his father's voice, "be ready to run . . . do it now. . . ."[38]

And Harry runs, dragging Cedric's body with him, dodging behind tombstones, using his wand and a spell to bring the Triwizard Cup within his grasp, and suddenly being whisked away by the Portkey, Cedric's body in tow, back to Hogwarts and safety. It is one of the most dramatic scenes in all the Potter stories, and one of the most revelatory of the spiritual structure behind them. Harry has been saved by what Christians call "the communion of the saints," the fellowship of love that grows out of the divine love and binds all believers' hearts together in holy unity!

At the somber end-of-term dinner in the Great Hall of Hogwarts, Dumbledore tells the assembled faculty and students about Cedric's death and Harry's heroism in resisting Voldemort and returning with Cedric's body. "He risked his own life to return Cedric's body to Hogwarts," says Dumbledore. "He showed, in every respect, the sort of bravery that few wizards have ever shown in facing Lord Voldemort, and for this, I honor him."[39]

Dumbledore turns to Harry and raises his goblet to him. Nearly everyone in the hall follows suit. They murmur Harry's name and drink to him. (Given the eschatological tone of all that has happened, can this be reminiscent of the way Christians lift their cups to Christ in the sacrament of the Lord's Table?) Dumbledore continues, saying that the Triwizard Tournament was organized with the intention of promoting closer ties among wizards all over the world—ties that now "are more important than ever before."

"Every guest in this Hall," he says, "will be welcomed back here at any time, should they wish to come. I say to you all, once again—in the light of Lord Voldemort's return, we are only as strong as we are united, as weak as we are divided. Lord Voldemort's gift for spreading discord and enmity is very great. We can fight it only by showing an equally strong bond of friendship and trust. Differences of habit and language are nothing at all if our aims are identical and our hearts are open."[40]

The Lord of Darkness spreads discord and enmity. The Lord of Light brings love and unity. And, in the final analysis, cleaving to the Light, to love, to unity, is the essence of the good life. Humility, decency, fair play, doing to others as one would have them do to you, being ready to sacrifice self for others, are all part of it. But it is the love of God and the unity of the spirit that raise them all beyond mere individual acts and impart to them a sense of transcendent meaning, that convert them into what the Apostle Paul in the Letter to the Galatians called "the fruit of the Spirit."

And what is the fruit of the Spirit? It is the opposite of what Paul denominated "the works of the flesh":

> Now the works of the flesh are obvious: fornication, impurity, licentiousness, idolatry, sorcery, enmities, strife, jealousy, anger, quarrels, dissensions, factions, envy, drunkenness, carousing, and things like these. I am warning you, as I warned you before: those who do such things will not inherit the kingdom of God.
>
> By contrast, the fruit of the Spirit is love, joy, peace, patience, kindness, generosity, faithfulness, gentleness, and self-control.[41]

Love—above everything!

A MATTER OF CHOICE

One thing Rowling makes abundantly clear, time and again, is that people are the product of the choices they make. To be sure, there seems to be innate goodness or badness in people—it would be hard to imagine Dudley Dursley or Draco Malfoy ever being very reflective about his life and thus doing anything to improve it. But the Harrys, Hermiones, and Rons are constantly weighing the consequences of their actions, *deciding* how they will behave, and contemplating what the results of their decisions may be.

Rowling doesn't preach to her characters. She tends instead to reflect on their nature at the ends of the novels. At the conclusion of *Harry Potter and the Chamber of Secrets,* for example, Harry and Dumbledore are discussing what happened to Harry when he was attacked by the basilisk and Voldemort in the chamber. Harry recalls that Tom Riddle, who is Voldemort's alter ego, said that the two of them were alike. Harry is obviously troubled by this, because even though he is a Gryffindor and Riddle was a Slytherin, the Sorting Hat almost put him in the Slytherin House. And, like Riddle, he speaks Parseltongue, or serpent language.

Dumbledore suggests that Voldemort may have put a little of himself in Harry the night he tried to kill him as a baby—that some of Voldemort's powers were unintentionally transferred to Harry when he received his scar. Harry is thunderstruck by this. "So I *should* be in Slytherin," says

Harry. "The Sorting Hat could see Slytherin's power in me, and it—"

"Put you in Gryffindor," says Dumbledore. "Listen to me, Harry. You happen to have many qualities Salazar Slytherin prized in his hand-picked students. His own very rare gift, Parseltongue—resourcefulness—determination—a certain disregard for rules . . . Yet the Sorting Hat placed you in Gryffindor. You know why that was. Think."

"It only put me in Gryffindor," says Harry in a defeated voice, "because I asked not to go in Slytherin. . . ."

"*Exactly,*" says Dumbledore, beaming. "Which makes you *very different* from Tom Riddle. It is our choices, Harry, that show what we truly are, far more than our abilities."[42]

Our choices, far more than our abilities. This has always been an important theme in the Judeo-Christian faith. "I call heaven and earth to witness against you today," said God to the Israelites, "that I have set before you life and death, blessings and curses. Choose life so that you and your descendants may live, loving the Lord your God, obeying him, and holding fast to him."[43]

"Simon, son of John," said the resurrected Christ to his disciple Simon Peter, "do you love me more than these?" "Yes, Lord," said Peter; "you know that I love you." Jesus said to him, "Feed my lambs."[44] Throughout the history of the Christian church, there has been an emphasis on the believer's choice as the all-important factor in his or her conversion and transformation as a person. Billy Graham's radio and TV programs, the most widely heard and watched evangelical services in the history of the world, were known as *The Hour of Decision.* God is also a chooser, selecting special persons for various tasks that need doing. But the character of those who adhere to the faith is finally determined by the decisions they themselves must make in the course of a lifetime.

Goethe's *Faust* is one of the flowerings of this tradition, and it is Faust's tragedy that he accepts the blandishments of Mephistopheles, thus indenturing himself to the evil one instead of making the harder choice he might have made.

Some have argued that "what will be will be," and that people are predestined or foreordained to become what they do eventually become. Many believe that race or class or family or DNA or some other given is the strongest determining factor in a person's character or behavior. This is the position of Cornelius Fudge, the Minister of Magic, in *Harry Potter and the Goblet of Fire,* when Dumbledore insists, after Voldemort's revitalization, that the ministry must send envoys to the giants and enlist their support in the future contest with darkness. Fudge knows that most wizards are suspicious of the giants and that they would strongly object to his approaching them. It might even mean the end of his career as minister.

"You are blinded," Dumbledore accuses, "by the love of the office you hold, Cornelius! You place too much importance, and you always have done, on the so-called purity of blood! You fail to recognize that it matters not what someone is born, but what they grow to be! Your dementor has just destroyed the last remaining member of a pure-blood family as old as any [Barty Crouch]—and see what that man chose to make of his life! I tell you now—take the steps I have suggested, and you will be remembered, in office or out, as one of the bravest and greatest Ministers of Magic we have ever known. Fail to act—and history will remember you as the man who stepped aside and allowed Voldemort a second chance to destroy the world we have tried to rebuild!"[45]

Rowling is acutely aware of the importance of choices in her own life. She speaks of studying French and Classics instead of English Literature as a mistake she made because her parents said that languages would make her more employable, and of going to London to take a bilingual secretarial course as "an even bigger mistake" because she was totally unsuited to secretarial work.[46] She has also said that she considers her first marriage, to a Portuguese journalist named Jorge Arantes, a mistake.[47]

She says that the writer who has had the most influence on her is Jessica Mitford, who instantly became her hero when she read *Hons and Rebels* at the age of fourteen. She admired Mitford for running away from home to fight in the civil war in Spain, and for charging her father's account for a camera she took with her to record events in that important struggle. "I wished I'd had the nerve to do something like that," says Rowling. "She had tremendous moral courage and did some physically brave things as a human rights activist. . . . She stood up against her family—they were very rich indeed and didn't believe in educating girls—and showed her passion by acting on what she believed, not preaching."[48] Rowling even named her daughter Jessica after Mitford.

But Rowling did make some hard and courageous choices that turned out right for her. One was to continue writing after she had written two unpublished novels and a number of stories. Another was to move to Edinburgh and continue to work on her first Harry Potter story while she strove to meet the qualifications for a postgraduate certificate in education. And yet another was to risk everything on the success of her work and not "waste" her time trying to earn a living while she was writing the second Harry Potter novel. She is clearly a determined woman, and has confirmed in her life story the truth she reiterates constantly in the novels—that people *choose* who they will be, they do not have to accept the characterizations thrust on them by background and happenstance.

Rowling obviously loves certain characters in her stories—wise old Professor Dumbledore, steady Professor McGonagall, huggable Hagrid, the gentle giant, faithful Ron (who is modeled on her friend Sean Harris, the one with the turquoise Ford Anglia), sometimes prickly, sometimes tender, always disciplined and determined Hermione (a lot like herself as a girl, she has confessed), and of course good, stubborn, nerdish Harry Potter. But it is also clear that she deeply admires some other characters, such as Professor Lupin, who has struggled against his history as a werewolf; Sirius Black, who withstood twelve years among the dementors at Azkaban (Rowling has said that the dementors are related to depression and that she has fought against them in her own life)[49]; and even—or especially—the unlikable Professor Severus Snape, who at one time allowed himself to receive the mark of Voldemort but decided to oppose him and continues valiantly to resist the latter's claim on his life.

The good life, however obvious it may appear to the casual observer or the reader of a novel, is not as easy to achieve and maintain as we might think. Often, it must be won again and again through the hard decisions we make about who we will follow and what we wish to become. It is never an assumable possession. Even the Apostle Paul, a stalwart convert to the Christian way of life if there ever was one, confessed that he frequently did the evil he did not want to do instead of the good he wanted to do,[50] and said that in spite of all his successes in following the way of Christ he still had not attained the goal and must continue to press toward it.[51]

It is part of what we like and admire about Harry Potter and the other good characters in J. K. Rowling's stories that, over and over, they are offered choices for their lives and decide to take the high road. Sometimes Harry and his friends compromise their principles on small matters and ignore the rules set down by their superiors. But they are never in error about the things that matter most. When the chips are down, and character lies in the balance, they always make the right decisions, even if those decisions will be punishing to them.

They usually are.

THE MAGICAL,
MYSTICAL WORLD

CHAP. 4.

ONSERVATIVE CHRISTIANS frequently object to the world of wizardry in the Potter novels—all the tricks, potions, spells, and enchanted objects. And, to be sure, there are plenty of these. They abound in the stories, tumbling over one another like jelly beans cascading out of a dime-store dispenser.

There are strange, magical objects, such as the Sorting Hat that places Hogwarts students in their respective houses, the Mirror of Erised ("desire" spelled backward), in which viewers see what they wish to see, a Sneakoscope that lights up when untrustworthy people are around, and a *Monster Book of Monsters,* that snaps at whoever tries to open it. There are fantastic and wonderful candies, such as exploding bonbons, levitating sherbet balls, and bubble gum that fills the air with bubbles that won't pop for days.

There is the famous platform nine and three-quarters at King's Cross Station, used only by the wizards as they are taking the special train to or from Hogwarts, and requiring them to walk directly into the wall between platforms nine and ten— but which Dobby the house-elf closes against Harry and Ron in *Harry Potter and the Chamber of Secrets*. And the glorious Great Hall at Hogwarts, peopled by ghosts as well as wizards, with a ceiling bewitched to look exactly like the sky outside, and twelve great trees at Christmas decorated with hundreds of candles and real hanging icicles. (In Harry's fourth year, the decorations are the most fabulous he has yet seen: everlasting icicles hanging from the marble banisters, the twelve trees adorned by "everything from luminous holly berries to real, hooting, golden owls," and all the usual suits of armor bewitched to sing carols when anybody passes them.) And the wonderful living statues and portraits everywhere, that move and sing and speak and cry, such as the painting described in *Harry Potter and the Prisoner of Azkaban*, in which a short, squat knight in a suit of armor looks out, sees Harry, Ron, and Hermione, and brandishes his sword at them, saying, "Draw, you knaves, you dogs!"[1] But the sword is too long for him, so that when he swings it, it topples him over into the grass.

Nor must we fail to mention the Forbidden Forest, full of deadly, entangling plants, centaurs, unicorns, and gigantic spiders, at whose edge stands the gamekeeper's cottage and the great Whomping Willow, which severely thrashes anybody or anything that comes within reach of its powerful branches. And there is the famous Polyjuice Potion, which allows people to change themselves into other people's forms, and gillyweed, which Harry eats to grow gills and fins when he must rescue

Ron from the merpeople under the lake, and bubotuber pus, a yellowish green liquid that covers Hermione's hands with painful sores, so that she looks "as though she were wearing a pair of thick, knobbly gloves," and dozens of other magical potions and substances. And Wizard Chess, which we have already mentioned, in which the larger-than-life-size chess pieces come alive and play the game violently. And a golden egg that sings underwater. And Mad-Eye Moody's magical eye that rotates constantly, surveying everything in a room. And wands. . . .

Much of the magic performed by wizards is done with the aid of a wand—and not just any wand, but a wand especially suited to its bearer. One of the most charming scenes in all the Potter novels is the one when Harry is first taken by Hagrid to Diagon Alley, the wizards' shopping center in London, and they enter the narrow little shop with the peeling gold letters on the door that read "Ollivanders: Makers of Fine Wands since 382 B.C." Old Mr. Ollivander himself, a small man with silvery, creepy eyes, appears. He recalls exactly every wand he has ever sold, including the one that belonged to James Potter, Harry's father, and, he is sorry to say, the one taken by Lord Voldemort, which was used to kill Harry's parents and then turned on Harry himself.

Measuring Harry very carefully, Mr. Ollivander ("old wander") tells him that every wand contains a magical core—either a unicorn hair, a phoenix tail feather, or the heartstring of a dragon—and that no two wands are exactly alike. After trying several wands, they arrive at precisely the right one for

Harry. Ollivander is struck by the fact that the phoenix that provided a feather for it is the same one that gave a feather for the wand that dealt Harry his scar. Later, of course, we learn that the donor was Fawkes, Dumbledore's pet phoenix that saves Harry's life in the *Chamber of Secrets*. And it is the kinship of the two wands that causes them to react strangely when Harry and Voldemort attempt to use them simultaneously on each other in the cemetery scene in *Harry Potter and the Goblet of Fire*.

(Perhaps it isn't important, but Voldemort's wand is made of oak, while Harry's is fashioned of holly, a wood often associated with Christ, and even, according to one legend, called "Christ's thorn" because it sprang from Christ's footsteps on earth, and its thorny leaves and berries like drops of blood were believed to be symbolic of his suffering.)

The wands are of course used to cast spells of various kinds, and Harry Potter's education at Hogwarts is an induction into a world of spells and curses that is amazing and often bewildering to him. There isn't any room for disbelief in such a world—one simply learns how to control the magical powers that reside in the wand and the nature of things in general. It is interesting that in all of Western legends and fairy tales since Christ, the usual language for spells has been Latin, the language of the Mass and until recent times the official language of Roman Catholicism. There is good reason for this. Clerics in the Middle Ages learned to read Latin in order to perform the sacraments of the church, but ordinary people did not. Hence Latin came to be the language of mystification, and, in the eyes of those who were more cynical, of mumbo jumbo. Even Martin Luther attacked the Mass as a "dumb show" because it was conducted in Latin, and insisted, as a principle of reformation, that both the Bible and the Mass should in the future be translated into the vernacular so that even the plowman in the fields could understand them!

Among the spells we encounter in the Potter stories are *Accio,* the summoning charm (Harry uses it to summon the Triwizard Cup and escape from Voldemort in *Harry Potter and the Goblet of Fire*); *Aparecium,* from the root word *appareo,* which causes invisible messages to appear; *Deletrius,* from the Latin *deleo,* which deletes or causes things to disappear; *Obliviate,* from "oblivion," which makes a person forget; *Riddikulus,* which causes things to seem funny; and *Wingardium Leviosa,* "take wings and levitate," which makes people or objects fly through the air.

In *Harry Potter and the Goblet of Fire,* we learn that there are three Unforgivable Curses, and that any wizard who performs them on another human being is liable to lifetime imprisonment at Azkaban. They are *Crucio,* which causes excruciating pain in the victim, *Imperio,* which puts the subject under the wizard's complete command or control, and *Avada Kedavra,* the so-called Killing Curse, which is usually fatal to the subject. It is the *Avada Kedavra* curse that Vordemort employed to destroy Harry's parents, and that he attempts to use on Harry in the cemetery scene in *Harry Potter and the Goblet of Fire.* This curse has a long history of actual usage, and derives from the Aramaic phrase *abhadda kedhabhra,* which means "disappear like this word." It was usually written several times, rather than spoken, in inverted pyramidal form, so that a letter was omitted from each line until the word literally disappeared. The common magician's formula *abra cadabra* was borrowed from this phrase.

Readers will remember that Voldemort also used the *Crucio* formula on Harry in the cemetery scene, and caused Harry to experience extreme pain:

> Voldemort raised his wand, and before Harry could do anything to defend himself, before he could even move, he had been hit again by the Cruciatus Curse. The pain was so intense, so all-consuming, that he no longer knew where he was. . . . White-hot knives were piercing every inch of his skin, his head was surely going to burst with pain, he was screaming more loudly than he'd ever screamed in his life.[2]

Apropos of our discussion of Harry as a Christ figure, there is an obvious connection between the words *Crucio* or *Cruciatus* and *crucifixion*. They are all derived, of course, from the Latin word *crux* or "cross." Crucifixion appears to have been a form of torture invented by the Persians, from whom it passed to the Greeks and Romans. The latter, especially, used it widely throughout their empire as a warning and deterrent to crime, particularly against rebellious slaves and seditious factions in the various provinces. Because it was so terrible, it could not be used on Roman citizens. Always conducted in a public place, it usually included scourging, lashing, or nailing the arms of the victim to a wooden crossbar, an announcement of the person's crime, and slow death by hunger, pain, and exposure. Usually several days were required for persons to die in this manner, and their bodies were left hanging for several more days beyond death, so that people would see them and remember the horror with which they had died. This was considered the most extreme form of death meted out by Roman officials. Jewish historian Josephus called it "the most wretched of deaths." Harry's excruciating pain from Voldemort's curse is consonant with this kind of death, and should underline the possibility that Rowling was thinking about the crucifixion of Jesus when she described his suffering.

THE SOURCES OF ENCHANTMENT

From the sublime to the ridiculous and the serious to the frolicking, there is no question that the reader who enters the fiction of J. K. Rowling is stepping into a world of magic and enchantment, one in which portraits move and talk, trees take out their aggressions on people, ordinary objects fly through the air, strange, belligerent plants, animals, and insects share the planet, and wizards practice exceptional powers that Muggles or ordinary people don't understand and usually don't even see. For young readers, especially, this is part of the fun of a Harry Potter story, and critics who worry that Rowling is trying to herd them into the arms of the occult are probably far more sinister than she. As G. K. Chesteron once said, St. John in his Revelation saw many strange creatures, but none half so strange as some of his interpreters! We ought to remember that Rowling did not invent the world of the extraordinary. On the contrary, she merely stands in the vanguard of numerous writers who have either preceded her or are writing today about such fantastic things that readers must park their common, everyday sense at the door and be prepared for magic and marvel on every hand.

English literature from *Beowulf* to Shakespeare is filled with stories of monsters and supernatural events. The medieval Arthurian legends, stories of King Arthur and the knights of the Round Table, recount numerous battles with strange beasts and people. The fairy tales of both Britain and Europe boast of extraordinary creatures and miraculous powers. Lewis Carroll's *Alice in Wonderland* stories and Frank Baum's *The Wizard of Oz* feature magical settings, extraordinary creatures, talking animals, and animated plants. C. S. Lewis' Narnia tales, which were a favorite of Rowling when she was a child, fairly burst with unbelievable characters and occurrences. J. R. R. Tolkien's *The Hobbits* and *Lord of the Rings* trilogy, other favorites, provide settings and wizards with whom Harry Potter would feel right at home (it is often noted that Dumbledore is extremely similar to Gandalf, the wizard in *Lord of the Rings*). Roald Dahl's *Matilda, The Witches, Charlie and the Chocolate Factory*, and *James and the Giant Peach* all bear striking similarities to the Potter stories.

Elizabeth Schafer, in *Exploring Harry Potter*, lists a number of other works that also foreshadow the Potter oeuvres in noticeable ways: James Barrie's *Peter Pan,* P. L. Travers's *Mary Poppins,* T. H. White's *The Once and Future King,* Ursula LeGuin's *A Wizard of Earthsea,* several of Stephen King's stories, Ian Fleming's *Chitty Chitty Bang Bang: The Magical Car,* Mary Norton's *Bed-knob and Broomstick,* Jane Yolen's *Wizard's Hall, The Pit Dragon* trilogy, and *The Tartan Magic* series, Diane Duane's wizard series, Julie Edwards' *The Last of the Really Great Whangdoodles,* and many other novels and stories too numerous to mention here, including works of both fantasy and science fiction. Clearly, Rowling writes out of a long and respectable tradition of magical worlds.

And, more to our point in this book, what about the wondrous or magical nature of the Bible itself, and Christian history beyond the Bible?

Consider a few of the high points in the Bible. The world is created *ex nihilo* by the spoken fiat of an extraordinarily powerful being named Yahweh or Elohim (the prominent names given in the parallel accounts in the early chapters of Genesis). A woman is created from the rib of a man. A talking serpent beguiles the woman into eating fruit from a forbidden tree. The couple are expelled from Eden for disobedience and a flaming sword is set at the entrance to prevent their return. There are giants in the earth. An invisible divine being speaks audibly to Abraham and tells him he will father a great nation. When Abraham's hand is stayed from sacrificing his son Isaac, a ram is magically provided to take the son's place. Moses encounters a flaming bush that is not consumed. When God sends Moses to free the children of Israel from bondage in

Egypt, he pronounces a number of curses on the Egyptian people, including frogs, flies, locusts, water that turns to blood, boils, and the deaths of firstborn children. As the Israelites flee from the Egyptians, Moses lifts his staff (a wand?) over the sea and the Israelites walk through it on dry land, while the waves engulf the Egyptians behind them. Moses uses the same staff to strike a rock at Horeb and cause drinking water to spout from it. God designates Aaron to assist Moses by making his staff sprout buds, bloom, and bear almonds—all overnight! The prophet Balaam has a conversation with his donkey, which actually talks back. Joshua commands the sun and moon to stand still in their courses until the Israelites have slain all their enemies (did he have a Time-Turner?). The bearers of the Ark of the Covenant stand on dry ground in the middle of the River Jordan before the city of Jericho, and the walls of Jericho collapse as the Israelites march around it, blowing their trumpets.

The angel of God touches Gideon's offering of meat and unleavened cakes with his staff and fire consumes them. As another sign to Gideon, God makes a sheep's wool thick with water, while the ground around it is dry as a bone. A witch at Endor conjures up the dead Samuel for Saul, the king of Israel, and Saul talks with him. Because a widow in Zarephath has been kind to the prophet Elijah, God gives her a jar of meal and a jug of oil that cannot be emptied. Elijah drenches a bull on an altar with water, calls on God, and fire rains on the altar and consumes everything, including the water in the trenches around the altar. Elijah strikes the river with his rolled-up cloak and the water parts so he and Elisha can walk through on dry ground. Elijah is taken up to heaven in a chariot of fire drawn by horses of fire. Elisha raises a Shunammite woman's son from death. When a woodsman loses his ax head in the river, Elisha throws a stick into the water and makes the ax head float. Isaiah has a dramatic vision of God high on a throne and surrounded by singing seraphim. Ezekiel is set down in a valley filled with bones and sees them rise up and assume their flesh again. Shadrach, Meshach, and Abednego are thrown into a furnace so hot that it burns the men who throw them in, but the three survive the heat and are seen walking around in it with a fourth man; when they emerge, not even the hair on their heads is singed. The fingers of a human hand appear and write on the wall in the presence of King Balshazzar. Daniel spends the night untouched in a den of ravenous lions. When Jonah is thrown overboard in a sea storm, he is swallowed by a great fish, spends three days and nights in the fish's belly, and is regurgitated on dry land.

All of these stories are in the Old Testament. And what of the New Testament? Jesus goes everywhere, constantly healing the sick and raising the dead. A woman is cured of a long illness by touching the hem of his garment. One man he raises from the dead has been in the tomb for four days and his body is already rotting. He feeds thousands of people with a handful of bread and fish. He turns six enormous vats of water into the finest wine the wine steward ever tasted. He commands sea storms to cease, and they do. He walks on the sea during a storm. He casts a legion of demons out of a man and into a herd of swine, and the swine rush headlong into the sea. He sends his servants to fetch a coin for taxes from the mouth of a fish. When he is crucified, the sun stops shining for three hours at midday and the graves of Jerusalem open and their dead walk through the city. The women who go to his tomb the third day after his death find it empty and hear from an angel that he has been raised from the dead. He suddenly materializes before his disciples in a room where the doors are locked.

At the Feast of Pentecost, tongues of fire appear on the foreheads of Jesus' followers and they understand languages from all parts of the world (perhaps they would even have understood Parseltongue!). Peter and John heal a man who has been lame from birth. Ananias and Sapphira fall over dead because they lied to the apostles. Saul is struck blind on the road to Damascus and then receives his sight again when touched by another man named Ananias. Peter resuscitates a dead woman named Tabitha. Saul, now called Paul, casts a spell of blindness on a magician named Elymas. A violent earthquake knocks down a prison, freeing Paul and Silas. On the island of Malta, Paul is bitten by a poisonous viper but shakes it off and suffers no ill effects.

These miracles are small compared to some that are reported among the saints of the Middle Ages. For example, St. Basil prayed for a hermit who wished to speak Greek and the man immediately spoke the language perfectly. St. Julian, confronted by a horde of demons in the form of huge Ethiopians, made the sign of the cross and they all disappeared. St. Thomas of Canterbury saw a bird being chased by a hawk. Suddenly it cried out to him, "Saint Thomas, help me!" He prayed for the bird and the hawk fell dead at his feet. When a wolf carried off a poor widow's pig, St. Blaise told her not to be sad, it would be restored to her. Within minutes, the wolf returned and gave the pig to the woman. St. Juliana had molten lead poured over her head, but was unharmed because of her faith. Cast into prison in chains, she was confronted by a demon. Stepping out of the chains, she bound the demon and flogged it with her chains until it cried, "My lady Juliana, have pity on me!"

When a woman laughed at the idea that Christ could be in the bread of the eucharist, St. Gregory prayed and the bread was transformed into a human finger. He prayed again and it was restored to the appearance of bread. The woman instantly became a believer and received communion. In Ireland, a man stole a sheep, cooked it, and ate it. Informed of the theft, St. Patrick called on the thief to come forward. When he didn't, St. Patrick commanded the sheep to bleat in the belly of the man who stole it. When the sheep bleated loudly, the man confessed, accepted his penance, and was restored to the church.

A priest at dinner spoke ill of St. Ambrose, the bishop of Milan. The words were barely out of his mouth when he fell ill, was carried to his bed, and died. St. Theodora revived a dead man who had been mauled by a wild beast. Then she tracked down the beast and cursed it, whereupon it died instantly. St. Margaret was swallowed by an enormous dragon. But she made the sign of the cross from inside it, and immediately it exploded into pieces, setting her free. St. Apollinaris was taken to a temple of the Greek god Apollo and forced to his knees before a statue of the god. He uttered a curse on the statue and it instantly crumbled to pieces.

St. Gregory told his steward to invite twelve pilgrims to dinner. When he saw a thirteenth guest at table, he asked the steward about it. The steward said, "No, my lord, there are only twelve." Taking the thirteenth guest aside, St. Gregory asked the man who he was. "Don't you recognize me, my lord?" he said. "I am the shipwrecked seaman to whom you once gave a silver bowl in which your mother had sent you some vegetables." "How did you know about the vegetables?" asked St. Gregory. "Because I am that seaman's angel," said the man, "and the Lord sent me back so that I might always protect you, and through me you might obtain from him whatever you ask." And immediately the man vanished.

St. Anastasia had three Christian maids who were locked up in a kitchen by a prefect who desired to have sexual relations with them. When he let himself into the kitchen, a spell fell over him, and in his confusion he made love to the stoves, pots, and pans. He came out of the kitchen panting and covered with soot. His servants, who had been waiting outside, thought he was a demon and beat him with rods to drive him away. He went to complain to the emperor, and on his way was set upon by robbers who beat him again, making him blind. Angrier than ever, he had the three maids brought before him and stripped of their clothing, so that his servants could see and describe their beauty to him. But because the maids were under the power of St. Anastasia, their clothing stuck to them like skin and could not be peeled away.

Such stories often grew bigger with the telling, and each province of the Christian world was keen to repeat legends that glorified its own particular saint. Other tales concerned Christians who drove serpents away by making the sign of the cross, preached sermons after all their teeth were knocked out, lived unscathed through hours of burning at the stake, commanded lions, tigers, and elephants to devour their opponents, flew through the heavens like birds, were fed by birds and wild beasts, survived drowning at sea, changed a few crumbs into sumptuous feasts, caused arrows to turn back upon those who shot them, stood up and witnessed after being trampled by horses, brought plagues upon the houses of their enemies, and quoted the entire Bible (including the apochrypha) while standing on one foot!

Are these things wild, or aren't they?

HOW "MAGICAL" IS HARRY POTTER'S WORLD?

The simple fact is, the only newness about Rowling's fictional world is the freshness with which she treats old themes and invents new ones. The world of magic and miracle has been around for a long, long time, and is an intrinsic part of the Judeo-Christian heritage, whatever explanations conservative Christians may wish to offer for it. Rowling herself reminds us of this by the way she intermingles magic and science in the students' curriculum at Hogwarts. "Magic," after all, is related to the word *magi*, the name for those mysterious wise men from the East who came seeking the baby Jesus. They were probably Persian priests who studied the heavens for signs of important events. So the students at Hogwarts study Astrology, among other early sciences, and learn to interpret the influences of the stars and planets. They also study Arithmancy, Herbology, Potions, and a kind of Animal Husbandry that includes strange insects and mythical beasts—all derivatives of ancient sciences with counterparts in modern times.

Rowling's world, in other words, is more whole than a lot of contemporary versions of human existence, for it is more continuous with the real history of understanding as it has developed through the ages. It may also reflect more accurately the nearness of fantasy and fact in modern life—the way a Buck Rogers world actually springs out of the dreams and imaginations of the past. As Arthur C. Clarke, one of the greatest scientific minds of the twentieth century and the man often credited with first envisioning global TV satellites, once said, "Any sufficiently advanced technology is indistinguishable from magic." The reason for this is that skillfully designed technology is basically an outgrowth of the imagination, and *magic* and *imagination* contain the same root meaning. It isn't any wonder that natives who have never seen electric lights, cameras, or television sets regard them as marvels—for, in a way, they are. As Elizabeth Schafer points out, Thomas Edison was known as "the Wizard of Menlo Park" and George Washington Carver was called "the Wizard of Tuskegee."[3]

One of the most provocative books about the nature of reality I have ever read is Lawrence LeShan's *The Medium, the*

Mystic, and the Physicist, first published by Viking Press in 1975. LeShan, a pioneer in paranormal research, explores the relationships among the worlds of clairvoyance, spiritual mysticism, and modern physics, and demonstrates how their territories converge, so that they are actually "three roads to the same reality." We are prone to dismiss single paranormal events as they occur, one by one, because we do not discern any pattern of verifiable relationships among them. The same is true of mystical experiences. But the truth is, says LeShan, that all modern science has sprung from some isolated event or events that spurred the imagination of a curious observer. It is the atypical case, the unusual incident, that, when seriously examined, teaches us about all the others.

It is the one substance in Madame Curie's workshop that glows in the dark that teaches us about the basic structure of all the others. It is the one Petri dish in Fleming's laboratory in which the germs die unexpectedly that leads us to the discovery of the antibiotics. It is the one set of flasks in Pasteur's experiments in which life does *not* appear that teaches us the source of life in the others. It is the atypical paralysis in which neurology can *not* find the lesion that leads Freud to the discovery of the unconscious. It is the one problem in physics (the addition of velocities problem) that cannot be solved in the usual way that leads to an Einsteinian revolution and gives us a deeper understanding of the problems we had been able to solve in the old way.[4]

Proceeding, then, on the premise that we should not dismiss evidences of paranormal occurrences too quickly, without supposing that there must be somewhere a key to the way they are related—albeit too few scientists ever try to find it—LeShan develops his thesis that the basic assumption of all three of his areas of interest, the paranormal, mysticism, and physics, is the *inner unity* of all reality. It is this inner unity that makes their very existence possible. That is, there are *paranormal* occurrences because all psychic phenomena are interrelated and people can be visited by the souls of people from other times and places. Certain persons have *mystical* experiences because either they are preternaturally disposed to be in harmony with invisible spiritual forces or they have learned to position themselves to be receptive to those forces. And the modern physicist believes that the only way to understand the *physical* truths of the universe is to regard them all as interrelated and interdependent, so that time and space and matter must be studied together and not separately.

Is it possible, asks LeShan, that the three worlds and their unities actually overlap? More than that, that they are concentric and coextensive? That reality, far from being the hardheaded, commonsense thing we once believed it to be, is at its core magical and mystical in nature? He cites W. R. Inge, the dean of St. Paul's Cathedral in London, who said in a book called *Christian Mysticism,* "One test is infallible. Whatever view of reality deepens our sense of the tremendous issues of life in the world wherein we move, is for us nearer the truth than any view which diminishes that sense."[5]

The goal of contemporary scientists, like that of both the original scientists and the original religionists, is to provide an understanding of life that is sufficiently broad and unified to describe, not discrete occurrences or experiences, but *everything that is*. As Stephen Hawking, perhaps the most respected theoretical physicist in the world today, says in *A Brief History of Time*, "The eventual goal of science is to provide a single theory that describes the whole universe."[6] Today there are two basic partial theories, the general theory of relativity and quantum mechanics. The first describes the large-scale structure of the universe, from anything the size of a few miles to a million million million million miles, the size of the entire universe; the second deals with phenomena on extremely small scales, such as a millionth of a millionth of an inch. But the two are unfortunately not compatible with each other, which means that one must be wrong. Hawking has said on many occasions that he believes scientists are on the verge of discovering a single theory that will explain everything; and, if that is found, it will answer all the questions that perplex us about not only *how* things work but *why* as well. If we do find that theory, says Hawking at the conclusion of *A Brief History of Time*, it will be "the ultimate triumph of human reason—for then we would know the mind of God."[7]

In view of all this, Harry Potter's world is perhaps not as arbitrary and fantastic as it might appear. Of course it is strange and bizarre. It is a hodgepodge of magic, dreams, and imagination, and constantly assaults the boundaries of credibility. But many of its weird practices and ideas are no wilder than those of ancient and medieval science—or, for that matter, some of the practices and ideas of a considerably more recent science, in, say, Newtonian physics or twentieth-century medicine. In other words, the fact that we have not yet arrived at a unified understanding of the world and how things work and what they mean does much to legitimize the fantastical approach of a Tolkien or a Dahl or a Rowling; the world as they describe it is in some ways as warrantable as any other partial view of life in the universe.

What the magical, mystical world of an Alice, a Frodo, or a Harry Potter does do for us is remind us of how exciting it is to live in a universe where we are still discovering things, where the absolutely worst thing that can happen to us is to surrender to the dementors and become soulless, mirthless beings staggering around amid all this beauty and wonder. As Schafer says:

> Magic seems to be an intrinsic part of human behavior. Humans want to be tricked and astounded so that they can question the natural order of their world and their basic beliefs. As society has become more industrialized and reliant on technology, many people sense their community has been demythologized, or stripped of mystery and wonder, and they feel empty. Magic helps fill their spirits with a sense of surprise, astonishment, and bewilderment about their external surroundings and internal self.[8]

A REKINDLING OF SPIRITUAL CONSCIOUSNESS

Nowhere in modern literature is this recovery of "surprise, astonishment, and bewilderment" more talked about than in the writings of Christian spiritualists. The spiritual tradition in Christianity has very ancient and venerable roots, of course, going all the way back to the *Confessions* of St. Augustine. It reemerged with power in the writings of Ignatius of Loyola, Teresa of Avila, and John of the Cross in the sixteenth century; and it has continued to be a phenomenon more Catholic than Protestant through Thomas Merton in the midtwentieth century. As the popularity of Asian studies, especially Buddhism, grew in America during the time of the Vietnam War, it merged with a general admiration of Merton to produce a new, widespread fascination with the idea of spirituality as an almost transreligious experience. While Christianity bought into the fascination with hundreds of books and conferences on the so-called Jesus prayer and a specifically Christian content to spirituality, there continues to be a vast secular interest in what it means to be a finely tuned, sensitively adjusted human being who is open to the divine currents in the galaxy and indeed regards the fulfillment of human nature as something virtually impossible apart from such an alignment with higher forces.

One exemplar of this "higher consciousness" is a woman named Julia Butterfly Hill, who in her twenties spent two years living in an ancient redwood tree in Northern California to prevent the Pacific Lumber Company from cutting down the tree for lumber. She gave the tree a name—Luna—and later called her autobiography *The Legacy of Luna*. Charles Hurwitz, chairman of the corporation that owned Pacific Lumber, spent hours trying to talk Hill out of the tree. He threatened to take her to court and have her removed from the forest. Hill believed she was serving the power of love in the world, and prayed to the "Universal Spirit" to give her the strength to serve it by protecting the wonderful tree. Eventually, she and Pacific Lumber Company reached an accord that was supposed to spare the tree, although the company later found a way to proceed with its logging operations in the area.

Many people did not understand Hill's devotion to the redwood. Spending so many months of her young life in a tree, they thought, was crazy. They said she was right to call the tree Luna, because she herself was displaying signs of lunacy. But Hill became a heroine to the real spiritualists of the age because she represented a sensitivity to all life they were seeking for themselves. Like the Buddhists of the 1970s who set themselves aflame for world peace, she was prepared to sacrifice herself for the good of the whole, for the sacredness of life itself.

Matthew Fox, the controversial Catholic priest who became an Episcopalian when his bishop refused to let him continue saying Mass, says in the introduction of his book *One River, Many Wells*:

> My thoughts turn to the subject of our various religions.
> None of them is mother of the ocean, rather the ocean is
> mother of all things. Our religions are so recent in relation

to the lifetime of the sea and to most other creatures—
including humanity itself. What religions did our ancestors
practice for the two million years that preceded the forms
we now recognize as 'world religions'? How humble our
religions ought to be before all creatures. As Mechtild of
Magdeburg said, 'the truly wise person kneels at the feet of
all creatures.'[9]

Maybe this is why, as Schafer notes, the Christian holidays
in the Potter stories—Halloween, Christmas, and Easter—
have become secularized and are not treated from a Christian
perspective at all. They reflect the reality of the new global
society in which, for many people, attachment to a particular
religious faith has been superseded by a more generalized spirituality in which people are no longer divided from one
another by the walls of sectarianism. The old holidays remain,
but as vestiges of a particularized, sectarian faith, and the new
ones have not yet emerged. One suspects that eventually they
will—Earth Day and Global Awareness Day and Love Day and
Isn't It Good to Be Alive Day.

Writer Anne Lamott describes the new spirit in her book
Traveling Mercies when she talks about why she makes her little son Sam go to church with her even though he hates to get
cleaned up and go:

> The main reason is that I want to give him what I found
> in the world, which is to say a path and a little light to see by.
> Most of the people I know who have what I want—which is

to say, purpose, heart, balance, gratitude, joy—are people with a deep sense of spirituality. They are people in community, who pray, or practice their faith; they are Buddhists, Jews, Christians—people banding together to work on themselves and for human rights. They follow a brighter light than the glimmer of their own candle; they are part of something beautiful.[10]

Most of the students and faculty at Hogwarts School of Witchcraft and Wizardry would understand this. They feel this sense of community, of following "a brighter light than the glimmer of their own candle," in their assemblages in the Great Hall, especially at beginnings and ends of terms. The Slytherins appear to feel it least, for they belong to a tradition inaugurated by Salazar Slytherin, who was devoted to the Dark Arts, and are less open to other ways. But the other students and faculty, particularly the Gryffindors, gather in a sense of unity and joy, and their celebration of Harry's victories is at least a little like the celebration at Christian communion of the victory of Christ.

As I have commented before, it is no accident that the position Harry Potter plays on the Gryffindors' Quidditch team is that of Seeker, for that is the title given to those in our time who seek this higher sense of the spiritual in their lives, who wish especially to remain open and attentive to the wonder and beauty of human existence. Wonder, in any religious tradition, lies at the heart of its sense of discovery and worship. What did Dag Hammarskjöld, the popular

United Nations secretary general who died in a plane crash, write in his diary?

> God does not die on the day when we cease to believe
> in a personal deity, but we die on the day when our lives
> cease to be illumined by the steady radiance, renewed daily,
> of a wonder, the source of which is beyond all reason.[11]

A distinguished Brit, Michael Mayne, who was dean of Westminster in London, wrote a book called *This Sunrise of Wonder,* which is filled with a vibrant and delicate sensitivity to the life of the world around him. He went to Switzerland to write the book, and penned it as a series of letters to his grandchildren, to remind them of the importance of being attentive to their rich environment. Early on, he says, "My subject is wonder, and my starting point so obvious it often escapes us. It is me, sitting at a table looking out on the world. It is the fact that I exist, that there is anything at all. It is the *givenness* that astonishes: the fact that the mountains, the larch tree, the gentian, the jay, *exist,* and that someone called *me* is here to observe them."[12] Later, he cites Meister Eckhardt, the medieval mystic, who wrote of how each of us must discover "our own ground," so that little by little we begin to detach ourselves from our egos and reflect the divine purpose at the center of all life. "That suggests," says Mayne, "that the deepest mystery about me is that I can find God in the depths of myself; and having begun to do so I am then enabled to find him everywhere."[13]

Givenness—haecceity—quidditas. The *this*ness or *what*-ness or particularity of things, of every thing, that participates finally—had we but the vision and understanding to perceive it—in the unity of the ALL, so that there is at last wonder and marvel in everything, breathing and nonbreathing, in the universe. It is this to which Rowling's world of magic and mysticism witnesses, this which she invites us to see by showing us talking portraits and exploding candies and almost-headless ghosts and ugly trolls and nipping hippogriffs. And if we don't see—*can't see*—then we are unfortunately like the Muggles in her stories, who live drably in everyday surroundings without ever knowing about the real color and magic and adventure around them. We are like the Dursley family, whose greatest concerns are for generous-sized slabs of breakfast bacon and vacations in Majorca and making a good impression on Mr. Dursley's boss.

OF GHOSTS AND GOBLINS
AND THE LIFE AFTER DEATH

CHAP. 5.

 BELIEVE IN . . . the resurrection of the body, and the life everlasting." Millions of Christians repeat these words from the Apostles' Creed every week in their services of worship. Not all of them believe the words, of course. Bryant Kirkland, long-time minister of Fifth Avenue Presbyterian Church in New York City, loved to tell about the slightly inebriated parishioner who phoned him one night to say she was at a party where several of her friends were animatedly discussing what they believed, and, embarrassed by her inability to join in, she wanted to know, "Doctor, what is it exactly that we Presbyterians believe?" But belief in the resurrection and everlasting life has been a cardinal tenet of the Christian church since the days of the apostles themselves. Christianity simply would not be Christianity were it denuded of this doctrine.

Yet in recent years it has become harder and harder for the average Christian to accept life after death as a fact, or even a reasonably sure bet. The more urban and technological the globe has become, and the more impersonal its parishes, the more difficult it has been to think of mortality with any sense of triumph, the way Christians usually did in previous eras. The Bible calls death "the last enemy"—sort of like Lord Voldemort, whose name is so appropriate—and the majority of Christians today probably agree with that assessment without experiencing any consolation of faith in eternal life. Just as most of the wizards in the Potter stories prefer not to have Voldemort actually named in conversation, but refer to him as You-Know-Who, most people today avoid really facing the fact of death, which is personally quite threatening, and support a collective effort to disguise it with cosmetics, canned music, and canapes. We are much more subdued and evasive at funerals than we are at cocktail parties.

Two hundred fifty years ago, Jonathan Edwards, now regarded as the finest preacher in eighteenth-century America, assaulted his congregation with constant remembrances of their mortality, and spoke in the most graphic terms of the kind of afterlife awaiting them. Today, from the staid old sanctuaries of Boston and New York to the hip churches of the California coast, death is seldom mentioned, and it is a rare preacher indeed who dares to speculate about the nature of the soul's survival after death. Surveys have shown that even on Easter, the Day of Resurrection, when it would be most natural for clergy to tackle the subject of an afterlife, most of them demur, preferring to talk instead about the beauties of nature or the importance of a life of faith.

In light of this absence of plain talk about death, readers ought to be happy with the prominence J. K. Rowling assigns to the interaction between the living and the dead, and the way her wizards are never fully separated from those who have died. Her novels are peopled by ghosts, goblins, and poltergeists as well as living persons, and the members of the Hogwarts community, who represent the more sensitive and understanding element of the British populace, accept these spectral presences as matter-of-factly as they do the presence of one another. Interestingly, the subject of death never comes up in the Dursley household, and we can guess without any trouble what the Dursleys' reactions would be if it did. They are like the majority of people in our own world who shun the topic of mortality as completely as possible, while the wizards at Hogwarts, who are far more in the know about things, deal with it in every story.

It is all related, in a sense, to the openness to wonder we considered in the last chapter. Life and death are part of the magic of the universe, but we understand this only as we draw aside from the hurly-burly of our busy existence and learn to marvel at everything. Macrina Wiederkehr puts it beautifully in her book *A Tree Full of Angels:*

> Spending your days in the fast lane of life impairs the quality of your seeing. If you want to see to the depths, you will need to slow down. You live in a world of theophanies. Holiness comes wrapped in the ordinary. There are burning bushes all around you. Every tree is full of angels. Hidden

beauty is waiting in every crumb. Life wants to lead you from crumbs to angels, but this can happen only if you are willing to unwrap the ordinary by staying with it long enough to harvest its treasure.[1]

THE THIN LINE

J. K. Rowling treats death as a reality—a *harsh* reality that separates families from loved ones. Her mother died of multiple sclerosis while she was still revising her first novel, and she has said that it had an enormous impact on her. Harry Potter lives with sadness and regret for the parents he barely knows, and Cedric Diggory's family, in *Harry Potter and the Goblet of Fire*, is truly grief-stricken when Cedric is murdered by Voldemort. Yet Rowling also treats the dead as if they are never all that far from the living, as if a very thin line divides the realms of the mortal and immortal. Her novels are peopled by innumerable ghosts as well as living creatures, and for the wizards, who are more sensitive to these matters than Muggles are, there is often some form of communication with them.

Rowling distinguishes between three kinds of spirits: ghosts, goblins, and poltergeists. The most prominent ghosts are Sir Nicholas de Mimsy-Porpington, also called Nearly Headless Nick, the resident ghost of Gryffindor Tower, who can seize his ear, pull off his once nearly decapitated head, and lay it on his shoulder; and Moaning Myrtle, who was murdered in one of the women's bathrooms and continues to live there, although she appears in other places, too. The best known of the poltergeists is Peeves, an irascible spirit (hence his name) who behaves like a spoiled child, throwing food at the table, playing practical jokes on students, messing up the halls, and generally making a nuisance of himself. But these are only the best known of countless spirits who inhabit the premises of Hogwarts.

Harry, along with other first-year students, is startled at his initial encounter with them:

> He gasped. So did the people around him. About twenty ghosts had just streamed through the back wall. Pearly-white and slightly transparent, they glided across the room talking to one another and hardly glancing at the first years. They seemed to be arguing. What looked like a fat little monk was saying: "Forgive and forget, I say, we ought to give him a second chance—"[2]

The ghosts are often seen frequenting the halls this way, and apparently are always present in the Great Hall for meals and festivities. In *Harry Potter and the Chamber of Secrets*, Harry and Nearly Headless Nick are walking together in the hall, when Nick suddenly stops and Harry walks right through him. He wishes he hadn't, for it feels "like stepping through an icy shower." Nick has just thought to invite Harry and his friends to his five-hundredth "deathday party," which will be held on Halloween in one of the roomier dungeons.

As Harry, Ron, and Hermione approach the party, they

almost wish they hadn't promised to attend. The way is lit by black tapers that cast a dim, hazy light over everything. When they enter the dungeon, they see hundreds of pearly, translucent figures drifting around a crowded dance floor, waltzing to "the dreadful, quavering sound of thirty musical saws." The youngsters' breath hovers visibly in the air. They feel as if they are standing in a freezer. The food table, covered with such revolting "delicacies" as maggoty haggis, furry green cheese, and rotten fish, bears a large gray cake resembling a tombstone. An inscription on the cake, in tarlike icing, says:

SIR NICHOLAS DE MIMSY-PORPINGTON
DIED 31ST OCTOBER, 1492

Later, as Nick is about to notify the orchestra and start the speech he has prepared for the occasion, the party is interrupted by the sound of a hunting horn. A dozen ghost horses, each ridden by a headless horseman, clatter onto the scene. The lead horseman, a ghost named Sir Patrick, leaps down, holds his head aloft, and taunts Nick about his still partly attached head. And when Nick mounts the podium and attempts to give his speech, he is interrupted again by Sir Patrick and his friends, who have just started a game of Head Hockey, causing the audience to follow the movement of the head and lose all interest in Nick.

This is rollicking good fun—no one doubts Rowling's sense of humor—but is it justifiable treatment of the dead? American readers, especially, have to remember the long and varied history of ghosts and ghost behavior in Great Britain, where numerous houses, hotels, and public buildings are reputedly inhabited by deceased spirits and there are many stories about the humorous idiosyncrasies of some of them. If people were inclined to be noisy, boisterous, or sportive in life, their shadows are often likely to reflect those characteristics in the afterlife.

Rowling follows this boisterous scene with Harry's hearing, for the second time, the strange voice he heard earlier in Professor Lockhart's office, growling, ". . . rip . . . tear . . . kill." It will turn out to be the voice of the basilisk from the hidden chamber, controlled by Voldemort, although Harry, who speaks Parseltongue, is the only one who actually hears discernible words. The effect of turning from the hilarity of Nearly Headless Nick's party to this chilling reminder of the presence of evil is little short of stunning! It says, in essence, that we live in a very spiritual universe where some spirits are benign and others are dark and threatening, and sensitive people, who are aware of both, will often careen wildly between them.

The ghosts apparently lead parallel lives with the students and faculty, discussing school events and even maintaining their old house loyalties. In *Harry Potter and the Goblet of Fire,* Harry and his friends are sitting by Nearly Headless Nick at the opening banquet of the school year, when the Sorting Hat decides which houses the new students will join. Nick belongs to Gryffindor House, while another ghost, the Bloody Baron, is a Slytherin. Nick and the Baron are discussing a recent ghosts' council meeting in which the topic of Peeves' antisocial behavior was hotly debated. Peeves has been wreaking havoc in the kitchen, hurling pots and pans everywhere, inundating the place with soup, and terrifying the house-elves out of their wits. Harry, Ron, and Hermione enter the conversation as naturally as if there were no distinction between them and the ghosts, the living and the dead.

Many writers on the subject of life after death stress the incredible nearness of the dead, especially the recently dead, to those who are living. Edgar Cayce, the American spiritualist, wrote many times of cases in which he experienced the presence of dead persons with messages for the living. Hans Holzer, whose *Life After Death: The Challenge and the Evidence* was one of the first immensely popular books in the genre, insists that the dead continue to move among us, not only attempting to communicate with us but actually relocating objects and interfering in our actions to affect the decisions we make. Moreover, he says, it isn't merely the deceased with whom we have had close emotional ties who try to contact us or interface with our lives. Sometimes it is distant relatives or persons we didn't even know—friends of friends, so to speak, who are part of a network of spirits on the other side.

When Bishop James Pike's son died from a fall in New York City, Pike, who up to that time was a very practical, hardheaded realist who had nothing to do with spiritualism, began consulting mediums in the attempt to contact the boy. Convinced that he and his son did have several conversations with the assistance of mediums, he wrote a book called *The Other*

Side. Once, he said, his son told him about meeting Paul Tillich on the other side. Tillich, the leading existential theologian of the twentieth century, whom Pike had known but his son had not, gave the boy a characteristic message to pass on to his father. This convinced Pike that spirits of the dead continue to monitor our thoughts and actions and to care about what we do.

Is Rowling flouting any Christian understanding of life after death with her fun-loving accounts of ghosts at Hogwarts? Not really, because there isn't any orthodox viewpoint about the nature of life after death. Among Christians, there is only the insistence that life after death exists, and beyond that there is little agreement about what it might entail. In fact, today there is very little discussion of the matter at all. Theologians sometimes argue over the question of "soul-sleeping"— whether references in the Bible to the thousand-year reign of Christ before the final judgment mean that there will be no resurrection of the dead until then and they remain meanwhile in a state of suspended animation. And Oscar Cullmann wrote an engaging study a few years ago, called *Immortality of the Soul or Resurrection of the Dead?*, in which he drew a careful distinction between the Greek notion of general immortality and the Hebrew-Christian idea of the individual's being raised by God, the latter concept recognizing divine sovereignty in the matter. But on the whole there is a kind of acceptable pandemonium regarding the subject. Beyond the agreement that the church should retain the assertion about resurrection of the body and life everlasting in its creed, there is very little official superintendence over exactly what we do believe about life after death.

THE MEMORY OF THE DEAD

Rowling flirts with one curious idea in her treatment of the dead, and that is the relationship between a ghost and a memory. It occurs in Harry's confrontation with Tom Riddle, a.k.a. Voldemort, in the Chamber of Secrets below Hogwarts. Tom, whose full name, Tom Marvolo Riddle, is an anagram for "I am Lord Voldemort," was a student at Hogwarts fifty years earlier; it is his diary with which Harry has been conversing for a number of weeks. Yet when Harry finally encounters him in the chamber, he looks the way he did fifty years ago, as though he were only sixteen.

"Are you a ghost?" asks Harry, uncertainly.

"A memory," says Riddle quietly. "Preserved in a diary for fifty years."[3]

Harry's friend, Ginny Weasley, found the diary and had been writing in it for months, pouring out her innermost secrets to Riddle. Now he has used those accumulated secrets, the strength of Ginny's life, to reassemble himself and leave the pages of the diary, and he stands before Harry as the embodiment not just of Tom Riddle but of Lord Voldemort himself. As we shall discover again in *Harry Potter and the Goblet of Fire,* the evil Lord Voldemort depends on the strength of others for his own vitality.

Is there any significance to Riddle's comment that he is a "memory" and not a "ghost"? Does he mean that the student Tom Riddle is only a memory because he is now actually Voldemort? Or is there a valid distinction between being a memory and being a ghost?

Common imagination suggests that a ghost is a more collected, vital entity than a memory. That is, a memory is scattered, fleeting, part of a generalized mosaic of impressions we bear of someone who died, while a ghost is a more specific, gathered impression, even a personality that continues to exist with some force, albeit diminished from that of the original. Christians hold services in memory of the dead. All Saints' Day is a specific occasion each year when honor and reverence are paid to those who have died, and Memorial Day exists to pay homage to those who died in military service for their country. But the appearance of an actual ghost, on either of those occasions, would prove extremely unsettling to those merely "remembering" the dead.

Michael Mayne, in *This Sunrise of Wonder,* offers a fascinating thought about remembering people and things. He is writing to his grandchildren, as we have noted before, and discusses the mystery of memory—specifically how the hippocampus, which is thought to be the residence of memory in the human brain, is related to the reality of daily life.

In *Moon Tiger* by Penelope Lively, the 67-year-old Cludia *[sic]*, smelling eucalyptus leaves in post-war Cairo, is overwhelmed by *wonder that nothing is ever lost, that everything can be retrieved, that a lifetime is not linear but instant. That, inside the head, everything happens at once.*

That takes us again to the heart of the mystery. One day, when you are looking back on your lives, you will find that all the people you have ever been (and we play many parts), all the bodies you have worn, all the faces of people and the look of places you have loved, still live inside your skin; they are still lodged in that part of your brain that is the memory.[4]

Perhaps if there were really such a device as the Time-Turner which Hermione used in *Harry Potter and the Prisoner of Azkaban* to reverse the hours so she can attend two classes that meet at the same time, and then by Harry and Hermione to turn back the clock long enough to rescue Sirius Black from the tower before the executioner can reach him, it would bear a key relationship to this philosophical question. It would make it possible for us to revisit our memories when they were at their most forceful, in their original existence.

But is a memory really less powerful than the thing it recalls? We generally assume it is. Yet what if the memory becomes a powerful motivation in real life? Suppose, for example, the recollection of Todd Beamer, one of the passengers on United Airlines flight 93 that was hijacked and crashed on September 11, 2001, inspires millions of people to live their lives more sacrificially and to give vast sums of money to various service organizations. Could Beamer possibly have had such influence while he was alive? Memories are not the same thing as ghosts, certainly. But they are obviously forceful in their own way.

Harry Potter's parents are both memories and ghosts in his life. He cherishes everything he can learn about them, because he was too young to remember them before they were killed, and he depends on the descriptions of Hagrid, Dumbledore, Sirius Black, Professor Lupin, and others to assemble memories that will surely influence him all his life. But his parents also appear to him as definable personalities—first in the Mirror of Erised, in *Harry Potter and the Sorcerer's Stone,* and then in freer, more "real" encounters—and he interacts with them not as memories but as living beings.

The whole question of the relationship of memory to life, merely touched on by Rowling, suggests Einstein's idea of relativity and the pursuit of theoretical physicists today for a unified theory of matter. If time is not linear, as we tend to presume, but is somehow cyclical or telescoped, so that all things happen coevally even though we perceive them as individuated, then there is a far more intimate relationship than we usually imagine between memory and reality. And it is all part of the sheer wonder of existence, the magic of being, that we touched on in the last chapter. Rowling is a mistress of wonder. It is her stock in trade, so to speak, and she may well have dropped the hint about memory and ghosts merely to provoke our speculation.

She has confessed that Elizabeth Goudge is one of her favorite writers, so she is doubtless aware of this passage from

Pilgrim's Inn where Jill and her twin children have followed an old familiar path through the woods in search of Christmas holly:

> When she had filled her basket with holly Jill sat down on the rock and waited happily for the twins. She did not find the waiting irksome, for she had been born one of those fortunate people who are never in a hurry and never restless. She had never felt restless in her life. In all that she did, in all that she saw, she was aware of a deep upspringing wonder, as though she did it or saw it for the first time. She was blessed with a mind neither retrospective nor anxious; the past and the future did not pull her two ways with remorse and dread, and the lovely freshness of each new-made moment was apparent to her focused vision.[5]

By her own confession, Rowling is often filled with anxiety, especially about getting her writing done. But, like Jill, she is "aware of a deep upspringing wonder," and her "focused vision" is able to hold both past and present in easy suspension, so that memories are real life and real life is already in the process of becoming memories.

RECOGNITION OF THE DEAD

The Christian faith has always alternated between the belief that those who have died have gone to be with the Lord—

really *gone*—and the belief that they remain somehow in the vicinity of the living, at least part of the time, and continue to reveal themselves to the people who mattered to them. John Calvin, for example, whose *Institutes* is one of the most formidable treatises on the church and its faith ever written, held that it is the sovereignty of God that is most important in the discussion of any tenet of faith, and was therefore ill disposed to consider that souls remain in any personal relationship with those they have left behind; their business in the afterlife is merely to join the chorus of saints who sing constant praises to the deity. Popular experience, however, appears to weigh heavily on the other side, and many Christian thinkers are of the firm opinion that the dead not only remain accessible to the living but are instantly recognizable to them.

Here, for example, is a passage from Leslie D. Weatherhead's popular *The Christian Agnostic,* which was published as Weatherhead's summa after his years as a well-known minister in London during and following World War II:

> As the last shadows fall, again and again the watcher by the bedside will see a strange, new light in eyes now opening easily, and the expression of those eyes is one of supreme joy and happiness. Then, in a way almost startling, the patient will sit up—he who could not raise his head—stretch out his arms and call the name of a beloved, dead it may be, a score of years before.
>
> My beloved father-in-law, when dying, was sure that a

daughter who had been dead for years was with him in his bedroom. Some of my own experiences in the death-chamber support this conclusion. Rosalind Heywood, watching a dying man, saw him suddenly sit up. She writes, "His face lit up. 'It's Annie,' he cried, gazing in joyous recognition at someone I could not see, 'And John! . . . Oh the Light! the Light!' "

If that is a trick of the patient's brain or nervous system, if it is the hallucination of a disordered mind, all I can say is that it is strangely convincing to the watcher. Having seen that more than once, I for one am in no doubt about man's survival of death or of his reunion with those he loves.[6]

Weatherhead's conclusion is supported by mountains of evidence from students of the life-after-life experience, such as Dr. Raymond Moody (*Life After Life* and *Reflections on Life After Life*), Dr. Maurice Rawlings (*Beyond Death's Door*), and Drs. Karlis Osis and Erlendur Haraldsson (*At the Hour of Death*). The well-known priest, sociologist, and writer Andrew Greeley tells in *Death and Beyond* about a poll of almost fifteen hundred persons he conducted in 1974, in which one of the questions was: "Have you ever felt that you were really in touch with someone who had died?" More than 25 percent of those asked testified that they had had such an experience, half of these more than once or several times. Among persons over the age of seventy, 39 percent had had the experience. A similar poll conducted two years later in Great Britain showed very similar results.

There is also biblical evidence behind this view. In the Old Testament, when King Saul consults the medium of Endor and bids her to summon the deceased prophet Samuel for him, both she and Saul recognize the old man who emerges from the ground, his robe pulled around him.[7] When Jesus appears to the disciples in the upper room following his crucifixion, and again at the Sea of Galilee where they are fishing, they know him.[8] The two disciples traveling to Emmaus do not recognize him immediately, but finally realize who he is as they are breaking bread together.[9] And the Apostle Paul, delivering the *kerygma*, or essentials, of the faith commonly held in the early church, refers to the occasion when more than five hundred people were with Christ and recognized him.[10]

There is no speculation in the Potter novels about where people go after death or what their afterlife experiences are like. But the dead are very certainly recognizable to the living, and continue to manifest essentially the same personalities they had in life. Nearly Headless Nick still appears in courtly dress and behaves very much as he did when he was a knightly warrior, although he has been dead half a millennium. James and Lily Potter are essentially as they were in life and continue to show parental interest in their son. And Professor Binns, the professor of the History of Magic whom we meet in *Harry Potter and the Chamber of Secrets,* is actually a ghost who has gone on teaching. As Rowling says, the most exciting thing about Binns' rather dull classes is that he enters the room through the blackboard. Because he was an ancient and shriveled man for many years, some people admit they hadn't even noticed he was dead. He simply got up to teach one day and left his body sitting in an armchair in front of the staff-room fire, and his routine has not varied an iota since.

Near the end of *Harry Potter and the Prisoner of Azkaban,* when Harry and Dumbledore are having the conversation that helps Harry to understand and come to terms with all that has transpired, Harry talks about the Patronus in the form of a stag that saved him from the dementors. Harry says he thought it was his father who had conjured the Patronus. "I mean, when I saw myself across the lake . . . I thought I was seeing him." Dumbledore says it was an easy mistake to make, because Harry does look amazingly like his father.

Harry shakes his head and says it was stupid of him to think it was his dad. "I mean, I knew he was dead."

"You think the dead we loved ever truly leave us?" asks Dumbledore. "You think that we don't recall them more clearly than ever in times of great trouble? Your father is alive in you, Harry, and shows himself most plainly when you have need of him. How else could you produce that *particular* Patronus? Prongs rode again last night."[11]

IN AID OF THE LIVING

This brings us to another point of the discussion, and an important one for many Christians: That the dead not only continue to have an existence of some kind but actually intervene in our affairs to help us when we need them. Apart from the work of

Christ himself, and an image in the Apocalypse of the saints in heaven praying for the souls of the living, there is not any biblical warrant for the opinion that the dead actively assist the living. But there is no doubt at all in popular Christianity that those who have died are valuable allies to the living. The idea of applying to the saints for assistance probably had its origin in praying for Christ's intercession, then Mary's, and finally that of other holy persons. Claudius, the ninth-century bishop of Turin, vigorously opposed the saying of prayers to the dead, but history took little notice of him. The idea that those who have already died can help us in our continuing struggle in this earthly existence is deeply enmeshed in all the Christian traditions—Roman Catholic, Orthodox, and even Protestant. Most saints have become particularly identified with different kinds of needs—Christopher is the patron saint of travelers; Anthony of Padua, Martin of Tours, and Vincent de Paul are patron saints of horses, and Brigid, Drogo, and Perpetua, of cows; Brendan, of whales; Ursula, Gregory the Great, and Catherine of Alexandria, of teachers; Angela and Gerard, of mentally or physically challenged persons; Anne and Anthony of Pavoni, of people who have lost things; Luke, Damian, and Pantaleon, of doctors; Catherine and Genesius, of secretaries; and Matthew, of security guards. Saint Paul the Apostle is the patron saint of poisonous snakes. But most Christians believe that even a godly parent, godparent, aunt, uncle, teacher, or acquaintance is a valuable friend in the life beyond.

J. K. Rowling appears firm in this belief as well. Moaning Myrtle is a good example. We first meet Myrtle in *Harry Potter and the Chamber of Secrets,* when Hermione confesses to Harry and Ron that she doesn't like to use the girls toilet where Myrtle lives because she is always "having tantrums and flooding the place." It is through Myrtle that Harry first discovers the diary of Tom Riddle and later realizes that the way to the secret chamber under the school must lie through her bathroom. When he asks her how she died, she isn't really certain. She remembers that she was in the toilet, hiding because another girl had been teasing her about her glasses, when she heard a boy's voice speaking a language she didn't understand. She unlocked the door and came out to tell him to use the boys toilet, when she suddenly died. The only thing she recalls about it is that she saw "a pair of great, big, yellow eyes"—those of the basilisk. Harry, Ron, and Professor Lockhart, the latter unwillingly, find the bathroom entrance to the basilisk's chambers below and descend there to face Voldemort and the mythical beast.

In *Harry Potter and the Goblet of Fire,* Myrtle appears to Harry out of one of the water taps when he is taking a bath in the prefect's room and trying to figure out the secret of the golden egg for the second task in the Triwizard Tournament. She complains that he hasn't been to see her lately—an indication that she likes him—and he says he was reprimanded for going to the women's toilet. She tells him to try putting the egg underwater—that that is what Cedric Diggory did that led him to its secret. He lowers the egg, but hears only a gurgling sound. "You need to put your head under too," she urges. "Go on!"[12] Harry submerges himself three times, until he has memorized the song being sung by the egg, but he still doesn't understand. So Myrtle chats with him about the clue until he figures out that the task is to rescue someone or something he will miss from the merpeople beneath the lake. When he leaves the bathroom, Myrtle asks him if he will come and visit her again in her bathroom, and he says he'll try.

Harry encounters Myrtle again under the lake when he is trying to find the village of the merpeople. He has just encountered a band of grindylows and managed to extricate himself from them when he hears her speak to him. He tries to speak too, but can only manage a bubble out of his mouth, which amuses Myrtle. "You want to try over there," she says, pointing. "I won't come with you. . . . I don't like them much, they always chase me when I get too close. . . ."[13] Harry follows her directions, and soon finds himself among the merpeople and their captives. So once more Myrtle has helped Harry in his competition for the Triwizard Cup.

But it is Harry's deceased parents who are his most persistent helpers. Even in death, they continue the kind of love and concern for his welfare that marked their attempt to protect him when they were murdered by Voldemort.

Harry first gets sight of them in the Mirror of Erised, in *Harry Potter and the Sorcerer's Stone.* As he looks into the magical mirror, he sees a crowd of people standing behind him. He whirls around, but the room is empty. He looks again. There are at least ten people standing behind him. Are they really in the room with him, but invisible? Or are they in the mirror? He looks again. There is a woman standing immediately behind his reflection, and she is smiling and waving at him. She is a pretty woman, with green eyes that look exactly like his. He notices that she is crying—smiling and crying at the same time. And behind her stands a tall, thin, black-haired man who wears glasses and whose hair is untidy and sticks up in the back just like Harry's.

Harry is so close to the mirror now that his nose is almost touching it. "Mom?" he whispers. "Dad?"

He looks at the other people in the group behind him. There are other pairs of green eyes like his, other noses like his, even a little old man who appears to have his own knobbly knees. Harry is looking at his family. He remains standing there a long time, staring at them. When he finally tears himself away to return to bed, he whispers, "I'll come back."[14]

In *Harry Potter and the Prisoner of Azkaban*, Professor Lupin, the Defense Against the Dark Arts teacher, shows Harry how to summon a Patronus, or guardian spirit, to scatter the boggarts that attack one and cause depression. Boggarts are called "shape-shifters" because they change their appearance to assume the shape of whatever the viewer fears most. For Harry, the shape they assume is that of the dementors, the hideous creatures from Azkaban that suck the souls out of the prisoners. When Harry asks what a Patronus will look like if he manages to accomplish the spell Professor Lupin is teaching him, Lupin says it is always unique to the boggart. And in Harry's case, when he pronounces the spell *"Expecto patronum!"* he at first hears loud voices shouting, and realizes they are his parents' voices as they try to fend off Voldemort and save Harry's life. Then, out of a white fog, his Patronus appears. It is a huge, silver shadow that comes between him and the boggart, forcing the boggart to retreat. Later in the same novel, when Lupin has turned into a werewolf, Harry looks across the lake and sees a great crowd of dementors, at least a hundred of them, gliding around the lake in his direction.

"Expecto patronum!" he shouts. *"Expecto patronum!"*

He shouts it again and again. For a moment, a silver mist arises between him and the nearest dementor. Then the dementor lowers its hood and he can see its eyeless face with its scabby, gray skin, and its mouth, a gaping, shapeless hole, sucking in air with the sound of a death rattle. His Patronus flickers and disappears. He tries again to summon it, but feels strong, clammy hands around his neck. He can hear his mother's voice screaming in his ears, as he must have when he was a baby and she was trying to save him from Voldemort. He seems to be drowning in fog. Then a silvery light grows brighter and brighter, and he realizes that the dementor has released him. He is too weak to stand, but he looks around. Something is driving the dementors away. It is circling him. With every ounce of strength he can muster, he lifts his head in time to see a great silver animal amid the light, galloping away across the lake. It returns to someone there, and someone is patting it, as if to say it has done a good job.

When Harry discusses it all with Hermione, she wants to know who conjured the Patronus. Harry thinks about it and realizes who he *thought* it was. "I think—" he says, hesitantly, knowing it will sound strange to her, "I think it was my dad." Hermione reminds him that his father is dead. He says he knows it. She wants to know if it was his father's ghost. "I don't know," he says, ". . . no . . . he looked solid. . . ."[15]

Later, near Hagrid's cottage by the Forbidden Forest, he hears yelping in the distance and knows the dementors are closing in on Sirius Black, who has transformed himself into the big black dog. In a minute, they will be coming toward him as well. He yearns to know if it was his dad who helped him before. "Come on!" he mutters. "Where are you? Dad, come on—"[16] But his dad doesn't come. And suddenly it hits him— he realizes it wasn't his father he saw on the other side of the lake, it was himself. *He* had summoned the Patronus, and the Patronus was his father's spirit, a huge stag known to his intimate friends, Lupin, Black, and Pettigrew, as Prongs.

"Expecto patronum!" yells Harry. And this time, out of the end of his wand comes not a faint silvery mist as before but "a blinding, dazzling, silver animal." It looks like a horse, galloping around the lake, but it isn't. He sees it lower its head and charge at the dementors, and watches them fall back, scattering and retreating into the darkness until they are gone. The enormous stag stops by the water, stares at him with its huge silvery eyes, then lowers its head and vanishes.

Is it a ghost, as Hermione suggested? Or a memory, one so strong it is able to dispel the horrible dementors? Or a reincarnation of the great Prongs, summoned to help Harry in his hour of need? Elizabeth Schafer suggests that the Patronus "could be a magical descendant of the Roman patronus who protected selected individuals in Britannia."[17] Regardless, we can be sure that the derivation of the word from the Latin *pater* ("father") or Greek *patrowos* ("paternal, received from one's ancestors") is important. Harry's father, though dead since Harry was a year old, is somehow instrumental in protecting and saving him.

The silvery light that occurs with the Patronum is an interesting touch. One of the distinguishing marks of the life-after-life experience, according to Morton Kelsey in *Afterlife: The Other Side of Dying,* is the appearance of a bright light or of "a being of light" which is experienced somewhat as the disciples of Jesus appear to have experienced his transfiguration. Betty J. Eadie, in the immensely popular account of her afterlife adventure called *Embraced by the Light,* remembers the doctor's declaring her dead and pulling the covers over her head. Yet she was still seeing the doctor and the nurse standing by her bed.

> I looked around the room and noticed that it was filled with brighter light than before. The bed seemed huge to me, and I remember thinking, "I'm like a little brown bug in this big white bed." Then the doctor walked away and I became aware of another presence nearby. Suddenly I wasn't lying on the bed but found myself in someone's arms. I looked up and saw a man with a beautiful white beard looking at me. His beard fascinated me. It seemed to sparkle with a bright light, a light that came from within the beard.[18]

In the Tibetan Book of the Dead, it is said that the *bardo* body (literally, the body "between two") takes three or four days to detach itself from the physical body and proceed on its journey. During this time it is surrounded by an intensely bright light, blinding even, which is the "Radiance of the Clear Light of Pure Reality." If the person who has died is ready utterly and completely to abandon ego existence and become one with the Light, then it attains salvation and never returns to the life it has left. But only those who have come close to the total purification of the self in this life are really prepared to make this transition. The majority of souls passing through the bright Light are unwilling to be absorbed by it and remain in a state of Nirvana forever.

When Harry sees the bright light in connection with his father's presence, it is a symbol of the beyond, and the purity of the state from which he returns. By contrast, the atmosphere around the Death Eaters and the dementors is always dark and foreboding. It is a classical dualism, in which the good is always bright and shining, the evil, somber and menacing.

Again in *Harry Potter and the Goblet of Fire* we see Harry's parents coming to his aid, when he is in the life-and-death battle with Voldemort in the cemetery. Five ghosts appear out of the end of Voldemort's wand after his wand and Harry's have had a "reverse effect" on each other. First comes Cedric Diggory, Voldemort's most recent victim. Then Frank Bryce, the Muggle who stumbled unwittingly on Voldemort and Wormtail at the old Riddle mansion in Little Hangleton. Then Bertha Jorkins, a witch from the Ministry of Magic. And finally Harry's father and mother. His father first, "the smoky shadow of a tall man with untidy hair," and then his mother, "a young woman with long hair" and also in "smoky, shadowy form."

The voices with which they speak to Harry are "distant" and "echoing." They urge him to hold on, not to let go, to fight Voldemort to the end. His mother, walking close to him, speaking low so that Voldemort does not hear, tells him to get to the Triwizard Cup, the Portkey, and return to Hogwarts. And when his father gives him the signal, Harry breaks his wand's connection with Voldemort's and runs as fast as he can, zigzagging behind headstones, dodging curses and graves, until he reaches Cedric's body. He points his wand back over his shoulder and bellows, *"Impedimenta!,"* stopping at least one of the Death Eaters in pursuit. In the nick of time, he raises his wand toward the Triwizard Cup and shouts, *"Accio!"* The cup sails into the air and soars toward him. He grabs its handle and presto, he and Cedric's body are speeding back toward Hogwarts, out of the grasp of the Dark Lord!

The writer of the ancient book of Hebrews, faced with the need to stanch the flow of fearful believers abandoning the Christian faith, addressed a circular epistle to the early churches in which he cataloged the great line of the faithful all the way from Abel, Noah, and Abraham, through Moses, Rahab, David, and Samuel, to the courageous believers of his own day. Time would fail him to tell, he wrote, of all who had "conquered kingdoms, administered justice, obtained promises, shut the mouths of lions, quenched raging fire, escaped the edge of the sword, won strength out of weakness, become mighty in war, put foreign armies to flight."

Others were tortured, refusing to accept release. . . .
Others suffered mocking and flogging, and even chains and
imprisonment. They were stoned to death, they were sawn in
two, they were killed by the sword, they went about in skins
of sheep and goats, destitute, persecuted, tormented—of
whom the world was not worthy. They wandered in deserts
and mountains, and in caves and holes in the ground.[19]

These, says the writer, lived by faith even before they knew
Christ, who was the fulfillment of all the promises made to
them. "Therefore," he concludes his peroration, "since we are
surrounded by so great a cloud of witnesses, let us also lay
aside every weight and the sin that clings so closely, and let us
run with perseverance the race that is set before us, looking to
Jesus the pioneer and perfecter of our faith, who for the sake
of the joy that was set before him endured the cross, disregarding its shame, and has taken his seat at the right hand of the
throne of God."[20]

The ghostly personalities around Harry Potter are *his*
cloud of witnesses, his encouragers in the struggle against
Voldemort. They have suffered at Voldemort's hand but do
not flinch in the continued battle against the evil one. They
are Harry's helpers in a conflict as old as persecution itself.
There can be no doubt that they will be there all the way,
whether the end comes with the seventh novel in the series or
lies beyond it. They belong to the forces of good, and good
will always be pitched against evil, until the last syllable of
recorded time.

IS THERE A RESURRECTION IN THE STORIES?

Harry Potter is a wounded hero, carrying Voldemort's scar on his forehead the way Christ bore the marks of the nails in his hands. But can he be said in any way to be resurrected, as Christ was resurrected? We noted earlier how, in *Harry Potter and the Sorcerer's Stone,* Harry lies in a trance or coma for three days following his violent struggle with Professor Quirrell and Voldemort. Is this in itself a symbol of resurrection? And if so, is it in any way connected with the continued vitality of the dead persons in the stories?

Our answer, in the absence of more definitive clues, must of course be tentative. Even if Rowling were consciously working with the core beliefs of the Christian faith, she would preserve the shadow and mystery of creativity, refusing to make the relationship over-plain. And the truth is that even in biblical faith the relationship between Christ's resurrection and the redemption of the dead is not as clear as Christians would often like it to be.

Professor John Hick of Cambridge University, in his scholarly *Death and Eternal Life,* cites the problems inherent in ascertaining exactly what the New Testament means by its use of the word *resurrection.* "There is a spectrum of possibilities," he says:

> Did the dead body of Jesus come forth from its grave to resume a fully physical life? Or was it somehow changed in

the tomb so that whilst retaining some physical attributes—including shape, solidity, and the capacity to speak and eat—it took on other contra-physical attributes such as the capacity suddenly to materialize and dematerialize at points in space? Should we draw upon the stories of supernatural powers developed by great spiritual masters of the east enabling them to exert an extraordinary control over their own bodies and even to materialize and dematerialize at will, and think of Jesus' resurrection as exhibiting an extreme form of this kind of psychic power? Or did the resurrection consist in visions seen by some of Jesus' disciples shortly after his death? If so, were the visions produced in their minds by the living spirit of Jesus? Did the resurrection appearances thus belong to the category, familiar in the annals of psychical research, of 'veridical hallucinations' in which telepathically received information is presented to consciousness in the form of visions? Or—moving further along the range of possibilities—instead of there having been either perception or visions, did the resurrection take place entirely on the inner plane of the disciples' faith? Was it a resurrection of their faith, or its elevation from a faith in Jesus as their earthly leader to faith in Jesus as God's chosen messenger, later becoming expressed in more readily comprehensible stories of visions and voices? And if so, is this powerful resurgence of faith to be attributed to the activity of the living spirit of the Lord; or to purely natural causes, such as wishful thinking and self-deception? Or to his spirit working through some such psychological mechanism?[21]

Before this bewildering array of possibilities, cited by Professor Hick not to discourage belief but to remind us of the problems we often face when attempting to reach absolute certainty about anything as metaphysical and significant as the resurrection, we can surely conclude that it is not necessary to specify exactly *how* resurrection and the afterlife are related in the Harry Potter stories in order to believe that they *are* somehow related—that Harry, as a Christ figure, brings the hope and assurance of the resurrection into the arena of human mortality and the whole question of an existence beyond the grave.

Voldemort, the Death Eaters, and the dementors represent the power and nature of death, in whose presence we constantly live. The dementors, especially, recall the shadowy world of the dead in Greek mythology, where ghosts are mere shades of their former selves, no longer empowered for living, and also the gloomy region of *Sheol* in Hebrew-Christian thought, which is likewise a place of sadness, darkness, unfulfilled longing, nagging regret, and utter powerlessness. When the boggarts appear to Harry, it is the dementors he sees; his fears take the form of their gray, scabby exteriors, with skin stretched over the holes where their eyes should be and mouths that suck hungrily at the very souls of others, wanting to devour everything that has feature and personality. This is because Harry is the hero of the opposite of death. He represents life and hope to all the good wizards and witches. Every time he survives a battle with Voldemort, it is an eschatological achievement, equal to a resurrection.

J. K. Rowling has said that her favorite painting is "perhaps" Caravaggio's *Supper at Emmaus,* which features Christ revealing himself to the disciples as the one who has just been raised from the dead. "I love it," she commented. "Jesus looks very likeable—soft and rounded—and the painting captures the exact moment when the disciples realize who this man is, blessing their bread."[22]

This is very revealing of an inner attitude we don't often get in interviews with Ms. Rowling. It seems to radiate a quiet reverence for the resurrection and all it stands for, which can explain a lot about her understanding of life and death and how they are related in the plots of her novels. If this is correct, it means that a great deal is riding on the faithfulness of Harry as a Christ figure, and what happens to him in future stories will essentially parallel what happened to Jesus.

AND NOW ABIDETH
FAITH, HOPE, AND LOVE

N CHRIST CHURCH, Oxford, there is a beautiful window in the pre-Raphaelite style depicting *FIDES*, *SPES*, and *CARITAS*—faith, hope, and love. *Faith* is holding one of those little clay lamps common in biblical times. At her feet writhe dragon-snakes. One serpent is even entwining the hand not supporting the lamp. But she looks completely unafraid. *Hope* has a light, airy appearance. She is standing on tiptoe and gazing upward, as if she were dancing. *Love* is a mother with a small child in her arms and two others peering around her skirt. In her free hand she holds a flame burning high—a flame representing both the hearth and the future.

Rowling may well prefer Caravaggio's painting of Christ with the disciples at Emmaus. But this window, with its dragon-snakes, its mother protecting her children, and its indomitable sense of hope and expectancy, is a perfect tableau for the Harry Potter stories. The reptilian character of Voldemort and the Slytherins is there. So is Lily Potter's undying care for her son. And so is joyous hope—an undying confidence in the human enterprise—represented by the students at Hogwarts and especially by Harry Potter himself, who, despite all obstacles and punishments, tackles life the way he does a match of Quidditch, with an ever-growing sense of destiny and excitement!

Why have the Potter novels struck such a resonant chord in hearts around the world? The question must be asked. There are even Harry Potter Withdrawal Clubs, to console avid readers between the dates when the novels appear. Is Harry Potter only a trend like Pet Rocks, Hula-Hoops, and Frisbees? Or is there some deeper reason, something that strikes to the heart of who we are as human beings living on the cusp of two centuries, one recently concluded and the other barely opened?

The answer may lie in a book by Phil Cousineau called *Once and Future Myths: The Power of Ancient Stories in Modern Times*. Cousineau describes an exchange with psychiatrist Rollo May at May's home in Tiburon, California, shortly before his death in 1991. He asked May whether the current authorities on the way the world works—science, media, and technology—can ever satisfy the human need for meaning. With a sadness in his voice that Cousineau found startling, May said it was precisely a *nothingness,* a *lack* of meaning in contemporary life, that had driven most of his clients into therapy. He described what he heard from them as "a cry for myth," for great, overarching patterns that explain why things are the way they are. Cousineau asked if May believed what Joseph Campbell was alluding to when he said, "People are always talking about looking for the meaning of life, when what they're really looking for is a *deep experience* of life." "Yes, yes," responded May, "but not only deep. Numinous."[1]

The Potter stories are rich with the human past—the wounded hero, the hero's journey, the quest for the Grail, mythical beasts, spells and incantations, exciting contests, noble tournaments, people who turn into animals, community rituals, learning that leads to power, the determined struggle against evil and darkness. The books are vivid, dynamic mosaics of all our dreams, hopes, and fears of whatever it is that has made us so uniquely human, but told with a freshness and transparency that permit us to enter the stories without being conscious of the fragments themselves, and *live* the dreams, hopes, and fears all over again, so that, without actually thinking about it, without feeling our pulses, we enjoy "a *deep experience* of life."

But not only deep—*numinous!*

Rowling's books put us in touch once again with the magic and mystery of life, the dimension beyond the ordinary, the sense of wonder that makes even commonplace experiences shine with the brilliance of celestial bodies. Everyday games become eternal contests, and run-of-the-mill children, the kind found on any playground or in any classroom, are metamorphosed into adolescent heroes and heroines. Ordinary animals sprout wings, grow horns, become mixed with other animals, to become the beasts of fairy tales and legends. Owls descend from all directions, bearing letters and packages, like fluttering, angelic messengers from heaven. A school is transformed into a mysterious castle with secret passageways, code words, hidden chambers, and a population of personable ghosts and goblins. Simple knowledge, the kind gained from books and teachers, translates directly into practical usage. Children battle with the enemies we have all faced—unbearable cousins, taunting classmates, mean and overbearing teachers, *dull* teachers, loneliness, unattractiveness, failure, intractable evil—and *win!*

What isn't to like? What isn't to be mesmerized by?

"I'm not a child," one adult told me, "but I love Harry Potter. I think I can become as engrossed in the stories as a child can, because they put me in touch with all the feelings I had as a child. And not only that, but with all the feelings I have as an adult. When I lay down one of the Harry Potter stories, I look at life differently. It has more color, more brilliance, more pizzazz! I don't become Harry Potter. Maybe more Hermione. But I think I feel a lot more youthful, and have a spring in my step that wasn't there before. It's been a long time since I read or watched anything that did that for me. In fact, I'm not sure if anything ever did it before."

Probably what happens to Potter readers is what writer Diane Ackerman calls "deep play"—an involvement in life that is so complete, so absorbing, that it promotes great relaxation and enables the very cells of the mind and heart to renew themselves. It even involves "rapture and ecstasy," two qualities human beings need in order to feel whole and truly alive.

And it *always*, Ackerman says, "involves the sacred and holy, sometimes hidden in the most unlikely or humble places— amid towering shelves of rock in Nepal; crouched over print in a dimly lit room; slipping on Astro Turf; wearing a coconut-shell mask."[2]

This is what I have been insisting about the presence of Christian mythical structure in the Harry Potter literature. It isn't all that's there—not by any means. There are ancient Greek, Persian, Egyptian, and Roman mythologies, archaic British and European lore and legend, simple folktales and fairy stories from all over the world, all thrown together like the stuff in a child's locker, so that some of it is bent and some is jammed into other objects and most of it would be almost impossible to restore to its original shape. But also there, as a conscious or unconscious framework for everything, is the worldview without which none of it would really work for Rowling's readers because it is, after all, *the* worldview of the Western hemisphere, the basic structure of the Christian faith.

That faith is multifold and complex. Scholars and leaders have been working on it since its simple beginnings, if indeed they were simple, in first-century Palestine, coaxing and caressing the texts until the books, scrolls, tapes, and films about it, all gathered together, would probably fill the Bibliothèque Nationale in Paris, the Bodleian Library in Oxford, and the Library of Congress in Washington, D.C. Now the Christian faith is a lot like the Hebrew religion, which preceded it, as described by a legend about the simple shepherd's pipe once played by Moses when he kept his father-in-law's flocks.

When the pipe was discovered, many years after Moses' death, it was decided that it should be put on display for the benefit of his admirers. But it looked far too common for such an important purpose, so someone suggested that it be embellished by an artist. A few centuries later, when the pipe was given a new home in an upscale museum, a committee said it needed improving yet again. So another artist was employed to overlay it in fine gold and silver filigree. The result, in the end, was a breathtaking piece of art, a marvelous sight indeed. It was so beautiful, in fact, that no one ever noticed that it was no longer capable of the clear, seductive notes once played upon it by Moses.

That is the way of all religions. With the best of intentions, they become increasingly complicated until they lose the enchantment that was once their divine warrant. But of all the creeds in Christendom—Apostles', Nicene, Anti-Nicene, and all the rest—there is probably no truer or more dynamic one than the brief statement of faith St. Paul wrote to the Corinthians early in Christianity's history: "And now faith, hope, and love abide, these three; and the greatest of these is love."[3]

The window in Christ Church, Oxford, is a picture of this creed. And so are the Harry Potter novels!

FAITH

Faith is shown, in the window, heedless of the dragon-snakes around her. In other words, faith lives amid evil as if the evil were not there. It lives as seeing beyond evil, as though evil, powerful and destructive as it is, is only temporary. In the end, good will prevail; faith believes this, utterly and completely. Faith, in the classic definition from the book of Hebrews, is "the assurance of things hoped for, the conviction of things not seen."[4] It is a fundamental assumption that makes life both bearable and enjoyable.

We can sense this in the Potter stories as Harry, like St. George in the medieval stories, sticks it to the dragons. There is an implicit belief in the world order conceived by the good wizards, and this belief governs all their actions. They often brush with disaster, yet always with the confidence that their way is right. Any alternative is inconceivable. Another way would lead to death.

Lord Voldemort—"You-Know-Who"—and his followers serve only to assure the good people that they view the world in the correct way. The very name of Voldemort's disciples—Death Eaters—is symbolic of their position. They swallow death the way fire-eaters swallow fire. It is not a normative, faithful way to live. It is negative, the shadow side of all that is good and holy, and exists only as the counterpoint to the way of Dumbledore and his friends.

Albus Dumbledore, Gandalf-like, is the nearest thing to a true father figure in the novels. He is almost like God presiding over the affairs of the faithful. He is there when the infant Harry is brought to the Dursleys' house, turning out the street lamps and then turning them on again, as if he is in charge of the light. He is gentle, knowing, wise, unflappable, kind, and tolerant. Like a merciful heavenly Father, he overlooks Harry's boyish propensity for bending rules and getting into scrapes, and sees instead his inner nature and his importance in the overall scheme of things. He can become strong and wrathful (again like the heavenly Father), as he does with Cornelius Fudge, the Minister of Magic, near the end of *Harry Potter and the Goblet of Fire*. His eyes are said to blaze as he and Fudge disagree over what must be done to save the world from Voldemort and his minions. Knowing that Voldemort will try to enlist the giants for his dark purposes, he insists that Fudge make overtures to the giants and win their allegiance. Like a true bureaucrat, Fudge becomes visibly nervous about the consequences of such a step.

"If the magical community got wind that I had approached the giants," he gasps, shaking his head, "—people hate them, Dumbledore—end of my career—"

"'You are blinded,' says Dumbledore forcefully, *his voice rising now, the aura of power around him palpable, his eyes blazing once more,* 'by the love of the office you hold, Cornelius! You place too much importance, and you always have done, on the so-called purity of blood! You fail to recognize that it matters not what someone is born, but what they grow to be!'"[5]

Rowling's treatment of bureaucracy is scathing. When the Quidditch World Cup matches are played in *Harry Potter and the Goblet of Fire,* the Ministry of Magic officials are in their element, arranging the venue, the seating, the camping, the amenities, the Portkeys to transport people, and everything else that must be seen to for a smoothly run show. Percy

Weasley, who aspires to ministry work, is ecstatic at the opportunities for serving the organization and becoming known to the various ministers. His father, Arthur Weasley, who already works at the ministry, gives Harry and Hermione, new to most of it, a rundown on the people they see passing them—Cuthbert Mockridge, Head of the Goblin Liaison Office, Gilbert Wimple, with the Committee on Experimental Charms, Arnold Peasegood, member of the Accidental Magic Reversal Squad, and Bode and Croaker, who are Unspeakables. When Harry and Hermione want to know what Unspeakables are, Weasley replies that they're from the Department of Mysteries, which is top secret, and that he has "no idea what they get up to."[6]

Fudge, as head of the Ministry of Magic and therefore chief bureaucrat, appears from time to time through the novels, almost always as the beneficent administrator, the superintendent who strolls through his provinces making sure that things are running efficiently and no one is unhappy with the Ministry's efforts. A shallow and generally benign man, he is concerned above all with avoiding gaffes and cock-ups, and with appearing to be managing everything well. When Sirius Black escapes from Azkaban, in *Harry Potter and the Prisoner of Azkaban,* and everybody thinks he is planning to kill Harry, Fudge seeks out Harry in Diagon Alley, where he and the Weasleys have gone to purchase their school supplies before the opening of the term. Harry is upset, because back at the Dursleys' he cast a spell on Aunt Marge that inflated her monstrously, and he thinks Fudge will tell him he is expelled from Hogwarts for unauthorized use of wizardry around Muggles. But Fudge behaves avuncularly, tut-tutting what has happened, feeding him buttered crumpets, and securing him a room at the Leaky Cauldron hostelry for the remainder of his vacation time. Harry doesn't realize until much later that Fudge is only trying to make sure he is okay so there won't be any chance of a screwup before Black is recaptured and returned to Azkaban. Like most experienced managers, Fudge is a slick politician who keeps his post by trying to quell trouble before it starts.

In *Harry Potter and the Goblet of Fire,* Fudge and the other bureaucrats are thrown into instant panic by the unexpected appearance of Voldemort's sign, "the Dark Mark," a large skull with a serpent for a tongue, in the night sky over the World Cup site. The area from which it emanated is instantly surrounded by a kind of wizard SWAT team, with police crashing through the underbrush in search of the perpetrator or perpetrators. The bureaucracy is on the side of goodness and decency and must always be seen to be upholding law and order. But, like all bureaucracies, it operates more out of concern for self-preservation than out of any deep commitment to moral order in the universe.

Dumbledore, on the other hand, is quietly, deeply, and passionately committed to the moral order, and presides over Hogwarts as the unshakable foe of darkness and evil. Harry seems to know this automatically, as a given in his nature.

When everybody, including himself, thinks Black is after him, he agrees wholeheartedly with Mrs. Weasley that "the safest place on earth" for him to be is wherever Dumbledore happens to be. "Didn't people always say that Dumbledore was the only person Lord Voldemort had ever been afraid of?"[7] And when Harry faces Tom Riddle in *Harry Potter and the Chamber of Secrets,* and Tom tells him he fashioned a new name for himself, Lord Voldemort, so that one day, when he had become the greatest wizard of all, other wizards would be afraid to speak it, Harry's mind turns instinctively to Dumbledore as his salvation:

> Harry's brain seemed to have jammed. He stared numbly at Riddle, at the orphaned boy who had grown up to murder Harry's own parents, and so many others. . . . At last he forced himself to speak.
>
> "You're not," he said, his quiet voice full of hatred.
>
> "Not what?" snapped Riddle.
>
> "Not the greatest sorcerer in the world," said Harry, breathing fast. "Sorry to disappoint you and all that, but the greatest wizard in the world is Albus Dumbledore. Everyone says so. Even when you were strong, you didn't dare try and take over at Hogwarts. Dumbledore saw through you when you were at school and he still frightens you now, wherever you're hiding these days—"[8]

And Harry's relation to Dumbledore is almost like that of a son to a father, for Dumbledore takes the deepest interest in

Harry and his development. There is a strong paternal feeling on his part for this remarkable child, and he seems to guide Harry with the right saying or the right gesture at precisely the right moment of his need.

I have not said this until now, for it could appear extremely far-fetched and ridiculous, and I have not felt like taking the risk. But suppose—just suppose—there is more significance to Harry's name than Rowling's casual remarks about it have led us to suspect. She once had some childhood friends named Potter, she says—Ian and Vikki Potter. And Harry—Harry's merely "a good, British name," isn't it? But consider—H.P. could stand for *huios pater*, Greek for "son" and "father" (the genitive of *pater* is *pateros*), something Rowling with her classics background would surely know. And Potter, as she would also know from her easy familiarity with European romance languages, is pronounced *pot-ter* in them, with an almost equal accent on both syllables, so that it sounds nearly identical to the Greek *pater*. Her hero could hardly be called Huios—it would be too obvious and would summon unwanted attention to itself. Huey, perhaps. But Harry is indeed a good old British name. One of two kings named Harold died at the Norman invasion of England in 1066. And isn't Harry the name of the youngest son of Prince Charles and Princess Diana? Born in 1984, he was about the same age as Harry Potter when the first Potter novel appeared.

As I said, it sounds far-fetched. Why make so much of Harry Potter's simple name? But the possibility is there— Harry, the Christ figure, and Albus Dumbledore, the Father figure. Rowling has said a number of times how excited she became when she first got the idea of the Potter stories while stalled on a train between London and Manchester for several hours. Could this symbolism have had anything to do with her excitement?

The strong sense of faith in the novels doesn't require such an identification to confirm it. It is there, whether the Son-Father thing is true or not. But I can't entirely dismiss the notion of its being true. Rowling is extremely clever, and it wouldn't be unlike her to disguise the religious meaning in her writings. She is also a very intuitive writer—which means that she could have introduced the meaning without thinking about it.

HOPE

Mainline Christianity has never made very much of the apocalyptic and eschatological elements in the New Testament because, as mainline and established, it doesn't have much interest in changing the status quo. It has focused instead on the structural and moral aspects of Jesus and the Apostles' teachings—on how Christians should behave, how they should regard non-Christians and the "world," and how they should pray and conduct their spiritual affairs. But objective scholarship is forced to admit that there is a very heady strain of apocalypticism in the Gospels, certain of the Epistles, and the book of Revelation, which is of course also known as the Apocalypse.

On the face of the evidence, Jesus apparently believed that the world would end soon after his death—perhaps even simultaneously with it—and that the kingdom of God would immediately appear. It is possible, of course, that most of the eschatological talk was put into Jesus' mouth by his followers after he died. But regardless of how they got there, there are large segments in the Gospels—notably Matthew 24–25 and Mark 13—that deal almost exclusively with the cataclysmic end of civilization.

That this bracing theme still holds a great deal of power for some is witnessed by the extraordinary popularity in recent years first of Hal Lindsey's book *The Late Great Planet Earth* and its spin-offs, and then of the Tim Lahaye–Jerry Jenkins *Left Behind* series, about the rapture of the faithful before God destroys the world and the universe. (At last count, the latter had sold approximately 30 million copies.) Both *The Late Great Planet Earth,* which is nonfiction, and the Lahaye–Jenkins books, which are novels, stem from a Pentecostalist emphasis on Revelation, with apocalyptic elements from the Old Testament book of Daniel thrown in. Largely ignored by mainline clergy and teachers, they have nevertheless won an enormous following among fringe churches and charismatic groups.

In the early church, Jesus was undeniably associated with the Eschaton, or end-time, when God would bring all history to a conclusion and the dramatic events symbolized in the book of Revelation would occur. His messiahship brought fresh hope and expectation to many who had begun to believe that the promises of the prophets would never be fulfilled.

This is the reason for the ecstatic speech of Simeon, the aged prophet who beheld the infant Savior in the temple. "Master," he said, "now you are dismissing your servant in peace, according to your word; for my eyes have seen your salvation."[9] The coming of Christ embodied the centuries-old hopes and aspirations of the Jewish people.

As John Sanford, the internationally known Jungian analyst, has written, the story of Christ's victory on the cross over the dominion of evil is "the most hopeful statement in the spiritual lore of humankind. It makes of Christianity an ultimately hopeful religious faith: no matter how great the darkness, no matter how powerful are the forces of senseless destruction, there is an essential divinity at the core of life that no power in heaven or earth can destroy."[10]

A similar sense of hope centers on Harry Potter in the Potter narratives. There is something electric in people's voices when they meet him. The story of his first encounter with Lord Voldemort, and the reflex action of Voldemort's Avada Kedavra curse, so that it nearly finished off Voldemort himself, has quickly become part of the wizard community's general knowledge. Good wizards everywhere, even in France and northern Europe, as we learn when the champions from those areas descend on Hogwarts for the Triwizard Tournament, recognize Harry's name and know of his special stature in the war with the Dark Lord. Just as Jesus was important to his followers in the first century as the symbolic opponent of evil and darkness in the world, Harry is important to the good people who know him in Rowling's fictional world.

There is a strong eschatological flavor to all of Rowling's novels. However funny or trivial the things that are going on in the foreground may be, they are set against the dark backdrop of conflict and potential disaster in the wizard realm. Voldemort is dangerous and threatening, even in a state of half-life, and there is always the worry that he will gather power again and disrupt everything. This is why there is so much panic and consternation when the Dark Mark appears in the sky over the Quidditch World Cup field near the beginning of *Harry Potter and the Goblet of Fire*. The sign has not been seen for years, and people had hoped it would never be seen again. Later in the novel, Professor Karkaroff interrupts Professor Snape's class because he is profoundly alarmed at the intensification of the Dark Mark on his arm, the one with which Voldemort branded his disciples. He and Snape both know it means that Voldemort is staging a return to power, and they dread it because it throws their lives into jeopardy. The Dark Lord never lets former disciples go. Part of them is bound to him forever.

Death and its minions are always ugly and menacing in the novels. Voldemort himself, when we meet him in *Harry Potter and the Sorcerer's Stone*, occupies the back of Professor Quirrell's head, like a ghoul, and forces Quirrell to drink the unicorn blood in order to make him stronger. The unicorn is a symbol of Christ and purity, so the act has something of the grotesque and witches' sabbath about it. When Frank Bryce stumbles upon Voldemort, Wormtail, and the snake "curled up on the rotting hearth rug, like some horrible travesty of a pet dog," in the first chapter of *Harry Potter and the Goblet of Fire*, he dares Voldemort to "turn 'round and face me like a man." Wormtail scoots the chair around so Bryce can see what is in it. The snake lifts its ugly head and hisses. And when Bryce sees the sight in the chair, his walking stick falls to the floor with a clatter and he screams so loudly that he doesn't even hear the words of the death curse spoken by "the thing in the chair" lifting its wand.

Voldemort's followers are also menacing and hateful. The Death Eaters, some of whom occupy important positions in the wizard government, are bitter and negative. The dementors, or soul-suckers, are utterly hideous. Harry's first encounter with one, on the train to Hogwarts in *Harry Potter and the Prisoner of Azkaban*, is shocking and unsettling. The lights on the train have gone out, and Professor Lupin, who is in the compartment with Harry, Ron, Hermione, and Neville, kindles some flames in his hand and starts for the door to see what is the matter. But the door slides open before he reaches it, and Harry sees a cloaked figure outside, so tall that it appears to reach the ceiling. Its face is completely hidden by the hood. Harry's eyes slide downward, and what they fall upon makes his stomach contract. There is a hand protruding from the cloak, and it is "glistening, grayish, slimy-looking, and scabbed," as if it were "something dead that had decayed in the water." The hand is withdrawn, and there is a long, slow, rattling sound, as if the creature were trying "to suck something more than air from its surroundings."[11]

Lupin later describes the Dementor's Kiss to Harry—how

the awful figure sucks the mind and soul out of its enemies, the way Tydeus, in the Greek myth, sucked the brain from the severed head of Melanippus (though Lupin doesn't mention Tydeus). He says he supposes there must be some kind of mouth under the hood, because the creature clamps its jaws on the mouth of the victim and sucks out the victim's soul.

"What—," says Harry, "they kill—?"

"Oh no," says Lupin. "Much worse than that. You can exist without your soul, you know, as long as your brain and heart are still working. But you'll have no sense of self anymore, no memory, no . . . anything. There's no chance at all of recovery. You'll just—exist. As an empty shell. And your soul is gone forever . . . lost."[12]

Voldemort, the Death Eaters, the dementors, the basilisk, the huge, ugly trolls, the dragons, snakes, spiders, grindylows, Blast-Ended Skrewts, and manticores, together with the Devil's Snare and other threatening plants, all paint an extraordinarily dark and threatening background for the Potter stories. They are one reason some parents won't let their children read Rowling's books. But they represent the shadow side of human existence, the horrible evil that contaminates and destroys people's souls, that binds and constricts them until, like the dementors' victims, they simply give up and live as the walking dead, no longer aware of a better way.

Harry, in the face of this, is fresh, strong, resourceful, and utterly resistant to evil. The lightning-shaped scar on his forehead, left by his original encounter with Voldemort, aches and throbs when something foul or malignant is about to occur—

sometimes so badly that it blinds him. It is an unfailing alarm to notify him of Voldemort's growing strength or threatening presence. It is Harry and his scar that Voldemort must destroy if he would possess the earth. Dumbledore, the wise and patient Father figure, realizes this, and casts all his power and knowledge behind Harry to defeat the Dark Lord. Harry is not only the knight-errant, he is the battleground. Like Christ on the cross, he suffers Voldemort's Cruciatus Curse, which makes him writhe on the ground in pain and distress. And twice, by the end of the fourth novel, he has been the target for Voldemort's Avada Kedavra curse. Everything is centered on him—the venom of Voldemort and the hope of the good wizards' survival. He is the eschatological figure of the novels, as Christ is of the Gospels, and all depends on him.

Not too long ago, Yale professor Henri J. M. Nouwen wrote a popular book called *The Wounded Healer*, whose thesis is that the best healers are those who have suffered wounds of their own but are prepared to take on the sufferings of others. This is essentially what Harry Potter is in the novels that bear his name: a wounded healer. Unlike Christ, whose wounding came at the end of his life, Harry's comes at the beginning, or very near the beginning. He already has the scar when we are introduced to him in the first story. Somehow, his power is tied up with the scar, just as Christ's was tied up with the nail holes in his hands; at least the scar bears evidence to his power. And he and his scar are the symbol of hope to the entire world of wizardry—the hope that, in the end, evil will be put down and good will triumph. Even at the end of the fourth novel, when things look so bleak for the good wizards, there is a sense of hope permeating everything. It is implicit even in Harry's gift of the Triwizard Cup prize money to Fred and George Weasley so they can buy a joke shop, and in his comment, "We could all do with a few laughs. I've got a feeling we're going to need them more than usual before long."[13]

I haven't commented much on the rich vein of humor running through the novels. But it is not unrelated to the business of eschatological hope. The thing that makes real humor possible—that is, true fun, joy, laugh-out-loud humor—is a strong confidence that everything is going to turn out okay. Humor doesn't work in dark or sad situations. For weeks after the tragic events of September 11, 2001, American humorists carefully toned down their monologues and certain funny movies were delayed for release because it was felt that the time wasn't right for the kind of frivolity and lightheartedness they purveyed. But humor is a wonderful tonic for tough times and bad days when we know that everything is going to come out all right in the end.

This is what Harry is talking about. Fred and George's practical jokes—Ton-Tongue Toffees, Canary Creams, fake wands—can make people laugh because there is light at the end of the tunnel. And much of that light is owing to Harry.

LOVE

Good and *evil* are nouns or adjectives. The verb forms of *good* are "to love" and "to help." The verb forms of *evil* are "to hate" and "to destroy." The cosmic struggle of good and evil therefore pit loving and helping against hating and destroying. Voldemort, Lucius Malfoy, and their associates are bent on hating and destroying the stability and structures of the wizard world. Dumbledore, Hagrid, Harry, and their friends are committed to saving them. The eschatological nature of the struggle arises from the fact that it is a struggle to the death. Evil takes no captives.

The ultimate goal of loving and helping is the essential unity of everything, while the goal of hating and destroying is the dismantling and dissolution of that unity. Lovers enjoy and celebrate. Haters scheme, besmirch, and try to overthrow. Lovers sacrifice themselves for the good of all. Haters destroy others for their own good. Lovers regard others as better than themselves. Haters have no consideration at all for others. Lovers tend to forgive offenses in others. Haters never forgive. They make a point of remembering.

Dumbledore is known for his forgiving nature. A wise and generous man, he has befriended the bumbling gamekeeper Hagrid for years, even though Hagrid was blamed for releasing the murderous creature from the Chamber of Secrets and dismissed from Hogwarts as a student. He brings Remus

Lupin back as a Professor of Defense Against the Dark Arts even though he knows Lupin is a werewolf and there would be outcries if others knew. He employed Severus Snape and trusts him as a colleague even though he knows that Snape was once branded by Voldemart's mark. He welcomes Professor Karkaroff from Durmstrang and displays every hospitality toward him although he knows that he too was once a servant of Voldemort. He repeatedly forgives Harry and his friends when they bend or break the rules of the school. He insists to Cornelius Fudge, the Minister of Magic, that they should send envoys to the giants, even though most wizards do not accept them.

Voldemort, on the other hand, is always full of bitterness and recriminations and forgives no one for anything. He hated Harry's parents from the time when they were students together and murdered them out of vengeance. He hates Harry because his Killing Curse on him failed and left Voldemort himself almost fatally wounded. He treats his servant Wormtail with loathing and contempt, frequently inflicting pain and humiliation on him, and requiring him in *Harry Potter and the Goblet of Fire* to cut off his hand in penance for not having been as faithful as he might. He berates Lucius Malfoy for not being a more visible, attentive servant. "I smell guilt," he hisses as he walks among the Death Eaters at the cemetery scene in *Harry Potter and the Goblet of Fire*. "There is a stench of guilt upon the air."[14] One of the Death Eaters flings himself at Voldemort's feet and shrieks, "Master, forgive me!

Forgive us all!"[15] Voldemort laughs, raises his wand, and pronounces the Cruciatus Curse on the follower, causing him to writhe in torment on the ground.

Voldemort raises his wand and stops the curse. The poor creature lies there, gasping.

"Get up, Avery," says Voldemort. "Stand up. You ask for forgiveness? I do not forgive. I do not forget. Thirteen long years . . . I want thirteen years' repayment before I forgive you."[16]

Thirteen is the number of years since his curse on Harry nearly destroyed himself, and is also an appropriate number for a Dark Lord, as it is popularly associated with nefariousness and evil. And perhaps it reminds us of another number, one from the Gospels denoting extreme fullness:

> Then Peter came and said to him, "Lord, if another member of the church sins against me, how often should I forgive? As many as seven times?" Jesus said to him, "Not seven times, but, I tell you, seventy-seven times."[17]

In *Harry Potter and the Goblet of Fire*, Harry's power to forgive is tested by his friend Ron's refusal to believe that Harry didn't put his own name into the goblet as a candidate for the Triwizard Tournament and the thousand-galleon prize. Hermione tells Harry that Ron is only jealous, but Harry has trouble forgiving a close friend who won't accept his word without question. Like the two schoolboys they are, they continue to exchange rude remarks until the rift between them is difficult to repair, and for several weeks they go their separate ways. Once, Harry hurls a "Potter Really Stinks" badge at Ron—one of Draco Malfoy's inventions—and hits him in the forehead. "There you go," says Harry. "Something for you to wear on Tuesday. You might even have a scar now, if you're lucky. . . . That's what you want, isn't it?"[18]

Their rapprochement occurs after Harry's hair-raising battle with the Horntail dragon in the first competition for the Triwizard Cup. It was a squeaker, and Harry could very well have lost his life. When Hermione and Ron come up to Harry afterward, Ron is white as a ghost. "Harry," he says, "whoever put your name in that goblet—I—I reckon they're trying to do you in!" "Caught on, have you?" Harry says, still smarting from Ron's earlier doubt. "Took you long enough." Hermione watches them both, fearful of what may happen. They stare at each other for a minute. Ron starts to open his mouth. Knowing what he's going to say, Harry stops him. "It's okay," he says. "Forget it." "No," says Ron, "I shouldn't've—" "*Forget it,*" says Harry.[19]

The whole episode is over, and the two boys begin to chatter together with the same affection they have always shared. Would it be pushing the envelope too much to say it is reminiscent of the reunion of Jesus and Simon Peter in Galilee after the crucifixion? Peter denied Jesus three times on the eve of his master's death. Three times, afterward, Jesus asked him, "Do you love me?" And three times Peter answered, "Lord, you know I love you."

Love also accounts, in the Potter narratives, for the way Harry, Hermione, and others accept people who are different from themselves. The Malfoys, father and son, are unyielding toward Muggles and Mudbloods—people who have any Muggle blood in them and aren't purebred wizards. But Harry and his friends are like Dumbledore, who says that it isn't how one is born that is important but what one makes of one's life. And Hermione, of course, mounts a campaign, in *Harry Potter and the Goblet of Fire*, to give the house-elves their freedom and compensation for their work, because she regards them as being of equal value with the wizards themselves. It is a sentiment that has its noble origins in a statement by St. Paul about the new regime in Christ: "There is no longer Jew or Greek, there is no longer slave or free, there is no longer male or female; for all of you are one in Christ Jesus."[20]

Real love, biblical love, is completely unselfish. The Greek word for love in the New Testament is always *agape* (generous love) or *philia* (love for a friend or sibling), never *eros* (sexual or acquisitive love). When asked what is the greatest commandment people are to live by, Jesus said:

"The first is, 'Hear, O Israel: the Lord our God, the Lord is one; you shall love the Lord your God with all your heart, and with all your soul, and with all your mind, and with all your strength.' The second is this, 'You shall love your neighbor as yourself.' There is no other commandment greater than these."[21]

The use of the word *agape* here indicates a complete selflessness—basking in adoration with a delight beyond desire, and then loving the neighbor, or the other, in the same way. It is the height of spirituality, a merging of the soul in what Emerson called the Oversoul, a total surrender to the beauty and splendor of God and the creation. It is a love that overcomes all barriers, accepts and dissolves all opposites, embraces all contrarieties. It is what Frederick Buechner expresses in *The Alphabet of Grace* when he says:

> The language of God seems mostly metaphor. His love is like a red, red rose. His love is like the old waiter with shingles, the guitar-playing Buddhist tramp, the raped child and the one who raped her. There is no image too far-fetched, no combination of sounds too harsh, no spelling too irregular, no allusion too obscure or outrageous. The alphabet of grace is full of gutturals.[22]

In the mystical oneness of everything, that is, even the dissonances are absorbed and heard as something else. There is a shining, otherworldly quality to everything. The lover is embraced by it all, disappears in the folds of its embrace, dies of ecstasy in the arms of the other, which of course is no longer the other, because now they are one, and there is only the sound of one hand clapping left ringing in the air.

Lord Voldemort could not endure such talk. He would ridicule it as the sheerest idiocy.

But Harry would understand—and Dumbledore—and Hermione—and even Hagrid, who cares for baby dragons and Blast-Ended Skrewts and other aberrations of nature. They belong to the fellowship of loving, kindred spirits. They are open to the world as magic and mystery, as a field of delight for all who live in it. But because they are realists—because they see things with open eyes and are not blinded by romanticism—they are ready to sacrifice themselves to oppose the Dark Lords and dementors and Malfoys who would rob them and others of their simple pleasure in life. They know how imperiled the world is and will do whatever is required to stop Voldemort—even if it kills them.

But we are confident that it won't. Not all of them, at any rate. And the reason we're confident is that we already know the overarching plot of the novels. It is the plot of orthodox Christianity, now written into the unconscious of every Westerner, and perhaps even Easterners as well. Christ may die, but Christ will live, because in the end evil is less powerful than good, and Satan will lose out to God. It is that simple. It is the text to which all life resonates. "God was, in Christ, reconciling the world to himself."[23] God was making all things one—bundling all the magic and mystery into a unity, a single existence.

Harry—and all his readers, for that matter—must make the hero's journey and battle the evil forces in order to come to the full realization of this. As John Sanford says,

> Good and evil will be curiously intermingled in any meaningful life process. If we are to become whole, life will send us, not what we want, but what we need in order to grow. The forces of evil will have to touch our lives, for without the dark Luciferian power, consciousness does not

emerge, as Mephistopheles seems to be saying in Goethe's play *Faust* when he declares of himself that he is "part of that Force which would do evil ever, yet forever works the good."

Individuation is a work, a life opus, a task that calls upon us not to avoid life's difficulties and dangers, but to perceive the meaning in the pattern of events that form our lives. Life's supreme achievement may be to see the thread that connects together the events, dreams, and relationships that have made up the fabric of our existence. Individuation is a search for and discovery of meaning, not a meaning we consciously devise, but the meaning embedded in life itself. It will confront us with many demands, for the unconscious, as Jung once wrote, "always tries to produce an impossible situation in order to force the individual to bring out his very best."[24]

Once we have made the pilgrimage and slain the dragons along the way, as Harry does, we arrive at the kind of genteel wisdom possessed by Dumbledore, which is characterized by an extreme wariness of evil and, at the same time, a profound love for life and people. We accept life on its own terms—the evil with the good—and, like God in the creation narrative in Genesis, pronounce it "very good." We understand the mystical oneness of everything, and cherish it with a deep passion. We wish we could even embrace the Voldemorts and Malfoys and love them into unity with everything else, though we are realistic enough to know that they persistently choose damnation and would never agree to reunification. This is the one point at which the Christian vision sticks and can go no further, but must finally remain dualistic; it recognizes that evil cannot be entirely absorbed by good. The devil and his angels must be cast into the lake of everlasting fire, for they will never repent and become part of the beloved community.

But this does not allay the power of faith, hope, and love in our lives. Especially love. We see the world as miracle—Rowling has only just touched on its real magic—and adore it. We understand fellowship, and crave it. We feel the presence of God, and bow down. All life is sacrament, and, through the journey to individuation, our hearts are purged to receive it. With Harry Potter in his finest moments, we feel a sense of deep and quiet reverence, an obligation to all that is, and we know—we *know*—that evil cannot finally win. God—and Dumbledore?—are too great for that!

ABOUT THE AUTHOR

John Killinger, who holds doctorates in both theology and literature, has taught courses in the theological aspects of contemporary literature at Vanderbilt University, the University of Chicago, City College of New York, and Samford University. An ordained clergyman, he has been minister of the First Presbyterian Church in Lynchburg, Virginia, and the First Congregational Church of Los Angeles, California. He is presently a freelance writer and for the past seven years has served as minister of the Little Stone Church, a resort parish on Mackinac Island, Michigan. Among his many publications are several books in the field of literary criticism, including *Hemingway and the Dead Gods* (Lexington, Kentucky: University Press of Kentucky, 1960; Citadel, 1965); *The Failure of Theology in Modern Literature* (Nashville: Abingdon Press, 1963); *The Fragile Presence* (Philadelphia: Fortress Press, 1973); and *World in Collapse: The Vision of Absurd Drama* (New York: Dell, 1970). He has also written two novels, *Jessie* (New York: McCracken Press, 1993) and *The Night Jessie Sang at the Opry* (Centreville, Virginia: Angel Books, 1996), which feature Christ as a woman in modern times.

NOTES

Note: All quotes from the Harry Potter books are from the standard (hardcover) American edition, Arthur A. Levine Books, Scholastic Publications. All quotes from the Bible are from the New Revised Standard Version.

INTRODUCTION

1. Richard Abanes, *Harry Potter and the Bible* (Camp Hill, Pennsylvania: Horizon Books, 2001), 97.

2. Ibid., 241.

3. Ibid., 271.

4. Connie Neal, *What's a Christian to Do with Harry Potter?* (Colorado Springs, Colorado: Waterbrook Press, 2001), 50.

5. Ibid., 88.

6. Margo Jefferson, "Harry Potter for Grown-Ups," *The New York Times* (January 20, 2002).

7. Elizabeth Schafer, *Exploring Harry Potter* (Osprey, Florida: Beacham Publishing Co., 2000), 163.

8. Ibid., 164.

NOTES

1. Mysterious Births and Miraculous Childhoods

1. J. K. Rowling, *Harry Potter and the Sorcerer's Stone* (New York: Scholastic, 1998), 2.

2. Ibid.

3. Luke 2:48.

4. Matthew 12:46–50; Mark 3:31–35; Luke 8:19–21.

5. John 19:26–27.

6. *Sorcerer's Stone*, 13.

7. Ibid., 17.

8. Ibid., 12.

9. Luke 2:25–38.

10. *Sorcerer's Stone*, 16.

11. A. N. Wilson, *Jesus: A Life* (New York: W. W. Norton, 1992), 73.

12. Ibid., 84.

13. *Sorcerer's Stone*, 53.

14. Luke 4:1–11.

2. The Struggle Between Good and Evil

1. Matthew 13:24–30.

2. *Sorcerer's Stone*, 298.

3. Revelation 12:7–9, 13–17.

4. Acts 2:2–3.

5. Romans 8:19, 21.

6. J. K. Rowling, *Harry Potter and the Prisoner of Azkaban* (New York: Scholastic, 1999), 427.

7. J. K. Rowling, *Harry Potter and the Goblet of Fire* (New York: Scholastic, 2000), 733.

3. The Game of Life

1. *Sorcerer's Stone,* 144.

2. Ibid., 167.

3. Abanes, *Harry Potter and the Bible,* 205–206.

4. Micah 6:8.

5. *Sorcerer's Stone,* 100.

6. J. K. Rowling, *Harry Potter and the Chamber of Secrets* (New York: Scholastic, 1999), 15.

7. Ibid.

8. Ibid., 110.

9. Matthew 19:17.

10. John 6:15.

11. Marcus Borg, *Meeting Jesus Again for the First Time: The Historical Jesus and the Heart of Contemporary Faith* (San Francisco: HarperSanFrancisco, 1994).

12. *Chamber of Secrets,* 328.

13. Luke 9:51.

14. *Chamber of Secrets,* 166–172.

15. *Sorcerer's Stone,* 291.

16. Ibid., 185.

17. Ibid., 188.

18. *Goblet of Fire,* 341.

19. Ibid., 139.

20. Ibid., 223.

21. Ibid., 224.

22. Ibid., 238.

23. Matthew 7:12.

24. John 15:12–13.

25. Matthew 20:28.

26. Jaroslav Pelikan, *Jesus Through the Centuries—His Place in the History of Culture* (New Haven, Connecticut: Yale University Press, 1985), 95.

27. *Sorcerer's Stone,* 177.

28. Ibid., 270.

29. Ibid., 283.

30. *Chamber of Secrets,* 179.

31. Ibid., 194.

32. Ibid., 301.

33. *Goblet of Fire,* 500.

34. John 15:13.

35. John 3:16.

36. 1 John 4:7–12.

37. *Sorcerer's Stone,* 299.

38. *Goblet of Fire,* 666–668.

39. Ibid., 722–723.

40. Ibid., 723.

41. Galatians 5:19–23.

42. *Chamber of Secrets,* 333.

43. Deuteronomy 30:19–20.

44. John 21:15.

45. *Goblet of Fire,* 708.

46. Lindsey Fraser, *Conversations with J. K. Rowling* (New York: Scholastic, 2000), 34–35.

47. Speaking of her marriage and divorce, Rowling said: "I've

made my mistakes in that area. Just because you've got a good brain doesn't mean you're any better than the next person at keeping your hormones under control." In Marc Shapiro, *J. K. Rowling: The Wizard Behind Harry Potter* (New York: St. Martin's Press, 2001), 60–61.

48. Fraser, *Conversations with J. K. Rowling*, 28.

49. Speaking to an interviewer, J. K. Rowling confirmed that Dementors represent the mental illness known as depression: "That is exactly what they are. It was entirely conscious. And entirely from my own experience. Depression is the most unpleasant thing I have ever experienced." In David Colbert, *The Magical Worlds of Harry Potter* (Wrightsville Beach, N.C.: Lumina, 2001), 57.

50. Romans 7:19.

51. Philippians 3:12.

4. THE MAGICAL, MYSTICAL WORLD

1. *Prisoner of Azkaban*, 100.

2. *Goblet of Fire*, 660–61.

3. Schafer, *Exploring Harry Potter*, 185.

4. Lawrence LeShan, *The Medium, the Mystic, and the Physicist* (New York: Ballantine Books, 1975), 5.

5. W. R. Inge, *Christian Mysticism* (Greenwich, England: Meridian Books, 1950), 24.

6. Stephen Hawking, *A Brief History of Time: From the Big Bang to Black Holes* (New York: Bantam, 1990), 10.

7. Ibid., 175.

8. Schafer, *Exploring Harry Potter*, 193.

9. Matthew Fox, *One River, Many Wells* (New York: Jeremy P. Tarcher/Putnam, 2000), 16.

10. Anne Lamott, *Traveling Mercies: Some Thoughts on Faith* (New York: Pantheon Books, 1999), 100.

11. Dag Hammarskjöld, *Markings* (London: Faber and Faber, 1964), 64.

12. Michael Mayne, *This Sunrise of Wonder: Letters for the Journey* (London: HarperCollins/Fount, 1995), 15.

13. Ibid., 22–23.

5. OF GHOSTS AND GOBLINS AND THE LIFE AFTER DEATH

1. Macrina Wiederkehr, *A Tree Full of Angels* (New York: HarperCollins, 1990), xii–xiii.

2. *Sorcerer's Stone*, 115.

3. *Chamber of Secrets*, 307–08.

4. Mayne, *Sunrise of Wonder*, 106.

5. Elizabeth Goudge, *Pilgrim's Inn* (New York: Coward-McCann, 1948), 314.

6. Leslie D. Weatherhead, *The Christian Agnostic* (Nashville: Abingdon Press, 1965), 266–67.

7. 1 Samuel 28:3–25.

8. John 20:19–23; 21:4–8.

9. Luke 24:13–27.

10. 1 Corinthians 15:6.

11. *Prisoner of Azkaban*, 427–28.

12. *Goblet of Fire*, 462.

13. Ibid., 496–97.

14. *Sorcerer's Stone*, 208–09.

15. *Prisoner of Azkaban,* 407.

16. Ibid., 411.

17. Schafer, *Exploring Harry Potter,* 177.

18. Betty J. Eadie, *Embraced by the Light* (Placerville, California: Gold Leaf Press, 1992), 5.

19. Hebrews 11:32–38.

20. Ibid., 12:1–2.

21. John Hick, *Death and Eternal Life* (London: William Collins Sons, 1976), 172–73.

22. Fraser, *Conversations with J. K. Rowling,* 30–31.

6. And Now Abideth Faith, Hope, and Love

1. Phil Cousineau, *Once and Future Myths: The Power of Ancient Stories in Modern Times* (Berkeley, California: Conari Press, 2001), 13.

2. Diane Ackerman, *Deep Play* (New York: Vintage Books, 1999), 13.

3. 1 Corinthians 13:13.

4. Hebrews 11:1.

5. *Goblet of Fire,* 708 [italics in the original].

6. Ibid., 86.

7. *Prisoner of Azkaban,* 67–68.

8. *Chamber of Secrets,* 314.

9. Luke 2:29–30.

10. John Sanford, *Mystical Christianity* (New York: Crossroad, 1994), 330.

11. *Prisoner of Azkaban,* 83.

12. Ibid., 247.

13. *Goblet of Fire,* 733.

14. *Goblet of Fire,* 647.

15. Ibid., 648.

16. Ibid., 649.

17. Matthew 18:21.

18. *Goblet of Fire,* 335–36.

19. Ibid., 358.

20. Galatians 3:28.

21. Mark 12:29–31.

22. Frederick Buechner, *The Alphabet of Grace* (New York: Seabury Press, 1970), 13.

23. 2 Corinthians 5:19.

24. John Sanford, *Healing and Wholeness* (Ramsey, New Jersey: Paulist Press, 1977), 20.